THE BOOK AND THE SWORD

THE BOOK
AND
THE SWORD

A Martial Arts novel
by
Louis Cha

Translated
by
Graham Earnshaw

Edited
by
Rachel May *and* **John Minford**

OXFORD
UNIVERSITY PRESS

OXFORD
UNIVERSITY PRESS

Oxford University Press is a department of the University of Oxford.
It furthers the University's objective of excellence in research, scholarship,
and education by publishing worldwide. Oxford is a registered trade mark of
Oxford University Press in the UK and in certain other countries

Published in Hong Kong by
Oxford University Press (China) Limited
39th Floor, One Kowloon, 1 Wang Yuen Street, Kowloon Bay, Hong Kong

© Oxford University Press (China) Limited 2004

The moral rights of the author have been asserted

First edition published in 2004

First edition published in paperback 2018

ISBN: 978-0-19-097428-2

Impression: II

British Library Cataloguing in Publication Data
available

Library of Congress Cataloging-in-Publication Data
available

CONTENTS

IMPORTANT DATES IN THE HISTORICAL BACKGROUND

The action of the novel takes place during the reign of the Emperor Qian Long, around the years 1758–1760.

1723 Yong Zheng Emperor, Fourth Son of Kang Xi, and third Emperor of the Manchu Qing dynasty, comes to the throne.

1735 Qian Long Emperor, Fourth Son of Yong Zheng (according to official historical sources), and fourth Emperor of the Manchu Qing dynasty, comes to the throne. His reign ends in 1799.

1751 The Manchus occupy Tibet.

1756–8 Extermination of the Dzungars and their leader Amursana by the Manchu armies. Some authorities (including the *Encyclopedia Britannica*) claim that 'the Chinese perpetrated an appalling massacre, the victims being estimated at one million.' The French historian René Grousset puts the figure at 600,000.

1758–9 Conquest of the Tarim Basin (sometimes known as Kashgaria, or Western Turkestan) and the defeat of the Muslim theocracy of the Hodjas by the Manchus under the Manchu general Zhao Hui. Capture of the Central Asian cities of Aksu, Kashgar, and Yarkand. Annexation of Turkestan, as Xinjiang (the New Territory).

1759 Battle of Ili.

1781–4 Later revolt of Muslims in Gansu Province, following the creation of a new sect by Ma Mingxin.

GLOSSARY OF PEOPLE AND PLACES

AFANTI Eccentric bewhiskered Uighur wise man, riding a donkey.

BAI ZHEN Commander in the Imperial Guard, charged with protecting Qian Long's person in Hangzhou; a legendary kungfu expert, skilled in the Songyang Martial Arts style.

BALD VULTURE Chen Zhengde, one of the legendary Twin Eagles of Heaven Mountains, jealous but adoring husband of Lady Guan.

BAOJUNLONGA Despotic ruler of the Secret City at the foot of White Jade Peak; father of Sanglaba.

BEAUTIFUL JADE West Lake courtesan with Red Flower connections.

CAO, Doctor Small town doctor who sees to Mastermind Xu's wounds.

CHEN SHIGUAN, Chief Minister (1680–1758) Father of Chen Jialuo.

CHEN JIALUO Helmsman of the Red Flower Society; son of the prominent Haining Chen family. Specialist in the use of Go-piece projectiles, also using as weapons a barbed shield and a set of five cords, each tipped with a steel ball, known as the Pearl Strings.

CHEN, Lady Wife of Chief Minister Chen, and mother of Chen Jialuo; former lover of Yu Wanting, the Old Helmsman. It was she who was forced to give up her newborn son (the future Qian Long Emperor) in exchange for the Emperor Yong Zhen's baby girl.

CHENG HUANG One of the Imperial Guards.

DONGFANG, Mr Qian Long's alias in Hangzhou.

FATHER SPECKLESS The one-armed Taoist Priest Wu Chen, prominent (second-ranking) member of the Red Flower Society. He has a longsword slung across his back. His face is pale and sickly and he has only one arm: his left sleeve is tucked under his belt.

FOUR TIGERS Four giant attendants of the Manchu military envoy sent to dictate terms of surrender to the Uighur Hodja Muzhuolun.

FRAGRANT PRINCESS *see* Hasli

FU DE Prominent Manchu military officer.

FU KANGAN A historical person. One of Emperor Qian Long's favourites, a young Manchu who held the posts of Military Governor of Manchuria and Commander-in-Chief of the Nine Gates of Peking, as well as Commander of the Imperial Guard.

GREAT HARDSHIP Monk at Shaolin Monastery, Fujian; Guardian of the First Hall.

GREAT IDIOCY Monk at Shaolin Monastery, Fujian; Guardian of the Third Hall.

GREAT INSANITY Monk at Shaolin Monastery, Fujian; Guardian of the Second Hall.

GU JINPIAO One of the Six Devils of Manchuria; bearded and lecherous.

GUAN, Lady Shifu of Huo Qingtong, one of the Twin Eagles of Heaven Mountains.

HAHETAI A Mongol, one of the Six Devils of Manchuria.

HAN WENCHONG One of the guards in the Zhen Yuan Security Agency, a practitioner of Iron Piba kungfu, and the owner of an extremely fast white horse.

HASLI Younger sister of Huo Qingtong; white-robed daughter of the Khozi Hodja Muzhuolun; a young lady of exceptional beauty. Named the Fragrant Princess by Emperor Qian Long.

HE SHEN (1750–1799) A historical person. One of Emperor Qian Long's favourites. He began his career as a guard of the Imperial Ante-chamber, and a deputy lieutenant of the Manchu Plain Blue Banner, and eventually rose to be the most powerful (and corrupt) of the Emperor's subjects. After the death of Qian Long, he was arrested and 'permitted to commit suicide'.

HEAVEN MOUNTAINS The great snow-capped mountain range in northwest Xinjiang (Turkestan).

HEAVENLY MIRROR Monk at Shaolin Monastery, Fujian; Guardian of the Fourth Hall.

HEAVENLY RAINBOW Abbot of Shaolin Monastery, Fujian; Guardian of the Fifth Hall.

HEAVEN'S EYE Mountain An extended range west of Hangzhou, on the borders between Zhejiang and Anhui Provinces.

HERDA, Colonel Manchu officer in General Zhao Hui's army.

HODJA *see* Muzhuolun

HUO QINGTONG Beautiful yellow-robed daughter of the Khozi Hodja Muzhuolun. She is about the same age as Li Yuanzhi, eighteen or nineteen, carries a dagger at her waist, and has long braids hanging down over her shoulders. She wears a full-length yellow gown, leather boots, and a small hat embroidered with gold silk, on the side of which is fastened a turquoise feather. She learned her kungfu from her Shifu, Lady Guan.

HOU YAYI Son of the Khozi Hodja Muzhuolun, and brother of Huo Qingtong and Hasli.

JIANG, CROCODILE One of the Red Flower heroes (thirteenth-ranking), who uses an iron oar as a weapon. Of Cantonese origin.

JIAO WENQI One of the Six Devils of Manchuria and a formidable fighter. He was killed five years before the story begins, while on an errand to the Uighur area. (He was sent by the Chen family of Haining, to find their missing son, Chen Jialuo.)

KAIBIEXING Uighur envoy.

LI E (1692–1752) Prominent poet of the Qing dynasty.

LI KEXIU Military Commander-in-Chief serving the Manchu throne; father of Li Yuanzhi.

LI YUANZHI Daughter and only child of Li Kexiu; passionate student of the Martial Arts and disciple of Hidden Needle Lu. Often appears in boy's clothing. She falls in love with Scholar Yu.

LIANG Wealthy Hangzhou merchant.

LITTLE ROSE Small town prostitute.

LU, HIDDEN NEEDLE Lu Feiqing, tutor and Shifu of Li Yuanzhi; a scholar in his fifties, adept at Wudang and Dart-throwing kungfu, former member of the anti-Manchu Dragon Slayers' Society. Brother-in-arms of the Wudang Masters, Fire Hand Zhang and Ma Zhen.

LUO, DIVINE KNIFE Luo Yuantong, father of Luo Bing; old friend of Hidden Needle Lu.

LUO BING Wife of Rolling Thunder Wen, the two of them senior members (joint fourth-ranking) of the Red Flower Society; a specialist in knife-throwing kungfu.

MA SHANJUN Hangzhou Lodge Master of the Red Flower Society; a wealthy merchant and brave fighter.

MA DATING Son of Ma Shanjun.

MA ZHEN Master Ma, Wudang Master, brother-in-arms of Fire Hand Zhang and Hidden Needle Lu, Shifu of Scholar Yu.

MAMI Young Uighur woman captured by Sanglaba, ruler of the Secret City, and mother of his child. Her last testament, telling the story of her life and tragic death, is found in the city.

MENG Senior Steward at Iron Ball Manor.

MUZHUOLUN The Khozi Hodja, Uighur leader; father of Huo Ayi, and the two sisters, Huo Qingtong and Hasli. A tall, thick-set man with a heavy black beard. Leader of one of the richest and most powerful of the nomadic Uighur tribes of the Heaven Mountains region, numbering nearly 200,000 people. A strong fighter, fair and just, greatly loved by his people.

QIAN Guard working for the Zhen Yuan Security Agency.

QIAN LONG, Emperor (1711–1799) Fourth Manchu Emperor. According to legend (on which the plot of *The Book and the Sword* is based) his natural parents are Chinese—the prominent minister Chen Shiguan and his wife—but he is swapped as a baby with Yong Zheng's baby daughter. He is thus the blood-brother of Helmsman Chen.

SANGLABA Son of Baojunlonga, tyrant of the Secret City.

SHI, MELANCHOLY GHOST One of the Red Flower Society heroes (twelfth-ranking); scar-faced, sinister Cantonese, with side-burns.

SIX DEVILS OF MANCHURIA A group of renowned if somewhat disreputable mercenary fighters, including Gu Jinpiao, Jiao Wenqi, Teng Yilei, the two Yan brothers, and the Mongol Hahetai.

SONG Junior Steward at Iron Ball Manor.

SUN Zhen Yuan Security Agency shouter.

TENG YILEI Eldest of the surviving Six Devils of Manchuria. A member of the gentry, and tall in stature.

TONG ZHAOHE One of the main guards of the Zhen Yuan Security Agency; a sneaky individual, responsible for the downfall of Iron Ball Manor.

TWIN EAGLES OF HEAVEN MOUNTAINS Bald Vulture and his wife Lady Guan, an elderly and somewhat eccentric Martial Arts couple living in the desert.

TWIN KNIGHTS OF WEST STREAM The Chang brothers from Sichuan, Black Death and White Death. Practitioners of Black Sand Palm kungfu, and skilled in the use of the projectiles known as Flying Claws. Both aged about forty, a frightening sight, tall and thin with faces as yellow as wax, sunken eyes, and long slanting eyebrows.

WANG WEIYANG North China Earth-Shaker, Founder and Head of the Zhen Yuan Security Agency. Over seventy years old. Adept at Eight Trigram kungfu.

WEI, LEOPARD One of the Red Flower Society heroes (ninth-ranking), the handsome fighter with the steel hooks. He has never been wounded and is consequently said to have nine lives.

WEN, ROLLING THUNDER Wen Tailai, elderly husband of Luo Bing; senior (fourth-ranking) member of the Red Flower Society, previously close comrade-in-arms of the Old Helmsman Yu Wanting; he knows of the secret concerning Qian Long's birth.

WU GUODONG Peking officer, deputed to pursue Rolling Thunder Wen and Luo Bing.

WU, Magistrate Friend of Lord Zhou's, in the town of Anxi.

XIBAO Girlfriend of one of the Yan Brothers.

XINJIANG Literally New Territory, the Chinese name for the huge Muslim area of Central Asia traditionally known in the West as Eastern Turkestan (Western Turkestan being the then Russian-controlled region to its west). The region was conquered during the earlier Han and Tang dynasties, and again by the Manchu Emperors, who incorporated it into Greater China in the eighteenth century. It includes the legendary cities of Kashgar (capital of the short-lived Turkish-Islamic Republic of Eastern Turkestan in 1933–4), Yarkand, and Khotan, and the desert oases of Hami (famous for its melons) and Turfan. It only became an official province of China in 1882–4. To this day it is the scene of frequent Muslim uprisings, which are ruthlessly suppressed by the central government.

XIN QIJI (1140–1207) Famous Song-dynasty poet.

XIN YAN Youth, page of Helmsman Chen Jialuo.

XU, MASTERMIND Xu Tianhong, prominent (seventh-ranking) member of the Red Flower Society, very short and slight in build, almost the size of a dwarf; but because of his wisdom and resourcefulness, he is the Society's chief tactician, dubbed the Kungfu Mastermind.

YAN BROTHERS Two of the gang known as the Six Manchurian Devils, working at various times for the Zhen Yuan Security Agency; one of them is carrying a valuable item (the Koran) in a red knapsack. They use weapons known as Five Element Wheels.

YANG, IRON PAGODA The fat man, prominent (eighth-ranking) in the Red Flower Society's hierarchy.

YONG ZHENG, Emperor (born 1711, reigned 1736–1796) Son of the second Manchu Emperor, Kang Xi (1654–1722). He was known as Yong Di while still a Prince. According to official versions of history, he was father of the fourth Emperor, Qian Long.

YU WANTING Former leader of the Red Flower Society, and referred to as the Old Helmsman. The lover of Minister Chen's wife, and privy to the secret of Qian Long's Chinese origins; he dies before the story begins.

YU, SCHOLAR Yu Yutong, a young, slender outlawed scholar and key member (fourteenth-ranking) of the Red Flower Society. Infatuated with the lovely (but married) Luo Bing. He plays on a Golden Flute, which he also uses as a Martial Arts weapon, sometimes wielding it like a staff, sometimes shooting darts with it. He is a disciple of the Wudang Master, Ma Zhen (brother-in-arms of Fire Hand Zhang and Hidden Needle Lu).

YUAN MEI (1716–1798) Famous Qing-dynasty poet. Judge at the courtesan competition on the lake.

YUAN SHIXIAO Master Yuan, the Strange Knight of the Heavenly Pool; Shifu of Helmsman Chen. Formerly the lover of Lady Guan.

ZENG TUNAN Energetic and trusted lieutenant of Li Kexiu.

ZHANG ANGUAN Emperor Qian Long's chef.

ZHANG, HUNCHBACK Zhang Jin, prominent member (tenth-ranking) of the Red Flower Society.

ZHANG, FIRE HAND (Judge) Zhang Zhaozhong, senior member of Wudang Martial Arts School, transcendent practitioner of the branch of Wudang kungfu known as Limitless Occult kungfu; now Major in the Imperial Guard, having gone over to the Manchu cause and betrayed his Wudang brothers. Former brother-in-arms of Hidden Needle Lu and Ma Zhen. His prime weapon is the sword (of irresistible hardness and sharpness) known as Frozen Emerald.

ZHAO, BUDDHA Zhao Banshan, Hidden Needle Lu's old friend from the Dragon Slayers' Society, now prominent member (third-ranking) of the Red Flower Society; a dart expert, sometimes using copper coins as missiles, nicknamed the Thousand Arm Buddha, or Buddha Zhao for short.

ZHAO HUI, General (1708–1764) Prominent Manchu general responsible for taking possession of the Koran, and quelling the Uighur uprising.

ZHEN YUAN SECURITY AGENCY Highly successful Wells Fargo-style North China enterprise, specializing in escorting valuable goods on long and dangerous journeys.

ZHOU, Lady Second wife of Zhou Zhongying.

ZHOU QI Daughter of Zhou Zhongying, a wild girl of eighteen always getting into trouble. She eventually falls in love with (and marries) Mastermind Xu.

ZHOU YINGJIE Ten-year-old son of Zhou Zhongying, by his second wife.

ZHOU ZHONGYING Lord of Iron Ball Manor, renowned Martial Arts practitioner; a well-respected man with a flowing white beard.

ZHUANGZI A legendary Taoist sage, most probably alive some time during the fourth century B.C.

GENERAL GLOSSARY OF TERMS

ART OF FLYING *see* Lightness kungfu

BANNERS, EIGHT (*baqi*) This was the system of military and social organization used by the Manchus. The three Higher Banners were the Plain White, and the Plain and Bordered Yellow; the five Inferior Banners were the Bordered White, the Plain Red, the Bordered Red, the Plain Blue, and the Bordered Blue. There were also Mongol and Chinese Bannermen.

BLACK SAND PALM KUNGFU (*heishazhang*) An esoteric form of kungfu in which the Twin Knights of West Stream specialized, leaving a black brand-like hand print on their victims.

BROTHER-IN-ARMS (*shixiong, shidi*) Term describing fellow disciples of the same Martial Arts Shifu.

CATTY (*jin*) A traditional Chinese measurement of weight, roughly equivalent to an English pound. A catty was divided into sixteen taels.

DHARMA Buddhist law or doctrine.

DRAGON SLAYERS' SOCIETY (*tulong bang*) A secret anti-Manchu organization whose power and influence had been widespread during the reign of Yong Zheng, the former Emperor. It was suppressed in the seventh year of Qian Long.

DRAGON WELL (*longjing*) A superior variety of tea, grown in the hills near Hangzhou.

DRUNKEN BOXING A somewhat eccentric style of kungfu, in which the movements of a drunken man are imitated.

EAGLE'S CLAW Slang expression for a thug employed by the Imperial Court.

EIGHT TRIGRAM KUNGFU Swordplay and boxing style used by Wang Weiyang. The Eight Trigrams were the eight basic symbols of the ancient divinatory classic *The Book of Changes*. Eight Trigram kungfu, like Wudang kungfu, was one of the softer, Inner Force Martial Arts traditions.

FIVE ELEMENT WHEEL A steel ring covered in knives, on the end of a handle, used as a Martial Arts weapon. The Five Elements in Chinese cosmology, with their associated colours and directions, were: Water (north, black), Metal (west, white), Fire (south, red), Wood (east, blue), Earth (centre, yellow).

FROZEN EMERALD The devastatingly sharp and hard sword belonging to Fire Hand Zhang.

GO-PIECE PROJECTILES These pebble-like objects were used with amazing accuracy and effect by Chen Jialuo, the Red Flower Helmsman.

HEAVEN MOUNTAINS (*Tian Shan*) A School of Martial Arts, to which the Twin Eagles and Huo Qingtong belong. Named after the Heaven Mountains range in northwest Turkestan.

HODJA (Turkish *khojah*) A term of respect for a Muslim teacher or leader, somewhat similar to Mullah. The Hodjas were often descended from saintly families. The Khozi Hodja, or 'Little' Hodja, Muzhuolun, for example, father of Huo Qingtong and Hasli, was a historical figure, a Sufi saintly ruler, descended from the Afaqi line of the Makhdumzada family that had ruled the area of Central Asia kown as Kashgaria for centuries. His family was originally descended from the famous sixteenth-century Naqshbandi saint known as Makhdum-I A'zam, in Bukhara. Muzhuolun's brother, the 'Big' or 'Greater' Hodja, Burhan-al-Din, was grandfather of Jehangir, the Muslim leader who was to make more trouble for the Chinese in the 1820s. For an excellent account of this Central Asian dimension of Chinese history in the Manchu dynasty, see Joseph Fletcher, 'Ch'ing Inner Asia, c.1800', in *Cambridge History of China*, volume 10, Part 1, pp. 35–106.

HUNDRED FLOWERS KUNGFU An elaborate kungfu style.

INNER FORCE (*neigong*) Literally 'inner work', this is the part of kungfu concerned not so much with particular techniques (moves, styles), but with the basic underlying physical (breathing, posture, etc.) and spiritual (meditation, concentration, consciousness) training, which gives the techniques their inner strength.

IRON PIBA KUNGFU A style of kungfu involving the throwing of piba-shaped missiles or darts, a speciality of the Han School of Luoyang.

KANG These heated bed-platforms, usually built out of brick, were (and are) very popular in northern China.

KARMA The Buddhist law of cause and effect, by which actions and thoughts in one life create a necessary response and due retribution in a subsequent life. Human destiny is determined by acts done in an earlier existence.

KAZAKHS Turkic-speaking Muslim ethnic group living on both sides of the Heaven Mountains range (i.e. some in present-day Kazakhstan, some in Xinjiang). They have always been renowned for their horsemanship.

KOUMISS Fermented mare's milk, drunk by nomads of Central Asia.

KUNGFU (*gongfu*) This is the general term used in the West and in Cantonese usage for all types of Martial Arts, and, in a broader (and more ancient) sense, a word for time spent in training and self-cultivation, and for all forms of skill and attainment. ('In this sense, Margot Fonteyn and Otto Klemperer are masters of kungfu.' Howard Reid and Michael Croucher, *The Way of the Warrior*, 1995). Traditionally the fighting arts were referred to in Chinese as Arts of the Fist (*quanshu*), and more recently as Martial Arts (*wushu*). The various Schools of kungfu developed many different styles of fighting.

LAMAISM This was the broad term for the Buddhism of Tibet and Mongolia, to which the Manchu Imperial House subscribed.

LIGHTNESS KUNGFU (*qing-gong*) A type of advanced (and semi-legendary) kungfu involving extra-fast running and super-human leaps of a levitational kind.

LIMITLESS OCCULT KUNGFU (*wuji xuangong*) A Wudang style of kungfu.

LONG ARM FIST Another Wudang style of kungfu.

MANCHUS This clan of the Jurched Tartars, from the north-eastern region now known as Manchuria, conquered and occupied China during the mid-seventeenth century, founding the dynasty known in Chinese as the Qing.

MOVE (*zhao*) This is one of the most basic elements in kungfu. A single move would have its own name, sometimes a graphic description of the move itself, more often a fanciful and poetic suggestion of it. A particular style or form of kungfu would consist of one or more series or sets of moves.

PIBA A Chinese musical instrument with four strings, in sound somewhat resembling the mandolin, but larger.

RED FLOWER SOCIETY An anti-Manchu secret society, with the overthrow of the Manchus and the restoration of a Chinese Emperor to the Dragon Throne as its twin main goals. When its members (or Brothers) function as a group, they are referred to in the text collectively, in almost Homeric fashion, as the Red Flower heroes.

SECURITY AGENCY (*biaoju*) These organizations, and the fearless fighters who served as escorts in them, became a standard feature of Martial Arts novels.

SHAOLIN KUNGFU This School of kungfu was named after the Shaolin Temple near the Central Sacred Peak (*zhongyue*) of Mount Song in central China, and is the oldest of the Martial Arts lineages, its origins dating back to the Indian Buddhist monk Batuo in the fifth century, and to the sixth-century Zen Patriarch Bodhidharma (also an Indian). Over the ages, it developed into countless styles and sub-divisions, the so-called Seventy-Two Arts of Shaolin. For example, the style made famous by the late Bruce Lee, Wing Chun, is a Cantonese development of the Southern Shaolin tradition. Many secret societies in Chinese history had links with Shaolin (e.g. the White Lotus sect, the Triads, the Boxers). The main Southern Shaolin Temple or Monastery (to which Helmsman Chen pays a visit towards the end of *Book and Sword*) was in Fujian Province.

SHIFU This is the traditional term of respect (meaning Master, or Guru) used of a Martial Arts adept by his disciples. 'A Teacher for a day is a Father for life,' goes the old Chinese saying.

SOFT CLOUD A style of kungfu known only to Red Flower Society members.

TAEL (*liang*) A traditional Chinese measurement of weight, roughly equivalent to an English ounce.

THREE PART A style of kungfu belonging to the Heaven Mountains School.

THREE THRUSTS AND SIX HOLES According to the Red Flower Society's code, a member who had committed an offence in a moment of confusion and sincerely regretted it could pierce his own thigh three times with a knife so that it penetrated right through, an act known as the Three Thrusts and Six Holes.

UIGHUR The Uighurs are the principal indigenous people of Muslim 'Chinese' Turkestan (now referred to by the Chinese as Xinjiang, or New Territory). There are at present some eight million of them. They are Turkic-speaking, turban-wearing people, who originally migrated westwards from Mongolia during the eighth and ninth centuries. Their written script is traditionally Arabic, and their physical features are almost Caucasian, with Indo-Iranian and

Mongoloid elements (many could be easily mistaken for Greeks or Southern Italians). In *Book and Sword*, Louis Cha refers to the Khozi Hodja Muzhuolun's people somewhat vaguely as Muslims. But he makes a point of differentiating between them and the Kazakhs. In this translation, they are always presumed to be Uighurs, although they may have included Tajiks and Uzbeks. As Joseph Fletcher points out in the *Cambridge History of China*, 'the people of Eastern Turkestan had no common ethnic designation for themselves other than *yerlik*, which merely means "local".'

VITAL POINT Nerve centres on the body which, when struck, can cause paralysis or even death. The same points are used for a different purpose in acupuncture.

WOLF'S TOOTH CLUB A Martial Arts weapon.

WUDANG A School of Martial Arts, based on Wudang Mountain, in Hubei Province. This lineage of kungfu was second only to the Shaolin School. Here on Wudang Mountain, in the later years of the Song dynasty, a Taoist Master named Zhang Sanfeng retreated deep into the mountains and developed a softer style of kungfu, based on Shaolin, but placing greater emphasis on meditation and on inner training of the *qi*. This was the forerunner of the Taiji (Grand Ultimate) kungfu so popular in the West today.

YAMEN Chinese term for a government office or compound.

NOTE ON PRONUNCIATION

In this book, Chinese names and place-names are in general spelled according to the Chinese system known as *Hanyu Pinyin*, which is now internationally accepted. (Occasional exceptions to this rule include well-established geographical names such as the Yangtze River, and the cities of Peking, Nanking, and Canton.) The following short list may help readers with some of the more difficult sounds used in the Pinyin system:

Letter	Pronunciation
c	*ts*
q	*ch*
x	*sh*
z	*dz*
zh	*j*

The following very rough equivalents may also be of help to readers.

Word	Pronunciation
Bo	*Boar* (wild pig)
Cai	*Ts'eye* ('It's eye', without the first vowel)
Cang	*Ts'arng*
Chen	*Churn*
Cheng	*Churng*
Chong	*Choong* (as in 'book')
Chuan	*Chwan*
Dang	*Darng* or *Dung* (as in 'cow dung')
Dong	*Doong* (as in 'book')
Emei	*Er-may*
Feng	*Ferng*
Gui	*Gway*
Guo	*Gwore*
Jia	*Jeeyar*
Jiang	*Jeeyung*
Kong	*Koong* (as in 'book')
Li	*Lee*

Long	*Loong* (as in 'book')
Lü	*Lew* (as in French 'tu')
Qi	*Chee*
Qian	*Chee-yenne*
Qing	*Ching*
Rong	*Roong* (as in 'book')
Shi	*Shhh!*
Si	*Szzz!*
Song	*Soong* (as in 'book')
Shun	*Shoon* (as in 'should')
Wen	as in 'forgot*ten*'
Xi	*Shee*
Xiao	*Shee-ow* (as in 'shee-cow' without the 'c')
Xing	*Shing*
Xiong	*Sheeoong*
Xu	*Shyeu* (as in French 'tu')
Yan	*Yen*
Yi	*Yee*
You	*Yo*-heave-ho
Yu	*Yew* tree (as in French 'tu')
Yuan	*You, Anne!*
Zha	*Jar*
Zhe	*Jerrr!*
Zhen	*Jurn*
Zhi	*Jirrr!*
Zhou	*Joe*
Zhu	*Jew*
Zhuang	*Jwarng*
Zi	*Dzzz!*
Zong	*Dzoong* (as in 'book')
Zuo	*Dzore*

CHAPTER 1

Golden Needles and Flies; Knights in Pairs;
Uighurs and Guards; Black Gold Gorge; The Thing;
Holed Up in the Inn; To the Manor; The Flower of Authority

Golden Needles and Flies

It was a hot summer's day in June, 1754, the eighteenth year of
Emperor Qian Long's reign. In the inner courtyard of the military
commander's Yamen in Fufeng, in the north-western province of
Shaanxi, a fourteen-year-old girl skipped towards her teacher's
study, eager for a history lesson. All was peaceful: not even a breath
of cool wind stirred. The girl hesitated, afraid that her teacher had
not yet woken from his afternoon nap. Quietly, she circled round
to the window, pierced a hole in its paper covering with one of her
golden hair clips, and peeped inside.

She saw her teacher sitting cross-legged on a chair, smiling.
His right hand waved slightly in the air, and there was a faint clicking
sound. Glancing over to where the sound came from, she saw
dozens of flies on a wooden partition opposite, all as still as could
be. Puzzled, she looked more closely and noticed a golden needle
as slender as a hair protruding from the back of each fly. The needles
were tiny and she was only able to see them because they reflected
the rays of the late afternoon sun slanting in through the windows.

Flies were still buzzing around the room. The teacher waved
his hand again, there was another faint click, and another fly was
pinned to the partition. Absolutely fascinated, she ran to the door
and burst in, shouting: 'Teacher! Show me how to do that!'

The girl was Li Yuanzhi, the only child of the local military
commander, Li Kexiu. Her fresh, beautiful face was flushed with
excitement.

'Hm,' said her teacher, a scholar in his mid-fifties named Lu
Feiqing. 'Why aren't you playing with your friends? I suppose you
want to hear some more stories?'

Moving a chair over to the partition, she jumped up to look,
then pulled the needles out of the flies one by one, wiped them

clean on a piece of paper, and handed them back to him. 'That was a brilliant bit of kungfu, teacher,' she said. 'You have to show me how to do it.'

Lu smiled. 'If you want to learn kungfu, there's no one better at it within a hundred miles of here than your own father,' he said.

'My father knows how to shoot an eagle with an arrow, but he can't kill a fly with a needle. If you don't believe me, I'll go and ask him.'

Lu thought for a moment, and then nodded. 'All right, come tomorrow morning and I'll teach you. Now go off and play. And you're not allowed to tell a soul about me killing the flies. If anyone finds out, I won't teach you.'

Yuanzhi was overjoyed. She knelt before him and kowtowed eight times. Lu accepted the gesture with a smile. 'You pick things up very quickly. It would be fitting that I should teach you this kind of kungfu. However…' He paused, deep in thought.

'Teacher,' said Yuanzhi hurriedly. 'I'll do anything you say.'

'I must be honest with you. I disapprove of much of what your father does,' he said. 'When you're older, I hope you will be able to think differently, to distinguish between right and wrong, good and evil. If you wish me to be your Shifu, you must also accept the strict rules of the Wudang Martial Arts Order to which I belong. Do you think you can?'

'I will always obey my Shifu's orders,' she said.

'If you ever use the skills I teach you to do evil, I will not have the slightest hesitation in taking your life.'

His face and voice had become stern and hard, and for a moment Yuanzhi was frightened. But then she smiled. 'Shifu,' she said, 'I'll be good. And anyway, I don't believe you could ever bring yourself to kill me!'

Knights in Pairs

The Wudang School, of which Lu Feiqing was one of the most famous members, stressed the use of Inner Force kungfu. In his prime, Lu had roamed China fighting for justice, and had become a famous member of the Dragon Slayers' Society, a secret anti-Manchu organization whose power and influence had been widespread during the reign of Yong Zheng, former Emperor and father of Qian Long. But the Society had been rigorously suppressed, and by the seventh or eighth year of Emperor Qian Long's reign (1743), it had disintegrated, and Lu had fled to the border areas of China. The Manchu Court dispatched men to look for him, but he was quick-witted and a good fighter and managed to avoid capture. Working on the old principle that 'small crooks hide in the wilderness, middling crooks in the city, and big crooks in the very midst of officialdom,' Lu eventually made his way to Commander Li's household and set himself up there as a teacher. It never once occurred to the Manchu military serving under Li that the softly-spoken, cultivated tutor teaching their commander's daughter was the redoubtable Wudang warrior, Lu Feiqing, known in the Martial Arts world of River and Lake as Hidden Needle Lu.

From that summer's day in 1754, Lu began teaching Yuanzhi the basic techniques of the Wudang School kungfu style, known as Limitless Occult kungfu. He taught her how to control her emotions and thoughts, and how to perform the series of moves known as the Ten Tapestries and the Thirty-Two Long-Arm Blows. He trained her to use her eyes and ears, and showed her the use of hand darts and other hidden projectiles.

More than two years passed. Yuanzhi was hard-working and clever, and made fast progress. Her father, Commander Li, was transferred even further north-west, to Gansu Province, as military commander at Anxi, one of the major towns in the north-west border regions, bordering on the great desert of central Asia. His family, including the tutor Lu, went with him.

Another two years passed during which Lu taught Yuanzhi the Soft Cloud sword technique and the secret of the Golden Needles. She did as her teacher had ordered, and did not tell a soul that she was learning any special sort of kungfu. Every day she practised by herself in the rear flower garden. When the young mistress was practising her kungfu, the maids (who knew that their young mistress had had an interest in the Martial Arts ever since she was a child) did not understand what they saw, and the menservants did not dare to watch too closely.

Commander Li was a capable man, and he advanced steadily through the ranks of officialdom. In 1759, the twenty-third year of Emperor Qian Long's reign, he distinguished himself in the battle of Ili, in which the largest of the tribes in the Muslim areas was defeated, and received an Imperial decree promoting him to the post of Commander-in-Chief of Zhejiang Province in the south-east.

Yuanzhi had been born and raised in the remote border areas of the north-west, and the prospect of travelling to new and beautiful lands filled her with excitement. She pressed her teacher to come as well, and Lu, who had been absent from the central areas of China proper for a long time, agreed with pleasure.

Li Kexiu went ahead with a small escort to take up his post and left his chief-of-staff and twenty soldiers in charge of his family, who were to follow him. The officer's name was Zeng, a vigorous and energetic man in his forties who sported a small moustache.

The entourage consisted of more than a dozen mules and a few horses. Lady Li sat in a mule-drawn carriage, but her daughter Yuanzhi couldn't bear to be cooped up and insisted on riding. It would have been improper for the daughter of a high official to be seen riding in public, so she changed into boy's clothes. These made her look so extraordinarily dashing and handsome that she refused to change back into her normal attire no matter what anyone said. All Lady Li could do was sigh and let her daughter have her way.

It was a late autumn day. Lu rode far behind the group, taking in the passing scenery as the colours of late afternoon merged into evening. But there was little to see along the ancient road except yellow sand, withered grasses, and the occasional crow flying homewards. A breeze sprang up from the west and Lu began to recite some verses he knew by heart, by the renowned patriot poet, Xin Qiji, of the Song dynasty:

> Broken by a hundred battles
> The exiled general turns
> To gaze across a river
> At his friend
> Left ten thousand miles behind.
> Cold were the waters of the River Yi,
> Cold the whistling west wind,
> White were the caps and gowns of those
> Who came to bid the warrior
> Farewell…

'The poet could have been writing of my own feelings,' he thought. 'He too had watched China fall to the barbarian tribes, and had no way of knowing when the old days would return. No wonder he sang such a sad song.'

The Li family entourage crossed the summit of a hill. Looking at the darkening sky, the muleteers said that another three miles would bring them to Twin Pagodas, a large town, where they planned to spend the night.

Just then, Lu heard the sound of galloping hooves and saw far up ahead two magnificent chestnut horses racing towards them in a cloud of dust. The two riders flashed by, one on either side of the line of mules, and were gone. Lu slapped his horse and caught up with Yuanzhi.

'Did you get a good look at those two?' he asked in a low voice.

'Were they bandits?' she replied excitedly. She would have liked nothing better than for them to be outlaws bent on robbery. It might give her a chance to display the skills she had worked so hard to attain over the past five years.

'It's hard to say,' said Lu. 'But they certainly did not look like ordinary highwaymen.'

'You mean they are kungfu masters?'

'From the way they ride their horses, I'd say it's unlikely they are novices.'

As the entourage neared the town, two more horsemen galloped past.

'Mm, this is very strange,' mused Lu. The country was desolate and the evening mist was thickening. He wondered why anyone would set out on a journey at this time of day.

Not long after, the mule-train entered the town. Officer Zeng led them to a large inn and Yuanzhi and her mother were shown to one of the best rooms. Lu was given a smaller room. After he had eaten dinner, a servant accompanied him to his room with a lantern. Lu was about to go to sleep when, in the stillness of the night, a dog barked and from far away he heard the faint sound of galloping horses approaching. He thought again about the four riders they had passed on the road.

The clip-clop of horses' hooves came closer and stopped right in front of the inn. There was a knock on the front door and Lu heard a servant open it and say: 'You've been riding hard. There's food and drink prepared for you.'

'Go and feed the horses quickly,' said a rough voice. 'We must start out again as soon as we've eaten.'

Lu considered the situation. Groups of men hurrying towards the north-west, and judging by the way they rode, all of them expert in the Martial Arts. In all his years in the border areas, he had never seen anything like it. He slipped quietly out of his room, crossed the courtyard, and went round to the back of the inn.

'All right, you say the new Helmsman is very young,' he heard the rough-voiced man say from inside. 'Do you think he will be able to control all the Brothers?'

Lu followed the voice and stationed himself underneath a window.

'He'll have to,' he heard the other say. 'It was the old master's wish.'

The man had a deep, sonorous voice, and Lu could sense the Inner Force resonating in it. Not daring to make a hole in the window-paper to peep through, he continued to listen from where he was, breathing as lightly as he could.

'Of course it was,' the rough-throated one replied. 'But we don't know if the new Helmsman will be willing to do it.'

'You don't have to worry about that,' said the other. 'He'll follow the old master's wishes all right.'

He said the word 'follow' with a peculiar southern Chinese accent, and Lu's heart jumped. 'Where have I heard that voice before?' he thought. He searched through his mind, and finally remembered: it belonged to his old friend Zhao Banshan, whom he had known twenty years before in the Dragon Slayers' Society. Zhao was about ten years younger than he was, but the two had often trained together, and had a great respect for each other. Lu had heard no news of him since the Dragon Slayers' Society had broken up and he was delighted at chancing upon an old friend in such an unlikely place. He was about to call out to Zhao, when the light in the room was suddenly doused and a dart shot out of the window.

But it was not aimed at Lu. Another figure shifted in the shadows nearby, caught the dart, and stood up, about to challenge the dart thrower. Lu leapt over and whispered fiercely:

'Don't make a sound! Come with me.' It was Yuanzhi.

No one chased them. Lu pulled Yuanzhi into his room. She was still wearing boy's clothing, and under the light Lu saw an expression of such eagerness on her face that he was both angry and amused.

'Yuanzhi, do you know what sort of men you are dealing with? What do you think you were doing, trying to pick a fight with them?' he asked sternly.

'What were *they* doing, shooting a dart at me?' she replied defiantly.

'They're either outlaws, or they're secret society men,' he said. 'I know one of them, and he is every bit as good a fighter as I am. They must be on very urgent business, to be travelling through the night like this. That dart was not meant to injure you, it was just telling you to mind your own business. If he had really wanted to hit you, I doubt if you would have been able to catch it. Now go and sleep.'

They heard a door open and the sound of horses' hooves as the two men galloped away.

The next morning, the Li family mule-train started out again, and travelled ten miles in just over two hours.

'Look, Shifu,' said Yuanzhi. 'There's someone coming.'

Two chestnut horses galloped towards them, and because of the previous night's incident, they paid particular attention to the riders. The horses were fine, spirited beasts, and identical in every respect. What was even stranger was that the two riders were also identical. They looked like twins. Both were aged about forty, tall and thin with faces as yellow as wax, sunken eyes, and long slanting eyebrows: the effect was frightening.

As they passed by, the two men glanced at Yuanzhi with their strange eyes. She reined in her horse and stared back belligerently, but they took no notice and raced on westwards.

'Where did that pair of ghosts come from, I wonder,' she said.

Lu glanced back at the receding figures. They looked for all the world like a couple of bamboo twigs on horseback. 'That's it!' he cried all of a sudden. 'Of course! It must be them!'

'You recognize them?' she asked excitedly.

'They must be the Twin Knights of West Stream. Everyone calls them Black Death and White Death.'

Yuanzhi laughed. 'Their nicknames really suit them. They look just like a couple of skeletons.'

'Young girls shouldn't say such things,' said Lu. 'They may be ugly but they are skilled fighters. I've never met them myself, but from what I've heard, they travel the country fighting evil and doing good. They have been inseparable ever since they were boys. They are widely known as outlaws, but they steal only from the rich and help the poor. They have made quite a name for themselves.'

'But if they are identical, why are they called Black and White?'

'From what I've been told, the only difference between them is that one has a black mole above the corner of one eye, and the other doesn't. There's probably no one better at Black Sand Palm kungfu than those two.'

'What are they doing out here in the border country?' Yuanzhi asked.

'I have no idea,' Lu replied. 'I've never heard of them operating here before.'

As he spoke, they heard more horses coming towards them. This time, the riders were a Taoist priest, and a hunchback dressed in brightly coloured clothes. The priest had a long-sword slung across his back. His face was pale and sickly and he had only one arm: his left sleeve was tucked under his belt.

Seeing the hunchback's ugly face and his garish attire, Yuanzhi laughed. 'Shifu,' she shouted before Lu could stop her, 'look at that hunchback!'

The hunchback glared at her angrily and, as he passed, stretched out his hand to grab hold of her. The one-armed priest seemed to have guessed what he was thinking of doing, and stopped his hand with a flick of his riding-whip. 'Don't go making trouble,' he growled.

Lu and Yuanzhi looked back and saw the two horses breaking into a gallop. Suddenly, the hunchback did a reverse somersault off the back of his horse, and with three bounds covered the distance to Yuanzhi. Yuanzhi's sword was in her hand, but the hunchback did not attack her. Instead, he grabbed the tail of her horse so that the animal, which had been cantering along, reared back on its hind legs, whinnying loudly. The hunchback's strength was frightening: the horse had not pulled him forward an inch. He chopped at the horse's tautly-stretched tail with his right hand, and snapped the end clean off as if with a knife. The horse lunged forward, and Yuanzhi was almost thrown. The hunchback turned and ran off, covering the ground swiftly despite his short legs and stocky frame. He looked just like a ball bouncing and tumbling through the sand. In a second, he caught up with his own horse, which was still galloping westwards, leapt onto its back, and soon disappeared from view.

'Shifu!' Yuanzhi called out in a plaintive voice, angry at having been humiliated in this way. Lu frowned and was about to berate her when he saw her eyes glistening with tears and stopped himself.

At that very moment, they heard a shout from behind: 'Weiyang! Weiyang!'

Yuanzhi was mystified. 'Shifu! What's that?' she asked.

'It's the call of a Security Agency shouter,' he said. 'Agencies like that hire out bodyguards, or provide escorts for valuable goods and important people, especially on long and dangerous journeys. Every Agency has a different call, and uses it to let both outlaws and friends know who they are. The Security Agency business is based much more on goodwill than on fighting ability. If the head of an Agency is generous and creates a lot of goodwill, he will make a lot of friends, and his business will prosper. Even outlaws, when they hear the call, will let them pass without attacking. "Making friends is more effective than joining fists," as the old saying goes. Now, if *you* were to try the Agency business...ha! That would be a real disaster! With all the people you've annoyed in less than half a day, you'd have trouble travelling an inch, even if you were ten times the fighter you are now.'

'Which Agency's call is that, Shifu?' she asked, ignoring his teasing.

'That's the Zhen Yuan Agency from Peking, probably the biggest in all of north China. The head of the Agency is Wang Weiyang, the North China Earth-Shaker. He must be seventy by now, but they're still calling out "Weiyang!", so apparently he hasn't retired yet. I sometimes think he ought to. The Zhen Yuan Agency has been making big profits for forty years now. That should be enough for anyone.'

'Have you ever met him, Shifu?' Yuanzhi asked.

'I've met him. He uses an Eight Trigram sword and the Eight Trigram boxing technique. In the old days, there was no one in north China who could beat him. That's why they called him the Earth-Shaker.'

Yuanzhi was elated by all this adventure and excitement. 'They're travelling very fast. When they catch up with us, you can point the old hero out to me.'

'He's hardly likely to come out on a trip like this himself!' Lu said. 'You really are a silly girl!'

Yuanzhi sulked. She was always being put down like this by her Shifu. It wasn't fair. She spurred her horse forward and caught up with the carriage, planning to talk to her mother for a while to cheer herself up a bit. Then she glanced round, and saw the stub of her horse's tail. She shuddered. There was nothing unusual about breaking a spear with one blow of the hand, but a horse's tail was pliable. How had the hunchback managed to snap it? She reined in her horse, meaning to wait for Lu to catch up so she could ask him, but changed her mind and galloped up the line to Officer Zeng instead.

'Officer Zeng,' she said, pouting. 'My horse's tail looks so ugly.'

'Why not take this horse of mine,' Zeng replied, guessing what it was that had upset her. 'He's in a bad mood today and won't do anything I say. You're such a good horsewoman, mistress. Perhaps you could help me teach him how to behave.'

'I probably won't be able to handle him either,' she said modestly. The two exchanged horses. Zeng's horse was of course very docile.

'Well done, mistress,' he complimented her. 'Even horses do your bidding.'

The Agency's call came closer and closer, and before long, a mule-train consisting of a score or more heavily laden animals began to file past.

Lu was afraid one of the Agency men would recognize him, so he covered the top part of his face with a large fur cap. As they trotted past, he heard one of them remark: 'According to Han, Jiao Wenqi's body has been found.'

Lu's heart missed a beat as he heard the name. Jiao was one of the group of fighters known as the Six Devils of Manchuria and a formidable fighter himself. Five years before, while on an errand to the Muslim regions, Jiao had discovered that Hidden Needle Lu was hiding in Commander Li's household and had come at the dead of night with two other fighters with the aim of capturing Lu and taking him back to Peking to claim the price on his head. After a hard fight, Lu had succeeded in killing all three of them and had hidden their corpses on a deserted hillside.

Lu looked round at the man who had spoken, but only had time to see that he had a full beard and a face as black as thunder. Once he had passed, Lu was able to see that he was carrying on his back a red knapsack and a pair of the weapons known as Five Element Wheels, steel rings covered in knives.

'Could it be that the Manchurian Devils have become Agency escorts?' he wondered. Of the Six Devils, Lu had only ever set eyes on Jiao, but he knew that the rest were excellent fighters, and that two of them, the Yan brothers, excelled in the Five Element Wheel.

Lu thought about the number of top fighters they had seen in the past two days and wondered if all this movement and activity could possibly have anything to do with himself. On the surface, the Zhen Yuan Agency men seemed to be on an escort assignment, so they did not pose a threat. As for the fighters travelling westwards in pairs, they did not seem to be looking for him. But where were they going and why?

Having exchanged mounts with Officer Zeng, Yuanzhi reined in her horse to wait for Lu to catch up.

'Shifu,' she smiled. 'How come no more riders have passed us? Since yesterday we must have seen five pairs. I want to see a few more of these heroes.'

Something about what she said jogged Lu's mind. He slapped his thigh. 'What an old fool I am!' he rebuked himself out loud. 'Why didn't I think of it before? They must be Greeting the Dragon's Head.'

'What's that?' she asked.

'It is the most solemn of the ceremonies held by the secret societies to honour an important personage. Usually, the six most senior men in the society are chosen to go to greet the guest, but for really important meetings, twelve are chosen and they go in pairs. Five pairs have passed us now, so there must still be one pair to come.'

'Which secret society do they belong to?' Yuanzhi asked.

'I don't know. But if the Twin Knights of West Stream and that hunchback are members, whichever society it is, its power and influence must be tremendous. These are very serious people we are dealing with. Whatever you do, don't provoke anyone else, do you hear?'

Yuanzhi nodded, and waited expectantly to see who else would pass them by.

Uighurs and Guards

Midday came, but there was no sign of anyone on the road ahead as they continued to travel eastwards. Lu was surprised and wondered if he could have guessed wrongly. Finally, instead of riders approaching from in front, they became aware of the sound of camel bells from behind and saw a dust cloud rising as a large desert caravan hurried towards them.

The caravan consisted of dozens of camels with twenty or thirty horses squeezed in between them, all ridden by Uighurs with high noses and sunken eyes. They had thick beards, and white cloths tied around their heads. Scimitars hung from their waists. Muslim traders were a common sight on the road back to China and Lu did not consider it unusual. What was unusual was the dazzlingly beautiful young girl he saw in their midst, dressed in yellow robes and riding a black horse. She was a truly poetic sight. Hers was the pristine beauty of the plum-blossom in the first days of spring; her soulful gaze called to mind the orchid flower chilled by the first frost of autumn. Her cheeks emanated the rosy glow of sunset clouds reflected in a crystal pond; her eyes shone with the clear, piercing light of the moon, casting its beams on the cold waters of the river.

Lu was impressed, but did no more than glance at her. Yuanzhi, however, stared in open-mouthed wonder. Growing up as she had in the north-west border country, she had seen few good-looking girls, let alone girls as beautiful as this one. She was about the same age as Yuanzhi, eighteen or nineteen, with a dagger at her waist and long braids hanging down her back. She wore a full-length pale yellow gown, leather boots, and a small hat embroidered with gold silk, on the side of which was fastened a turquoise feather. She was altogether an enchanting sight.

The girl trotted by, and Yuanzhi spurred on her horse and followed, gazing fixedly at her. The girl was annoyed at being stared at disrespectfully by a Chinese boy, and she whirled her whip above her head and wrapped it round the mane of Yuanzhi's horse. Giving it a sharp tug, she pulled out a large clump of hair, and the horse reared in pain, almost throwing Yuanzhi to the ground. The Uighur girl cracked the whip in the air and horse hair flew in all directions.

In a fit of pique, Yuanzhi pulled out a steel dart and threw it at the girl's back. But, not wishing to harm her, she also called out: 'Watch out for the dart!' The girl leant to one side, and the dart shot past her right shoulder. She waited until it was about ten feet beyond her, then flicked her whip, caught the dart by its tip, and effortlessly sent it flying back towards Yuanzhi, calling out: 'Hey, little boy! Here's your dart!' Yuanzhi caught it neatly.

The Uighurs in the caravan applauded loudly at the superb skill with which the yellow-robed girl handled her whip. A tall, thick-set man with a heavy black beard (whom she referred to as father) went over and said a few words to her. But she took no further notice of Yuanzhi. The procession of camels and horses moved on, overtook Lady Li's carriage, and gradually disappeared into the distance.

'That girl was impressive, wasn't she?' said Lu.

'Those people spend their lives on horseback. They ought to be good with their whips. But it doesn't mean she knows any real kungfu,' Yuanzhi replied.

Lu laughed. 'Really?'

Towards evening they arrived at the town of Bulongji. There was only one large inn in the town, outside which the Zhen Yuan Agency had already planted its flag. With all these travellers to look after, the inn's servants were very busy. Lu had a wash, and then strolled into the courtyard of the inn with a cup of tea in his hand. In the dining-hall, he saw two tables of Agency men drinking and talking loudly. One of the guards had placed his weapons, the pair of Five Element Wheels, down on the ground. He had the red knapsack on his back.

Lu took a sip of tea, and stood there in the courtyard gazing casually up at the sky.

One of the guards laughed. 'Yan, once you've delivered that red thing safely to Peking, General Zhao Hui will reward you with at least a thousand taels, won't he? Then you can go and have a good time with that girlfriend of yours, Xibao.'

So it really is one of the Yan brothers, Lu thought. He paid even closer attention to what was being said.

'Reward?' said Yan. 'Ha! I'm sure everyone will get something.'

'Your girl has probably gone off with some other man willing to make an honest woman of her,' added a strange, almost effeminate voice. Lu looked over out of the corner of his eye, and saw a man with a sly face and a slight figure, also dressed as an Agency guard.

Yan grunted, obviously displeased.

'Shut up, Tong,' the first guard retorted. 'You never have anything good to say.'

Tong laughed. 'All right,' he said, still speaking in the same feeble high-pitched voice. 'But Yan, fun is fun and serious is serious. Don't think about Xibao too much or you might find someone has stolen that red knapsack from off your back. No one minds if you lose your head, but the Agency's reputation has to be maintained.'

'Don't worry,' Yan replied angrily. 'If those Uighurs try getting it back, I'll soon put an end to their nonsense. I am not one of the Six Manchurian Devils for nothing! I got where I am with real kungfu, not like some weaklings I know in the Agencies. All they know how to do is eat and fart!'

Lu looked at the red knapsack on Yan's back: it wasn't big, and from the look of it, whatever was inside was very light.

'The Six Manchurian Devils are famous, I'll grant you that,' said Tong. 'It's a pity Jiao was done in. And we still don't even know who the murderer was.'

Yan banged the table. 'Who says we don't know? It's got to be the Red Flower Society!'

That's strange, Lu thought: I'm the one who killed Jiao. What's this about some Red Flower Society? He walked slowly around the courtyard pretending to inspect the flowers, moving closer to the group of guards.

Tong would not let the matter drop. 'If it wasn't for the fact that all I can do is eat and fart,' he said, 'I would have settled things with the Red Flower Society long ago.'

Yan shook with anger. One of the other guards broke in to mediate: 'The fact of the matter is, the Red Flower Society's leader died last month,' he said. 'They've lost their man in command, so who is there to settle with? And another thing, where's the proof that Jiao *was* murdered by the Red Flower Society? They'll simply deny the charge, and then what are you going to do?'

'Yes,' said Tong changing his tack. 'We daren't provoke them, but surely we've got enough guts to bully a few Uighurs. This little trinket we've snatched is as precious to them as life itself. In the future, if General Zhao ever wants money from them, or cattle and sheep, do you think they'd dare to refuse? I tell you, Yan, stop thinking about that girlfriend of yours. When we get back to Peking, you should ask General Zhao to give you a little Uighur girl for your mistress. Then you can really...'

Before he could finish, a piece of dried mud flew out of nowhere and lodged itself in his mouth. Tong began to choke. Two of the other guards snatched up their weapons and rushed outside while Yan picked up his Five Element Wheels and looked warily around. His younger brother came running in, and both of them stood there together, not daring to move for fear of falling into some trap. Tong spat out the mud and began uttering all manner of profanities, in his high-pitched squeaky voice.

Two other guards, whose names were Tai and Qian, rushed in through the door. 'The little bastard's gone,' one of them said. 'No sign of him.'

Lu had observed the whole incident and laughed inwardly at the helpless expression on Tong's face. Then he saw a shadow darting across the rafters in a corner of the dining-hall. It was already growing dark, but he spotted the same figure leap off the corner of the roof, land noiselessly, and speed off eastwards.

Lu wanted to know who had treated Tong to a mouthful of mud and, making use of his highly developed kungfu skills in the Art of Flying, he followed, the teacup still balanced in his hand. The pace was fast, but the person he was following was not aware of his presence.

Lu's quarry had a slim figure and moved daintily, almost like a girl. They crossed a hill and an ink-black forest loomed ahead. The person slipped into the trees with Lu close behind. Underneath, the ground was covered with dead leaves and twigs which crackled as he stepped on them. Afraid of giving himself away, he slowed down. Just then, the moon broke through the clouds and a shaft of clear light shone down through the branches, covering the earth with a jumble of ghostly shadows. In the distance he saw the flash of a yellow gown, and his quarry moved out of the forest.

He followed to the edge of the trees. Beyond was a large expanse of grass on which were pitched eight or nine tents. His curiosity got the better of him, and he decided to go and have a closer look. He waited until two guards had turned away, then jumped across with a leap known as Swallow Gliding Over Water and landed behind one of the camels grazing beside the tents. Crouching low, he ran behind the largest tent, pitched in the centre. Inside, he could hear people talking agitatedly in the Uighur language. He had lived in the border country for many years, and could understand some of what was said. Carefully, he lifted up a corner of the canvas and looked inside.

The tent was lit by two oil lamps, under which a large number of people were seated on carpets. He recognized them as the Uighur caravan that had passed them that day. The yellow-robed girl stood up and drew a dagger from her waist. She cut the index finger of

her left hand with the tip of the blade and let several drops of blood
fall into a cup of koumiss, the fermented mare's-milk wine drunk
by the inhabitants of Central Asia. Then, one by one, every Uighur
in the tent did likewise. The tall bearded man that the girl had
called father raised the cup and made a short speech of which Lu
could understand only something about 'the Koran' and 'our
homeland.' The yellow-robed girl spoke after him, her voice crisp
and clear. She concluded by saying:

'If the sacred Koran is not recovered, I swear never to return
to our homeland.' The Uighurs lustily repeated the oath. In the
dim light, Lu could see determination and anger written on every
face.

This group of Uighurs that Lu had stumbled across belonged to
one of the richest and most powerful of the nomadic Muslim tribes
of the great range known as Heaven Mountain, numbering nearly
two hundred thousand people. The tall bearded man was the Khozi
Hodja, known by the Chinese as Muzhuolun. He was the leader of
the tribe; a strong fighter, fair and just, he was greatly loved by his
people. The yellow-robed girl was his daughter, Huo Qingtong.

The tribe lived by nomadic herding and contentedly travelled
the great desert of Eastern Turkestan. But the power of the Manchu
Court had gradually extended into the Muslim lands, and its
demands for taxes had increased. At first, the Khozi Hodja had
gone out of his way to comply, and had worked hard to meet the
demands. But the Manchu officials were insatiable and made life
impossible for his tribe. On several occasions, the Hodja sent
missions to the Manchu Court to appeal for a reduction of taxes.
But far from achieving a reduction, the missions only served to
arouse the Court's suspicions. General Zhao Hui, a prominent
Manchu of the Plain Yellow Banner, was given orders to deal with
their insubordination. In the process he discovered that the tribe
owned an ancient manuscript of the Koran, originally brought all
the way from the sacred city of Mecca, which they had treasured
for generations. The General decided to use this Koran as a means
of blackmailing the Uighurs into submission, and he dispatched a
number of top fighters to steal it while the Hodja was away on a
long journey. On his return, the Hodja had convened a great
assembly in the desert, and had personally led a group of hand-
picked men to recover the Sacred Book. They had vowed to lay
down their lives if necessary.

Lu came to the conclusion that the Uighurs' plotting had nothing to do with him. Just as he was leaving to return to the inn, Huo Qingtong, the girl in the yellow robe, caught sight of him.

'There's someone outside,' she whispered to her father and shot out of the tent in time to see a shadow running fast for the trees. With a flick of her hand, she sent a steel dart speeding after him.

Lu heard the projectile whizzing through the air and leant slightly to one side. As it passed, he stretched out the index finger of his right hand and, carefully calculating the speed and direction of the dart, tapped it gently as it passed so that it fell into the teacup he was holding. Then, without looking back, he made use of his levitational skills once more, and virtually flew back to the inn, where he went straight to his room. He took the dart out of the cup and saw that it was made of pure steel with a single feather attached to it. He threw it into his bag.

Black Gold Gorge

The Agency group was the first to start out from the inn early the next day, the shouter shouting their call: 'Weiyang!' Lu noticed that most of the guards were stationed around Yan. The red knapsack on his back was clearly the real treasure being escorted.

Once the Agency men had left, Officer Zeng led his own column out onto the road. At noon, they rested briefly at a place called Yellow Crag after which the road rose steadily upward into the mountains. They planned to cross three ranges that day before stopping in the town of Sandaogou.

The mountain road became increasingly precarious and Yuanzhi and Officer Zeng kept close by Lady Li's mule-drawn carriage, afraid that if one of the animals lost its footing, it could send the carriage crashing into the gorge below. Around mid-afternoon, they arrived at the mouth of Black Gold Gorge, where they saw the Agency men seated on the ground resting. Officer Zeng directed his men to follow suit. Black Gold Gorge was flanked by high peaks with an extremely steep mountain track leading up between them. Stopping further on up the track would be difficult: the top of the gorge would have to be reached at one stretch. While they rested, Lu hung back at the rear and turned his back, not wishing to be seen by the Agency men.

Once they had rested, they all set off again and entered the gorge, the Agency men and the soldiers under Officer Zeng's command forming a long snaking column. Men and animals alike panted up the mountain. The shouts of the muleteers melded into a continuous drone.

Suddenly, Lu saw a figure darting across the crest of a peak to his right, and then seconds later he heard the jangling of camel bells from in front as a group of Uighurs mounted on camels and horses charged down towards them from the top of the gorge. Their hooves sounded like thunder, and the Agency men began shouting, calling on them to slow down.

In an instant, the Uighurs were upon them and four camels quickly encircled Yan, the guard carrying the red knapsack. Each of the four Uighur riders raised a large iron hammer with both hands and brought it smashing down viciously on his head. The mountain road was narrow, leaving little room for manoeuvring, and the camel-men had the advantage of height. Even if he had been a better fighter than he was, Yan would have been unable to avoid the four hammers, each weighing more than a hundred pounds. Both he and his horse were beaten to a bloody pulp.

The yellow-robed Uighur girl, Huo Qingtong, jumped down from her horse and with a flash of her sword cut one of the straps holding the red knapsack to Yan's corpse. But before she had time for a second stroke, she felt a rush of air at her back as a blade sliced towards her. She dodged to one side, then cut the other strap. Her assailant aimed a cutting stroke at her waist to stop her from picking up the knapsack. Unable to avoid the stroke, she raised her sword to block it, and the two blades clashed in a shower of sparks. Looking up, she saw that it was the handsome young boy who had stared at her so disrespectfully the day before. In a sudden fit of anger, she lashed out with three attacking sword strokes, and the two began a fierce duel.

Her assailant, Yuanzhi, was still dressed in boy's clothes. Without stopping to consider the rights and wrongs of the situation, she had decided to get her own back for the damage done to her horse's mane.

Huo Qingtong could see her chance of recovering the Koran slipping away and wanted to finish the fight quickly. She changed to the sword style known as Three Part, and in a few strokes had forced Yuanzhi into retreat. The Three Part sword style was the highest achievement of the Heaven Mountains School of kungfu. It was called Three Part because only a third of each stroke was completed. As the opponent moved to counter one stroke, it changed. It was an intricate and vicious style, with no defensive strokes: attacking and killing was all.

The two went through a dozen or more moves without their blades ever touching, Huo Qingtong completing only a third of each stroke, and then changing it without waiting for her opponent to defend. She cut and thrust at the air around Yuanzhi's body, and the Chinese girl, knowing she could not match her opponent's speed, leapt away. Huo Qingtong did not pursue her but turned back to the knapsack, which she found was already in the hands of a small, thin man standing beside Yan's body. It was the guard named Tong Zhaohe. She lunged at him with her sword.

'Oh dear,' the man squeaked. 'I'd better get out of here!' Tong jumped clear with three quick steps, Huo Qingtong following hard on his heels. She raised her sword to cut him down, but the stroke was blocked by a Five Element Wheel thrust forward by the surviving Yan brother.

Huo Qingtong fought briefly with Yan, whom she recognized as a strong and capable adversary. Then she heard a loud whistle coming from the hilltops, the signal for the Uighurs to retreat, and knew that help for the Agency men was on its way. She saw Tong scampering away with the knapsack so she quickly changed to the Three Part sword style again, forcing Yan to retreat, and then raced after Tong. The whistles became louder.

'Daughter! We must retreat quickly!' the Hodja shouted. She abandoned the chase and directed her comrades as they lifted their dead and wounded onto camels and horses. Then the Uighur column charged on up the mountain path, only to find, a little way further on, a large number of Manchu soldiers blocking their path.

Officer Zeng rode forward, his spear held crosswise. 'You insolent Muslims!' he shouted. 'What is the meaning of this insurrection?'

Two of Huo Qingtong's steel darts hit his hands, sending his spear clattering to the ground. The Hodja raised his sabre high and charged forward with some of his warriors, and the Manchu troops scattered. Boulders crashed down from the mountain tops, pulverizing more than a dozen Manchu troops, and in the midst of the mêlée, the Uighurs made good their escape.

Throughout the battle, Lu had remained on the sidelines, his hands folded inside his sleeves. Yuanzhi had been of great assistance to the Agency men even though she had been beaten by Huo Qingtong, and the Uighurs had been unable to get what they wanted. As the Agency men tended the wounded and carried off the dead, Lu gave Yuanzhi a severe lecture, criticizing her for interfering in the affairs of others, and needlessly making even more enemies.

'There are very few good men amongst the Security Agencies, and many bad ones. Why go siding with evil men?' he scolded her. She hung her head, not daring to look up.

They crossed through the pass and arrived in Sandaogou, a medium-sized market town, as dusk was falling. The muleteers said there was only one inn, called the Antong, and both the Agency men and Officer Zeng's column headed for it. The inn was crude and simple in the extreme, with earthen walls and mud floors. Seeing no servants coming out to greet them, the guard named Tong shouted: 'Are you all dead in there? A pox on eighteen generations of your ancestors!' Yuanzhi frowned. No one had ever dared to use such language within her hearing before.

Just then, they heard the sound of clashing swords from inside. Yuanzhi was delighted. 'Here's some more fun to watch!' she cried, and ran into the inn ahead of the others.

The entrance hall was empty and silent, but passing through to the courtyard, she saw a young woman fighting fiercely with four men. In her left hand was a sword, and in her right, a knife. She was obviously battling for her life. It seemed to Yuanzhi that the four men were trying to force their way into the room outside which the woman was standing. The four were all strong fighters, and well-armed: one wielded a whip, one a staff, one a sword, and one a Devil's Head cutlass.

Lu followed Yuanzhi into the courtyard. 'This is probably another of those secret society people,' he thought.

The woman dodged and parried, holding all four men at bay until suddenly the one wielding the cutlass swung his weapon towards her as another of the attackers thrust his sword at her heart. She fended off the sword with the knife in her right hand, but she could not dodge the cutlass and it struck her on the left shoulder. But she did not give up, and as she continued to fight, drops of her blood flew in all directions

'Don't kill her! We need her alive,' shouted the man with the whip.

Lu's chivalrous heart was moved at the sight of one woman being attacked by four men, and despite his own sensitive situation he could see he might have to lend a hand himself. He watched as the swordsman attacked with a slicing blow from the left. The woman parried it obliquely, but she was already wounded and out of breath. The two blades clashed, and the knife was jolted from her hand and clattered to the ground. The swordsman then thrust his blade at her again, and she frantically dodged to the right, creating an opening through which the man with the cutlass charged towards the door.

Ignoring all danger, the woman plunged her left hand into her gown and drew out two throwing knives which she slung at her enemy as he dodged past her. One of the knives embedded itself in the door-post but the other plunged into his back. Luckily for him, the woman's hand lacked strength (as a consequence of the wound in her left shoulder), and the knife did not kill him. He staggered back, screaming with pain, and pulled the knife out. Meanwhile, the woman was struck on her thigh by the man wielding the staff. She swayed unsteadily, but defiantly resumed her position blocking the doorway.

'Go and help her,' Lu said quietly to Yuanzhi. 'If you can't beat them, I'll come over as well.'

Yuanzhi was bursting to test herself. She leapt forward, her sword at the ready, shouting: 'Four men fighting one woman! You should be ashamed of yourselves!' Seeing someone coming to the aid of the woman, and one of their number already wounded, the four men turned and ran from the inn.

The woman's face was deathly pale and she leaned against the door, breathing heavily. Yuanzhi went over to her.

'Why were they doing that?' she asked, but the woman was temporarily incapable of speech.

At this moment Officer Zeng appeared. He walked over to Yuanzhi. 'Lady Li would like to see you, mistress,' he said, and added in a whisper: 'She's heard that you were involved in a fight on the road and is very upset. You'd better go quickly.'

The woman's expression changed as soon as she saw Officer Zeng's military uniform; she pulled her throwing knife out of the door-post, went back into her room, and banged the door shut without answering Yuanzhi.

Yuanzhi felt that she had been snubbed. She walked over to Lu. 'Shifu, what were they fighting about?' she asked.

'It was probably some kind of vendetta,' he said. 'But it isn't over yet. Those four will be back.'

Yuanzhi was about to ask another question when she heard someone inside the inn shouting and swearing.

'A pox on your ancestors, what do you mean no good rooms? Are you afraid we haven't got the money to pay?' It was Tong's high-pitched voice again.

'Please don't be angry, sir,' an employee of the inn answered. 'We'd never dare offend such an eminent person as yourself. But it is a fact that our few good rooms are all occupied.'

'Who have you got staying in them? I think I'd better go and have a look,' Tong said, walking out into the courtyard.

Just then a door opened, and the young woman who had been fighting leaned out. 'Please bring some hot water,' she called out to a servant.

Tong looked at the woman. He saw her smooth white skin and the beauty of her face and eyes, and noticed on her left arm a bracelet of pearls, each one perfectly formed. The pearls set off to perfection the jade-like delicacy of her wrist. His heart missed a beat, his mouth watered. The woman was speaking Mandarin with a strong southern Chinese accent, and the exotic edge this gave to her voice excited him even further.

'The name's Tong!' he shouted back to the inn employee. 'Tong Zhaohe of the Zhen Yuan Agency! I've passed along this road on business dozens of times, and I've never stayed in anything but the best rooms. If there are no good rooms vacant, you'd better *make* one vacant for me!' The door to the woman's room was still open and he walked straight inside.

'Ai-ya!' the woman exclaimed. She moved to obstruct him, but felt a stab of pain in her thigh and sat down.

As Tong entered the room, he could see that there was a man lying on the kang. The room was dimly lit but he could make out that the man's head was wrapped in bandages, his right arm was in a sling, and one of his legs was also bandaged.

'Who is it?' the man asked in a low voice.

'My name is Tong. I'm a guard with the Zhen Yuan Agency,' he replied. 'We are passing through Sandaogou on business, but there are no decent rooms available here. I was wondering if you could move. Who is this woman? Your wife, or your girlfriend?'

'Get out,' the man ordered hoarsely. His wounds were clearly serious; he was barely able to speak.

'One of them's just a woman, and the other's too badly wounded to even move,' thought Tong, who had not seen the woman fight. 'Now's my chance!'

'If you don't want to give up your room, that's all right by me,' he said with a grin on his face. 'We can all three snuggle up together on this kang. Don't worry, I won't push over onto your side.'

The man on the kang shook with anger.

'Don't get involved with this ruffian,' the woman urged him quietly. 'We can't afford to make any more enemies at the moment.' She turned to Tong: 'You stop your nonsense and get out.'

Tong laughed. 'Can't I stay here and keep you company, darling?'

'Come over here,' the man on the kang said hoarsely.

Tong took a step towards him. 'Why? Do you want to see how handsome I am?'

'I can't see clearly enough,' the man replied.

Tong laughed out loud and took another step towards him. 'Take a closer look. It's a bit like big brother choosing a husband for his sister—'

Before he could finish, the wounded man on the kang had sat up and, as fast as a lightning flash, pressed one of the Vital Points on Tong's ribs, following this up with a sharp blow to his back. Tong flew straight out of the door, and landed heavily in the courtyard. The Agency shouter, Sun, rushed over to help him up.

'Tong,' he whispered. 'Don't provoke them. It looks like they're members of the Red Flower Society.'

'Aagh! I can't move my leg,' Tong cried. 'The Red Flower Society?' he added suddenly. 'How do you know?' He broke into a cold sweat of fear.

'One of the porters told me,' said Sun. 'Those four Yamen officers were here just now to arrest the two of them, and there was quite a fight before they left.'

One of the principal Agency guards, the surviving Yan brother, Yan Shizhang, came over. 'What's going on?' he asked.

'Yan,' Tong shouted from the ground. 'Some bastard from the Red Flower Society's gone and closed one of my points!'

Yan frowned and tried to pull Tong up by his arm. 'We'll go back to their room and talk it over,' he said. His first thought was for the Agency's reputation. It created a bad impression when an

Agency guard was floored and couldn't even get up. Another of the guards, Qian Zhenglun, came over. 'Are you sure it was the Red Flower Society?' he asked Sun.

'When those four officers left, they told the porter that the couple in there were fugitives,' he whispered. 'They told the porter to inform them if they tried to leave. I overhead them talking.'

Qian glanced at Yan and helped him pull Tong up.

'If they're Red Flower Society, I think we ought to let it pass, ' Qian said. 'We'll wait till Tong is better. Did you see what happened when the four officers tried to arrest them just now?' he asked Sun.

'It was some fight,' said Sun, gesticulating wildly. 'The woman fought with a sword in her left hand and a dagger in her right hand. The four of them couldn't get the better of her.'

'Sounds like she's one of Luo's Divine Knife people,' replied Qian, surprised. 'She used throwing knives, I suppose?'

'Yes, yes, she's really deadly. It was incredible!' Sun exclaimed.

Qian turned to Yan. 'It's that fellow Wen of the Red Flower Society. He must be here,' he said. They carried Tong away in silence.

Lu had observed the whole incident, but the Agency guards had talked in low tones, and he had only managed to catch Qian's last two utterances. Yuanzhi walked over and asked him: 'Shifu, when are you going to teach me to close points like that? Did you see how fantastic that move was?'

Lu took no notice of her, but reflected to himself out loud: 'If it is one of Divine Knife Luo's people, I can't just stand by and do nothing.'

'Who's Divine Knife Luo?' Yuanzhi asked.

'A good friend of mine. I hear he passed away. All the moves used by the woman we saw fighting a minute ago belonged to his School.'

As he said this, the two guards Qian and Tai returned with Tong, and helped him stagger over to the woman's room. Sun, who had accompanied them, coughed loudly outside the door and announced in a low voice:

'Three guards of the Zhen Yuan Agency have come to pay their respects to Mr Wen of the Red Flower Society.'

The door creaked open and the woman stood in the doorway staring at them. 'What do you want?' she asked.

'Our friend here didn't know who you were,' Qian said. 'He has insulted you and we have come to apologize. Please be forgiving and don't be offended by what happened.' He bowed low and Tai and Sun followed suit.

'Mistress,' Qian continued. 'We have never met before, but I have heard a great deal about you and your husband. Master Wang, the head of our Agency, was always on very good terms with the leader of your honourable Society, Master Yu, and also with your father Divine Knife Luo. Our friend here is always losing his temper, and talking rubbish—'

The woman cut him short. 'The master has been wounded, and he has just gone to sleep. When he wakes, I will pass on your message. I am not trying to be rude, but his wounds are serious, and he hasn't slept well for two days.' There was an expression of apprehension on her face.

'What sort of wounds does Mr Wen have?' Qian asked. 'We have some Golden Wound Ointment with us.' He wanted to put them in their debt so that they would be obliged to help cure Tong.

'Thank you, but we have medicine of our own,' the woman replied, understanding his intention. 'Your colleague was not touched on an important point. When the master wakes, I will send one of the inn servants round to see to him.'

Seeing that she had agreed to cure Tong, Qian and the others started to retire.

'By the way,' said the woman. 'How did you know our names?'

'With your swords and throwing knives, it was easy to guess,' Qian replied. 'And only Mr Wen closes points like that. It had to be Rolling Thunder Wen Tailai and his wife Luo Bing.'

The woman smiled, flattered at having been recognized.

The Thing

Yuanzhi sat for a long time with her head in her hands, annoyed that Lu would still not teach her the kungfu of closing points. After dinner, she went to see her mother, who scolded her for causing trouble on the road, and told her she was not to wear boy's clothing any more.

'Mother, you're always talking about how you have no son,' she replied with a smile. 'Aren't you happy now that you have one?'

Lady Li gave up and went to bed. Yuanzhi also got ready for sleep, and was just about to take off her clothes when she heard a light tapping on the window-sill and someone saying: 'Come out, little boy! I want to ask you something.'

Yuanzhi picked up her sword and ran out to the courtyard where she spotted a figure standing in the shadows.

'Follow me if you dare!' the figure said and jumped over the courtyard wall. Like a young calf unafraid of a tiger, Yuanzhi followed without a thought for what might be waiting for her on the other side. As her feet touched the ground, she found a sword thrust towards her.

Yuanzhi raised her own sword and parried the stroke, shouting: 'Who is it?' The yellow-robed figure retreated two steps, and said: 'I am the Uighur girl Huo Qingtong. What were you doing helping the Agency men mess up our plans? Why don't you mind your own business?'

'I'll do whatever I please,' Yuanzhi replied. 'I happen to like meddling in other people's business. Let me give you another lesson in swordsmanship!' Her sword flashed out, and Huo Qingtong raised her own sword to parry it.

Yuanzhi knew that she couldn't beat the girl on equal terms, so she retreated steadily as she fought, heading towards Lu's room.

'Shifu! Shifu!' she called out suddenly. 'Someone's trying to kill me!'

A sneering laugh exploded from Huo Qingtong. 'Ha! You useless creature! You're not even worth killing!'

She began to walk away, but Yuanzhi attacked, forcing her to face her once more. Yuanzhi heard someone behind her and knew that her Shifu had emerged; seeing Huo Qingtong's sword bearing down on her, she jumped behind Lu's back.

Lu fended off her strokes with his sword and Huo Qingtong soon realized that his sword technique, while of the same School as Yuanzhi's, was far superior. She became anxious and attacked fiercely, waiting for an opportunity to retreat. But his strokes followed each other without pause, sticking to her closely.

Yuanzhi put her sword in its scabbard and joined the fray, this time using Limitless Occult Hand kungfu. Huo Qingtong was unable to beat Lu alone, so how could she manage against both of them? Yuanzhi displayed great cunning: a touch on one side, a hook with her leg on the other. She was not aiming to hurt the Uighur girl, but was intentionally having fun at her expense, to pay her back for the tuft of her horse's mane ripped out the day before.

Lu, for his part, had been impressed earlier that day by the Uighur girl's swordsmanship and simply wanted to test her. His sword thrust at her and she raised her own blade to ward it off. Meanwhile, Yuanzhi moved in towards her back, shouting 'Watch out for my fist!' and struck out at her left shoulder with the move known as Ferocious Rooster Snatching Grain. Huo Qingtong turned her left hand and diverted the blow by grasping for Yuanzhi's arm. With both the Uighur girl's arms now occupied, Yuanzhi seized the opportunity and used the flat of her hand to strike at Huo Qingtong's chest. If the blow had been in earnest, it would have caused serious injury, but there was no strength behind it. She ran her hand heavily over the girl's chest and then jumped back laughing. Huo Qingtong was consumed with fury and, ignoring Lu's sword, swung round and attacked Yuanzhi using the Heaven Mountains School Mirage style, a series of dazzling feints that left Yuanzhi utterly at a loss. Lu could not stand by. He raised his sword and accepted the brunt of the attack, while Yuanzhi stepped back.

'All right,' she laughed. 'Don't be angry. Just marry me, and we'll forget about it.'

Huo Qingtong had been deeply insulted, but she knew she could not overcome Lu. She threw her sword at Yuanzhi with all her strength, aiming to take the 'boy' to the grave with her.

Lu started in fright and threw his own sword at Huo Qingtong's. The two swords collided in mid-air with a clang and fell to earth together. He then pushed Huo Qingtong back five or six steps with a light touch on her left shoulder. 'Please don't take offence, miss,' he said. 'There's something I want to say.'

'Well?' she replied angrily. 'What are you waiting for?'

Lu looked over at Yuanzhi. 'Don't you think you ought to apologize to the lady?'

Yuanzhi walked over and bowed low, a wide grin on her face. Huo Qingtong replied with a fist.

'Oh, no! Don't hit me!' Yuanzhi laughed. She dodged away, and pulled off her cap, revealing her head of beautiful hair.

'Now look,' she smiled. 'Am I a boy or a girl?'

Seeing Yuanzhi's real face under the moonlight, Huo Qingtong was struck dumb. Her anger and shame evaporated, leaving only irritation.

'This is my pupil,' said Lu. 'She is always disobedient and I am unable to control her. I am sorry for what happened just now. Please don't be offended.'

He brought his hands together in salute and bowed. Huo Qingtong turned slightly away, refusing to accept the apology.

'What is your relationship with the Twin Eagles of Heaven Mountains?' he asked her. Huo Qingtong's eyebrows shot up and her lips quivered, but she maintained her silence. Lu continued: 'I have always been on good terms with the Twin Eagles, Bald Vulture and his wife Lady Guan, so we should not be enemies.'

'Lady Guan is my Shifu,' Huo Qingtong said. 'I will go and tell her how badly you treated me, that you told your pupil to attack me, and even joined in yourself.'

She gave them both a look of intense hatred, then turned to go.

Lu waited until she had gone a few steps, and then said: 'And when you go and tell your Shifu, who are you going to say did all these things?'

Huo Qingtong stopped and turned. 'Well, who are you?' she demanded.

Lu stroked his beard and laughed. 'You've both got the tempers of children,' he said. 'All right, all right. This is my pupil, Li Yuanzhi, and you can tell your Shifu and her husband that I am Hidden Needle Lu. Please convey my congratulations to them on having such an excellent pupil.'

'I've lost face, and I've made my Shifu and her husband lose face as well by allowing myself to be treated in such a fashion.'

'Miss, don't think that you have lost face by being beaten by me,' Lu replied seriously. 'There are few in the fighting community who could last as long as you did against me. I suspected you knew the Twin Eagles when I saw you fighting earlier today, but your use of the Mirage sword style just now decided it. Tell me, do they still argue all the time?' He laughed.

Huo Qingtong saw that Lu knew all about her Shifu's husband and his intense jealousy, which always led to disputes between him and her Shifu. But she was still unwilling to relent.

'If you are my Shifu's friend, why did you let your pupil interfere, and stop us from recovering our Sacred Book? I don't believe you are a good man.'

'Being beaten in a sword duel is not worth worrying about,' Lu said. 'But failing to recover your Sacred Book is a different matter.

That I understand. If your people are ill-treated and insulted, you must be prepared to risk even your own life to get satisfaction.'

Huo Qingtong was greatly taken aback to hear him say this. He clearly understood her predicament. His words dispelled her pride, and she bowed respectfully before him. 'Please tell me how the Sacred Book can be recovered,' she said. 'If you are willing to help, I and the rest of my tribe will be eternally grateful.' She fell to her knees.

'It was stupid of me to interfere like that,' said Yuanzhi. 'My Shifu has already given me a long lecture. Please forgive me. I'll help you get your Sacred Book back. It's in that red knapsack, isn't it?' Huo Qingtong nodded. 'Well, let's go,' Yuanzhi added.

'We must discuss the situation first,' said Lu. The three talked in low tones for a while; then, with Lu keeping a lookout, the two girls crossed over the wall into the inn.

They ran, crouching, over to the room occupied by the Agency guards, and squatted under the window in the shadow of the wall. Inside, they heard Tong crying and groaning for a while. Then he stopped.

'You are so gifted, Master Zhang,' one of the guards said. 'To be able to cure Tong so quickly.'

'If we'd known you were coming, we wouldn't have had to apologize to that Red Flower Society scab,' said another.

'I want you all to watch that pair,' a powerful voice replied. 'Tomorrow, when Wu and the others arrive, we'll make our move.'

'Once we've got him, I'm going to kick that bastard in the head a few times, very hard,' said Tong.

Yuanzhi rose to her feet and found a tear in the window-paper through which to look. She saw five or six people seated around the room. In the middle was an awe-inspiring man whom she decided must be the one they called Master Zhang. His eyes flashed like lightning and his temples were high and protruding, indicating a man of profound Inner Force.

'Tong, give me the knapsack,' said Yan. 'Those Uighurs won't give up so easily. I'm afraid we'll have more trouble on the road.'

Tong began to untie the knapsack hesitantly, as if unwilling to hand it over.

'Now don't worry,' Yan said. 'Once we've got this knapsack to Peking safe and sound, we'll all get our share.'

Yuanzhi thought swiftly. Yan was a powerful fighter, and once he had possession of the knapsack it would be difficult to recover it. She whispered a few words into Huo Qingtong's ear, took off her hat, and pulled her long hair over her face. Then she picked up two bricks lying nearby and hurled them through the window. They crashed into the room, and the lamp was instantly doused. The door opened and several men rushed out.

'Who's there?' one yelled.

Huo Qingtong whistled at them, then leapt over the wall, and the guards and Zhang chased after her. As soon as they had gone, Yuanzhi burst into the room.

Tong was lying on the kang when he saw the Thing come through the door, an unghostly ghost, and an inhuman human, with its hair dishevelled and wild. The Thing hopped towards him squealing loudly, and his body went limp with fright. It seized the red knapsack from his hands and ran from the room.

The guards chased after Huo Qingtong for a while, but Zhang suddenly stopped in his tracks. 'Damn!' he said. 'This is just a diversion to lure us away. Get back quickly!'

They returned to the inn to find Tong lying on the kang in a state of shock. It was a while before he managed to tell them how the ghost had stolen the knapsack.

'What ghost?' Zhang said angrily. 'We've been tricked!'

Meanwhile, Yuanzhi was hiding outside beside the wall, holding the knapsack tightly. She waited until all the guards had re-entered the room before jumping back out of the courtyard. She whistled softly, and Lu and Huo Qingtong appeared from the shadow of the trees.

Yuanzhi was feeling particularly smug. 'I've got the knapsack,' she laughed, 'so you can't ever—'

Before she could finish, Lu shouted: 'Watch out behind you!'

As she turned, someone slapped her on the shoulder. She quickly tried to grab the hand but failed and her heart jumped in fright as she realized how formidable her assailant was: he had followed her without her even being aware of it. She quickly looked around and in the moonlight saw a tall, powerful man standing beside her. She stepped backwards in fright, and threw the knapsack at Huo Qingtong.

'Catch!' she yelled, and brought her hands together to face the enemy.

He was extraordinarily fast. As the knapsack left her hand, he leapt after it and caught it in mid air. In that instant, Huo Qingtong attacked him, and with his left hand holding the knapsack, the man swung his arms out at her, using the Long Arm style. There was great power behind the blow, and both girls were forced back several paces. Yuanzhi now recognized him as the Master Zhang she had seen a short while earlier. The Long Arm style was one of the fundamental techniques of Wudang School kungfu, the very same style that she had studied with Lu. Yuanzhi gasped involuntarily at the effortless power with which Zhang used it. He was clearly a master. She glanced around, but her Shifu was nowhere to be seen.

Yuanzhi advanced a step and attacked bravely, using the same Long Arm technique. As their fists clashed, she felt a prickly numbness run through her arm followed by an unbearable ache. She stumbled, then jumped off to the left.

'Tell me, child!' Zhang said. 'Is your Shifu's surname Ma or Lu?'

'Ma,' she said to deceive him. 'How did you know?'

'Well, he's my brother-in-arms. Don't you think you ought to kowtow before me?' He laughed.

As soon as Huo Qingtong heard mention of a connection between them, she abandoned Yuanzhi. She could see that the Koran could not be recovered, and ran quickly away.

Yuanzhi chased after her a short way, but suddenly a cloud bank covered the moon, plunging her into pitch darkness. She started in fright as several thunder claps rolled across the sky, and she turned back to find that Zhang had disappeared too. By the time she leapt back over the wall into the inn, large droplets of rain were falling, and as she entered her room the downpour came.

Holed Up in the Inn

The heavy rain lasted all night. Next morning, having washed and combed her hair, Yuanzhi looked out of the window and saw that it was still pouring. Her mother's maidservant came in.

'Officer Zeng says the rain is too heavy and we can't leave today,' she announced.

Icy gusts blew in through a tear in Yuanzhi's window. She felt bored, particularly as the inn was in such a desolate spot. She walked over to the room occupied by Master Wen of the Red Flower Society hoping to catch a glimpse of him and the woman warrior who had defended him, but the door was firmly shut and no sound came from within. The Zhen Yuan Agency had not left that morning either, and several of the guards were lounging about in the dining-hall, chatting. Master Zhang was not among them. A gust of wind blew from the west and Yuanzhi began to feel rather cold. She was about to return to her room when she heard the sound of bells outside the front gate and a horse galloped in from the rain.

A young scholar dismounted and ran inside. As one servant led his horse off to be fed, another asked the scholar if he would be staying at the inn.

'I'll have to get back on the road again soon,' he replied, taking off his raincape. The servant invited him to take a seat and poured him a cup of tea.

The scholar was tall and slender with a handsome face. In the border country, such elegance was a rare sight, and Yuanzhi could not help staring at him. The scholar saw her too and smiled. She flushed and quickly looked away.

There was the sound of horses again outside the inn and four men came in. Yuanzhi recognized them as the Yamen officers who had attacked the young woman the day before and she quickly retired to Lu's room to ask what they should do.

'Let us go and have a look first,' Lu said, and the two peeped into the dining-hall through a hole in the window.

One of the four, the one with the sword, summoned a servant, quietly questioned him for a moment, then said to his companions: 'Those two Red Flower Society outlaws still haven't left. We'll deal with them when we've eaten.'

The scholar's expression changed slightly and he began to observe the four men out of the corner of his eye.

'Shall I help the woman again?' Yuanzhi asked.

'Do nothing until I tell you,' Lu said. He paid no further attention to the four officers, but focused his gaze on the scholar.

Once he had finished eating, the scholar moved his stool into the corridor leading to the courtyard. He pulled a flute from the bundle on his back and began to play a pleasant, lilting melody. The flute looked as if it was cast from pure gold. This in itself was puzzling. The road they were on was far from safe, and a golden flute openly displayed by a lone scholar was bound to attract thieves.

When the four men had finished eating, the swordsman jumped onto the table and announced in a loud voice:

'We are Yamen officers and we have come to arrest fugitives of the Red Flower Society. Peaceful citizens need not be afraid.'

He jumped down from the table and led the other three towards the courtyard. The scholar, who was still blocking the corridor and playing his flute, ignored them. The swordsman approached him. 'You are standing in the way of officers of the law,' he growled.

The scholar casually put down his flute. 'You gentlemen wish to arrest fugitives: tell me, what law have they broken?' he asked. 'Confucius said, "Do not do unto others what you would not wish done to yourself." Do you really have to arrest them?'

The officer with the staff stepped forward. 'That's enough of your nonsense!' he shouted. 'Get out of the way!'

'Please calm yourself, honourable sir,' the scholar replied. 'There's no need to get agitated. Let me be host. We'll all have a drink and become friends, what do you say?'

The officer stretched out his hand to push him away, and the scholar swayed to one side. 'Ai-ya,' he exclaimed. 'A gentleman uses words, not force.'

He fell forward as if over-balancing and put out the golden flute to steady himself, leaning, as he did so, on a Vital Point on the left thigh of the officer, who involuntarily fell to his knees as his leg went limp.

'Ai-ya!' the scholar exclaimed again. 'Kneeling! There's really no need for such courtesy.' He bowed before the officer.

Those watching could tell that the scholar was highly skilled in the Martial Arts, and Yuanzhi, who had originally been anxious on his behalf, was overjoyed to see him closing Vital Points so effectively and effortlessly.

'This character may be with the Red Flower Society as well!' cried one of the officers fearfully. The officer with the paralysed leg meanwhile collapsed on the floor, and the others pulled him to one side.

'Are you a member of the Red Flower Society?' the swordsman asked, a slight touch of fear in his voice.

The scholar laughed. 'I am indeed. My name is Yu Yutong. I play but a small role in the Society, ranking only fourteenth in seniority.' He waved the flute at them. 'Don't you recognize me?'

'Ah, you're Scholar Yu!'

'You are too kind,' said the scholar. 'That is indeed who I am. You sir, with the flashing sword, face of cunning, and rat-like eyes.

You must be the famous officer from Peking, Wu Guodong. I'd
heard you had retired. What are you doing getting involved in this
kind of game?'

Swordsman Wu's blade flicked out, steely yet smooth, and
Yu countered with his golden flute, fighting the three officers
simultaneously, working through a complex series of moves which
soon had them completely flustered. After a moment, Yuanzhi
turned to Lu in surprise.

'That's the Soft Cloud sword style, isn't it?' she said.

Lu nodded, thinking to himself: 'The Soft Cloud sword
technique is a secret style known only to our school. If this scholar
is a member of the Red Flower Society, then he must be a pupil of
my brother-in-arms, Ma Zhen.'

The Wudang School or Martial Arts lineage to which Hidden
Needle Lu belonged was represented by three disciples, or brothers-
in-arms, among whom Lu was placed second. The most senior
was Ma Zhen and the most junior Zhang Zhaozhong, the Master
Zhang with whom Yuanzhi had tangled the night before. Master
Zhang was a highly gifted and very diligent fighter, and was
commonly known in the River and Lake community by his *nom-
de-guerre*, the Fire Hand Judge, or Fire Hand Zhang for short. But
he had defected from the Wudang School and thrown in his lot
with the Manchu Court, and, rising swiftly in seniority, he had
already attained the rank of Major in the Imperial Guard. Lu
considered him a traitor and had long ago severed relations with
him.

His guess that Scholar Yu was a pupil of Elder Brother Ma
Zhen was correct. Yu came from a respected scholarly family in
southern China, and had already passed the first Imperial Civil
Service examination when his father became involved in a dispute
over a burial plot with a wealthy family. The ensuing law suit had
forced Yu's father into bankruptcy, and he was imprisoned on a
trumped-up charge and died in jail. Yu left home in anger and met
Ma Zhen, whom he accepted as his Shifu, abandoning his formal
studies in favour of the Martial Arts. He returned and sought
vengeance for his father's death. He killed the rich landlord and
then became an outlaw in the world of River and Lake, and later a
member of the Red Flower Society. He was an alert and intelligent
young man, and could speak several different dialects. On this
occasion, he was travelling on secret society business to the city of

Luoyang and had been unaware that his fellow Society members, Wen Tailai and his wife, were holed up in the inn.

Hearing that a fight was in progress, the Agency men all came in and stood to one side watching. Tong noticed a catapult strapped to the back of one of the officers, and shouted: 'If it was me, I'd leave the other two to take care of the bastard, and use the slingshot on him.'

The officer with the catapult realized Tong was right. He jumped onto a table, readied his weapon, and sent a shower of pebbles flying towards Yu.

Yu dodged them one by one while simultaneously parrying the other two officers. But his opponents soon gained the upper hand, and after a few more moves, one of the missiles struck Yu's cheek and the pain began to slow his movements.

'You might as well give up,' Tong called to Yu. 'Pull down your trousers and let them give you a taste of the cane.'

But Yu did not panic. With a sudden movement, he drove his left hand at a Vital Point on Swordsman Wu's chest. Wu quickly retreated two steps and Yu thrust the flute into the stomach of the other officer, who grunted loudly and buckled in agony. Yu moved to strike him again, but Wu intercepted him.

Fighting back the pain in his stomach, the third officer moved stealthily up behind Yu as he fought Wu, and raised his Devil's Head Cutlass to bring it down on Yu's skull. But before he could do so, a throwing knife plunged into his chest, killing him instantly. The Devil's Head Cutlass clattered to the floor.

Yu turned and saw a woman standing nearby, supporting herself on the table with her left hand, the slender fingers of her right hand clasping another throwing knife, delicately, as if it was the stem of a fresh flower. She was indescribably lovely. As soon as he saw her, Yu's spirits rose.

'Kill the Eagle's Claw with the catapult first!' he shouted. Eagle's Claw was their slang for a thug employed by the Imperial Court.

The officer with the catapult turned round frantically, just in time to see the flash of the blade as it flew towards him. In desperation, he held up the catapult to try to stop it, but the knife drove itself into the back of his hand.

'Help!' he screamed. 'This is too dangerous! Let's get out of here!'

He jumped off the table and fled. Wu forced Yu back with two more strokes from his sword, slung the officer with the paralysed leg over his shoulder, and rushed for the door to the hall. Instead of chasing them, Yu raised the flute to his mouth end-on instead of crosswise, and puffed. A tiny arrow shot out of the end and buried itself in the shoulder of the paralysed officer, who screamed with pain.

Yu turned to the woman. 'Where's Brother Wen?' he asked.

'Come with me,' she said. She was wounded in the thigh, and supported herself as she walked with a long door-bar.

Meanwhile, as the officers rushed out of the inn, they collided head-on with a man coming in, making Wu reel back several paces. He saw that it was Master Zhang, and his initial anger turned to delight.

'Master Zhang,' he cried. 'Things have gone very badly! One of our men has been killed by the Red Flower rebels and this one has been paralysed.'

Fire Hand Zhang grunted. He lifted the officer into the air with his left hand, then squeezed his waist and slapped his thigh, freeing the blood flow. 'Have they escaped?' he asked.

'They're still in the inn.'

Zhang grunted again. 'They've certainly got guts,' he said, walking into the inn courtyard. 'Resisting arrest, killing an official, then brazenly staying on here.'

They led Zhang towards Wen's room, but just as they reached the door, Yuanzhi slid out of a room nearby and waved a red knapsack at Zhang.

'Hey, I've stolen it again,' she laughed and ran towards the main gate of the inn.

Zhang was startled. 'These Agency men are truly useless,' he thought. 'No sooner have I got it back for them than they lose it again.'

He shot after her, determined to teach her a good lesson. It was still raining, and before long they were both soaking wet. Yuanzhi saw him closing in and ran off along the side of a stream, Zhang following stealthily. He increased his pace, closing the distance between them, then stretched out his hand and caught hold of the back of her jacket. Greatly frightened, Yuanzhi pulled away with all her strength, and a piece of the cloth tore off. Her heart pounding, she hurled the red knapsack into the stream.

'It's yours,' she shouted.

Zhang knew how vital General Zhao Hui considered the Koran to be and immediately leapt into the stream while Yuanzhi laughed and ran off. As he fished the knapsack out of the water, he saw that it was already soaked. Frantically, he opened it to see if the Koran was wet, and then let fly with a stream of coarse language. There was no Koran in the knapsack, only a couple of registers from the main desk at the inn. He opened one and read of money collected from rooms for meals, and of servants' wages. He groaned at how he had allowed himself to be fooled, and threw the registers and the fake knapsack back into the stream. If he took them back and someone asked about them, he would certainly lose face.

He returned to the inn and quickly found Yan with the red knapsack still safely fastened to his back.

'Where did Wu and the officers go?' he asked.

'They were here a moment ago,' Yan replied.

'What damned use is there in the Emperor employing people like that?' he demanded.

He walked up to Wen's door. 'You Red Flower Society rebels! Come out immediately!' he shouted. No sound came from the room. He kicked at the door and found it slightly ajar.

'They've escaped!' he yelled, and burst into the room to find it empty. There was a lump under the bed covers, and he flung them off, to reveal two of Wu's officers lying face to face. He prodded the back of one of them lightly with his sword, but there was no movement. He turned them over and saw they were both dead. Both their skulls had been smashed in. It was obviously the work of a master of Inner Force kungfu: his respect for Wen Tailai increased appreciably. But where was Wu? And in which direction had Wen and his wife escaped? He called for one of the servants and interrogated him, without learning anything.

Fire Hand Zhang had guessed wrong: the officers had not been killed by Rolling Thunder Wen.

To the Manor

What had actually occurred was as follows:

Lu and Yuanzhi had watched the whole fight through the window, and saw Master Zhang enter as the officers were leaving.

'That's the man who took the knapsack from me last night,' Yuanzhi said.

'Go quickly and draw him away, the further the better,' Lu whispered. 'If I'm not here when you return, start out tomorrow without me and I will catch up with you.'

He watched Zhang chase Yuanzhi out of the inn, then picked up a writing-brush and hurriedly wrote a letter which he placed inside his gown. He ran to Wen's room and knocked lightly on the door.

'Who is it?' a woman's voice called.

'Let's just say that I am a good friend of Divine Knife Luo,' said Lu. 'I have important news for you.'

There was no answer from inside. Wu and the other two officers appeared and stood at a distance keeping watch, obviously suspicious of Lu. The door suddenly opened and Scholar Yu looked out.

'May I ask who you are, sir?' he asked.

'I am your Shifu's brother-in-arms, Hidden Needle Lu.'

A look of hesitation appeared on Yu's face. He had heard of Lu but had never met him.

'I'll prove it to you,' Lu whispered. 'Stand aside.'

Scholar Yu's suspicions deepened, and he planted his foot firmly on the opposite door-post, blocking the way with his leg. Lu's left hand shot out, aiming to hit Yu's shoulder. Yu dodged, and Lu slipped his right hand underneath Yu's armpit and pushed him to one side using the first move in the Wudang School's Long Arm style. 'It really is Hidden Needle Lu!' Yu thought, both surprised and delighted. As Yu moved back, Luo Bing raised her sword and dagger ready to attack, but Yu stopped her. Lu waved his hands at them, indicating they should stand clear, then ran back outside into the courtyard.

'Hey, they've gone!' he shouted to Officer Wu. 'Come and see!'

Wu rushed into the room with the other two officers and Lu closed the door behind them.

Wu saw Yu and the others in the room and shouted frantically: 'It's a trap!' But before the officers could turn, Lu's two fists smashed into their heads, shattering their skulls and killing them instantly.

Wu was a little more quick-witted. He leapt onto the kang, and, with both hands raised to protect his head, was about to throw himself at the window; but Rolling Thunder Wen, who was lying on the kang, sat up and struck out with his left fist, breaking Wu's right shoulder with a sharp crack. Wu wavered, but steadied himself against the wall with his left foot, then broke through the window and escaped. Luo Bing launched a throwing knife after him which lodged itself in his back. But he ignored the pain, and fled for his life.

Yu and Luo Bing no longer harboured any suspicions about Lu. They both bowed before him.

'Sir, please forgive me for not being able to pay my respects to you properly,' Wen said from the kang.

'There's no need,' said Lu. He looked at Luo Bing. 'What is your relationship with Divine Knife Luo?' he asked.

'He was my father.'

'He was a very good friend of mine,' Lu said. He looked at Scholar Yu and added: 'You are a pupil of Ma Zhen's, I presume. How has my brother-in-arms been recently?'

'He is well,' said Yu. 'He has often expressed concern about you. He told me he hadn't seen or heard anything of you for more than ten years.'

'I miss him too,' Lu said regretfully. 'Did you know that another of your Shifu's brothers-in-arms has been here looking for you?'

Yu looked up in fright. 'Zhang Zhaozhong?'

Lu nodded. Wen Tailai shuddered slightly at the sound of Zhang's name, and then gasped in pain. Luo Bing quickly went over and supported him with her hand, her face full of love and pity.

Yu looked on, absorbed. 'To have a wife like that would be better than being a god!' he murmured. 'Even the worst wounds would be worth suffering for her sake!'

'Zhang has brought shame upon our School, but there's no denying that his kungfu is excellent,' Lu said. 'And I would guess that reinforcements will not be far behind him. With your Brother Wen so badly wounded, I think all we can do at the moment is to avoid them.'

'We will do whatever you suggest,' Luo Bing said. She looked down at her husband, who nodded.

Lu now pulled a letter from his gown and handed it to Luo Bing. On the envelope were written the words: 'Respectfully addressed to Lord Zhou Zhongying, of Iron Ball Manor.'

'Do you know him?' asked Luo Bing, delighted.

'I have never met him, but we have been friends from afar for a long time,' Lu said. 'I think your husband should hide there while one of us goes to your honourable Society to report what has happened.' He saw a hesitant look on Wen's face. 'What do you think, sir?'

'Your arrangements would be perfect, but I feel I have to tell you something. I am involved in a bloody feud with Emperor Qian Long. The Emperor won't be able to eat or sleep in peace until he sees me die with his own eyes. I know Lord Zhou would take us in, but I am afraid he would bring great trouble upon himself by doing so.'

'To men on River and Lake, there is nothing more important than helping a friend in need,' said Lu.

'But in my situation, the greater the friend, the less I should involve him.'

'Refusing to involve others in your problems is an upright and manly thing to do. But I do think you are making a mistake.'

'Why?' Wen asked quickly.

'If you refuse to go, then we will have to stay here and fight. I don't want to exaggerate the enemy's strength or denigrate our own, but who do we have to match Zhang? I am nearly sixty years old, my life is of little value. But my young friend with the flute here has a promising future and your wife is full of youth. Just because you want to play the hero, we will all surely die here.'

Wen began to sweat profusely.

'Husband!' Luo Bing exclaimed. She pulled out a handkerchief and wiped the beads of sweat from his brow, then held his hand.

Wen's affection for his wife outweighed his sense of duty and he relented. 'You are right,' he said. 'I will do whatever you say.' But then he sighed. 'Once we reach Iron Ball Manor, the Red Flower Society will be beholden to yet another person.'

The Red Flower Society always took care to repay its benefactors and to exact revenge on its enemies—hence the awe in which they were held by the Zhen Yuan Agency men.

'Tell me, what's the relationship between Zhao Banshan and you?' asked Lu.

'Buddha Zhao? He ranks third in our Society.'

'So that's it! Just what your Red Flower Society is involved in, I don't know. But Buddha Zhao is an old friend of mine, and he and

I would willingly die for each other. In the old days when we were both in the Dragon Slayers' Society, we were closer than natural brothers. If he is a member of your Society, then your affairs are certain to be just. What does it matter what great crimes you have committed? The biggest crimes are to assassinate officials and to rebel against the Throne. Ha! Well, I just killed two official running dogs!' He gave one of the corpses a kick.

'There's too much to explain,' Wen said. 'When this is over, if I live, I will tell you everything. But briefly, the Emperor sent eight Imperial Guards to arrest my wife and myself. I was wounded in a fight at Jinquan but we escaped and came here. They'll get me sooner or later. But the Emperor has a secret I must expose before I die. That is all I can say at present.'

Lu asked where the Red Flower Society leaders were.

'The Red Flower Society has twelve leading Brothers,' said Yu. 'All of them, apart from Brother Wen and Sister Luo Bing, are already gathered in Anxi. We have asked a new Helmsman to assume the leadership of the Society, but he is unwilling to do so. He says he is too young and inexperienced and insists that the Taoist priest, Father Speckless, should be leader: he ranks second in the Society. At present, the matter is unresolved. The meeting to elect a new Helmsman will not start until Brother Wen and Luo Bing arrive.'

Yu turned to Wen, his superior in the Society's hierarchy. 'Should I go ahead to Anxi and report?' he asked.

Wen hesitated, uncertain of what to say.

'Let us do it this way,' suggested Lu. 'You three start out immediately for Iron Ball Manor. Once you are settled there, Scholar Yu can continue on his business. Meanwhile, I myself will go on to Anxi to report.'

Wen pulled a red silk flower from his gown and handed it to Lu. 'When you arrive in Anxi, fasten this flower to your lapel and you will be met by someone from our Society,' he said.

Luo Bing helped her husband up while Yu lifted the two corpses from the floor onto the kang and covered them with the bedclothes. Then Lu opened the door and strode calmly out, mounted a horse, and galloped off westwards.

After a short while, the others also emerged from the room, Yu leading the way. Luo Bing supported herself with the door-bar in one hand and held up Wen with the other. The inn's staff shrank away as the three approached. Yu threw three taels of silver onto the front desk.

'There's money for the room and the food,' he said. 'We have left two very valuable items in our room. Don't touch them. If there's anything missing when we get back, there'll be trouble.'

The innkeeper nodded rapidly, almost too scared to breathe. Servants led out their horses. Wen could not lift his foot into the stirrups, so he placed his left hand on the saddle and vaulted lightly onto the horse's back.

'Excellent kungfu, Brother Wen!' Yu praised him. Luo Bing mounted her own horse with a delighted smile, and the three of them rode off.

In the town, Yu asked the way to Iron Ball Manor, and they galloped off southeast. Luo Bing was happy: she knew that once they got to the Manor, her husband would be safe. Lord Zhou commanded great respect throughout the border regions.

The road led them through terrain covered with loose stones and long grass, which gave it a rather desolate air. As they were riding along, they heard the sound of galloping hooves ahead and three horses raced towards them. The riders were all large, strong men, but one was particularly tall and impressive with silver-white whiskers and a smooth rosy face. In his left hand, he constantly jiggled two iron balls together. As they passed, the riders looked at Wen in surprise, but they were galloping fast, and flashed past in an instant.

'I'm afraid that was probably Lord Zhou himself,' Yu said.

'I was thinking the same thing,' replied Luo Bing.

'We'll find out when we get to the Manor,' said Wen.

A few miles further on, as evening drew near, Iron Ball Manor appeared before them. The wind was strong and the clouds low, and in the bright rays of the setting sun it was a desolate sight, set amidst an endless expanse of withered grasses and yellow sand. Seeking sanctuary as they were, the mood of the three was despondent, and the desolation of the area affected them all. They spurred their horses forward and found the Manor was surrounded by a moat, the banks of which were planted with willow trees. The bare branches whirled and danced in the strong west wind. Within the moat, the Manor was protected with fortifications and a watchtower: it was an imposing sight.

One of Lord Zhou's retainers invited them in, seated them in the great hall, and brought them tea. Then a middle-aged man with the air of a steward came out to receive them. He said his name was Song. He asked Wen and the others for their names.

'I have heard much about you,' he said, startled to hear that they were members of the Red Flower Society. 'But I had thought that your honourable Society was based in southern China. I wonder if you could tell me why you have come all this way to visit our Lord? I am afraid he went out a short while ago.' Song was carefully weighing up the visitors, wondering what their intentions were.

Wen, meanwhile, was becoming angry at Song's coolness. 'Since Lord Zhou is not at home, we will excuse ourselves,' he said. 'We have evidently come at an inopportune time.' He stood up, using a chair for support.

'There's no rush,' Song replied. 'Please stay and have a meal before leaving.' He turned and whispered a few words to an attendant.

Wen insisted they would go.

'Well, please wait a while first, otherwise our Lord may blame me for neglecting honoured guests.' As he spoke, the attendant reappeared carrying a tray on which were two large silver ingots. Song took the tray.

'Sir,' he said. 'You have come a long way to visit our humble Manor and we have not had a chance to look after you properly. Please be so kind as to accept this for your travelling expenses.'

Wen, filled with rage, picked up both of the ingots with his left hand. 'You underestimate us, friend Song,' he said. 'We did not come to your honourable Manor to extort money.'

Song quickly protested that he would not dare to suggest such a thing.

'Goodbye,' said Wen, laughing coldly and placing the ingots back on the tray.

Song looked down and started in fright. With just one hand, Wen had crushed the two ingots together into a flat cake of silver. He led the three out towards the gate, offering profuse apologies as he went. Wen ignored him. Attendants brought their horses, and they mounted immediately.

Luo Bing took out a gold ingot many times more valuable than the silver offered by Song and gave it to the attendant holding her horse. 'Thank you for your trouble,' she said. 'Here's a little something for you to have a drink.' The attendants could hardly believe their luck, and began thanking her profusely. Luo Bing smiled in reply.

Just as they were about to ride off, a rider galloped up, leapt off his horse, and saluted Wen politely with his fists clasped. 'Please come into our humble Manor and make yourselves comfortable,' he said.

'We do not wish to trouble you,' Wen replied. 'We will visit again another time.'

'We passed you on the road a while ago and our Lord guessed you were coming to the Manor,' the man continued. 'He would have liked to turn back, but he has important business to attend to. So he ordered me to come to receive you. He is eager to make your acquaintance. He said he would definitely return tonight. He insists that you must stay.'

Wen's anger melted as he heard the sincerity in the newcomer's voice, and they went back into the Manor. The man introduced himself as Meng, Zhou's steward and senior disciple. Song stood to one side looking very uncomfortable. Guests and host sat down and fresh tea was served. An attendant whispered something to Meng, who stood up and bowed before Luo Bing.

'Our Lady invites you to proceed to the inner hall to rest,' he said.

A maidservant led Luo Bing through a passageway and a woman in her forties came striding forward and grasped Luo Bing warmly by the hand.

'They told me just now that some members of the Red Flower Society had arrived and then left again. I'm so relieved you've come back. My Lord will be so happy! Now, don't rush away. You can stay for a few days. Look, all of you,' she said, turning to her maidservants. 'Look how beautiful this girl is! She puts our girls to shame.'

Luo Bing thought the woman was rather indiscreet. 'What is your name, madam?' she asked. 'My husband's name is Wen.'

The woman, it turned out, was Lord Zhou's second wife. His first had borne two sons, but both had died in fights. This second wife had given birth to a daughter, Zhou Qi, a wild girl of eighteen always getting into trouble, and it had seemed as if Zhou was destined to have no more sons. But in his fifty-fourth year, another was unexpectedly born to them. The couple were overjoyed to have gained a son so late in life.

'Call the young master in quickly,' Lady Zhou said after seating herself comfortably. 'Let the lady see him.'

A lively, good-looking child emerged from the inner rooms and kowtowed to Luo Bing, who judged from his bearing that he had already received several years of training in the Martial Arts. She took hold of his hand and asked him his name and age.

'My name is Zhou Yingjie and I'm ten this year,' the child replied.

Luo Bing unfastened the pearl bracelet from her wrist and gave it to him.

'I'm sorry I don't have anything nicer to give you, but you can put these pearls round the edge of your cap,' she said. Lady Zhou protested, but to no avail.

While they were talking, one of the maidservants rushed in crying: 'Mistress Wen! Master Wen has fainted!'

Lady Zhou quickly gave orders to fetch a doctor while Luo Bing ran back to her husband. Wen's injuries were already serious, and he had used up a great deal of his remaining strength when he'd squeezed the silver ingots together. He was now unconscious, his face drained of colour. Luo Bing ran to him, calling his name over and over again. Slowly, he regained consciousness.

Steward Meng dispatched a man to ride after Lord Zhou and report to him that the guests were settled in. As he turned back inside after seeing the man gallop off, he noticed a figure dart behind a willow tree. He made no sign that he had seen anything unusual, but slowly walked back into the Manor and ran up to the watchtower. After a while, he saw a short man creep furtively out from behind one willow tree and run behind another.

Meng called for Lord Zhou's young son and whispered some instructions to him. Then he ran out of the Manor gate, laughing and shouting: 'Come along little man, I'll pretend to be afraid of you, all right?'

The boy followed close behind, shouting: 'Where do you think you're running off to? You won't admit defeat, will you? Come here and kowtow before me!'

Steward Meng bowed and mockingly begged for mercy. The boy made a grab for him and Meng ran straight for the willow behind which the intruder was hiding. He charged straight into the man, knocking him flat.

It was the squeaky-voiced Zhen Yuan Agency guard, Tong Zhaohe. He had seen Wen and the others leave the inn and had followed them, determined to prove wrong those who said he was good for nothing but eating and farting. Tong had few abilities, but he was no fool and knew immediately that Meng had planned the collision to test his kungfu. So he let his whole body go loose, pretending that he knew none at all. His kungfu was in fact mediocre, and pretending to know none at all was not difficult.

'Excuse me,' said Tong. 'Is this the road to Sandaogou?' He tried to get up, but cried out in pain: 'Ai-ya! My arm!'

'I'm so sorry,' said Steward Meng. 'You're not hurt, are you? Please come into the Manor and I'll have a look at you. We have some excellent medicinal ointments.'

Tong was powerless to refuse. Meng helped him up and led him into an ante-room.

'Please undo your clothing and let me examine your wounds,' Meng said. He felt around Tong's body, testing him. When an enemy's fingers touch Vital Points, a kungfu initiate is sure to flinch.

'I'm not afraid to die,' thought Tong to himself. 'I'll act the innocent until the end!' Meng pressed the Sun points on his temples, and other points on his chest and armpits. All Tong did was giggle.

'Ai-ya! Stop that! I'm very ticklish!'

They were all fatal points, but Tong seemed unconcerned. Meng decided he really didn't know any kungfu. 'But from his accent, he isn't a local,' he thought, still suspicious. 'Could he be a petty thief, I wonder?'

Steward Meng could not detain Tong for no reason, so he walked him back towards the gate. Tong peered about him as they walked through the Manor, trying to discover where Wen and the others were. Meng decided he must be a scout for a gang of thieves.

'Be careful, my friend,' he said. 'Have you any idea where you are?'

Tong looked around in mock awe. 'Such a big place! It looks like a great temple. But there's no Buddha.'

Meng escorted him over the drawbridge and laughed coldly. 'Goodbye friend,' he said, clapping Tong heavily on the shoulder. 'Come and visit us again sometime.'

The pain from the blow went straight to Tong's marrow. Swearing profusely, he staggered to his horse and galloped back to the Antong Inn in Sandaogou. As he entered his room, he saw Fire Hand Zhang, Officer Wu, and the Agency men, together with seven or eight men he didn't know. They were in the midst of a discussion on where Wen Tailai might have escaped to. No one could think of an answer, and their faces were gloomy.

Tong smugly related how he had followed Wen, naturally omitting the part about his humiliating encounter with Steward Meng.

Zhang was delighted. 'Let's go,' he said, adding with uncustomary warmth: 'Friend Tong, you lead the way.'

The whole group immediately set out for Iron Ball Manor, rubbing their hands in anticipation as they went. Tong boasted extravagantly of how he had used Lightness kungfu, and of the risks he had taken in tracking Wen. 'This is an assignment from the Emperor himself, so I went all out against those bandits,' he said.

Officer Wu, who had already employed a bone-setter to help mend his fractured shoulder, hurriedly introduced Tong to the newcomers. Tong was most impressed to hear their names: they were all top fighters employed by the Court, famous Martial Arts specialists, both Manchu and Chinese, who had been sent specifically to arrest Wen Tailai.

The Flower of Authority

Lu Feiqing galloped westwards towards Anxi, braving the strong winds which whipped his face. Passing through Black Gold Gorge, he noticed that the blood spilled during the recent battle had already been washed away by the rain. He covered about twenty miles in one stretch and arrived at a small market fair, just as the sky was growing dark. He was impatient to continue on his way and complete his urgent mission, but his horse was exhausted, breathless, and foaming at the mouth. As he considered what to do, he saw a Uighur at the edge of the fair leading two large, well-fed horses and looking around as if waiting for someone.

Lu went over and asked if he could buy one of them. The Uighur shook his head. Lu reached into his cloth bundle and took out a large silver ingot, but the man shook his head again. Anxious and impatient, Lu turned the bundle upside down and six or seven more silver ingots fell out: he offered them all. The man waved his hand to indicate the horse was definitely not for sale, and Lu dejectedly began to put the ingots back into his bundle. As he did so, the Uighur glimpsed a dart amongst the ingots, which he picked up and examined closely. It was the dart Huo Qingtong had thrown at Lu after he followed her to the Uighur camp. He asked where the dart came from. In a flash of inspiration, Lu said Huo Qingtong was his friend and that she had given the dart to him. The Uighur nodded, placed the dart back in Lu's hand, and passed over the reins of one of the horses. Delighted, Lu pulled out an ingot of silver again, but the man waved his hand in refusal and walked away.

'I would never have guessed that such a pretty young girl would have such great influence among the Uighurs,' Lu thought to himself, as he rode off. In the next town, he came across more Uighurs. He pulled out the dart and was immediately able to trade his mount for another strong horse.

Lu continued to change horses in this fashion the whole way and, eating dry provisions as he rode, he covered two hundred miles in a single day and a night. Towards evening on the second day, he arrived at Anxi. Lu was a man of great strength, but he was getting on in years, and galloping for so long without rest had exhausted him. As soon as he entered the city, he took out the red flower Wen had given him and stuck it in his lapel. Only a few steps later, two men in short jackets appeared in front of him, saluted him, and invited him to accompany them to a restaurant. Once there, one of the men sat with him while the other excused himself and left. Lu's companion was extremely courteous, and ordered food and wine without asking any questions.

After three cups of wine, another man hurried in, came over to them, and saluted them politely with his fists clasped. Lu quickly stood up and returned the salute. The man, aged about thirty, wore an ordinary gown. He asked Lu for his name.

'So you are Master Lu of the Wudang School,' the man said. 'We have often heard Brother Zhao speak of you. I have great admiration for you. Our meeting today is very auspicious.'

'What is your honourable name?' Lu asked.

'My name is Wei. The Brothers all call me Leopard.'

'Please be seated, sir,' Lu's first companion said. He saluted both Lu and Wei, and then left.

'Our Society's new Helmsman and many of our Brothers are here in Anxi,' said Leopard Wei. 'If we had known you were coming, they would certainly have all been here to greet you. In a moment, if you don't mind, we will go and everyone can pay you their respects.'

They left the restaurant and rode out of the city.

'You have met Brother Wen Tailai and his wife,' Wei said.

'Yes. How did you know?'

'Brother Wen ranks fourth in our Society. The flower you are wearing is his. It has four green leaves.'

Lu was surprised at how openly Wei talked about their Society's secret signs, treating him not in the slightest like an outsider.

After a while, they arrived at an imposing Taoist monastery surrounded by tall, ancient trees. Over the main gate was a wooden tablet inscribed with four large characters: 'Jade Void Taoist Monastery.' Two Taoist priests standing in front of the monastery bowed respectfully. Leopard Wei invited Lu inside, and a young novice brought tea. Wei whispered in his ear, and the novice nodded and went inside. Lu was just about to raise his cup when he heard someone in the inner hall shout: 'Brother Lu! I've been worried to death about you!' It was Lu's old comrade, Zhao Banshan—Buddha Zhao.

Zhao's questions came thick and fast, but Lu brushed them aside.

'There is an urgent matter to be discussed first. Your Brother Wen is in serious trouble.'

He outlined the predicament of Wen and his wife. Even before he had finished, Leopard Wei ran inside to report. While he was still talking, Lu heard Wei arguing loudly with someone in the courtyard.

'Why are you holding me back?' the other shouted. 'I must go to help Brother Wen now!'

'You're too impatient,' Wei replied. 'This matter must be discussed by everyone first, and then it is up to the new Helmsman to decide who goes.' The other continued to protest.

Taking Lu by the hand, Buddha Zhao walked into the courtyard, and Lu saw before him the hunchback who had severed the tail of Yuanzhi's horse.

Wei gave the hunchback a push. 'Go and pay your respects to Master Lu,' he said. The hunchback walked over and stared dumbly at him for a moment. Lu knew the hunchback remembered his face and, uneasy at the thought of how Yuanzhi had laughed at him that day, he was about to apologize when the hunchback said:

'You have ridden more than two hundred miles in a night and a day to report on behalf of Brother Wen. I, Hunchback Zhang Jin, thank you!' He knelt down, and kowtowed to Lu four times, his head banging on the flagstones.

Lu wanted to stop him but it was already too late, so all he could do was to kneel down and return the gesture.

The hunchback stood up. 'I am leaving now,' he announced. As he went out through the circular doorway, a very short man coming in the other way caught hold of him. 'Where are you off to?' he asked.

'I am going to find Brother Wen and Sister Luo Bing. Come with me.' Without waiting for a reply, the hunchback pulled him along by the wrist.

This hunchback Zhang Jin had been born with a deformed body, but his strength was frightening. When talking to others, he often referred to himself as Hunchback Zhang, but anyone outside the Society calling him 'hunchback' was courting disaster. He ranked tenth in seniority in the Red Flower Society; his travelling companion was a man by the name of Xu Tianhong, who ranked seventh. Xu was very short and slight in build, almost the size of a dwarf, but his wisdom and resourcefulness made him the Red Flower Society's chief tactician, and the fighting community had dubbed him the Kungfu Mastermind.

One by one, the other members of the Red Flower Society came out and were introduced to Lu. They were all famous heroes and Lu recognized most of them, having passed them on the road several days before. The formal greetings were kept to a minimum, and after a moment the one-armed Taoist priest, Father Speckless, who ranked second within the Society, said: 'Let us go and see the new Helmsman.'

They went through to the rear courtyard and entered a large room. On one of the wooden walls a huge Go-board had been carved. Two men were sitting on a couch about thirty feet away, fingering Go-pieces and throwing them at the vertical board, each piece (or pebble) lodging itself in the lines which formed the squares. In all his wide experience, Lu had never seen Go played in this extraordinary fashion. Playing white was a young man with a refined face wearing a white gown who looked like the son of a nobleman. His opponent, playing black, was an old man dressed in farmer's clothes.

'I wonder who this old hero is,' Lu thought to himself. 'Never have I seen anyone with his strength and accuracy.' He could see black was in a dangerous position, and that with just one more successful move by white, all the black pieces would be lost. The young man threw a piece, but his aim was slightly off: the piece failed to embed itself in the intersection of the lines and fell to the floor. The old man laughed.

'You missed,' he said. 'Admit defeat!' He pushed the Go-pieces aside and stood up.

His opponent smiled. 'We'll have another game in a while, Shifu,' he said. The old man saw the group entering, and strode out of the room without so much as a greeting.

'Helmsman,' Zhao said. 'This is Brother Lu Feiqing of the Wudang School.' And to Lu: 'This is our new Helmsman. I hope you will get to know one another well.'

The young man brought his two fists together in salute. 'My name is Chen Jialuo. I would greatly appreciate your honoured counsel.'

Lu was surprised to find that this Helmsman gave every appearance of being a pampered young man from a wealthy family, the complete opposite of the rest of the bandit-like bunch.

Zhao informed the Helmsman of how Wen had taken refuge in Iron Ball Manor, and asked him for a plan of action. The Helmsman turned deferentially to the Taoist priest. 'Father Speckless,' he said. 'Please give us your advice.'

Standing behind the priest was a large, fat man, whom Zhao had introduced a moment before as Iron Pagoda Yang. He now stood up and shouted: 'Rolling Thunder Wen is badly wounded, someone we have never met before has ridden hard for a day and a night to report to us, and we are still deferring to each other. We'll be the death of Brother Wen with all our deference! Can we stop this nonsense? How can we disregard the last wishes of the old Helmsman? Helmsman Chen, if you do not respect the dying wish of your foster father, you are unfilial. If you despise us Brothers so much that you are unwilling to assume leadership, then the Red Flower Society's seventy or eighty thousand members may as well disband and go their separate ways.'

Everyone began talking at once: 'We cannot remain leaderless like this! The new Helmsman must hesitate no longer! Brother Wen is in trouble! The new Helmsman must issue orders for us to go to the rescue of Rolling Thunder!'

The young man, Chen, looked greatly distressed. His eyebrows drew together in a deep frown as he silently pondered the problem.

'Brothers!' shouted one of the Twin Knights of West Stream. 'Since the new Helmsman obviously holds us in such low regard, we two intend to return to our home in Sichuan as soon as Brother Wen has been rescued.'

Chen saw he had no alternative. He saluted the heroes with his fists. 'Brother Wen is in trouble and we can wait no longer. All of you insist that I become Helmsman, and because of the respect I have for you all, I will do as you say.'

The heroes of the Red Flower Society shouted and applauded with delight and relief.

'Well then,' said the Taoist priest. 'The new Helmsman should now pay his respects to his predecessor and accept the Flower of Authority.'

Lu knew that each society had its own special rites and ceremonies of which the initiation of a new leader was by far the most important. As an outsider, Lu felt uncomfortable about being present during such a ceremony, so he congratulated Chen and immediately excused himself. He was extremely weary after his journey, and Buddha Zhao led him to a room where he washed and slept. When he awoke, it was already night.

'The Helmsman has set off with the others for Iron Ball Manor,' Zhao said. 'But he left me here to keep you company. We can follow on tomorrow.'

After twenty years apart, the two friends had much to talk about. They talked of the doings of the fighting community over the years, the good and the bad, the living and the dead, until the east grew light.

'Your Helmsman is so young,' said Lu. 'He looks like any other rich man's son. Why are you all willing to follow him?'

'It would take a long time to explain,' Zhao replied. 'You rest for a while longer and we can talk again later when we're riding.'

CHAPTER 2

Eagle's Claws and Iron Balls; Love, Fever, Rescue;
Fighting Galore; Fire! Fire!; Talking in the Spinney;
On the Road; Spectacular Swordsmanship; Night Creepers

Eagle's Claws and Iron Balls

Tong set off from the inn at Sandaogou, and eagerly led Fire Hand Zhang and the others to Iron Ball Manor. This time, having some supporters with him, he walked brazenly up to the Manor gate.

'Tell your master to come out and receive Imperial officials,' he shouted to an attendant.

The attendant turned to go inside, but Zhang decided they could not afford to offend such a respected man as Lord Zhou. 'Say that we have come from Peking,' he called out, 'and that there is some official business we would like to consult Lord Zhou about.'

He glanced meaningfully at Officer Wu, who nodded and went round to the rear of the Manor with one of the officers, to prevent anyone escaping.

As soon as he heard what the attendant had to say, Steward Meng knew that the officers had come for Rolling Thunder Wen. He told Song to go out and keep them occupied, and then went immediately to Wen's room.

'Master Wen,' he said, 'there are some Eagle's Claws outside. There's nothing we can do. We'll just have to hide the three of you for a while.'

He helped Wen up, and led him to a pavilion in the garden behind the Manor. Meng and Scholar Yu pushed aside a stone table in the pavilion, exposing an iron plate beneath it. They worked free an iron ring on top of the plate and pulled it up. Underneath was a cellar.

Just then, they heard people outside the back gate, and at the same time shouting from in front, as Fire Hand Zhang forced his way through towards the garden. Wen saw that they were surrounded and hurried down the steps into the cellar. Steward Meng replaced the iron plate, and pushed the stone table back over it with the help of two attendants. Zhou's young son kept getting in the way as he tried to help. Meng looked round quickly to make sure nothing was out of place, then ordered the attendants to open the rear gate.

Fire Hand Zhang and the others entered the garden. Seeing Tong amongst the group, Steward Meng said coldly: 'So you are an official. I should not have been so impolite to you earlier.'

'I work for the Zhen Yuan Security Agency,' Tong replied. He looked round at Zhang. 'I saw the three fugitives enter the Manor. You should order a search.'

'We are peaceful citizens,' said Song. 'My master, Lord Zhou, is one of the most respected gentlemen west of the Yellow River. He would never dare to harbour bandits, and has no rebellious intentions himself.'

Steward Meng asked Zhang to explain the purpose of his visit. Zhang did so, and the steward laughed out loud. 'But the Red Flower Society is a secret society in south China,' he protested. 'Why would they come to the northwest border areas? This guard has let his imagination run away with him.'

Zhang and the rest were professionals, and they knew all too well that Wen was in the Manor. If they conducted a thorough search and found him, there would be no problem. But if the search failed to find him, the matter would certainly not rest there. Causing offence to a man such as Lord Zhou was no light matter, and they hesitated.

Tong was worried that he would be a laughing-stock if Wen wasn't caught that day, and decided to trick Zhou's son into talking. He smiled and took him by the hand, but the boy snatched his hand away.

'What do you want?' he demanded.

'My young friend,' Tong said. 'You tell me where the three visitors who came to your house today are hiding and I'll give you this to buy sweets with.' He took out a silver ingot and presented it to the boy.

The boy made a face at him. 'Who do you think I am? Do you think anyone in my family wants your stinking money?'

Zhang studied the child's face and guessed he knew where Wen was hidden. 'Just you wait until we find them,' he warned. 'We'll cut off your father's head, and yours, and your mother's as well.'

The boy raised his eyebrows. 'I'm not afraid of you, so why would my father be afraid of you either?' he replied.

Suddenly, Tong noticed the pearl bracelet on the boy's left wrist and recognized it immediately as Luo Bing's.

'Those pearls. They belong to one of the visitors,' he said. 'You must have stolen them from her.'

'Why should I steal?' the boy replied angrily. 'She gave them to me.'

Tong laughed. 'All right. She gave them to you. Well, where is she?'

'Why should I tell you?'

'Stop chattering with the child,' Zhang interrupted. 'He won't know anything. He would certainly have been sent away before they hid the three guests in their secret place.'

As he hoped, the child rose to the bait. 'How would you know?' he shouted.

Steward Meng was becoming anxious. 'Let's go inside, young master,' he said.

Zhang seized the opportunity. 'Yes, take the little boy away. He doesn't know anything.'

The boy could hold out no longer. 'I *do* know!' he shouted. 'They're in the garden, in the pavilion!'

Steward Meng tried to stop him, but it was too late. As soon as the words were out, the boy knew he had done something wrong. He flew indoors, panic-stricken and on the verge of tears.

Zhang looked at the pavilion. It was a wide building, and empty, and had red-painted railings around its sides. It provided no hiding-place. He leapt onto one of the railings and looked up into the roof, but saw no sign of a hiding-place there either. He jumped down again and stood silently, deep in thought. Then he had an idea.

'Steward Meng,' he smiled. 'My kungfu is unsophisticated, but I have some clumsy strength. Why don't we have a competition?'

'I wouldn't dare to be so presumptuous,' Meng replied. 'But if you insist. You choose: shall we fight with weapons or without?'

Zhang laughed loudly. 'There's no need for a fight, not between friends such as ourselves. No, I suggest we take turns at trying to lift this stone table. I hope you won't laugh at me if I can't.'

Meng gave a start. 'No, I don't think that would be…a good…' he stuttered.

The others were surprised at Zhang's desire to engage Meng in a test of strength, and they watched intently as he pushed up his sleeves and grasped one of the round legs of the stone table with his right hand. He shouted the word 'Lift!', and raised the forty-odd pound table off the ground using just the one hand.

They applauded him for his strength, but the shouts of applause quickly changed to cries of surprise as they noticed the iron plate that had been exposed. The officers lifted up the plate and at once saw Wen in the hole beneath them. But none dared go down and arrest him. They couldn't use darts either as they had been ordered to capture him alive, so all they could do was stand at the entrance to the cellar, weapons in hand, shouting at him.

'We've been betrayed by Iron Ball Manor,' Wen said quietly to Luo Bing. 'We are husband and wife, and I want you to promise me one thing.'

'What's that?'

'Whatever I tell you to do in a moment, you must do.'

Luo Bing nodded, her eyes full of tears.

'Wen Tailai is here,' Wen shouted. 'What's all the noise about?'

A sudden silence descended on the group above.

'My leg is wounded,' Wen added. 'Let a rope down and lift me up.'

Fire Hand Zhang turned round to ask Steward Meng to fetch some rope, but he had disappeared; so he ordered an attendant to go instead. A length of rope was brought, and one of the officers named Cheng Huang grabbed one end and threw the other down into the cellar and hauled Wen out.

As soon as his feet reached the ground, Wen jerked the rope out of Cheng Huang's hands, and with a roar, whirled it round and round his head. Zhang and the others were caught off guard. They ducked in panic as the rope swept towards them. Tong, who had already suffered at Wen's hands, had hidden behind the others, and didn't see the rope until it was too late. With the piercing force of an iron rod, the rope smashed solidly into his back, knocking him to the ground.

Two other officers, Rui and Yan, both members of the Imperial Guard, raced towards Wen from either side while Scholar Yu, wielding his Golden Flute, leapt up the stone steps and attacked Cheng Huang.

Cheng was wielding a brass staff, which was several times, the length of the flute, but Yu quickly forced him onto the defensive. Luo Bing limped up the steps, supporting herself with her sword, but found her way blocked by a tall, muscular man standing at the mouth of the cellar, with his hands on his hips. She pulled out a throwing knife and aimed it at him. The man was Fire Hand Zhang. He made no move until the knife was only an inch from his nose, then stretched out his hand and grabbed it by the hilt. Luo Bing saw his leisurely reaction, and drew a ragged breath.

Fire Hand Zhang now forced her sword to one side, and gave her a push which threw her off balance. She fell back down into the cellar.

Rolling Thunder Wen, meanwhile, was battling simultaneously with the two Imperial Guards, Rui and Yan. His mind was numb with the excruciating pain from his wounds, and he fought like a madman, striking out wildly. Scholar Yu, for his part, had gained the upper hand in his fight with Cheng Huang. Fire Hand Zhang noticed to his great surprise that Yu's technique contained many elements peculiar to the Wudang School. Yu suddenly jumped back into the cellar to help Luo Bing.

'Are you all right?' he asked her.

'It's nothing. Go and help my husband!'

'I'll help you up first,' Yu said.

Wen looked around and saw that his wife had not yet managed to get out of the cellar. He realized he himself could continue no longer. He threw himself at Cheng Huang, paralysed him with a blow to the kidneys, then grabbed him round the waist and fell into the cellar, dragging Cheng down with him.

They landed on the cellar floor with Wen on top of Cheng, neither of them able to move. Luo Bing quickly helped Wen up. His face was completely drained of colour and covered in sweat, but he forced a smile. There was a gulping sound, as he sprayed out a mouthful of blood onto the front of her tunic. Yu understood what Wen was planning, and shouted. 'Make way! Make way!'

With Cheng Huang in the hands of the enemy, Fire Hand Zhang decided against any precipitate action. He heard Yu's shout and waved his arm at the others, indicating they should clear a path for them.

The first one out of the cellar was Cheng Huang with Luo Bing grasping his collar and holding the point of a dagger to the small of his back. Next came Scholar Yu supporting Rolling Thunder Wen. The four shuffled slowly out.

'If anyone moves, this man dies,' Luo Bing shouted.

The four passed through the forest of swords and spears and made their way slowly towards the rear gate. Luo Bing silently thanked Heaven and Earth when she spotted three horses tied to the willow trees just outside.

Fire Hand Zhang could see that the fugitives were about to escape. He decided that capturing Wen Tailai and taking him back to Peking was more important than saving Cheng Huang's life. He picked up the rope Wen had thrown on the ground, fashioned it into a lasso, and flung it at Wen using all his Inner Force. The rope flew whistling through the air and encircled Wen. With a tug, Zhang pulled him out of Scholar Yu's grasp. Wen cried out and Luo Bing turned to help him, ignoring Cheng Huang. But her wound prevented her from moving, and she fell to the ground before she had taken two steps.

'Go! Go quickly!' Wen shouted.

'I'll die with you,' said Luo Bing.

'You agreed that you would do what I told you!' he replied angrily; but before he could finish, the officers swarmed over him. Scholar Yu raced over and picked Luo Bing up, then charged straight out of the gate. An officer moved to stop him, but one of Yu's legs flew through the air and kicked him so hard that he landed on the ground five or six paces away.

Yu ran with Luo Bing over to the horses and placed her on the back of one just as three officers raced through the gates after them.

'Use your throwing knives, quick!' he shouted.

Three blades flashed from her hand and there was a blood-curdling shriek as a knife planted itself in the shoulder of one of the officers. Yu freed the reins of the three horses, mounted one, and pulled the head of the third round so that it was facing the gate. He rapped it sharply on the rump with his flute and the horse charged straight at the officers, trapping them in the gateway. In the confusion, Yu and Luo Bing galloped off.

Luo Bing lay on the horse in a semi-delirious state. She tried several times to pull her horse round and return to Iron Ball Manor, but each time Yu stopped her. He slowed the pace only when he was sure there was no one chasing them.

Another mile further on, Yu saw four riders approaching led by a man with a flowing white beard: it was the Lord of Iron Ball

Manor himself, Zhou Zhongying. Seeing Yu and Luo Bing, he reined in his horse and called out:

'Honoured guests, please stop! I have called for a doctor.'

Full of hatred, Luo Bing flung one of her knives at him. Zhou had not been expecting this at all. He threw himself down flat on his horse, and the knife flew over his back. Behind him, one of his followers deflected the knife with a stroke from his sword, and it plunged into the trunk of a large willow tree beside the road. The blade reflected the rays of the blood-red setting sun, and the light flashed and danced all around them. Just as Zhou was about to question them, Luo Bing began cursing him.

'You vile creature!' she shouted, tears coursing down her face. 'You betrayed my husband! I will have my revenge on you!' She urged her horse forward, brandishing her pair of swords.

'Wait!' cried Zhou, fending her off with his hands. 'Let me explain.'

'We must save your husband first,' said Scholar Yu to Luo Bing, restraining her. 'We can raze Iron Ball Manor to the ground once we've rescued him.'

Luo Bing saw the logic in what he said, and pulled the head of her horse round. She spat on the ground in hate, slapped her horse, and galloped off.

Lord Zhou had always been a man of honour who stood by his friends, a man spoken of with respect on River and Lake. He wondered what was behind this young woman's anger and questioned the attendant who had been sent to the town to fetch a doctor. But the man said only that when he left, Lady Zhou and Steward Meng had been looking after the guests, and that there had been no disagreements.

Zhou galloped all the way back to the Manor, and strode quickly inside shouting: 'Call Steward Meng!'

'The steward is with her Ladyship,' one of the attendants told him. Then the rest all began talking at once, giving him accounts of what had happened, how the officers had arrested Wen Tailai and taken him away, and had left the Manor only a short while before.

'Who was it told the officers the three guests were hiding in the cellar?' Zhou asked.

The attendants looked at each other, not daring to speak. The sound of Zhou's two iron balls clacking together in his hand grew even louder than usual. 'What are you all standing there for?' he shouted. 'Go and get Meng immediately!'

As he spoke, Steward Meng himself ran into the room.

'Who let the secret out?' Zhou shouted hoarsely. 'Tell me!'

Meng hesitated, then said: 'The Eagle's Claws found it out for themselves.'

'Nonsense!' Zhou roared. 'How would that bunch of dog-thieves ever find a place as well-hidden as my cellar?'

Meng did not answer, not daring to meet his master's gaze. Lady Zhou came in hugging her son, but Zhou ignored her.

His gaze swung round to Song's face. 'It was you, wasn't it? As soon as you saw the officers, you took fright and talked, didn't you?' he shouted. Steward Meng he knew to be trustworthy, but Song was a coward and knew no kungfu.

'No...it wasn't me,' replied Song, scared out of his wits. 'It was...it was the young...the young master.'

Zhou's heart missed a beat. 'Come over here,' he said to his son.

The boy walked, cringing, over to his father.

'Was it you who told the officers that our three guests were in the garden cellar?' he asked.

The boy had never dared to lie to his father, but he could not bring himself to confess. Zhou brandished his whip.

'Will you speak?' he shouted.

The boy looked at his mother. He was so scared he wanted to burst into tears. Lady Zhou walked over and stood close beside him.

Steward Meng saw that deception was of no avail. 'Master,' he said. 'The officers were very cunning. They made out that if the young master did not talk, he would be a coward.'

'You wanted to be a hero, so you told them, is that correct?' Zhou shouted.

The boy's face was drained of colour. 'Yes, father,' he replied quietly.

Zhou could not control his anger. 'Is that any way for a brave hero to act?' he shouted. He threw the two iron balls in his right hand at the opposite wall in frustration, but at that very moment, his son threw himself into his father's arms to beg for mercy, and one of the balls hit the boy square on the head. Zhou had put all of his rage and might into the throw. Blood sprayed in all directions.

Zhou was appalled by what he had done. He took hold of his son and embraced him.

'Father,' the boy said. 'I...I won't do it again...Don't hit me...I...' He died even as he was speaking. Everyone in the room watched in stunned silence.

Lady Zhou grabbed her son, shouting: 'Child, child!' She saw he had stopped breathing, and stared dumbly at him for a moment. Then, like a crazed tiger, she struck out at Zhou.

'Why? Why did you kill the child?' she sobbed.

Zhou shook his head and retreated two paces. 'I...I didn't...'

Lady Zhou let go of her son's body, and grabbed a sword from the scabbard of one of the attendants. She leapt forward to strike out at her husband. He made no move to avoid the blow.

'It would be better if we were all dead,' he said, closing his eyes.

Seeing the state he was in, her grip loosened. She dropped the sword to the ground and ran out of the hall, sobbing.

Love, Fever, Rescue

Luo Bing and Scholar Yu kept to the back roads for fear of meeting Yamen officers, and rode on until the sky was completely black. The countryside was desolate: there were no inns and they were unable to find even a farmhouse. They stopped to rest beside a large rock. Yu released the horses to graze, then cut some grass with Luo Bing's sword and spread it out on the ground.

'At least we have a bed, even if we have no food or water,' he said. 'We must wait until tomorrow and try to think of something then.'

Luo Bing cared about nothing but her husband. She cried continuously. Yu comforted her, saying the Red Flower Society would certainly come in force to help them rescue Rolling Thunder Wen. Luo Bing was exhausted, and hearing his words, she was a little reassured and soon fell into a deep sleep.

In her dream, she seemed to meet her husband, who held her gently in his arms, and kissed her lightly on the mouth. She felt deliciously happy and lazily let him embrace her.

'I've been so miserable thinking about you,' she said. 'Are all your wounds healed?'

Wen mumbled a few words and held her even tighter, kissing her even more passionately. Just as she was beginning to feel aroused,

she suddenly started and awoke. In the starlight, she could see that
the person embracing her was not her husband, but Scholar Yu.

'I've been miserable thinking about you too!' he whispered.

Ashamed and angry, Luo Bing slapped him hard on the face,
fought her way free, and stumbled away a few steps. She fumbled
for her knives, and shouted harshly: 'What you're doing is totally
out of order!'

Yu was stunned. 'Listen to me—'

'No, you listen to me!' she replied angrily. 'Which four types
of people does the Red Flower Society put to death?'

'Tartars and Manchus; corrupt officials; landlords and tyrants;
and villains and scoundrels,' Yu recited quietly, his head hung low.

The space between Luo Bing's eyebrows closed. 'Which four
crimes by Red Flower Society members are punishable by death?'

'Death to those who surrender to the Manchu Court. Death
to those who betray the Society. Death to those who betray their
friends. And death to those who violate the wives and daughters
of others.'

'If you have the guts, you will deal with yourself quickly!'
Luo Bing shouted. 'You must punish yourself with the Three Thrusts
and Six Holes!'

According to the Society's code, a member who had
committed an offence in a moment of confusion and sincerely
regretted it could pierce his own thigh three times with a knife so
that it penetrated right through and came out the other side. This
was known as the Three Thrusts and Six Holes. The member could
then plead to the Helmsman for forgiveness, and hope that his case
would be dealt with leniently.

'I beg you to kill me,' Yu cried. 'If I die at your hand, I will still
die happy.'

Luo Bing's anger blazed even more intensely. She raised the
knife in her hand, her wrist steeled, ready to throw.

'You don't know anything,' Yu said in a shaky voice. 'You
don't know how much I have suffered for you over the last five or
six years. From the moment I first saw you, my heart...was...no
longer my own.'

'I was already married then,' Luo Bing said angrily. 'Do you
mean you didn't know?'

'I...I knew. I couldn't control myself, so I never dared to see
too much of you. Whenever the Society had any business to be

done, I always begged the Helmsman to send me to do it. The others thought I was just hardworking; no one knew that I was really avoiding you. When I was away working, there was never a day or an hour when I did not think of you.'

He took a step towards her and pulled up his left sleeve, exposing his arm. 'I hate myself,' he said. 'I curse my heart for the animal it is. Every time the hatred overcomes me, I cut myself here with a knife. Look!'

By the dim starlight, Luo Bing could see that his arm was covered in scars, and her heart involuntarily softened.

'I always think, why couldn't Heaven have allowed me to meet you before you married,' he continued. 'We are about the same age, but the difference in age between you and Brother Wen Tailai is huge.'

Luo Bing's anger surged up once more. 'What does the difference in our ages matter? My husband is loving and just, he is a great man. How could he be compared with someone like you, you—'

She gave a snort of contempt, then turned and walked over to her horse. As she struggled to mount it, Yu went over to help her up, but she shouted 'Keep away!' and got up on her own.

'Where are you going?' he asked.

'It's none of your business. With Rolling Thunder in the hands of the Eagle's Claws, I might as well be dead anyway. Give me my swords.'

Yu lowered his head and handed the pair of swords to her.

Seeing him standing there, so lost and bewildered, Luo Bing suddenly said: 'Work seriously for the good of the Society, never show me any disrespect again, and I won't tell anyone about what happened tonight. And I'll help you find a nice girl—a talented and beautiful girl!'

She smiled briefly, slapped her horse, and rode off.

Luo Bing rode on for a mile or so, then stopped, searching the sky for the North Star to get her bearings. If she rode west, she would meet up with the fighters of the Red Flower Society; to go east would be to follow after her captured husband. She knew that, wounded as she was, it would be impossible for her to save him single-handed. But with her husband heading eastwards, how could she possibly turn away from him? Broken-hearted, she let her horse wander unchecked for a few miles. Then, seeing that she had already travelled a long way from Scholar Yu, she dismounted and settled down to sleep in a spinney of small trees. Angry and bitter, she cried to herself for a while and then fell into a deep sleep.

In the middle of the night, she woke suddenly with a burning fever and called out in a slurred voice: 'Water! I must drink some water!' But there was no one at hand to hear her.

Next day, her condition was even worse. She managed with a struggle to sit up, but her head hurt so badly she was forced to lie down again. She slept, and awoke to feel the sun beating down on her head. She watched as it sank towards the west. She was thirsty and hungry, but remounting the horse was impossible.

'It doesn't matter if I die here,' she thought. 'Except that I will never see my husband again.' Her eyes glazed over and she fainted away. But after an interval, she heard someone say: 'Good. She's coming round!'

She slowly opened her eyes and saw a young, doe-eyed girl standing beside her. The girl was eighteen or nineteen years old with a tanned face and thick eyebrows. She looked very happy to see Luo Bing awaken.

'Go quickly and get some millet gruel for the lady to drink,' she told a maid.

Luo Bing realized she was lying on a kang in between the folds of a quilt. The room she was in was clean and tastefully furnished. She was obviously in the house of a very wealthy family.

'What is your family name, miss?' she asked the girl.

'My surname is Zhou. You sleep for a while. We can talk again later.'

The girl watched as Luo Bing drank a bowl of gruel and then quietly left her. Luo Bing closed her eyes and slept once more.

When she woke, the lamps had already been lit. Outside the door, she heard a girl's voice saying loudly:

'Father should never have allowed them to throw their weight around like that and run riot here in Iron Ball Manor! If it had been me, I would have taught them a good lesson!'

Luo Bing started in fright when she heard the words Iron Ball Manor. The girl and her maid walked into the room and looked through the curtains hanging over the kang, but Luo Bing closed her eyes and pretended to be asleep. The girl went over to the wall and took down a sword. Luo Bing noticed her own swords on a table close by and prepared herself. If the girl struck out at her, she would throw the quilt over her head, grab the swords, and fight her way out. But all she heard was the maid saying:

'Mistress, you mustn't make any more trouble. His Lordship is very distressed. Don't make him angry again.'

'Huh! I don't care,' the girl replied. She hurried out of the room, sword in hand, with the maid at her heels.

Luo Bing guessed correctly that the girl was Lord Zhou's daughter, Zhou Qi. She was a bold, straightforward person, very much like her father, and had a love of minding other people's business. On the day Wen was captured, she had wounded someone in the mêlée, and had spent the night away from home, planning to wait for her father's anger to subside before returning. On her way back, she came across Luo Bing unconscious by the road and brought her to the Manor, where she discovered to her horror that her father had killed her brother, and that her mother had run off.

'If they could betray my husband to the authorities, why did they save me?' thought Luo Bing darkly. 'There must be some other evil scheme afoot.'

The wound on her thigh had not yet healed, and she could not afford to make the slightest mistake. Having been in the Manor once before, she had a vague idea of its layout, and planned to make her way stealthily round to the garden, and then leave by the back gate. But as she passed by the great hall, she saw the lamps were burning brightly inside and heard someone talking very loudly. There was something familiar about the voice. She put her eye close to a crack in the door and saw Lord Zhou in conversation with two other men, one of whom she recognized as the Agency guard Tong. Seeing him, she thought again of her husband's cruel fate and immediately ceased to care whether she lived or died. She pushed open the door and slung one of her knives at Tong.

Fighting Galore

With his wife missing and his son dead, Zhou had spent two extremely wretched days. He paced up and down the halls of Iron Ball Manor, a tormented soul. After nightfall on the second day, one of his retainers reported that two visitors had arrived at the Manor gates, and Zhou ordered Steward Meng to receive them.

One was Tong, the other a member of the Imperial Guard named Pan, one of the officers who had helped to seize Wen. Meng guessed that no good would come of the visit, and tried to fob them off.

'His Lordship is not feeling well,' he told them. 'If you have any message, I will convey it for you.'

Tong laughed. 'Whether Lord Zhou sees us or not is up to him. But Iron Ball Manor is faced with a crisis that may destroy every member of the Zhou family. What is the point of putting on such airs?'

Meng had no option but to allow them through. The iron balls in Zhou's hand clacked sharply together as the visitors repeated their words.

'What do you mean, Iron Ball Manor is faced with a crisis?' he demanded.

Pan pulled a letter from his gown and spread it out on the table, holding it down with both hands as if afraid that Zhou would snatch it away. Zhou peered down at it and saw that it was a letter written to him by Hidden Needle Lu Feiqing of the Wudang School, asking him to come to the aid of some friends of the Red Flower Society who were in difficulties.

Rolling Thunder Wen had not been able to present the letter to Zhou, and it had been found when he was searched after his capture. Hidden Needle Lu was a well-known fugitive, and the letter clearly indicated that he was in league with Iron Ball Manor. The officers had discussed the matter, and had decided that reporting the existence of the letter to their superiors would not necessarily result in Lu's capture and could even increase their own workload. It would be more beneficial to use the letter to extort a sum of money from Zhou and divide it up amongst themselves.

Zhou was shocked at the sight of the letter. 'What do you gentlemen want?' he asked.

'We have long been admirers of yours, Lord Zhou,' said Pan. 'We know of your reputation for generosity and friendship. Friends are much more important than money, and I'm sure you would spend thousands of silver ingots for a friend without batting an eyelid. You of course realize, Lord Zhou, that if the authorities were ever to see this letter, the consequences would be disastrous. When we found it, we resolved to destroy it in the spirit of friendship, even though it meant risking our own heads. We all agreed never to say a word about Iron Ball Manor harbouring the fugitive Wen

Tailai. We decided to shoulder this monstrous responsibility and not to report it to our superiors.'

'That was very good of you,' Zhou replied dryly.

'But,' Pan continued, 'the thing is that we officers have had a lot of expenses on this trip out of the Capital. We have heavy debts to settle. If perhaps Lord Zhou could spare a thought for us, we would feel eternally grateful.'

Zhou was extremely angry. He had let down his real friends, his beloved son had died as a result, his wife was gone, and these officers were the ones to blame. And now they had come back to try and blackmail him.

'We are mere nobodies, it's true,' Tong said. 'We accomplish little, and bungle much. If we were ever asked to build a Manor like this one of yours, we'd have to confess that it was beyond our abilities. But if we were asked to destroy it—'

Before he could finish, Zhou's daughter, Zhou Qi, came running into the hall, and shouted harshly: 'Let me see you try!'

Zhou motioned to his daughter and the two of them walked out of the hall together. 'Go and tell Steward Meng that whatever happens, these two Eagle's Claws must not be allowed to leave the Manor!' he whispered.

'Good!' replied Zhou Qi, very pleased. 'I was getting angrier and angrier just listening outside.'

Zhou returned to the hall.

'Since you refuse to do us this favour, Lord Zhou, we will take our leave of you,' said Pan. He picked up Lu's letter and ripped it to shreds as Zhou stood by dumbfounded, completely taken aback.

'This is a duplicate of the letter,' Pan explained. 'The original letter is with the Fire Hand Judge, Zhang Zhaozhong.'

It was at that moment that one of Luo Bing's throwing knives came flying through the air towards Tong. Zhou detested and despised Tong, but he couldn't allow him to die in the Manor. He had no time to consider the matter carefully, and quickly threw one of the iron balls in his hand at the knife. There was a 'clang' as both knife and ball fell to the ground.

'Aha!' shouted Luo Bing. 'So you're all in this together. You vile creature! You've already betrayed my husband, why don't you kill me as well?' She ran into the hall, her swords held high, and struck out at Zhou.

With no weapon in his hand, Zhou hurriedly picked up a chair to deflect the blow. 'You are being too hasty!' he protested. 'Why don't we talk this over?'

But Luo Bing was in no mood for talk. Zhou retreated steadily as she attacked, heading for the wall. Suddenly, Luo Bing heard the sound of a blade swishing towards her back, and ducked as the blade cleaved over her head. She turned to find Zhou Qi standing behind her, seething with anger.

'You ungrateful woman!' Zhou Qi shouted, pointing her finger accusingly. 'I saved you, out of the goodness of my heart. What are you doing attacking my father?'

'You people of Iron Ball Manor,' Luo Bing replied bitterly, 'with your fake charity and fake generosity! Just keep away, and I won't harm you.'

She turned and resumed her attack on Zhou, who dodged left and right, shouting 'Stop! Stop!' In a fit of rage, Zhou Qi jumped in front of her father and began fiercely fighting with Luo Bing.

In terms of Martial Arts skill and experience, Luo Bing was far superior to Zhou Qi, but she was greatly handicapped by the wounds to her shoulder and thigh, and by her resentment and anger (such negative emotions are to be avoided at all costs in the Martial Arts). She gradually began to lose ground.

'Stop!' Zhou shouted repeatedly, but both girls ignored him. Pan and Tong stood to one side watching the battle.

Suddenly, they all heard a weird cry and saw a figure in black come lurching out of the shadows and lunge at Zhou's daughter. It was a little hunchback wielding a short-handled Wolf's Tooth club, the sharp teeth on the end of which sparkled and flashed as it swung wildly towards Zhou Qi. The girl jumped in fright and countered by chopping at his shoulder with her sword, with the move known as Magic Dragon Shakes His Scales. The hunchback blocked her sword with all his might. Under the intense shock of the impact, Zhou Qi's arm went numb and her sword nearly fell out of her hand. She leapt back. The hunchback did not press his attack, but instead turned to Luo Bing.

'Brother Zhang!' she cried. Tears coursed down her face.

'Where's Rolling Thunder?' he asked. The hunchback was Zhang Jin, tenth in seniority in the ranks of the Red Flower Society. In the light of the lamp, the ugliness of his physical appearance was now all too visible.

Luo Bing pointed at Zhou, Pan, and Tong. 'They betrayed him! Brother Zhang, avenge him for me!'

Without waiting for details, Hunchback Zhang threw himself onto the ground and rolled towards Lord Zhou. Zhou leapt up onto a table and shouted 'Stop!' again, but Hunchback Zhang was not interested in explanations. He aimed the Wolf's Tooth club at Zhou's thigh. Zhou jumped into the air, landing on the ground just as the club slammed into the sandalwood table. The fangs sank deep into the wood, and for a moment Hunchback Zhang was unable to pull the club free.

Just then, Steward Meng rushed into the hall and handed Lord Zhou his gold-backed sword. He had no idea of the hunchback's motives, but anyone attacking his master was an enemy. Lord Zhou and Steward Meng attacked the hunchback together, but Zhang held them off with his club, at the same time shouting out: 'May your ancestors be damned, Mastermind, if you don't get in here quickly and protect Sister Luo Bing!'

Hunchback Zhang and Xu Tianhong, the Kungfu Mastermind, had raced day and night without stopping to reach Iron Ball Manor. Hearing Hunchback Zhang's call, Xu now ran into the hall and made straight for Luo Bing. Her heart leapt for joy as she spotted him. She pointed at Tong and Pan.

'They are the ones who betrayed Rolling Thunder,' she cried.

Xu leapt at Tong. Xu was like a dwarf in stature, but his kungfu was transcendent and, in a second, he had his opponent on the run. Tong dodged to the left as Xu stabbed at him with his steel staff, then hit the floor with a thud as Xu kicked him off his feet.

Xu felt a current of air hit his back as Pan attacked him holding a pair of tempered iron hoops. Xu had no time to turn round; he stepped hard on Tong's chest with his left foot and did a somersault, flipping over to face his attacker. Tong yelled out in pain.

On the other side of the hall, Hunchback Zhang was battling furiously with Steward Meng, Lord Zhou, and Zhou Qi simultaneously.

'Go quickly and guard the Manor gate,' Meng shouted to an attendant. 'Don't let anyone else in.'

'Everyone stop!' Zhou called out. 'Listen to what I have to say!'

Meng and Zhou Qi immediately stepped back several paces. Mastermind Xu also retreated a step, and shouted to the hunchback: 'Hold it, Brother Zhang. Let's listen to him.'

But as he did so, Pan drove his hoops at Xu's back. Caught off his guard, Xu flinched, but his shoulder was struck. He stumbled, and called out angrily: 'You Iron Ball Manor people certainly know a trick or two.' He did not know that Pan was not of the Manor. He abandoned his staff for a short-sword, and fought furiously with Pan.

Tong stood at a distance, staring at Luo Bing. She had only one throwing knife left and was unwilling to use it rashly, so she raised her sword and chased after him. Tong raced nimbly about the great hall, dodging around the tables and chairs.

'Don't be rash,' he told her. 'Your husband is already dead. Why not play along with me?'

When she heard him say that Rolling Thunder was dead, everything went black before Luo Bing's eyes, and she fainted away. Tong raced over to her as she collapsed.

Zhou's anger surged within him as he saw what was happening, and he also ran towards Luo Bing, his gold-backed sword held high. He planned to stop Tong from molesting Luo Bing. But somehow, one misunderstanding followed another: he heard someone at the door to the hall shouting loudly:

'If you dare hurt her, I will fight you to the death!'

The newcomer (a man of handsome features and strong vigorous movements) charged at Zhou with a pair of hooks in his hands, aiming them at Zhou's throat and groin respectively. Zhou raised his sword, lightly deflected the hooks, then retreated a step.

'Who are you, sir?' he asked.

The man ignored him, and bent down to look at Luo Bing. Her face was white and her breathing very shallow. He helped her up into a chair.

The fighting in the hall was growing more furious all the time. Suddenly, there was a shout outside followed by the sound of weapons clashing. A moment later, one of the Zhou retainers came running into the hall closely followed by a tall, fat man holding a steel whip.

'Brother Yang! Brother Wei!' shouted Mastermind Xu. 'We must kill all of these Iron Ball Manor people today, or our work isn't over.'

The fat man was Iron Pagoda Yang, eighth in the Red Flower Society's hierarchy, while the one with the handsome face and the hooks was Nine Life Leopard Wei, who ranked ninth. Leopard Wei was a fearless fighter who had never once been seriously wounded, and was consequently said to have nine lives.

Zhou observed the ensuing battle, and was greatly impressed by the fighting skills of the newly arrived intruders. 'Heroes of the Red Flower Society!' he shouted at the top of his voice. 'Listen to me!'

By this time, Leopard Wei had taken over from Xu and was busy fighting Pan. He slackened off slightly as he heard Zhou's shout, but Xu called out: 'Careful! Don't be tricked.'

Even as he spoke, Pan raised his hoops and struck out at Wei. He was afraid of Iron Ball Manor and the Red Flower Society getting together, and couldn't allow them any opportunity to talk peace.

Mastermind Xu tried to assess the desperate battle in progress in the hall. Hunchback Zhang was fighting three people at once and was under pressure, although not yet ready to admit defeat. Leopard Wei, meanwhile, was also having difficulty maintaining his defence. Victory, Xu could see, was impossible.

'Set fire to the place, quick!' he shouted to disconcert the Manor people. 'Brother Shi, go and seal the rear gate. Don't let anyone escape!'

On hearing the shout, Zhou Qi ran for the door of the hall planning to look out for the arsonists.

'So you want to escape, do you?' a deep voice outside said as she reached the doorway.

She started backwards in fright. In the flickering candlelight, she saw two men blocking the doorway. The face of the one who had spoken looked as though it was covered in a layer of frost. Gleaming shafts of light shone from his two eyes, sapping the very life from those they fixed upon. Zhou Qi wanted to look at the other man, but her eyes were caught by the first man's stare.

'A ghost!' she cried softly.

'That's right,' he replied. 'I'm Melancholy Ghost.'

It was the Red Flower Society's Superintendant of Punishments, Melancholy Ghost Shi. There was no warmth in his words. Zhou Qi had never been afraid of anything before, but she shuddered at the sight of this sinister man.

'Do you think I'm afraid of you?' she shouted to bolster her own courage, and struck out at him with her sword.

The man countered with his own sword, his eyes still fixed on her, and, in only a few moves, had completely out-manoeuvred her.

On the other side of the hall, Steward Meng was battling Hunchback Zhang, but it had already become obvious that he was no match for him. Tong, meanwhile, had not been sighted for some time. Only Lord Zhou, fighting against Mastermind Xu and Leopard Wei, had managed to gain the upper hand. But just as he was on the point of winning, someone else leapt forward shouting: 'I'll take you on, old man!'

Lord Zhou's new adversary was using an iron oar as a weapon. It swung up from behind his back, over his right shoulder, and smashed down towards Zhou with astonishing ferocity. This man was known as Crocodile Jiang, and ranked thirteenth in the Red Flower Society's hierarchy.

Zhou noted Crocodile Jiang's mighty strength and dodged to the left. Then he began to retreat as he fought him off, keeping constantly on the move. He could see that Pan was being routed by Iron Pagoda Yang, and as Pan ran close by him, Zhou struck out at him with his great sword.

Lord Zhou knew that the Red Flower Society had utterly misunderstood the situation, and that it would take more than a few words to explain matters. Furthermore, his several attempts to halt the battle had been sabotaged by Pan. With the Red Flower Society's fighters becoming increasingly numerous, and the fighting fiercer and fiercer, it was only a matter of time before someone was wounded, if not killed, and when that happened, the misunderstanding would have become a matter for true vengeance. The situation would be irretrievable.

Seeing Zhou's sword slicing towards him, Pan started in terror and frantically dodged out of the way. He fully realized Zhou's intention.

'We joined forces to capture Wen Tailai but it was you who killed him,' he shouted at Zhou. 'What are you planning now? You want to murder me and keep the whole Manchu reward for yourself, is that it?'

Hunchback Zhang howled and smashed his Wolf's Tooth club at Lord Zhou's thigh. But Mastermind Xu, who was altogether subtler and more attentive, finally realized what was happening. Fighting with Lord Zhou earlier, he had noticed how the old man had several times stayed his hand, and he knew there had to be a reason for it. 'Brother Zhang!' he shouted. 'Not so fast!'

The Hunchback's blood lust was up, however, and he paid no attention. Crocodile Jiang's iron oar swung forward, aimed at Zhou's midriff. Zhou leant to one side to avoid it, but just at that moment Yang swung his steel whip down towards his shoulder from behind. He heard the gust of wind behind his ear and blocked the blow with his sword, causing both Yang's and his own arm to go numb for a second. The physical strength of the three Red Flower fighters was frightening and, battling all three single-handed, it was obvious that Zhou was gradually being worn down. Then Jiang's iron oar struck upwards at Zhou's great sword: Zhou lost his grasp, and the sword flew up out of his hand and impaled itself in a beam in the roof of the hall.

The Red Flower Society fighters pressed in closer around Zhou, who was now weaponless, and Hunchback Zhang and Crocodile Jiang's weapons converged towards him. Zhou knew he had no time to lose. He picked up a table and heaved it at the two of them. As he did so, the candlestick on the table fell to the floor and the flame went out.

In a flash of inspiration, Steward Meng pulled out a catapult and—pa-pa-pa!—shot out a string of pellets at the other candles, extinguishing them all.

An inky blackness descended on the hall.

Fire! Fire!

Everyone held their breath and stayed completely silent, not daring to make any sound that would give away their position.

In the midst of the silence, footsteps sounded outside the hall. The door was thrown open and a shaft of light struck their eyes as a man carrying a burning torch strode in. He was dressed in the robes of a scholar and, in his left hand, he held a golden flute. As soon as he had passed through the door, he stood to one side and raised the torch up high, lighting the way as three other men entered. The first was a one-armed Taoist priest with a sword slung across his back. The second man, wearing a light gown loosely tied around the waist, looked like the son of a nobleman. He was followed by a young boy in his teens who held a bundle in his hands. The four were in fact Scholar Yu, Father Speckless, and the newly appointed Helmsman of the Red Flower Society, Chen Jialuo. The young boy was Chen's page, Xin Yan.

Scholar Yu presented Zhou with a letter of introduction, bowed, and then announced in a loud voice: 'The Helmsman of the Red Flower Society has come to pay his respects to Lord Zhou of Iron Ball Manor.'

Zhou put his hands together in salutation. 'Honoured guests,' he said. 'Welcome to my humble Manor. Please be seated.'

The tables and chairs in the great hall had all been overturned and thrown about during the fight and everything was in great disorder.

'Attendants!' Zhou roared. The tables and chairs were quickly rearranged, the candles relit, and the guests and hosts seated. Helmsman Chen took the seat of honour on the eastern side of the hall and was followed, in order of seniority, by the other Red Flower heroes. Zhou took the seat of honour on the western side, followed in order by Steward Meng, Zhou Qi, and his various retainers.

Scholar Yu stole a glance at Luo Bing's beautiful, drawn face. He had no idea if she had told anyone of his misdemeanour. The night she had left him, he had not known where to go, but after two days of roaming around aimlessly, he had run into Helmsman Chen and Father Speckless, who were on their way to Iron Ball Manor.

With the Red Flower heroes and the Manor people being so polite to each other, Pan knew his game was up and began to sidle towards the door in the hope of slipping out unnoticed. But Mastermind Xu leapt over and blocked his path.

'Please stay here,' he said. 'There is a great deal of explaining to be done.'

Pan did not dare to object.

'Brother Wen Tailai, fourth in our humble Society, was attacked by the Eagle's Claws and suffered a serious injury,' Helmsman Chen said coldly, addressing Lord Zhou. 'He came to you for refuge, and we are much indebted to you for the assistance extended to him. All the Brothers of our Society are grateful, and I take this opportunity to offer our thanks.'

He stood and bowed deeply.

Zhou hurriedly returned the bow, extremely embarrassed.

'Helmsman, you don't understand!' shouted Hunchback Zhang, jumping up. 'He is the very man who betrayed Brother Wen!'

Leopard Wei, who was sitting next to Zhang, gave him a push and told him to shut up.

'Our Brothers have travelled through the night to call on you,' Helmsman Chen continued, ignoring the interruption. 'We have all been extremely anxious about Brother Wen. We are unaware of the state of his injuries, but I imagine you would have invited a doctor to treat him. If it is convenient, Lord Zhou, we would like you to take us to him.'

He stood up, and the heroes of the Red Flower Society followed suit.

Zhou stammered, momentarily unable to answer.

'They killed him!' Luo Bing shouted, her voice choked with sobs. 'Helmsman, we must kill this old man in payment for Brother Wen's life!'

Helmsman Chen turned pale. Hunchback Zhang, Iron Pagoda Yang, and a number of the others drew their weapons and moved forward threateningly.

'Your Brother Wen did indeed come to our humble Manor—' Steward Meng began.

'Well then, please take us to see him,' Xu broke in.

'When he, and Lady Luo Bing, and your Brother Yu arrived here, our Lord was not at home,' Meng replied. 'It was I who dispatched someone to fetch a doctor: Lady Luo Bing and your Brother Yu saw that with their own eyes. Later, the Court officers arrived. We are extremely ashamed to say that we were unable to protect our guests, and that your Brother Wen was captured. You blame us, sir, for not looking after him properly and for failing to fulfil our responsibility to protect friends. We admit it. If you wish to kill us, go ahead. But do not point your finger at our Lord and accuse him of betraying a friend!'

Luo Bing jumped forward a step and pointed at Meng accusingly. 'You tell us!' she shouted. 'We were in the cellar. It was a good hiding-place. You must have been in the pay of the Eagles's Claws, or they would never have known where we were!'

Steward Meng was speechless.

'Lord Zhou, at the time of the incident, you may not actually have been at home,' Father Speckless added. 'But just as a dragon has a head, men have masters. As this concerns Iron Ball Manor, we must ask you to account for what happened.'

Pan, cowering to one side, suddenly spoke up. 'It was his son that talked,' he shouted. 'Why doesn't he just say so?'

'Lord Zhou, is this true?' Helmsman Chen asked.

Zhou nodded slowly. The heroes of the Red Flower Society roared in anger and moved in even closer, some glaring at Zhou, some looking at Chen, waiting for his signal.

Chen gave Pan a sidelong glance. 'And who are you, sir?' he asked.

'He's an Eagle's Claw,' Luo Bing said. 'He was one of the ones that seized Brother Wen.'

Helmsman Chen slowly walked over to Pan, then suddenly snatched the iron hoop out of his grasp, whipped both his hands behind his back, and held them together. Pan gave a shout and struggled unsuccessfully to break free.

'Where have you taken Brother Wen?' shouted Chen. Pan kept his mouth shut, an expression of proud insolence on his face. Chen's fingers pressed the Central Mansion point below Pan's ribs. 'Will you talk?' he asked.

Pan yelled out in agony. Chen touched his Tendon Contraction point. This time, Pan could bear the pain no longer.

'I'll talk...I'll talk,' he whispered. 'They're taking him to Peking.'

'So he...he isn't dead then?' Luo Bing asked quickly.

'Of course he isn't dead,' Pan replied. 'He's an important criminal. No one would dare to kill him!'

The Red Flower heroes all breathed a sigh of relief; Luo Bing's heart overflowed with happiness, and she fainted away, falling backwards to the floor. Scholar Yu stretched out his hand to catch her, but then suddenly pulled it back again. Her head hit the ground, and Hunchback Zhang hurriedly knelt down beside her.

'Sister!' he called, giving Yu a sidelong glance full of disdain. 'Are you all right?'

Helmsman Chen relaxed his grip on Pan's hands. 'Tie him up,' he said to his page-boy, Xin Yan. 'Brothers!' he went on loudly. 'It is vitally important that we save Brother Wen. We can settle our scores here another time.'

The heroes of the Red Flower Society voiced their assent in unison. Luo Bing was now sitting on a chair crying with joy. Hearing the Helmsman's words, she stood up, supported by Hunchback Zhang. The heroes then walked to the door of the hall, escorted by Steward Meng. Helmsman Chen turned and said to Lord Zhou. 'Our apologies for the inconvenience we have caused you. We will meet again.'

Zhou knew from his tone what he really meant: the Red Flower Society would be back to seek vengeance.

'Once we've saved Brother Wen, I, Hunchback Zhang, will be the first to return to do battle with you, old man!' shouted Zhang.

Zhou Qi leapt forward. 'What sort of creature are you that you dare speak to my father like that?'

'Huh!' he replied. 'Go and call your big brother out and tell him I wish to meet him.'

'My big brother?' she asked, puzzled.

'Yes, your big brother—the one who betrayed Rolling Thunder. Where's he hiding?'

'This hunchback's talking nonsense,' Zhou Qi said. 'I don't have an elder brother.'

'Very well,' Lord Zhou said angrily. 'I will hand over my son to you. Follow me!'

Suddenly, there were shouts from outside of 'Fire! Fire!', and flames began to cast a glow in the great hall. But Zhou paid no attention. He strode out and Helmsman Chen and the others followed him through two courtyards. The fire was already burning fiercely and the heat from the flames was oppressive. In the dark of the night, the red glow reached up through the billows of smoke and far into the sky.

'Let's all put the fire out first,' called out Mastermind Xu.

'First you tell someone to burn the place down, and then you pretend to be a good man!' cried Zhou Qi indignantly. She remembered how he had threatened earlier to set fire to the Manor, and was convinced that the Red Flower Society was responsible. Full of grief and resentment, she struck out at him with her sword, but Xu nimbly dodged out of the way.

Lord Zhou appeared not to notice any of this, and continued to lead them towards the rear hall of the Manor. As they entered the hall, they could see that it was arranged for a funeral. A pair of lighted candles had been placed on the altar before the Spirit Tablet bearing the name of the deceased, along with white streamers and piles of 'funeral money' for the deceased to spend in the other world. Zhou parted a set of white curtains, revealing a small black coffin with its lid still open.

'My son revealed your Brother Wen's hiding-place, it is true,' he said. 'If you want him...then take him!' His voice suddenly broke.

In the sombre candlelight, the heroes looked into the coffin and saw the corpse of a boy.

'My brother was only ten years old,' cried Zhou Qi. 'He didn't understand what was going on. He was tricked into letting out the secret. When father returned, he was very angry and killed my brother by mistake. That's why my mother has left home. Are you satisfied yet? If not, why don't you kill my father and me as well?'

The Red Flower heroes realized they had unjustly accused Lord Zhou. It had all been a misunderstanding. Hunchback Zhang, who was temperamentally the most direct of them all, leapt forward and kowtowed before Zhou, his head hitting the floor with a resounding thump.

'I have wronged you, sir!' he cried. 'Hunchback Zhang begs your forgiveness.'

Helmsman Chen and the others all came forward one by one to apologize. Lord Zhou hastened to bow to them in return.

'Never will we forget the assistance that Lord Zhou has extended to the Red Flower Society,' declared Chen. 'Brothers, the important thing now is to put out the fire. Everyone lend a hand quickly.'

The Red Flower heroes ran out of the hall. But the flames were already lighting up the sky. The sound of roof tiles smashing to the ground, and of rafters and pillars collapsing, mingled with the frantic shouts and cries of the servants. The Anxi region is notorious throughout China as a 'wind storehouse', and the wind was now stoking the flames. It was soon clear that the fire could not be extinguished, and that the great Iron Ball Manor would soon be completely razed to the ground.

The heat in the rear hall was intense, and the cloth streamers and paper money on the altar were already smouldering. But Lord Zhou remained beside the coffin.

'Father, father!' Zhou Qi shouted as the flames started to curl into the hall. 'We must leave!'

Lord Zhou took no notice. He continued to gaze at his son in the coffin, unwilling to leave him there to be consumed by the fire.

Hunchback Zhang bent over and shouted: 'Brother Yang, put the coffin on my back.'

Iron Pagoda Yang grasped hold of the two sides of the coffin, lifted it up, and placed it on Zhang's hunched back. Maintaining his crouching position, Zhang Jin then charged out of the hall. Zhou

Qi supported her father, and with the others gathered around to protect them, they too ran outside. It was a matter of minutes before the roof of the rear hall collapsed. They all shuddered at the thought of how close a shave it had been.

'Ai-ya!' Zhou Qi suddenly shouted. 'That Eagles's Claw Tong may still be inside!'

'If he is, so be it!' commented Melancholy Ghost Shi. 'Someone as evil as him deserves to be burnt alive.'

Steward Meng explained to the Helmsman how Tong had come to Iron Ball Manor, first to spy, next as a guide for the officers when they came to seize Wen, and finally to engage in blackmail.

'Yes!' shouted Mastermind Xu. 'It must have been him who started the fire.' He glanced furtively over at Zhou Qi and saw that she was also looking at him out of the corner of her eye. As soon as their eyes met, they both turned their heads away.

'We must catch this man Tong and bring him back with us,' said Helmsman Chen. 'Brothers—Xu, Yang, Wei, and Zhang—the four of you go and search along the roads to the north, south, east, and west. Come back to report within two hours whether you find him or not.'

The four left, and Helmsman Chen went over to apologize to Lord Zhou once again.

'Lord Zhou,' he said. 'The Red Flower Society is responsible for this tragedy that has come upon you. Our debt to you will be difficult to repay. But we will find Lady Zhou and bring her back to you. Iron Ball Manor has been destroyed, and we undertake to have it completely rebuilt. All your people will receive full compensation from the Society for whatever they have lost.'

'What kind of talk is that, sir?' replied Lord Zhou. 'Wealth and riches are mere worldly things. Any more of that sort of talk, and I shall begin to wonder if you consider me your friend.'

He had been greatly upset to see Iron Ball Manor burn down, but friendship was more important to him than such worldly considerations. Above all, now that the misunderstanding had been cleared up, he was happy to have established relations with such well-known fighters as the Red Flower heroes. But a moment later, he caught sight once more of his son's little coffin and another wave of sorrow flooded his heart.

The four Red Flower heroes sent out to look for Tong eventually returned with nothing to report. They guessed that he must have taken advantage of the fire and confusion to escape.

'Luckily we know that the fellow is with the Zhen Yuan Security Agency,' said Chen. 'We will catch up with him one day no matter where he runs to. Lord Zhou, where should your servants and their families go for temporary refuge?'

'I think they should all make their way to Chijinwei, the town to the east of here, as soon as it gets light,' Zhou replied.

'I have a small suggestion, sir,' Xu said.

'It is not for nothing that Brother Xu is nicknamed the Kungfu Mastermind,' Chen explained to Zhou. 'He is the wisest and most resourceful of us all.'

Zhou Qi gave Xu a look of contempt and cleared her throat noisily.

'Please speak, Brother Xu,' said Zhou hurriedly, embarrassed by his daughter's behaviour.

'When that fellow Tong gets back, he is certain to embellish his story with a lot of nonsense, accusing Your Lordship of many more crimes,' Xu replied. 'I think it would be best for your people to go west and lie low for a while until we have evaluated the situation. It may not be safe for them to go to Chijinwei now.'

Zhou agreed to this immediately. 'Yes, you're right,' he said. 'I will send them to Anxi first thing tomorrow. I have friends there they can stay with.' He turned to his junior steward, Song. 'Take them all to Anxi,' he said. 'When you get there, you can stay temporarily at the residence of Magistrate Wu. All expenses are to be paid by us. I will contact you when I have completed my business.'

'Father, aren't we going to Anxi too?' Zhou Qi asked.

'Of course not. This Red Flower Society hero Rolling Thunder Wen was seized in our Manor. How can we stand by and do nothing when he has still to be rescued?'

Zhou Qi and Steward Meng were delighted at the news.

'We are greatly moved by your gesture of goodwill, Lord Zhou.' Chen said. 'But saving Brother Wen is an act of rebellion. You and your family are peaceful law-abiding citizens. It would be best to leave this to us.'

'You needn't worry about implicating us,' Zhou replied, stroking his beard. 'And if you won't allow me to risk my life for a friend, then you are not treating me as a friend.'

Chen thought about this for a second, then agreed.

'Time is pressing,' Zhou added. 'Please issue your orders, sir.'

The embers of Iron Ball Manor were still smouldering, and the smell of burning wood hung heavily in the air. As they listened solemnly to Helmsman Chen's orders, the flames crackled to life again, fanned by the wind.

The Twin Knights of West Stream, the Brothers Chang, had been sent on ahead to discover Wen's whereabouts, and Scholar Yu was told to link up with them, while the rest of the Red Flower heroes split up into groups of two and three.

'Please start out immediately,' Chen said to Scholar Yu. 'Everyone else can rest or sleep here on the ground. We will meet up again inside the Great Wall. The Eagle's Claws on the Jiayu Gate will most probably be examining everyone rigorously, so we must be careful.'

Yu saluted the heroes with clasped fists, and mounted his horse. As he rode off, he glanced furtively round at Luo Bing, but she was deep in thought with her head bowed. He sighed, whipped his horse, and galloped wildly off.

'Brother Xu,' Chen said quietly to Mastermind. 'You go with Luo Bing and Lord Zhou. Take extra care that no officials recognize him. Sister Luo is wounded and she is greatly feeling the absence of Brother Wen, so you must be careful not to let her do anything rash. There is no need for you to travel fast. Just avoid getting involved in any fighting.'

Xu nodded.

They settled down to sleep, but less than four hours later, dawn broke. Buddha Zhao, with Hunchback Zhang and Melancholy Ghost Shi, were the first to leave. Luo Bing, who had not closed her eyes the whole night, called Hunchback Zhang over.

'Brother Zhang, you are not to cause any trouble on the road,' she said.

'Don't worry,' he replied. 'Rescuing Rolling Thunder is the important thing, I know.'

Steward Meng and a number of other Zhou family retainers covered the body of Zhou's son with shrouds and buried it beside the Manor while Zhou Qi wept bitterly and her father Lord Zhou stood tearfully by. The Red Flower heroes paid their respects before the grave.

Talking in the Spinney

Zhou Qi continued to be hostile towards Mastermind Xu as they
travelled along. No matter how often or how sternly her father
reproved her, or how often Luo Bing tried to mediate with smiles,
or how calmly tolerant Xu was, Zhou Qi continued to jeer at him
and insult him. In the end, Xu became angry as well.

'I've only been nice to her for her father's sake,' he thought.
'Does she think I'd really be afraid of her?' He reined in his horse
and dropped behind.

On the third day, they passed through the Jiayu Gate, which
marks the western end of the Great Wall.

Seeing his daughter so disobedient, Zhou several times called
her over and tried to reason with her. Each time she would agree,
but as soon as she saw Xu, she would start arguing with him again.
His wife might have been able to discipline their daughter, reflected
Zhou, but she had gone he knew not where.

They arrived in the nearby town of Suzhou, and found rooms
in an inn near the east gate of the city. Xu went out for a while, and
when he returned he said:

'Brother Yu hasn't met up with the Twin Knights yet.'

'How would you know?' Zhou Qi demanded. 'You're just
guessing.'

Xu glanced at her in contempt.

Lord Zhou was afraid that his daughter would say something
else equally impolite. 'Brother Xu,' he said, addressing him as if he
himself was a member of the Red Flower Society. 'This place was
called Wine Spring Prefecture in ancient times. The wine here is
very good. Let's you and I go to the Apricot Blossom Tavern on
Great East Street and drink a cup.'

'Good idea,' said Xu.

'Father, I want to go too,' Zhou Qi said. Xu stifled a laugh.
'What are you laughing at? Why shouldn't I go?' she asked angrily.
Xu turned away and pretended he hadn't heard.

'We'll go together,' Luo Bing said with a smile.

Being a chivalrous man, Zhou did not object.

The four of them arrived at the Apricot Blossom Tavern and
ordered wine and food. The spring water of Suzhou is clear and
cold, and the liquor distilled with it is fragrant and rich. It is
considered to be the best in all the northwestern provinces. The

waiter brought a plate of Suzhou's famous roasted cakes, as soft as spring cotton and as white as autumn silk. Zhou Qi couldn't stop eating them. The tavern was crowded and it was inconvenient to discuss Wen's coming rescue, so instead, the four talked about the scenery they had passed through, among other things.

'Your Helmsman Chen is very young,' said Zhou. 'What was that strange style of kungfu he was using towards the end?'

'It is a style invented by his Shifu,' Xu replied. 'When he was fifteen years old, the Helmsman was sent by our former Helmsman to the Muslim regions, to Heaven Mountains, to become the disciple of the Strange Knight of the Heavenly Pool, Master Yuan. After that he never returned to southern China. Only Father Speckless and some of the other senior members of the Society saw him when he was young.'

'He is certainly a remarkable man,' said Zhou. 'When I first set eyes on him, I thought him a typical rich gentleman's son. Then I discovered that not only is he a fighter of the first rank, he is also a man of great knowledge and judgement. Truly, a man's worth cannot be measured by his looks.'

Xu and Luo Bing were very pleased to hear Zhou praising their leader in such glowing terms.

'In these last few years, there have been many new heroes on River and Lake,' Zhou continued, addressing Xu. 'The rear waves of the Yangtze River push forward the front waves, as the saying goes. It is rare to find someone who combines the qualities of intelligence and bravery as you do, my friend. It is important that such skills are not wasted, but are used to achieve something worthwhile.'

'Yes,' said Xu, meaning that he agreed with Zhou's view that his skills should be put to good purpose; but Zhou Qi grunted and thought: 'My father praises you and you agree! What modesty!'

Zhou drank a mouthful of wine. 'I once heard that Old Helmsman Yu of your Society belonged to the Shaolin School of kungfu, and had a style of fighting very similar to my own,' he remarked. 'I had long wanted to meet him and learn from him, but with him in southern China and myself in the north-west, my wish was never fulfilled and he has now passed away. I enquired about the origins of his Martial Arts skills, but everyone had a different story, and I never heard a reliable report.'

'Old Helmsman Yu hardly ever talked about his Shifu, replied Xu. 'It was only just before he died that he revealed that he had once studied kungfu in the southern Shaolin Temple in Fujian Province.'

'I myself studied in the northern Shaolin Temple,' said Lord Zhou, 'in Henan Province. That would account for the similarity between our styles. Tell me, what illness did Old Helmsman Yu die of?' Zhou asked. 'He would only have been a few years my senior, I believe.'

'The Old Helmsman was sixty-five when he passed away,' Xu replied. 'The cause of his illness is a long story. There's a very mixed bunch of people here at this tavern. Perhaps we should travel on another few miles this evening. We'll find a more deserted place and talk at length there.'

'Excellent!' said Zhou. He asked the keeper of the tavern to make up the bill.

'I'll just go downstairs for a second,' said Xu.

'I am the host,' Zhou warned. 'Don't you go and try paying the bill.'

'Certainly not,' Xu replied, but still went down to the ground floor.

'He's always so furtive!' Zhou Qi said with a pout.

'Mind your tongue, girl!' her father scolded her.

'It's true,' said Luo Bing with a smile. 'Brother Xu is always full of strange tricks. If you make him angry, you'll have to be careful he doesn't play some of them on you.'

'Huh!' she said. 'He's no bigger than I am. Why should I be afraid of him?'

Lord Zhou was about to berate her again, but hearing footsteps on the stairs, he said nothing.

'Let's go,' said Xu, walking up.

The four covered ten miles at one go. They noticed a spinney of a dozen or so large trees to the left of the road screening rocks and boulders behind. They tied their horses to the trees and sat down, leaning against the tree-trunks. The moon was bright, the stars in the sky few, and the night air cool as water. The wind blew through the grass with a low whistling sound.

Xu was about to speak when he heard the muffled sound of horses galloping from far off. He lay down with his ear to the ground and listened for a while, then stood up.

'Three horses coming this way,' he said.

Zhou waved his hand and they untied their horses and led them behind the boulders. It seemed a good place to hide. The sound of hooves came gradually closer, and three horses passed heading east. In the moonlight, they could see only that the riders all wore white turbans and long striped gowns—typical Uighur clothing—while sabres hung from their saddles. They waited until the riders were a long way off, then sat down again. Zhou proceeded to ask why it was the Manchu Court had arrested Wen.

'They have always considered the Red Flower Society to be a thorn in their side,' Luo Bing replied. 'But they had another reason for dispatching so many Martial Arts masters to catch my husband. Last month, Old Helmsman Yu went to Peking, and Rolling Thunder and I went with him. Helmsman Yu told us that he intended to break into the Imperial Palace and see Emperor Qian Long face to face. We were very surprised, and asked what he wanted to see the Emperor about, but he wouldn't say. Rolling Thunder warned him that the Emperor was very dangerous and cunning and advised him to enlist our best fighters and to get Brother Xu here to devise an absolutely foolproof plan.'

Zhou Qi studied Xu. 'That dwarf?' she thought to herself. 'Is he so talented that others come to him for help? I don't believe it!'

'Helmsman Yu said that he had to see the Emperor on a matter of great importance, and that only one or two people could accompany him or there could be problems. So Rolling Thunder agreed to go with him. That night, the two of them crossed the wall into the Palace while I kept watch outside. I was really frightened. More than two hours passed before they came back over the wall. Very early next day, the three of us left Peking and returned to the south. I asked Rolling Thunder if they had seen the Emperor and what it was all about. He said they had seen him, and that it concerned driving out the Manchus and restoring the Throne of China to the Chinese people. He said he couldn't tell me more, not because he didn't trust me, but because the more people who knew, the greater the danger of the secret getting out.

'After we returned to the south, Old Helmsman Yu parted from us,' Luo Bing continued. 'We returned to the Society's headquarters at Lake Tai, while he went on to Haining. When he returned, his whole appearance had changed. It was as if he had suddenly aged more than ten years. He never smiled, and a few days later he contracted the illness from which he never recovered.

'Just before he passed away, he called together the Society's Lodge Masters, and said that it was his last wish that Brother Chen should succeed him as the new Helmsman. He said this was the key to the Restoration of the Throne to the Han people. He said it was not possible to explain the reasons then, but that we would all find out the truth one day.'

'What was your Brother Chen's relationship with Old Helmsman Yu?' Zhou asked.

'He was the Old Helmsman's foster son,' Luo Bing said. 'Brother Chen is the son of the Emperor's former Chief Minister Chen from Haining. When he was fifteen, he passed the provincial civil service examination. But soon after that, the Old Helmsman took him to the border country, to live among the Uighurs, to learn the Martial Arts from the Strange Knight of the Heavenly Pool, Master Yuan. As to why the son of a Chief Minister, a young man from one of China's noblest families, should choose to enter the world of River and Lake, and honour a member of the fighting community as his foster father, we don't know.'

'I imagine one of the reasons your husband Wen was seized is that he knows something about all this,' suggested Zhou.

'Perhaps,' replied Luo Bing. 'At the time of Old Helmsman Yu's death, there was one important piece of unfinished business on his mind and he wanted very badly to see Brother Chen once more. When he first returned from Peking, he had sent a messenger to the Muslim border country with instructions for Brother Chen to go to Anxi and wait there for orders. The Old Helmsman knew he wouldn't last long enough to see his foster son again, so he urged us all to hasten to Anxi to work out a plan of action together with Brother Chen. He entrusted all the secret information to my husband to pass on personally to the new Helmsman when they met. But now he—' Her voice choked with sobs. 'If anything should happen to my husband...no one will ever know what Old Helmsman Yu hoped to achieve.'

'You mustn't worry,' Zhou Qi consoled her. 'We'll soon rescue him.'

Luo Bing squeezed her hand and smiled sadly.

'How was your husband wounded?' Zhou asked.

'We travelled in pairs to Anxi, and Rolling Thunder and I were the last pair. While we were in Suzhou, eight officers, members of the Imperial Guard, came to our inn and said they had orders from the Emperor to accompany us back to Peking. Rolling Thunder knew that he had to see the new Helmsman before he could comply with such a demand, and a fight broke out. It was a hard battle, two against eight. Rolling Thunder killed two of them with his sword and three more with his bare hands, while I hit two with my throwing knives. The last one sneaked away. But Rolling Thunder was badly wounded.'

'We knew we couldn't stay in Suzhou,' she continued, 'so with difficulty we made our way through the Jiayu Gate. But my husband's wounds were serious and it was really impossible for us to go much further, so we stopped at an inn to give him a chance to recover quickly. Little did we guess that the Eagle's Claws would find us again. What happened afterwards, you already know.'

'The more the Emperor fears and hates Brother Wen, the less his life is in danger in the immediate future,' Xu said. 'The officials and the Eagle's Claws know he's important so they won't dare to harm him.'

'That's very shrewdly observed, Brother Xu,' Zhou said.

'If only you'd all arrived a bit earlier,' Zhou Qi suddenly said to Xu. 'Then your Brother Wen wouldn't be in trouble now, and you wouldn't have had to go venting your anger on Iron Ball Manor—'

'You stupid girl!' cried Zhou. 'What are you talking about?'

'We were held up by the delay in the new Helmsman accepting his position,' said Xu. 'Besides, Brother Wen's and Sister Luo Bing's kungfu is so excellent, no one would have guessed that they would be attacked!' Xu replied.

'You're supposed to be the Kungfu Mastermind,' Zhou Qi said. 'Surely you could have guessed!'

Her father tried to reason with her: 'If Brother Xu *had* guessed it, we wouldn't have become acquainted with these good people from the Red Flower Society.' He turned to Luo Bing. 'By the way, who is Helmsman Chen's wife? Is she the daughter of some great family perhaps, or a famous Martial Arts fighter herself?'

'Helmsman Chen hasn't married yet,' Luo Bing replied. 'But Lord Zhou, when are we going to be invited to *your* daughter's wedding reception?'

'This girl of mine is crazy,' Zhou answered with a smile. 'Who would want her? She might as well stay with me for the rest of her life.'

'Wait until we've rescued Brother Wen, then I'll be matchmaker for her,' Luo Bing said. 'You're sure to be satisfied with my choice.'

'If you're going to keep on talking about me, I'm leaving,' Zhou Qi said quickly, deeply embarrassed. The other three smiled.

A moment passed, then Xu suddenly stifled a laugh.

'What are you laughing at now?' Zhou Qi asked him angrily.

'Something personal,' he countered. 'What business is it of yours?'

'Huh,' she replied. 'Do you think I don't know what you're laughing at? You want to marry me to that Helmsman Chen of yours. But he's the son of a chief minister; how could we possibly be matched? Besides, you all treat him like some precious treasure. Can't see anything special about him myself.'

Soon Zhou suggested that they all get some sleep, and set out again at first light. So they took their blankets off the horses' backs, and lay down beneath the trees.

'Father,' whispered Zhou Qi. 'Did you bring anything to eat? I'm starving.'

'No, I didn't,' replied Zhou. 'But we'll make a move early tomorrow and stop when we reach Twin Wells.'

Not long after, he began snoring lightly. Zhou Qi tossed and turned, unable to sleep for hunger. Suddenly, she noticed Xu stealthily get up and walk over to the horses. She saw him take something out of his saddle-bag, then go back and sit down. He wrapped the blanket around himself, and started eating something noisily and with relish. She turned over away from him and shut her eyes, but finally she could bear it no longer, and glanced at him out of the corner of her eye. She wished she hadn't. Next to him she saw a pile of what were obviously the famous Suzhou roasted cakes. So that was why he had gone downstairs at the tavern—to buy some cakes! Her mouth started watering, and she felt hungrier than ever. But having spent the whole time arguing with him, she could hardly start begging him for food.

'Go to sleep and stop thinking about eating,' she told herself. But the more she tried to sleep, the less she was able to. Then the fragrant smell of wine assailed her nostrils, as Xu took a swig from his drinking-gourd. She could suppress her anger no longer.

'What are you doing drinking wine at two o'clock in the morning?' she demanded. 'If you've got to drink, don't do it here!'

'All right,' said Xu. He put down the gourd without re-corking it and settled down to sleep, letting the fragrance of the wine drift over towards her.

She buried her face angrily in her blanket, but after a while, it became too stuffy. She turned over again and, in the moonlight, she saw her father's two Iron Balls glistening beside his pillow. She quietly stretched her hand over, picked one of them up, and threw it at the wine-gourd. It shattered and the wine spilled over Xu's blanket.

He appeared to be asleep, and paid no heed to what had happened. Zhou Qi saw that her father and Luo Bing were sleeping peacefully and crept over to retrieve the Iron Ball. But just as she was about to pick it up, Xu suddenly turned over, trapping it beneath his body, and then proceeded to snore noisily.

She started and pulled back her hand, not daring to try again. Despite her bold character, she was still a young lady, and could not possibly allow her hand to come into contact with a man's body. There was nothing she could do, so she went back and settled down to sleep. Just then, she heard a laugh escape from Luo Bing. Completely flustered, she didn't sleep well all night.

On the Road

Next day, Zhou Qi woke early, and curled up into a ball hoping that the dawn would never come. But before long, her father and Luo Bing were up. A moment later, Xu awoke, and she heard him exclaim in surprise: 'What's this?'

Zhou Qi pulled the blanket over her head.

'Ah, Lord Zhou!' she heard him say. 'Your Iron Ball has rolled all the way over here! Oh, no! The wine-gourd is smashed! That's it, a monkey in the hills must have smelt the wine and come down to have a drink. Then it saw your Iron Ball and took it to play with. One careless slip and the gourd was smashed to pieces. What a naughty monkey!'

Zhou laughed heartily. 'You love to jest, don't you, Brother,' he said. 'There are no monkeys in this area.'

'Well then, maybe it was a fairy from heaven,' Luo Bing suggested with a smile.

Now that Xu had called her a monkey, Zhou Qi was even more furious than before. Xu pulled out the roasted cakes for everyone to eat but, out of spite, she refused to eat even one.

They reached the town of Twin Wells, and had a quick meal of noodles. Then, as they were leaving, Mastermind Xu and Luo Bing stopped suddenly and began closely examining some confused charcoal markings at the foot of a wall. They looked to Zhou Qi like the scribblings of an urchin.

'The Twin Knights have found out where Rolling Thunder is and are following him,' Luo Bing announced joyfully.

'How do you know? What are these signs?' Zhou Qi asked.

'They are a code used by our Society,' she said, rubbing the marks off the wall with her foot. 'Let's go!'

Knowing that Wen had been found, Luo Bing's face was suddenly wreathed in smiles. Their spirits rose and they covered nearly fifteen miles at one go. At noon the next day in the town of Seven Road Ditch, they came across more markings left by Scholar Yu, telling them that he had caught up with the Twin Knights. The wound on Luo Bing's thigh was now just about healed, and she no longer had to use a walking-stick. She was constantly thinking about her husband, and found it increasingly hard to control her impatience.

Towards evening, they arrived at the town of Willow Springs. Luo Bing wanted to keep going, but Mastermind Xu remembered Helmsman Chen's orders not to travel fast. 'Even if *we* aren't tired, the horses just can't do it!' he pointed out.

Luo Bing reluctantly agreed, and they found rooms in an inn for the night, but she tossed and turned, unable to sleep. In the middle of the night, she heard a pitter-patter sound outside the windows as it started to rain and suddenly remembered the time she and Wen had received an order from Old Helmsman Yu soon after their marriage to go to the town of Jiaxing, to the aid of a widow who was being persecuted by a local ruffian. When they had completed the assignment, they spent the evening at Misty Rain Tavern on the South Lake, drinking wine and enjoying the rain. Wen had held his new wife's hand and sung songs at the top of his voice as he tapped out the rhythm with his sword on the severed head of the ruffian. Her memories of the scene flooded back as she listened to the rain on the window.

'Brother Xu does not want to travel fast because of Lord Zhou and his daughter,' she thought. 'Perhaps I should go on ahead?'

Once the idea had occurred to her, it was impossible to put it out of her mind and she immediately got up, picked up her swords, and left a message for Xu in charcoal on the table. Zhou Qi was sleeping on the kang in the same room and, afraid of awakening her, she opened the window as quietly as she could and jumped out. She went to the stables and found her horse, then threw on an oil-skin raincoat and galloped off eastwards. She hardly noticed the rain as it struck her hot cheeks.

At dawn, she stopped briefly in a town. Her mount was exhausted, and she had no alternative but to rest for an hour. Then she raced on another ten or fifteen miles. Suddenly the horse stumbled on one of its front hooves. She frantically pulled in the reins, and luckily the animal did not fall. But she knew that if she kept up this pace, it would die from exhaustion, and so she was forced to proceed much more slowly.

She hadn't gone far when she heard the sound of a horse behind her. She turned and saw a white horse which caught up with her almost as soon as she heard it and flew past. It was so swift, she had no opportunity to even see what the rider looked like.

Soon after, she arrived in a small village and saw the snow-white horse standing under the eaves of a house as a man brushed its coat, its hoar-frost coloured mane stirring in the wind. It was a large, long-legged beast, with a fiery spirit, and as Luo Bing approached, it neighed loudly, causing her own mount to retreat a few steps in fright.

'If only I had this fine horse to ride,' she thought, 'I would catch up with Thunder in no time at all. Its master will never sell it, so I'll just have to take it.'

She slapped her mount and charged forward, hurling one of her throwing knives, which embedded itself in a wooden column of the house and severed the rope that tethered the white horse. Then, holding her bag with her left hand, she vaulted from her own horse onto the back of the white horse. It was the move known as the Hidden Dragon Soars into the Heavens. The magnificent animal reared in fright and neighed loudly again, then, like an arrow loosed from a bow, galloped off down the road.

The horse's owner was taken completely by surprise, but after a second's hesitation, he raced after her. Luo Bing had already gone some distance, but seeing him give chase, she reined in the horse, took a gold ingot out of her bag, and threw it at him.

'We've exchanged horses,' she shouted. 'But yours is better than mine, so I'll give you this gold to make up the difference!' She gave one of her captivating smiles, and with a slight squeeze of her thighs, urged the white horse on. It shot forward. The wind whistled by her ears and the rows of trees on either side flashed past her. She rode for over an hour, and the horse still showed no signs of fatigue, his hooves prancing high as he galloped along. Soon, fertile fields began to appear along the side of the road, lined with poplars, and she arrived in a large town. She dismounted and went to a tavern to rest for a while. She was told the town was called Sandy Wells, and that it was more than twenty miles from the place where she had stolen the horse.

The more she looked at the animal, the more she liked it. She fed it hay herself and stroked its coat affectionately. As she did so, she noticed a cloth bag hanging from the saddle. Opening it up, she found a weapon inside, one of the metallic missiles known as an Iron Piba, formed in the shape of a piba lute.

'So the horse belongs to someone from the Iron Piba School of Luoyang,' she thought. 'This could cause some trouble.'

She put her hand into the bag again and pulled out twenty or thirty taels of silver coins and a letter inscribed with the words: 'To be opened only by Master Han Wenchong. Sealed by Master Wang.' The envelope was open and, as she unfolded the letter, she saw it was signed: 'Yours sincerely, Weiyang'.

She started slightly in surprise. 'So the fellow is connected with Wang Weiyang of the Zhen Yuan Security Agency. We still have to get even with them, so stealing this horse could be considered part payment. If I had known earlier, I wouldn't have given him that gold ingot.'

She looked again at the letter. It urged Han to meet up as soon as possible with the Zhen Yuan Agency's Yan brothers (two of the Manchurian Devils who worked for Wang's Agency) and assist them in protecting an important item being brought back to Peking. Then Han was to help escort something to south China. It added that Han should suspend his investigation into whether or not the Manchurian Devil Jiao Wenqi had been killed by the Red Flower Society, and resume it at some future time. Luo Bing knew that Jiao Wenqi was also a member of the Iron Piba School in Luoyang.

'It's rumoured that he was killed by the Red Flower Society, but in fact he wasn't. I wonder what the important item is that the Zhen Yuan Agency is escorting? After Thunder is rescued, we can go and collect it together.'

Very happy at this thought, she finished her noodles, mounted up, and sped off again. The rain continued to fall, sometimes light, sometimes heavy. The horse galloped like the wind, and she lost count of how many horses and carts they overtook.

'This horse is going so fast that if the others ahead are resting for a while, I might miss them if I so much as blink!' she thought to herself.

Just then, someone slipped out from the side of the road and waved. The horse stopped instantly in mid-gallop and backed up several paces. It was a boy who bowed before her.

'My lady,' he said. 'The Helmsman is here.' It was Helmsman Chen's young page, Xin Yan.

Xin Yan walked over and took the horse's reins. 'Where did you buy such a good horse?' he asked in admiration. 'I nearly didn't see you, you were going so fast.'

Luo Bing smiled. 'Is there any news of Brother Wen?' she asked.

'The Twin Knights say they have seen him. Everyone's in there.' He pointed to a small, decrepit temple by the side of the road.

'Look after the horse for me,' she said. Inside, seated in the temple's main hall, were Helmsman Chen, the Twin Knights (the Chang brothers—Black Death and White Death), and several other Red Flower heroes. They all stood and warmly welcomed her as she came in. Luo Bing bowed before Chen and explained that she had been too impatient to wait for the others, and hoped that he would forgive her.

'Your concern for Brother Wen is understandable,' Chen said. 'As for your failure to follow orders, we will discuss a penalty when we have rescued him. Brother Shi, please make a note of it.' Melancholy Ghost Shi nodded.

Luo Bing smiled sweetly and turned to the Twin Knights. 'Have you really seen my husband? How is he? Is he suffering?'

'We caught up with him and his escort last night at Twin Wells,' one of them replied. 'But he was surrounded by guards, and we didn't take any action for fear of alerting them. There were turtles everwhere!' The Twin Knights were from the western province of Sichuan, and often used this Sichuan term of abuse. 'I went to a window to have a look and saw Brother Wen lying on a kang resting. He didn't see me.'

'The Zhen Yuan Agency turtles and the Eagle's Claws are all
in this together,' said the other Knight. 'By my reckoning, they have
ten first-class Martial Arts masters among them.'

As they were speaking, Scholar Yu came into the temple. He
flinched on seeing Luo Bing, then made a report to Helmsman Chen.

'The Uighurs have set up tents beside the stream ahead of us,'
he said. 'Their guards are carrying swords and spears and look very
formidable. I couldn't get close during daylight, but we could go
and investigate again when it gets dark.'

Suddenly, they heard the sound of a column of men and
animals pass by outside the temple. Xin Yan dashed in and reported:
'A large train of mules, horses, and carts has just gone by, escorted
by twenty government soldiers with a military official in command.'
As soon as he had finished, he left to resume his watch.

Helmsman Chen discussed the situation with the others. 'There
are very few people in the area to the east of here, which makes it
perfect for our rescue operation. But we don't know what the Uighurs
and this column of government troops are doing. When we make
our move to rescue Brother Wen, they may try to interfere.'

'We have all heard a great deal about the famous Fire Hand
Judge, Zhang Zhaozhong,' said Father Speckless, the Taoist Priest.
'He was in command of this operation to capture Brother Wen. I
should like to have the pleasure of fighting him in person.'

'Very well,' Chen said. 'We certainly cannot let him escape.'

'It's lucky that my friend Hidden Needle Lu isn't here yet,'
said Buddha Zhao. 'It might be difficult for us to kill Fire Hand
Zhang before his very eyes. After all, they are brothers-in-arms.'

'Well then, we should act quickly,' one of the Twin Knights
added. 'I estimate we should catch up with them by early tomorrow
morning.'

'Right,' said Chen. 'Please tell us in detail what you've found
out so that we will know what to expect tomorrow.'

'At night, Brother Wen sleeps wherever the Eagle's Claws
sleep, and during the day, rides in a carriage with his hands and
feet manacled,' one replied. 'The carriage curtains are kept tightly
closed, and two Agency turtles ride on either side.'

'What does this man Fire Hand Zhang look like?' asked Father
Speckless.

'He's about forty years old, a big tall fellow, heavily built, with a
thick short beard. He looks pretty impressive, damn his ancestors!'

They were all eager for the fight, but there was nothing they could do but wait. They ate some dry rations and then asked the Helmsman to give his orders.

'That group of Uighurs is most unlikely to be working with the Eagle's Claws,' he said. 'Once we have rescued Brother Wen, we won't need to worry about them. Brother Yu, you and Brother Jiang will take care of that military official and his twenty troops. Bloodshed isn't necessary. Just don't let them interfere.' Scholar Yu and Crocodile Jiang nodded.

Chen then turned to Leopard Wei and Melancholy Ghost Shi. 'You two are to overtake the Eagle's Claws, and set up guard at the mouth of the gorge as early as possible tomorrow. They must not be allowed to escape.' Wei and Shi left the temple and rode off.

'Father Speckless and the Twin Knights: the three of you deal with the members of the Imperial Guard escorting the carriage; Buddha Zhao and Iron Pagoda, you two deal with the Agency men. Sister Luo and Xin Yan will make straight for the carriage. I will coordinate and give assistance to whichever group encounters problems. Brother Zhang Jin, you stay here and keep guard. If any government troops come by heading east, you must think of some way to stop them.'

The forces having been divided up, the heroes left the temple, mounted up, and waved farewell to Hunchback Zhang.

When they saw Luo Bing's white horse, they all made approving noises. 'I should have presented it to the Helmsman,' she thought to herself. 'But Thunder has suffered so much, I'll give it to him after he's been rescued.'

'Where are the Uighurs camped?' Chen asked Scholar Yu. 'We can circle round and have a look.'

Yu led the way, but as they approached the wide space where the Uighurs had been, they could see that the tents and people were gone, leaving only piles of mule and horse droppings.

'Let's go!' said Chen. They spurred their horses forward and galloped off along the road. Luo Bing's horse was so fast that she had to stop occasionally to let the others catch up with her. As dawn broke, they came to the bank of a small stream.

'Brothers,' said Helmsman Chen. 'We will stop here and let the horses drink some water and recover their strength. We should be able to catch up with Brother Wen in another two hours.'

Luo Bing flushed. Scholar Yu saw her expression and he walked slowly over to her.

'Sister Luo,' he said quietly. 'I am willing to give up my life to rescue Brother Wen for you.'

She smiled slightly. 'That's right and proper,' she sighed.

Yu quickly turned away.

'Sister Luo,' said Chen, 'Lend your horse to Xin Yan and let him go on ahead to investigate.'

Xin Yan mounted the white horse and flew off.

The others waited until their horses had drunk their fill, then mounted up and followed swiftly. Not long after, when the sky was already light, they saw Xin Yan riding back towards them.

'The Eagle's Claws are just ahead,' he shouted.

Xin Yan and Luo Bing exchanged horses and galloped forward with renewed vigour and spirit.

'Did you see Brother Wen's carriage?' she asked.

Xin Yan nodded excitedly. 'Yes! I rode close to the side of the carriage hoping to get a look inside but the Eagle's Claws raised their swords to scare me off.'

The group galloped on, the horses' hooves sounding like thunder. A long column of men and horses came into sight ahead, and they saw that it was the column escorted by government soldiers.

'Brother Wen's carriage is another two miles further on,' Xin Yan said to Helmsman Chen. They spurred on their horses and overtook the column. Once past it, Crocodile Jiang and Scholar Yu turned their mounts around to block the road.

Yu saluted the government troops as they caught up, engaging them in light banter about the fine weather and the beautiful scenery.

'Out of the way!' shouted one of the Manchu soldiers at the front. 'This is the family of Commander-in-Chief Li.'

'His family? Well, I think you should all stop and have a good rest. There's a pair called Black Death and White Death in front of us, and we wouldn't want to frighten the ladies.'

Another of the soldiers flourished his horsewhip and cracked it in Scholar Yu's direction. 'That's enough of your nonsense!' he shouted.

Yu laughed and dodged out of the way. The commanding officer rode forward and asked in a loud voice what was going on.

It was Zeng Tunan, the officer who had been entrusted with escorting Commander Li Kexiu's family to Hangzhou.

Yu brought his hands together in salute. 'What is your name, sir?' he enquired.

Officer Zeng had his suspicions about Yu and Jiang, and hesitated to answer.

Yu took out his golden flute. 'I have a rudimentary knowledge of music,' he said. 'I often lament how rarely I come across people with discerning musical tastes. You, sir, have a dignified appearance. Please dismount and rest while I play you a tune to while away the loneliness of the journey.'

Officer Zeng started in surprise when he saw the golden flute, and remembered what he had heard of the fight in the inn that day between the four Yamen officers and a scholar with a golden flute. 'Let each go his own road,' he shouted. 'Please make way!'

'I know ten songs,' said Yu. 'Some are passionate and rousing, some are sweet and captivating. But they all have beautiful tunes. I haven't played them for a long time. This chance meeting with such an esteemed gentleman as yourself has made me eager to show off my talents.'

He lifted the golden flute to his mouth and a series of beautiful notes rose clear and sharp into the sky.

Officer Zeng could see that the affair was not going to be concluded amicably. He raised his spear and threw it straight at Yu who continued to play until the tip was almost upon him. Then his left hand shot out and grabbed the spear, and he struck it with the golden flute, snapping it in two.

Zeng was completely taken aback. Reining in his horse, he retreated several paces, snatched a sword from one of the soldiers, and charged forward again. He fought Yu through seven or eight moves, then Yu found an opening: the golden flute struck Zeng's right arm, and the sword flew out of his hand.

'You really ought to listen to these ten songs of mine,' said Yu. He put the flute to his lips, and started to play once more.

Zeng waved his hand at his soldiers. 'Seize this fellow!' he roared. The soldiers swept forward, shouting and yelling as they came.

Crocodile Jiang leapt off his horse brandishing his iron oar, and with a move known as Stirring the Grass to Find the Snake, he tapped the first soldier lightly on the legs, toppling him onto the

oar, then swung the oar upwards, and deposited him into the crowd
of his comrades. He scooped and dumped one Manchu soldier after
another as if he was doing no more than shovelling earth, and the
soldiers behind yelled out in fear and retreated.

Just then, the curtains on a large carriage the soldiers were
escorting suddenly parted, and a girl dressed in red and holding a
glistening sword lunged at him. Jiang's oar struck powerfully at the
blade, and the girl, seeing the strength behind it, leapt back. Jiang
was a Cantonese with a thick accent, and he had found that few
people outside his native province understood what he said. As a
result, he had never been a great talker. This certainly did not seem
an occasion for small talk. He flourished his oar and began to fight
with her without saying a word. He was surprised to discover that
her swordsmanship was excellent.

Yu looked on from the side. He had forgotten all about playing
the flute and was engrossed in watching the young girl who was
using the traditional Soft Cloud sword style of his own School.

He leapt forward and inserted his golden flute between their
weapons, separating them. 'Stop!' he shouted.

The girl and Jiang both retreated a step. By this time, Officer
Zeng had found another spear and was spurring his horse forward,
but the girl ordered him to stay back.

'What is your name, mistress, and that of your Shifu?' Yu
asked.

'I don't feel like telling you,' the girl replied with a smile. 'But
I do know that you are Scholar Yu, and that you are a member of
the Red Flower Society.'

Yu and Jiang looked at each other in surprise. Officer Zeng
was even more astonished at the sight of his commander-in-chief's
daughter joking with these notorious bandits.

All three men were looking at the smiling girl, and could not
think what to say, when they heard horses approaching. The Manchu
soldiers parted and six horses raced up from the west. The front
rider was Hidden Needle Lu. Scholar Yu and the girl (who was of
course Li Yuanzhi) both greeted him, one calling him Uncle (because
his Shifu, Ma Zhen, was Lu's brother-in-arms) and the other Shifu.

Behind Lu came Lord Zhou, the two groups having met on
the road.

'Yuanzhi, what are you doing here with these two gentlemen?'
Lu asked.

'Brother Yu insisted on us listening to him play the flute,' she replied with a smile. 'We didn't feel like listening but he wouldn't let us leave.'

'There is danger ahead,' Lu said to Yuanzhi. 'It would be best if you all stayed here so as not to frighten Lady Li. When this business is finished, I will come and find you.'

Yuanzhi pouted angrily at being forbidden from going to watch the fun, but Hidden Needle Lu took no further notice of her. He saluted the others, and rode on eastwards.

Spectacular Swordsmanship

The heroes galloped on after Wen's carriage. After a while, they noticed in the distance a column of men and horses strung out over the flat plain. Father Speckless drew his sword and roared: 'Chase them!' The figures ahead of them gradually grew larger. Luo Bing's white horse raced round to the front, and in an instant, she had caught up with the column. With her twin swords in hand, she prepared to overtake it, then block its path. But suddenly, shouts rose from in front, and several dozen Uighurs riding camels and horses raced towards them from the east.

This was completely unexpected. Luo Bing reined in her horse and stopped to see what the Uighurs were doing. By now, the officers and Agency men had also halted, and gazed in consternation at the Uighurs as they bore down on them, sabres glinting in the sun.

Helmsman Chen ordered the Red Flower heroes to halt to watch the fight. Suddenly, they saw a rider skirt round the battle and race straight towards them. As he approached, they recognized him as Leopard Wei. He rode up to Chen.

'Helmsman,' he said breathlessly. 'We set up guard at the mouth of the gorge, but this group of Uighurs broke past us. There was no way of stopping them, but now they're attacking the Eagle's Claws. It's all very strange.'

'Father Speckless, Brother Zhao, and the Twin Knights,' Chen said. 'The four of you go and get Brother Wen's carriage away. The rest of us will wait and see how things develop.'

The four heroes galloped off.

'Who are you?' the officers shouted as they approached. Buddha Zhao didn't bother to answer. Two steel darts left his hands, and two of the officers fell dead from their horses. Zhao was nicknamed the Thousand Arm Buddha because he had a serene, kindly face and a soft heart; he was also a master of all types of darts and kept a number of them secreted around his body.

As the four heroes approached the carriage, a white turbaned Uighur struck out at them with his spear, but they dodged past him and attacked the Agency guards who were securing the carriage. One of the guards swung his sword at Father Speckless, who blocked the stroke with his own sword, which slid down the other's blade as fast as lightning and sliced off all his fingers before plunging into his heart. He heard the sound of another blade cleaving towards his back and, without turning, drove his sword up and back so that the blade sliced his attacker clean in half from left armpit to right shoulder.

Seeing Father Speckless' terrifying swordsmanship, and two of their own men killed before completing even one move, the other guards' courage broke and they scattered.

Buddha Zhao raced up to the carriage and drew open the carriage curtains to look inside. In the darkness, he could dimly make out a figure wrapped in a coverlet.

'Brother Wen!' he shouted happily.

'You take Brother Wen back, and I'll go and look for Fire Hand Zhang to settle accounts with him,' cried Father Speckless, riding up. He spurred his horse forward and charged into the crowd of fleeing Agency guards and officers.

'Fire Hand Judge Zhang! Come out and face me!' he cried repeatedly, but no one answered him.

The Red Flower Society heroes were overjoyed to see Buddha Zhao accompanying the carriage back, and all raced up to meet him. Luo Bing galloped into the lead and up to the carriage, jumped off her horse, and pulled aside the carriage curtains.

'Thunder!' she called out shakily, but the figure inside made no sound. Startled, Luo Bing leapt in and pulled off the coverlet. By this time, the heroes had all dismounted and were standing closely about, watching.

Meanwhile, a fierce battle was raging between the Uighurs on one side and the officers and Agency guards on the other. Father Speckless continued to weave his way backwards and forwards through the crowd, searching for Zhang. All of a sudden, a horse charged out in front of him, its rider a huge Uighur with a bushy beard.

'Where has this wild priest sprung from?' he shouted.

Father Speckless replied with a stroke from his sword, and the Uighur raised his sabre to parry the blow. The priest countered with two strokes to left and right, the second following the first with incomparable speed. The Uighur lunged frantically backwards, hooked his right foot in his stirrup, and swung beneath his horse's belly. Then he urged his horse forward and escaped, clinging on beneath the animal.

'You did well to avoid three strokes from my sword,' Father Speckless smiled. 'I'll spare your life.' He charged back into the battle.

Meanwhile, Luo Bing pulled the man out of the carriage and threw him on the ground. 'My husband!' she shouted. 'Where's my husband?' Even before she had finished speaking, tears were coursing down her face.

The man on the ground was old and wizened, dressed in an officer's uniform, with his right hand in a sling. Luo Bing recognized him as Wu Guodong, the officer sent from Peking to pursue them and capture them. His right arm had been broken by Wen at the inn. She gave him a kick, and wanted to question him again, but her voice failed her.

Leopard Wei held one of his fearsome steel hooks close to Wu's right eye, and shouted: 'Where is our Brother Wen? Talk, or I'll put this eye of yours out for a start!'

'Fire Hand Zhang took him off a long time ago,' Wu replied sullenly. 'He told me to ride in the carriage. I thought he was being considerate, and giving me a chance to rest my arm, but he was just using me, setting me up while he himself goes to Peking and takes all the credit. Damn him!'

Helmsman Chen called out to the Red Flower heroes standing round the carriage: 'Gather all the Eagle's Claws and Agency guards together! Don't let any of them get away!'

The heroes encircled the officers and Agency men, who were still fighting furiously with the Uighurs. Buddha Zhao waved both his hands and three darts shot through the air, simultaneously felling two officers and one guard.

The Uighurs by now realized that the Red Flower Society heroes were on their side. They gave a great cheer. The large Uighur with the thick whiskers galloped forward and shouted: 'I don't know who you are, but you have drawn your weapons to assist us, and I thank you.' He raised his sword in salute.

Helmsman Chen returned the salute. 'Brothers, let's all join in!' he shouted, and the Red Flower heroes rushed at the enemy, all except for Luo Bing, who was too confused to care.

By this time, most of the good fighters amongst the officers and Agency guards were either dead or seriously wounded, and many of their number were kneeling on the ground begging for mercy as the battle continued.

Suddenly, Father Speckless galloped out of the mêlée, and shouted to the other Red Flower heroes: 'Come and have a look at this young girl's swordsmanship! It's not bad!'

They all knew that the Priest's own skill with the sword was unrivalled throughout the land, so hearing him praise another's swordsmanship, and a girl's at that, they all pressed in to watch. The thickly whiskered Uighur shouted a few phrases in his own language, and the other Uighurs gave way and made a place in the circle for the Red Flower Society fighters.

Helmsman Chen looked into the centre of the circle and saw a girl in yellow robes fighting closely with a short, stocky man wielding a pair of Five Element Wheels. On his back was a red knapsack.

'The girl's name is Huo Qingtong,' said Hidden Needle Lu to Helmsman Chen. 'She's a pupil of the Twin Eagles of Heaven Mountains. The man using the Five Element Wheels is Yan. He's one of the Six Devils of Manchuria, and works for the Agency.'

Chen started in surprise. He knew that the Twin Eagles of Heaven Mountains were leading members of the fighting community in the Uighur border regions, and also that for some reason relations between them and his own teacher, Master Yuan, were strained. Focusing his attention on the duel, he saw the yellow-robed girl attack ferociously with her sword, but Yan withstood the onslaught with the help of his Five Element Wheels. The Uighurs shouted their support and some edged in closer, obviously eager to intervene on the girl's behalf.

Yan parried and attacked, then suddenly retreated a step. 'Wait!' he shouted. 'There's something I want to say.'

The Uighurs moved up even closer. It looked as though he would be carved up before he had a chance to say anything. Yan shifted both wheels to his left hand and grabbed the red knapsack off his back. He held the wheels up high.

'If you are going to gang up on me,' he shouted, 'I'll cut up the knapsack now.'

The razor-sharp teeth of the Five Element Wheels flashed. The Uighurs retreated, anxious to preserve their holy book intact.

'There are so many of you!' he shouted. 'It would be the easiest thing in the world for you to kill me. But I will never surrender except in a one-to-one fight. If any one of you can defeat me single-handed, I will freely hand over the knapsack. Otherwise I prefer to take it with me.'

Zhou Qi leapt into the circle. 'Very well,' she cried. 'Let it be between the two of us.' She brandished her sword, ready to charge forward, but Huo Qingtong shook her head.

'Thank you, sister, but I will fight first,' she said. 'If I cannot beat him, I'll ask you to lend me a hand.'

'The knapsack contains something that is very precious to this Uighur tribe,' Lu Feiqing explained to Zhou Qi. 'This lady wishes to recover it with her own hands.'

Yan slung the knapsack onto his back. 'Who's it going to be, then?'

'No matter what the outcome, you will give up the Sacred Book,' Huo Qingtong said to him. 'If you win, you will be allowed to leave. If you lose, you will forfeit your life as well.'

Her sword cut in from the side, thrusting at his left shoulder, and Yan countered using the sixty-four moves of the combined Five Elements and Eight Trigrams styles, which are designed to wrest away an opponent's weapon while maintaining a very tight defence.

Helmsman Chen motioned Scholar Yu over. 'Brother Yu, go immediately and find out what has happened to Brother Wen. We will follow after you,' he said.

Yu nodded and retreated from the circle. He glanced over at Luo Bing and saw her looking dazed. He wanted to go and comfort her, but thought better of it and galloped off.

Huo Qingtong attacked again, this time using a slightly faster sword style. Yan, who had been trying to block her sword with his wheels, now found this impossible. After another twenty or so moves, Huo Qingtong's cheeks began to flush slightly and small beads of sweat appeared on her forehead. But she was full of spirit and her footwork never faltered. Her sword style suddenly changed to the Heaven Mountain School Mirage technique, combining feint with force. The heroes held their breaths, completely absorbed. Suddenly, Huo Qingtong's blade slashed forward and struck Yan's right wrist. He cried out in fright and dropped the wheel in his right hand. The crowd roared in unison.

Yan leapt backwards. 'I accept defeat! The Sacred Book is yours!' he cried and began to undo the red knapsack on his back. An expression of joy filled Huo Qingtong's face and she replaced her sword in its scabbard, as she moved forward to accept the Koran which her people held so sacred. But as she approached, Yan flicked his right hand and three darts flew towards her chest. She had no time to dodge out of the way. Instead, with the move known as the Iron-Plated Bridge, she bent straight over backwards and the darts flew just over her face. Yan quickly followed with three more darts. As he unleashed them, Huo Qingtong was still facing the sky, and was unaware of the impending disaster. The onlookers gasped in fear and anger.

As she straightened up again, she heard the sound—ding-ding-ding—as the three darts were intercepted by three projectiles and fell to the ground at her feet. She broke into a cold sweat and quickly re-drew her sword. Yan lunged forward now with all the power of a crazed tiger. His Five Element Wheel smashed straight down at her. She had no time to escape, and all she could do was to raise her sword and block the stroke with all the force she could muster. For a while, they were deadlocked. But Yan was the stronger of the two, and his Five Element Wheel slowly pressed down towards her head until the sharp blades on the wheel were touching the turquoise feather on her cap. The Red Flower heroes were about to move forward and come to her aid, when there was a flash of blue as Huo Qingtong drew a dagger from her waist with her free hand and rammed it straight into Yan's belly. He cried out once, then toppled over backwards, dead. The crowd cheered as one man.

Huo Qingtong untied the knapsack from Yan's back. The big black-whiskered Uighur walked over to her, praising her and calling her 'good child'. She held the knapsack in both her hands and presented it to him with a modest smile. 'Papa,' she said. He took the knapsack and the cheering crowd of Uighurs pressed forward.

Huo Qingtong saw a boy jump off his horse, retrieve three round white objects from the ground, and present them on the palm of his hand to a young man in the crowd, who took them and put them in his bag.

'It must have been him who deflected that villain's darts and saved my life,' she thought. She took a closer look at the young man. He cut a graceful figure, dressed in a light gown tied loosely around the waist, and fanning himself with a folding fan. Their eyes met, and he smiled at her. Blushing, she lowered her head. She ran over to her father and whispered into his ear. Her father, Muzhuolun, the Khozi Hodja, nodded, walked over to the young man, and bowed before him. The young man hurriedly dismounted and returned the bow.

'Thank you sir, for saving my daughter's life,' said the Hodja. 'I am extremely grateful to you. May I be so bold as to ask your name?'

'My name is Chen Jialuo,' he said. 'We have a sworn brother whom we thought was being held captive by this band of Eagle's Claws and came here to save him. But he is not here. However, we are very pleased that you have recovered your tribe's Sacred Book.'

The Hodja called his son, Huo Yayi, and his daughter over, and the three bowed before Helmsman Chen in thanks.

The son had a full face, large ears, and a thick beard. His sister, on the other hand, was graceful and delicate as a spring flower. Earlier, Helmsman Chen had concentrated on watching her sword style, but now with her standing close to him, he found his heart beating fast. He wondered that such a vision of a girl could exist in this world.

'You saved me from a terrible fate, sir,' said Huo Qingtong quietly. 'Such great kindness, I will never forget.'

'Please, there is no need for thanks,' Chen replied. 'I count myself fortunate that you were not offended by my interference. I have long heard that the Three Part sword style of the Twin Eagles of Heaven Mountains was the most advanced of our time. Now I have seen it for myself: the style truly lives up to its reputation.'

Huo Qingtong spoke in barely audible tones to her father, who nodded rapidly. 'Yes, yes,' he said. 'That is what we should do.' He walked over to Helmsman Chen.

'Thanks to your assistance, our business has now been completed,' he said. 'I heard you mention that you came here to rescue one of your number. I would like to put my own son and daughter at your disposal, together with several companions. Their kungfu may be poor and they will probably be of little use, but they could be helpful running errands and the like. Will you accept this offer, sir?'

'That is very good of you,' Chen replied, and immediately introduced the other members of the Red Flower Society to him.

'Your swordsmanship is extraordinarily fast,' said the Hodja to Father Speckless. 'I have never seen anything like it in my life. It's lucky your hand was stayed by mercy, or I might not be here...'

'I must beg your pardon,' the priest replied with a smile. 'I hope you didn't take offence.'

While they were talking, a horse galloped up from the west. A youngster dismounted and went up to Hidden Needle Lu, addressing him as Shifu. It was Li Yuanzhi who by this time had changed into her boy's clothes. She caught sight of Huo Qingtong, and ran over and grasped her hand.

'Where did you go that night?' asked Yuanzhi. 'I was worried to death about you! Did you get the Sacred Book back?'

'We have just recovered it,' Huo Qingtong said happily. 'Look.' She pointed at the red knapsack now on her brother's back.

'Have you opened it to have a look? Is the Sacred Book inside?'

Huo Qingtong nodded, and hurriedly undid the knapsack. Inside, was nothing but a pile of waste paper.

The Hodja grabbed an Agency shouter who was squatting on the ground and boxed his ears. 'Where has the Sacred Book gone?' he roared.

'I don't know anything about what the guards do,' mumbled the man, and pointed to one of the guards named Qian, who was sitting with his head in his hands. Qian had received several light wounds in the confused battle, and had surrendered after most of the others were killed. The Hodja dragged him over.

'Friend,' he said. 'Do you want to live or die?'

Qian said nothing. The Hodja angrily raised his hand to strike him.

'The other guards took the book with them,' Qian said.

The Hodja was sceptical and ordered his subordinates to search the mule-train thoroughly, but they found no trace of it. He now realized why Yan had been unwilling to hand over the knapsack.

Meanwhile, Yuanzhi was questioning Lu as to what had happened since they had parted. 'I'll tell you about it later,' he replied. 'Go back now, your mother will be worried about you. Don't say anything about what you've seen here.'

'Of course,' she said. 'But who are these people? Introduce me to them.'

Lu considered Yuanzhi's position as the daughter of a

provincial commander-in-chief and decided it would be better not to. 'I don't think it's necessary,' he said.

Yuanzhi pouted. 'I know you don't like me,' she said. 'You prefer that Golden Flute Scholar, or whatever he's called. The one who studied with your brother-in-arms. Anyway, I'm leaving.'

She mounted her horse, galloped over to Huo Qingtong, bent down and embraced her, then whispered a few words into her ear. Huo Qingtong laughed, and Yuanzhi spurred her horse forward and raced off back the way she had come.

Chen had watched the whole incident, and was astonished to see Huo Qingtong being so familiar with this handsome youngster. He stared abstractedly at her, his heart a prey to conflicting emotions.

'Helmsman,' said Mastermind Xu, walking over. 'Let's discuss how we are going to save Rolling Thunder.'

Chen started from his reverie. 'That's right,' he said. 'Xin Yan, take Sister Luo Bing's horse and go and get Brother Zhang.'

'Brother Wei,' Chen continued, turning to Leopard Wei. 'Scout around and look for any signs of where the Eagle's Claws are. Come back this evening to report.'

'We will camp here tonight,' Chen said to the rest. 'We can resume the chase early tomorrow morning.'

Night Creepers

After all the hard riding and fighting they had done that day, they were all hungry and tired. The Hodja directed his men to erect tents by the side of the road, and set aside several for the use of the Red Flower Society; he also sent over cooked beef and mutton for them to eat.

When they had finished, Helmsman Chen gave orders that Wu Guodong be brought in, and questioned him closely. Wu cursed Fire Hand Zhang bitterly. He said that at first, Rolling Thunder Wen had been seated in the carriage, but that once Zhang realized they were being followed, he had told Wu to sit in the carriage instead, as a decoy. Helmsman Chen also interrogated the other Agency guards, but failed to learn anything new.

Mastermind Xu waited until the prisoners had been led out of the tent and then said to Chen: 'Helmsman, that guard Qian has a cunning glint in his eye. Let's test him out.'

'Very well,' Chen replied.

Night fell, but still Leopard Wei and Melancholy Ghost Shi had not returned to report. The others became worried about them.

'They have probably discovered which way Brother Wen is being taken and are following after him,' Xu said. 'It may not be such bad news.' The others nodded, and soon went off to sleep in their tents. The Agency guards and officers were all bound hand and foot and placed outside with Crocodile Jiang keeping watch over them.

When the moon rose, Xu emerged from his tent and told Jiang to go in and sleep. He walked round in a great circle then went over to where the Agency guard Qian was sleeping. He sat down and wrapped himself in a blanket, treading heavily on Qian's thigh as he did so. Qian woke with a start. Not long after, Xu began snoring lightly, and Qian's heart leapt for joy. The rope binding his upper body had not been knotted tightly, and after a short struggle, he managed to wrench himself free. He held his breath, not daring to move. Xu's snoring grew heavier, so he quietly undid the rope binding his legs, stood up, and tip-toed away. He went behind the tents, untied the reins of a horse from a wooden post, and walked slowly to the road. He stood listening very carefully, but there was not a sound to be heard. He started walking again, gradually quickening his pace, until he arrived beside the carriage in which Wu Guodong had sat.

Zhou Qi woke with a start as she heard a noise outside her tent. She lifted the bottom of the canvas and saw a figure walking stealthily towards the road. She picked up her sword and raced out of the tent, and was just about to call out when someone grabbed her from behind and covered her mouth.

Very frightened, she struck backwards with her sword. But her assailant was very agile and grabbed her wrist, forcing the sword away and whispering: 'Don't make a sound, Miss Zhou. It's me, Mastermind Xu.'

Zhou Qi no longer tried to make use of the sword, but she thumped him really hard on the chest with her fist. Half in pain and half play-acting, Xu grunted and toppled over backwards.

'What did you do that for?' she hissed. 'Someone's trying to escape, can't you see?'

'Don't make any noise,' he whispered back. 'Let's watch him.'

They crawled slowly forward and watched as Qian lifted up the cushions in the carriage. There were two sharp cracking sounds as if he was prying planks apart, then he emerged with a small box which he stuffed into his gown. He was about to mount his horse when Xu slapped Zhou Qi's back and shouted: 'Stop him!' Zhou Qi leapt to her feet and raced after him.

Qian already had one foot in the stirrup when he heard the shout but did not have enough time to mount properly. He gave the horse a savage kick on the rump, and the animal, startled by the pain, went galloping off. Qian started to laugh triumphantly, but then all of a sudden he tumbled off the horse and onto the ground.

Zhou Qi ran up to him, placed a foot on his back, and held the point of her sword to his neck.

'Take a look at that box in his gown,' said Xu as he ran up. Zhou Qi pulled out the box, opened it up, and saw inside a thick pile of parchment pages bound in the form of a book. She flipped through it in the moonlight, but the pages were completely covered in strange characters that she did not recognize.

'More of your Red Flower Society scribblings,' she said, throwing it casually at Xu. 'I wouldn't understand it.'

Mastermind Xu caught it and looked at it. 'Miss Zhou,' he exclaimed. 'This is a great achievement on your part. I think it's the Uighurs' Sacred Book. Let's go and find the Helmsman quickly.'

'Really?' she asked. She saw Chen coming up to meet them. 'Helmsman Chen,' she said, 'what do you think this thing is?'

Xu passed the wooden box over, and Chen looked inside. 'It is almost certainly their Sacred Book,' he said. 'It's fortunate that you managed to stop that fellow, Miss Zhou.'

Zhou Qi was very pleased to hear them praising her. After a moment, she asked Xu: 'Did I hurt you when I hit you just now?'

'You are very strong,' he replied with a smile.

'It was your own fault,' she said, and turned to Qian. 'Get up, we're going back!'

She took her foot off Qian's back, but he did not move. 'Stop playing dead! I didn't hurt you,' she scolded him. She kicked him lightly once, but Qian still didn't budge.

Helmsman Chen pinched him beneath his armpit. 'Stand up!' he shouted. Slowly Qian clambered to his feet. Zhou Qi stood thinking for a second, and then realized what had happened. She searched around on the ground and found a white Go piece.

'I think this is yours!' she said, handing it back to Chen. She knew that he specialized in throwing Go-pieces at a distance. He was clearly the one who had brought Qian to the ground. 'You cheated me. You beat me to it! Huh! I might have known it!'

'It was you that heard this fellow and chased after him,' said Chen with a smile.

Zhou Qi was happy to accept this. 'Well, all three of us can share the credit,' she said.

The three of them, escorting Qian and carrying the Koran, walked over to the Hodja's tent. As soon as the four sentries passed on their message, the Hodja came out, hastily throwing on his robes, and invited them inside.

Chen told him what had happened and handed over the Koran. The Hodja was overjoyed. A moment later, all the Uighurs crowded into the tent and bowed respectfully before Xu, Chen, and Zhou Qi.

'Master Chen,' said the Hodja. 'You have recovered my people's Sacred Book. To express our thanks is not enough. If there is ever anything you want us to do, simply let us know, and even if it means crossing a thousand mountains and ten thousand rivers, we will still hurry to your assistance. There is no task we would refuse. Tomorrow I will return home with the Sacred Book and will leave my son and daughter here under your direction. Please allow them to return after your Brother Wen has been rescued.'

Helmsman Chen hesitated for a second before replying. 'It would be best if your son and daughter went home with you. We are very moved by your goodwill, sir, but we really have no right to impose on them in such a way.'

The Hodja was surprised by Chen's refusal, and tried several times to convince him to change his mind, but Chen was adamant.

The rest of the Red Flower heroes now entered the tent and congratulated the Hodja. The tent was full to bursting, and many of the Uighurs retired outside.

Mastermind Xu saw Lord Zhou enter. 'In the recovery of the Uighurs' Sacred Book, it was your daughter who earned the greatest merit,' he said.

Zhou looked at his daughter approvingly. Suddenly Xu pressed his hand to his chest and cried out in pain. Everyone turned to look at him.

'What's the matter?' Lord Zhou asked. Zhou Qi looked on, panic-stricken, afraid that Mastermind Xu was about to let on that she'd punched him hard in the chest not long before. Xu hesitated, then smiled and said: 'It's nothing.'

'Right,' Zhou Qi thought. 'I'll find a way to get back at you sooner or later.'

Early next morning, the Uighurs and the Red Flower heroes bade farewell to each other. Zhou Qi took Huo Qingtong's hand. 'This young lady is a nice person and a powerful kungfu fighter as well,' she said to Chen. 'Why won't you let her help us?' Chen was silent for a second.

'The Helmsman doesn't want us to risk our lives, and we appreciate his good intentions,' Huo Qingtong said. 'Besides, I have been away from home a long time and I miss my mother and sister very much. I would like to get back soon. Goodbye, we will see each other again.'

She waved, pulled round her horse's head and galloped off.

'Look at her,' Zhou Qi said to Chen. 'She's even crying because you won't let her come with us. You're despicable.'

Helmsman Chen silently watched Huo Qingtong as she galloped away. Suddenly, she reined in her horse and turned round. She saw him still standing there and bit her lip, then beckoned to him. Chen hesitated for a moment, then went straight over to her. She jumped off her horse and they stood facing each other for a second, unable to speak.

Huo Qingtong steadied herself. 'You saved my life, and we are indebted to you for recovering our tribe's Sacred Book. No matter how you treat me, I will never blame you,' she said.

She undid the dagger tied to her waist. 'This dagger was given to me by my father. It is said that a great secret is hidden in it, but it has been passed down from hand to hand over the centuries, and no one has ever been able to discover what that secret is. I would like you to keep it. Perhaps you will be able to unravel the mystery.'

She presented the dagger to him respectfully with both hands, and Chen stretched out both his hands to receive it.

'I would not normally presume to accept such a precious object,' he said. 'But since it is a present from you, it would be disrespectful of me to refuse.'

Huo Qingtong could not bear to see the desolate look on his face. 'In my heart I know why you do not want me to go with you to rescue your Brother Wen. You saw yesterday how that young man acted towards me, and you despise me as a result. The truth is that the young man is Master Lu Feiqing's disciple. Go and ask Master Lu about him—then you can decide whether or not I really am the sort of girl you think I am!'

She leapt onto her horse and galloped away in a cloud of dust.

CHAPTER 3

The Helmsman keeps the Peace; The Demon's Mark;
Yellow River Night Battle; Needles, Prostitutes, Poison,
Cure; A Packet of Medicine; Dog-Officials and Refugees

The Helmsman keeps the Peace

Chen held the dagger in his hands and stood gazing into the distance
as Huo Qingtong caught up with the Uighur column and
disappeared over the horizon. He was about to go and ask Hidden
Needle Lu about his young disciple when he saw a horse galloping
towards him. As it came closer, he was disappointed to see that it
was only his page Xin Yan returning on the white horse.

'Master!' he shouted excitedly. 'Brother Zhang has a prisoner.'

'Who is it?' Chen asked.

'I went to the old temple and found Hunchback Zhang arguing
with a man who wanted to pass. The man saw the horse I was
riding and began cursing me as a horse-thief and then he struck out
at me with his sword. Hunchback Zhang and I fought with him.
His kungfu was really good. He fought the two of us single-handed
until finally I picked up some stones and started throwing them at
him, and Hunchback Zhang clubbed him on the thigh. It was only
then that we managed to capture him.'

Chen smiled. 'What is his name? What was he doing?'

'We asked him, but he wouldn't say. Brother Zhang says he
must be a member of the Han School of Luoyang because he was
using Iron Piba kungfu.'

Presently Hunchback Zhang galloped up, dismounted, and
bowed before Chen. He pulled a man off the horse's saddle. The
man was tied hand and foot, but he stood there haughtily, with an
air of defiance.

'I understand you are a member of the Han School of Luoyang,'
said Helmsman Chen. 'May I be so bold as to ask your name?'

The man said nothing.

'Xin Yan, undo this gentleman's bonds,' Chen said.

Xin Yan drew his knife and cut the rope that bound the man's
hands and feet, then stood behind him, his knife at the ready.

'My friends have wronged you, but please do not take offence,' Chen said. 'Come into my tent and sit down.'

Chen and the man sat on the ground while the other Red Flower heroes came in and stood behind Chen.

When he saw Luo Bing enter, the man's anger flared up and he jumped to his feet. 'She's the one who stole my horse,' he shouted, pointing at her.

'So it's Han the guard,' Luo Bing replied with a smile. 'We exchanged horses and I compensated you with a gold ingot. You did very well out of the deal. What are you angry about?'

Chen asked what had happened, and Luo Bing recounted how she had taken the white horse. The others laughed as they listened.

'In that case, we will return you your horse,' Chen said. 'There is no need to give back the gold ingot. Consider it a token of our respect, and payment for the rental of your horse.'

Han was about to reply when Luo Bing said: 'Helmsman, this won't do. Do you know who this man is? He's a Zhen Yuan Agency guard.' She pulled out Wang Weiyang's letter and handed it to him.

Chen's eyes flashed down the lines. 'The great name of Wang Weiyang has long been known to me, but regrettably I have never met him,' he said. 'So, you are a member of the Han School of Luoyang. What relation are you to Fifth Lady Han?'

Han did not answer the question, but instead said: 'May I in turn be so bold as to ask you *your* name, sir?'

Chen smiled. 'My surname is Chen, my given name, Jialuo.'

Han stood up. 'You mean...you are the son of Chief Minister Chen?' he asked in a quavering voice.

'This is Helmsman Chen of our Red Flower Society,' said one of the Twin Knights.

Han slowly sat down again. He seemed to be sizing up this young Helmsman.

'Someone in the underworld started the rumour that our Society was connected with the death of one of your School's members,' Chen said. 'In fact, we know nothing of it. I dispatched one of our Brothers to Luoyang to explain the matter, but something came up and he was forced to postpone the trip. So your arrival could not have been better timed. I don't know how this rumour started. Can you tell me?'

'You...you're really the son of Chief Minister Chen of Haining?' Han asked.

'Since you already know my identity, why should I try to deny it?' replied Chen.

'When you left home, your family offered a large reward for anyone who could succeed in finding you,' Han said. 'Some people said that you had joined the Red Flower Society and gone to the Uighur border regions. My late comrade Jiao Wenqi was engaged by your family to look for you, but he mysteriously disappeared on the way. That was five years ago. Recently, in Shanxi Province, someone found the Iron Piba darts that Brother Jiao used, and we now know for certain that he was murdered. No one knows the exact circumstances of his death. But consider, sir: it must have been the Red Flower Society. Who else could it have been?'

'I am the man who killed Jiao Wenqi,' interrupted Hidden Needle Lu. 'And I am not a member of the Red Flower Society. So this matter has nothing to do with them.'

The others were greatly taken aback by this announcement. Lu stood up and told the story of how Jiao, who had been searching for him, had found him one night; how Lu had fought one against three, and had been injured, but had still managed to kill them on the deserted hillside. The Red Flower heroes listened and then cursed Jiao, saying he was shameless and deserved to die. Han's face darkened but he said nothing.

'If Master Han wishes to avenge the death of his brother-in-arms, there is no reason why he should not do so now,' Lu said. He turned to Luo Bing. 'Mistress Wen, return Master Han's weapon to him please.'

Luo Bing pulled out the Iron Piba and handed it to Lu.

'Since your friend Jiao was commissioned by the Chen family to find their son, he should have stuck to his mission and not come after me,' Lu said. As he spoke, he absent-mindedly exercised his Inner Force kungfu on the body of the hollow Iron Pipa, slowly flattening it. 'Why did he want to come and give me trouble? We of the fighting community may not be able to save our country from the Manchu barbarians, but we should still fight for justice and join together in opposing those who oppress the people.'

Lu's Inner Force was extraordinary. His hands had now rolled the flattened iron into a tube, and then with a few deft squeezes, transformed it into an iron club.

'The people I detest most of all are the ones who work for the Manchu Court: the Eagle's Claws and the Security Agency running dogs. They use a smattering of Martial Arts knowledge to assist the wicked with their evil deeds. Take my advice, and work for someone else.'

His voice suddenly hardened and he twisted the iron club into an iron ring.

As Lu talked, Han watched him effortlessly twist and squeeze his School's famous iron weapon as if he were making noodles. He was terrified by this display of sheer force. He knew that Jiao's kungfu had been about the same standard as his own, and realized that fighting with this old man Lu would mean certain death.

Han's courage had already evaporated. He did not dare challenge Lu. But although shocked and humbled, he did not wish to appear too cowardly.

'This whole business was my fault to start with,' said Helmsman Chen. 'I will write a letter to my elder brother in Haining, telling him that Jiao did in fact succeed in finding me, but that I was not willing to return home; and that on his way back, Jiao met with an accident and passed away. I will ask my brother to pay the reward and compensation money to Jiao's family.'

Han continued to hesitate, and Chen's eyebrows rose. 'But if your heart is set upon revenge, then I will fight you myself.'

Han shuddered. 'I will do exactly as you say, sir,' he replied.

'Good,' said Chen.

He told Xin Yan to hand him his writing-brush, inkstone, ink, and writing-paper, and in his vigorous calligraphic style, wrote a letter exactly as he had described, which Han took from him with words of humble apology.

'Master Wang asked me,' he began, 'to help escort a certain cargo back to Peking, and then to escort some treasures from the Emperor to your honourable family down in the south. The Agency shouter who brought me the letter said the Emperor is always extremely generous towards your family. Every few months, he bestows upon them a certain quantity of precious stones and treasures. There is now a large accumulation of these that must be sent south to your home. Your family asked us to escort them, but I would not dare to continue earning my daily rice in this profession. You have put me to shame, with your superb demonstration of kungfu prowess. I will make suitable arrangements for Jiao's dependants, and then return home.'

'I am happy that you are willing to follow Master Lu's invaluable words of advice,' Chen said. 'Xin Yan, please bring in the other gentlemen from the Zhen Yuan Agency.'

Xin Yan went out and led in Qian and the other guards. Han and the guards exchanged a puzzled stare.

'Master Han, please take these friends with you,' said Helmsman Chen. 'But if we ever catch them making trouble again, do not blame us if our hands are not stayed by mercy.'

Chen did not mention the return of the white horse, and Han did not dare to bring it up.

'We will go now,' said Chen. 'All of you rest here for a day before making a start.'

The Red Flower Society heroes mounted their horses and started off, leaving the Agency men and officers standing silently behind.

'Helmsman Chen,' said Hidden Needle Lu after they had travelled for a while. 'My young disciple is sure to meet up with those Agency men before long. They have been humiliated and have been unable to get their revenge, so they may cause trouble. I would like to stay behind and keep an eye on them for a while before following after you.'

'Please do as you wish, Master Lu,' Chen replied.

Lu saluted, then galloped back the way they had come. Chen realized as Lu disappeared that he had still not asked him about his young disciple.

The Demon's Mark

Scholar Yu, under orders to investigate the latest whereabouts of Rolling Thunder Wen, made discreet enquiries along the road as he went, but discovered no clues. In less than a day he arrived at Liangzhou, a prosperous, bustling city and one of the largest in Gansu Province. He found a room in an inn, then went to a tavern and drank alone, reflecting in a somewhat maudlin fashion on his present predicament. He kept thinking of Luo Bing's enchanting voice and captivating smile, and a wave of longing rose within him. He knew it was a hopeless case, and the more he drank, the more melancholy he became.

He was just about to leave the tavern when two men came in. Yu knew he had seen one of them before and quickly turned his head away. He searched frantically in his memory, and finally placed him as one of the officers he had fought at Iron Ball Manor. Luckily, the man and his companion paid him no attention.

They chose a table near the window which happened to be just next to Yu's and sat down. Yu sat with his head on the table, pretending to be drunk.

The two men chatted for a while, then one said:

'Friend Rui, it's amazing how you managed to capture that fellow. I wonder what sort of reward the Emperor will give you?'

'I'm not bothered about the reward,' Rui replied. 'I just want to get him to Hangzhou safe and sound. When we left Peking, there were eight of us on this mission, and now I'm the only one left. It was that fight in Suzhou. I still get the shivers just thinking about it.'

'You've got Fire Hand Zhang to help you now,' the other said. 'I'm sure nothing more will go wrong.'

'That's true,' Rui replied. 'But it means that he and the Emperor's special forces—you and the others with you—will get all the credit. What do we ordinary officers get out of it? But tell me, friend Zhu. Why are they sending him to Hangzhou instead of to Peking?'

'As I think I told you,' Zhu replied, lowering his voice, 'my younger sister married into the Shi family. They are very highly placed at Court. She told me in private that the Emperor plans to go down south. Perhaps he wants to question your man himself.'

Rui grunted and drank another mouthful of wine. 'So the six of you came rushing out here from Peking to see that the Imperial command was carried out?'

'And to give you people some help. The Red Flower Society is known to be very powerful in the south. We have to be especially careful.'

As he listened, Yu gave silent thanks for the sheer luck of having overheard this snippet of conversation. If he had not happened to be there and hear what they were saying, the Red Flower heroes would have gone racing to Peking to save Rolling Thunder Wen, when in actual fact he was being taken south to Hangzhou.

Zhu spoke next: 'Exactly what crime has this fellow committed that the Emperor wants to question him personally?'

'How would we know?' Rui replied. 'We were just told that if we didn't catch him, we'd all get the sack. I just want to keep my head on my shoulders!'

The two laughed and drank, and their conversation turned to the subject of women. Peking women had the cutest little feet, they both agreed, whereas girls from the south had the softest skin and the lightest complexion. Finally, they paid the bill and stood up to leave. Rui looked over at Yu slumped prostrate on the table.

'Scholars!' he said and laughed harshly. 'Three cups of wine and they can't even walk.'

Yu waited until they had gone, then hastily threw five silver coins onto the table and dashed out of the tavern. He spotted the men entering the city Yamen. He waited for a long time but didn't see them reappear, and decided they must be lodging there.

He returned to his room and, as soon as it was dark, changed into some dark clothes, stuck his Golden Flute into his belt, then ran over to the Yamen. Making his way round to the back, he clambered over the wall.

All was pitch-black in the courtyard save a shaft of light coming from a window in the eastern hall. As he crept closer, he heard voices coming from inside. He wet the tip of his finger with a drop of saliva, then lightly moistened the window-paper and made a small hole. Looking through, he was surprised to find that the hall was full of people. He could see Fire Hand Zhang sitting in the middle, with various officers—some attached to the local Yamen, some sent from Peking—on either side of him. A man standing with his back to Yu was shouting and cursing angrily, and Yu knew from his voice that it was Rolling Thunder Wen.

'You can curse to your heart's content,' a voice off to the side said darkly. 'I may not be your match in the Martial Arts, but you will still get a taste of my hand.'

Yu was distressed to hear these words. 'They are going to ill-treat Brother Wen,' he thought. 'He is the person Sister Luo respects and loves most. I cannot stand by and allow him to be insulted by these wretches!'

Next he saw a tall, thin middle-aged man wearing a blue gown advancing on Wen with his hand raised. He had a sinister face, and a nasty smile. Just as the man was about to strike Wen, Yu poked his flute through the hole in the window-paper and, with a puff, shot a small dart into the man's left eye. He fell to the ground in agony and there was a moment of confusion in the hall. Yu shot a second dart at the right cheek of one of the officers, then kicked open the main door of the hall and ran straight in.

'Nobody move!' he shouted. 'The Red Flower Society has come to the rescue!'

He raised his flute and shot at the officers standing beside Wen. Then he pulled out the dagger concealed in the cloth binding his trouser-leg and cut the ropes securing Wen's hands and feet.

Fire Hand Zhang thought a large-scale attack of some sort was in progress and immediately drew his sword and went to the hall door to prevent Wen and Yu from escaping, and to prevent anyone outside from getting in.

As soon as Wen's hands were free of the bonds, his spirits surged. One of the Peking officers lunged towards him and Wen struck him hard with his fist, sending him reeling away. The others were so afraid of Wen's power that for a while they did not dare to get too close to him.

'Brother Wen, let's get out of this place!' Yu said.

'Are the others here?'

'No,' Yu replied *sotto voce*. 'There's only me.'

Wen nodded once. The wounds on his right arm and thigh had not yet healed, but he was able to run for the door with his right arm resting on Yu's shoulder.

Fire Hand Zhang strode forward a step. 'Halt!' he shouted, and jabbed at Wen's stomach with his long-sword. Wen was slow on his feet, and so was obliged to use a hand-attack as his defence. He struck out swiftly at his opponent's eyes with the index and middle fingers of his left hand, and Zhang was forced to retract his sword.

The two men fought with incredible speed, but Wen only had the use of his left arm and after a few more moves, Zhang landed a powerful blow on his right shoulder. Unable to keep his balance, Wen sat down heavily on the floor.

'I should never have done this,' Yu thought as he fought off a number of officers. 'I will save Brother Wen, then I will let the Eagle's Claws kill me! At least that way Sister Luo Bing will know that I, Yu Yutong, stand for something!'

When he saw Wen fall to the ground, he flipped round and struck out desperately at Zhang.

'Brother Wen, get out quick!' Yu shouted. Wen rested a moment and then with difficulty clambered to his feet. Scholar Yu's Golden Flute flew and danced wildly through the air. Yu was completely unconcerned for his own safety. Even with his superb swordsmanship, Fire Hand Zhang was forced to retreat several paces in the face of this suicidal attack. Wen saw an opening and shot out of the door. The mob of officers came howling after him in hot pursuit.

Ignoring his own safety, Yu valiantly blocked the door to stop them. Two swords had already found their way into his body.

'Are you mad?' shouted Zhang. 'Don't you want to live? Who taught you that kungfu style?' Yu was using the traditional style of the Wudang School, the very School to which Zhang himself belonged. It was for this reason that so far Zhang had spared him.

'It would be best if you killed me,' cried Yu, smiling sadly. After a few more moves, Zhang's sword struck him once more, this time on the right shoulder. Yu shifted the Golden Flute to his left hand and continued the fight without retreating a step.

The body of officers charged forward again, and once more Yu's flute danced, whistling strangely as the air whipped through it. One officer chopped at him with his sword, and gashed his shoulder. Yu's body was now spattered in blood, but he continued to hold his own in the fierce battle. There was a sudden crack as the jawbone of another officer was shattered. The massed officers pressed forward, knives, swords, whips, and clubs all thrusting towards Yu simultaneously. Yu's thigh took a hit from a club, and he fell to the ground. His Golden Flute kept up its dance for a few moments, then he fainted away.

It was at this moment that a sudden shout came from the doorway: 'Stop! All of you!'

The officers turned and saw Rolling Thunder Wen walking slowly back into the hall. He ignored them entirely, and went straight over to where Yu lay. The sight of his bloodied body brought tears to his eyes. He bent down and was greatly relieved to find that Yu was still breathing.

'Treat this man's wounds at once,' he ordered.

The officers were in such awe of this man's power, that they did exactly as he said. Wen watched them bind Yu's wounds and carry him through to the inner hall. Then he placed both of his hands behind his back.

'Now tie me up,' he said. One of the officers looked over at Fire Hand Zhang, then walked slowly over.

'What are you afraid of?' Wen asked. 'If I was going to hurt you, I would have done so long before now.'

The officer bound his hands and took him down to the dungeon. Two men were left to guard him.

Early the next morning, Fire Hand Zhang went to see Yu and found him in a deep sleep. He was told by a guard that a doctor had visited Yu and prescribed some medicine. When Fire Hand Zhang visited him again that afternoon, Yu appeared more alert.

'Tell me, is your Shifu's surname Lu or Ma?' Zhang asked him.

'My Shifu's name is Ma Zhen.'

'So that's it. Ma was my brother-in-arms. My name is Zhang Zhaozhong.'

Yu nodded slightly.

'And tell me,' continued Zhang, 'are you a member of the Red Flower Society?'

Yu nodded again.

'You seem such a nice young man,' Zhang sighed. 'What a pity that you should have come to this. What relation is Wen Tailai to you? What were you doing risking your life to save him?'

Yu closed his eyes and was silent. A moment passed.

'At least in the end I did save him,' he finally said. 'So now I can die in peace.'

'Huh! Did you really think you could snatch him away from me?'

Yu was startled. 'Didn't he escape?' he asked.

'How could he? Stop day-dreaming!'

Zhang tried to interrogate him further, but Yu paid him no heed. After a while he began to sneeze.

Zhang smiled slightly. 'You stubborn boy,' he said, and left.

He proceeded to give orders for the officers to organize an ambush, using Wen as bait. After dinner, Wen was brought out of the dungeon and interrogated once more, in the same manner as the night before, when Yu had unexpectedly burst in and disrupted the proceedings. This time, however, heavily armed troops were hidden all around the Yamen, waiting to catch any Red Flower Society would-be rescuers. But they waited in vain.

The next morning, Fire Hand Zhang received a report that the water of the Yellow River—which flows to the east of Liangzhou, and which they would need to cross on their way south to Hangzhou—was rising rapidly. The current at the point where they intended to cross was already very strong. He ordered an immediate departure. He had Wen and Yu placed in separate carriages and was just about to start out when his subordinate Wu Guodong and the Zhen Yuan Agency guards raced into the Yamen. Wu breathlessly told him how they had been attacked and captured by the Uighurs, who were now working together with the Red Flower Society, and that Yan had been killed by a young Uighur girl.

'Yan was a very tough fighter,' commented Fire Hand Zhang. 'How extraordinary that he should have died at the hands of a girl!' He raised his hand in parting. 'We have no time to lose. We will meet again in Peking.'

Zhang was concerned at this new alliance between the Uighurs and Red Flower Society. It was going to make his job harder. He immediately went to inform the Liangzhou military commander that he needed four hundred crack troops transferred to his command to help escort a number of criminals wanted by the Emperor. The commander did not dare refuse. He dispatched two of his senior officers, Colonel Cao Neng and Lieutenant–Colonel Ping Wangxian, to lead the escorting soldiers as far as Lanzhou, the provincial capital, where provincial troops would take over.

Zhang's column surged out of the town, stealing and pilfering from the common people in the usual way as they went.

They travelled without incident for two days. Then, about ten miles from the village of Twin Wells, they came upon two men, naked to the waist, sitting beneath a tree by the side of the road, with a pair of fine horses standing nearby. Two of the soldiers went over to them.

'Hey!' one of them shouted. 'These look like official horses. Where did you steal them from?'

'We are law-abiding citizens,' replied one of the men. 'We wouldn't dare to steal horses.'

'We are tired of walking. Lend them to us,' the second soldier said.

The two men stood up, went over to their horses and untied the reins.

The soldiers walked haughtily over and were just about to take hold of the reins when the two men leapt onto the horses and galloped over to one of the carriages.

'Is that Brother Wen in there?' one of them shouted.

'Ah, is that you, Melancholy Shi!' answered Wen from within the carriage.

'Brother Wen, we must leave now,' the man replied. 'But don't worry, we'll be back soon to rescue you.'

The two men galloped away before the carriage guards could attack.

The column lodged that night at a town called Clear Water Store. Early the following morning, while most of the soldiers were still asleep, a scream was heard, and there was a moment of confusion. The two troop commanders, Colonel Cao and Lieutenant–Colonel Ping, went to investigate and found the bodies of more than a dozen soldiers lying where they had slept, each with a gaping gash in the chest. There was no indication of who had killed them.

The next evening, they rested at Hengshi, a large town. The column filled three inns, and a large number of private houses had to be commandeered besides. During the night, one of the inns caught fire. Zhang ordered the guards to watch Wen closely and to be on the look-out for any sort of ruse. The flames rose higher and higher.

'Bandits!' Colonel Cao cried as he ran into Fire Hand Zhang's room. 'We are being attacked!'

'Please go and direct operations yourself, Colonel Cao,' Zhang replied. 'I am unable to leave this place.'

Cao nodded and left.

From outside the inn came the sound of screams and shrieks, galloping horses, the crackle of the flames, and the smash of roof-tiles as they hit the ground. Zhang ordered two guards onto the roof to keep watch, but instructed them not to get involved unless the enemy attacked the inn. The fire did not get out of control, and before long it was extinguished. The agitated clamour continued for a while, then gradually died down to the point where the sound of hooves could be heard as horses galloped off eastwards.

Colonel Cao, his face covered in soot, grease, and blood, ran in to report to Fire Hand Zhang again.

'The bandits have retreated!'

'How many of our men have been killed or wounded?' asked Zhang.

'I don't know yet. Dozens.'

'How many bandits were captured?'

Cao's mouth fell open. After a moment, he said: 'None.'

Zhang grunted.

'Their faces were covered with cloth, and their kungfu was awe-inspiring,' Cao added. 'But it's very strange: they didn't steal anything. All they did was kill our men. Just before they left, they threw down two hundred taels of silver for the innkeeper saying it was by way of compensation for starting the fire.'

'So you think they were bandits, do you?' Zhang said. 'Tell everyone to get some rest. We will start out again early tomorrow.'

Cao left and went to see the innkeeper, whom he accused of being in collusion with the bandits and of being responsible for the murder of the soldiers. The innkeeper kowtowed and begged for mercy and finally handed over the two hundred taels of silver to Cao—which was the point of the exercise.

It was noon the next day before the soldiers finally made a fresh start on their journey. They now passed through beautiful country—lush green hills and sparkling blue water, surrounded by dense vegetation on all sides. Then, after they had travelled about four hours, the road began to grow gradually steeper and high peaks rose on either side.

Presently a horse came galloping down the road towards them and halted about ten paces in front of the column.

'Listen to me, all of you!' the rider called out. 'You have offended the demons. Turn back quickly and you will be spared. Continue eastwards, and each one of you turtles will surely die.'

The soldiers shuddered as they looked at the man. He was dressed in rough hempen clothes bound at the waist with grass rope. His face was pale yellow and his eyebrows slanted upwards, just like the images they had seen of life-stealing spirits in the temples. The man spurred his horse forward, galloped on past them down the mountain, and was gone. Suddenly, one of the soldiers in the rear-guard gave a cry and fell to the ground, dead. The rest looked on aghast. But there was no wound visible on his body. Terrified, they all began talking at once.

Colonel Cao assigned two soldiers to stay behind and bury the dead man, and the column continued on its way up the mountain. Before they had gone very far, another horse approached them from in front, ridden by the very same man they had seen earlier.

'Listen to me, all of you!' he called out once again. 'You have offended the demons. Turn back quickly and you will be spared. Continue eastwards, and each one of you turtles will surely die.'

The soldiers wondered fearfully how the man (or demon) could have made his way round so that he now stood in front of them once more. They had clearly seen him go down the mountain, and a cursory glance was enough to establish that there were no short cuts back up the slope. There was something very strange going on. The man spurred his horse forward and the soldiers shrank from him as if he was a real demon.

One of the officers from Peking, the man named Zhu (whom we have already encountered in conversation with Rui, the sole surviving member of the original eight-man-mission), was brave (or foolhardy) enough to stick out his sword and obstruct the man's progress. 'Slow down, friend,' he said.

The man-demon promptly struck Zhu on the shoulder with his right hand, and Zhu's sword clattered to the ground. Then he rode off down the mountain. As he passed the end of the column, once again, the last soldier gave a shriek and fell to the ground, dead. The other soldiers stood there staring foolishly, scared out of their wits. Fire Hand Zhang rode down to the end of the column to investigate.

'What is this fellow, a man or a ghost?' stammered Zhu. He pressed his wounded right shoulder, his face by now deathly pale. Fire Hand Zhang told him to undo his clothes, and examined the large black swelling on his right shoulder. He ordered the troops to strip the dead soldier bare and examine him for wounds. When they turned him over, they found a similar black swelling on his back, on which the shape of a hand could be vaguely discerned. 'The Demon's Mark!' shouted the terrified soldiers. 'The Demon's Mark!' Total panic was beginning to set in. Fire Hand Zhang ordered that two soldiers stay behind and bury the dead man. But the two men chosen, even when threatened with death, absolutely refused to carry out the order. Zhang had no alternative but to order a general halt and wait until the body was buried before continuing.

'Master Zhang, that creature is very strange,' said the officer named Rui. 'How was he able to pass us by, and then make his way back and appear in front of us again?'

Zhang stood deep in thought for a while. 'Officer Zhu and the two soldiers were obviously victims of Black Sand Palm kungfu,' he said. 'There are very few masters of that kungfu in the underworld.'

'The greatest master of Black Sand Palm is the Taoist priest Hui Lü, from Sichuan in the west. But he's been dead for many years,' Rui said. 'Could it have been his ghost?'

Zhang slapped his thigh. 'That's it!' he cried. 'They're Hui Lü's disciples. The Twin Knights of West Stream. The Chang brothers. People call them Black Death and White Death. I was trying to think of one person. That's why I couldn't work it out. So now we know we're up against them as well.'

What he had no way of knowing was that the Chang brothers were also members of the Red Flower Society.

That night, the column stayed at Black Pine Village. Colonel Cao posted guards all around the village to keep careful watch, but next morning, not one of these guards returned to report, and a detail sent to investigate found them all dead, with a string of paper money tied round each of their necks. The rest of the soldiers were now more terrified than ever, and more than a dozen immediately deserted, slipping stealthily away.

Next they had to cross the Black Scabbard range, one of the most precipitous spots on the road going east from Liangzhou. Colonel Cao gave orders for the men to have a hearty meal before starting uphill, in an effort to raise their morale. The air became colder and colder as the road climbed ever more steeply upwards, and despite the fact that it was only September, snowflakes were floating down around them. The road narrowed and deteriorated to the point where there was little more than a track winding between a steep mountain face on one side and a sheer cliff on the other, falling into a deep ravine, so deep that they could not see the bottom of it. The soldiers moved slowly hand in hand, terrified of slipping on the snow and plunging to their deaths. Several of the guards dismounted and helped to push Wen's carriage along.

Just as they were gingerly inching their way forward, they heard a peculiar chirping sound coming from behind a rock-face in front of them. A moment later, the sound became an unearthly, ghostly wailing noise, a tragic, harsh howl, which echoed through the ravine, causing everyone's hair to stand on end. The soldiers all stopped in their tracks.

Then came a shout: 'Those who continue will meet the King of Hell! Those who turn back will live!'

Colonel Cao led a few brave soldiers forward, all of whom were struck dead by arrows and fell tumbling to their deaths at the bottom of the ravine. Then a man appeared around a curve in the road ahead. 'Those who continue will meet the King of Hell! Those who turn back will live!' he boomed in deep, chilling tones.

The soldiers recognized him as the demon that they had seen twice the day before and that had killed with his naked hand. Not one of them dared continue. They turned and fled with squeals of fear. Colonel Cao shouted to them to halt, but his deputy, Lieutenant–Colonel Ping, had to raise his sword and slay one of the soldiers before some of them steadied. Sixty or seventy had already disappeared.

'Guard the carriage,' said Fire Hand Zhang to Rui. 'I'll go and talk to these Chang brothers.' He leapt past the soldiers. 'Is that the Twin Knights up ahead?' he called out in a loud, clear voice. 'I am Zhang Zhaozhong, the Fire Hand Judge. I greet you. There is no enmity between us. Why are you playing this game?'

The man laughed coldly. 'Ha! So, the Twin Demons meet Fire Hand Judge,' he said. He strode over and struck out at Zhang with such power that his hand made a whistling sound as it cut through the air.

The road at that point was extremely narrow and Zhang was unable to dodge to either left or right. He countered the blow with his left hand, using all of his Inner Force, while simultaneously striking out with his right palm. His opponent parried with another devastating blow from his left hand. Their four hands met, and they stood there almost motionless for a while, testing each other's strength. Suddenly, Zhang swept his left leg crosswise in the move known as Level Clouds Slicing the Peak. The man had insufficient time to evade the blow, and he was obliged to bring his hands together and drive them viciously at Zhang's temples, aiming for his Greater Yang points. Zhang veered to one side, hastily withdrew his leg, then moved forward; his opponent did likewise. With the precipice looming beneath them, the two glided past each other. They had exchanged positions.

Zhang suddenly became aware of someone attacking him from behind. He dodged out of the way and saw that his new assailant was another pale, skeleton-like figure, his face exactly the same as the first.

Zhang still had more than two hundred soldiers with him, but they were powerless to assist because of the narrowness of the mountain path leading through the ravine.

The three fought more and more fiercely. In the midst of the battle, one of the Twin Knights hit the rock-face by mistake and a small avalanche of loose stones rattled down off the precipice followed by a boulder which plunged down into the depths of the ravine. A long time passed before they finally heard the distant crash as it hit the ground below.

The battle continued for a long time. Suddenly, one of the Twin Knights struck out in an unexpectedly forceful manner with his fist, obliging Zhang to dodge to one side. The other Twin then leapt over and occupied Zhang's former position against the rock-face, and both attacked him at the same moment, attempting to force him into the ravine. Zhang saw one of the Twins sweeping his leg forward, and he stepped back a pace, so that half of his own foot was now perched over the edge of the precipice. A cry of terror went up from the troops. Then Zhang felt a gust of wind as the other Twin swung his fist towards his face. Zhang knew he could not retreat any further. He also knew that there would be great strength behind the oncoming blow. He could not attempt to counter it. If he did, his opponent would simply be thrown back against the rock-face by the force of the collision, while he himself would certainly fall to his death. So, with the wisdom born of fear, he seized hold of his attacker's wrist, and with a great shout hurled him into the ravine.

Even as his body vaulted through the air, Black Death stayed utterly calm. He drew in his legs and performed a flying somersault in mid-air, in order to slow down the force of his fall. Halfway through the circle, he pulled a Flying Claw Grappling Hook from his belt and threw it straight up above him. His brother White Death had also meanwhile taken out his Flying Claw. The two hooks locked tightly, almost as if they were shaking hands. White Death jerked on the rope before the full force of his brother's fall could take effect, and swung him up and over, bringing him flying back to earth more than thirty yards further along the mountain path.

White Death saluted Fire Hand Zhang with clasped fists. 'Your skill is indeed transcendent! Excellent kungfu!' With these words, without even bending down to concentrate his strength, he sprang into the air, and landed further down the path. He grabbed hold of his brother's hand, and the two disappeared round the bend.

The soldiers now clustered round Fire Hand Zhang, some praising his kungfu, others lamenting that Black Death had not fallen to his death. Zhang said not a word, but leaned against the rock-face and slowly sat down. He looked at his wrist and saw the jet-black impression of five fingers branded on his flesh. He was seized with a sense of terror.

Yellow River Night Battle

The column crossed the Black Scabbard range. That night another thirty or forty of the soldiers deserted. Fire Hand Zhang discussed the situation with Rui and the other officers.

'These bandits are not going to give up even though this is the main road east to the provincial capital, Lanzhou,' he said. 'There's going to be a lot more trouble ahead. We had better make our way round by the backroads, and cross the river at Crimson Bend.'

Colonel Cao had been looking forward to getting to Lanzhou so that he could transfer his burden of command to other shoulders, and was very unhappy with Zhang's new plan. But he did not dare to disagree.

'So many soldiers have deserted on the way,' said Zhang. 'When you get back, Colonel Cao, you can report that they were killed during an attack on bandits, and died courageously fighting for their country. I will write out a note to that effect in a moment.'

Cao's spirits rose again. According to the military regulations of the time, if a soldier was killed in action, he was awarded a pension (much of which naturally made its way into the pockets of the officer in command).

They heard the roar of the mighty Yellow River long before it came into view, and travelled more than half a day further before arriving at the Crimson Bend crossing. At this bend on the Yellow River, the rocks along the banks are blood-red, hence its name. Dusk was already approaching, but through the evening mist, they could see the fury with which the Yellow River surged eastwards and southwards, its muddy waters bubbling and boiling against the banks.

'We must cross the river tonight,' said Fire Hand Zhang. 'The water is dangerous, but if we delay, we may run into more trouble with the bandits.'

With the river running so fast, the crossing could not be made using ordinary boats. Only light, inflated sheepskin rafts would be buoyant enough for the purpose. Soldiers were sent out to search for such rafts, but none could be found. Darkness fell, and Zhang was growing more and more anxious when he spotted two sheepskin rafts shooting down the river towards them. His soldiers hailed them, and the two rafts edged towards the bank.

'Hey, boatman!' shouted Colonel Cao. 'Ferry us across and we'll pay you well.'

A big man stood up on the raft and waved his hand as he approached the bank.

'Well? Are you mute or something?' yelled Cao.

'A pox on your ancestors!' the man called back in a thick, barely comprehensible Cantonese accent. 'Pickle the lot of 'em alive! If you're coming, come! If you're not, then bugger off! But whatever you do, stop pissing me around!' Colonel Cao and the others were solid northerners, and could barely understand a word he was saying. Cao invited Fire Hand Zhang and the guards escorting Wen to climb aboard the rafts first.

Zhang weighed up this boatman. He sported a wide-brimmed hat, which hid half his face. It was impossible to distinguish his features clearly. But the bulging muscles on his arms spoke of great strength, while the oar in his hands was of a very dark colour and appeared to be made of something other than wood. Zhang felt there was something strange about him. He himself could not swim, and he simply could not afford to fall victim to some trick.

'Colonel Cao,' he said. 'You go ahead first with some of the men.'

Cao ordered a number of the soldiers onto the rafts. The current was rapid, but the boatmen on the two rafts were both of them evidently highly skilled and experienced, and they delivered the troops safely to the opposite bank, before returning to load another batch.

Colonel Cao now boarded one of the rafts himself with another group of soldiers. Just as they were pulling away from the bank and into the current, a long whistle sounded behind them. It was answered by a whole series of other whistles from all around.

Fire Hand Zhang hastily ordered the remaining troops on his bank to surround Wen's carriage and guard it closely. By the light of the crescent moon which hung low in the sky, he made out a dozen or so horses coming towards them. He galloped forward.

'What's the meaning of this?' he shouted.

The riders spread into a straight line as they approached, then the one in the middle spurred his horse on ahead of the others. In his hand he held a white folding fan. 'Is that the Fire Hand Judge, Zhang Zhaozhong?' he asked, fanning himself.

'It is,' replied Zhang. 'And who are you, sir?'

The man with the fan laughed. 'Thank you for escorting our Brother Wen this far. We don't want to trouble you any further.'

'Are you from the Red Flower Society?'

'Everyone on River and Lake praises the Fire Hand Judge for his superlative mastery of the Martial Arts,' the man replied, smiling, 'but he is obviously gifted with divine powers of perception as well. You are correct. We are from the Red Flower Society.' He gave a long whistle.

Zhang started slightly as he heard the two boatmen on the rafts whistle back. Colonel Cao was seated on one of the rafts. As he had seen the horsemen approaching on the shore, his face had turned a deathly grey. With a deft stroke of his oar, the boatman stopped the raft in midstream.

'Crocodile Jiang!' Colonel Cao heard a crisp woman's voice call from the other raft. 'Ready when you are.'

'Right!' replied Jiang. He said a lot more, but he was speaking in Cantonese again, and Colonel Cao was unable to follow him. He raised his spear and thrust it at Jiang, who deflected it deftly with his oar and then knocked Cao and all the other soldiers on board into the raging torrent. Both boatmen then rowed back to the shore.

Fire Hand Zhang was glad he had been cautious. 'This is not the first time you and your men have killed government troops!' he shouted at Helmsman Chen. 'You have committed many unpardonable acts. What is your position in the Red Flower Society, sir?'

'I hardly think you need to ask my name,' said Helmsman Chen, putting away his fan. 'Xin Yan, give me my weapons.'

Xin Yan opened his bag and placed two weapons in Chen's hands. Normally, the other Red Flower heroes should have fought first, but Chen was unable to resist the opportunity to demonstrate his skills.

Fire Hand Zhang jumped off his horse and strode forward. But just as he was preparing himself for the fight, Zhu, the officer who had accompanied him from Peking, ran up behind him and said: 'Fire Hand Zhang, let me deal with him.'

Zhang decided to let his subordinate test out the enemy first. 'Very well. But be careful.'

Zhu charged forward, sword raised, and chopped at Helmsman Chen's thigh. Chen jumped lightly off his horse and lifted the shield in his left hand to parry the blow. In the moonlight, Zhu saw the nine glistening, sharp hooks protruding from the face of the shield, and knew that if his sword collided with them, it would be caught in their grasp. He hastily retracted his sword. Chen now brandished the weapon in his right hand: it consisted of five cords, each one tipped with a steel ball especially designed for striking Vital Points on the human body. Terrified by the mere sight of this ferocious-looking weapon, Zhu leapt backwards, but the cords were already circling round behind him. He felt a sudden numbness on his back, as the point known as the Hall of the Will was closed. Then the cords entwined his legs and, with a single tug, Chen pulled him off his feet, swung him round and round through the air, and sent him flying straight towards a rocky outcrop nearby.

If he had hit the outcrop, he would have been instantly smashed to pieces. But Fire Hand Zhang, seeing that Zhu was completely outclassed, had raced over and was able to catch him by his pigtail and pull him down just in front of the rock-face, opening his closed point as he did so.

'Rest for a while,' he said. Zhu was too paralysed by fear to be able to answer.

Zhang now brandished his precious Frozen Emerald sword in the air and leapt in front of Chen, thrusting at his right shoulder. Chen flipped his five cords towards the blade, while holding the barbed shield steady in his left hand.

As the two of them battled on, the boatmen, Crocodile Jiang and Luo Bing, jumped ashore and ran towards the carriages guarded by the soldiers. Jiang charged straight into the enemy ranks, immediately killing two of the soldiers nearest him. The others frantically gave way. Luo Bing raced over to one of the carriages, and lifted up the carriage-curtain.

'Husband, are you in there?' she called. But the man inside the carriage was not Rolling Thunder Wen; it was Scholar Yu, still seriously wounded and delirious. Suddenly hearing Luo Bing's voice, he thought it must be a dream, or that he had died and was meeting her in the other world.

'You've come at last!' he cried happily.

Luo Bing knew that the voice was not her husband's and ran to the next carriage. But before she could pull aside the curtain, a saw-toothed sword chopped at her from the right. She parried with her own sword, and looking up at her attacker in the watery moonlight, recognized him as Rui, the sole survivor of the eight officers who had first attacked Wen and herself in Suzhou. The memory brought a surge of hatred, and she redoubled her attack. Rui was aware of her skill with throwing knives and accelerated his strokes to avoid giving her an opportunity to use them. Two other officers joined in the fray, while the mass of soldiers closed in from all sides.

Four more of the Red Flower heroes led by Leopard Wei came galloping towards Luo Bing through a hail of arrows. One arrow planted itself in the neck of Wei's horse. The pain made it gallop even more furiously, and the animal kicked one of the soldiers in the chest with its hooves. Leopard Wei leapt from the horse with his hooks raised and, amid a chorus of screams, he gouged them into the breasts of two other soldiers. Wei then aimed his hooks at Rui, forcing him to abandon his attack on Luo Bing. Hunchback Zhang and the others hurled themselves into the fight, and presently the soldiers scattered.

Free once more, Luo Bing threw herself into the second carriage and flung her arms round Wen's neck. Then she burst into tears.

After a while, Hunchback Zhang stuck his head in through the carriage-curtain. 'Brother Wen,' he grinned. 'We've come to take you back.'

He climbed onto the driver's seat and the carriage moved off northwards away from the river. It stopped by the side of a mound, from which they had a commanding view of the battle.

Suddenly, they saw Fire Hand Zhang break away from his duel with Helmsman Chen and run after them. He had soon reached the carriage. Luo Bing saw him coming and went out to meet him, brandishing her sword. But she had not reckoned with the extraordinary strength of Zhang's sword, Frozen Emerald. The two blades clashed with a great 'clang', and hers snapped clean in two. Concentrating all his strength, Zhang then leapt up into the carriage, dragging Luo Bing in with him. Greatly concerned for her, the other Red Flower heroes raced up to save her. Zhang lifted her up and threw her into the arms of the Twin Knights. Then he turned and grabbed Wen, pulling him to the carriage door. 'I have Wen Tailai!' he shouted. 'If anyone dares to come any closer, I'll kill him!'

The cold gleaming point of Frozen Emerald was poised at Wen's neck.

'Husband!' Luo Bing wailed, and tried to throw herself at the carriage, but Hidden Needle Lu held her back. He took a step forward himself.

'Zhang!' he called out. 'Can you see who I am?'

Zhang and he had not met for a long time, and anyway it was difficult to see clearly in the moonlight. Lu drew his own sword, known as White Dragon, took hold of the tip of the blade with one hand, and bent the whole sword until it formed a circle. Then he let the tip go and the blade sprang back, quivering in the air. It was the sort of feat of Inner Force kungfu for which he was renowned. Zhang needed no further clues to enable him to recognize his old brother-in-arms.

'Ah, so it's you, Hidden Needle,' Zhang grunted. 'Why have you come looking for me?'

'You are wounded,' Lu replied. 'All the heroes of the Red Flower Society are here, as well as Iron Ball Zhou. You'll never escape alive today. But in memory of our beloved Shifu, I will give you a way out.'

Zhang grunted again, but said nothing.

Suddenly they heard shouts and cries drifting over from the east, as if some huge army was racing towards them. The Red Flower heroes were filled with apprehension, but Fire Hand Zhang was even more surprised and worried than they were.

'These Red Flower people are truly resourceful,' he thought. 'Even here in the northwest, it seems they can still call up huge reinforcements.'

'Release Wen,' Lu continued, 'and I will ask the Red Flower heroes, out of respect for me, to let you go. But there is one thing you must swear to.'

Zhang eyed the strong enemy force surrounding him. 'What is that?' he said.

'Swear that you will immediately retire from public life, and never be a running dog for the Manchus again.'

For years Fire Hand Zhang had pursued glory and wealth with absolute dedication and every ounce of his energy. Since going over to the Manchus, he had risen high in the ranks of officialdom, swept upwards in the world as if by some unstoppable whirlwind. For him, giving up his position would be like giving up his life. He released Wen from his grip, pushing him back inside the carriage, and tugged at the mule's reins. The carriage surged forward.

The Red Flower heroes held back for fear of risking Wen's life. But Luo Bing could not stand by and watch her husband taken away from her again. 'Just release him,' she called desperately, 'and we'll let you go without making you swear anything.'

Fire Hand Zhang took no notice. He drove the carriage on towards the safety of his own troops, who had by now regrouped.

Rui saw Zhang approaching and ordered the soldiers to fix arrows to their bows in readiness. The roar of the approaching army (wherever they might be) was meanwhile growing louder. Both the Red Flower Society and Zhang's soldiers were afraid that they were reinforcements for the other side.

'Leopard Wei, take three men and scatter the Eagle's Claws,' Chen shouted.

Wei and his chosen men raised their weapons and charged into the enemy ranks, slaughtering as they went.

A youngster darted out from behind Hidden Needle Lu, crying: 'I'm going too!' Helmsman Chen frowned: it was Li Yuanzhi, once more dressed in boy's clothes. Some days earlier, when Lu had met up with her again, she had pestered him to take her with him to help rescue Wen. Lu had finally given in to her demands, but had made her promise to do as she was told. Yuanzhi then wrote a letter to her mother in which she said she had decided to go on ahead alone to see her father in Hangzhou.

Chen quickly issued his orders, and Buddha Zhao raced after Wen's carriage, sending two darts flying at the eyes of the mule that was pulling it along. The mule gave a long scream and reared up on its hind legs. The Twin Knights ran to either side of the carriage and flung their Flying Claws at Zhang, who fended them off with his sword. Simultaneously, Father Speckless and Mastermind Xu leapt onto the carriage and attacked Zhang from behind.

'Now!' Chen shouted to Xin Yan. The two of them soared through the air and landed on top of the carriage.

When Zhang heard them land, he threw a handful of his Golden Needles at them. Chen saw the darts moving through the air and, pushing Xin Yan off the carriage, he protected himself with his shield. There was a metallic patter as the needles hit it, but despite the extraordinary speed of his reflexes, he heard Xin Yan cry out and knew that the boy had been hit. He jumped down to help him. Zhang threw another handful of the needles from short range at Father Speckless and Mastermind Xu. The priest leapt away from the carriage with the speed of an arrow, moving faster and further than the needles, but Xu only had time to protect himself with a cotton coverlet that was lying in the carriage. His left shoulder was exposed and, when the needles struck, he experienced a sudden feeling of numbness, and tumbled from the carriage.

Hunchback Zhang raced over to where he lay. 'Brother Xu, are you all right?' he shouted, bending down to help him. Suddenly he himself felt a searing pain in his back as he was hit by an arrow and stumbled forward.

'Brothers! Everyone regroup!' shouted Chen. Arrows were flying towards them in thick clouds, like locusts. Hunchback Zhang rested his left hand on Father Speckless' shoulder and struck out at the arrows with the Wolf's Tooth Club he held in his right hand.

'Brother Zhang, you mustn't move!' the priest said. 'You must stay calm.' He halted the flow of blood from Zhang's wound with a firm touch to the artery, and carefully extracted the arrow. Then he ripped a corner off his robe and bound up the wound.

It was now that they were able to see that the mighty army surging towards them from the east was a huge pitch-black mass of Manchu soldiers.

Fire Hand Zhang was, needless to say, ecstatic at the sight of reinforcements arriving. But his breathing was becoming more and more difficult and he knew that his injuries were serious. Helmsman Chen and his men attacked the carriage once more. Fire Hand Zhang lifted up Wen's body, and was swinging it round and round in the air, when a detachment of cavalry came charging towards the Red Flower Society fighters with sabres raised. Chen could see that Wen would certainly be killed if they continued with their attempt to recapture him by force. They would have to let him go yet again. He gave a loud whistle and raced behind a nearby mound. The others followed.

Chen conducted a headcount. He found that Mastermind Xu, Zhou Qi, Lu's young disciple, Lord Zhou, and Steward Meng were all missing.

'Has anyone seen Brother Xu and Lord Zhou?' Chen asked.

Hunchback Zhang, who was lying on the ground, raised his head and said: 'Brother Xu was injured. Isn't he here? I'll go and find him.'

He stood up, but the arrow wound on his back was too serious, and he swayed unsteadily.

'Don't you move,' said Melancholy Ghost Shi. 'I'll go.'

'I'll go too,' added Crocodile Jiang, but Chen held him back. 'You and Sister Luo Bing make your way to the river-bank and prepare the rafts,' he said. Jiang and Luo Bing, her hopes dashed again, went to carry out this command.

Melancholy Ghost Shi meanwhile leapt onto a horse and galloped off around the mound with sword in hand. He rode up onto higher ground and looked around, but could see no sign of Mastermind Xu and the others, so he rode on to search for them, and was soon lost in the enemy ranks.

Not long after, Lord Zhou and Steward Meng rejoined Helmsman Chen.

'Have you seen your daughter?' Chen asked. Zhou shook his head. Chen could see that he was sick with anxiety.

'My young disciple has disappeared too,' Hidden Needle Lu said. 'I'll go and look for them.'

As Lu rode out into the open, the ranks of enemy soldiers suddenly parted and several horses came charging towards him. In the lead was Father Speckless followed by Leopard Wei, his whole body spattered with blood and dirt. Helmsman Chen was shocked to see the state he was in, and immediately moved forward to obstruct any pursuers. But the soldiers did not dare to stand in the way of these ferocious-looking men and let them retreat behind the mound.

Wei was shouting deliriously: 'Kill the bastards!'

'Brother Wei has worn himself out with all this killing,' said Father Speckless. 'His mind is a little confused. It's nothing serious.'

'Have you seen Brother Xu and Brother Shi?' Chen asked.

'I'll go and look for them,' replied the priest.

'We are also looking for young Miss Zhou and Master Lu's disciple,' Chen said.

Father Speckless mounted up again, sword at the ready, and rode back into the enemy ranks. An officer spurred his horse forward and charged at him with spear raised, but the priest dodged the spear thrust and drove his sword into the officer's heart. The officer slumped from his horse and the soldiers under his command howled and scattered in all directions. Father Speckless was unstoppable. He continued his onslaught and soldiers fell wherever his sword went. As he galloped along a stretch of the road, he saw a crowd of soldiers surrounding Melancholy Ghost Shi, who was fighting fiercely against three officers.

'Get away,' shouted Father Speckless. 'I'll cover you!'

The two raced back to the mound, but there was still no indication of what had happened to Mastermind Xu and the others. A commander led his company in an attack on the mound occupied by the Red Flower Society, but the heroes immediately killed more than a dozen of them, and the rest retreated.

Helmsman Chen led his horse up onto the top of the mound. 'Steward Meng,' he said, handing Meng the reins of his horse. 'Hold my horse steady and make sure it doesn't get hit by a stray arrow.' He himself leapt up onto the horse's back and stood on the saddle. Looking around, he saw the huge Manchu column heading towards them, stretching away to the east and north. A bugle sounded and the column turned into a fiery dragon as each soldier raised a torch. Lit up in the glow, he saw a large banner fluttering in the wind on which he could just make out the words 'General Zhao Hui' written in large characters. The whole army presented a fearsome sight, with its serried ranks of infantry in clanking armour and cavalry mounted on sturdy horses.

Chen jumped down from the horse. 'Armoured troops will soon be upon us!' he shouted. 'Everyone head down to the river.'

Lord Zhou was still very concerned for his daughter, but it would be impossible to find her among such a huge body of troops. The Red Flower heroes helped up Leopard Wei, Hunchback Zhang, and the other wounded, and galloped towards the banks of the Yellow River with the Manchu cavalry now in hot pursuit. Luo Bing and Crocodile Jiang punted the sheepskin rafts up to the shore and took the wounded on board first.

'Everyone get on the rafts quickly!' yelled Helmsman Chen. 'Father Speckless, Brother Zhao, Lord Zhou, we four will hold—'

Before he could finish, a wave of crossbow arrows flew towards them.

'Charge!' roared the indomitable Father Speckless, and the four of them threw themselves at the first ranks of cavalry. Lord Zhou's huge sword rose and fell, slicing Manchu soldiers down from their horses, while Buddha Zhao slung lethal copper coins at the eye-slits in their armour. It was impossible to see clearly in the dark, but he still managed to blind five or six men. By this time, everyone except Helmsman Chen and the other three had boarded the rafts.

Helmsman Chen spotted a mounted officer directing the newly arrived troops, and raced over to him. He pulled the officer from his horse and dragged him down to the river. The Manchu troops rushed forward to try to save their commanding officer, but they didn't dare to fire any arrows. Chen and the three others leapt onto one of the rafts and pulled their horses on board. Crocodile Jiang and Luo Bing began to move the rafts out towards the middle of the river.

The Yellow River was in full flood, and the powerful current pulled the two large sheepskin rafts swiftly downstream. The hubbub of the great armed column slowly faded into the night as the river roared around them.

The Red Flower heroes set about tending to their wounded. Leopard Wei's mind gradually cleared and his body was found to be free from serious wounds. Buddha Zhao was an expert physician (as well as being a superb thrower of darts), and he bound up Iron Pagoda Yang's and Hunchback Zhang's wounds. Zhang was more seriously injured, but was in no immediate danger. Xin Yan had been hit by several Golden Needles, and was in such pain that he cried out continually. The needles had penetrated right through the flesh to the bone. Buddha Zhao took a magnet from his medicine bag and drew them out one by one. Luo Bing rowed silently on. Things had not gone well. Not only had they failed to rescue Wen, but Mastermind Xu, Zhou Qi, Hidden Needle Lu, and his young disciple had all gone missing as well. And as for Scholar Yu, no one knew where had got to.

Helmsman Chen began questioning the captured Manchu officer. 'What the hell was your column doing travelling through the night like that?' he asked.

The officer said nothing. Iron Pagoda Yang slapped him on the face. 'Are you going to talk?' he shouted.

'I'll talk...I'll talk,' the officer said quickly, holding his cheek. 'What do you want to know?'

'What was your column doing travelling at night?'

'General Zhao Hui received an Imperial command ordering us to attack the Uighur areas and subdue them before a certain date. He was afraid we wouldn't complete our mission in the time allowed, and also that the Uighurs would hear of our approach and make preparations. So we've been marching day and night.'

'The Uighurs are very law-abiding people,' said Chen. 'What do you want to attack them for?'

'That...that, I don't know,' the officer said.

'If you are heading for the Uighur areas, why did you come interfering in our business?'

'General Zhao heard that there were some bandits making trouble in this area and ordered me to lead a detail to deal with them. The main army didn't stop—'

Before he could finish, Iron Pagoda Yang gave him another slap. 'Damn you!' he shouted. '*You're* the bandits!'

'Yes, yes! You're right!' cried the officer.

Chen was silent for a while, then questioned the officer closely regarding the army's troop strength, the route it was taking, and the quantity of rations it was carrying. Some of this the officer didn't know, but he did not dare to hide what he did know.

'HEAD...FOR...THE...SHORE!' Chen shouted at the top of his voice. Luo Bing and Jiang steered the rafts towards the bank and everyone stepped ashore.

Chen called the Twin Knights over.

'Go back as fast as you can and find out what happened to the others,' he said. 'If they have fallen into the hands of the Manchus, they will certainly be taken back to Peking along the Great Road. We can intercept them further east and work out some way of rescuing them.'

The Twin Knights nodded and set off on their mission.

'Brother Shi,' Chen continued, turning to Melancholy Ghost. 'I want you to do something for me.'

'Whatever you say, Helmsman.'

Chen wrote a letter under the light of the moon.

'You are to take this to the Hodja Muzhuolun, in the Uighur regions,' he said. 'We have only met him and his people once, but they showed us the greatest friendship. We must warn them of the Manchu army's arrival. Sister Luo, please lend your white horse to Brother Shi for the trip.' Luo Bing had kept the animal aboard the raft throughout the battle.

Melancholy Shi mounted, and minutes later disappeared in a cloud of dust. With the horse's phenomenal speed, he estimated he could overtake the army in a day and warn the Hodja in time.

Helmsman Chen then directed Crocodile Jiang to tie the Manchu officer's hands behind his back. They placed him on one of the rafts and pushed it out into the river, leaving it for Fate to decide whether he should live or die.

Needles, Prostitutes, Poison, Cure

Zhou Qi had been separated from the others in the midst of the battle. The Manchu troops surged around her, and she galloped blindly off trying to escape them. In the darkness, her horse suddenly tripped, and she tumbled to the ground, her head crashing heavily against the hard earth. She passed out. Luckily it was still dark, and the soldiers did not find her.

She had been unconscious for she did not know how long when there was a sudden bright flash before her eyes and a great roar followed by a wave of coolness on her face. She opened her eyes and saw the sky full of black clouds, and torrential rain sweeping down.

She jumped up. Someone beside her sat up as well. She started in fright and frantically grabbed for her sword. Then she gasped in surprise: it was Mastermind Xu.

'Miss Zhou, what are you doing here?' he called out above the roar of the rain.

Zhou Qi had never liked Xu and had always gone out of her way to quarrel with him. But he was at least one of her own people, and she burst into tears.

'What's happened to my father?' she asked, biting her lip.

Xu motioned her to lie down. 'Soldiers,' he whispered.

Zhou Qi threw herself to the ground, and they slowly crawled behind a small mound of earth.

The sky was by now growing light and, through the rain, they saw several dozen Manchu soldiers hastily burying corpses, cursing as they worked. 'You two, have a look round for any more bodies,' an officer shouted, and two soldiers climbed up onto higher ground. Looking around, they spotted Zhou Qi and Xu and called out: 'Two more over there!'

'Wait for them to come over,' Xu whispered.

The soldiers walked over carrying shovels, and as they bent over them, Zhou Qi and Xu simultaneously thrust their swords into their bellies. They died without a sound.

The officer waited for a while, but with no sign of the soldiers returning and the rain getting heavier, he rode over to investigate, cursing and swearing all the while.

'Don't make a sound. I'll steal his horse,' Xu whispered. As the officer rode closer, he saw the bodies of the two soldiers, but before he could call out, Xu leapt up and slashed at him with his sword. The officer raised his horsewhip to counter the blow, but Xu's sword sliced clean through both his whip and his head.

'Mount up quickly!' Xu called, holding the horse's reins. Zhou Qi leapt onto the horse and galloped off with Xu running along behind.

The Manchu troops began to give chase on foot. After only a few paces, the pain in Xu's shoulder where he had been hit by Fire Hand Zhang's Golden Needles became unbearable and he fell to the ground with a cry. Zhou Qi reined the horse round and galloped back. Leaning over, she hoisted him across the saddle, then slapped the horse's haunches and raced off again. The soldiers had soon dropped far behind.

When they had gone some distance, Zhou Qi stopped and had a closer look at Xu. His eyes were tightly closed, his face white, and his breathing shallow. Greatly frightened, she sat him properly on the horse, then with her left arm around his waist to keep him from falling, she galloped on, keeping to lonely, deserted tracks. After a while, she saw an inky-black section of forest ahead and rode in amongst the trees. The rain had stopped, and she dismounted and continued on foot, leading the horse with Xu on it behind her until she came to a clearing. Xu was still unconscious, and Zhou Qi lifted him down from the horse and laid him on the grass. Then she sat down herself, letting the horse wander off to graze. Here she was, a young girl not yet twenty, alone in a strange forest. She began to sob, her tears falling onto Xu's face.

As Xu slowly recovered consciousness, he thought it must be raining again. He opened one eye a fraction and saw a beautiful face before him with both big eyes red from crying. His left shoulder began hurting again and he cried out in pain.

Zhou Qi was overjoyed to see that he was still alive, and asked how he felt.

'My shoulder is extremely painful. Please look at it for me, Miss Zhou,' he replied. He forced himself to sit up and, holding a knife in his right hand, cut a hole in the shoulder of his jacket.

'I was hit by three Golden Needles here,' he said, examining the shoulder out of the corner of his eye. The needles were small, but they had penetrated deep into the flesh.

'What shall we do?' Zhou Qi asked. 'Should we go to a town and find a doctor?'

'We can't do that,' replied Xu. 'After last night's battle, going to see a doctor would be like walking straight into a trap. What we really need is a magnet to draw the needles out, but we don't have one. Do you think you could cut away the flesh and pull them out?'

During the night battle, Zhou Qi had killed quite a number of enemy soldiers without losing her composure once. But now, faced with the prospect of cutting away the flesh on Xu's shoulder, she hesitated.

'I can't stand the pain! Do it now...' he pleaded. 'No, wait. Do you have a tinder-box with you?'

Zhou Qi felt around in her bag. 'Yes. What do you want it for?'

'Collect some dry grass and leaves and burn them up to make some ash. When you've pulled the needles out, you can cover the wound with the ash and then bandage it.'

She did as he said and made quite a large pile of ash.

'That's fine,' said Xu with a laugh. 'There's enough there to stop a hundred wounds bleeding.'

She pressed on his shoulder beside the needle holes. As her fingers came into contact with male flesh, she involuntarily pulled back and her whole face turned bright red. Xu noticed her blushing, but misinterpreted her reaction. Perhaps he was not such a Mastermind after all.

'Are you afraid?' he asked.

'What have I got to be afraid of?' she replied, suddenly angry. 'You're the one who's afraid! Turn your head away and don't look.'

Xu did as he was told. Zhou Qi pressed the skin around the needle holes tightly, then slipped the tip of the knife into the flesh and slowly began to turn it. Blood flowed from the wound. Xu silently gritted his teeth, his whole face covered in beads of sweat the size of soya beans. She cut away the flesh until the end of a needle appeared, then grasping it tightly between her thumb and forefinger, pulled it out.

Xu forced himself to treat his 'operation' in a light-hearted fashion.

'It's a pity the needle doesn't have an eye, or I'd give it to you to embroider with,' he said.

'I can't embroider,' Zhou Qi replied. 'Last year, my mother told me to learn, but I kept snapping the needle or breaking the thread. She scolded me, and I said: "Mother, I can't do it, you teach me." But she said she had no time. Afterwards I discovered that she can't embroider either.'

Xu laughed. As they had been talking, another needle had been removed.

'I didn't really want to learn,' Zhou Qi continued with a smile. 'But when I found out that mother couldn't do it either, I insisted on her teaching me. But I couldn't catch her out. She just said: "If you don't know how to sew, I don't know how you'll ever—"'

She stopped in mid-sentence. 'Don't know how you'll ever what?' asked Xu.

'I don't feel like telling you.'

What her mother had said was: 'I don't know how you'll ever find a husband.' As they talked, her hands never stopped, and the third needle was finally out as well. She covered the wound with ash, then bandaged it with strips of cloth. She couldn't help but admire him for the way he continued to smile and chat to her despite the pain.

'He may be short, but he's a brave man,' she thought. By this time, her hands were covered in blood.

'You lie here and don't move,' she said. 'I'll go and find some water for you to drink.'

When she came to the edge of the forest, she studied the lie of the land before running out from the trees. Several hundred paces away, she found a small stream which was flowing swiftly after the heavy rain. As she bent down to wash her hands, she caught sight of her reflection in the water—her dishevelled hair, her wet and crumpled clothes, and her face, covered in blood and dirt.

'How can I let him see me looking so terrible?' she thought to herself.

She washed her face clean, and combed her hair with her fingers. Then, scooping water from the stream, she drank deeply. She knew Xu would certainly be thirsty too, but had nothing in which to carry water. After a moment's thought, she took a piece of clothing from the knapsack on her back, dipped it in the stream so that it was soaking wet, then ran back.

Zhou Qi could see from his face that he was in great pain, although he was trying to appear unconcerned, and feelings of tenderness stirred within her. She told him to open his mouth and squeezed water into it from the cloth.

'Is it very painful?' she asked softly.

Mastermind Xu's whole life had been spent amidst mountains of knives and forests of spears, or else in the shady world of plots and traps; no one had ever spoken to him with the warmth and softness he detected now in Zhou Qi's voice. Deeply moved, he steadied himself. 'I am a little better now. Thank you.'

'We can't stay here,' Xu said after he had drunk some water. 'And we can't go to a town either. All we can do is find a secluded farmhouse and pretend that we are brother and sister—'

'You want me to call you brother?' asked Zhou Qi, astounded.

'If you feel that I'm too old, you could call me uncle,' he suggested.

'Pah! Do you think you look like my uncle? I'll call you my brother, but only when there are other people around. When we're on our own, I refuse.'

'All right, you don't have to,' he replied with a smile. 'We'll say that we met the army on the road and were attacked by the soldiers who stole all our possessions.'

Once they had agreed on their story, Zhou Qi helped him to mount the horse. The two made their way out of the trees, and chose a small track heading straight towards the sun.

The northwest can be a very desolate place. Hungry and tired, they had to travel for more than two hours before finally spotting a mud hut. Xu dismounted and knocked at the door. After a moment, an old woman came out. Seeing the strange clothes they were wearing, she looked at them suspiciously. Xu told her some of the story they had concocted, and she sighed.

'These government troops, always making trouble,' she said. 'What is your name, sir?'

'My name is Zhou,' said Xu.

Zhou Qi glanced at him but said nothing. The old woman invited them inside and brought out some wheatcakes. They were black and rough, but Zhou Qi and Xu were so hungry that they found them delicious.

'Old woman,' said Xu, 'I am wounded and unable to travel. We would like to spend the night here.'

'There's no problem about your staying here, if you will put up with the discomfort of a poor person's home.'

'We are eternally thankful that you are willing to take us in,' Xu replied. 'My sister's clothes are all wet. If you have any old clothes, I would appreciate it if you would allow her to change into them.'

'My daughter-in-law left some clothes behind. If you don't mind, mistress, you could try them on. They'll probably fit.'

Zhou Qi went to change. When she came out, she saw Xu was already asleep in the old woman's room.

Towards evening, Xu began babbling incoherently. Zhou Qi felt his forehead and found it feverish. She decided his wounds must be festering. She knew such a condition was extremely dangerous, and asked the old woman if there was a doctor in the neighbourhood.

'Yes, there is, in the town of Wenguang about seven miles east of here,' the old woman replied. 'The best one is Doctor Cao, but he never comes out to country places like this to see patients.'

'I'll go and fetch him,' Zhou Qi said. 'I'll leave my...my brother here. Please keep an eye on him.'

'Don't you worry about that, miss,' the old woman replied. 'But honestly, the doctor won't come.'

Undeterred, Zhou Qi attached her sword to the saddle and galloped off. Night had already fallen when she reached the town. She asked a passerby where Doctor Cao lived, then galloped straight on to his residence. She knocked on the door for a long time before a manservant finally opened it.

'It's already dark. What are you banging like that for?' he demanded.

Zhou Qi was angered by his manner, but remembered that she was appealing for help. 'I've come to ask Doctor Cao to visit a patient,' she said, controlling herself.

'He's not in,' said the man. Without another word, he turned and began to close the door.

Zhou Qi could restrain herself no longer. She pulled him out of the doorway and drew her sword. 'Where's he gone? Quickly!'

'He's gone to Little Rose's,' the man replied in a quavering voice.

Zhou Qi brushed the blade over his face. 'What's Little Rose's?'

The man was frantic with fright. 'Your Majesty... My lady...' he stammered. 'Little Rose is a prostitute.'

'Prostitutes are bad people. What's he gone to her place for?' Zhou Qi asked.

The manservant wanted to laugh at this girl who looked so ferocious and yet was so ignorant of worldly matters, but he did not dare. 'She is a good friend of my master,' he said.

'Well, take me there at once.'

Her sword was resting on his neck, and he dared not disobey, but led her off down the street.

'This is it,' he said, pointing to a small house.

'Knock on the door. Tell the doctor to come out.'

The man did as she said, and the door was opened by the Madame of the house.

'This lady wants my master to go and visit a patient,' the man said. 'I told her the master was busy, but she wouldn't believe me and forced me to come here.'

The Madame gave him a look of contempt and slammed the door.

Zhou Qi rushed forward to stop her, but was too late. She beat noisily on the door for a while, but there was no response from inside. In her anger, Zhou Qi kicked the servant to the ground.

'Get out of here!' she shouted.

The man picked himself up and ran off.

Zhou Qi waited until he had disappeared then leapt over the wall into the courtyard of the house. She saw light coming from a room nearby, and stealthily made her way towards it. Crouching down, she licked the tip of her finger and made a small hole in the window-paper. Putting her eye to the hole, she saw two men lying on a couch, talking. One was stout, and the other thin and tall. A seductive-looking tart was pummelling the thin man's thighs. The stout man waved her away, and the girl stood up.

'I can see the two of you are up to some mischief,' she tittered. 'You really ought to be careful, you know, or you'll end up having sons without proper holes in their bums!'

'Filthy little slut!' the stout man shouted back with a laugh. The girl smiled and walked out, locked the door, then turned and went into an inner hall.

'That must be Little Rose,' Zhou Qi thought. 'She's a dirty little whore, but there's some truth in what she said.'

She watched as the stout man pulled out four silver ingots and placed them on the table.

'Doctor Cao,' he said. 'There's two hundred taels of silver. We're old business partners, and that's the old price.'

'Friend Tang,' the thin man replied. 'Take these two packets of medicine, and have a good time. The red packet you give to the girl, and in less time than it takes to eat a meal, she will be unconscious to the world and you can do whatever you like with her. You don't need me to teach you anything about that, do you?'

The two men had a good laugh.

'This black packet you give to the man,' Cao continued. 'Tell him it will speed his recovery. Soon after he takes it, his wounds will start bleeding and he'll bleed to death. It will look as if his wounds have simply reopened and no one will suspect you. What do you think of the plan?'

'Excellent, excellent,' Tang replied.

'So, my friend, you will have gained both the girl and her fortune. Doesn't two hundred taels seem like rather a small reward for such a service?'

'I would never try to deceive a friend such as yourself,' the other said. 'The girl certainly has a pretty face. I could hardly keep my hands off her, even when I thought she was a boy—because of the way she was dressed. There's nothing particularly special about the man, except that he's with the girl—so he'll have to be got rid of.'

'Didn't you say he had a flute made out of gold?' Cao asked. 'That flute alone must weigh several catties.'

'All right, all right, I'll add another fifty taels,' Tang said, and pulled out another lump of silver.

Zhou Qi was growing angrier and angrier as she listened to this exchange. She ran to the door, kicked it open, and charged straight inside. Tang gave a shout and aimed a flying kick at her sword wrist. Zhou Qi simply flipped her sword over, cut off his right foot with one slice, then stabbed him in the heart.

The thin man stood to one side, struck dumb with fright. His whole body shook and his teeth chattered. Zhou Qi pulled her sword out of Tang's dead body and wiped the blood off the blade onto his clothes. Then she grabbed the thin man.

'Are you Doctor Cao?' she shouted. The man's legs folded beneath him and he fell to his knees.

'Please...young lady...spare my life...'

'I'm not interested in your life! Get up.'

Cao stood up shakily, but his knees were still wobbly, and he had to kneel down again. Zhou Qi put the five silver ingots and the two packets of medicine on the table into her pocket.

'Out,' she ordered.

She told him to fetch his horse, and the two mounted up and galloped out of the town. In less than two hours, they arrived at the old woman's hut. Zhou Qi ran to the kang where Xu was lying and found him still unconscious. In the candlelight, she could see his whole face was bright red and knew he had a high fever. She dragged Cao over.

'My...brother here has been wounded. See to him at once,' she ordered.

Hearing that he was expected to give medical treatment, Cao's fears eased slightly. He looked at Xu's complexion and took his pulse, then undid the bandage round his shoulder and looked at the wound. He shook his head.

'The master is deficient in both blood and breath,' he said. 'His body heat is rising—'

'No one wants to hear all that!' Zhou Qi interrupted him. 'You just see to him at once. If you fail, you can forget about ever leaving here.'

'I'll just need to go to town to get some medicine,' Cao said. 'Without medicine I can do nothing.'

Xu awoke and lay listening to the two of them talking.

'What do you take me for—a three-year-old child?' Zhou Qi demanded. 'You make out the prescription and I'll go and buy the medicine.'

Cao had no alternative but to ask for a pen and paper. But where were things like that to be found, in such a poor hut in such a desolate place? Zhou Qi frowned, at a loss what to do.

'Your "brother's" condition will not allow delay,' said Cao with an air of complacency. 'It really would be best if you let me return to town to get the medicine.'

'Sister,' Xu said. 'Take a small piece of firewood and char it in the fire. Then let him write on any old piece of rough paper. You can even write on a piece of wood.'

'What a good idea!' Zhou Qi exclaimed happily, and set fire to a piece of firewood as he had said. The old woman searched out a piece of yellow paper originally meant to be burnt in worship of Buddha, and Cao made out the prescription. When he had finished, Zhou Qi found a length of grass rope and tied his hands behind his back, bound his legs together, and made him sit on the floor next to Xu.

'I'm going to the town to buy medicine,' she told the old woman as she placed Xu's sword beside his pillow. 'If this dog of a doctor tries to escape, wake up my brother and he can kill him.'

Zhou Qi rode back to the town and found a medicine shop. She shouted for the shopkeeper to open up and got him to make up the prescription, which was for a mixture of more than ten different types of medicinal herbs.

The sky was growing light. She saw village constables patrolling the streets and guessed that the dead body at Little Rose's had been discovered. She shrank into a street corner and waited until they had passed before galloping off.

As soon as she returned to the hut, she hastily brewed up the medicine, then poured it into a rough bowl and took it over to Xu. She shook him awake and told him to drink it.

Xu was extremely moved at the sight of her dishevelled appearance, the result of all her recent adventures. Her face was streaked with sweat and ash, and her hair full of twigs and grass. He knew she was the daughter of a rich family and would never before have experienced anything like this. He sat up and took the bowl from her. He passed it over to Cao.

'You drink a bit,' he said. Cao hesitated slightly and Zhou Qi realized Xu's meaning.

'Yes, yes,' she said. 'He must drink some first. You never know how evil this man is,' she added to Xu.

Cao drank two mouthfuls.

'Rest for a while, sister,' said Xu. 'I'll wait before drinking the medicine.'

'Yes,' said Zhou Qi. 'Let's see if he dies first.'

She moved the oil lamp next to Cao's face and watched him with her big, black, unblinking eyes to see whether he would die or not.

'We doctors have the best interest of our patients at heart. Why would I want to harm him?' said Cao, smiling bitterly.

'Really?' said Zhou Qi angrily. 'And what about that secret discussion you had with that man Tang—about harming some girl and getting hold of someone's golden flute. I heard it all. Do you deny it?'

Xu's ears pricked up at the mention of a golden flute and he quickly asked her about it. Zhou Qi related the conversation she had heard, and told him how she had killed the fat man at Little Rose's.

Xu asked Cao: 'Who is the person with the golden flute? And who is the girl dressed as a boy?'

Zhou Qi drew her sword and stood by him threateningly. 'Tell us everything you know, or I'll run you through with my sword this minute!'

'I...I'll tell you,' said Cao, absolutely terrified. 'Yesterday my friend Tang came to see me and said that two people had asked to take lodgings at his home. He said one was very badly wounded and the other was a very good-looking young man. At first he was unwilling to take them in, but when he saw how extraordinarily beautiful the young man was, he agreed to let them stay for one night. He noticed the young man's voice and manner were just like a girl's. Also, he observed that the young man wasn't willing to share a room with the other, so he came to the conclusion that it must be a girl dressed in boy's clothes.'

'So you sold this man Tang some poison,' Zhou Qi said.

'I deserve to die,' replied Cao.

'What was the wounded man like?' Xu asked.

'Tang asked me to examine him. He was about twenty-three or four years old, dressed as a scholar, and had sword and club wounds in seven or eight places.'

'Were the wounds serious?' asked Xu.

'Very serious. But they were none of them fatal. None of his Vital Points had been affected.'

Xu saw he would not gain much by continuing the questioning, and gingerly raised the bowl of medicine to his lips. But his hands shook and some of the medicine slopped out. Zhou Qi took the bowl from him and held it to his mouth. He drank the brew down, then thanked her.

'These two are not brother and sister,' Cao thought as he watched. 'Whoever heard of a brother thanking his sister!'

After drinking the medicine, Xu slept for a while, his whole body sweating profusely, and towards evening, his condition began to improve. The next day, Xu was almost recovered and could get up. After another day, he decided he could just about manage to ride a horse.

'The man with the golden flute is clearly Scholar Yu,' he said to Zhou Qi. 'He was at Iron Ball Manor. You must have seen him there. I wonder why he should seek lodgings with such a man? Even though you've already killed Tang, I'm still a little worried. Let's go tonight and investigate.'

'If I had known it was Scholar Yu, I would have fetched him and brought him along with me, then the two of you could have convalesced together.'

Xu smiled. 'But who could this girl dressed in boy's clothing be?' he wondered out loud, mystified.

That evening, Zhou Qi gave the old woman two of the silver ingots, which she accepted with effusive blessings and thanks. Zhou Qi then pulled Cao up, and with a swish of her blade, cut off his right ear.

'I'm only sparing your worthless life because you cured my brother,' she shouted. 'If I ever catch you up to your evil tricks again, I'll stick my sword straight into your heart.'

'We'll visit you again in three months' time, to check up on you,' threatened Xu.

'You ride his horse,' Zhou Qi said to Xu. The two mounted up and galloped off towards Wenguang.

'Why did you say we would be coming back in three months' time?' Zhou Qi asked.

'I just didn't want the doctor to give the old woman any trouble,' Xu replied.

Zhou Qi nodded and they continued on for a while.

'Why are you always so crafty with people?' she suddenly asked. 'I don't like it.'

'You don't realize how many evil people there are in the world,' he said after a long silence. 'When dealing with friends, love and justice should always come first, of course. But when dealing with bad people, you must be very careful otherwise you will be tricked and will suffer.'

'My father wouldn't agree,' said Zhou Qi. 'He says it's better to suffer yourself than to cheat other people.'

'That is what makes your father the great man that he is,' replied Xu. 'That's why he has such a reputation on River and Lake, as a true man of justice and honour.'

'Well, why don't you imitate my father?'

'Lord Zhou is a generous and good man by nature. I am afraid I'm much too inferior a person ever to be able to be like him. I'm far too sneaky and sly!'

'That's what I like least about you—your sly nature. My father says that if you treat others well, they will naturally treat you well in return.'

Xu didn't reply.

The two waited until it was dark before entering the town. They found Tang's residence and climbed over the wall to investigate. Xu caught a watchman and, threatening him with a knife, asked him about Scholar Yu's whereabouts. The watchman said Doctor Cao had killed his master at Little Rose's, and that in the confused aftermath the two lodgers had left.

'We'll go after them,' Zhou Qi said.

A Packet of Medicine

In less than a day, they had got beyond Lanzhou. Two days further on, Mastermind Xu discovered markings on the road left by Helmsman Chen saying that everyone should meet further east, in Kaifeng, the capital city of Henan Province. Zhou Qi was delighted to hear that the main group was all right. She had been very worried about her father, but she now relaxed and drank some wine to celebrate. The wound on Xu's shoulder had by now healed up and he was fully recovered. They chatted as they travelled, Xu telling her all sorts of stories of the River and Lake community and explaining all its taboos and rules. She took it all in eagerly.

'Why didn't you talk about these things before, instead of always quarrelling with me?' she asked.

That day they arrived at Tongguan, a gateway town between central China and the north-west, and searched for lodgings. They heard that the old Yuelai Inn was the best, but when they got there, they were told there was only one room left. Until this moment, Zhou Qi had been impressed with how refined and polite Xu had been towards her, a real gentleman. But now, suddenly faced with the prospect of having to share a room with him, she was both embarrassed and suspicious. No sooner were they in the room, than Xu barred the door. Zhou Qi's face went bright red and she was just about to speak when Xu hurriedly silenced her with a wave of his hand.

'Did you see that Zhen Yuan Agency scoundrel just now?' he whispered.

'What?' said Zhou Qi, startled. 'You mean the one who led the other guards to Iron Ball Manor, to capture Rolling Thunder Wen—the one who caused the death of my brother?'

'I only caught a glimpse of him so I can't be absolutely sure. I was afraid he would see us, which is why I rushed us into the room. We'll go and investigate in a while.'

The servant came in with some hot tea and asked if they wanted anything to eat. Xu ordered a few dishes, then said:

'Several gentlemen from the Zhen Yuan Agency are also staying here, I think?'

'Yes,' replied the servant. 'Whenever they pass through Tongguan, they always give us their custom.'

Xu waited for the servant to leave. 'That Agency guard Tong is definitely the ringleader and chief troublemaker,' he said. 'We'll finish him off tonight. That way we can properly avenge the death of your young brother, and all that Brother Wen has suffered.'

Zhou Qi thought once again of her brother's tragic death and the burning of her family home at Iron Ball Manor, and her anger surged within her anew.

'Lie down for a while and rest,' said Xu, seeing her impatience. 'We can wait until nightfall before making our move and still have plenty of time.'

He sat down at the table and settled himself for sleep without so much as glancing further in Zhou Qi's direction. Zhou Qi had no option but to suppress her anger. She sat down on the kang and tried to rest. The time dragged by until the bell sounded for the second watch. There was only one hour to go before it was midnight. She decided she could control herself no longer.

'Let's go,' she said, drawing her sword.

'There are a lot of them, and some may be good fighters,' Xu whispered. 'We should investigate first. We'll think of some way to lure Tong out, then deal with him alone.'

Zhou Qi nodded.

They went out into the courtyard and saw a lamp shining in a room on the eastern side. They walked stealthily over. Zhou Qi found a tear in the window-paper and looked through it while Xu stood behind her keeping a lookout. Suddenly, she stood up and began to aim a kick at the window. Quick as a flash, Xu shot in front of her, blocking her way. Zhou Qi quickly retracted her leg so as not to kick him in the chest, and the sudden movement overbalanced her. He knelt down close to her.

'What is it?' he whispered.

'Do something, quick!' she hissed. 'That's my mother in there. They've got her tied up.'

Xu looked shocked by this piece of information. 'We must go back to the room quickly. We can discuss it there,' he said.

Once they were back in the room, Zhou Qi demanded desperately: 'What is there to discuss? They've captured my mother. We must do something.'

'Control yourself,' Xu replied. 'I will rescue her for you. How many people were there in the room?'

'About six or seven.'

Mastermind Xu lowered his head, deep in thought.

'What are you afraid of?' Zhou Qi asked. 'If you won't do it, I'll go by myself.'

'I'm not afraid. I'm thinking of a way to save your mother and kill that man at the same time. It would be best if we did the two things together.'

Just then, footsteps passed by the door, and they heard a servant's voice muttering: 'Midnight, and those Agency guards are still at it. Ordering more drinks at this hour of the night! A pox on their mothers! May Lord Buddha make sure they meet up with robbers on the road.'

Suddenly, Xu had an idea. 'That Doctor Cao had two packets of medicine, didn't he?' he said to Zhou Qi. 'Quickly! Give me the one he said would make a person unconscious.'

Zhou Qi gave him the packet. 'What are you going to do?' she asked. Xu said nothing in reply, but opened the window and jumped out with Zhou Qi close behind. They ran along the corridor. Suddenly Xu whispered: 'Get down, don't move.'

Zhou Qi wondered what trick he was up to. A moment passed, then suddenly they saw a flicker of light as the servant came back towards them carrying a candlestick and a tray. Xu picked a pebble off the ground and threw it, extinguishing the candle.

The servant started in surprise. 'That's bloody ridiculous!' he cursed. 'There's no wind at all, and the candle goes out on me.'

He put down the tray and turned to relight the candle. While his back was turned, Xu darted out and, in a flash, he had tipped the medicine into the two pots of wine on the tray and slipped away without the servant noticing.

'Now let's go and wait outside their room,' he said to Zhou Qi.

They made their way round to the exterior of the guards' room and settled down to wait. Xu looked in through the hole in the window-paper and saw a middle-aged woman seated on the floor with her hands tied behind her back. There were several men sitting around her, including Han, the white horse's former owner, and the Agency guards Qian and Tong. They were engaged in a lively discussion.

'When people talked of Iron Ball Manor,' boasted Tong, 'they always said it was as impregnable as if it had walls of iron. But with just my one torch, I razed it to the ground. Ha ha!'

Outside the window, Xu shook his hand at Zhou Qi, afraid that she would have another fit of rage.

'Stop bragging, Tong,' Han replied. 'I've met Lord Zhou and I doubt if all of us together would be a match for him. If he ever comes looking for you, you'll be done for!'

'We don't need to worry!' replied Tong. 'We've got Zhou's old woman! Now there's a stroke of luck! With her in our hands, he wouldn't dare do anything to us!'

Just then, the servant entered with the food and wine, and the guards immediately began eating and drinking. Han seemed quiet and dispirited and Tong continually urged him to drink the wine, saying, 'Even heroes are helpless when they're outnumbered. Next time, we'll take on the Red Flower Society one to one and see who's the better.'

'And who are you going to take on, old Tong?' asked another of the guards.

'Me? I'm going to find that daughter of Zhou's—' Before he could finish, he slumped to the floor. The others all looked on aghast, but as they jumped up to help him, one by one they too dropped to the floor unconscious.

Xu prised the window open with his sword, then leapt into the room. Zhou Qi hurriedly cut the ropes which bound her mother's hands. Lady Zhou was speechless at the sight of her beloved daughter, and thought she must be dreaming.

Xu lifted Tong up from the floor. 'Miss Zhou,' he said. 'Avenge your brother.'

Zhou Qi did not hesitate. One sweeping slice of her sword, and Tong was dead. She raised her sword again to kill the other guards, but Xu stopped her.

'The crimes of the others do not deserve death,' he said. 'Spare them.'

She nodded and put away her sword. Lady Zhou, knowing her daughter's temper, was surprised at how she obeyed Xu.

Xu searched the bodies of the guards and found several letters which he placed in his gown, planning to examine them later.

The three of them returned to the room that Xu and Zhou Qi had taken for the night. Xu picked up their knapsacks and left a small silver ingot on the table in payment for the room and the food. Then they went to the stables, led out three horses, and galloped off eastwards.

When she realized her daughter was not only travelling with a man but had shared a room with him, Lady Zhou's surprise turned to suspicion and displeasure. Her temper was as explosive as her daughter's.

'Who is this gentleman anyway?' she asked accusingly. 'What are you doing with him? You lost your temper with your father and left, didn't you?'

'It was you that lost your temper and left,' Zhou Qi replied. 'Mother, I'll talk to you about this later.'

It looked as if an argument was about to start, and Xu quickly tried to mediate.

'It's all your fault,' Zhou Qi told him angrily. 'Do you want to make it worse?'

Xu smiled and walked away. Mother and daughter pouted silently, each thinking her own thoughts.

That night, they took lodgings in a farmhouse, and once mother and daughter were in bed together, Zhou Qi finally told her everything that had happened. Lady Zhou kept up a constant bombardment of questions and the two were crying one minute and laughing the next. It was past midnight before they had each told the story of events since they'd parted.

Lady Zhou told her daughter how, heartbroken and angry over the death of her young son, she had gone to Lanzhou to stay with relatives. After a few days, she had begun to feel restless, and left. On reaching Tongguan, she had seen the Zhen Yuan Agency's flag outside the Yuelai Inn. She remembered that the man responsible for her son's death was one of the Agency guards called Tong, and that evening she had gone to the inn to investigate. She listened to the guards talking, and discovered Tong among them. Unable to control her anger, she attacked him, but the Agency men had the superiority of numbers and she was captured.

The next day on the road, Lady Zhou asked Xu to tell her something about his family background.

'I am from Shaoxing in Zhejiang Province,' Xu replied. 'When I was twelve, all the members of my family were killed by Yamen guards. I was the only one who managed to escape.'

'Why did that happen?' asked Lady Zhou.

'The magistrate of Shaoxing prefecture liked my sister and wanted her as his concubine. But she had already been promised to someone else, so my father naturally refused to agree. The magistrate then accused my father of being in collusion with bandits and put him and my mother and brother in prison. He told my sister that all she had to do was agree, and my father would be released. My sister's husband-to-be went to assassinate the magistrate, but he was caught and beaten to death by the guards. When my sister heard, she drowned herself in the river. After that, what chance did the rest of the family have of being spared?'

'Did you ever get revenge?' Zhou Qi asked.

'When I was grown up and had learned the Martial Arts, I went back to look for the magistrate, but he had been promoted and transferred somewhere else. In the last few years, I've been everywhere looking for him, but I've never tracked him down.'

Lady Zhou also asked him if he was married. She said that travelling about so much, he must surely have seen some girl he liked?

'He's much too cunning for that,' Zhou Qi said with a laugh. 'No girl would want him.'

'Enough of your remarks, young lady,' Lady Zhou scolded her.

'You want to become his matchmaker, don't you?' Zhou Qi said with a smile. 'Have you got a girl in mind? One of your relatives in Lanzhou?'

When they lodged at an inn that night, Lady Zhou spoke plainly to her daughter.

'A virgin like yourself,' she said, 'travelling alone with a young man and staying in the same room! How do you expect to ever be able to marry anyone else?'

'He was wounded,' Zhou Qi replied angrily. 'Did I do wrong to look after him? He may be full of all sorts of cunning tricks, but he has been a real gentleman towards me all along.'

'*You* know that, and so does he. And I believe you, and I'm sure your father would believe you too. But what are other people going to think? If your husband ever suspected, you would never be able to face him again. That is the difficulty we women have.'

'Well then, I shall never marry,' shouted Zhou Qi.

'Sh! He's right next door,' Lady Zhou said. 'It would be very embarrassing if he should hear.'

'Why should I be afraid? I haven't done anything wrong. What are you trying to hide?'

When they arose next morning, a servant brought them a letter.

'The gentleman next door told me to give this to your Ladyships,' he said. 'He said he had some affairs to attend to and had to go on ahead. He rode out early this morning.'

Zhou Qi snatched the letter from him.

'Dear Lady Zhou and Miss Zhou,' it said. 'Miss Zhou Qi saved my life when I was wounded and I am very grateful to her. You are now reunited and can make your way from here to Kaifeng, which is not far. Please do not be offended that I have gone on ahead. I will naturally never forget how Miss Zhou saved me, but please rest assured that I will never say a word about our journey together to anyone. With respect, Xu Tianhong.'

Zhou Qi finished reading and stood there dumbfounded for a second. Then she threw down the letter and lay back down on the kang. Lady Zhou told her to get up and eat, but she took no notice.

'My daughter, we are not at home in Iron Ball Manor now,' Lady Zhou said. 'What are you losing your temper for?' Zhou Qi still took no notice.

'You're angry at him for leaving, aren't you?' Lady Zhou said.

'He did it for my sake. Why should I hold it against him?' Zhou Qi replied angrily. She turned over and covered her head with the coverlet.

'So you'll hold it against me instead?' said Lady Zhou.

Zhou Qi suddenly sat up.

'He must have heard what you said last night. He was afraid other people would gossip and make it impossible for me to marry, so he left. But why all this concern about whether I marry or not? I refuse to marry anyone. I refuse to marry *anyone*!'

Lady Zhou saw she was crying as she spoke. It was obvious to her that her daughter had fallen in love with Xu. The girl had unwittingly revealed her feelings before she even fully understood them herself.

'You are the only daughter I have,' Lady Zhou comforted her. 'Do you think I don't love you? Don't worry yourself. I'll see to everything.When we get to Kaifeng I'll speak to your father and get him to take charge of this matter so that you can be betrothed to Mr Xu.'

'Who said I ever wanted to marry him?' Zhou Qi replied hurriedly. 'The next time I see someone dying in front of me, I won't do anything to save him, not the slightest thing.'

Dog-Officials and Refugees

Mastermind Xu followed Chen's secret directions to Kaifeng and met the Red Flower heroes at the home of the local Society Lodge Master there. They were very happy to see that Xu was alive and well, and a banquet was held to welcome him. By this time, Hunchback Zhang, Leopard Wei, and Xin Yan had all recovered from their wounds. Melancholy Ghost Shi had not yet returned from the Uighur border regions, and the Twin Knights were still trying to find out what had become of Rolling Thunder Wen.

Xu did not mention anything about Lady Zhou or Zhou Qi to Lord Zhou. He was afraid that if he were too closely questioned, he would not know how to word his answers. And anyway, he thought, they would be there within a day. So he only passed on to the Red Flower heroes the news they had gleaned of Scholar Yu: that he was badly wounded and travelling with a girl dressed as a boy. They discussed the matter for a while but could not think who the girl might be. They were all worried for Yu's safety. But he was quick-witted, and ultimately they felt confident he would know what to do.

Early next morning, Zhou Qi arrived by herself. Her father and the others were delighted to see her. After they had exchanged greetings, she drew Xu quietly to one side, telling him that she had something to say to him. He walked hesitantly after her: he thought she wanted to berate him for leaving them behind. But he was wrong.

'My mother won't see my father,' Zhou Qi whispered. 'Think of something.'

'Well, ask your father to go to her,' said Xu, surprised at this turn of events.

'She still wouldn't be willing to see him. She goes on and on about the death of my brother, and says that my father has no conscience.'

Xu thought for a moment. 'Very well,' he said finally. 'I have an idea.' He quietly gave her instructions.

'Do you think that will work?' she asked.

'Definitely. You'd better go immediately.'

Xu waited until she had left, then returned to sit with the other Red Flower heroes. When the appointed hour arrived, he quietly said to Lord Zhou: 'I understand the Bamboo Garden Restaurant next to the Iron Pagoda Temple here in Kaifeng is famous for its excellent wine. Let's go and try it.'

'Good idea! I'll be host,' replied Zhou, who was always interested when it came to wine. 'We can all go and drink our fill.'

'The eyes and ears of officials are numerous in this city. It would not be a good idea for all of us to go,' Mastermind Xu replied. 'Perhaps it would be better if just the Helmsman and I accompanied you. What do you think?'

'Certainly,' Zhou replied. 'You always think things through so carefully.'

They proceeded to invite Helmsman Chen, and the three of them then went directly to the Iron Pagoda Temple. The Bamboo Garden was as good as its reputation. The three men talked, ate fresh Yellow River carp, and downed the establishment's excellent wine until they were well and truly drunk.

Xu raised his cup to Zhou. 'I drink to you, Lord Zhou, and to your reunion today with your daughter,' he said.

Zhou drank a mouthful and sighed.

'You are still not happy,' Xu continued. 'Is it because Iron Ball Manor was burned to the ground?'

'A material possession such as Iron Ball Manor is not something worthy of regret,' Zhou replied.

'Well then, you must be thinking of your deceased son?'

Zhou said nothing but sighed once again.

'Brother Xu, I think we should be going,' said Helmsman Chen. 'I've had enough wine.'

Xu ignored him. 'Why did Lady Zhou leave home?' he asked.

'She blamed me for killing the child,' replied Lord Zhou. 'Ah, where could she have run to, all alone? She loved him as dearly as her own life. I have truly failed her. I had no intention of killing him. It was a stupid mistake, something done in anger. Once we have rescued your Brother Wen, I will search the farthest ends of the earth to find her and bring her back.'

As he spoke, the door-curtain parted and Lady Zhou and Zhou Qi walked in.

'I heard what you said,' said Lady Zhou. 'I'm glad to hear that you admit your mistake. I'm here now, so there's no need to go searching for me anywhere.'

Zhou was so surprised and delighted at the sudden appearance of his wife that he was momentarily speechless.

'Helmsman Chen, this is my mother,' Zhou Qi said. 'Mother, this is Helmsman Chen of the Red Flower Society.' The two greeted each other formally.

'Father, what a coincidence this is,' the girl added. 'I had heard that the wine here was good and decided to come here and try it. Mother didn't want to come and I had to drag her along. Who would have guessed that you would be here too?'

They all laughed and drank. Zhou Qi was exuberantly happy, and, without thinking, she began to talk elatedly about how the Agency guard Tong had been killed, and how both the death of her young brother and the burning of the Manor had therefore been avenged. Xu surreptitiously tried to stop her, but she took no notice.

'Mastermind Xu was very clever to think of a way of dealing with them,' she exclaimed. 'After all the guards had passed out, we jumped in through the window and saved mother. Then he lifted Tong up and let me kill the bandit myself.'

Lord Zhou and Helmsman Chen toasted Mastermind Xu.

'You have saved my wife and taken revenge on my behalf,' Zhou said to him. 'I am eternally grateful to you.'

'How did the two of you meet up on your travels?' asked Helmsman Chen, and Xu mumbled a few sentences by way of explanation.

Zhou Qi seemed to become greatly distressed. Her face flushed and with a clumsy movement of her arm she knocked her chopsticks and wine-cup to the ground. The wine-cup smashed loudly, increasing her embarrassment.

Chen examined both their faces carefully. When they had returned to the house where they were staying, he called Xu over to one side.

'Brother Xu, what is your opinion of Miss Zhou?' he asked.

'Helmsman,' Xu replied hastily. 'Please don't mention what she said in the restaurant to anyone. She is such a good person and has such a pure heart. The trouble is, if other people start talking and spreading malicious rumours, we would never be able to face Lord Zhou again.'

'I too think Miss Zhou is an extremely nice person,' said Chen. 'How would you like me to be your matchmaker?'

'That's impossible,' said Xu, jumping up. 'I would never be good enough for her!'

'You must not be so modest. You are the Kungfu Mastermind, renowned throughout the fighting community. Lord Zhou always speaks of you with the greatest respect.'

Xu stood dumbfounded for a second.

'What do you think?' Chen repeated.

'Helmsman, you don't understand. She doesn't even like me.'

'How do you know?'

'She said so herself. She said she hated my peculiar ways. She's always saying that I'm too sly and cunning. We've done nothing but quarrel and argue ever since we met.'

Chen laughed. 'So you're certain?'

'Helmsman, there's no point even talking about it. And anyway, we cannot risk being turned down.'

Just then, a servant entered.

'Master Chen,' he said. 'Lord Zhou is outside and wishes to speak to you.'

Chen smiled at Xu and walked out of the room. He saw Zhou pacing up and down the corridor with his hands behind his back and quickly went up to him.

'Lord Zhou, you should have sent for me. Surely it wasn't necessary for you to come to me in person?'

'Think nothing of it,' Zhou replied. He took Chen by the arm, led him into one of the reception rooms, and sat down.

'I have something on my mind and want to ask your help,' he said. 'My daughter is nineteen this year. She has been a good-for-nothing since the day she was born, but she is basically a good and sincere person. Her faults are more than anything the consequence of my teaching her something of the Martial Arts. She has wasted much time in her life, and still has no husband.' He hesitated a moment before continuing. 'Everyone respects your comrade-in-arms Brother Xu. I would like to ask you to be the matchmaker and to arrange for my daughter's betrothal to him. But I am afraid that with her temper and her impulsive ways, she would not be good enough for him.'

Chen was delighted. 'Leave this matter completely in my hands,' he said. 'You are a pillar of the fighting community, Lord Zhou. It is a great honour for the Red Flower Society that you are willing to give up your daughter to one of our Brothers. I will go and see to it immediately.'

He hurried back to Xu and told him the news. Xu was so delighted, his heart beat wildly.

'Well,' said Chen. 'Are you willing?'

'Of course!'

'I thought so,' said Chen with a smile. 'But there is something else. All three of Lord Zhou's sons are dead, and the youngest died as a result of the family's involvement with the Red Flower Society. It looks as if the Zhou family line is finished. Would you be willing to become not just his son-in-law, but his son?'

'You mean, become a member of the Zhou family?'

'Yes. The first of your sons would have the surname Zhou, and the second Xu. It would be a small repayment of our debt to Lord Zhou.'

Xu agreed. The two of them went to Lord Zhou. They also asked Lady Zhou to come over. Unaware of what was happening, Zhou Qi followed her in. As soon as Lord Zhou saw the expression on the faces of Helmsman Chen and Mastermind Xu, he knew the matter was decided.

'Daughter, go outside for a moment,' he said with a smile.

'You are doing something behind my back,' she protested. 'I won't have it!' She turned and left the room.

Chen brought up his idea of Xu becoming a member of the Zhou clan, and Lady Zhou and her husband beamed with delight.

'We are away from home,' Zhou said to Xu, 'and I have nothing suitable to present to you. But later I will teach you how to use the Iron Balls.'

Mastermind Xu was overwhelmed. He was about to acquire both a beautiful wife and a wise Shifu. He knelt down to kowtow in thanks.

As soon as the news leaked out, the other Red Flower heroes came to offer their congratulations, and that night a great banquet was held to celebrate. But Zhou Qi hid herself away and refused to come out.

During the drinking, Melancholy Ghost Shi returned from his journey to the Uighur regions with the Hodja's answer to Helmsman Chen's letter.

Chen took the letter. Just then, Crocodile Jiang raced in shouting: 'The Yellow River has broken its banks!'

They clustered round and questioned him on the extent of the disaster.

'The river has already broken through at seven or eight points. In many places the roads are completely impassable,' he replied.

They were all concerned about how country folk were faring in the wake of this disaster. Furthermore, the Twin Knights had still not returned to report on what had happened to Rolling Thunder Wen.

'Brothers, we have already waited here in Kaifeng several days,' said Helmsman Chen. 'Conditions on the road ahead have probably changed by now, and I am afraid these latest floods will have ruined our plans. What do you all think we should do?'

'We can't wait any longer,' Hunchback Zhang called out. 'Let's head on to Peking quickly. Even if they are holding Brother Wen in the Heavenly Prison, we'll still get him out.'

The others voiced their agreement, and it was decided to start out without any delay. They thanked the local Society Lodge Master and headed off in a north-easterly direction.

Once they were on the road, Chen opened and read the Hodja's letter. In it, the Hodja thanked the Red Flower Society for its warning and said he had called his people together and was preparing for war, determined to fight the enemy to the end. The mood of the letter was grimly heroic and Chen's anxiety showed on his face.

'Did the Hodja have anything else to say?' he asked Shi.

'He asked after Brother Wen. When he heard we had not yet rescued him, he expressed great concern.'

'Did you meet the Hodja's family?' Chen asked.

'I met his wife, his son, and two daughters. You know the eldest daughter. She asked after your health.'

Chen hesitated. 'She didn't say anything other than that?' he asked with some hesitation.

Shi thought for a second. 'Just as I was leaving, there appeared to be something else she wished to say to me, but in the end she only asked about the details of our attempt to rescue Brother Wen.'

Chen was silent. He put his hand into his gown and felt for the dagger that Huo Qingtong had given him. The blade was eight inches long, bright and dazzling, and the handle was entwined with gold thread. It was old and worn, and clearly a thing of great antiquity. Huo Qingtong had said that it concealed a great secret. He had examined it closely over the past few days, but had been unable to find anything unusual about it. He turned and looked back westwards. The host of stars were shining brightly in the night sky. Out there, somewhere on the great expanse of desert, the same stars were shining on Huo Qingtong.

They travelled all night, and when morning dawned, they were already close to the places where the Yellow River had broken through its banks. The great plain had been turned into a vast lake. Fields and homes in low-lying areas had long since been submerged. Many local people were camping out in the open on hilltops.

The Red Flower heroes made their way round the flood, keeping to the high ground and heading north-east. Occasionally, they spotted a cluster of corpses bobbing along beside pieces of driftwood. That night, they camped out in the open, and the next day had to make a long detour.

Zhou Qi had been riding with Luo Bing the whole way, but suddenly she could restrain herself no longer. She spurred her horse on and caught up with Mastermind Xu.

'You're the one with all the ideas,' she said. 'You must think of a way to help these poor people.'

During the two days since they had become engaged, they had been too shy even to speak to each other. Now, the first thing

Zhou Qi did when she opened her mouth was to present him with a problem of mammoth proportions.

'It's all very well to say that,' he replied, 'but how can we possibly help so many refugees?'

'Would I come and ask you if I knew of a way myself?'

'First thing tomorrow I'm going to tell all the others never to call me Kungfu Mastermind ever again. Then you won't be able to put me on the spot like this.'

'When did I ever put you on the spot?' Zhou Qi asked quickly. 'All right, I was wrong to say that. It would be better if I'd said nothing.' She pouted silently.

'Sister, we're one family now,' said Xu. 'We can't continue to argue like this.' Zhou Qi ignored him.

'I'm the one who's in the wrong,' he coaxed. 'Forgive me this time. Go on, give me a smile.' Zhou Qi turned her head away.

'Ah, so you won't even smile. You are so bashful in front of your new fiancé.'

She burst out laughing. 'You talk such nonsense,' she said, raising her horsewhip.

The road was packed with refugees, dragging their sons and carrying their daughters, crying and wailing as they went on their way. Suddenly a horseman appeared, galloping towards them through the crowd. The road was very narrow and as the rider careered from side to side, he knocked a woman carrying a child into the water. But he took no notice, and continued to gallop on. The Red Flower heroes were furious, and as the rider passed by, Leopard Wei pulled him from his horse and punched him hard in the face. The man screamed and spat out a mouthful of blood and three teeth.

He was a military official.

'I am here on important official business,' he shouted as he scrambled to his feet. 'I'll deal with you hooligans when I come back.' He mounted his horse again, but this time it was Hunchback Zhang Jin who pulled him off.

'What sort of important official business?' he roared.

'Search him,' ordered Helmsman Chen. Zhang frisked him quickly and found an official document. Chen saw that the document had a singed corner and a chicken's feather stuck to it indicating that it was an urgent report which the courier would be required to travel day and night to deliver. On the wrapper were written the words: 'Extra Urgent Dispatch for Border Pacification General Zhao Hui.' He broke the seal and took out the document.

The courier went white with fear. 'That's a secret military document,' he cried feebly. 'Aren't you afraid of having your head chopped off?'

'If anyone should be afraid, it's you,' said Helmsman Chen's page Xin Yan with a laugh. As Chen read he discovered that the letter was from a certain commander in charge of military provisions reporting to General Zhao that rations for the Great Army had reached the city of Lanfeng, some thirty miles east of Kaifeng, but that because of the floods, there might be a delay of several days before they could be delivered.

Chen handed the letter to Mastermind Xu. 'It has nothing to do with us,' he said.

But as Xu read the document an expression of delight came over his face. 'Helmsman,' he cried. 'This is truly a wonderful stroke of good fortune! With this, we can both assist the Hodja *and* save the refugees.'

He jumped off his horse and, walking over to the official, tore the document up in front of him.

'What are you going to do now?' he asked. 'Losing a military document is a capital offence, isn't it? If you want to stay alive, you'd better run for it.'

The official was startled and angry, but he saw the truth of Xu's words. He took off his military uniform, threw it in the water, then ran off, melding into the mass of refugees.

'You mean, we should steal the army's provisions and hand them out as disaster relief? Yes, that would certainly kill two birds with one stone,' said Chen, nodding gravely. 'The only problem is that the provisions for the Great Army are bound to be heavily guarded, and we are few in number. What do you suggest, Brother Xu?'

Mastermind Xu whispered a few words in his ear, and Chen nodded in agreement. 'Good, we'll do it that way,' he said, and ordered the Red Flower heroes to disguise themselves and disperse. Their instructions were to spread certain rumours.

The next morning, tens of thousands of refugees descended on Lanfeng out of the blue. When the county magistrate, Wang Dao, saw the crowd outside his Yamen gates, he ordered his officers to seize a number of the refugees and question them. They all said they had heard the same thing: that there would be a distribution of relief money and provisions in the city that day. Wang immediately ordered that the city gates be barred, but by then, a huge crowd of refugees had already gathered inside with many more outside waiting to get in. Wang sent someone to announce to the crowd that there would be no distribution of relief, but the numbers continued to grow. Wang began to feel nervous, and went personally to see the Provisions Commander, Sun, who was stationed in the Stone Buddha Temple in the eastern part of the city. He asked if some of the commander's troops could be assigned to help control the situation in the city.

'I have my orders from General Zhao Hui,' Sun replied. 'Any slip-up on my part, no matter how small, before these provisions reach the Great Army, will be a capital offence. It is not that I am unwilling to help, but my responsibilities are heavy. Please forgive me, Magistrate Wang.'

Wang pleaded with him, but Sun was adamant. Back on the streets, he saw the refugees creating an uproar everywhere.

Night fell, and fires broke out simultaneously in several parts of the city. Magistrate Wang hurriedly dispatched men to put them out. In the confusion, an officer ran in to report that the west gate had been forced by the refugees and thousands more were streaming into the city.

Wang was desperate, completely at a loss what to do.

'Bring me a horse!' he shouted frantically, and set off on horseback, leading his guards towards the western part of the city. But before they had gone half a street, they found the way completely blocked by refugees. He heard someone in the midst of the crowd shout: 'Stone Buddha Temple! The food and money are to be distributed at Stone Buddha Temple! Everyone to Stone Buddha Temple!' The refugees surged forward.

Wang could see the road to the west was impassable. He decided there was nothing for it but to try and make his way east to Stone Buddha Temple and seek refuge there. When he arrived, the temple gate was already tightly shut, but the guard recognized him and let him in. Outside, the refugees had already surrounded the temple. Someone in the crowd was shouting that all the relief cash and the food rations issued by the Court had been swallowed by the 'dog-officials'.

A cry went up. 'Money and food! We want money and food!'

The mass of refugees took up the chant and their roar rattled the roof-tiles.

Wang shook with uncontrollable rage. 'Rebels!' he bellowed. 'Rebels!'

For a military official, Commander Sun was quite brave. He ordered his soldiers to place a ladder against the wall and climbed up onto the wall to address the crowd.

'Those of you who are peaceful citizens, leave the city quickly and do not put faith in rumours,' he shouted. 'If you do not leave, we will be forced to fire on you with arrows.'

Two of his officers led a group of archers onto the top of the wall and a roar of defiance went up from the crowd.

'Fire!' shouted Sun. A wave of arrows flew through the air and a dozen or more refugees fell to the ground. The crowd turned and fled in panic and the cries of women and children could be heard as the refugees trampled each other.

Sun laughed out loud. But even as he laughed, someone in the crowd threw two stones at him, one of which hit his cheek. He felt a sharp pain and rubbed the spot only to find his hand covered in blood.

'Fire again!' he ordered in a great rage. 'Fire!' The archers let loose another wave of arrows and another dozen refugees were hit.

Suddenly, two tall, thin men leapt up onto the wall, grabbed several of the archers, and threw them to the ground. Incensed by the way they had been fired on in cold blood, the refugees meanwhile were surging back, and began beating the archers viciously.

The Red Flower Society heroes in the crowd were greatly surprised by the sudden reappearance of the Twin Knights (for that is who the two thin men were). More refugees jumped up onto the wall and into the temple courtyard, and a moment later, the temple gates opened and Crocodile Jiang ran out.

'Everyone come in and get some food,' he shouted, beckoning to the refugees. But the soldiers guarding the temple were still many and the refugees did not dare to press in too close. Commander Sun's great sword danced as he fought desperately along the top of the wall, retreating steadily before the Twin Knights. Suddenly, his arms went numb, and his sword clattered to the ground at the foot of the wall. His hands were forced behind his back, and he felt the icy coldness of a blade on his neck.

'You turtle!' the man behind him shouted. 'Order your troops to throw down their weapons and retreat inside the temple!'

Sun hesitated for a second. He felt a sharp pain on his neck as the man lightly pressed his sword, breaking through a layer of skin. Not daring to disobey further, Sun shouted out the order. Seeing that their commanding officer had been captured, the soldiers did as they were ordered and retired inside the temple as the refugees roared their approval.

Helmsman Chen now walked into the main hall of the temple and saw the altar piled high with bags of food and cash. Melancholy Ghost Shi pulled County Magistrate Wang in for the Helmsman to dispose of.

'Are you in charge of this county?' Chen asked.

'Y-yes…your Majesty,' Wang replied in a quavering voice.

Chen laughed. 'Do I look like a king?' he asked.

'I deserved to die. I spoke incorrectly. What is your name, sir?'

Chen smiled slightly and ignored the question. 'You're an official,' he said. 'Presumably you have some ink in your veins. I'm going to set you a little test. I'm going to give you the first lines of a rhyme, and I want you to give me a rhyming ending for it.' He waved his fan in the air. 'Do it properly, and your life will be spared. But if you fail, I'm afraid things will start going rather badly for you.'

The refugees gathered round, a circle of thousands of eyes all focused on Wang's face. It was certainly a novel experience for them, to see their Magistrate put to the test like this in public—and even more novel that it should be at the hands of a Red Flower chief.

'It begins like this,' said Helmsman Chen.

> *Will any man among us*
> *Live long enough to see*
> *The Yellow River flow green?*
> *Will any man among us*
> *Be old enough to see*
> *Our rulers' guilt washed clean?*

Wang's face broke out in beads of sweat. He was a scholar of sorts, and had been obliged to write rhyming verses for his exams. But he was simply too shaken to be able to think of anything at all.

'Your Highness,' he finally stammered. 'You've completely stumped me, I'm afraid…'

'That's all right,' said Chen. 'Let me put the question to you in a plainer form, and ask you for a plain answer. Which do you think would take longer to clean up in this country of yours—the muddy waters of the Yellow River, or the stinking sewer of officialdom?'

Wang suddenly had (what seemed to him to be) an inspiration.

'If the day ever dawned, Your Highness, when our officials were clean and guiltless, that would certainly be a miracle! And by the same miracle, the muddy waters of the Yellow River might flow green too!'

Chen laughed. 'Well said! That will do. Your life is spared. Now you can call together your guards and distribute the money and food to the refugees. Oh, and Commander Sun, you can help too.'

The refugees cheered thunderously for the Red Flower Society heroes. As they filed past to collect the food and money, they jeered and laughed at Sun and Wang, who pretended not to notice.

'Listen everyone!' Chen called out. 'If the authorities ever send people to investigate, you can say it was the Commander and your own County Magistrate who personally authorized the distribution.'

The refugees roared their approval.

The Red Flower heroes supervised the operation late into the night until the last bit of food and money had been distributed.

Xu then shouted to the refugees, 'Take the soldiers' weapons and hide them in your homes. If the dog-officials know what's good for them, they'll leave you alone. But if they come after you, you'll be able to fight back.'

A number of stalwart men came forward and collected up the swords and spears that had been discarded by the soldiers.

Helmsman Chen walked out of the temple with Commander Sun and the other Red Flower heroes as the refugees continued to roar their thanks. They mounted their horses and rode out of the city. After travelling a few miles, Chen pushed Sun off his horse.

'Commander, thank you for your help,' he said. 'The next time you escort provisions, be sure to write to me.' He laughed and saluted, then galloped off in a cloud of dust with the other Red Flower heroes.

'Do you have any news of Brother Wen?' Chen asked the Twin Knights after they had ridden on a little way.

'We found a message left by Scholar Yu which said Brother Wen was being taken to Hangzhou,' one of them replied.

Chen was greatly surprised. 'Why is he being sent to Hangzhou and not Peking?' he asked. 'I thought the Emperor wanted to question him personally.'

'We thought it strange too. But Scholar Yu is always very particular about details. It's certain to be reliable information.'

Chen told the others to dismount, and they sat round in a circle and discussed the situation.

'Since Brother Wen is being sent to Hangzhou, we should turn around and head south,' Mastermind Xu said. 'We must try to work out some way of saving him. Hangzhou is our territory. The power of the Court is not as great there as in Peking, so it should be easier to rescue him. But we should still send someone to Peking to see if there is any news, just in case.'

The others agreed. Chen looked over at Shi. 'I wonder if I can trouble you to go once more,' he said.

'All right,' replied Melancholy Ghost. He rode off northwards alone towards Peking, while the other heroes headed south.

Chen enquired further of the Twin Knights about Yu's movements, but they said they had no further information. They had returned to report as soon as they had seen the markings. Passing through Lanfeng, they had come across the refugees and met up with the other Red Flower heroes.

'With the provisions gone, Sister Huo Qingtong and her Uighur people should have no trouble beating the Great Army,' Zhou Qi said.

'That girl's sword style wasn't at all bad,' added Father Speckless, 'and she seemed a pleasant enough person. She deserves our help. I hope she does succeed in beating them. It would be something everyone could be pleased about.'

CHAPTER 4

*Lute and Fan; A Pleasant Outing on the Lake; At the Grave-side;
The Dwarf Magician and the Jade Vases*

Lute and Fan

In less than a day, the Red Flower heroes arrived in the town of
Xuzhou. The local Society Lodge Master was immediately rushed
off his feet making arrangements for them. After a night's rest, they
continued on south. Every place they passed through now, big and
small, had a Red Flower Society lodge, but the heroes maintained
their anonymity and sped onwards. They reached Hangzhou several
days later and took up residence in the home of the Hangzhou
Lodge Master, Ma Shanjun. Ma's residence lay at the foot of Lonely
Mountain beside the West Lake, on the outskirts of Hangzhou.

Ma was a merchant who owned two large silk factories. He
was about fifty years old and portly, and in his flowered silk robe
and black woollen jacket, he was the picture of a wealthy man
used to luxury. But the appearance was deceptive: he was also a
brave fighter. That night at a welcoming banquet in the rear hall,
the heroes told him of their plan to rescue Rolling Thunder Wen.

'I will dispatch men at once to find out which prison Brother
Wen is being held in, and then we can decide on a plan of action.'
He told his son Ma Dating to send one of his men to investigate.

The next morning, the son reported that his men had discreetly
asked about Wen at all the prisons and barracks in the area, but had
failed to find any trace of him. Helmsman Chen called a meeting of
the Red Flower heroes to discuss the situation.

'We have Brothers in all the Yamens and barracks,' said Ma.
'If Brother Wen were in a public prison, we would know about it. I
am afraid the authorities are guarding him somewhere secretly.'

'In that case, our first step is still to find out where Brother
Wen is,' said Chen. 'Please continue to dispatch capable men around
all the Yamens, Lodge Master Ma. This evening, I will ask Father
Speckless and the Twin Knights to go to the Commander-in-Chief's
Yamen to see what they can find out. It is important that we don't

alert the Manchus to what we are doing. So whatever happens, there must be no fighting.'

Father Speckless and the Twin Knights set out at midnight and returned four hours later to report that the Commander-in-Chief's Yamen was tightly guarded by at least a thousand soldiers with torches on guard duty. Several of the officers on patrol were second and third level Mandarins wearing red caps. The three had waited a long time, but the troops showed no sign of dropping their vigilance and they'd had no option but to return.

'I've noticed that the patrols have been particularly strict around Hangzhou over the past few days,' Ma said. 'Yamen officers have been visiting every gambling den and every brothel, and a lot of people have been rounded up for no reason at all. Could it have something to do with Brother Wen?'

'I don't think so,' replied Mastermind Xu. 'Most probably the local officers are making an extra effort to impress some top-level officials visiting from Peking.'

'I haven't heard of any visit by a high official,' said Ma.

The next day, Zhou Qi asked her parents to take her to see the famous West Lake. Lord Zhou agreed and asked Mastermind Xu to accompany them. Because Xu had lost his parents when he was very young and had had no family of his own ever since, to be suddenly treated as a son by Lord and Lady Zhou, and to be betrothed to such a lovely young woman, filled his heart to overflowing with a great sense of joy. His Red Flower Brothers were very happy for him.

Helmsman Chen also went down to the lake for a stroll with Xin Yan. They walked for a while, then sat alone on a bridge and gazed at the panorama of water and mountains. In the dense forests of bamboo and trees that ran along the hillsides, a myriad leaves glistened brightly. The air was moist and hazy and the mountain peaks were beautiful, wreathed in clouds. Chen had been to the West Lake several times in his youth, but this was the first time he had been able to appreciate its beauty.

As he gazed out at the scene, he spotted a carriage heading towards the Hidden Spirit Temple on Flying Peak, some five hundred feet above them.

'Let's go up there,' he said to Xin Yan. There was no road leading straight up to the peak, but they both excelled in the levitational kungfu known as the Art of Flying and were soon speeding up and across the open ground. In next to no time they reached the top. There they gazed up at the sky, enjoying the peace and seclusion of the forest.

Suddenly, they saw two large men wearing blue gowns walking towards them. The two weighed them up as they passed, expressions of surprise on their faces.

'Master, they must surely be kungfu experts,' whispered Xin Yan. Then two more men came walking towards them dressed in exactly the same way. They were discussing the scenery, and from their accents, they sounded like Manchus from Peking. All the way along the path, they kept passing men in blue gowns, perhaps thirty or forty of them in all. They all looked like well-trained fighters, and they all seemed greatly surprised when they set eyes on Helmsman Chen.

Xin Yan was positively dizzy at the sight of so many obviously top-ranking fighters. Helmsman Chen for his part was more than a little curious. He wondered whether some secret society or Martial Arts School was holding some sort of gathering in Hangzhou.

'But Hangzhou is Red Flower Society territory. If anything of that sort were happening, we would surely have been informed. I wonder why they all stare at me with such a surprised look?'

As they rounded a bend, the sound of a lute accompanied by chanting and the soft tinkle of a waterfall drifted across towards them. The voice recited:

> *Peace and tranquillity*
> *Prevail 'twixt Heaven and Earth,*
> *And no blot stains the purity*
> *Of our blessed realm.*
> *Prosperity and good fortune*
> *Extend over four reigns.*
> *The people greet their Liege,*
> *The wine banners fly in every village,*
> *As the Imperial cortège*
> *Draws nigh.*

They strolled across in the direction of the music, and saw a man dressed in the robes of a nobleman seated on a rock playing the lute. He must have been aged about forty. Two strong fighters and one stooped old man, all three wearing blue gowns, stood beside him.

Helmsman Chen suddenly trembled. He was struck with a vague feeling of recognition as he looked at the lute-player. There was something strangely familiar about his aristocratic bearing. The more Chen looked at him, the more familiar he seemed. The group eyed Chen and Xin Yan warily. The lute-player's fingers performed a final swirl over the strings and the lute was silent.

Helmsman Chen saluted with clasped fists. 'I could not help overhearing the song you just played, sir,' he said. 'I have never heard it before. Did you write it yourself?'

The man smiled. 'Yes. It is a recent composition of mine. Since you are a music lover, I would be grateful of your opinion.'

'Oh, it was excellent! Excellent!' said Chen. 'I especially liked the phrase "The wine banners fly in every village."'

An expression of delight lit up the man's face. 'So you remember the words. Won't you come over here and sit down, sir.'

Helmsman Chen had refrained from adding that he disapproved of the way the song flattered the Emperor. He walked over, bowed, and sat down.

The man studied Chen carefully and with curiosity.

'On our way up the peak,' said Chen, 'we met a large number of other men out strolling, all of whom looked surprised when they saw me. Now you are looking at me in the same way. Is there something strange about my face?'

The man laughed.

'It's something you wouldn't know about,' he said. 'You see, I have a friend who bears a striking resemblance to you. The people you met on the path are also my friends, so they would have noticed the same similarity, and were naturally puzzled.'

'So that's it,' Chen smiled. 'The funny thing is, I also find *your* face very familiar. It's almost as if we had met before, but I can't remember when. I wonder if you can?'

The man laughed again. 'How strange,' he said. 'What is your name, sir?'

'Lu Jiachen,' Chen told him. 'And yours, sir?'

The man hesitated for a moment, as if in thought. 'My name is Dongfang. I am from Hebei Province. From your own accent, I would guess you are from around these parts.'

'That is correct,' said Chen.

'I had long heard that the scenic beauty of the south was incomparable,' continued this man who called himself Dongfang (an obvious alias, since the words simply meant 'Orient'). 'Now I can see for myself that it is true. Not only is the scenery superb, but the area is also obviously blessed with talented gentlemen such as yourself.'

Helmsman Chen could tell from the way he spoke that this was no ordinary man. He watched the reverential way in which the old man and the other two attendants treated him, and wondered just who this 'Orient' was.

'Someone with your outstanding appreciation of music is certainly a virtuoso himself,' Dongfang said. 'Will you not play a song for us?' He pushed the seven-stringed lute towards Chen.

Chen stretched out his hand and lightly strummed the strings. He found the lute's tone to be matchlessly crisp and clear. It looked like a genuine antique.

'I am really not worthy to play such a fine instrument,' he said. He checked the tuning, then began to play an air named 'The Goose Lands on the Flat Sands'.

Dongfang listened attentively. 'Have you ever been to the border regions yourself?' he asked when the tune finished.

'As a matter of fact I have just returned from there,' Chen replied. 'How did you know?'

'Your playing conjures up so poignantly the vast emptiness of the great desert. I have heard that tune many times in my life, but never have I heard it played with such feeling.' Helmsman Chen could tell that this 'Orient' indeed had a great appreciation of music and was very pleased.

'There is something I would like to ask you,' Dongfang continued.

'Please feel free.'

'I would guess that you are from the family of an official,' he said. 'What post does your respected father hold? And what is your rank?'

'My father has unfortunately passed away. I myself am a man of little talent and no official rank,' Chen replied.

'On the contrary, you are obviously greatly talented. Could it be that your examiners failed to appreciate your abilities?'

'No, it is not that.'

'The Commander-in-Chief of Zhejiang Province is a personal

friend of mine. If you were to go and see him tomorrow, things could change.'

'Thank you for your kind thought, but I have no wish to be an official,' Chen replied.

'But do you intend to hide yourself away like this forever?'

'I would rather live in seclusion than oppress the common people.'

Dongfang's expression suddenly changed and the two blue-gowned attendants both took a step forward. He was silent for a second, then laughed out loud. 'You are, I see, a man of principle and of noble character,' he said. 'More so than a simple person such as myself.'

The two weighed each other up, each aware that there was something special about the other.

'You must have heard much news on your long journey from the Uighur regions,' said Dongfang. 'And you must have seen a great deal of beautiful scenery.'

'When I arrived at the Yellow River, I found great flooding and vast numbers of homeless, destitute people. I had no heart for appreciating the scenery after that.'

'I am told that the refugees in Lanfeng looted grain stores meant for the western army. Did you hear anything about that?'

Helmsman Chen was taken aback that the man should have known about this. They themselves had hurried south after the Lanfeng riot without stopping to rest. 'I understand there was such an incident,' he said. 'The refugees had no clothes and no food and the local officials did nothing to help them. They were forced to break the law in order to survive, an action which under the circumstances is pardonable.'

Dongfang was silent for a while. 'I gather it was not quite as simple as that,' he said nonchalantly. 'What I heard was that the Red Flower Society incited the refugees.'

'What is the Red Flower Society?' asked Helmsman Chen, innocently.

'It is a rebellious underground society. Have you never heard of it?'

'I divide my time between my lute and my chessboard. I have little time for the affairs of the world.'

'That's nothing to be ashamed of. These people are in any case no great problem.'

'What basis do you have for saying that?'

'What basis? The Emperor is secure on his Throne, and the administration of the country is in enlightened and orderly hands. One or two capable men will be assigned to the job, and the Red Flower Society will be wiped out in no time at all.'

'I know nothing of matters of government, so please do not laugh if I should say something stupid. But in my humble opinion, most of the officials at Court are nothing more than drunkards and gluttons. I very much doubt if men such as they would be able to succeed in doing "the job", as you call it.'

As he said this, Dongfang and his three attendants turned pale.

'That is simply the view of a scholar,' Dongfang replied. 'I must beg to differ. These friends of mine here, for example, are certainly of more than mediocre ability. If you were a student of the Martial Arts, you would know that I was not exaggerating.'

'I myself lack the strength to so much as truss a chicken,' said Chen. 'But I have always had the greatest respect for heroic fighters. Are these your disciples? I wonder if you could ask them to demonstrate their abilities for me?'

'Show this gentleman one of your tricks,' Dongfang said to the attendants.

One of the attendants stepped forward. 'The magpie in that tree is much too noisy,' he said. 'I'll bring it down so we can have some peace.'

He waved his hand, and a sleeve dart went through the air towards the magpie. But then, just as it was homing in on its target, it suddenly veered off to one side and fell to the ground.

Dongfang looked surprised and his attendant's face flushed with embarrassment. He threw another dart. This time everyone was watching closely. The same thing happened. They could see that a piece of earth knocked the dart off course.

The stooped old man standing by Dongfang's side noticed that Xin Yan's hand had moved slightly and realized he was responsible. 'This young man's kungfu is excellent. We must get to know one another,' he said, and grasped at Xin Yan's hand with his fingers bent into the shape of a steel claw.

Helmsman Chen was greatly surprised to see the old man using Great Force Eagle's Claw kungfu of the Songyang School. He knew that there were only a handful of Claw practitioners alive with that degree of concentration and skill. He wondered to himself why such a distinguished fighter would agree to be Dongfang's servant.

Chen flicked open his fan in front of Xin Yan as the old man lunged at the boy, and the old man quickly retracted his Claw. His master was treating this gentleman in a friendly manner, and it would be extremely disrespectful to damage one of his possessions. He glanced at Chen, wondering if he knew kungfu. Chen began fanning himself lightly, in a completely relaxed manner, as if his move with the fan a second earlier had been a pure coincidence.

'This boy's kungfu is very good despite his youth,' said Dongfang. 'Where did you find him?'

'He doesn't really know any kungfu at all,' replied Chen. 'He has just been throwing things at insects and birds ever since he was small, and has become quite good at it.'

Dongfang knew that this was untrue, but chose not to pursue the matter. He looked at Chen's fan.

'Whose is the calligraphy on your fan? May I look?' he asked. Chen handed the fan over to him. Dongfang immediately recognized the calligraphy as being from the hand of the great Manchu poet Singde, friend of the Emperor Kang Xi.

'Only a man of such noble character as yourself would be worthy of something like this. Where did you get it?'

'I bought it in a bookstore for ten gold pieces.'

'If you had paid ten times as much, I would still consider it a bargain,' Dongfang replied. 'Possessions such as this are usually passed down from generation to generation in the great families. They are priceless heirlooms. It is certainly amazing that you were able to buy it so easily in a bookstore.'

Chen knew Dongfang didn't believe him, but he didn't care. He smiled lightly.

'I like this fan very much,' Dongfang said. 'I wonder if I could ask you to sell it to me?'

'I would be pleased to give it to you,' Chen replied.

Dongfang accepted the fan. He lifted up the ancient lute and presented it to Chen. 'Just as a heroic fighter should be presented with a treasured sword, so should this lute belong to you.'

Chen knew the lute was an extremely valuable instrument, and he wondered why the man wanted to exchange gifts so soon after they had met. But as the son of a prominent official, he had seen many such treasures in his youth and was not dazzled by them. He saluted Dongfang with clasped fists in thanks, and told Xin Yan to carry the lute for him.

'If there is ever anything I can do for you in the future, just come to Peking with that lute and ask for me,' said Dongfang. 'Shall we walk back down the hill together?'

'I should be delighted,' said Helmsman Chen, and the two started off, arm in arm.

As they reached the Hidden Spirit Temple, several people came towards them, led by a handsome man wearing an embroidered gown. The man bore a striking resemblance to Chen and was even about the same age, but he lacked Chen's imposing air. Chen and he stared at each other in surprise.

'He's very like you, isn't he, my friend?' said Dongfang. 'He is my nephew. Kang, come and meet my new friend.'

The man referred to as Kang bowed towards him, and Chen quickly returned the courtesy.

All of a sudden, they heard a girl's voice calling out in surprise. Chen turned and saw Zhou Qi with Mastermind Xu and her parents emerging from the temple. He knew she must have been taken aback to see two men both of whom looked just like Helmsman Chen. He saw Xu hustling her away, and himself turned back, pretending to have noticed nothing.

'My friend,' said Dongfang. 'We seem to have taken a liking to each other on our very first meeting. We will surely meet again. Goodbye.' They bowed to each other and Dongfang walked off, surrounded by his blue-gowned guards.

Helmsman Chen turned and attracted Mastermind Xu's attention with a barely perceptible nod. Xu hurriedly made his apologies to Lord Zhou and to Zhou Qi and followed after Dongfang and his companions.

Towards evening, Xu returned to make his report. 'The gentleman you met spent a long time boating on the lake and then went to the Yamen of the Provincial Commander-in-Chief,' he said.

Helmsman Chen told him all about his meeting with Dongfang, and the two decided that this man must be a very senior official, either an Imperial Envoy or a member of the Emperor's close family. From his appearance, he did not look like a Manchu, and so they concluded he was probably an Envoy.

'Could his arrival have anything to do with Brother Wen's capture, I wonder,' Helmsman Chen mused. 'I think I had better go over to the Commander-in-Chief's Yamen personally this evening to investigate.'

'It would be best to take someone with you just in case,' Xu replied.

'Ask Buddha Zhao to come with me,' said Chen. 'He's from Zhejiang Province so he should know his way around Hangzhou.'

A Pleasant Outing on the Lake

At nine o'clock that night, Helmsman Chen and Buddha Zhao started out for the Commander-in-Chief's Yamen and, using the Art of Flying, they soon found themselves approaching the Yamen wall. They spotted two figures patrolling on a rooftop close by and crouched down to watch for a while. Zhao waited for the men to turn their backs, then sent a pellet shooting off towards a tree about fifty yards away. Hearing a suspicious noise in the branches, the guards quickly went over to investigate, which gave Chen and Zhao an opportunity to slip silently over the wall and into the Yamen precinct.

They hid in the shadows and looked out across the Yamen's main courtyard, which, to their surprise, was brightly lit with torches. There were several hundred troops standing guard. Another strange thing was that so many soldiers could manage to be so quiet. When they moved, they walked lightly on tiptoe, and the only sounds to be heard were the occasional call of a cicada, and the constant crackle from the burning torches.

Chen could see there was no way of getting past this silent force of guards. He gestured towards Zhao and the two retreated, avoiding the guards posted on the rooftop. They stopped behind a wall to discuss what to do.

'We don't want to alert them,' Chen whispered. 'We'll have to go back and think of some other plan.'

But luck was on their side. Just then, a side-gate of the Yamen creaked open and an officer emerged followed by four soldiers. The five marched down the street a few hundred yards and then turned back, obviously on patrol.

'Get them,' Chen whispered. Zhao slipped out of the shadows and threw three darts. Three of the soldiers immediately dropped to the ground. Helmsman Chen followed with two of his Go-piece missiles, hitting the officer and the remaining soldier. They quickly dragged the five bodies into the shadows, stripped the uniforms from two of them, and put them on.

They waited once more for the rooftop guards to turn away, then jumped over the Yamen wall and strode nonchalantly into the torch-lit courtyard. This time they were able to pass through into an inner courtyard which was being patrolled exclusively by senior military officials, commanders, and generals. Waiting for the right moment, they leapt up under the eaves of one of the buildings, then hung onto the rafters not daring to breathe. Once it was clear they had not been discovered, Helmsman Chen hooked his legs over a beam and hung down over a window. He moistened the window-paper and looked inside, as Buddha Zhao kept guard beside him.

Chen found himself looking in at a large hall. Five or six men wearing the gowns of high officials stood in the centre facing another man who was seated with his back to Chen. Another official walked in and kowtowed nine times towards the seated man.

Chen was surprised. He knew that this was the ceremonial salutation reserved for use when entering the presence of the Emperor, and wondered if somehow this was the Emperor Qian Long himself who had come to Hangzhou.

'The Zhejiang Province Civil Administrator Yin to see His Highness the Emperor,' announced one of the officers.

So it *was* the Emperor, Chen thought to himself. No wonder security was so tight.

'I have sent troops to quell the Uighur regions,' the Emperor said. 'I hear you object to this idea.'

Chen frowned: the Emperor's voice was strangely familiar.

'Majesty, upon my life, I would never dare think such a disloyal thought,' said the mandarin referred to as Yin, continuing to kowtow.

'I asked Zhejiang Province to supply six thousand tons of grain to meet the needs of the army. Why did you disobey my orders?'

'Majesty, truly I would never dare do such a thing,' Yin replied. 'But the harvest in Zhejiang has been very poor this year. The common people are suffering greatly, and it is temporarily impossible to supply such an amount.'

'So the common people are suffering, are they? What about the army? The army is in urgent need of food supplies. Am I to let them starve out there?'

'I am sure Your Majesty knows best,' Yin quavered, continuing to kowtow.

'No, I want you to tell me,' replied the Emperor.

'Your Majesty's ability to spread enlightenment and civilization is far-reaching. The Uighur barbarians are in fact not worth such a large military expedition. As the Ancients said: "War is an instrument of violence which a man of virtue should use only as a last resort." If Your Majesty were to cancel the campaign, the whole world would be thankful for your benevolence.'

'So the people are discontented because I have decided to wage this campaign, is that what you are trying to say?' Qian Long replied coldly.

Yin kowtowed even more energetically. His forehead was by now covered in blood.

Qian Long laughed shortly. 'You have a hard skull,' he said. 'If you hadn't, you wouldn't dare contradict me.'

As he said this, he turned round, and Helmsman Chen started violently: the Emperor Qian Long was the man he had met earlier that day—the man who had called himself 'Orient', or Dongfang!

'Get out!' he heard Qian Long shout. 'And leave your cap here!' Yin kowtowed a few more times and then retired.

'There must certainly be some irregularities in Yin's affairs,' Qian Long said to the remaining officials. 'I want the Commander-in-Chief to conduct a thorough investigation and inform me of the results. The man must not be protected out of any sense of personal favouritisim. Whatever his crimes are, they must be exposed.' The officials assented in chorus.

'Now I want you to leave me. And arrange for six thousand tons of grain to be collected and dispatched immediately.' The officials kowtowed and retired.

'Tell Kang to come,' the Emperor ordered. An attendant left and returned a moment later with Helmsman Chen's look-alike, the man he had met earlier that day. He stood close to Qian Long with an air of composure and familiarity very different from the cringing manner of the officials.

'Call for Commander Li Kexiu,' Qian Long ordered, and a military officer quickly appeared, kowtowing his way into the Emperor's presence.

'Li Kexiu, Commander-in-Chief of Zhejiang Province, pays his respects to Your Majesty,' he said.

He was, of course, Yuanzhi's father.

'How is that Red Flower Society bandit, Wen Tailai?' asked Qian Long.

'The man was arrested after a fierce struggle and he was very seriously wounded,' Li replied. 'I have assigned doctors to treat him. We will have to wait until his mind is clear before we can question him.'

'You must be careful,' Qian Long said.

'Your servant would not dare to be negligent in even the slightest detail,' replied Li.

'Go now,' said the Emperor, and Li retired.

'Let's follow him,' Chen whispered, but as they dropped quietly to the ground, someone inside the hall must have spotted them. The shout went up: 'Intruders!'

Helmsman Chen and Buddha Zhao ran back into the outer courtyard and mingled with the troops. Bamboo clappers sounded loudly and the stooped old man Chen had seen earlier that day guarding the Emperor began giving orders for a search.

Chen and Zhao strolled casually towards the gate.

'Who are you?' the old man shouted at them, and reached for Zhao. Zhao deflected his hand, and he and Chen made a run for it with the old man chasing. For his age, he was extraordinarily nimble. As they reached the gate, the old man lunged at Zhao again. Helmsman Chen ripped off the uniform he was wearing and flung it over the old man's head, then they raced out of the Yamen gate. The old man cast the uniform off to one side and chased after them. But the slight delay had made all the difference.

Hundreds of troops swarmed out behind the old man like bees from a hive.

'All of you go back!' he shouted. 'Protecting the Emperor is of the utmost importance! You five, come with me.' He ran off down the street with five guards, following the two black shapes as they flew over the rooftops ahead. The old man gradually closed the distance between himself and the 'intruders'. Suddenly, the two figures leapt down and stood stock-still in the middle of the street right in front of the old man, who immediately lunged at Helmsman Chen.

'I am your master's good friend,' Chen laughed, not bothering to retreat or defend himself. 'You are certainly an audacious old fellow!'

The old man looked at his face under the moonlight and started in surprise.

'So it's you,' he said, retracting his hand, 'Come along with me.'

'Or *you* follow *me*, if you dare!' countered Helmsman Chen with a smile.

The old man hesitated for a second. In that second, as the five guards ran up from behind, Chen and Zhao raced off westwards towards the West Lake.

'After them!' shouted the old man. The guards reached the lake in time to see Chen and Zhao jumping into a boat and pushing off from the shore. The boatman punted the craft out several yards from the bank.

'Gentlemen!' cried the old man. 'Before you go, please tell me who you are.'

'I am Zhao Banshan from Wenzhou,' Zhao roared. 'You must be a member of the Songyang Martial Arts School.'

'Ah, so you are the one they call the Thousand Arm Buddha?'

'That's just a nickname. I don't really deserve it. And your name, sir?'

'My surname is Bai, my first name Zhen.'

Buddha Zhao and Helmsman Chen gasped in surprise. Bai Zhen was a legendary kungfu Master, who had not been seen or heard of for years. And now, it seemed, he had become the personal bodyguard of the Emperor!

'So you are Master Bai,' said Buddha Zhao. 'No wonder your kungfu is so superb.'

'I hear you are a leading member of the Red Flower Society, Mr Zhao,' replied the old man. 'Who is your companion?' Suddenly, the answer came to him without his having to be told. 'Oh, of course, he must be Chen Jialuo, the Helmsman of the Society. Is that right?'

Chen opened his fan. 'The moon is clear and the wind is fresh,' he said. 'Why not come and drink a cup of wine with us, sir?'

'You have intruded into the Commander-in-Chief's Yamen, and disturbed the official household. You must accompany me to see my master. He is well-disposed towards you, and would not do you any harm.'

'Go back and ask your master to come here instead and have a talk with me,' replied Helmsman Chen. 'We can have a drink together if he wishes. I will wait for him here.'

Bai had seen the solicitude with which the Emperor had treated Chen earlier, and he dared not offend him. But after such an intrusion into the quarters of the Emperor, he was also loath to return without them. There were, however, no other boats nearby, and with no way of chasing after them across the lake, he was forced to return to report to Qian Long.

'Why not!' Qian Long said after a pause. 'It would be a pleasure to go to the lake and enjoy the moonlight. Go and tell him I will come immediately.'

'But Majesty, these are dangerous bandits,' replied Bai. 'In my humble opinion, you should not risk such danger.'

'Go!' insisted Qian Long. 'Do as I say.'

Bai did not dare to disagree, and rode swiftly back to the lake. Crocodile Jiang was sitting at the stern of a boat with his arms round his knees, waiting for him.

'My master will be here soon,' Bai shouted.

He hurried back to resume his guard of the Emperor's person. Qian Long was in high spirits, and talked and laughed with Commander Li Kexiu, who was waiting on him. He had changed into an ordinary gown, while his bodyguards had also put on civilian clothes. Once at the lakeside, he gave his orders.

'My host probably knows who I am by now, but I still want all of us to keep up the pretence that we are just common people.'

Imperial Guard units had been hidden all around the lake, supported by local troops hand-picked by Commander Li. In the flickering lantern light, they saw five boats gliding towards them across the water. Leopard Wei stood at the bow of the middle boat.

'I have been sent by my master to invite you onto the lake to enjoy the moon,' he announced. Then he jumped onto the bank and bowed before Qian Long.

Qian Long nodded slightly. 'Excellent,' he said, and stepped onto the boat. Commander Li, Bai, and thirty or forty Imperial Guards promptly boarded the boats with him. More than a dozen of the guards were expert swimmers, and Bai ordered them to keep their wits about them.

They started out across the lake, which was a fairyland of lights, with pleasure boats everywhere, bedecked with lanterns that filled the darkness like stars in the night sky. The sound of music floated across towards them. A small sampan darted into view then turned and led the boats across the water to a large flotilla of other craft. Despite the huge number of troops they had stationed around the shore, Bai and the other guards were uneasy at the sight of such a powerful force, and all covertly felt for the weapons they had hidden on their persons.

'So you decided to come, my friend,' Helmsman Chen called from a nearby boat. 'Please come aboard!' He too was keeping up the 'incognito' pretence, indulging the Emperor's charade.

The two boats drew alongside each other and Qian Long, Commander Li, Bai, and several other guards jumped across. Bai and the others relaxed when they saw that Chen and his attendant, Xin Yan, were the only other people on the boat. The cabin was spacious, with exquisite murals decorating the walls. The table in the centre was set with wine-cups, bowls, and chopsticks, and was covered with dishes of fruit, a wide variety of wines, and all manner of delicious-looking things to eat.

Helmsman Chen and his guest shook hands and smiled broadly, then sat down facing each other. Commander Li, Bai, and the others stood behind Qian Long.

Helmsman Chen smiled briefly at Bai and noticed a handsome-faced youth standing behind Commander Li, whom he recognized to his surprise as Hidden Needle Lu's young disciple. He wondered what the youth was doing in the company of all these court officials.

Xin Yan poured some wine, and Helmsman Chen, afraid that Qian Long would be suspicious, drained his own cup first, then began eating. Qian Long picked at a few of the dishes that Chen had already tried, then put down his chopsticks. He heard a flute on a neighbouring boat playing the tune 'A Welcome to the Honoured Guest.'

'You are truly a man of culture,' he said to Chen. 'It is amazing that you have managed to lay on such a sumptuous reception at such short notice.'

Chen dismissed the praise. 'One cannot drink wine without music,' he said. 'I understand that the Lady Beautiful Jade has the finest voice in all Zhejiang Province. Shall I ask her to sing for us?'

Qian Long clapped his hands in approval. 'Tell me, who is this Beautiful Jade?' he asked, turning to Commander Li.

'She is one of Hangzhou's most famous courtesans,' replied Li. 'I have heard that she is very haughty by nature and if she doesn't feel like it, she won't even show herself in public, let alone sing, no matter how much she is offered.'

'Have you ever seen her yourself?' Qian Long asked.

'I… As a matter of fact, no, Majesty, I haven't,' Li replied, extremely embarrassed.

Leopard Wei escorted Beautiful Jade out. Qian Long looked admiringly at the perfect whiteness of her skin and her deliciously petite figure, though he found her face not particularly to his liking. It was her eyes that caught his attention the most forcefully. They were so full of life. As she looked around the cabin, her glance contained an intimate greeting for every person there.

Helmsman Chen stretched out his hand towards Qian Long. 'This is my new friend Dongfang,' he said. Beautiful Jade greeted him, then sat down next to Chen and cuddled up to him.

'I hear you sing very well,' said Helmsman Chen. 'I wonder if you would allow us the pleasure of enjoying your talent?'

'If you want to hear me sing, I will gladly sing for three days and three nights without stopping. But I am afraid you'd only tire of me.' An attendant handed her a piba and, with a light strum, she began:

> *Outside the window all is quiet and still;*
> *You kneel before the bedstead eager for a kiss.*
> *I scold you, call you heartless, and I turn away,*
> *But despite my words I'm still half inclined to love.*

Helmsman Chen applauded enthusiastically. Qian Long, hearing her smooth, clear voice, felt a warm feeling rising in his chest. Beautiful Jade smiled, then began strumming the piba again. This time she turned to Qian Long:

> *I want to beat you!*
> *Don't think I'm joking,' sang the girl.*
> *'I clench my teeth;*
> *This time I really will.*
> *But if I hit you softly,*
> *You won't fear me.*
> *And I cannot bear*
> *To hit you hard.*
> *Oh, my lover,*
> *Perhaps I won't hit you after all…*

The Emperor was completely carried away by the song. 'If you want to hit me,' he cried, 'then hit me!'

Qian Long had been born and raised deep in the stuffy confines of the Imperial Palace. He had come across many girl singers, but all of them had been dignified and monotonous, nothing like this southern Chinese courtesan. He was entranced by her eyes and captivated by her seductive charm. Everything—the song, the perfumed lake, the moon's reflection—it all conspired to make the scene more and more dreamlike, so much so that gradually he forgot entirely that he was the Emperor, and that he was in the company of a gang of notorious bandits.

Beautiful Jade poured some wine for Helmsman Chen and for Qian Long and the two drank three cups in quick succession while Beautiful Jade drank one to keep them company. Qian Long took a jade ring from his finger and gave it to her.

'Sing another song,' he said. Beautiful Jade looked down and giggled, revealing two adorable little dimples. Qian Long's heart melted.

'All right,' she said. 'For you.' She fluttered her eyelids at him, then struck up another tune on the piba. This time, the rhythm was fast and light with a complex melody, and Qian Long shouted out his approval.

She sang of a poor man with ambitions who gradually climbed his way up in the world, first obtaining clothes, then a house, then a wife and concubines, and then power. Finally, he began to covet the throne of the Emperor himself.

Helmsman Chen laughed heartily, but as the song progressed, Qian Long's expression became increasingly dour.

'Could this girl know who I really am,' he wondered to himself. 'Is she singing this song to make fun of me?'

Beautiful Jade finished the song and slowly put down her piba.

'The song makes fun of poor men,' she said with a smile. 'Both of you, sirs, are wealthy gentlemen with large mansions, lovely wives, and beautiful concubines. You would not know of such things.'

Qian Long laughed, and his eyes travelled over her, taking in her softness, the fun-loving spirit that radiated from her eyes. He wondered how he should go about telling Commander Li to have her brought to the Yamen, and how he could ensure the affair remained secret.

He suddenly heard Helmsman Chen speak. 'The great Emperor Xuanzong of the Tang dynasty had a great interest in beautiful women. That in itself is not significant. But he should never have allowed himself to put his weakness for women above the interests of the nation.'

'The Emperor Xuanzong,' Qian Long replied, 'was at first a wise ruler, but he became muddle-headed in his later years. He was far inferior to his ancestor, Emperor Taizong.'

'Taizong was certainly a very capable ruler,' agreed Chen.

The two men Qian Long most venerated throughout history were Emperor Wu of the Han dynasty and Emperor Taizong of the Tang dynasty. Both had greatly expanded the Empire, and their reputations had carried far beyond their country's borders. Ever since he had ascended the Throne, Qian Long had worked single-mindedly to emulate them and had sent armies out on long expeditions to the Muslim border regions with the intention of carrying on their work. He saw himself very much as an empire-builder in their mould.

'Emperor Taizong was a wise and courageous man,' he said. 'The barbarians cringed in fear at the sound of his name. He was proficient in both letters and war. Such talent would be hard to equal.'

'I have read Emperor Taizong's works,' said Helmsman Chen. 'He makes some points which I feel are very true.'

'Such as?'

'He said: "The ruler can be compared to a boat, and the common people to water. The water can either support the boat or it can sink it."'

Qian Long was silent.

'Sitting as we are in this boat, the metaphor could not be more apt,' continued Helmsman Chen. 'If we row smoothly, we will have a very smooth ride. But if we row about in a frenzied, disorderly manner, or if the water should rush by in a raging torrent, the boat will certainly capsize.'

His words contained not only the implication that the people could overthrow the Emperor whenever they wished, but also the more immediate threat of throwing Qian Long into the water there and then. Never in his life had Qian Long had such threatening words addressed to him. His anger surged up and, unable to control himself, he threw his wine-cup to the floor.

The cup flew downwards, but just as it was about to hit the deck, Xin Yan shot out and caught it. He presented it to Qian Long on bended knee. 'Sir,' he said, 'you seem to have dropped your cup.'

The speed of his move startled Qian Long. Commander Li took the cup from Xin Yan and watched for some sign from the Emperor's eyes. But Qian Long composed himself and laughed.

'My friend, this young helper of yours is certainly a very agile little fellow,' he said. He turned to one of his guards. 'Play with him,' he said.

The guard, who was named Fan, bent down and struck out at Xin Yan with his pair of large swords. Xin Yan performed a nimble backward somersault and landed on the bow of the boat.

'Let's play chase,' he said to Fan with a smile. 'You catch me; then I'll have lost and I'll have to chase you.'

Fan was furious at having missed his target and bounded after him, but the boy soared off through the air like a great bird, landing on a small sampan nearby. The two chased each other across more than a dozen boats before Fan finally cornered Xin Yan at the end of a string of three boats. He thrust the sword in his left hand at Xin Yan's chest. Xin Yan countered by striking out with his fist at Fan's stomach. Fan then leapt up in the air, aiming to fall on Xin Yan from above. But as he jumped, the boatman, Crocodile Jiang, twirled his oar and spun the boat around. Fan shouted in fear as the boat disappeared from under him, and he splashed heavily into the lake. Xin Yan clapped in delight.

Two of Qian Long's guards dived into the lake to save Fan, who was desperately thrashing about in the water. Meanwhile, Crocodile Jiang placed his oar in front of him. Fan grabbed it and held on tight. Jiang then swung the oar up, tossing Fan back towards Qian Long's boat. 'Catch!' he shouted. A guard ran to the bow and caught him. Another guard, named Long, stepped forward.

'I understand this young lad is also very proficient with missiles,' he said darkly as Xin Yan moved back to Chen's side. 'Does he want to try me out for size?'

'You and I are already friends,' Chen said to Qian Long. 'We should not allow our servants to disturb the pleasant atmosphere with their bickering. As this gentleman is an expert in the use of darts, let us ask him to display his talent on something other than my page-boy. What do you think?'

'Fine, except we don't have a target,' Qian Long replied.

Xin Yan leapt over onto the boat on which Iron Pagoda Yang was sitting and whispered something in his ear. Yang nodded, waved to Hunchback Zhang in the next sampan, and pointed to another boat nearby. 'Grab the end of that boat,' he said, and took hold of the other end himself. 'Up!' he shouted and the two lifted the little boat out of the water while their own boats sank lower. The others gasped at this awesome display of strength.

'Master, will this do as a target?' Xin Yan shouted. 'Please come and make a bullseye on it.'

Helmsman Chen raised his wine-cup, drained it, then flung it at the boat. It sliced into the wood without shattering, embedding itself neatly in the keel. The onlookers clapped and cheered. Bai and the other guards frowned at the sight of such phenomenal power: a man whose Inner Force kungfu allowed him to drive a porcelain cup into a boat keel as if it were a steel dart was a formidable opponent.

'Use the cup as the target,' Helmsman Chen suggested, smiling. The guard Long silently pulled five spiked balls from his bag and threw them one after the other. They struck the target with a quick rat-a-tat, and slivers of porcelain flew in all directions.

Xin Yan slipped out from behind the boat. 'Not bad!' he shouted.

The guard Long was suddenly overcome by a malicious impulse, and he threw another five of the spiked balls at Xin Yan himself.

A shout of surprise went up from the others. In his fright, Xin Yan lunged to one side, but one of the spiked balls struck his left shoulder. There was no pain, but the shoulder immediately went numb. The Red Flower heroes now edged their little boats forward, all eager to match themselves against the offending guard.

The other Imperial Guards were ashamed that one of their number should have used such a low trick against a boy in the presence of the Emperor. But protecting His Majesty was of overriding importance, and they immediately pulled out their weapons. Commander Li gave a sharp whistle, signalling the troops on the shore to mobilize.

'Brothers!' Helmsman Chen called. 'We cannot show any impoliteness towards my honoured guest. Move back, all of you.'

The Red Flower heroes rowed back several yards. Iron Pagoda Yang and Hunchback Zhang had already put the target boat back into the water, and Luo Bing was busy inspecting Xin Yan's wound. Mastermind Xu also jumped over to see how he was.

'Don't worry, it's not painful,' Xin Yan said. 'Just very itchy.'

He moved his hand up to scratch the wound and Mastermind Xu quickly stopped him. He could see that the spiked ball had been dipped in a very powerful poison.

'Let go of me!' Xin Yan began yelling. 'It's unbearably itchy!' He struggled with all his might to break free.

'Be patient for a moment,' said Xu, trying not to look as worried as he felt. He turned to Luo Bing. 'Ask Brother Zhao to come over.'

Another boat moved swiftly up alongside with the Red Flower Society's Hangzhou Lodge Master, Ma Shanjun, standing at the prow. He leapt over next to Xu and whispered: 'Brother Xu, the whole lake is surrounded by Manchu troops, including several crack units from the Imperial Guard.'

'How many men altogether?'

'Seven or eight thousand. And that's not counting the reserve forces waiting further away.'

'Go and call together all the Brothers in Hangzhou and surrounding areas,' said Xu. 'Tell them to gather near the lake and await orders. Also tell them to have a red flower hidden on their persons.'

Ma nodded.

'How many can you get together immediately?' Xu asked.

'Including the workers from my factories, about two thousand,' he replied.

'Two thousand of our Brothers should be enough to deal with fifteen thousand of them,' said Xu, 'considering a lot of the Chinese troops are Society members. We have no time to lose.'

Ma nodded and left.

Meanwhile Buddha Zhao's boat glided over. He examined Xin Yan's wound and frowned deeply. He carefully pulled out the poisonous spiked ball, then took a large bolus from his bag and placed it directly into the open wound. He looked up at Mastermind Xu.

'There's nothing more I can do,' he said in a despairing voice. 'The poison is extremely potent. No one can save him now except the man responsible.'

'How long can he hold on?' asked Xu, greatly frightened.

'At the most, six hours.'

'Brother Zhao, let's force the man to deliver the antidote.'

In three great bounds Zhao leapt over to the boat in which Helmsman Chen and Qian Long were sitting, with each bound touching down on the deck of a different boat. He spoke to Chen, and as he spoke he pointed to the guard Long.

'Sir,' he said. 'I would like to ask this gentleman here to acquaint me with some of his tricks.'

Helmsman Chen, who was himself furious at the wounding of Xin Yan, turned to Qian Long.

'This friend of mine is also quite good with projectiles,' he said. 'It would be interesting to see him and your man matched against each other.'

The Emperor was always game to watch any spectacle—the more dangerous the better. 'Go on,' he said to the guard Long. 'But make sure you don't lose.' Long bowed.

'That's Thousand Arm Buddha,' whispered Bai. 'Be careful.'

Guard Long knew the name well, and shuddered at the thought of facing him. But at the same time he had confidence in his own ability. He had never yet met his equal in the field of projectiles. 'This is just between you and me,' he said to Buddha Zhao.

'Do you think we mean to trick you?' protested Zhao angrily.

Guard Long leapt onto the prow of a boat nearby.

Zhao sent off a flurry of darts and sleeve arrows after him, and Long's heart froze at the sight of the speed with which Zhao operated. He threw himself down onto the deck and the darts struck the boat with a quick succession of popping noises.

Guard Long jumped up again and, spotting Zhao's figure in the moonlight, flung a dart at him. Zhao dodged to the right to avoid it, and suddenly found three poisoned spiked balls winging towards him. He leant over backwards and the spiked balls whizzed past the tip of his nose. Three more spiked balls followed in quick succession. Zhao deflected two of them into the water with darts of his own, then caught the third and placed it inside his gown.

Guard Long leapt towards another boat and Zhao threw a boomerang-shaped blade after him. The guard ducked and watched in surprise as the blade swirled over him and returned to Zhao's hand. Fascinated by the sight of the strange weapon, the guard failed to notice two other darts flying towards him which simultaneously struck both his shoulders. His body went limp and he fell to his knees.

The Imperial Guards were astounded to see him fall. One of Long's comrades, a man named Chu who earlier in his life had been a monk, raced over to defend him, but another swordsman intercepted him. Chu saw in the moonlight that the man was dressed in Taoist robes.

'Who are you?' he barked.

It was Father Speckless. 'Do you mean to say you are a swordsman and you don't know me?' he asked with a smile.

The guard Chu attacked with a move known as Buddha Ambushing the Tiger, followed by a stroke from the sequence known as the Nine Successions.

'That's very good,' said Father Speckless, still smiling. 'Now continue with a Golden Wheel stroke.'

As he spoke, Chu was indeed following through with a Golden Wheel stroke. He wondered how the old priest could possibly have known. The priest went on to guess his next two moves correctly, just as if he was a teacher instructing a pupil. Chu retreated two paces and stared at him, embarrassed.

Meanwhile, Buddha Zhao had grabbed Long and was pressuring him to hand over the antidote. Long closed his eyes and said nothing, thinking to himself that as long as he did not give in, the Emperor would be sure to reward him when they got back.

Father Speckless continued his game of forcing Chu to counter with the moves he called out. Qian Long, although no more than a mediocre fighter himself, had a thorough knowledge of kungfu, and found the whole spectacle entertaining. He also felt a little anxious for his own men. Chu was one of his top guards, he thought to himself. What use were guards if these bandits were able to play with them in such an effortless fashion? He watched a few more moves and then decided he had had enough.

'Tell him to come here,' he said to Bai.

'Guard Chu,' Bai shouted. 'The Master asks you to come here.'

Chu breathed a sigh of relief. The Emperor's order was like a reprieve from a death sentence, and he prepared to jump away. Father Speckless, however, had other ideas.

'Just a moment,' he said. He struck forward with his sword and Chu felt a cool breeze course across his face and body as the sword flashed about him. The courtesan Beautiful Jade suddenly laughed out loud, and Chu looked down and saw that his clothes had been cut to shreds by the priest's sword. Not only that: he felt his head and found his hair and queue had been shaved completely off. As he shook with fear and shame, his trousers suddenly fell down.

'These friends of yours are extraordinarily skilled in the Martial Arts, my friend,' Qian Long said to Helmsman Chen. 'Why don't you all offer your services to the Court? It seems such a pity to waste all this talent.'

Helmsman Chen smiled. 'We prefer to do just as we please,' he said. 'But thank you. We are very grateful for the offer.'

'Since that is how you feel, I will take my leave. It is getting late.' Qian Long looked meaningfully over at the guard Long who was still in Buddha Zhao's hands in the other boat.

'Brother Zhao,' Chen called. 'Set my guest's man free.'

'Absolutely not!' Luo Bing answered. 'He poisoned Xin Yan, and he refuses to hand over the antidote.'

Qian Long whispered some instructions to Commander Li, then turned to Long. 'Give him the antidote,' he ordered.

'I'm afraid I didn't bring the antidote with me,' replied Long. 'I left it in Peking.'

'Brother Zhao,' said Mastermind Xu, 'give me those two spiked balls.' Buddha Zhao pulled them out of his bag and handed them over. Xu ripped Long's gown off his chest and drove the balls into his flesh. Long cried out in pain and terror.

'Master,' shouted Mastermind Xu. 'Please send over some wine. We want to drink a toast with our friend here to seal our friendship, and then we will let him go.'

'Very well,' said Helmsman Chen. Beautiful Jade filled three cups with wine, and Chen threw them one by one over to the other boat. Buddha Zhao calmly stretched out his hand and caught them. Not a drop of the wine was spilled.

Mastermind Xu took one of the cups. 'Let us drink a toast,' he said. Long knew that the alcohol would greatly accelerate the effects of the poison and clamped his mouth shut.

'Go on, have a drink,' said Mastermind Xu with a smile. 'There's no need to stand on ceremony.' Zhao grabbed Long's nose between two of his fingers, then pressed strongly on his cheeks with his thumb and forefinger, forcing him to open his mouth. He poured all three cups of wine down his throat.

Long decided his life was more important than his reputation. 'Let me go,' he said. 'I...I...I'll get the antidote.' Zhao laughed and loosened his grip. Long pulled three packets of medicine from his bag.

'The red one should be swallowed, the black one sucks out the poison, and the white one closes the wound,' he said and promptly fainted away.

Buddha Zhao hurriedly poured the red medicine into one of the wine-cups, mixed it with some lake water for Xin Yan to drink, then spread the black medicine onto the wound. A moment later, black blood welled out of the gash. Luo Bing wiped it up as it appeared, and gradually the blood regained its red colour. Xin Yan cried out in pain as Zhao administered the white medicine.

'Please forgive my friends for their rough and ready ways,' Helmsman Chen said to Qian Long.

Qian Long laughed. 'It has certainly been an interesting evening. I will take my leave now.'

'My guest wishes to go home,' Helmsman Chen called out. 'Head back to the shore!'

The flotilla glided slowly off, and soon reached the lakeside. Commander Li jumped ashore and helped Qian Long across onto land as the guards formed a protective semi-circle. Then Li pulled out a pipe and blew three sharp notes on it. Several hundred Imperial troops appeared.

'You insolent wretches!' Li shouted at the Red Flower Society fighters. 'You are in the presence of His Majesty the Emperor and still you don't kowtow?'

At this very moment, at a gesture from Mastermind Xu, Lodge Master Ma and his son fired flares up into the air above the lake. Seconds later, a great roar went up on all sides, and a huge host of men rushed out from the trees, from behind the buildings that stood by the lakeside, and from under bridges. Each man had a red flower on his lapel and a sword in his hand.

'Brothers!' shouted Mastermind Xu. 'The Helmsman is here!' The Red Flower Society men roared their approval and surged forward.

The Imperial Guards and troops now drew their swords, fixed arrows to their bows, and the two sides turned to face each other, both determined not to yield. Commander Li mounted a horse and waited for Qian Long's order to launch the attack and seize the Red Flower Society fighters.

Helmsman Chen walked calmly over to an officer of the Imperial Guard and pointed to the horsewhip the man was holding. Hypnotized by Chen's gaze, the officer meekly dismounted and handed the whip over. Chen then leapt onto his horse and pulled a red flower from his pocket which he fixed to his gown. The flower was made of the finest silk stitched with gold thread, and the green leaves around it were studded with jewels which glittered and sparkled in the torchlight. It was the Helmsman's personal badge, and the Red Flower heroes bowed before him in respect.

Suddenly, a large number of government troops broke ranks and swarmed forward despite shouts from their officers. They raced over to Helmsman Chen, bowed, then ran back to their ranks as another batch ran out to pay their respects. The Red Flower Society's influence was widespread in the South, and large numbers of soldiers, especially those in units under Chinese command, were Society members.

Qian Long was flabbergasted at the sight of so many of his own troops breaking ranks to bow before this bandit chief. The Imperial Guard units he had brought with him from Peking were clearly the only men he could trust. Considering the danger of his position, he decided a fight had to be avoided at all costs.

'So these are the men you call your trusted soldiers,' he said coldly to Commander Li. 'Tell them to withdraw.'

'Yes, Majesty!' replied Li, trembling with fear. He ordered his troops back to camp.

'Brothers!' cried Mastermind Xu, when he saw that the soldiers were retreating. 'Thank you all for your trouble. You may all go home now.'

An answering roar thundered from the mass of the Society followers: 'Helmsman, farewell!' The roar echoed out over the lake.

Qian Long had the courtesy to remain civil to his host despite the débâcle. He bade Chen farewell. 'Thank you for a very pleasant outing on the lake,' he said. 'We will surely meet again.'

At the Grave-side

Helmsman Chen and the Red Flower heroes returned to the boats and ate and drank to their hearts' content. They had handed out a crushing defeat to the Imperial Guard, and were in good spirits.

'Brother Ma,' said Mastermind Xu to the Society's Hangzhou Lodge Master, Ma Shanjun. 'After such a setback, the Emperor certainly won't let matters rest. You should advise all the Red Flower Brothers in Hangzhou to be very careful, especially those serving as soldiers.'

Ma nodded and finishing off his cup of wine, departed with his son.

Helmsman Chen also drained his wine-cup and sighed as he watched the broken reflection of the moon floating on the lake between the lotus leaves.

'What date is it today?' he asked Mastermind Xu, looking up. 'We have been so busy lately, I've completely lost track of time.'

'It's the seventeenth. It was the Mid-Autumn festival the day before yesterday. Don't you remember?'

Helmsman Chen was silent for a moment, then said: 'Brothers, please go and get some sleep now, all of you. I will stay here for a while. Tomorrow, I have some private business to attend to, but the day after that we will begin preparations for rescuing Brother Wen.'

'Would you like anyone to accompany you?' asked Mastermind Xu.

'No, there's no need. There is no danger. I just want to be by myself and think things over.'

The boats moved to shore, and the Red Flower heroes bade farewell to Helmsman Chen. Some of them were already more than a little drunk, and they walked through the deserted streets of Hangzhou arm in arm, singing loudly into the darkness.

Helmsman Chen watched them go, then jumped into a small sampan and skulled the boat out over the mirror-smooth surface of the lake. The shore receded, and he stowed the oar and let the boat drift. He stared up at the moon. The next day was his mother's birthday. For ten years he had been away from home; and for much of that time, his mother had been dead. Now that he was back in southern China, and close to his home town of Haining, he remembered her kind, smiling face, and the thought of her death— the common fate that awaits all men—made the tears trickle down his face.

At first light, Helmsman Chen plucked the red flower from his gown and placed it in his bag. Then he strolled towards the eastern gate of Hangzhou. The guard on duty stared at him, then saluted: he was a Red Flower Society man himself. Chen nodded to him.

'Since you are leaving the city, will you be needing a horse, Helmsman?' the guard asked.

'Yes, I would be most grateful for one,' answered Chen. The guard went off, delighted to be able to serve his Helmsman, and came back a short time later with a horse. Following behind were two minor officials who both bowed respectfully before Chen. They also felt fortunate to have an opportunity to render a service to the Helmsman.

Chen mounted up and galloped off. The horse was a fast one and he reached the western gate of Haining city by noon. It had been ten years since he left his home town, but little had changed. He was afraid of meeting someone who might recognize him and, rather than enter the city, he turned his horse northwards and rode two or three miles further on. There he stopped at a farmhouse, where he was welcomed and served with a midday meal. Having eaten, he lay down to sleep. He had been up the whole of the previous night, and now he slept very deeply.

Noting the traveller's gentlemanly attire and the fact that he spoke the local dialect, the farmer and his wife treated Chen with great courtesy, and killed a chicken for the evening meal. Helmsman Chen questioned them about events of the past few years and the farmer said: 'The Emperor has ordered that the whole of Haining county be exempt from taxes for three years. It's all out of respect for the late Minister Chen.'

Chen reflected on the many years that had passed since his father had died, and wondered again why the Emperor had suddenly begun to bestow such handsome favours on his family. It was not the first time he had heard of such a thing. That evening, when he had eaten dinner, he gave three taels of silver to the farmer in thanks and rode back towards his family home in the northwest of the city.

As he reached the main gate of the house, he stopped in surprise. In the old days, it had been named Secluded Garden, but the old name board had been taken down and replaced with one which read Peaceful Pool Garden. The characters were rounded and flowing, and he recognized the calligraphy at once as being that of Emperor Qian Long himself. Perplexed, he leapt over the wall into the compound. Next to the old house that he remembered so well, new structures had been erected, an endless series of pavilions and platforms, mansions and chambers.

He passed along a covered walkway towards the compound he knew as Jade Bracelet Hall, but again found a new name board over its door, inscribed with the words Hall of Beloved Days, also written in Qian Long's hand. Chen frowned. The words 'Beloved Days' were always used to refer to the filial affection of children for their parents. What was the Emperor doing writing such a thing here?

He emerged from the hall and walked across a zig-zagging bridge with red railings into a thick bamboo grove towards the little hermitage that had always been known as Fragrant Bamboo Lodge, the former residence of his mother. This name board had also been changed, to Spring Sunshine Hall. 'Spring Sunshine' was another poetic allusion, this time used to describe a son's gratitude for his mother's love. It could have no other meaning.

Chen sat down on a rock, greatly confused in his mind. What did all this mean? Why had Qian Long written this name board for *his*—Chen's—mother's lodge?

'Surely he wouldn't have been so thoughtless,' Chen mused, perplexed. 'Could he have done it in an attempt to befriend me, knowing that I would come back here one day?'

That seemed far-fetched. He tiptoed up the steps, and looked through a window into the main room of the lodge. It was arranged exactly as it had been when his mother was alive, with redwood furniture, a large carved bed, a clothes chest inlaid with gold, all as he remembered them from ten years before. A red candle flickered on the table. Suddenly, he heard the sound of footsteps from an adjoining room and an old woman entered. It was his mother's personal maid, Nanny Huan. The woman had reared him, and Chen felt closer to her than to any of the other servants.

He jumped into the room through the open window and hugged the old woman.

Greatly frightened, she opened her mouth to scream, but Chen covered it with his hand and whispered: 'Sh! It's me!' She stared at him, too shocked to speak. In fact, he had changed so much in the ten years since he had left that at first she didn't know who he was.

'It's me, Jialuo. Don't you recognize me?' he asked.

'You...you're Master Jialuo? Have you come back?' the woman asked, completely confused.

Helmsman Chen smiled and nodded. She gradually came to her senses and could see the features of the mischievous child she had known in the past. At once she threw her arms round him and began to sob loudly. Chen hastily quietened her.

'Stop crying!' he said. 'No one must know that I've returned.'

'It doesn't matter,' she replied. 'They've all gone to the new compound. There's no one else here.'

'What new compound?'

'The one that was built earlier this year. Heaven knows what it cost, or what it's for.'

Chen knew that Nanny Huan had little understanding of such worldly matters. 'How did my mother die? What was her illness?' he asked.

The woman pulled out a handkerchief and wiped her eyes. 'Mistress was very unhappy, I don't know why. She didn't eat properly for days, and she became ill. It dragged on for more than a week before she passed away.' She began to cry quietly again. 'She kept calling for you. "Where's my Jialuo?" she used to say. "Hasn't he come yet? I want to see Jialuo!" She was calling out like that for two whole days before she died.'

Chen began to weep too. 'Where is her grave?'

'Behind the new Sea Goddess Temple,' she finally replied.

'Sea Goddess Temple?' Chen echoed.

'Yes, they built that in the spring too. It's huge, right on the embankment, by the sea front.'

'I'm going to have a look. I'll be back in a little while,' he said.

'No...no, you mustn't!' she interrupted hastily, but he had already leapt out through the window.

He knew the path down to the embankment well and was soon there. Looking west, he saw a huge structure that had certainly not been there before. This, he decided, must be the Sea Goddess Temple. He ran towards the main entrance.

Suddenly, he heard the sound of light footsteps, and darted behind a willow tree. Two men dressed in black clothes emerged from either side of the temple wall, saluted each other, and continued on in opposite directions around the temple. Chen was mystified. Just then, two more men appeared dressed in exactly the same fashion as the first pair and followed the same path round the temple wall. Even more curious, Chen waited for them to disappear around the corners of the building, then jumped silently up onto the wall. Another pair passed down below. He waited for a while and counted about forty men constantly circling the temple, all of them alert and silent, and all of them obviously kungfu experts. Could there be some very special religious ceremony going on inside, he wondered? Full of curiosity, he jumped quietly down into the courtyard and crept into the main temple building to investigate.

Incense smoke curled up from in front of the central altar, and candles flickered and danced. He wondered which god the altar was dedicated to, but when he looked up to see, he gasped out loud involuntarily. The handsome-faced statue standing on the altar was a likeness of his father.

He spotted an open door to the left and crept over. Looking out, he saw a long covered walkway paved with white flagstones. He knew that if he went along the white-stoned path he would easily be spotted, so he leapt onto the roof of the walkway and flitted silently down to its end. In front of him was another hall of worship, outside which was written in huge characters: The Palace of the Empress of Heaven. The doors to the hall were open and he went inside. As he caught sight of the statue on the central altar, he started again, this time even more violently. It had the face of his mother.

He felt lost in a thick fog of bewilderment and ran back outside, looking for his mother's grave. He saw a long yellow tent that had been erected behind the hall. He shrank into a corner as a sturdy black-clothed man passed by on patrol.

He had seen things that evening that beggared the imagination. Despite the strict guard being kept on the place, he was determined somehow to get to the heart of the matter. He crept slowly over to the yellow tent and crawled inside, then lay absolutely still and listened carefully. There were no sounds outside, and he concluded that he had not been discovered. He looked round and saw that the vast tent was completely deserted. The ground had been carefully flattened and the grass cleanly cut. The tent was joined to a string of others, forming a long tunnel that stretched back from the temple buildings. Two large lanterns burned brightly in every tent and, looking down the tunnel, the two rows of lights stretching away into the distance looked like fiery coiling dragons. He stood up and walked forward, as if in a dream.

Suddenly he heard the rustle of clothing up ahead and quickly hid to one side. After a moment, he continued making his way forward again until finally he spotted a man seated in front of two graves at the very end of the tunnel. The graves must have been those of his mother and father. He was about to run forward and prostrate himself when the seated man stood up, gazed at the graves for a while, then knelt down and bowed several times. The man had his back to him, but Chen could see that he was shaking, as if he was crying.

Chen's fears and suspicions evaporated: the man was clearly either a relative or one of his father's former subordinates. He walked quietly over and tapped him on the shoulder.

'Please get up,' he said.

The man started, but did not turn round.

'Who is it?' he cried harshly.

'I too have come to pay my respects,' Chen replied. He knelt before the graves.

'Mother, father,' he sobbed uncontrollably. 'I have come too late. I will never see you again.'

As he said this, the man beside him gasped. Chen turned, to find himself looking at none other than his newly made friend Dongfang, 'Orient', the Emperor Qian Long.

'What…what are you doing here in the middle of the night?' Qian Long asked in surprise.

'Today is my mother's birthday,' Chen replied. 'I have come to pay my respects to her. And you?'

Qian Long ignored the question. 'You mean…you are the son of Chen Shiguan?' he exclaimed incredulously.

'Yes. Didn't you know?'

Qian Long shook his head.

In the past few years, Qian Long had been bestowing extraordinary favours on the Chen family of Haining. Although some of his ministers were aware that the new leader of the Red Flower Society was a son of the late Minister Chen, none had dared to mention it because of the Emperor's unpredictable temper.

Chen could not understand why on earth the Emperor would come secretly to kneel and cry before the grave of a former minister. It was all completely inexplicable.

Qian Long took Helmsman Chen's hand. 'You must think it strange, seeing me here paying my respects in the middle of the night,' he said. 'Your father and I had great affection for each other, so I took advantage of this visit to the south to offer my thanks to him.'

Chen made a noncommittal sound. He was still totally in the dark.

'If word of this should get out, it would be extremely inconvenient,' Qian Long continued. 'Can you give me your word that you will not reveal it to anyone?'

Chen was deeply moved by Qian Long's reverence for his own mother and father. 'Set your mind at rest,' he replied. 'I will not mention this evening to anyone.'

Qian Long immediately breathed easier. The two men—one the Emperor of China, the other the leader of the country's largest secret society—shook hands. They were silent for a while, each occupied with his own thoughts. Far off, they heard a low roar like thunder.

'The tide is coming in,' said Chen. 'Let's go to the embankment and look at the tidal bore. It has been ten years since I saw it.'

'Very well,' replied Qian Long, still holding Chen's hand. They walked out of the tent.

As the two of them emerged from the tent, the guards outside rushed forward to wait on the Emperor, wondering how his companion could have entered without their being aware of it. The old man Bai Zhen, chief of the Emperor's guard, and the other officers shook with fear when they saw that the man in question was none other than the notorious Helmsman of the Red Flower Society. One of the guards led the Emperor's horse across.

'You take my horse,' Qian Long said to Chen. The guards hurriedly led over another horse and the two men rode out of the temple gate side by side.

The roar of the ocean filled their ears. They dismounted and gazed out at the pale silvery moonlight reflected off the water.

Qian Long stared at the waves for a long time, then said: 'Fate seems determined to throw us together. Tomorrow, I will return to Hangzhou, and after three more days there, I will continue back to Peking. Why don't you come with me? I'd like to have you always by my side. Seeing you is almost like seeing your father.'

Chen was surprised by the warmth of his words.

'You have distinguished yourself both in scholarship and in the Martial Arts,' Qian Long continued. 'It would be easy to promote you to your father's former post, which would be ten thousand times better than you hiding yourself away in the underworld. Give up your life of crime, and come with me. I will make it worth your while.'

'I am extremely grateful to you for your goodwill,' Chen said. 'But if what I coveted was great wealth, I would never have left home in the first place.'

'Why *did* you leave? Why did you insist on mixing in the underworld, instead of following the path that every nobleman follows, the path of officialdom and success? Was it that you couldn't get on with your father and brother?'

'No, it wasn't that. It was the wish of my mother. My father and elder brother knew nothing of it. They spent a lot of time and effort looking for me.'

'Your *mother* told you to leave home? That is truly strange. Why would she do such a thing?'

Helmsman Chen hung his head. 'It was the result of some tragedy she suffered. I am not too clear about it myself.'

'The Chen family has distinguished itself through many generations,' said Qian Long. 'During the last three hundred years alone, more than two hundred members of your family have done well in the Imperial examinations. Three have served as prime ministers, and eleven have filled other senior official posts. The number is extraordinary. Your father was an honest and hard-working man. He often used to plead before my father on behalf of the common people, weeping tears of compassion as he did so. My father sometimes used to joke and say: "Minister Chen Shiguan was sobbing again today. I suppose I'll have to agree to what he says."'

Hearing of his father's conduct as an official, Chen was both saddened and pleased, both angry and proud. 'He wept before the Emperor, and I steal military grain,' he thought. 'Our methods are different, but our goals are the same.'

They stood and watched the tide thunder in at the bore.

'I would like to give you a piece of advice,' Qian Long said. 'The actions of the Red Flower Society have come very close to rebellion. Past behaviour I can ignore, but from now on you must not continue to disregard the law like that. I will not tolerate it.'

'Everything we do is for the good of the country and the common people,' replied Helmsman Chen.

Qian Long sighed. After a moment, he continued: 'As a result of our meeting tonight, I promise you one thing: when we destroy the Red Flower Society, you will be spared.'

'In that case, I too will make you a promise: if you should ever fall into the hands of the Red Flower Society, we will not harm you either.'

Qian Long laughed. 'You refuse to give an inch, even before the Emperor. All right, it's been said now. We should put our fists together and swear that from today onwards neither shall harm the other.'

The two men stretched out their arms and touched fists three times.

'With such a strong tide, if the sea embankment is not renovated, the homes and graves of the common people will sooner or later be flooded,' Qian Long said. 'I must arrange for it to be reconstructed.'

'That would be the act of a ruler who loves his subjects,' Chen replied. 'They will be very grateful to you.'

Qian Long nodded. 'Your father performed great services for his country. I could not bear to see his grave swallowed up by the sea.'

He took Chen's hand and started walking along the embankment with him. The guards wanted to follow, but he waved them back.

'I can see from your expression that you are still unhappy,' he said as they strolled along. 'Apart from your grief for your parents, what else is there that troubles you? You may be unwilling to become an official, but if you have any requests, I will do my best to comply with them.'

Chen was silent for a moment. 'There is one thing…but I doubt if you would agree.'

'Any request you make will be granted.'

'Really?'

'I promise. I never joke about such things.'

'Then I ask you to release my sworn brother, Wen Tailai.'

Qian Long stared at him in utter dismay. This was certainly not the sort of request he had in mind. For a moment, he was at a loss.

'How has Brother Wen offended you?' asked Helmsman Chen.

'I cannot release him,' replied the Emperor. 'But since I have made you a promise, I cannot go back on my word. I will agree never to kill him, whatever the circumstances.'

'Then we shall have no choice but to use force to rescue him,' replied Helmsman Chen. 'I asked you to release him not because we are unable to rescue him, but simply to avoid the use of force, and the damage it would do to our friendship. If we wish to rescue him, have no doubt, we can.'

Qian Long had witnessed the might of the Red Flower Society, and he knew this was no empty boast.

'I respect your devotion to your friend,' he said. 'But I tell you in all honesty, I simply cannot allow this man out of my grasp. If you go ahead with this threat of yours, if you insist on trying to rescue him, then three days from now I will have no choice but to kill him.'

Helmsman Chen could feel his blood boiling. 'Kill Brother Wen, and you will never sleep easy again,' he threatened.

'And if I don't kill him, I will never sleep easy either.'

'Now I see that being Emperor must be a heavy burden to bear. Heavier by far than the carefree life that I lead.'

'How old are you?' Qian Long asked.

'Twenty-five.'

'It is not your carefree life I envy you. It is your youth. But that is of no consequence. One day we will all of us turn to dust, no matter what our achievements.'

The two strolled on for a time.

'How many wives do you have?' Qian Long asked. Without waiting for an answer, he plucked a piece of jade from his gown and offered it to Chen, saying: 'This is a priceless piece of jade. Give it to one of your wives.'

Chen did not take it. 'I am not yet married,' he said.

Qian Long laughed. 'You always set your sights too high. Give it to the lady you love as a wedding present, then.'

Chen accepted the stone. The jade emanated a pale radiance in the moonlight and holding it in his hand he found it slightly warm to the touch. He realized it was a piece of the incalculably valuable variety of jade known as 'warm jade'. 'I thank you for the present,' he said, placing it in his pocket. 'We will meet again.' He saluted with clasped fists, mounted his horse, and started off.

Qian Long waved goodbye to him. 'Take good care of yourself!' he shouted.

The Dwarf Magician and the Jade Vases

Forcing himself to put aside thoughts of family and home, Helmsman Chen rode back to the Red Flower Society's mansion near Hangzhou where he found everyone gathered around Melancholy Ghost Shi, who had just arrived back from Peking. Shi immediately broke free from the group and bowed before Helmsman Chen.

'I found out in Peking that the Emperor had come south,' said Shi, 'and travelled day and night to get here to tell you only to find that the Brothers had not only seen him, but had clashed with his men as well.'

'You've had a hard trip, Brother Shi,' replied Chen. 'Did you hear any other news while you were there?'

'Once I heard that the Emperor was here,' replied Shi, 'I disregarded everything else.'

Chen deduced from his haggard look that he was worn out after the hard ride. 'Go and get a good sleep,' he said. 'We'll talk again later.'

Shi bowed and took his leave. As he passed Luo Bing, he said: 'That white horse of yours is very fast. But don't worry, I took good care of him. Oh—' He stopped again. 'I saw the horse's previous owner, Han Wenchong, on the road.'

'What? Did he want his horse back?'

'He didn't see me. I came across him at a tavern in Yangzhou with several other guards from the Zhen Yuan Agency. I heard them cursing our Red Flower Society, so I went across and eavesdropped. They said all sorts of insulting things about us, and accused us of killing that guard called Tong.'

Mastermind Xu and Zhou Qi smiled at each other. 'What is the Zhen Yuan Agency up to this time?' Xu asked.

'I gathered that they were escorting a consignment of valuable gifts presented by the Emperor to the Chen family of Haining.' Melancholy Ghost Shi turned to Chen. 'It was for your family, Helmsman, so I told the local Society leader to discreetly make sure it was delivered safely.'

'Thank you,' Chen replied, smiling. 'For once we can work together with the Zhen Yuan Agency.'

'The head of the Agency is with them, which shows the importance they attach to the consignment.'

Helmsman Chen and the others were astonished to learn that the North China Earth-Shaker Wang Weiyang was escorting this consignment personally.

'Wang hasn't escorted a consignment like this for more than ten years,' said Lord Zhou. 'Helmsman, your family obviously has enormous prestige.'

'I thought it strange too at first,' added Shi. 'But later I learned that apart from the valuables for the Helmsman's family, they were also carrying a pair of jade vases.'

'Jade vases?' asked Helmsman Chen.

'Yes, treasures from the Uighur regions. The Uighurs scored a victory over General Zhao Hui's army, but with the Manchu forces so powerful, they know they can't hold out against them for much longer. So they have sent the vases as a peace offering.'

The heroes excitedly asked Shi for details of the Uighur victory.

'What I heard was that General Zhao Hui's troops starved for several days as a result of our stopping their new supplies from reaching them, and finally had to retreat. The Uighurs organized an ambush on the road and killed two or three thousand of them.' At this the Red Flower heroes clapped and laughed. 'The Manchu army finally did receive more supplies,' Shi continued, 'and began to advance again, but I didn't hear any further news. The Uighurs sent an envoy to Peking with the peace offering, but the court officials there didn't dare to make a decision. They sent him and the vases down south for the Emperor to deal with.'

'The vases won't make any difference,' said Helmsman Chen. 'No matter what valuable treasures they send, he will never agree to peace.'

'I heard the Agency men say that if peace was agreed to, the vases were to be kept,' Shi added. 'If not, they were to be returned. So it's vital that they should not be damaged in any way.'

Chen glanced at Mastermind Xu, and the two walked away from the main group into a side chamber.

'Brother Xu, last night I saw the Emperor. He told me that he would be returning to Peking in three days' time, and that before he left he intended to kill Brother Wen.'

'Then we must lose no time,' replied Xu.

'The Emperor is probably not back in Hangzhou yet. Most of the top fighters are with him, so it should be relatively easy to rescue Wen if we make a move now.'

'The Emperor isn't in Hangzhou?'

Chen told him about their meeting in Haining. Xu fiddled meditatively with the writing-brushes and paper on the tabletop in front of them. He was thinking hard.

'The only plan I can see at the moment is to steal the jade vases,' said Xu finally. 'Since the Emperor has already sent a huge army out west, he is certain to be unwilling to talk peace, which means he will have to return the vases. If he is unable to do so, then his word will lose all credibility, and the Emperor, as we know, is obsessed with his own prestige.'

'Yes!' exclaimed Helmsman Chen. 'Once we have the jade vases, we can go to him and say that if he touches a single hair on Brother Wen's head, we will smash them.'

'Exactly! We may not be able to exchange the vases for Brother Wen, but we can at least delay things for a few days, which will also help the Hodja and his Uighurs.'

'Very well then,' said Chen. 'So we must go after the North China Earth-Shaker, Wang Weiyang.'

Wang Weiyang was sixty-nine years old. The Zhen Yuan Security Agency, which he had built up with his own hands, had prospered in North China for more than thirty years in spite of strong and sometimes violent opposition. Everywhere they went Wang's Eight Trigrams swordplay and his Eight Trigrams fist kungfu were a byword. There was a saying in the fighting community: 'You'd be better off bumping into the Devil than into old Wang.' He had planned to retire from business altogether and live a quiet life. But after the fiasco with the Koran, which General Zhao Hui had commissioned them to transport safely, and which had then been stolen from them, when the Agency was entrusted with the task of escorting these priceless jade vases to the Emperor himself, he decided to accompany the consignment personally. In view of the diplomatic sensitivity of the mission, he gave it top priority. From each of his Agency branches, he detailed six top fighters, while the Court also supplied a number of Imperial Guards to accompany the Uighur envoy on his journey south. Precautions along the way were extremely strict, and so far there had been no incidents of any kind.

Noon was approaching as the contingent arrived at a town less than three miles from Hangzhou. The Agency men went into the largest restaurant and ordered food. They were jubilantly discussing how they planned to celebrate once they got to Hangzhou, when a horse neighed outside.

The Agency guard Han pricked up his ears. He ran out to find his own beloved white steed walking slowly past with a heavy load of firewood on its back. He tried to grab the reins, but the peasant with the horse gave the animal a rap on the rump and it cantered off down the street. Unwilling to give up, Han ran after them. Once outside the town, the horse turned off the road and galloped into the trees with Han following as best he could.

'Old Han's gone crazy thinking about that white horse of his,' laughed another of the Agency guards. 'Every time he sees a horse on the road with so much as a couple of white hairs, he has to chase after it to see if it's his. When he gets home tomorrow and sees his old lady's snow-white skin, I expect he'll think she's his horse too and jump straight in the saddle...'

The others exploded with laughter.

Just then, one of the waiters welcomed a new customer: 'Please sit over here, sir.'

A man who looked like a rich merchant entered, followed by four servants, one of them carrying a water-pipe. He seated himself at the table and a waiter hurriedly poured him a cup of tea, chattering: 'Try this Dragon Well tea, sir. It's made with fresh spring water brought in only yesterday.'

The merchant, whose name was Liang, grunted and said in a thick Hangzhou accent: 'Bring me a few slices of meat, a bowl of eel soup, and three catties of the best rice wine.'

The waiter bowed and a moment later the fragrance of hot wine assailed their nostrils as he returned with a large jug of it.

'Why is Han away so long?' asked Wang Weiyang.

Suddenly the main door of the restaurant was kicked open, and a dwarf shuffled in followed by a girl and a strong-looking young man, all three dressed in rough clothes.

The dwarf bowed in all four directions and announced: 'Ladies and gentlemen, I am a humble travelling player. I should like to do a few tricks to amuse you. If you are impressed, I'd be happy to accept your contribution. If you are not, please accept my apologies.'

He picked up a teacup from a table and covered it with his tattered hat. 'Change *this instant!*' he shouted, and whisked the hat away: the cup had disappeared. He waved the hat around in the air to show that the cup was not inside it.

Intrigued, Liang the merchant stood up and walked over to get a closer look.

'May I borrow your snuffbox for a moment, sir?' the dwarf asked him. Liang laughed and handed the snuffbox over. The dwarf placed it in his hat and made it disappear in the same way.

'You be careful, that snuffbox's very precious,' one of Liang's servants warned. 'Don't you go damaging it now.'

The dwarf smiled at the servant. 'Please be so kind as to look in your pocket, sir,' he replied. The servant felt in his coat pocket and pulled out the snuffbox.

Liang and his servants were amazed, as were the Agency guards and Imperial Guards. Everybody now crowded round to watch the dwarf's conjuring. Liang pulled a jade ring off his left hand and handed it to him saying: 'Make this disappear too.'

The dwarf put the ring on the table, covered it with his hat, and blew on it.

'West is east and east is west! Topsy-turvy like the rest!' he shouted and whipped away the hat. The ring had disappeared. The onlookers gasped.

'Please be so good as to feel in your pocket, sir,' the dwarf said. Liang put his hand in his pocket, pulled the ring out, and stared at it in surprise.

'Excellent, excellent!' he cried.

Several dozen people had entered the restaurant by this time, to see what was going on, including a number of army officers.

'There's nothing so special about a trick like that!' complained one of the officers. 'Let's see if you dare to make *this* disappear.' He slapped an official document down on the table. The onlookers could see that it was marked 'Urgent Dispatch for Excellency Wang, Board of War, Peking.' It had been sent from the Yamen of the Zhejiang Provincial Commander-in-Chief Li, and was being taken north to Peking by a military escort.

'Please don't be offended if I say no, sir,' the dwarf replied. 'I may earn my living in a rather disreputable way, but I'd never dare touch something official like that.'

'Oh go on!' Liang urged the dwarf. 'It's only a game. Go on, make it disappear.' He turned to his servants. 'Give me five taels of silver,' he said. One of the servants pulled an ingot of silver from a bag and handed it to Liang, who placed it on the table. 'Make that thing on the table disappear, and this silver ingot is yours,' he said to the dwarf.

The dwarf looked at the ingot, then turned and held a whispered conversation with the girl behind him.

'I seem to have found some more courage,' he finally said. He proceeded to cover the document with his hat, and shouted the words: 'Change! Change *this instant*!' His hand pointed left and right, up and down, and finally settled on the leather case that contained the Uighur jade vases. 'In you go! In you go! Into *that case*!' he cried, and picked up the hat. The document had indeed disappeared.

'He's really got quite a talent, this turtle,' the officer commented. The dwarf bowed before Merchant Liang.

'Thank you for your contribution,' he said, then picked up the ingot and handed it to the girl standing behind him. The crowd clapped in approval.

'All right, now let's have the dispatch back,' said the officer.

The dwarf smiled. 'It's in the leather case. Just open the case and have a look,' he replied. All the Agency men jumped up in shock as he said these words. The case was sealed with the Imperial seal. No one dared to break it open. The officer went over and felt the case with his hand.

'Excuse me, my man,' said Wang Weiyang. 'The object in that case is a treasure belonging to the Imperial Court. It can on no account be touched.'

'You must be joking,' the officer replied and continued to feel the case.

'Who's joking? Back off a bit!' one of the Imperial Guards warned.

'Very well, sir,' the officer said. 'But be so good as to return the dispatch to me at once.'

'Enough of your tricks!' the Imperial Guard shouted at the dwarf. 'Give him back his dispatch, quick!'

'It's in the leather case. If you don't believe me, open it and see,' insisted the dwarf.

The officer flew into a rage. 'Hand it over!' he roared, punching him on the shoulder.

The dwarf assumed a sorrowful expression. 'Do you really think I would dare deceive you?' he said. 'The dispatch is there, inside the leather case. But I'm afraid I can't spirit it back out again!'

It was Merchant Liang who now intervened. He walked over to the Imperial Guard. 'What is your name, sir?' he asked politely.

'My name is Lin.'

'Well sir, these market-place scoundrels clearly have no sense of propriety. I would be obliged if you were to take this matter in hand and return the dispatch to its rightful owner.'

'This case is the property of the Emperor,' replied Guard Lin. 'No one would dare open it without the Emperor's express permission.'

Liang gave a tortured frown.

'If you don't return that dispatch to me,' said the officer, 'you will be guilty of delaying important government business, and that is a capital offence. What do you say, my friends?'

Seated around the room were another dozen or so of his fellow army officers and guards, who now began to edge towards Lin.

Wang Weiyang, with his decades of experience, felt there was something decidedly odd about what was going on. He guessed that the dwarf was the key to the affair and reached out to grab his arm. The dwarf shrank away, crying: 'Master, master, have mercy on me!'

Wang noted the dwarf's extraordinary agility and became even more suspicious. He was just about to go after him when he saw the military men beginning to brawl with the Agency guards and the Imperial Guards. Wang clutched the leather case to his chest. He had a guard protecting him on either side. Guard Lin pulled out his dagger and slammed it into the table.

'Enough of this!' he roared at the soldiers. 'Back off, all of you!'

The officer in command of the escort delivering the dispatch drew his sword. 'Give me back the dispatch, or I'll finish you off, even if I die in the attempt!' he shouted. 'All together!'

He lunged forward and threw himself at Lin. The other officers seized their weapons and charged into the fray, and a great battle ensued. Guard Lin was one of the best fighters in the Imperial Guard, but after a few strokes he found this humble army officer gaining the upper hand.

Wang Weiyang shouted repeatedly for them all to stop but no one listened. In the midst of the confusion, another group suddenly surged in through the door.

'Seize the troublemakers!' cried a voice.

The officers all stopped in their tracks. Guard Lin took a deep breath and looked at the young official who had entered surrounded by several dozen soldiers. He immediately recognized the man as the Emperor's current favourite, the young Manchu Fu Kangan, who held the posts of Military Governor of Manchuria, Commander-in-Chief of the Nine Gates of Peking, as well as Commander of the Imperial Guard. Lin hastily pushed his way forward and greeted Fu as the other Imperial Guards bowed before him.

'What's going on here?' asked Fu.

'They started making trouble, Commander,' Lin replied, and gave an account of what had occurred.

'And where is this magician?' asked Fu. The dwarf, who had hidden himself in a far corner, now came forward.

'This is a very strange business,' said Fu. 'You are all to come with me to Hangzhou. I wish to conduct a thorough investigation.'

'Yes, sir. A wise decision, sir,' said Guard Lin.

'Let's go,' said Fu, then walked outside and remounted his horse. The soldiers under his command gathered together the Agency men, the army officer who had started the trouble, and even the Uighur envoy, and herded them all out after him.

'Lord Fu,' said Lin. 'This is the head of the Zhen Yuan Security Agency, Wang Weiyang.'

Wang went over and bowed in greeting, but Fu merely looked him up and down and grunted. 'Let's go,' he said again.

The column of men soon entered Hangzhou city and made its way to a huge private residence by the West Lake.

'This must be where Commander Fu is staying,' Wang thought to himself. 'He's one of the Emperor's favourites, so it's not surprising he has such a strong force of men with him.'

They entered the rear hall of the residence. 'Please be seated,' Fu said to Guard Lin, and continued on into an inner chamber by himself.

A short while later, an officer of the Imperial Guard came out and escorted the army officer who had started the trouble, the conjuring dwarf, and Merchant Liang and his servants inside.

'I was getting a bit worried during that brawl,' said one of the Agency guards. 'There was something strange about those army men. I thought they might try to damage the jade vases.'

'Yes, their kungfu was surprisingly good for army officers,' Guard Lin replied. 'It's lucky Lord Fu turned up or we might have had some serious trouble.'

'Lord Fu's Inner Force kungfu is superb,' said Wang Weiyang. 'It's very unusual for such a senior nobleman to be so accomplished in the Martial Arts.'

'What?' said Lin. 'Commander Fu's kungfu is good? How do you know?'

'You can see it in his eyes.'

As they were talking, an officer came out. 'Wang Weiyang of the Zhen Yuan Agency, come with me,' he said. Wang stood up and followed him out.

They passed through two courtyards and into another hall in which sat Commander Fu Kangan on a dais. He had changed into an official gown with a huge plume in his cap, and the imposing atmosphere was enhanced by the long official desk in front of him and the serried ranks of Imperial Guards standing on either side.

As he walked in, two officers shouted in unison: 'Kneel!' Wang did as he was told.

'So you're Wang Weiyang, are you?' Fu said shortly.

'I am sir,' said Wang.

'I hear you have the nickname North China Earth-Shaker.'

'That is just what some of my friends call me.'

'Both the Emperor and I live in Peking,' Fu said coldly. 'We dwell in North China. Are you trying to suggest that you can shake *us* off our feet too?'

Wang felt a sudden wave of fear. He hastily kowtowed and said: 'Your Lordship, I would never dare suggest any such thing! I will immediately abolish the nickname.'

'Insolent fellow!' roared Fu. 'Take him away!'

Two soldiers marched up and led him off, and Wang, in spite of his legendary kungfu skills, did not dare to resist.

The Imperial Guards and Agency guards were brought in one after the other, and one after another they were taken away and thrown manacled into the dungeons. Finally, an army officer marched up to Fu's table carrying the leather case in both hands, knelt down on one knee, and raised the case high in the air in presentation, saying: 'Lord Fu, here are the jade vases.'

Fu laughed out loud, and stepped down off the dais. The dwarf and the others kneeling on the ground also stood up and started laughing.

'Brother Xu,' Fu said to the dwarf, 'that was magnificent! You truly deserve the nickname Kungfu Mastermind!'

The conjuring dwarf was in fact Mastermind Xu, while the Hangzhou Lodge Master, Ma Shanjun, had played (very convincingly) the part of the wealthy Merchant Liang. Helmsman

Chen had taken the role of his own double, the Emperor's favourite, Lord Fu Kangan, and the Twin Knights and some of the other Red Flower heroes had played the troublemaking army officers. Xu had remembered that Han Wenchong would be able to recognize some of the Red Flower heroes and so had arranged for him to be lured away into the forest, using the white horse as bait.

Helmsman Chen now broke the seal on the leather case and lifted the lid. Inside was a pair of jade vases about one foot in height. On each was drawn the picture of a girl dressed in Uighur clothes, her long hair plaited. The girl was extraordinarily beautiful. She had strangely bewitching eyes, and cherry-red lips that almost seemed to move. The pictures were so lifelike, it was as if the girl (or both versions of her) was about to walk off the vase, out of the picture, and into the room.

Everyone gathered round to admire.

'When I saw Huo Qingtong, I thought she must be the most beautiful girl on this earth,' said Luo Bing. 'But this girl is even lovelier.'

'It's just a picture,' Zhou Qi protested. 'You don't think there's really anyone that beautiful, do you?'

'I don't think any artist could have invented a face like that,' Luo Bing replied.

'Let's bring the Uighur envoy in and ask him,' Xu suggested.

As he entered, the envoy bowed respectfully before Helmsman Chen, in the belief that he was a senior court official.

'You have had a long hard journey, sir,' said Chen. 'What is your name?'

'My name is Kaibiexing. May I ask your name?'

Helmsman Chen smiled but did not reply.

'This is General Li, Commander-in-Chief of Zhejiang Province,' said Mastermind Xu.

The others stared at him in surprise, wondering what was going through his mind this time.

'I trust your master the Hodja Muzhuolun is well?' said Helmsman Chen to the envoy.

'Thank you for asking, sir. Our leader is very well.'

'I wonder if you could tell me something,' continued Chen. 'Who is this beautiful girl on the vases? Is she a real person, or did the artist draw her from his own imagination?'

'The vases originally belonged to Hodja Muzhuolun's third daughter, Hasli. She was the model for the girl in the picture.'

'So she must be Huo Qingtong's sister,' said Zhou Qi. 'Is she older than Huo Qingtong, or younger?'

'Do you know Lady Huo Qingtong?' said the envoy, evidently greatly surprised.

'I have met her,' she replied.

Helmsman Chen wanted to ask how Huo Qingtong was, but stopped himself. 'Please go and rest now,' he said to the envoy. 'We will talk again later.'

The envoy bowed. 'Thank you, Commander. Where are the vases to be kept?'

'Don't you worry. We have made arrangements,' said Chen.

The envoy was led away.

CHAPTER 5

*Foiled Again; A Cunning Plan; Earth-Shaker meets
Fire Hand Judge; A Gunpowder Plot; Beautiful Jade's Boudoir;
The Emperor's New Clothes; Death by Dog?*

Foiled Again

Presently, Mastermind Xu went to see the Uighur envoy Kaibiexing.

'I will take you to see the Emperor now,' he said, and they left, accompanied by Steward Meng carrying the leather case containing the jade vases. Without the envoy knowing, one of the vases had already been carefully removed.

When they arrived at the Commander-in-Chief's Yamen, where the Emperor's temporary lodgings were situated, Meng handed the leather case to the envoy and pointed to the main gate.

'You may proceed on your own,' he said. He and Mastermind Xu returned to join the Red Flower heroes.

That same afternoon, a gateman came in with a visiting-card for Helmsman Chen. It was signed 'Your servant Zeng Tunan'. Zeng was the trusted lieutenant of Commander Li Kexiu.

'It seems that your plan has worked, Brother Xu,' said Helmsman Chen. 'Brother Wei, please go and receive the man.'

Leopard Wei went to the reception room and saw a large man seated in a chair. 'What is it you wish to see our master about?' he asked.

'I have come with instructions from Commander-in-Chief Li to talk to the Helmsman of your Society about a certain matter,' replied Zeng stiffly.

'Our master is not free at present. You can talk to me.'

'It concerns a certain Uighur vase,' he said. Zeng was clearly not at all happy about having to negotiate with a man he considered a bandit.

Leopard Wei merely grunted.

'The Uighurs dispatched a peace envoy with a case containing a pair of vases for His Majesty the Emperor,' Lieutenant Zeng went on to explain. 'But when His Majesty the Emperor opened the case, there was only one vase. He was very angry and questioned the envoy closely. The envoy said that he had already had an audience with my master, the Commander-in-Chief of Zhejiang Province. The Emperor called in Commander Li, who denied having had the meeting and was naturally mystified by the whole affair. Luckily, the Emperor knew that my master Commander Li would not have done anything improper, and that there must be some reasonable explanation.'

'So far so good,' said Leopard Wei, nodding casually.

'But His Majesty said that my master would be held responsible for the affair and has given him three days to find and return the missing vase. This presents a great difficulty.'

'You mean,' replied Leopard Wei, 'your master is afraid that if he doesn't find the vase, he will be removed from office, is that it? It's certainly tough being an official. The thought that at any moment one's whole family could be executed and all one's possessions seized must be rather distressing.'

Zeng ignored his sarcasm. 'Let's not play games with each other. I have come to ask you and your associates to return the vase.'

'Unfortunately we have not heard of any such vase,' replied Leopard Wei. 'But as your master Commander Li has run into this difficulty, we will naturally do our best to help him find it. I dare say we may come across some clue as to its whereabouts sometime during the next year or two.'

'My master Commander Li says he has the greatest respect for your superior, the person you refer to as Helmsman Chen. He has sent me today to ask you for your assistance. He would feel easier if he could do something for you in return. Please do not hesitate to inform us of your "Helmsman" Chen's wishes.'

'Thank you for being so frank. That is excellent,' replied Leopard Wei. 'Our Helmsman Chen has two wishes that he wants me to share with you. The first is this: he knows that the Red Flower Society has offended Commander Li, and he would like to ask him to let bygones be bygones.'

'That goes without saying. I can guarantee that the Commander will never make difficulties for your Society over this matter. And the second thing?'

'The second is this: our Brother Wen Tailai is imprisoned in the Commander's Yamen.'

Zeng grunted.

'We know that in the eyes of the law, he has committed a crime,' Leopard Wei continued. 'We understand that no matter how courageous Commander Li may be, he would never dare to release him. But our Helmsman Chen misses Wen Tailai greatly and would like to be able to meet with him alone tonight.'

Lieutenant Zeng thought about this for a second. 'This is a very serious matter. I will have to consult my master and return with the reply.'

Zeng took his leave. He returned two hours later.

'My master says that Wen Tailai's crimes are extremely serious, and that normally no one would be allowed to visit him,' he said.

'*Normally?*' exclaimed Leopard Wei.

'But given that your Helmsman Chen is willing to return the vase, my master will risk his neck and allow your Helmsman Chen to meet with the prisoner. However, there are two small conditions he must agree to. First, it must be understood that my master has agreed to this purely in order to cement his friendship with your Helmsman Chen. If anyone else were to find out about it, it would be disastrous.'

'You mean, Commander Li wants Helmsman Chen to agree not to reveal a word about the affair to anyone, is that it?'

'Exactly.'

'I can agree to that on our Helmsman's behalf,' said Leopard Wei.

'The second condition is that your Helmsman Chen must make the visit unaccompanied.'

Leopard Wei smiled. 'Commander Li is naturally afraid that we will take advantage of the meeting to try to rescue our Brother Wen. Very well, we agree to this condition. Our Helmsman Chen will go by himself. But that does not mean we have agreed not to attempt a rescue.'

'You are a man of honour,' replied Zeng, 'and I value your word. Please ask your Helmsman Chen to come to the Yamen this evening.'

'If Zhang the Fire Hand Judge were to be there when Helmsman Chen and Brother Wen meet,' said Leopard Wei, 'it would naturally be impossible to preserve the secrecy of the agreement, which could be extremely inconvenient for Commander Li.'

'That is true,' Lieutenant Zeng replied. 'My master will think of some excuse for getting Zhang out of the way.'

When Lieutenant Zeng had left, the Red Flower heroes gathered in the Great Hall to await their orders for Wen's rescue.

'Brother Xu, I delegate the detailed arrangements to you,' said Helmsman Chen.

Xu was silent for a moment. 'We know Fire Hand Zhang will be elsewhere and that the Helmsman can get inside. That will of course make it much easier to rescue Brother Wen,' he said. 'But Commander Li is also certain to take precautions. We must first work out what he intends to do and then do something unexpected ourselves, to disrupt his plans.'

It was Iron Pagoda Yang who spoke next. 'He will station a large contingent of troops around the entrance to the dungeon; he may even enlist the support of some of the outstanding fighters from among the Imperial Guards. They will allow only the Helmsman in, and only the Helmsman out.'

'We had better be waiting outside the Yamen just in case those turtles try anything against the Helmsman,' said one of the Twin Knights.

'Of course we'll be waiting outside,' agreed Mastermind Xu. 'But I don't think Commander Li will dare to harm the Helmsman while the missing vase is still in our hands.'

'I have an idea!' said Helmsman Chen suddenly. 'When I go to see Brother Wen, I will wear a wide cape and a large hat that covers my face—'

Mastermind Xu knew what he was planning: to change places with Wen. 'But that way,' he protested, 'we would gain one man only to lose another. It's not a good idea.'

'Finish what you were saying, Helmsman,' said Father Speckless.

'Once I am in the dungeon, I will exchange clothes with Brother Wen and then let him leave first. The guards will think it's me. You can be waiting outside to help him get away.'

'But what about you?'

'The Emperor and I have a special relationship. Once they discover the switch, they'll let me go.'

The Red Flower heroes were unhappy at the thought that their leader was about to place himself in such danger, but they were forced to agree that in the circumstances it was probably the best plan.

When all the arrangements were completed, Helmsman Chen threw on a large cape with the collar turned up, donned a hat pulled well down over his face, and set off for the Commander-in-Chief's Yamen accompanied by Leopard Wei. By the time they arrived, it was already close to dusk and the first stars had begun to appear in the sky. A man came out to meet them.

'Is that your Helmsman Chen?' he whispered. Leopard Wei nodded. 'Please come with me,' the man said to Chen. 'The other gentleman must stay here.'

Leopard Wei stood and watched as Helmsman Chen followed the man into the Yamen. A flight of ravens flew overhead through the evening mist on their way home, cawing as they went. It seemed an omen, and Leopard Wei's heart beat wildly as he wondered what fate awaited the Helmsman. After a while, the rest of the Red Flower heroes arrived and spread out around the outside of the Yamen.

As he entered the gate, Helmsman Chen could see that the compound was filled with hundreds of soldiers on guard. The man led him through a series of three courtyards, and finally into a room.

'Please take a seat,' he said, and left. A moment later, Commander Li entered and saluted Helmsman Chen. 'It is an honour to meet you,' he said.

'We met the day before yesterday on the lake,' Chen answered with a smile, opening his cape and removing his hat.

'You may now see the prisoner,' said Li. 'Please follow me.'

As they reached the door, an attendant came running breathlessly towards them.

'Commander Li, His Majesty the Emperor has arrived!' he reported in a great fluster. 'Lieutenant Zeng has gone out to meet him.'

Li started in surprise and turned to Helmsman Chen. 'You had better wait here for the time being,' he said.

Li hurried through to the front courtyard, just in time to see Qian Long entering it with a large contingent of Imperial Guards. He hastened to kneel down before him and kowtowed.

'Make ready a well-guarded room,' said Qian Long. 'I wish to personally interrogate the prisoner Wen Tailai.'

Li invited the Emperor into his own study, and the Imperial Guards established themselves on all sides of it. Some of them even took up positions up on the roof.

'I have important matters of a confidential nature to discuss with this prisoner. No one else must hear. Not even yourself,' said Qian Long to his senior guard, the elderly kungfu master Bai Zhen, before dismissing him.

A moment later, four guards entered carrying a stretcher on which lay the sleeping figure of Rolling Thunder Wen, handcuffed and chained. The guards deposited Wen, and then retired.

'How are your injuries?' Qian Long asked after a long silence. Wen's eyes opened and he sat up. His wounds had not yet healed, but his mind was clear. He had seen Qian Long once before when he had entered the Imperial Palace with Old Helmsman Yu, but was surprised at suddenly meeting him again here in Hangzhou.

'I am still alive,' he said coldly.

'I asked my men to bring you here because there is something important I wish to discuss with you.'

Wen grunted.

'When you visited me with that leader of yours, your Helmsman Yu, I discussed a serious matter with him. Unfortunately, I hear he fell ill and died very soon afterwards. It was a great pity.'

'If Old Helmsman Yu had not died, I dare say he would be imprisoned here with me now,' replied Wen.

Qian Long laughed. 'You underworld fighters are certainly frank. You say whatever you are thinking. Now, sir, I have only one question for you. Answer me honestly, and I will immediately release you.'

'Release me? Ha! What do you take me for? A three-year-old? I know that you cannot rest easy while I'm still alive. You have stayed your hand until today only because you wish to interrogate me first.'

'You're much too suspicious,' said Qian Long with a smile. He walked forward two paces.

'Did your Helmsman Yu ever tell you what it was he talked to me about on that occasion?' he asked.

'No. What was it?' Wen knew he had to play for time.

Qian Long stared at him, and Wen returned the gaze unflinchingly. After a while, Qian Long turned his head away.

'It concerned my origins,' he said quietly.

'He didn't say anything in particular. *Origins*? You are the Emperor, the son of the late Emperor and Empress. Everyone knows about your origins. What more is there to say?'

Qian Long breathed a sigh of relief. 'That night you visited me, you must have known what the reason was?'

'Old Helmsman Yu told me that once in the past he had helped you with some important matter. The Red Flower Society was short of funds, and he wanted to ask you for a favour in return: three million taels of silver. But you refused the request. And now you have even had me seized and thrown into jail. If I ever get out of this, I will tell the world how ungrateful you are.'

Qian Long laughed out loud. He glanced at Wen: the man's anger and indignation seemed sincere enough. 'In that case, I had better have you killed,' he said, half-believing him. 'Otherwise, if I let you go, my reputation will be ruined.'

'Why didn't you kill me earlier? If you had, you could have blamed everything on me. Then you wouldn't have had to feel so guilty every time you saw your own mother.'

'What about my own mother?' Qian Long asked, turning pale.

'You know what I mean.'

'So you know everything?' Qian Long's voice sounded chilling, almost sinister.

'No, not *everything*. Old Helmsman Yu just said the Empress Dowager knew that he had once helped you. She knew that he had asked you to repay him, but that you hadn't wanted to part with the silver. You've got mountains of money. Three million taels would be nothing to you. But you refused.'

Qian Long laughed nervously. He pulled out a handkerchief and wiped away the beads of sweat on his brow, then began pacing the room to steady himself. 'You show no fear at all before your Emperor.' He smiled. 'You are indeed a man of steel.'

'What have I got to be afraid of? I doubt if you would dare to kill me straight away,' said Wen.

'Not dare?'

'You want to kill me because you're afraid your secret will get out. But that's the whole point.' Wen smiled. 'If you *do* kill me, that's precisely when your secret *will* be revealed!'

'Are you trying to tell me that dead men talk?'

'No.' Wen hardly seemed to be answering Qian Long. He almost seemed to be talking to himself. 'As soon as I die, someone will open a certain letter and reveal the evidence contained in it to the world. Then you'll be in real trouble.'

'What letter?' asked Qian Long.

'Before we came to the Palace to see you, Old Helmsman Yu wrote down every detail of the affair. He sealed the document in an envelope, together with two important pieces of evidence, and left it with a friend.'

'Was he afraid that something untoward might happen?'

'Of course he was! Why should he trust you? Old Helmsman Yu told his friend that if he and I were both to die, he should open the letter and carry out the instructions contained in it. So long as one of us was still alive, he was not to open it under any circumstances. The Old Helmsman has already passed away, so I don't think you'll dare kill me.'

Qian Long wrung his hands, anxiety written all over his face.

'Wouldn't it have been worth giving him the three million taels of silver, just to buy that letter and the two pieces of evidence?' Wen asked.

'The silver was never a problem. I had always planned to hand it over and then let you go. I want you to write a letter to your friend telling him to bring the letter you just mentioned to me. Then I will pay you the money straight away.'

'Ha ha! I am not that stupid. If I tell you his name, you'll just send your guards to kill him or capture him. No, I'm very comfortable here. I'd happily stay here the rest of my life. You see, you and I share one and the same fate. I may die first, but when I do, you won't live much longer.'

Qian Long bit his lip. 'If you won't do as I say, it is of no importance,' he said after a pause. 'I give you two days. If you persist in your obstinacy, I will have no alternative but to have you secretly killed. No one else will even know. Your friend will think you're still alive. And even if I don't kill you, I can still have your eyes gouged out, your tongue removed, your arms cut off... Think about it over the next couple of days.'

He pushed open the door and walked out. His guards reassembled around him, and Commander Li escorted him out of the Yamen.

Rolling Thunder Wen was carried back to the dungeon by the Commander's own guards, with the formidable Fire Hand Zhang providing an escort. Once they were in the cell, one of the guards handed Zhang a letter.

'Commander Li asked me to give you this,' he said. Zhang opened and read the letter, then left.

Rolling Thunder Wen lay there on the bed thinking about his wife and his Red Flower friends. He hoped none of them would be harmed if a rescue was attempted (which he knew was only a matter of time).

Just then, the iron door to his cell opened with a clang and a man walked in. Wen thought it must be Fire Hand Zhang returning and did not even bother to open his eyes.

The man walked over to the bed. 'Brother Wen,' he murmured.

Wen was stunned. He looked up to see Helmsman Chen gazing down at him. 'Helmsman!' he exclaimed, sitting up. Chen smiled and nodded. He took two steel files from his pocket, and began filing vigorously at Wen's manacles. After a moment, a series of light scratches appeared on the surface, but the file was ruined. The manacles were made of a specially cast steel and an ordinary file was useless against it.

'Helmsman, only the hardest blade in the world will ever break through these chains,' said Wen.

Helmsman Chen remembered the battle with Fire Hand Zhang at the Yellow River crossing and how sharp Zhang's Frozen Emerald sword had been.

'Does Fire Hand Zhang guard you night and day?' he asked quickly.

'He's never more than a step away. He left only a short while ago.'

'Good. We'll wait for him to return and steal his sword.' Helmsman Chen threw the files under the bed.

'I'll never get out of here,' said Rolling Thunder Wen. 'The Emperor wants to silence me. I know a secret, and he's afraid I will reveal it. I had better tell you what it is, Helmsman, in case I should die.'

Chen nodded.

'That night, when I went to the Imperial Palace with Old Helmsman Yu, the Emperor was very surprised to see us. Old Helmsman Yu said that a certain lady from the Chen family in Haining had asked him to come, and handed him a letter. The Emperor's face went pale as he read it. He told me to wait outside. The two of them then talked in private for about two hours before Old Helmsman Yu finally came out. On the way back, he told me the secret. Now I'm telling you. It's this. The Emperor is not really a Manchu at all. He is Chinese. And he is your elder brother.'

Helmsman Chen looked utterly devastated. 'But that's impossible,' he said firmly. 'My brother is in Haining.'

'Old Helmsman Yu told me that on the very day the late Emperor Yong Zheng's wife gave birth to a baby girl, your mother also gave birth—to a boy. Emperor Yong Zheng heard of this, and gave orders that the newborn baby boy of the Chen family should be brought for him to look at. When the baby was returned to the Chens, it had become a girl. The baby boy grew up into the man who is now the Emperor Qian Long—'

Before he could finish, they heard the sound of footsteps in the corridor and a guard came in.

'What is it?' asked Helmsman Chen.

'Fire Hand Zhang is on his way back. Commander Li says he can't detain him any longer and asks you to leave at once.'

'Thank you,' replied Chen. His left hand shot out and pressed a Vital Point on the guard's body. The guard toppled to the floor without a sound, and Chen pushed him under the bed.

'Since Zhang is on his way, I shall have to be brief,' Wen continued. 'Old Helmsman Yu knew all along that the Emperor was Chinese. His aim in going to the Palace was to win him over to our cause, to urge him to overthrow the Manchus and restore China to the Chinese, while remaining Emperor himself. The Emperor appeared moved by the appeal, but asked the Old Helmsman to bring him further evidence of the truth of his claim, before he could make a decision. As soon as Old Helmsman Yu returned home, he fell ill and never recovered. His last wish (as you know) was that you should succeed him as Helmsman. He said to me that this secret offered us a wonderful opportunity to restore the honour of the Chinese people. The Emperor is your blood brother. If he himself is unwilling to overthrow the Manchus, then everyone will support you in taking his place.'

His words left Chen too stunned to speak. He thought back to when he had first seen Qian Long by the lake, and afterwards crying before the tomb of his parents. Could it really be true that the Emperor was his own blood brother, the son of his own mother and father?

'I understand your mother wrote down the full details of how Emperor Yong Zheng swapped his baby girl for the baby that was your older brother. This is contained in a letter which Old Helmsman Yu entrusted along with several other pieces of evidence to your Shifu, Master Yuan, for safe keeping.'

'So when the Twin Knights went to see my Shifu this summer,' said Helmsman Chen, 'they were carrying these things to him on the Old Helmsman's orders?'

'That's correct. It was such an important and secret mission that not even you could be told. All that your Shifu knows is that these documents are of the utmost importance. Even he does not know what they are. Just before Old Helmsman Yu passed away, he gave me new orders, that when you became Helmsman, you should open the letter yourself and make your own plans accordingly. But I stupidly allowed myself to be captured and failed to carry out these orders, thus jeopardizing the whole enterprise. Helmsman, if you can't get me out today, you must go to the Uighur regions as quickly as possible to see your Shifu. You must not endanger our great cause just for my sake.'

Rolling Thunder Wen was clearly relieved to have finished saying what he had to say. He was about to add something further, when footsteps sounded in the corridor again. He signalled quickly with his hand, and Helmsman Chen hid under the bed. Wen then draped himself over the side of bed with his head resting on the floor.

When Fire Hand Zhang entered the cell, by the faint light of the room's single candle he saw Wen half lying on the floor, almost as if he were dead. Shocked, he leapt forward and touched Wen's back, but there was no reaction. He started to lift Wen's body back onto the bed, but as he did so, in that very instant, Wen leapt up and attacked him. Zhang fell back in surprise, feeling a sudden numbness in his lower abdomen. He knew he had been hit by someone waiting in ambush under the bed and roared angrily, sidestepping two paces and drawing breath in an attempt to control the spreading paralysis. Helmsman Chen, who was startled to see Zhang still standing upright at all, leapt out from beneath the bed and struck Zhang's face with his fists seven or eight times.

If he responded to this attack, Zhang knew his control would be lost and the paralysis in his abdomen would spread even further through his body. He retreated, and as he did so, Helmsman Chen's foot flew through the air and struck him on another Vital Point. This time, Zhang could no longer sustain his control. His whole body went limp and he slumped to the ground.

Helmsman Chen searched him. To his great disappointment he discovered that he did not have Frozen Emerald with him. He pulled a piece of paper out of Zhang's pocket and saw by the candlelight that it was a note from Commander Li asking Zhang to show his sword to an important official who was waiting to see it. This must have been the excuse Li had used to draw Zhang away. He guessed that Zhang must have been anxious to get back to the dungeon to resume his guard duties, and had returned as quickly as possible, without the sword.

Helmsman Chen continued his search of Zhang's body, and suddenly leapt up jubilantly.

'What is it?' asked Wen. Helmsman Chen raised his hand and displayed a set of keys. He tried one on the manacles and they opened immediately.

Wen was free at last! As he began stretching his arms and legs, Chen took off his cape and hat.

'Put these on and get out quickly,' he said.

'What about you?'

'I'll wait here for a while. You go first.'

Wen understood his intentions. 'Helmsman, I appreciate what you have in mind, but we cannot do it that way.'

'Brother Wen, you don't understand. I am in no danger if I stay here.' He told Wen about how the Emperor and he had sworn an oath together.

'I still cannot allow it,' said Wen.

Chen frowned. 'I am the Helmsman. All members of the Red Flower Society must follow my orders, is that not correct?'

'Of course.'

'Fine. Then this is my order. Put these clothes on quickly and get out. The Brothers are outside waiting for you.'

'This one time I am forced to disobey your order,' Wen said. 'I will gladly accept whatever punishment you decide upon.'

They were deadlocked. Helmsman Chen pursed his lips thoughtfully.

'Very well then, we'll have to risk going out together. Put on *his* clothes,' he said pointing at Fire Hand Zhang.

'Excellent!' Wen exclaimed.

The two stripped off Zhang's clothes and exchanged them for Wen's, then locked up Zhang in the chains and manacles. Zhang shook with rage, his eyes blazing blood-red with hate, but he was unable either to offer the least resistance or to utter a sound.

The two walked quietly out through the door and along the corridor. As they reached the top of a flight of stone steps, a bright light assailed their eyes and they saw that the whole courtyard was filled with torches. Forty or fifty soldiers stood directly ahead of them, with shining spear-tips pointed at the dungeon entrance. Behind them were two or three hundred archers in serried ranks, with bows drawn. Commander Li stood to one side with his right hand held high. The slightest move from him, and the spears and arrows would be loosed, and Chen and Wen would be dead.

Helmsman Chen stepped back a pace. 'How are your wounds?' he whispered to Wen. 'Do you think you are up to charging through?'

'No, my leg is too weak,' Wen replied with a rueful smile. 'You go by yourself, Helmsman. Don't worry about me.'

'Very well then,' said Helmsman Chen, 'you carry on pretending that you're Zhang and we'll see how it goes.'

Wen pulled his hat down to his eyebrows and strode out into view. Commander Li's heart sank at the sight of Fire Hand Zhang and Helmsman Chen together. He assumed that Zhang had arrested him. But he himself had express orders from the Emperor to let Chen go unharmed. He turned to his daughter Yuanzhi.

'Give Zhang back his sword. Do something to distract him so that Chen can get away,' he said.

Yuanzhi walked over with Frozen Emerald in her hand and held it out to Wen (whom she took to be Zhang), positioning herself between the two men.

'Uncle Zhang, here is your sword,' she said, as she did so giving Chen a slight nudge with her elbow. Wen grunted and made a move to accept the sword. Suddenly in the torchlight she recognized him.

'You're not Uncle Zhang!' she cried. 'You're Wen Tailai! So you think you can escape do you!' She drew Frozen Emerald from its scabbard and thrust it at his chest.

Wen feinted to one side and caught the blade with his fingers while his right hand struck out at the Greater Yang Vital Point on her forehead. Yuanzhi tried quickly backing away, but with Wen still holding the blade of her sword, she was totally unable to move. She herself let go of the sword and tried to slip away, but Wen struck her left shoulder and a searing pain surged through her. She cried out and squatted down. Helmsman Chen had already begun to move forward. He glanced back and saw that Wen was surrounded, but still fighting fiercely.

'Stop fighting or the archers will shoot,' Commander Li roared.

Blood was pouring from the old wounds on Wen's thigh, which had burst open with the sudden exertion. He knew he lacked the strength to break through the circle of soldiers.

'Helmsman, catch the sword!' he shouted. 'Make a dash for it!' He tried to throw Frozen Emerald, but a sudden pain in his shoulder made his hand go limp and the sword clattered to the ground only a few feet from him. He had been hit by an arrow.

Helmsman Chen turned to Commander Li. 'Stop the shooting! ' he shouted. Li waved his hand and the archers stopped.

'Fetch a doctor quickly to deal with Wen Tailai's wounds,' said Helmsman Chen. 'I'm leaving now.' And so saying, he hurried out of the Yamen. Commander Li gave the necessary orders, and the guards pretended to give chase, without really obstructing him.

Once he was out in the open, Leopard Wei and Luo Bing came up to meet him. Helmsman Chen smiled bitterly and shook his head. Their plan had failed. The eastern sky was already pale as with heavy hearts the Red Flower heroes returned home.

A Cunning Plan

They gathered later in the Great Hall to discuss the situation.

Helmsman Chen spoke to Leopard Wei first: 'Brother Wei, you had better deliver the second vase to Commander Li and let him put it back in the case with the other one. We cannot go back on our word.' Leopard Wei bowed and left.

Lodge Master Ma's son entered the hall and walked over to Helmsman Chen. 'Helmsman, Fire Hand Zhang has sent you this letter.'

Chen opened the letter. It angrily accused him of deception and plotting, of behaviour unbefitting an honourable man, and challenged him to a duel at a time and place of his choice. 'He wants revenge for last night,' Helmsman Chen told the others. 'Huh, a duel! Does he think I'm scared?'

'We have to rescue Brother Wen in the next two days,' said Mastermind Xu. 'I have in mind digging a tunnel, and getting him out that way. We must make an immediate start. Why don't you postpone the meeting with Zhang for a few days? We should not allow this matter to interfere with our real purpose.'

'That is true,' said Chen. 'Today is the twentieth, so I will set the meeting for noon on the twenty-third.'

He immediately wrote a letter inviting Zhang to meet him alone on that day and ordered one of his men to take it to the Commander-in-Chief's Yamen.

One of Lodge Master Ma's men entered and said: 'Master, the old man Wang Weiyang still refuses to eat and does nothing but shout abuse and insults.'

'Who is he insulting?' asked Ma.

'The Imperial Guards. He says he doesn't understand why they have thrown him into prison.'

'The North China Earth-Shaker has finally met his match,' Father Speckless chuckled. 'On his very first trip to the south, he gets given a hard time.'

Mastermind Xu's face suddenly brightened. 'I have a plan that should make it easier for you to deal with Fire Hand Zhang, Helmsman,' he said. He told them his idea, and they were all delighted.

'Excellent! Very cunning,' said Father Speckless. Zhou Qi smiled and shook her head.

'Once again Miss Zhou thinks that Brother Xu is not being straightforward enough,' said Helmsman Chen with a smile. 'But when dealing with dishonourable men, one does not have to be completely honourable. Steward Meng, go and have a talk with the North China Earth-Shaker.'

In forty years of Agency business, Wang Weiyang had never suffered a set-back like this. Now, on his first trip to the south, he was in dire straits. He was yelling and shouting, insisting that he should be allowed to see the commander of the Imperial Guard to settle the matter, when the door to his cell opened and Steward Meng walked in wearing the uniform of an officer in the Imperial Guard.

'So you are the North China Earth-Shaker?' Meng said brusquely.

Wang raged inwardly. 'Yes,' he said. 'That is a nickname given to me by my friends. If Lord Fu finds it unpleasing, I will change it immediately.'

'Lord Fu is a close friend of the Emperor,' said Meng coldly. 'He has no interest in such trifles.'

'I am escorting a number of precious articles to Hangzhou for the Imperial Court. Why are you detaining me here?'

'Do you really want to know?'

'Of course!'

'It's just that at your age, I'm afraid you may not be able to stand the shock.'

Wang hated references to his age more than anything. He lost his temper again, and struck the corner of the table with his fist. Splinters of wood flew around the room.

'I may be old, but my heart is still strong,' he shouted. 'Why should I be afraid?'

Meng laughed. 'You're a truly remarkable man! You may have heard the saying in the fighting community: "You'd be better off bumping into the Devil than into old Wang; you'd be better off bumping into a spear than into Fire Hand Zhang." There's some truth in it, isn't there?'

'That's the reputation I have amongst bandits.'

'Certain people are wondering why the saying puts "old Wang" before "Fire Hand Zhang"? Does it mean that old Wang's kungfu is better than Zhang's? And is that truly the case?'

Wang stood up. 'Aha!' he exclaimed. 'So the Fire Hand Judge wants to test me. He thinks I'm getting too slow in my old age. I never thought it would come to that.'

'Fire Hand Zhang is my superior in the Imperial Guard, did you know that?'

'I knew that your master was serving in the Imperial Guard.'

'Would you recognize him if you saw him?' asked Meng.

'We both live in Peking, but he is an official and I am an ordinary citizen. I have heard a great deal about him, but I've never had the good fortune to meet him.'

'He has also heard a great deal about you,' said Meng. 'He says there are three matters he wants to raise with you. If you agree to them, you will be allowed to leave immediately.'

'Well? What are they?'

'Firstly, he wants you to abandon the nickname North China Earth-Shaker.'

'Huh! What's the second thing?'

'He wants you to close down the Zhen Yuan Agency.'

'What? Close down my Agency? It's been operating for more than thirty years,' Wang protested angrily. 'I have never suffered a single loss at the hands of bandits and highwaymen and other members of the fighting community, and now your master Zhang wants me to retire? And the third thing?'

'He wants you to issue a proclamation instructing members of the fighting community to reverse the order of the saying about you and Fire Hand Zhang. His name must come first. Fire Hand Zhang also says that as you are now getting on in age, your Eight Trigram sword is probably no longer of much use to you, and suggests that you donate it to the Imperial Guard.'

Wang's anger reached boiling point. 'I don't owe Zhang any favours! He's carrying this too far!' he shouted.

'You have enjoyed a great name for forty years. Perhaps it *is* time to retire. A single mountain is not big enough for two tigers, as the saying goes. Surely you understand the sense of that?'

'So he wishes to humiliate me, and to promote his own name. Huh! And what if I don't agree. Will he continue to hold me prisoner here?'

'My master is an honourable man. He would not do such a thing,' said Meng. 'Instead he invites you to duel with him at noon today on Lion Peak. If you win, the three conditions will not be mentioned again. If you lose, then he asks you to agree to all three. He says it would be rather inconvenient if the Emperor were to find out about this, and asks you to go to the duel alone. That is, if you are not too scared to go.'

Wang spluttered with rage. 'Scared? Even if I am to die there, I'll still go. And I don't need anyone with me.'

'Then please write it down in a letter and I will take it back to my master,' said Meng. He pulled out some paper and a writing-brush.

Wang, his hand shaking in anger, wrote:

'To His Excellency Fire Hand Zhang Zhaozhong, the Fire Hand Judge. Your insolent words and behaviour have gone too far. I will meet you today at noon on Lion Peak. If I lose, I will be at your disposal. Wang Weiyang.'

Steward Meng smiled, picked up the letter and walked out, closing the door of the cell behind him.

That same morning, Han Wenchong, the Agency guard who had once owned the white horse, was moved to a new cell. Having fallen into the hands of the Red Flower Society once more, he was afraid he would not be able to escape so easily again. As he morosely considered his predicament, he heard someone shouting in the cell next to his, and recognized the voice of Wang Weiyang. He could hear him cursing Fire Hand Zhang. Greatly curious, he was just about to call out to Wang when his cell door opened and two men walked in.

'We'd like you to come with us to the Great Hall for a chat,' one of them said.

As they entered the hall, Han saw three men sitting on the left. In the middle was the Red Flower Society's Helmsman Chen. On one side of him sat a dwarf, and on the other a man with a flowing white beard. Han bowed silently and sat down.

'Mr Han, I never thought that we would meet again here,' said Helmsman Chen. 'Our fates seem somehow to be tied together.'

Han hesitated for a moment. 'I know I agreed to lay down my sword and return home,' he said finally. 'But my master Wang insisted that I do this one last job. Out of loyalty to him, and because I knew the valuables were for your family, I—'

'Mr Han,' Mastermind Xu interrupted harshly. 'We of the fighting community set great store by two things: trust and honour. By your own word, you have proved to be untrustworthy. How do you think you should be dealt with?'

Han steeled himself. 'What is there to say? If you're going to kill me then kill me.'

'There's no need to talk like that,' said Helmsman Chen. 'Your master Wang has been grossly insulted by Fire Hand Zhang, and says that no matter what, he must fight it out with him. We of the fighting community are very annoyed over this affair. What is your own relationship with Fire Hand Zhang?'

'I've met him a few times in Peking, but we are from two different worlds. You couldn't say we had any relationship exactly.'

'As I thought. Have a look at this letter,' said Helmsman Chen, and handed him the note Wang had written.

Han knew that Wang had always showed the greatest respect for officialdom in the past. But he also knew that if Fire Hand Zhang had really insulted Wang, the old man would have been unable to swallow it. He himself had heard Wang cursing and now seeing the letter, there was no room for doubt.

'I would like to see my master Wang and discuss the situation with him,' he said.

'There is no time for that,' Helmsman Chen replied. 'I want

you to take this letter to Fire Hand Zhang now. You can see your master Wang when you return.' Helmsman Chen then called Melancholy Ghost Shi and introduced him to Han. 'Brother Shi here will accompany you to see Fire Hand Zhang. I realize you are not familiar with the circumstances. You do not know how Zhang has caused your master to lose face. But I'm afraid there is no time to give you the details now. When you see Fire Hand Zhang, you can just say that Brother Shi here is a guard with the Agency. Do exactly as Brother Shi says.'

Han was starting to grow suspicious. He hesitated once more.

'Do you have any doubts, Mr Han?'

'No, no,' he answered hastily.

Mastermind Xu could tell that Han suspected something. 'Please wait a moment,' he said. He left the hall and returned with a flask of wine and a wine cup into which he poured some wine.

'I was too abrupt in what I said just now about trust and honour,' he said, offering the cup to Han. 'Please accept this token of my apology. Let there be no hard feelings between us.'

'Well said!' Han replied. He drained the cup, picked up the letter, and walked towards the door.

'Oh no!' Mastermind Xu suddenly exclaimed. 'Come back! I've made a terrible mistake. That cup of wine had poison in it!'

Han went pale as he turned back towards them.

'I am truly sorry,' said Mastermind Xu. 'That flask of wine had poison in it for use whenever needed and one of the servants must have given it to me by mistake. I didn't realize it until I smelt it. You've already drunk a cupful. Ah Mr Han!' Xu turned to an attendant. 'Go and fetch the antidote quickly!'

'The antidote is in the east city residence,' the attendant replied.

'You fool! Ride over there then and get it!' Xu shouted at him. The attendant bowed and left.

'I have been very careless,' Xu said apologetically to Han. 'Please go ahead and deliver the letter to Fire Hand Zhang first. Do exactly as Brother Shi says. You can take the antidote when you get back. Don't worry. Everything will be fine.'

Han knew he had no choice. Either he did as the Red Flower Society ordered, or he was a dead man. He gave Xu a bitter look, then turned and walked out without a word. Melancholy Ghost Shi followed him.

Lord Zhou frowned as the two men left. 'That fellow Han doesn't seem to me to be all that bad a person,' he said. 'Poisoning him like that was not a very honourable thing to do.'

'But I didn't. There was no poison in the wine,' replied Xu.

'No poison?'

'None.' Xu proceeded to pour himself a cup from the same flask and drank it down.

'I was just afraid he was getting a little too suspicious, and might mess up our plan in front of Fire Hand Zhang, so I decided to scare him a little. When he comes back, he can drink another cup and it will all be over.'

The others laughed.

Fire Hand Zhang was sitting beside Wen Tailai keeping watch when the cell door opened and a guard came in, bearing a visiting-card inscribed with the words: North China Earth-Shaker, Wang Weiyang.

'Go and tell him that I cannot see visitors,' he said.

The guard left, but returned a moment later to say: 'The visitors won't leave. They have a letter for you.'

When Fire Hand Zhang read the letter, he was both angered and perplexed by it. He had never had any disputes with Wang, and wondered why the old man should challenge him to a kungfu duel.

'Tell Commander Li that I have to see a visitor, and ask him to send someone to stand watch in my place,' he said to the guard.

Four guards arrived to replace him, and Fire Hand Zhang went to the reception hall. He recognized the Agency guard Han and saluted him with his fists.

'Isn't your master Wang here with you?' he asked.

'This is my Agency colleague, the guard Shi,' Han replied, pointing to his companion. 'There are a number of things my master wants him to say to you.'

Fire Hand Zhang threw Wang's letter onto the table. 'I have respected old Wang from afar for a long time, but I have never had any personal dealings with him whatsoever,' he said. 'How can he say that I have been insolent, that my words and behaviour have gone too far? There appears to be some misunderstanding here.'

'Our master is a leading member of the fighting community,' said Shi coldly. 'When that community produces a rotten element, all other members are dishonoured. My master therefore considers it to be his business to deal with the matter, regardless of whether there is a direct connection.'

Fire Hand Zhang stood up, fury written on his face. 'So I am to deduce from what you say that old Wang Weiyang considers me to be a rotten element?'

Melancholy Ghost Shi said nothing, but his silence confirmed Zhang's deduction.

'Please enlighten me as to just how I have dishonoured the fighting community,' demanded Fire Hand Zhang.

'Members of the fighting community abhor disrespect for superiors above all else,' Shi replied. 'You, sir, are a senior member of the Wudang School. The charge is that you have not only turned against your own former brothers-in-arms, but have also attempted to arrest one of them on behalf of the Manchu Court. Is this true?'

'What may or may not happen between myself and my brothers-in-arms is of no concern to outsiders such as yourself!' cried Zhang angrily.

'Secondly,' continued Shi, 'there are no grounds for personal emnity between yourself and the Red Flower Society, and yet purely to further your own career, you seized the Red Flower Brother Wen Tailai, and in the process caused the death of the young son of Lord Zhou of Iron Ball Manor. Do you feel no guilt for such things?'

'I am employed by His Majesty the Emperor and I am loyal to him. What has all of this got to do with the Zhen Yuan Agency?'

'Did you not work to implicate our Agency in your schemes, as a result of which many of our men were killed and wounded?' said Melancholy Ghost Shi.

'You really did do wrong there, sir,' Han added. 'You can't blame our master Wang for being angry.'

'Let us leave other matters aside for the moment,' Melancholy Ghost Shi continued coldly. 'How do you think these three matters should be dealt with?' He rolled his eyes and struck an expression of dignified authority.

Fire Hand Zhang was incensed at being treated like a criminal in the dock. 'You're obviously looking for trouble!' he shouted, striding forward.

Melancholy Ghost Shi retreated a pace. 'What's this?' he asked. 'You want to take me on instead? Is that because you are afraid to accept the North China Earth-Shaker's challenge?'

'Who says I'm afraid?' Zhang roared. 'Very well. I will be there on Lion Peak at noon today.'

'If you change your mind and decide not to go,' said Shi, 'then never again can you consider yourself to be a member of the fighting community. Our master says that if you have any guts at all, you will go alone. There will be no one else from the Agency there.'

'You think I need help? You think I am afraid of that egotistical, muddle-headed old man?'

'Our master does not fight with words,' Shi continued, ignoring Zhang's comment. 'When you meet him, the issue will be decided by kungfu alone. So if you wish to curse and swear, please feel free to do so now.'

Fire Hand Zhang was speechless with rage. Melancholy Ghost Shi laughed coldly, then turned on his heel and left with Han following.

While the two had argued, Han's mind had been on the poison he had taken. He supposed it must have already started to work on him, and just wanted Shi to hurry up and finish so that he could get back and take the antidote.

'Fire Hand Zhang has agreed to meet at noon,' reported Shi, when the two of them returned to the mansion at Solitary Peak. Han collapsed into a chair with what appeared to be agonizing stomach cramps. Xu coolly poured out a cup of wine and handed it to him.

'This is the antidote. Drink it up, my friend.'

Han quickly stretched out his hand to take it, but Lord Zhou snatched the cup away first and drank it down at one draught. Han stared at him in amazement.

'We have toyed with you enough, Mr Han,' Zhou said with a smile. 'You didn't swallow any poison at all. Brother Xu, come and apologize.'

While Mastermind Xu made his apologies, Steward Meng went in once more to see Wang Weiyang. 'Fire Hand Zhang has accepted your challenge,' he said. 'You can go now. And by the way, he does not like people who nag and complain, so if you have anything to say, say it now. When you get to Lion Peak, the matter will be decided with fists and blades, not words. If you try talking to him then, even to beg for mercy, I doubt if he will so much as listen to a word you say. If you are afraid, there is still time to pull out.'

'Afraid? I am prepared to die today if need be,' Wang shouted, angrily stroking his beard. As he made to leave, an attendant handed him his Eight Trigram sword and a bag of projectiles.

Han was standing by the door. 'Please be careful Master Wang,' he said.

'You know about this too?'

Han nodded. 'I have seen Fire Hand Zhang.'

'What did he say about me?'

'It was demeaning. You would not wish to hear it.'

'Speak,' ordered Wang.

'He called you...an egotistical, muddle-headed old man.'

Wang grunted angrily. 'We shall see. If anything should happen to me, please look after the Agency and the affairs of my family for me.' He hesitated. 'And tell my two sons not to rush into taking revenge. Their kungfu is still not good enough, and they would lose their lives to no good purpose.'

He then started out for Lion Peak and the duel.

Earth Shaker meets Fire Hand Judge

The slopes of Lion Peak produce abundant quantities of tea. Lion Peak Dragon Well is one of the most exquisite varieties of the leaf under heaven. The mountain itself is high and precipitous, and few people ever venture to the very top.

Wang Weiyang, his great sword slung across his back, clambered up the steep slope and emerged through the tea bushes onto an expanse of open ground on the very summit. He saw walking towards him a tall, burly man wearing a short jacket. The man stared at him for a moment.

'Are you Wang Weiyang?' he asked.

'Yes. And you must be the Fire Hand Judge, Zhang Zhaozhong?'

'I am. Do you wish to fight bare-handed or with weapons?' Fire Hand Zhang was a very thorough man. He had looked around him carefully during his climb up the peak, but had detected no sign of anyone lying in ambush.

Wang was startled to see that Zhang's mouth and nose were swollen and his right eye ringed in black. (These injuries had been caused by Helmsman Chen the night before.)

'We have no great grudge against each other,' thought Wang. 'Why risk killing him with a sword-stroke? The consequences of killing an official of his rank are unthinkable. It will be enough to humiliate him with my Eight Trigram kungfu. I'll show him I'm not egotistical!'

Out loud he said: 'I would be honoured to pit myself against your famous Limitless Occult kungfu.'

'Very well,' Zhang replied. He brought his fists together in salute and waited for Wang to launch his attack.

'If I may—' As Wang spoke these words, his left fist shot out and his right hand sliced across towards Zhang's right shoulder. Then in a flash, his left fist flipped over and aimed for the right shoulder while the right hand went for the chest. Zhang retreated three paces and fended off the blows. The two circled around, each surprised at the extent of the other's ability.

'His moves are fast and powerful,' Fire Hand Zhang thought. 'He's a strong adversary.'

'He avoided those blows of mine with ease,' Earth-Shaker Wang thought. 'Fire Hand Judge is no misnomer.'

Suddenly, Zhang stepped forward and swept his left leg across at Wang, who jumped clear off the ground to avoid it and countered with a fist aimed at Zhang's face.

They were evenly matched and fought close and fast. The sun was riding high. Their two shadows danced on the ground, merging and separating with lightning speed. Wang knew that at his age, a long drawn-out battle would finish him. So he quickly changed his style, and, with one hand protecting his body and the other facing outwards, he raced round Zhang, his feet following the ancient pattern of the Eight Trigrams.

The style dictated that he keep moving, circling round Zhang to the left and right, waiting for an opportunity to strike. It would make even a kungfu master dizzy after a few circuits.

Zhang knew how ferocious this style was, and lunged at his opponent. But Wang had already circled round the other way. Suddenly he struck at Zhang with both fists, one of which slammed into his shoulder. Zhang caught hold of Wang's wrist and struck out at his elbow in retaliation. With his free hand, Wang swung at Zhang's other shoulder and the two leapt apart.

Zhang had had the worst of the encounter. 'Excellent kungfu!' he shouted. 'Let us duel with swords.'

He drew Frozen Emerald. Wang also drew his sword, and the two stood facing each other.

Zhang's mind was bent on restoring his dignity, and he struck out with a series of fast and vicious sword-strokes. Wang could tell from the way the light glinted on Frozen Emerald that it was a superb weapon, and knew that if their two swords clashed, his own blade would come off the worst. So he did not dare to parry the strokes directly.

They whirled round and round. Wang began to sweat. He secretly worked a number of darts into his palm and then swapped his sword over to his left hand. Slashing out with a left-handed stroke, he simultaneously flung the darts at Zhang. Zhang managed to dodge both blade and darts, but he was becoming more and more flustered by the onslaught. He swept his sword across at Wang's waist. As the two swords clashed, Wang's blade snapped clean in two.

Wang roared and hurled the remaining half of the blade at Zhang, following it with his last three darts. With a cry, Zhang fell over backwards and Frozen Emerald dropped to the ground.

'Forgive me!' Wang cried out anxiously. 'I have some Golden Wound Ointment here.'

Zhang was silent. Wang feared he was dead. Killing a court official was no laughing matter. He rushed across and bent down to examine Zhang.

As he did so, he saw flashes of gold before his eyes. Cursing himself, he leant over backwards as fast as he could, but it was too late. He felt stabs of pain in his left breast and shoulder as the deadly needles plunged home. He gave another angry roar and jumped up ready to fight Zhang to the death. But the pain in his chest and shoulder was so extreme that he could only fall back to the ground with a groan. Zhang laughed out loud. He pulled Wang's dart from his wrist, ripped a strip of cloth from his jacket, bound the wound, then stood up.

'You attacked me when I was coming to see if you were injured!' Wang cried angrily. 'What a despicable thing to do! You'll never be able to look the fighting community in the face after today.'

'We are alone up here. No one else knows anything about it!' exclaimed Zhang with a smile. 'Come on, old man. You've lived to a ripe old age. It's about time you went to meet your forefathers.'

He picked up half of Wang's snapped sword and began digging a large hole in the ground with it. Then he heaved Wang to the edge.

'So, North China Earth-Shaker,' he said, 'here's some real earth to shake!' He kicked Wang down into the hole and began to bury him alive.

Even as he was working away, he heard a long, cold laugh from somewhere behind him. He spun round in fright and saw the Agency guard Han standing there with an Iron Piba missile in his hand.

'So that's how you Agency people operate!' Zhang shouted angrily. 'You arrange a one-to-one duel, and secretly set up an ambush. Do you have no shame?'

'*You* are the shameless one!' Han replied, pointing to where Wang lay half-buried.

'All right, let's see your Iron Piba kungfu then!' Zhang roared. He flew through the air at Han, using Lightness kungfu, and thrust his sword at him. Han retreated two steps and another sword struck out at Zhang from amongst the bushes. Zhang parried the stroke. He saw that the second swordsman was the other 'Agency guard' who had accompanied Han to see him earlier.

'Come on, I'll take you all on!' he shouted. 'I'm not called the Fire Hand Judge for nothing!'

Just as he was about to strike, he heard a noise behind and turned to see eight or nine men walking towards him, led by the Red Flower Society's Helmsman, Chen Jialuo. A shiver of panic passed through him, and he glanced about, looking for some avenue of escape.

'Mr Han, go and see to your master,' said Helmsman Chen. Han ran over to the hole and helped Wang out. Fire Hand Zhang did not try to stop him. Old Wang was trembling all over.

'Earth-Shaker Wang told me he wanted a private duel with no observers or seconds!' shouted Zhang.

'My Brothers and I came to admire the scenery and happened to come across the two of you,' replied Helmsman Chen. 'It was a very impressive display, but you did not win very honourably, Fire Hand Zhang.'

'We were matching our strength and our wits. All is fair in war. What was wrong with my victory?'

'Indeed.' Helmsman Chen smiled as he walked slowly

forward. 'You certainly seem quite a strategist. I suppose you know that we want to rescue our Brother Wen Tailai?'

'Well?'

'His manacles are made of the finest steel which no file will ever get through. I therefore have no alternative but to ask you to lend us your excellent sword. As a member of the fighting community, I am sure you will be happy to oblige.'

Fire Hand Zhang looked at the number of his adversaries. He was going to have a hard time getting out of this.

'If you want to borrow my sword, you will have to take it by force,' he said. He turned and sprinted towards the path that led down the southern side of the mountain. Suddenly, he saw in front of him the one-armed Taoist priest. He slung two Golden Needles at him. He knew there was no chance of hitting the priest, but he hoped that the needles would occupy him long enough for him to get past. But Father Speckless deftly dodged out of the way, then crouched down and thrust his sword at Zhang's right leg. Zhang brought his own blade down to parry the stroke and the two fought fiercely. Fire Hand Zhang could feel his strength beginning to wane. The priest gave a shout and Frozen Emerald was jolted out of Zhang's hand. In that split second, as Zhang stared at his sword in surprise, the priest aimed a flying kick at his groin, knocking him to the ground. Hunchback Zhang and two of the other Red Flower fighters then jumped on him while Luo Bing pulled out some rope and bound his hands. Remembering that it was Fire Hand Zhang who had been responsible for the capture of her husband at Iron Ball Manor, she punched him hard on the nose.

'You have only won because there are more of you!' Fire Hand Zhang shouted angrily. 'If you're going to kill me, then get it over with.'

'He ought to be buried in the hole he dug,' suggested Melancholy Ghost Shi. The others shouted their agreement. Fire Hand Zhang broke into a cold sweat.

'What do you say?' asked Helmsman Chen. 'Admit defeat and swear never again to go against the Red Flower Society, and we will spare you for the sake of your brother-in-arms, Hidden Needle Lu.'

'You're wasting your breath!' Zhang shouted stubbornly. 'After all your crafty tricks, how can you expect anyone to admit defeat to you?'

'Very well then,' said Chen. 'I will kill you, and spare you the horror of being buried alive.' He pulled out his dagger and walked over to Zhang. 'Aren't you afraid of death?' he asked.

'Do your worst,' Zhang replied, and laughed bitterly. He closed his eyes and waited for death.

Suddenly they heard shouts from lower down the mountain, and turned to see two men running towards them, moving as fast as the wind with superb Lightness kungfu.

As they approached, the Red Flower heroes saw that one of the men was Hidden Needle Lu, and the other a kindly-looking old Taoist priest.

Just as Lu was about to introduce the old man, Fire Hand Zhang went up to him and bowed.

'Brother Ma,' he said, 'we have not seen each other for many years. How fares it with you?'

The Red Flower heroes realized that this must be the celebrated Wudang Master Ma Zhen, Scholar Yu's Shifu. They all bowed before him.

'We came as fast as we could when we heard about the duel,' said Hidden Needle Lu. He looked round and saw with relief that no one had been fatally injured.

Ma Zhen had long heard of Fire Hand Zhang's unsavoury record, but seeing his bloodstained clothes and swollen face, he now found himself feeling almost sorry for him. 'Brother Zhang, how did you get into such a mess?' he asked.

'I was one against so many. How could things have ended any differently?' Zhang replied indignantly.

The Red Flower heroes were furious at his insinuation.

'So you're blameless are you?' shouted Zhou Qi. She brandished her sword and made as if to charge at Zhang, but her father held her back.

'His two brothers-in-arms are here now,' Lord Zhou said. 'Let us see what they have to say.' His words put the onus of dealing with Zhang squarely on Ma Zhen's shoulders. Ma Zhen looked at Lu, and then at Zhang. Suddenly, he went down on his knees before the Red Flower heroes. Greatly surprised, Helmsman Chen helped him up again.

'My friends,' Ma began, his voice choked with sobs. 'This useless brother-in-arms of mine has committed terrible crimes. To the shame of our Wudang School, we have failed to discipline him

and have lost face before all our brothers in the fighting community.
I…I…' He was overcome with emotion. 'Brother Lu,' he added.
'Tell them what it is I am trying to say.'

'Brother Ma is very angry about Zhang's behaviour. But in
memory of our late Shifu, he wishes you to spare him.'

The Red Flower heroes looked at Helmsman Chen and then
at Lord Zhou, waiting for their decision.

'Let Lord Zhou be the arbiter,' said Helmsman Chen. 'We will
do whatever he says.'

'Considering it was this man who had Iron Ball Manor burnt
to the ground, I ought not to rest until I am revenged,' said Zhou,
then paused. 'But having heard your words, Master Ma, I will hand
him over to you and let bygones be bygones.'

'Father!' Zhou Qi cried, horrified.

Zhou stroked her hair. 'Don't worry, child,' he said softly.

'Out of respect for your wishes, Master Ma, the Red Flower
Society will also let bygones be bygones,' added Chen.

Both Ma and Hidden Needle Lu bowed to the heroes. 'We
will be eternally grateful,' said Ma.

'What do you intend to do if he turns to evil ways again?'
Father Speckless asked sternly.

'I will discipline him. I will make sure that he turns over a
new leaf,' Ma replied. 'I will now take him back with me to my
hermitage on Wudang Mountain so that he can reflect on his
misdeeds in solitude. Brother Lu, once Rolling Thunder Wen is out
of danger, please write and inform me so that my mind can rest
easy. By the way, where is my pupil, Scholar Yu?'

'He was separated from us at the Yellow River,' replied
Helmsman Chen. 'We later heard that he had been rescued by a
girl, but we have no further information. As soon as we have saved
Brother Wen, we will go and investigate. Please don't worry, sir.'

'That disciple of mine is very clever, but he is not steady enough.
Please give him whatever instruction is necessary, Master Chen.'

'We treat our Brothers as blood relations,' replied Helmsman
Chen. 'Brother Yu is part of our family. He is a capable man. We
place great faith in him.'

'I am very grateful for what you have done today,' said Ma.
'Friends! Next time any of you are in Hubei Province, please come
to stay with me on Wudang Mountain.' The Red Flower heroes all
thanked him.

'Very well! Let's go!' Ma spoke curtly to Fire Hand Zhang. Zhang noticed that Luo Bing had already slung Frozen Emerald across her back. He knew that to try to retrieve it would only result in more punishment. So he bit his lip and followed after Ma Zhen, his head bowed.

When they had gone, the others asked Hidden Needle Lu for an account of what had happened to him since they had parted. He told them that for a time he had searched unsuccessfully for his young disciple Li Yuanzhi. Then, realizing that Fire Hand Zhang was the key to the affair, he had gone south and asked his brother-in-arms Ma Zhen to help him. They had hurried to Peking together only to discover that Fire Hand Zhang had already set out for Hangzhou, so they had travelled south once more.

The Red Flower heroes walked slowly down from the peak, talking as they went. Helmsman Chen turned to old Wang and Han.

'You are both free to go,' he said.

'Master Chen, I will never forget how you saved my life today,' Wang replied.

Helmsman Chen laughed. 'I must ask your forgiveness, Master Wang,' he said and related how it was they who had stolen the jade vases and provoked the duel between himself and Fire Hand Zhang. Wang was so relieved to have escaped from the jaws of death, he did not seem to blame him for the deception.

'You are certainly a born leader,' he said to Helmsman Chen, and laughed. 'So young and already a hero. I may be old, but I still have much to learn.'

'When our affairs have been successfully concluded, we will drink a few cups of wine together,' Chen replied.

They arrived at the lake and returned to Lonely Mountain by boat. Hidden Needle Lu extracted the needles from Wang's wounds with the use of a magnet, and then treated them with Golden Wound Ointment.

By this time, evening was approaching.

'Most of the work on the tunnel has been completed,' the Hangzhou Lodge Master Ma reported. 'We should be finished in another six hours.'

Helmsman Chen nodded his thanks, and sent Crocodile Jiang off to supervise the work. He then turned once more to old Wang and Han.

'We have been looking after a few members of your Agency,' he said. 'Why don't you take them to the lake for some recreation?'

As Wang watched the Red Flower Society fighters hurrying to and fro, he guessed they were preparing to rescue Wen Tailai. He decided that if he were to leave by himself now and the plan should go wrong, they could easily suspect that he had informed the authorities.

'I am getting old, and what with these wounds, I am not feeling at all well,' he replied. 'I would like to rest here for a day.'

'As you wish,' said Chen.

A Gunpowder Plot

The Red Flower heroes ate a hearty meal and then returned to their rooms to rest. At six o'clock that evening, one of their men reported that the tunnel diggers were already under the Commander-in-Chief's Yamen, but that a large rock was blocking their path, and they were trying to dig around it. Helmsman Chen and Mastermind Xu delegated their men: some were to attack from the left, some from the right, and some would be held in reserve. At about eight o'clock, the same man returned to report that the diggers had come up against a large iron plate and had decided to stop work for a while for fear of alerting the guards on duty inside.

'We will wait another two hours and then make our move,' said Helmsman Chen.

Those two hours passed slowly. The Red Flower heroes could hardly control their impatience. Luo Bing kept restlessly sitting down and standing up, while Hunchback Zhang paced up and down the hall mumbling curses. The Twin Knights took out some cards and began playing with Iron Pagoda Yang and Leopard Wei (who were not concentrating on their game, and were well and truly cleaned out). Zhou Qi was examining their new toy, Frozen Emerald, watched from a distance by a smiling Mastermind Xu. Lodge Master Ma kept taking a large gold watch out of his pocket and checking the time. Hidden Needle Lu and Buddha Zhao were deeply absorbed in a conversation about all that had happened since they last met. Father Speckless and Lord Zhou sat down to a game of chess. Helmsman Chen picked up a book of poems by the famous Song-dynasty poet Lu You, and began reciting them quietly to himself. Melancholy Ghost Shi just sat there motionless, gazing up at the night sky.

'The time has come,' Lodge Master Ma finally announced.

The Red Flower heroes all made for the door. They donned various disguises and made their way separately through the darkened streets of Hangzhou to a house just outside the Commander-in-Chief's Yamen, where Crocodile Jiang was waiting for them. 'The place is absolutely crawling with soldiers,' he said. 'Be as quiet as possible.'

He stood at the entrance of the tunnel with his Iron Oar at the ready, as the Red Flower heroes filed through one by one. The tunnel had been dug deep, and since Hangzhou is situated in such a low-lying area, they found themselves ankle-deep in water. By the time they reached the big rock, the muddy water was up to their chests, while several dozen yards further on, it rose to their necks.

Seven or eight of their scouts were already waiting near the iron plate with torches and spades in hand.

Helmsman Chen gave the order to start work, and watched them as they worked like demons. Soon they had shifted the rock to the side of the iron plate. Another spurt of furious digging and the iron plate itself was dislodged, and Leopard Wei, his pair of hooks at the ready, went through first with the rest of the Red Flower heroes following behind.

The men held the torches high to illuminate the way as Leopard Wei ran along a corridor towards Wen's cell. But they found the way blocked by a locked iron gate.

'Iron Pagoda, Leopard,' said Mastermind Xu quickly. 'Go and guard the exit to the dungeon just in case the Manchus have plotted a secret attack.'

The scouts meanwhile worked to loosen the stones to the side of the gate, and then, with the help of several of the Red Flower heroes, lifted the gate out of position. Luo Bing ran through and into Wen's cell. It was empty.

This was the latest in a series of heartbreaking disappointments. Luo Bing crumpled onto the floor and began to sob. Zhou Qi wanted to comfort her, but her father held her back.

'Let her be,' he said. 'A cry will do her good.'

'Clearly Commander Li predicted a jailbreak, and has moved Brother Wen somewhere else,' said Mastermind Xu.

'But we're in the Yamen now, so we will find him no matter what,' replied Helmsman Chen.

They went back to the door of the dungeon and saw Iron Pagoda Yang fighting fiercely with a group of Manchu soldiers. Father Speckless gave a shout, charged out, and finished off two Manchu soldiers on the spot. Further on, they found Leopard Wei battling six or seven officers.

In view of his long-standing relationship with Commander Li, Hidden Needle Lu thought it inadvisable to reveal himself. He tore a strip off his gown and covered his face so that only the eyes were showing. Just then, the Manchu soldiers broke away and retreated up to the Yamen courtyard in confusion, with Leopard Wei and the others in hot pursuit.

Mastermind Xu leapt up onto a nearby wall. From that vantage point he could see soldiers standing guard throughout the whole Yamen complex. A drum sounded, and Xu interpreted this to mean that the commanders were still positioning their soldiers. Then he spotted a two-storey building standing all on its own in the southern part of the main courtyard, surrounded by several hundred troops. There was nothing special about the building except for the tight security around it, and Xu decided that this was probably where Rolling Thunder Wen was being held. He jumped down from the wall and whirled his sword around his head.

'Brothers, follow me!' he shouted, and charged towards the building.

The further they went, the more soldiers appeared. But despite their numerical superiority, the Manchu troops were no match for the Red Flower Society fighters, each of whom was an experienced practitioner of the Martial Arts. In only a short while, the Red Flower heroes had fought to within a few yards of the building.

'Buddha, let's you and I go and have a look inside,' Father Speckless said to Zhao.

They sprang over to the doorway with two long strides. A sword came swerving towards them, but with one thrust from the one-armed priest's blade, the Manchu swordsman screamed and his weapon clattered to the ground. They raced on into the building with Luo Bing and the others close behind.

As the fighting continued, the Red Flower heroes found the numbers of Manchu soldiers diminishing. Suddenly they heard Father Speckless yell from upstairs: 'Brother Wen is here! We've got him!' The Red Flower heroes gave a cry of joyful excitement.

Zhou Qi raced up the stairs and saw everyone gathered round an iron cage. Helmsman Chen was sawing at the bars with Frozen Emerald. Zhou Qi went closer and saw that within the first iron cage was another smaller cage. And there, within this second cage, sat Wen Tailai, with his arms and legs manacled like a captured wild animal. Helmsman Chen sawed through two bars of the outer cage, and Hunchback Zhang used brute strength to twist them apart. Luo Bing was slim enough to wriggle through into the outer cage. She took Frozen Emerald from Helmsman Chen and began to saw away at the lock on the small cage. The Red Flower heroes were all smiling in jubilant expectation. Then suddenly they heard a bugle sounding. The remaining Manchu troops had retreated about a hundred feet and had formed themselves into ranks all around the building.

'Chen Jialuo!' someone shouted from amongst the Manchu ranks. 'I wish to speak with your Helmsman!'

Helmsman Chen went to the window and spotted Commander Li outside. 'I am here. What is it, Commander Li?'

'Come out quickly now, or you will all die.'

'We will not come out without our Brother!' replied Helmsman Chen. 'We would rather die than do that. Today we are determined to leave here with Brother Wen, or not at all.'

'Since you are so stubborn,' Li shouted, 'you leave me no choice.' He gave the order to start the fire.

The troops pushed huge piles of firewood and grass right round the building. The firewood was soaked in oil and seconds later a torch was thrown into it, and a fiery ring blazed up into the sky. The Red Flower heroes were trapped inside.

Helmsman Chen could see how dangerous the situation was, but he remained outwardly calm. 'We must all work together,' he said quietly. 'Cut through some more of the bars as quickly as you can.'

Another Manchu gesticulated angrily at Chen. 'Death is staring you in the face and still you don't go down on your knees and beg for mercy?' he boomed. 'Do you realize what we have stored in that building?'

As Chen stood there, pondering this remark, he heard Mastermind Xu exclaim in their Red Flower secret code: 'Oh no! The place is packed with gunpowder! We're in real trouble!'

It was then that Chen noticed the row of wooden barrels around the room they were in. He quickly smashed one of them open and a black powder flew out in all directions. The smell of saltpetre assailed their nostrils. His heart froze. They were all going to be blown to pieces! He turned and saw that the lock on the inner cage had now been forced open, and Luo Bing was helping Wen out.

'Sister Luo Bing, Brother Zhao!' shouted Helmsman Chen. 'You two protect Brother Wen. Everyone follow me.' He charged down the stairs. Hunchback Zhang bent down and heaved Wen onto his back, making his way down to the ground floor, escorted by Luo Bing and Buddha Zhao, Hidden Needle Lu, Lord Zhou, and the others. As they reached the door, they saw swarms of arrows flying at them like locusts. Leopard Wei and the Twin Knights tried several times to break out of the building, but each time they were driven back inside.

'You are standing in a gunpowder keg, and I have the fuse!' Commander Li shouted. He raised a fiery torch and waved it. 'The minute I light the fuse, you will all be burnt to a cinder. Put that man Wen down immediately.'

Helmsman Chen knew that what he said was true. But at the same time he calculated that because of Wen's importance to the Emperor, Li would not dare to light the fuse.

'Put Brother Wen down!' he shouted. 'Let's get out of here!' He brandished his long-sword and charged out with Leopard Wei and the Twin Knights at his side.

Hunchback Zhang was charging forward with his head down, and did not hear a word of what Chen had said.

'Put Brother Wen down!' cried Buddha Zhao. 'It's too dangerous. We don't stand a chance. We've got to get out or he'll be killed too.'

Hunchback Zhang placed Wen on the ground near the door. Luo Bing hesitated, but Hunchback Zhang grabbed her by the arm and hurtled on out after the others. Li saw in the firelight that they had abandoned Wen, and with a wave of his hand ordered his archers to stop firing to prevent him being hit by mistake.

Having made it out of the building, the Red Flower heroes regrouped by the wall.

'Brother Yang, Brother Wei, Brother Zhang, and the Twin Knights, you five are to lead an attack on the Manchu troops and disperse them,' ordered Helmsman Chen. 'Brother Xu, you must somehow come up with a way to cut the gunpowder fuse. The rest of you, as soon as that's done, we go back and rescue Brother Wen.'

Commander Li was just about to order someone to go and mount guard over Wen when he spotted the Twin Knights and three others storming towards him. He hastily shouted to a detachment of Imperial Guards to intercept them.

Hidden Needle Lu, the first to spot a way out of the dilemma, ran like the wind straight for Commander Li. Li's personal guards moved to stop him, but Lu dodged to the left and right and slipped past them all, darting like a bird, wriggling like a fish. In a moment, he was at Li's side. Yuanzhi, wearing boy's clothes, was standing next to her father. Seeing this strange masked man charging forward, she cried out shrilly 'How dare you!' and thrust her sword straight at his chest. It was the move known as Spring Clouds Suddenly Unfold, taught her by her Shifu—Hidden Needle himself! Lu saw it coming and ducked under the stroke, then slipped round behind Commander Li and gave him a powerful shove which sent him reeling forward. Full of fear for her father, Yuanzhi struck out again with her sword, but Lu dodged out of the way once more, picked Li up in his arms, and ran inside the circle of fire. The Manchu troops shouted in alarm, but the heat from the flames was so intense that none of them dared follow him. Li Yuanzhi herself was held back by Leopard Wei and his whirling steel hooks.

When the Red Flower heroes saw Hidden Needle Lu carrying Commander Li into the danger zone, Hunchback Zhang and Crocodile Jiang went in after them. Helmsman Chen gave orders that no one else was to follow them.

The Manchu troops completely ignored Helmsman Chen and the other Red Flower fighters, and only stared anxiously at the men inside the ring of fire. Suddenly, a man with a torch leapt over to the gunpowder fuse and lit it. Zeng Tunan, a lieutenant under Li, recognized him as one of the Imperial Guards.

The thread of sparks whirled off at an incredible speed. Once the lighted fuse reached the circle of fire and passed through it into the building, it would ignite the gunpowder. Disaster would be inevitable. The Manchu troops began to scatter in panic. In the midst of the confusion, a figure wearing a long blue gown, his face covered with a blue silk mask, raced forward and began thrashing at the sparks with the whip he had in his hand. Seeing that this was of no avail, he threw himself bodily down onto the burning fuse itself. His clothes burst into flames, but the fuse was stopped.

The immediate danger had been averted. Hunchback Zhang and Crocodile Jiang now charged out through the circle of fire carrying Wen Tailai. The flames were blazing more fiercely than ever. The Twin Knights went racing forward to meet them, and told them all to roll about on the ground until all the flames had been extinguished. First they rolled Wen on the ground, then they saw to themselves. Luo Bing ran up to attend to Wen.

The Twin Knights meanwhile ran over to rescue the masked man in blue, who had collapsed on the ground. All three of them caught fire. By the time the flames had been extinguished, the man's body was a mass of burns.

Once Wen was out of danger, Hidden Needle Lu slung Commander Li over his shoulder, took a deep breath, and leapt back out of the circle like a great bird.

'We've done it!' shouted Helmsman Chen, and gave the order to beat a hasty retreat.

Father Speckless led the way, brandishing his sword, and the others followed—the Twin Knights carrying the masked man, Hunchback Zhang carrying Wen, and Hidden Needle Lu with Commander Li still thrown over his shoulder.

The Manchu troops chased after them, shouting and yelling. But not one of them dared get too close. The eight hand-picked Imperial Guards, who had been instructed to protect Wen, were frantic to see him escape like this: his loss could cost them their heads. Among them was the man who had lit the fuse. Chen handed Frozen Emerald to Buddha Zhao, saying, 'Cover the others as they retreat, Brother Zhao. I'm going to deal with this fellow.' He pulled out his Pearl Strings, the ropes with steel balls fastened to the ends, and with a flick of his hand, tossed them at the man.

The man tried to leap out of the way, but he was not quick enough, and the strings wrapped themselves round his legs. He was caught. Chen tugged fiercely, and dragged him into the heart of the roaring flames.

By this time, almost all of the heroes had escaped over the Yamen walls. Chen raised his hand and shouted to the rest: 'Retreat!'

Leopard Wei raced over to the gunpowder fuse and relit it, and the Manchu troops cried out in fear as the remaining Red Flower fighters retired.

Suddenly, there was a blinding flash and a roar as the gunpowder stacked in the building ignited. Explosion followed explosion, black smoke swirled up into the air, and bricks flew in all directions. The soldiers threw themselves on the ground but, despite their distance from the building, several dozen of them had their heads smashed to pieces by stray bricks and pieces of wood. By the time the rest crawled back onto their feet, the Red Flower heroes were gone.

Only when they were certain they were not being chased did the Red Flower heroes relax. They rode out of Hangzhou and came to a river where more than a dozen boats were lined up along the bank. The heroes joyfully boarded the craft.

'Master Chen,' whispered Hidden Needle Lu. 'Commander Li and I have an old connection. Now that Brother Wen is safe, why don't we let him go?'

'If that is your desire,' Chen replied, and, on his orders, an attendant untied Li's bonds and released him. As he did so, he gave the order to weigh anchor.

'Head for Jiaxing!'

The rivers and canals of Zhejiang Province are an endless maze of twists and turns, and in a moment the boats were lost to view.

'Now we can turn around and head west,' said Chen. 'We can take Brother Wen to Heaven's Eye Mountain to convalesce. Commander Li can go chasing after us to Jiaxing!'

The heroes burst out laughing and, in that moment, all the accumulated oppression and frustration of the past several months was swept away.

Dawn was just breaking. Luo Bing wiped her husband's body clean. She had already sawn off his manacles with Frozen Emerald, and he was now in a deep sleep.

'Helmsman,' said Mastermind Xu. 'That masked man who saved Rolling Thunder is very badly wounded. Shall we have a look at him?'

'From the way he keeps his face covered, I should say he doesn't want to be recognized. I think we should let him be,' said Lord Zhou.

Nonetheless Xin Yan gently applied white soy sauce to the masked man's burns. His whole body had been blistered by the flames, and he screamed out incessantly in pain, his hands clawing about uncontrollably. Suddenly, he inadvertently ripped the mask off. As he did so, the Red Flower heroes all cried out in unison: 'Brother Yu!'

It was Scholar Yu, the man with the Golden Flute. They were horrified when they saw his face—it was red-black, raw and swollen, with countless blisters all over it. Luo Bing brought a wet cloth and lightly wiped the dirt and gunpowder from his face, then applied more of the white soy sauce. Whenever she thought about his provocative behaviour that night near Iron Ball Manor she still felt angry, but having seen what he was willing to go through to save her own husband, she knew that his infatuation was more than just lust. As she looked down at him, she wondered how she could ever repay him.

The boats docked and Lodge Master Ma sent someone hurrying off to find a doctor. When he came, the doctor first examined Wen. 'This gentleman's wounds are only superficial,' he said. 'He is strong and healthy, and with several months of convalescence he should make a good recovery.' Then he pointed at Yu, and went on: 'This gentleman, however, has some extremely serious burns. There is a danger that the fire poison will attack his heart. I will make out a prescription to counter the effect of the fire, and examine him again later.' From his tone, he appeared to consider it a hopeless case.

The doctor went ashore. A while later, Wen opened his eyes and looked at everyone standing around him.

'What are you all doing here?' he asked wearily.

Luo Bing burst into tears. 'Thunder!' she cried happily. 'You're back! You're alive!'

Wen nodded slightly and closed his eyes again.

As for Yu, none of the Red Flower members had any idea how he had come to be at the Yamen that night. What had happened was this. During the night battle at the Yellow River crossing, Yuanzhi had somehow been cut off from the Red Flower fighters. She had spotted a carriage and jumped onto it, urging the mules to go and racing blindly away. She did not stop to rest until the next morning, when she had put a great distance between herself and the Manchu army. Then, upon opening the carriage curtain, she had found Scholar Yu lying inside unconscious and badly wounded. After carefully considering the situation, she climbed back onto the carriage and drove on to the nearby town of Wenguang.

As the daughter of an official, she was used to doing things in style. She chose the largest residence in the town and knocked on the door to ask for lodgings. The residence turned out to be that of the evil landowner, Tang, who took them in. (This was the fat man who had procured the drugs from Doctor Cao, to stupefy his beautiful guest.) When subsequently Tang was found murdered, Scholar Yu realized immediately that they could be implicated, and they escaped in the confusion. Yuanzhi was planning to go to Hangzhou anyway to be with her parents; and Yu, knowing that Hangzhou was also where Wen was being held, decided they might as well travel together. He was still seriously wounded, and Yuanzhi nursed him on their journey.

When they reached Hangzhou, Yuanzhi told her parents that her companion had been wounded while saving her from bandits, and her father, Commander Li, allowed him to stay in the Yamen as an expression of his gratitude. A doctor was called to treat his injuries. When Commander Li saw what a refined person Yu was, skilled in both scholarly and martial pursuits, he decided that once his wounds had healed he would invite Yu to become his son-in-law. Little did he know that Yu was also a key member of the Red Flower Society.

Beautiful Jade's Boudoir

When Qian Long was informed that the Red Flower Society had escaped with Wen, he was both surprised and angry. But he decided there was nothing to be gained by punishing the Imperial Guards. He could see from their wounds that they had fought bravely, and to their enormous relief he let them off leniently.

A while later, when Commander Li went to see the Emperor, he was told that a decision on whether or not he would lose his post would be deferred until later. Li was overjoyed at this unexpected clemency.

After Li had left, Qian Long continued to think about Wen's escape, wondering if his secret would now get out. From what Wen had said, it did not appear that he knew everything, but there was something about his manner which suggested there was still much he did know and could tell. Wen had said there were two important pieces of evidence hidden somewhere, and Qian Long wondered what this evidence could be. He was himself by now almost certain that he was of Chinese blood, and not a Manchu. But what good could possibly come of such knowledge leaking out? He paced about the room, extremely angry that he, the Son of Heaven, should have been outwitted like this by a band of brigands. If they discovered his secret, would he be forced to submit to them for the rest of his life, on pain of having the secret revealed to the world at large? The more he thought about it, the angrier he became. He picked up a large blue-and-white porcelain vase, decorated with a floral pattern, and threw it violently to the floor. The guards and eunuchs waiting outside heard the crash clearly and trembled in their boots, not daring to enter.

Qian Long passed most of that day in a state of great mental confusion. Then, towards evening, he heard the sound of gentle music drifting in from somewhere outside. The music came closer and closer, passed by the gates of the Yamen, then gradually receded. A moment later, another musical troupe passed by. He had always been very fond of music, and the sound had the effect of softening his mood.

He called for service, and a young chamberlain named He Shen, who had recently come to favour, hurried in.

'What is that music outside?' Qian Long asked. 'Go and find out.'

After a while, He Shen came back to report: 'I made enquiries, Majesty, and learned that all of the famous courtesans of Hangzhou will gather on the West Lake this evening to choose what they call the "First Champion Graduate of the Boudoir", as well as Second and Third Champions.'

'How dare they make fun of the Imperial Civil Service Examinations like that!' said Qian Long, amused despite himself. 'How ridiculous!'

Seeing the smile on the Emperor's face, He Shen advanced a step and added in a low voice: 'I understand that the Four Beauties of Qiantang River will be there.'

'And who are the Four Beauties of Qiantang River?'

'Apparently they are the four most famous singsong-girls of Hangzhou. Everyone out on the streets is trying to guess which one will be this year's Champion.'

'The Champion Graduate in the Imperial Examinations is chosen by me personally. Who chooses the Champion of the Boudoir? Don't tell me there is an Emperor of the Boudoir as well?'

'Each singsong-girl sits in a flower-boat, and on the boat are displayed the gold and jewels presented by her customers. Then the winner is chosen by some of Hangzhou's most eminent gentlemen.'

'When do they play this game?' Qian Long asked, fascinated.

'Soon,' He Shen replied. 'As soon as it starts to get dark, the judging will begin. If Your Highness is interested, you could go and watch.'

Qian Long smiled. 'I'm afraid people would laugh at me,' he said. 'If the Empress were to hear that I had been choosing the Champion of the Boudoir, she might not be too pleased!'

He laughed.

'If Your Majesty dressed up in ordinary clothes, no one would know,' He Shen suggested. He knew the Emperor's weakness for mingling 'incognito' with his subjects.

'Very well, we'll go and have a quiet look and then come back. But tell anyone who comes with me that they're not to do anything to attract attention,' instructed Qian Long.

He Shen quickly helped Qian Long change into the attire of a member of the gentry—a long silk gown and a finely embroidered jacket—and then they left for the West Lake, together with the old kungfu master Bai Zhen and several dozen Imperial Guards.

Once at the lakeside, a guard steered a boat up to meet them. Music and singing could be heard coming from different parts of the lake, while the multitude of lanterns provided a sumptuous sight. They watched as more than twenty flower-boats glided lazily back and forth over the water, each boat draped with silk curtains and lanterns. Qian Long ordered the oarsman to steer close to the flower-boats. Some of them were decorated with flowers and animals cleverly constructed out of silk and lit with lanterns. Others had lanterns with elaborate illustrations of stories picked out on the silk, forming delicate traceries of light. It was a magical sight. Qian Long sighed at this gorgeous spectacle, so characteristic of southern China, and so far outdoing anything the north had to offer. As many as a hundred other small boats moved to and fro on the water, carrying well-to-do pleasure-seekers who appraised each of the flower-boats as they glided past.

A gong sounded and the music from the boats ceased. One rocket after another now soared up into the air and exploded into a dazzling array of colour before falling into the lake with a hiss. As the firework display ended, the curtains on the flower-boats were drawn apart at exactly the same moment, to reveal a gorgeously attired woman seated inside each one. Thunderous cheering and applause arose from every part of the lake.

Servants produced wine and food for the Emperor to partake of while enjoying the scene. His boat glided slowly over the lake past the flower-boats. Qian Long kept three thousand concubines in his Palace in Peking, and had seen countless beauties in his time. But the reflections of the lanterns on the water, the splash of the oars, and the slight waft of perfume had completely captivated him. As they neared the boats of the Four Beauties of Qiantang River, they saw that they were different from the other flower-boats. One was decorated entirely with paper water lilies, while the second was topped by two pagodas. The third was decked out as the Lunar Palace and lit with lanterns shaped as toads and hares, the animals which are supposed to inhabit the moon. Qian Long gasped in delight. As they glided towards the fourth, he saw that it was decorated entirely with real shrubs and flowers, whose branches criss-crossed each other and created a thick panoply of foliage: it was as simple as nature, and yet as beautiful as a painting. The courtesan was dressed all in white, and she was seated with her back to them. But even viewed from the back, she had an air of other-worldliness about her. She was like a goddess.

Qian Long was overwhelmed. He could not restrain himself from bursting audibly into song. It was a much-quoted line that he sang, from the romantic opera *The Western Chamber*:

'Oh, will you not turn your face to me?'

The courtesan, hearing these famous words, did indeed turn. And then she smiled. Qian Long's heart leapt: it was the girl he had met on the West Lake several days before, Beautiful Jade.

He heard the tinkle of a feminine voice as the courtesan on the water lily boat began to sing. At the end of her song, the crowd applauded and a pile of ingots, big and small, mounted on the table in front of her. Then the courtesan in the twin-pagoda boat picked up a piba-lute and lightly strummed a tune, following which the third played a melody on the flute. Qian Long ordered He Shen to give her ten taels of gold.

The pleasure launches then crowded round Beautiful Jade's boat. She parted her ruby lips, flashing her sparkling white teeth, and began to sing a song, accompanied by a flute.

It was the middle of the eighth month, and it was already cool on the lake, but Beautiful Jade's voice had a warmth that conjured summer breezes and fragrant flowers.

'Such talent!' sighed Qian Long.

To his great delight, Beautiful Jade's dewdrop eyes constantly looked over in his direction as she sang. She was evidently drawn to him. Qian Long loved to be admired. He was fond of demonstrating his own talents in art, calligraphy, and poetry, and his ministers, not surprisingly, praised everything he did. But this was a different sort of encounter. Beautiful Jade did not know who he was. For a beautiful woman to favour him not out of reverence for his position and power as Emperor, but out of genuine recognition of some real quality of his, must mean that she had been struck by his spirit, his good looks, and talent. Famous courtesans are truly discerning, he thought. He immediately ordered He Shen to present Beautiful Jade with fifty taels of gold.

The boats of all the courtesans were piled high with gifts, especially those of the Four Beauties. Midnight approached and the chief judge, a famous Hangzhou poet by the name of Yuan Mei, began the job of inspecting the gifts. As with the Imperial Examinations, not only the courtesans, but also the spectators on the lake, were on tenterhooks as to the outcome.

Qian Long said a few quiet words to He Shen, who nodded and hurried back to the Yamen. He returned a while later with a package.

The inspection over, the boats all clustered round the launch on which the judge sat, to hear him announce the winners.

'The gifts presented to Miss Twin Pagodas are the most numerous,' he announced. There was a roar from the other boats as some applauded and some groaned.

'Not so fast,' cried a voice. 'I wish to present one hundred taels of gold to Miss Water Lily.'

'And I wish to present Miss Lunar Palace with a jade bracelet and ten pearls,' another wealthy gentleman called out. When the crowd saw the lustrous green bracelet and the large round pearls sparkling under the lantern light, they knew that they must be worth well over a hundred taels of gold. They all concluded that Miss Lunar Palace was certain to be chosen as that year's Champion.

Suddenly He Shen called out: 'My master has a number of items he would like to present to Miss Beautiful Jade!'

A servant carried the package over to the judge, who opened it to find three scrolls. He ordered the servants to unroll them.

As the first scroll was unrolled, the judge and his colleagues started in surprise: it was a poem by the great poet of the late Tang dynasty, Li Shangyin, written in the hand of the famous Ming-dynasty calligrapher, Zhu Yunming.

'This is an extremely valuable piece of calligraphy,' exclaimed one of the judge's colleagues, another celebrated Hangzhou poet by the name of Li E. Another of the assistant judges, the poet Zhao Yi, hurriedly opened the second scroll and saw that it was a painting of a beautiful lady with flowers in her hair, done by the great Ming painter Tang Yin. It carried the Imperial vermilion seal of Qian Long. The judge was puzzled and turned to ask his various colleagues if they knew who the benefactor was. They looked at the scrolls and pondered silently.

'Why don't we go over and meet him?' suggested one, another celebrated local poet called Shen Deqian.

'If we do that, people will accuse us of being unfair,' replied another. 'With such treasures as these two scrolls, the Champion is obviously Beautiful Jade.'

'Let's have a look at the third scroll,' suggested a third.

They unrolled it and saw that it was a piece of unsigned calligraphy, 'in the manner of' Zhao Mengfu, the great calligrapher of the Song dynasty.

'Not very graceful,' remarked one of the experts, himself a Yangzhou-born calligrapher of distinction by the name of Zheng Banqiao. 'Lacks strength.'

'Sh! That is the Emperor's hand,' whispered Shen Deqian urgently.

This put an end to their discussion.

'The judging of the gifts has been completed,' the chief judge announced in a loud voice. 'This year's Champion is Miss Beautiful Jade, second is Miss Lunar Palace, third is Miss Water Lily.'

Applause sounded from all corners of the lake.

Beautiful Jade began to sing again, and her tender voice penetrated Qian Long to the core, moving him deeply.

'Go and tell that girl to come over,' he said to He Shen. 'But don't say who I am.'

The boat glided over to Beautiful Jade's boat and He Shen leapt across. After an interval, he returned with a piece of paper and handed it to Qian Long, saying: 'She told me to give this to you.'

Qian Long peered at the note under the lamplight. It simply read: 'Tomorrow.'

The calligraphy was very poor, but the paper was heavily scented with a fragrance that made his heart quiver.

'Why wait until tomorrow? I am here now,' he said. But when he looked up again, he saw that Beautiful Jade's boat was already moving off. The concubines of his harem tried every trick they could think of to win his favour. When had a woman ever rejected his advances? But the more she kept him at arm's length, the more he desired her. He hurriedly issued an Imperial command: 'Chase after that boat!'

Qian Long stood silently at the prow, his heart pursuing the boat ahead. The lights on the lake were beginning to go out now, but the music had not yet ceased. He indistinctly heard what he thought was the sound of soft laughter and conversation from the boat in front.

The distance between the two boats gradually closed. Suddenly the curtain on the flower-boat parted for a second and an object was flung in the direction of Qian Long. Bai Zhen, the ever-present elderly superintendant of the Emperor's guard, lunged forward to intercept it, and as it hit his hand he noticed that it was not a dart as he had expected, but a red handkerchief knotted into a little bundle. He quickly presented it to the Emperor.

Qian Long untied it and inside he found a lotus sweet and a lily bulb: both were time-honoured symbols of love. How could he fail to catch the meaning of such a romantic message?

The flower-boat reached the bank, and Beautiful Jade stepped off and into a small horse-drawn carriage. She looked out of the carriage window and smiled seductively at Qian Long, then closed the curtain.

'Hey! Wait a moment! Don't go!' He Shen yelled, but the driver took no notice and, with a clatter of horses' hooves, the carriage moved off south.

'Get another carriage quickly!' He Shen called. The guards soon found a carriage and forced its occupants out. Qian Long stepped inside and it raced off in pursuit.

Bai Zhen saw that they were heading towards the fashionable pleasure-quarter of the city, and concluded to his relief that it was no more than a harmless whim of the Emperor's to spend the night with a courtesan. But at the same time, he had seen this same woman only days before with the Red Flower Society men. He needed to take certain precautions against a possible trap. He quickly ordered one of his subordinates to call in extra men to help protect the Emperor.

Beautiful Jade's carriage passed along several streets, then turned into an alley and stopped in front of a pair of black-painted gates. A carriage attendant jumped down and knocked on them just as Qian Long was descending from his carriage. There was a long squeak as the gates opened, and an old woman came out, pulled aside the carriage curtain, and greeted Beautiful Jade. She stepped out of the carriage and, seeing Qian Long standing to one side, hurried over to greet him.

'Thank you so much for your gifts just now,' she said. 'Please come in and have some tea.' Qian Long smiled and walked in after her. A guard rushed in ahead of him, his hand on the hilt of his sword, to make sure that all was safe. Beyond the gates was a courtyard. The scent of flowers assailed their nostrils, emanating from two cassia trees in full bloom. The moon was still shining brightly, and the shadows of the branches danced on the ground. Qian Long followed Beautiful Jade into a small, elegantly decorated chamber lit by two tall, red candles. A maid brought in wine and food. Qian Long looked at the plates of delicacies, which included marinated chicken and 'thousand-year-old' eggs, and marvelled at how exquisite they were compared to the heavy food he was served in the Imperial Palace. The maid poured two cups of deeply fragrant vintage rice wine through a strainer.

Beautiful Jade took a sip and smiled. 'Mr Dongfang, how can I ever thank you?' she said.

Qian Long raised his cup and drained it in one draught. 'Sing me a song first,' he said, returning her smile. 'We will discuss at our leisure how you can thank me.'

Beautiful Jade picked up a piba-lute and began to play softly. It was a lilting, romantic lyric by Zhou Bangyan, the great song-writer of the Song dynasty.

While the Emperor drank and enjoyed himself with Beautiful Jade, Commander-in-Chief Li arrived and encircled the alley with ring after ring of soldiers. His officers searched every nearby house thoroughly, leaving only Beautiful Jade's room unchecked. Bai Zhen also ordered a group of hand-picked guards to patrol the rooftops with bows and arrows at the ready.

The guards and soldiers were kept busy the whole night. Dawn finally broke without anything untoward having happened. The sun rose, and He Shen tiptoed over to Beautiful Jade's bedchamber to peek through a crack in the window. He spied Qian Long's boots lying by the bed and retreated. Eight o'clock passed, nine o'clock, and ten o'clock, and still there was no sign of the Emperor. Growing more and more anxious, He Shen returned to the window and called quietly: 'Majesty, would you like some breakfast?' He called several times, but there was no response. He then went to the door and gave it a push, but it was barred from the inside. 'Majesty!' he called out loudly. Still no answer from the room. He Shen was now very concerned, but he didn't dare break the door down. Instead, he went to discuss what to do with Commander Li and Bai Zhen.

'Why don't we tell the old bawd to go and knock on the door with some breakfast? His Majesty won't be offended,' suggested Li. This seemed an excellent idea to Bai Zhen, and the three went off to look for the old woman, but they found the whole establishment deserted. Greatly alarmed at the situation, they began banging frantically on Beautiful Jade's door.

'Force it open!' ordered Li. Bai Zhen put both of his palms to the door, and, with a slight push, snapped the door-bar.

He Shen went in first and carefully pulled apart the bed-curtains. The bedclothes were in total disarray, but there was absolutely no sign of either Qian Long or Beautiful Jade. He almost fainted to the floor in fright.

Bai Zhen hastily called in some guards and searched the establishment, but they failed to find so much as half a clue. How could the Emperor have disappeared? The guard they had mounted was so tight that not even a sparrow could have escaped without being noticed! Bai Zhen scoured the room once more looking for a secret door, but he knocked and banged for a long time without finding anything suspicious. The Commandant of the Imperial Guard, Lord Fu Kangan, and the Provincial Governor arrived having received news of Qian Long's disappearance. They all gathered in the middle of Beautiful Jade's boudoir, pale, frightened, and completely at a loss what to do.

The Emperor's New Clothes

What had happened the previous night was this:

After listening to Beautiful Jade sing for a while and drinking a few cups of wine, Qian Long had begun to feel a little sleepy.

Beautiful Jade smiled. 'Would you like to lie down?' she asked. He nodded in answer, and she helped him take off his clothes and boots, led him over to the bed, and covered him with the bedclothes.

'I'm just going out for a second, then I'll come back to you,' she said.

Feeling lulled and drowsy from the scented pillow and sheets, Qian Long heard faint sounds coming from in front of the bed.

'You mischievous girl,' he said with a smile. 'What's keeping you?'

The bed-curtains opened and a head appeared between them. In the candlelight Qian Long could see that it was a pock-marked face, with thick sideburns. It was very different from Beautiful Jade's fair features. He rubbed his eyes in disbelief and looked again just in time to see the intruder hold a shining dagger to his neck and say quietly in Cantonese: 'A pox on your ancestors, you bastard Emperor! One sound and I'll use this!'

Qian Long's mood of drowsy lust vanished in a flash. It was as if he had been doused with a bucket of icy water. The man said nothing more, but stuffed a handkerchief into Qian Long's mouth, then rolled him up tightly in the quilt and carried him off.

Unable to move or make a sound, Qian Long stared at the suffocating blackness all around him and felt himself being carried down a flight of steps. He caught the musty smell of mud and dank humidity, then after a moment he felt himself being carried upwards again. He realized the man must have emerged from a hidden tunnel in the room.

He felt himself being jolted from side to side and heard the sound of wheels starting to move. He was in a carriage. In his terror, he kept asking himself who had kidnapped him and where they were taking him.

The carriage travelled for a long time. After a while the road became more uneven, and the carriage shook and bumped about more violently, indicating that they had left the city. Finally they stopped, and Qian Long felt himself being lifted out of the carriage and carried upwards, one step after another, endlessly, until he thought they must be ascending a high peak. He was so frightened, his whole body trembled. From within the stifling darkness of the quilt, he almost began to cry.

Finally, he was put down with a bump. He waited quietly, not daring to speak, but a long while passed without anything happening. He slowly pushed his head out of the quilt in which he was wrapped and looked out. Everything was still in total darkness. He fancied he could hear the sound of waves breaking a long way off. He listened more closely, and could hear the wind rippling through pine trees and the clear, steady chime of a brass bell. The wind became stronger and stronger, gusting angrily, and he thought he felt the structure he was in rocking slightly. He was more afraid than ever, and made a move as if to stand up.

'If you want to live, don't move,' a deep voice growled close by. Qian Long started in fright and stayed as still as he could.

Gradually the wind subsided and it began to grow light. He could now see that he was in a small room. The people carrying him had climbed for so long to reach it, he thought it must be a house on the peak of some mountain. He heard a series of snuffling noises, and, listening carefully, realized it came from the guards, who were eating noodles. From the sound of it there were two of them, chewing great mouthfuls with relish. Qian Long had been awake all night. He felt hungry and his appetite sharpened as the smell of the noodles wafted over to him.

The two finished eating. One of the guards walked over and placed a full bowl of prawn and eel noodle soup near him. Qian Long wondered if it was intended for him. But the guards said nothing, and despite his hunger he did not dare to open his mouth to ask.

'That bowl of noodles is for you,' one of the guards finally said. 'There's no poison in it.'

Qian Long was overjoyed. He loosened the quilt and sat up to get the bowl, but then a wave of cold struck his body and he remembered that he was naked. He hastily lay down again and wrapped himself in the quilt again. How could he stand up in front of strangers without a stitch on?

'A pox on your ancestors! So you're afraid of poison are you?' one of the guards said. 'All right, I'll eat it to show you.' He picked up the bowl and guzzled its contents down.

Qian Long looked at the man's scar-covered face in fright. 'I am not wearing anything,' he said. 'Please get me some clothing.'

Even though he said please, his words still smacked of an Imperial order. The man grunted. 'I haven't got time,' he replied. It was Melancholy Ghost Shi.

Qian Long could feel himself growing angry. But he remembered that his life was in their hands, and swallowed his Imperial pride.

'Are you Red Flower Society men?' he asked. 'I want to see your leader, Chen.'

'You had our Brother Wen treated so badly, his body is a mass of wounds. The Helmsman is busy finding a doctor for him. He hasn't got time to see you,' Shi replied. 'Maybe when Brother Wen has recovered, we'll think about it.'

Qian Long wondered how many months or years it might take for Wen to recover.

'And if Brother Wen doesn't recover,' said the other guard, who was Iron Pagoda Yang, 'that's it for you. A life for a life.'

Qian Long pretended he hadn't heard.

The two guards began talking volubly, cursing the Manchu invaders for having seized the lands of the Chinese people, and the officials and landlords for the way they oppressed the common folk. Qian Long was shocked by the hatred and bitterness evident in their every word. At noon, two other guards arrived to relieve them, and as the new pair ate, they discussed the sadistic ways in which magistrates punished and tortured honest citizens, describing in great detail how slivers of bamboo were forced under fingernails, buttocks were branded with red-hot iron bars, and bodies were stretched on the rack.

'We'll get our hands on all those corrupt officials sooner or later,' said one, 'and give them a taste of their own medicine.'

'First we have to deal with their leader,' replied the other.

To Qian Long, that single day lasted a year. Towards evening, the Twin Knights took over the watch. First, they sat there drinking in dour silence. Then, when they were slightly drunk, they began discussing the cruel and unusual methods used by members of the fighting community to take vengeance on enemies: how Black Tiger had once been arrested, and how later he had gone back and gouged out the eyes of the official responsible; how White Horse had avenged his brother's death by burying the murderer's entire family alive.

Hungry and frightened, Qian Long covered his ears, but every word still found its way in. The twins displayed great staying power, and talked until morning, cursing the pro-government turtles an untold number of times. The candlelight flickering on their gaunt features made them look like living ghosts, and Qian Long was unable to close his eyes once the whole night.

The next morning, Buddha Zhao and Leopard Wei came on duty. Qian Long looked at the kindly face of Zhao and the handsome face of Wei. They were very different from the skeletal demon-like guards they had replaced, and he relaxed slightly. But his hunger was becoming too much to bear.

'I want to see your leader, your Helmsman Chen,' he said to Zhao. 'Please pass on the message for me.'

'The Helmsman is busy today,' Zhao replied. 'Maybe in a few days.'

Qian Long wondered if he would still be alive after a few more days of this kind of treatment. 'Well, please get me something to eat first to ease my hunger.'

'All right,' replied Zhao. 'His Imperial Majesty wants a banquet!' he shouted at the top of his voice. 'Jump to it!' Leopard Wei bowed and left.

Qian Long was overjoyed. 'And while you're about it, get me some clothes,' he said.

'His Imperial Majesty wants some clothes! Bring him a gown at once!' Zhao bawled out again.

'You're a good man,' said Qian Long. 'What's your name? I will reward you well later.' Zhao smiled slightly but did not answer. Qian Long suddenly recognized him. 'Ah, now I remember,' he said. 'You're the one who is so good at throwing darts.'

Steward Meng now came in, bearing a suit of clothes which he placed on the quilt. Qian Long sat up. Then he saw that they were Chinese clothes in the style of the overthrown Ming dynasty. He hesitated.

'These are the only clothes we've got,' said Zhao. 'Wear them or not, as you like.'

Qian Long considered the situation. How could he, the Emperor of the Manchu dynasty, possibly wear a set of Ming-dynasty Chinese clothes? But if he didn't put something on, he would get nothing to eat. One day and two nights of hunger gave him the courage to overcome his misgivings, and he donned the garments without further delay.

The clothes felt unfamiliar, but at the same time there was something quite dashing and elegant about them. He walked the few steps over to the window and looked out. He started involuntarily. Forests and fields were spread out before him like a great chessboard, and in the far distance was a great river spotted with sails. He realized he was at the top of a tall pagoda and, from its position and design, knew it to be the famous Six Harmonies Pagoda near Hangzhou.

Several more hours passed before someone came to announce: 'The banquet is ready. Please come down and eat.'

Qian Long followed Zhao and Wei down one floor of the pagoda to a room where a large round table had been set up in the centre. All the seats around the table were already occupied except for three, and as Qian Long descended, the diners stood up and saluted him. Qian Long was secretly delighted at this sudden display of respect.

'Our Helmsman says that Your Majesty and he have been close friends ever since you first met,' said Father Speckless. 'That is why he has invited you here to stay for a few days, so the two of you can have an opportunity to talk things over. However, something important has suddenly come up which requires the Helmsman's attention and he has asked me to convey his sincere apologies.'

Qian Long grunted noncommittally. Father Speckless invited him to take a seat, and Qian Long took the guest's place of honour.

A servant brought up a flask of wine and the priest took it from him.

'We lot are very uncouth. We would never be capable of waiting on Your Majesty properly. Please do not be offended,' he said, pouring wine into Qian Long's cup. But as it reached the rim, his face darkened.

'His Majesty must have the very best wine,' he shouted angrily at the servant. 'How dare you bring us this weak stuff?' He picked up the cup and threw its contents into the servant's face.

'This is the only wine we have here, sir,' replied the servant apologetically. 'I will go to the city straight away and buy some better wine.'

'And be quick about it!' shouted Father Speckless. 'Wine like this may be all right for coarse people like ourselves, but how can you offer it to His Majesty?'

Mastermind Xu took the wine flask from him and poured out a cup for everyone else, leaving only Qian Long's cup empty, and apologizing profusely as he did so.

A moment later, another servant brought in four steaming dishes of food: some lightly-fried shrimps, a plate piled with salted pork spare-ribs, a steamed fish, and a plate of fried chicken slices. Qian Long breathed in the fragrant aroma of the food, but Father Speckless frowned.

'Who cooked this food?' he demanded. A man took two steps forward. 'I did,' he said.

'What sort of simpleton are you? Why didn't you arrange for His Majesty's favourite cook, Zhang Anguan, to come and prepare some food? How can you expect His Majesty to eat this rough Hangzhou cooking?'

'These dishes look absolutely delicious,' protested Qian Long. 'They certainly cannot be called rough.' He picked up his chopsticks and leant over to help himself. Hidden Needle Lu, who was sitting next to him, stretched out his own chopsticks and caught Qian Long's between them.

'These dishes are too coarse for Your Majesty. You wouldn't want to go getting an upset stomach,' he said, and applying the slightest pressure, snapped Qian Long's chopsticks clean in two.

Qian Long's face flushed deep red and he slammed the chopstick ends down onto the table. The others pretended not to notice and began eating.

'Go and fetch His Majesty's personal cook and tell him to prepare some food at once,' Mastermind Xu shouted. 'His Majesty is hungry, do you hear?'

The cook hastily retired. Qian Long knew they were playing with him. Hunger gnawed at his stomach as he watched the others eating and drinking voraciously. He was livid with rage, but he could not risk displaying his feelings. When they had finished, a servant came in with some tea.

'This tea is not too bad,' said Xu. 'Your Majesty may like to drink a cupful.'

Qian Long drank the cup dry in two gulps, but it only served to aggravate his hunger. Crocodile Jiang rubbed his belly appreciatively. 'I'm full!' he said.

'We are making arrangements for a proper banquet for you, Your Majesty,' said Buddha Zhao.

Father Speckless stamped his foot and exclaimed that the Helmsman would be very displeased to learn that his honoured guest had been kept waiting.

Lord Zhou began clicking his Iron Balls together. 'Are you hungry, Your Majesty?' he asked. Qian Long said nothing.

'What do you mean, hungry?' asked Crocodile Jiang. 'I'm full!'

'The trouble is, the well-fed never appreciate the misery of the hungry,' put in Mastermind Xu. 'There are countless millions of ordinary people starving, but when have the officials in power ever spared a thought for them? You've been a little bit hungry today, Your Majesty, so perhaps in future you'll understand more how the common people suffer when they starve.'

'Some people go hungry for months and years on end. Some never eat their fill once in a whole lifetime,' said one of the Twin Knights. 'What's so terrible about eating nothing for a day or two?'

Most of the Red Flower heroes had been born into poverty. Their anger rose as they thought of the hardships of the past, and they all began talking at once, swapping stories. Qian Long's face went pale as he listened. He found himself moved by their sincerity. 'Can such misery really exist in the world?' he asked himself. The more he heard, the more embarrassed he felt, and finally he rose and went back upstairs. The Red Flower heroes did not try to stop him.

A few hours later, he smelt the aroma of mutton with onions and green peppers wafting up from below. This was a speciality of his personal chef, Zhang Anguan, and just as Qian Long was wondering if it could really be him, Zhang Anguan ran up and kowtowed, saying: 'Please come and eat, Your Majesty.'

'What are you doing here?' Qian Long asked in amazement.

'I was watching an opera performance in a park yesterday, Your Majesty, when I was kidnapped. Today, they asked me to wait on you, and I was delighted to have the opportunity.'

Qian Long nodded and went downstairs again. This time the table had been set with a number of dishes including the mutton, all of which were his personal favourites. In addition to the main dishes, there were a dozen or so plates of small delicacies, and his heart leapt for joy at the sight of the feast. Chef Zhang filled a bowl of rice for him.

'Please enjoy your meal, Your Majesty,' said Father Speckless.

Qian Long wondered whether they would really allow him to eat this time. He was just about to raise his chopsticks when a young woman came in carrying a cat.

'Father,' she said to Lord Zhou. 'Kitty is hungry.'

The cat struggled to free itself, and jumped onto the table. It ate a couple of mouthfuls from the dishes spread before Qian Long, then it suddenly went rigid, and dropped down dead on the tabletop.

Qian Long's face went white. Chef Zhang, shaking with fright, knelt down before him: 'Your Majesty...Your Majesty...the food...it's them... They've poisoned the food... Don't eat it!'

Qian Long gave a loud, bitter laugh. He looked round at the Red Flower men. 'You are already guilty of rebellion and other heinous crimes! And now you wish to assassinate me!' he said. 'If you are going to kill me, do it cleanly. Why go to all the trouble of poisoning the food?' He pushed his chair back and stood up.

'Your Majesty, are you sure this meal is inedible?' asked Father Speckless.

'You are traitors and criminals, all of you!' Qian Long shouted, his anger breaking through. 'We'll see what sort of an end you all come to!'

Father Speckless slammed his hand down on the table. 'For a real man, life and death are decided by Heaven!' he shouted. 'If you won't eat, then I will! Has anyone got the guts to join me?'

He picked up his chopsticks, took some food from one of the dishes the cat had tried, and began chewing noisily. The other Red Flower heroes sat down again too and tucked into Qian Long's food, all saying: 'If we die, we die. What does it matter?' Qian Long was stunned at the sight of these men eating poisoned food.

The truth was that the Red Flower heroes had fed the cat poison in advance. They now ate all the dishes up in a trice, and suffered no ill effects. Qian Long, who had failed to eat even one mouthful, had lost yet another round.

Death by Dog?

While Qian Long went hungry, the entire official administration of Hangzhou was turned upside down. News of the Emperor's disappearance had not yet leaked out, but the whole city had been searched. All exits from Hangzhou by both land and water were heavily guarded, and several thousand 'suspected bandits' had been arrested, until every prison in the city was full to bursting. The local officials were extremely concerned, but they also took advantage of the situation to seize a number of rich businessmen and merchants and extort large sums of money from them.

Lord Fu Kangan, Commander Li, and old Bai Zhen jumped about like ants on a scalding hotplate, completely at a loss what to do.

Early on the morning of the third day, Lord Fu Kangan called a meeting in the Provincial Governor's residence. Glum-faced and powerless, Fu and his colleagues argued about whether or not the Empress should be informed. But none of them dared consider the consequences once such a report had been sent.

As they sat there paralysed by indecision, one of the Imperial Guards ran in, his face deathly pale, and whispered something in Bai Zhen's ear.

Bai Zhen went white and stood up. 'How could this happen?' he demanded. Lord Fu Kangan hurriedly asked what was wrong.

'The six guards protecting the Emperor's bedchamber have been killed,' said the man. Far from being alarmed, Fu seemed positively pleased by this news.

'Let's go and see,' he said. 'This event must be connected with His Majesty's disappearance. We may even find some clues.'

They hurried to the bedchamber that had been set aside in the Governor's residence for Qian Long. Six corpses lay sprawled at all angles around the room. Some had had their eyes gouged out, some had gaping holes in their chests: all had died a horrible death.

'These six men were good fighters,' said Bai Zhen. 'How could they have been finished off without even being able to utter a sound?'

They stared in open-mouthed horror, incapable of deciphering the scene. Bai Zhen examined the corpses. The assassins had moved so fast, some of the six had not even had time to draw their swords.

He frowned. 'This room is not big enough for a large number of people to fight in, so at the very most there cannot have been more than two or three intruders,' he said. 'Their kungfu must have been extraordinary.'

'Since they already have the Emperor, why should they come here and kill these guards?' asked Commander Li. 'From the look of it, last night's assassins and the people who kidnapped the Emperor are not the same bunch.'

'That's right!' exclaimed Lord Fu Kangan. 'The assassins came, planning to kill the Emperor, but found he wasn't here.'

'Supposing you are right,' said Bai Zhen, 'and the men who killed these guards were from the Red Flower Society, then that means the Emperor has fallen into someone else's hands. But other than the Red Flower Society, who else is there whose kungfu is so good?'

The Red Flower Society's fighters were difficult enough to handle, he was thinking to himself: the possibility of there being yet *another* group of powerful enemies suddenly appearing on the scene was chilling.

Bending over to look at the corpses again, Bai Zhen noticed that some of the wounds appeared to have been made by the claws and teeth of a dog. He hurriedly asked Commander Li to send someone to find some hunting hounds.

A couple of hours later, a soldier appeared with three dog-handlers and six hounds. Bai Zhen ordered the men to let their charges sniff around the corpses, and after no more than a second the dogs charged out of the chamber on the trail of a scent. They ran straight to the lake and barked madly across the water. After another moment, they raced off again around the edge of the lake to where Qian Long had stepped ashore following the courtesan contest, then turned towards the city. The streets were crowded and the scent confused, and the dogs were forced to slow down, but they continued to head towards Beautiful Jade's establishment.

There should have been troops on guard outside the entrance, but none were to be seen, and as they entered the courtyard they found a dozen corpses lying on the ground. The ruthless assassins, whoever they were, had left not one of Qian Long's guards alive. Some seemed to have had their throats ripped out by dogs. To Bai Zhen's eyes, the wounds seemed to have been inflicted by very large animals, possibly a cross between dogs and wolves such as were bred in the northwest. Could the assassins have come from there?

The dogs sniffed their way around Beautiful Jade's chamber several times. Then they began scratching and pawing at a certain point on the floor. Bai Zhen ordered the soldiers to prise up the floorboards with their swords and underneath they found a stone slab.

'Lift it up!' Bai Zhen ordered urgently. The soldiers heaved the slab up, to reveal a deep hole. The dogs immediately leapt into it. Commander Li and Bai Zhen looked down at the tunnel glumly. So that was how it had been done! The kidnappers had simply avoided the heavy guard altogether, by coming and going via the tunnel. Full of shame, they led their troops down into the darkness.

CHAPTER 6

Brother!

After two days and nights of being starved, frightened, and angered, Qian Long's resistance was virtually worn away. On the morning of the third day, a young lad appeared and said: 'Mr Dongfang, our master invites you to come and talk with him.' Qian Long recognized him as Helmsman Chen's page, Xin Yan, and followed him down to the floor below.

As he entered, Helmsman Chen, smiling broadly, advanced to greet him, and bowed. Qian Long returned the bow, and the two sat down. Xin Yan served some tea.

'Bring something to eat,' Chen ordered. A moment later, Xin Yan carried in a tray piled high with plates of spring rolls, prawns, chicken, and ham. He set out bowls and chopsticks and poured wine for them both.

'Please forgive me for not being able to see you sooner. I had to go and visit a friend who was wounded,' said Chen.

'It doesn't matter.'

'There is something I wish to talk to you about,' Chen added. 'But please eat first.' He chose a morsel from each plate, then put down his chopsticks and watched Qian Long wolf down the food. When he had finished, Qian Long sat back, unspeakably contented, and raised his teacup. He examined the tiny Dragon Well tea-leaves and took a leisurely sip, savouring the pleasant sensation of the warm liquid seeping into his stomach.

Helmsman Chen walked over to the door and pushed it open. 'The others are all downstairs standing guard,' he said. 'There could not be a more convenient place for us to talk. No one will hear us.'

Qian Long's expression hardened. 'Why did you have me brought here?' he asked. 'What is it you want?'

Chen stepped forward and stared into his face.

'Do you still not recognize me, *brother*?' he asked after a moment's silence. The words were soft, the tone intimate, but they hit Qian Long's ears with the force of a thunderclap. There was an expression of deep sincerity on Chen's face, as he slowly extended his hand and took Qian Long's.

'We are blood-brothers,' he said. 'There is no need to continue the deception. I know everything.'

Helmsman Chen pulled a cord beside a painting hanging on the wall and the painting rolled up to reveal a large mirror. 'Take a look at yourself,' he said.

Qian Long stood up and gazed at himself in the mirror, in his Chinese clothes. It was true: his face bore not the slightest likeness to a Manchu. He looked at Chen standing beside him. Despite their difference in age, their faces were similar. He sighed and sat down.

'Brother, we were not aware of the truth until now,' said Chen. 'We even took up arms against each other. The spirits of our father and mother in heaven must have been mortified. Luckily neither of us was hurt and nothing happened which cannot be rectified.'

Qian Long felt a rasping dryness in his throat, and his heart began to beat rapidly. A moment passed in utter silence. 'I asked you to come to Peking with me, but you refused,' he said finally. Chen said nothing, but turned and gazed out at the great river flowing in the distance.

'With your intelligence and your abilities,' Qian Long continued, 'you would rise rapidly as a mandarin at Court. That would be of great benefit to our family and to the nation and it would bring us both honour. Why be so disloyal and unfilial, why continue to behave in such an unforgivable manner?'

Chen spun round. 'I have never accused *you* of being disloyal or unfilial, and yet you accuse *me* of these things!'

'Don't you see?' replied Qian Long. 'Ministers and subjects are bound by loyalty to their emperor. But I am already Emperor. I am not bound to anyone. How could I possibly be disloyal to you?'

'Don't *you* see?' protested Chen. 'You are obviously a Chinese, and yet you submit to the Manchus. Can you call that loyalty? When our father and mother were alive, you never attended to them properly. Can you call that filial behaviour?'

Beads of sweat dripped from Qian Long's forehead. 'At the time, I knew nothing of all this,' he said quietly. 'I first heard about it when the leader of your Red Flower Society, Helmsman Yu, visited me last spring. Even now, I'm not sure whether to believe it or not.'

'You only have to look at yourself,' Chen said. 'You don't even look like a Manchu. How can you have any further doubt?'

Qian Long stood there, brooding in silence, filled again with feelings of remorse at the freshly revived memory that he'd had his own nurse put to death in order to preserve the secret of his birth.

'You are Chinese through and through,' continued Chen. 'There's no denying it. And the Chinese homeland—your homeland—has fallen into the hands of the Manchus. And yet you yourself lead them in the oppression of your own people. Is that not the most disloyal, the most unfilial, the most unforgivable behaviour?'

For a moment, Qian Long was at a loss for a reply. 'And now,' he finally said, with a haughty air, 'to make matters worse, I have had the misfortune to fall into your hands. Well, if you are going to kill me, then kill me. There is no point wasting words.'

'Have you forgotten?' Chen replied softly. 'We made a pact on the embankment at Haining. We said we would never do anything to hurt one another. I can never go back on my word. And anyway, now that we know we are blood-brothers, we have even less reason to do each other harm.' A tear trickled unbidden down his cheek.

'Well, what do you want me to do? Are you trying to force me to abdicate?'

'No,' said Chen, wiping his eyes. 'We want you to stay on as Emperor. But as the wise, enlightened founder of a new dynasty.'

'Founder of a *new dynasty*?' Qian Long echoed in surprise.

'Yes. You will be a Chinese Emperor, not an Emperor of the Manchus.'

Qian Long suddenly understood. 'So you want me to drive out the Manchus?' he said.

'Yes! You will be Emperor just the same, but instead of being regarded as a traitor and cursed by future generations, you can establish a new and lasting Chinese dynasty of your own!'

Chen saw from Qian Long's expression that his words were beginning to have the desired effect.

'The way things stand, you are simply basking in the glory of the former Manchu rulers,' Chen continued. 'What is so special about that? Come here. Look at that man.'

Qian Long went over to the window and looked down in the direction Chen was pointing. He saw a peasant in the distance hoeing the ground.

'If that man had been born in the Imperial Palace and you had been born in his farmhouse, he would have been Emperor, and you would have had no choice but to hoe the field.'

Qian Long started at the strangeness of the idea.

'A man is born into the world and his life is gone in a flash,' said Chen. 'If he achieves nothing worthwhile in his lifetime, he will decay and rot like the grass and the trees and leave no trace behind him. Those Chinese emperors of the past who established their own noble dynasties—the Han, the Tang, the Ming—were truly great men. Even Tartars like Genghis Khan and Nurhachi were outstanding in their own way. It is their achievement that is remembered. Do you want just to be forgotten, along with all the other lesser emperors of history?'

Every word he spoke stabbed deep into Qian Long's heart. 'If I really do as he says,' he was thinking to himself, 'if I throw the Manchus out and restore the Chinese homelands to the Chinese people, I would truly be the founder of a dynasty and a man of great achievement.'

Just as he was considering an answer to Helmsman Chen's question, he heard the sound of dogs barking in the distance.

The Twin Eagles

Seeing Chen frown slightly, Qian Long looked out and spied four massive hounds galloping towards the pagoda with two figures following. In a flash, they had reached the pagoda and there was a sharp challenge from below. Qian Long and Helmsman Chen, from where they stood on the second-highest floor of the thirteen-storey pavilion, could not hear distinctly what was being said, but they could see the two newcomers and their dogs forcing their way into the building. A moment later, there was a loud whistle indicating danger.

Qian Long was overjoyed. He assumed that help had arrived at last. Helmsman Chen looked around carefully, but could see no other signs of movement outside: the two intruders had clearly come on their own. He heard the shouts of young voices interspersed with the barks and growls of the dogs, which told

him that down on the second floor Zhou Qi and Xin Yan were
doing battle with the hounds. All of a sudden, there were two
screams, and two swords went hurtling out of the window. Just
then, Crocodile Jiang, wielding his mighty Iron Oar, could be seen
chasing the four dogs out of the pagoda and beating them
mercilessly. Someone on the sixth floor gave an ear-splitting whistle.
The four dogs turned and raced away.

The intruders had now reached the sixth floor, Chen thought
to himself. That meant that Brothers Shi, Wei, and Yang had been
unable to stop them. He groaned inwardly.

Suddenly, he saw Mastermind Xu leap from the seventh-floor
window out onto the narrow eaves, pursued by a tiny old woman
with a head of white hair and a sword slung over her back.

'Watch out for the dart!' Xu yelled with a flick of his hand,
and his opponent hastily withdrew. But it had been merely a feint,
enabling Xu to escape round the corner.

The old woman chased after him.

'Watch out!' Xu yelled.

'You bastard monkey!' the old woman cursed. 'Don't think
you can fool this old grandma a second time!'

She made a grab for him, but this time Xu's move had been
no feint: he had picked up a piece of tile from the roof and sent it
hurtling towards her. The woman was unable to avoid it. She
blocked the tile with her hand and it shattered. The Twin Knights,
standing guard on the eighth floor, appeared to be fully occupied
dealing with the old woman's partner, for they were unable to give
Xu any help. In the end Xu's kungfu was no match for the old
woman's, and after a few moves, he was forced to dodge out of the
way again.

Qian Long watched with pleasure as the two newcomers
fought their way up. Helmsman Chen seemed strangely
unconcerned. He pulled a chair to the window so that he could sit
and observe the battle. After all, there were only two of them, he
reasoned: in the end, they could not overcome all the Red Flower
Society fighters.

Then he heard the sound of more dogs barking in the distance
intermingled with shouts and galloping horses. Footsteps sounded
on the stairs and Xin Yan raced in.

'The guards outside report that more than two thousand
Manchu troops are approaching, heading straight here,' he told

Chen. Chen nodded and Xin Yan raced back downstairs. Qian Long had not understood what Xin Yan had said, since the boy had used the Red Flower secret language, but seeing Chen's anxious expression, he knew it was unwelcome news. He looked into the distance and to his delight spotted amongst the maple trees a white flag on which was written one large word: 'Li'. Commander Li had come to the rescue.

Helmsman Chen leaned out of the window and was shouting to Lodge Master Ma to retreat into the pagoda and prepare the bows and arrows, when suddenly the white-haired old woman rushed into the room with the Red Flower heroes in hot pursuit. Lord Zhou attacked her with his great sword, while Helmsman Chen pulled Qian Long into a corner. Mastermind Xu motioned some of the others to guard the windows.

'Throw down your sword,' shouted Chen, 'and we'll spare you!'

The old woman could see she was surrounded, but she continued to fight, completely unafraid. There was something strangely familiar about her sword style. The old woman forced Lord Zhou back a pace, then shouted at Qian Long: 'Are you the Emperor?'

'Yes, I'm the Emperor,' he replied hastily. 'Are all the rescue forces here?' The woman leapt onto the table, then, with her sword pointing straight ahead, flew at Qian Long like some great bird, thrusting the blade at his heart. The Red Flower heroes had assumed her to be one of Qian Long's underlings come to rescue him, and were caught completely unaware by this fast move. Helmsman Chen, who was standing by Qian Long's side, thrust his fingers at a Vital Point on the old woman's arm. Her sword slowed, giving Chen time to draw his dagger and counter its onward movement. Their two blades clashed, then both combatants retreated two paces. Chen pulled Qian Long back and, placing himself in front of him, saluted.

'What is your honourable name, madam?' he asked.

'Where did that dagger of yours come from?' she asked, having failed to hear Chen in the noisy confusion. He was surprised by her question. 'A friend gave it to me,' he said.

'What friend?' the woman demanded. 'I thought you were a servant of the Emperor. I know perfectly well who this dagger belonged to. What I don't know is why she would have given it to you. What is your relationship with Master Yuan, the Strange Knight of the Heavenly Pool?'

'He is my Shifu,' said Chen, answering the last question first.

'Is he now?' the woman muttered. 'Your Shifu may be strange, but he's a gentleman. How could you have dishonoured him by becoming a lackey of the Manchus?'

'Excuse me, ma'am, but this is our Helmsman Chen,' shouted Iron Pagoda Yang. 'I'd ask you to show a little respect.'

The old woman's face took on a puzzled expression. 'So you are the Red Flower Society?' she asked.

'We are,' said Yang.

She turned on Chen and screeched in rage: 'Have you surrendered to the Manchus?'

'The Red Flower Society stands for justice and honour,' he replied. 'How could we ever bend our knees before the Manchu court? Please sit down, madam, and let us discuss this calmly.'

Her expression softened slightly. 'Where did that dagger of yours come from?' she asked again.

From observing her kungfu style, and from hearing these questions of hers, Chen had already almost solved the puzzle.

'It was given to me by a Uighur friend,' he said. Such an exchange of presents between a young man and woman was no everyday occurrence, and Chen was reluctant to discuss the matter in front of everyone.

'So you know Lady Huo Qingtong?' the old woman demanded. Chen nodded.

'It was she who gave him the dagger,' Zhou Qi interjected impatiently. 'Do you know her? If you do, then we're all on the same side!'

'She is my disciple,' the old woman said. 'Since you say we are all on the same side, I don't understand what you are doing helping the Emperor, and stopping me from killing him.'

'On the contrary, ma'am, we are doing the very opposite,' said one of the Twin Knights. 'We captured the Emperor in the first place. If he is to be killed, it will not be you who does it.'

'This is clearly a big misunderstanding,' said Chen. 'We assumed the two of you were Palace Guards coming to rescue him. That is why we tried to obstruct you.'

The old woman went over to the window and stuck her head out. 'Come down, husband!' she bellowed at the top of her lungs.

There was a moment's silence, and then an arrow came flying in through the window from below. The old woman grabbed it, then turned in one movement and threw the arrow so that it drove itself into the tabletop.

'You treacherous rascal!' she screeched at Chen as the arrow quivered. 'What are you trying to do to me?'

'Don't be angry, madam,' replied Chen hastily. 'Our Brothers at the bottom of the pagoda are not yet aware of the situation.' He walked to the window to tell the Red Flower heroes to hold their fire, and saw that the pagoda was already surrounded by Li's troops.

He turned to Buddha Zhao. 'Tell the others to guard the doorway, but not to go outside.' Zhao nodded and went downstairs.

'You must be Lady Guan,' said Lord Zhou to the old woman. 'I have long respected you.'

Lady Guan nodded slightly.

'This is Lord Zhou Zhongying,' Chen told her.

'Ah, I have heard about you too,' she said, then suddenly screeched out: 'Husband, come on down! What are you doing?'

The others all jumped at this unexpected outburst.

'I believe your husband is fighting with Father Speckless,' said Lord Zhou. 'We should go and explain the situation to them quickly.'

Chen motioned to the Twin Knights to guard Qian Long, and the rest of them raced up the stairs to the thirteenth floor.

'Husband!' shouted Lady Guan. 'These are Red Flower Society people!'

Her husband, who was universally referred to on River and Lake as Bald Vulture, was locked in fierce combat with Father Speckless. He started in surprise, and hesitated in his attack. 'Is that really so?' he said.

There was a sudden laugh from up above their heads and Hidden Needle Lu dropped to the floor, separating the two combatants.

'Excellent swordsmanship,' he chuckled, 'most excellent!' He nodded appreciatively at both Bald Vulture and at Father Speckless. 'And do you recognize *me*?' he asked Bald Vulture.

Bald Vulture looked at him closely for a moment, then gave a shout.

'Why, it's Hidden Needle Lu!' he exclaimed. 'What brings you here?'

Without answering this question, Lu turned to the old woman and bowed to her. 'My Lady Guan, it has been many years since I last saw you, but your kungfu is more impressive than ever!'

'Why!' exclaimed Bald Vulture again, staring at Lu's blade. 'That's a very precious sword you have there!'

He was talking of Frozen Emerald, the treasured heirloom of the Wudang School, that had been in the hands of Fire Hand Zhang.

Lu smiled. 'It really belongs to someone else,' he said. 'I'm just borrowing it. But let me introduce you to everyone.' He introduced all the Red Flower heroes one by one to Bald Vulture and his wife Lady Guan, the legendary couple known as the Twin Eagles of Heaven Mountains.

'I thought you two were living happily in Heaven Mountains,' Lu said. 'And here you are, trying to kill the Emperor.'

'You have all met my young disciple, Lady Huo Qingtong,' replied Lady Guan. 'This whole affair started with her. The Emperor sent an army to attack the Uighurs. They were unable to match the Manchu troops' strength and lost several battles in a row. Later, the Manchu grain supplies were ransacked—'

'That was the Red Flower Society,' interrupted Lu. 'They did it to help the Hodja.'

'Yes, I heard about that,' said Lady Guan. She glanced at Chen. 'No wonder she gave you that dagger.'

'She gave it to me earlier, when we helped them recover their sacred Koran.'

'Yes, I knew you'd helped them get that back. The way the Uighurs talk of you, one would think you were all great heroes!' Her tone suggested that she thought otherwise. 'Anyway, after the Manchu troops lost their grain, they also lost a battle and the Hodja suggested peace talks. But just as the talks were getting under way, the Manchu general got hold of some rations and attacked again.'

'Manchu officers have no sense of honour,' said Lu, shaking his head.

'One thing is for certain: the ordinary people in the Uighur lands have been brutally treated by the Manchu troops,' Lady Guan continued. 'It was the Hodja who asked us to help. We originally didn't want to have anything to do with this—'

'On the contrary! It was your idea!' Bald Vulture butted in accusingly. 'Now you're trying to act all innocent.'

'What do you mean, my idea? Look at the way the Manchus behave, burning and pillaging their way across Uighur lands, treating the people as if they were no better than animals. Don't you care?'

Bald Vulture grunted in indignation and was about to argue further when Lu raised his hand.

'You two haven't changed,' he said with a smile. 'The minute you open your mouths, you start arguing. Don't take any notice, madam, please continue.'

She eyed her husband angrily, then said: 'First we thought of assassinating the Manchu general, Zhao Hui, but there didn't seem much point in killing one general, because the Emperor would just send another and it would go on for ever. So we decided to kill the Emperor instead. We went to Peking, but on the way there we heard that he had come down south. We followed him out of Hangzhou with our dogs, using the tunnel. It must be the one you people dug. At the time, we were very puzzled as to why the Emperor was suddenly so keen on travelling around in tunnels.'

'What? So you mean to say that these people captured the Emperor?' said Bald Vulture. Helmsman Chen nodded. 'Good work!' Bald Vulture commented.

Suddenly, there was a roar from the Manchu troops down below, around the base of the pagoda.

'I'd better go and tell the Emperor to shut them up,' said Mastermind Xu, and ran downstairs. A moment later they saw Qian Long stick his head out of the window on the seventh floor and shout: 'I'm up here! All is well!'

'His Majesty is up there! All is well!' repeated Bai Zhen down below. The troops promptly all prostrated themselves on the ground.

'I'm safe and sound!' Qian Long added. 'I'm busy up here. There's no need for such a lot of noise.' There was a pause, then he added: 'You can all move thirty paces away from the building!'

They complied immediately.

'Mastermind commands the Emperor, and the Emperor directs the troops,' said Chen with a smile. 'That's the way! Much better than having to charge out and kill and slaughter. The Emperor is the greatest treasure under heaven. It's much better to use him than to kill him.' The others laughed.

Leopard Wei, who was watching the Manchu soldiers withdraw, saw several men in their midst with hunting dogs on leashes.

'Ah, I was wondering how they found their way here,' he said. He took a bow from one of the Red Flower scouts, and let fly two arrows. There were two protracted yelps and two of the dogs fell to the ground, dead. A roar went up from the Manchu troops, and they accelerated their retreat.

'Master Lu, Lord Zhou,' said Chen. 'Please look after the Twin Eagles while I go and continue my conversation with the Emperor.'

As Helmsman Chen reached the twelfth floor, the Twin Knights and Mastermind Xu bowed to him and retired. Qian Long had come up from the seventh floor, and was sitting despondently in a chair.

'Have you made a decision yet?' asked Chen.

'You have me in your power. You might as well kill me if you are going to. What is the point of talking?'

Chen sighed. 'It is such a pity,' he said.

'What's a pity?'

'I have always thought of you as a person of talent and vision. I was proud that my parents should have produced such a good son. But...'

'But what?'

Chen was silent for a moment. 'But although outwardly you appear to be a man of courage, it turns out you are hollow inside. Not being afraid of death is the easiest thing in the world. But conceiving grand designs, making great decisions, those are things that can only be undertaken by a man with true courage. And that is precisely what you are incapable of.'

Qian Long was silent, but he appeared to have been moved by Chen's words.

'All you have to do is to decide to restore the Chinese nation, and we will immediately follow your every instruction. You will have all the heroes of the underworld on your side,' Chen added. 'I can vouch for them. They will not dare to do anything disrespectful towards you.'

Qian Long nodded several times, but there was still a degree of doubt in his mind which made it impossible for him to speak out. Chen guessed his thoughts.

'All I want is to see you throw the Tartars out of China,' he said. 'Then, with your permission, I will retire to the seclusion of the Western Lake and live out the rest of my life in peace with my friends.'

'What sort of talk is that?' said Qian Long. 'If this Grand Design you speak of is ever to be achieved, you cannot possibly retire: your assistance will be required more than ever in planning affairs of state.'

'We are getting ahead of ourselves,' replied Chen. 'Very well. But later, once the Grand Design has been completed, then you must allow me to retire.'

Qian Long slapped his hand down on the table. 'All right,' he said. 'We'll do as you say.'

Chen was overjoyed. 'You have no further doubts?' he asked.

'None. But there is one thing I would like you to do for me. Your former Helmsman Yu had certain items of evidence that were deposited for safety in the Uighur lands. He said they constituted proof of my birth. Go and get them so that I can see them. Only then will my last doubts disappear. Then we will discuss the details of our plans.'

Chen felt this was reasonable. 'Very well,' he replied. 'I will start out tomorrow and get them myself. In return, you must promise to send orders to your army under General Zhao, to retreat from the Uighur lands.'

'I promise to do so,' said Qian Long. 'When you return, I will first assign you to the Imperial Guard, then promote you to be commander of the Peking garrison. I will gradually transfer military power in every province into the hands of Chinese officers we can trust. I'll make you President of the Board of War, with orders to disperse the key Manchu Banner units. Then we can act.'

Chen knelt down and performed the ritual act of obeisance of a vassal before his lord, but Qian Long hurriedly helped him up.

'An oath must be sworn in front of the others over this,' Chen said. 'There must be no going back.'

Qian Long nodded.

Chen clapped his hands once and ordered Xin Yan to help Qian Long change back into his original clothes.

'Please ask everyone to come to pay their respects to the Emperor,' he said.

The Red Flower heroes crowded in. Chen told them that Qian Long had agreed to expel the Manchus and restore the Chinese throne. Then, in a clear voice, he swore an oath: 'In future, we will assist Your Majesty, and together we will plan and execute the

Grand Design. If anyone should reveal this secret, he will be damned by Heaven and Earth.'

He drank a draught of a specially prepared brew of Covenant Wine to seal the pact, and Qian Long did likewise.

'Bald Vulture, Lady Guan,' said Hidden Needle Lu. 'Come and drink a cup of the Covenant Wine as well.'

'I have never believed the word of a Manchu official, so why should I trust their leader?' said Bald Vulture.

With his right hand he suddenly struck the wall, reducing a section of it to rubble. He pulled out a brick.

'May whoever breaks the covenant, betrays his friends, and destroys the Grand Design be crushed like this!' he shouted harshly. He exerted a slight pressure, and the brick crumbled into a thousand pieces. Qian Long looked in consternation, first at the hole in the wall and then down at the fragments of brick lying scattered on the floor.

'Even though you decline to take the oath, we are all friends, and in this together,' said Helmsman Chen. Then, turning to Qian Long: 'I trust Your Majesty will never vacillate or forget the covenant established today.'

'Please rest easy on that account,' replied Qian Long.

'All right. Let us escort His Majesty out,' said Chen. Leopard Wei raced out of the pagoda, shouting: 'Come and meet His Majesty!'

Commander Li and Bai Zhen half suspected something. They ordered their troops to move slowly forward, afraid that this was yet another Red Flower Society ruse. Suddenly, they saw Qian Long emerge from the pagoda unharmed, and prostrated themselves on the ground. Bai Zhen led a horse over and Qian Long mounted.

'I have been enjoying myself, drinking and composing poetry with them here,' he said to Bai Zhen. 'I merely wanted a few days' peace and quiet. Trust you to make a mountain out of a molehill and rob me of my pleasure!'

The Red Flower heroes returned to the pagoda.

'Lady Guan and I are extremely happy to have met you all today,' said Bald Vulture. 'Especially Lord Zhou, whom we have respected for so long, and Master Lu, whom we have not seen for many years. But now my wife and I have some other minor affairs to deal with, and will take our leave.'

Lady Guan pulled Helmsman Chen over to one side. 'Are you married yet?' she asked.

Chen blushed deep red. 'No,' he replied.

'Engaged?'

'Not engaged either,' he said. Lady Guan smiled to herself. Then suddenly she gave one of her screeches: 'If you are ever so ungrateful as to turn your back on the one who gave you that dagger, I will never forgive you.' Chen was so shocked by her outburst, he was completely lost for a reply.

'You scorpion!' her husband shouted from the other side of the room. 'Let him be! Let's get going!'

Lady Guan turned, emitted an ear-splitting whistle, and four dogs raced out of the trees. The couple bowed before the Red Flower heroes and took their leave.

Helmsman Chen led the others back up to the top floor of the pagoda.

'I promised the Emperor that I would go to see my Shifu and bring back certain things from him,' said Chen. 'But first let's go to Heaven's Eye Mountain to see how Brother Wen and Brother Yu are doing.'

Lodge Master Ma and his son returned to Hangzhou by themselves, while the rest of the Red Flower heroes galloped off westwards.

The Grand Design

The trees on the hillsides were dense and dark. It was already well into autumn and Heaven's Eye Mountain was covered in fiery-red leaves and yellowing grass. Lookouts sent word of the approach of Chen and his comrades, and Hunchback Zhang and the other Red Flower heroes came down to greet them.

Luo Bing was not among them, and Chen was concerned that something had happened to her.

'Where's Sister Luo?' he asked. 'And how are Brother Wen and Brother Yu?'

'They're fine,' replied Hunchback Zhang. 'Sister Luo said she was going to get a present for Brother Wen. She's been away two days already. You didn't meet her on the road?'

Chen shook his head. 'What present?'

Hunchback Zhang smiled. 'I don't know. Brother Wen's wounds have healed well, but he spends all his time in bed moping. Sister Luo came up with this idea of going to get him a present.'

They made their way up the mountain and entered the courtyard of a large mansion. Wen Tailai was lying dejectedly on a rattan couch. They told him briefly about what had transpired at the pagoda and then went to the room next door to see Scholar Yu.

As they stepped inside, they heard the sound of sobbing. Chen walked over and pulled aside the bed-curtain to reveal Scholar Yu lying face-down on the bed, his back shaking uncontrollably. Even young women like Luo Bing and Zhou Qi rarely cried, and they were all shocked and embarrassed by his behaviour.

'Brother Yu,' Chen said quietly. 'We've come to see you. How do you feel? Are your wounds very painful?'

Yu stopped crying, but did not turn over. 'Helmsman, Brothers, thank you all for coming to see me. Forgive me for not getting up to greet you properly. My health has improved a lot over the past few days, but my face has been burnt so badly, it's so ugly that I can't face anyone.'

Zhou Qi smiled. 'What does it matter if a man has burn marks on his face?' she said. 'Don't tell me you're afraid you won't be able to find a girl willing to marry you?' Some of the heroes laughed at her uninhibited way of talking.

'Brother Yu,' said Hidden Needle Lu. 'Your face was burnt while saving Brother Wen and myself. When people hear of this act, they will all think you a hero. What need is there for such distress?'

'You are right,' said Yu, and burst into tears again.

The Red Flower heroes returned to the main hall. Helmsman Chen and Mastermind Xu talked together in low tones, then clapped their hands and everyone stood up.

'Brothers,' said Chen. 'So far, things have gone well for us. But in the future, we will be facing even tougher problems. I will now give you your assignments. Brother Wei, Brother Shi, you two are to go to Peking and see what you can find out about the Emperor's plans and if he intends to honour our pact or break it. This will be extremely difficult to execute. You must both exercise great caution.' Leopard Wei and Melancholy Ghost Shi nodded.

'Now, Twin Knights,' Chen continued. 'You are to go to the Southwest and make contact with the fighters in Sichuan, Yunnan, and Guizhou provinces. Brother Yang, you are to go to Anhui and Jiangsu provinces, Father Speckless to Hubei and Hunan. Brother

Jiang, I want you to join forces with Lodge Master Ma in Hangzhou and contact people in Zhejiang, Fujian, and Jiangxi provinces. I would like to ask Master Lu to deal with Shandong and Henan. I would like Lord Zhou, Steward Meng, Brother Xu, and Miss Zhou Qi to handle the northwest provinces. Brother Wen and Brother Yu will remain here convalescing, with Sister Luo and Brother Zhang to look after them. Xin Yan will accompany me to the Uighur lands.

'I am not asking you to begin preparations for an actual uprising,' he added, 'but simply to improve relations with other members of the fighting community in all areas and to provide a basis on which we can act later. Absolute secrecy is essential, so do not reveal anything to anyone no matter how close they are.'

'We understand,' they replied in unison.

'Exactly one year from now, we will all gather in Peking. By that time, Brother Wen and Brother Yu will be fully recovered and we can begin to execute the Grand Design!'

Cheers arose from the heroes. They followed Chen excitedly out of the hall.

Only Hunchback Zhang, assigned by the Helmsman to stay at Heaven's Eye Mountain, was unhappy. Rolling Thunder Wen guessed his thoughts, and went over to speak to Chen.

'Helmsman, my wounds are almost healed, and although Brother Yu's burns are serious, he too is recovering quickly,' he said. 'It is a bit much to ask us to stay cooped up here for a year. The four of us would like to accompany you to the Uighur lands. The trip would also help to take Brother Yu's mind off things.'

'All right, we'll do as you say,' Chen agreed. Hunchback Zhang was very pleased when he heard the news.

Lord Zhou took Chen aside. 'Helmsman,' he said. 'The fact that we have discovered through Brother Wen that you and the Emperor are blood relations is a matter worthy of great rejoicing. I would like to add to it one more happy event. What do you think it is?'

'You wish to hold a wedding for Brother Xu and Miss Zhou, is that right?'

'Exactly,' Zhou replied, smiling.

Chen walked over to Zhou Qi, his face wreathed in smiles, and bowed before her. 'Congratulations, young lady,' he said.

She blushed deeply. 'What do you mean?'

'Since your betrothed is my Brother, I should really call you Sister. Very well then. Congratulations, Sister!' He clapped his hands loudly and the Red Flower heroes immediately fell silent.

'Lord Zhou tells me he wants his daughter and Brother Xu to be married this evening. So we have something else to celebrate!'

The Red Flower heroes cheered loudly and congratulated Lord Zhou and Mastermind Xu. Zhou Qi hurried out to her room in embarrassment.

'Hunchback Zhang!' Leopard Wei called out. 'Stop her. Don't let the bride escape!' Zhang made as if to grab her and Zhou Qi chopped out with her left hand to fend him off.

'Help!' he cried in mock surprise, dodging to one side. 'The bride's attacking me!'

A laugh escaped from her as she ran out of the hall.

Just then, there was the tinkling of bells outside and Luo Bing ran in carrying a large box.

'Oh good, everyone's here!' she cried. 'What's happened to make you all so happy?' She looked enquiringly at Chen.

'Ask Brother Xu,' said Leopard Wei.

'What's happened, Brother Xu?' Luo Bing asked, but Xu was speechless for a moment. 'Mm? That's strange. Has the Kungfu Mastermind gone all silly?'

Crocodile Jiang dodged behind Xu and held up his two thumbs and made them bow to each other. 'Mastermind is getting married today,' he said with glee.

'Oh, how awful, how awful!' Luo Bing exclaimed, absolutely delighted.

The others laughed. 'What do you mean, awful?' asked Pagoda Yang.

'If I'd known, I could have brought a sheep and some nice things back with me. As it is, I have almost nothing to give them as a present. Isn't that awful?'

'Will you let us all see what you've got for Brother Wen?' asked Pagoda Yang.

Luo Bing smiled and opened up the box. Glinting inside were the two jade vases which the Uighurs had sent to the Emperor along with their request for a truce.

'Where did you get them?' the heroes asked in astonishment.

'The other day I was chatting with Thunder and I said how wonderfully beautiful the girl on the vases was, but he didn't believe me—'

'I'll bet I know what Rolling Thunder said to that,' interrupted Mastermind Xu. 'Something like: "She couldn't possibly be more beautiful than you." Am I right?'

Luo Bing smiled but did not answer. 'Did you go to Hangzhou and steal them from the Emperor?' Xu asked.

Luo Bing nodded, very pleased with herself. 'I got them so Thunder could have a look. The Helmsman can decide what should be done with them after that, whether we keep them or return them to Sister Huo Qingtong.' Wen proceeded to examine the vases, making admiring noises.

'I was right, wasn't I?' asked Luo Bing. Wen smiled and shook his head. Luo Bing realized that what her husband meant was that the girl on the vase could never be as beautiful as she was. Her cheeks flushed.

'The Emperor has a large number of top fighters around him at all times,' said Father Speckless, 'and such precious items as these vases must have been very well guarded. How did you manage to steal them?'

Luo Bing told them how she had sneaked into the Yamen, grabbed a eunuch, and forced him to tell her where the vases were. Then she had slipped poison into the food of some of the guards, made cat noises to distract the rest, and grabbed the vases. The Red Flower heroes praised her skill, all except Hidden Needle Lu.

'Sister Luo,' he said. 'I was your father's friend, so I hope you'll forgive me if I speak my mind. You are undoubtedly very brave, but was it wise to take such a risk, and all on your own, just for the sake of a remark you made to your husband? As it happened, the Imperial Guards were fully occupied that particular night searching for the Emperor. If they had been there, things could have turned out rather differently.'

Luo Bing accepted her scolding with a good grace.

The wedding ceremony took place amidst great merriment, and the next morning the Red Flower heroes made their way down the mountain, wished each other well, and went their separate ways.

Helmsman Chen and Lord Zhou were both ultimately heading for the northwest, and Chen suggested they travel together. But Zhou said he wished to take advantage of their presence in the south to visit the Southern Shaolin Monastery in Fujian Province, a Buddhist and Martial Arts centre whose style of kungfu was related to his own. So taking his wife and Steward Meng with him, he headed south.

Helmsman Chen, Rolling Thunder Wen, Luo Bing, Mastermind Xu, Zhou Qi, Hunchback Zhang, Scholar Yu, and Xin Yan all travelled north through Nanking. By the time they had crossed the Yangtze, Wen had completely recovered and Yu was progressing well. As they continued north, the weather became cooler, and the grass and trees turned yellow as early winter set in. Once they had passed through the ancient city of Kaifeng, Yu was well enough to ride a horse, and the eight of them galloped together along the highway. The north wind blew angrily, throwing dust and sand into their faces.

Wen, riding the white horse, galloped ahead of the others and stopped at an inn in a small village, telling the servants to kill a chicken and prepare a meal. Then he sat down near the door to await the arrival of his friends. He ordered a pot of tea and wiped his face with the hot flannel brought out to him. Suddenly, a figure darted out from a room to one side of the inn but immediately withdrew on catching sight of Wen.

About an hour later, Chen and the others rode up and Wen quietly informed them of what had happened. Xu looked round towards the side-room and saw that a section of the window-paper had been moistened. A black eyeball, pressed to the centre, immediately disappeared. He smiled.

'Whoever it is, he's a novice,' Xu said. 'The slightest move, and he reveals himself.'

'Go over and see,' Helmsman Chen said to Xin Yan. 'If it's money he needs, lend him some.'

Xin Yan went over to the side-room and said in a loud voice:

All streams under heaven flow from the same source,
Red Flowers and green leaves are all one family.

This was the Red Flower Society members' catch-phrase for identifying themselves to other members of the fighting community. Even if the other party was not a member of the Red Flower Society, as long as he knew the phrase and asked for help, he would receive it. But all was quiet in the room. Xin Yan repeated his call, and the

door creaked open. A figure dressed in black with a large hat pulled
down low came out and gave him a letter.

'Give this to your Brother Yu.'

The figure then ran out of the inn, jumped onto a horse, and
galloped away. Xin Yan gave the letter to Scholar Yu who opened
it and found the following words written inside:

'What do ugliness and beauty have to do with true love? I
will follow you even over a thousand mountains and across ten
thousand rivers. And tell your Helmsman that three of the Devils
of Manchuria are on their way to the Uighur lands to seek revenge
on Huo Qingtong for killing their brother-in-arms.'

Scholar Yu recognized the calligraphy as that of Li Yuanzhi.
He frowned and handed the sheet of paper to Helmsman Chen.

Chen studiously ignored the first part, which obviously dealt
with private romantic affairs. But he immediately informed the
others of the news about the three Devils of Manchuria.

'Those three will be tough fighters,' said Wen. 'I wonder if
she can handle them?'

'We once watched Lady Huo fighting with that Manchurian
Devil, Yan Shizhang, and she proved herself to be a somewhat better
fighter than he was,' replied Mastermind Xu. 'But if the Helmsman
hadn't stepped in to save her, I'm afraid she would have fallen victim
to his evil tricks.'

'The eldest of the Devils, Teng Yilei, is very strong, a
formidable man,' observed Rolling Thunder Wen.

'Since three Devils are already on their way, it would be best
if someone went on ahead on Sister Luo's horse,' Mastermind Xu
suggested. 'From the look of things, the military situation in the
Uighur lands is tense, and the Hodja and his people must be busy
making defensive preparations. We shouldn't let Lady Huo be
caught unawares by the three Devils.' Chen knew he was right,
and he frowned silently.

'Helmsman, I think it would be best if you were the one to go
on ahead,' said Xu. 'You speak their language, your kungfu is good,
and the three Devils have never seen you before. If General Zhao
Hui has not withdrawn by the time you get there, you can also
help the Uighurs.'

'Very well!' said Chen after only a moment's hesitation.

Ahmed, Ayesha, and the Fawn

Helmsman Chen was extremely concerned at the news that three
of the Devils of Manchuria were out to get Huo Qingtong. He kept
seeing her in his mind's eye, disappearing slowly into the dust of
the Great Desert. But then, remembering how intimate she had
been with Hidden Needle Lu's young disciple, he decided that he
was being a fool to think she might have romantic feelings for him.
Either way, he was unable to get her out of his mind.

The white horse carried him along with extraordinary speed,
and in less than two days he arrived at Jiayu Gate, at the western
end of the Great Wall. He climbed up onto the battlements and
looked out at the Wall snaking away into the distance, holding at
bay the great wilderness. He felt a sense of excitement at the thought
of once more entering the border regions, and followed custom by
throwing a stone at the Wall—the sandstorms beyond the Wall
were often perilous, the way was often hard, and, according to
tradition, if a traveller threw a stone at the Wall as he passed through
the Jiayu Gate, he would return alive.

He travelled on, riding by day, and resting by night. After he
had passed the Jade Gate and Anxi, the desert changed colour
gradually from pale to dark yellow, and then slowly to grey as he
skirted the Gobi. The region was uninhabited, there was nothing
but endless expanses of broad desert. He passed through the place
known as Stellar Gorge, the main link between Gansu Province
and the Uighur lands. It was already winter and the first
accumulations of snow could be seen along the gorge, providing a
thrilling contrast of black and white. Also, a perfect place for an
ambush, Chen thought.

That night, he lodged in a small hut and the next day found
himself at the edge of the Gobi Desert. The Gobi was as flat as a
mirror, there were no rolling sand-dunes. Gazing into the distance,
it seemed to him as if the sky and earth touched one another, and
as if he and his horse were the only beings in the universe. All was
silent.

As he rode, day after day, he considered the problem of how
to find Huo Qingtong. He was a Chinese, and the Uighurs could
suspect him of being a spy, so to gain their confidence he would
have to resort to deception. He decided to disguise himself as a
Uighur, and at the next settlement bought a small embroidered

cap, a pair of leather boots, and a striped gown. Riding on, he found a deserted place and changed into his new clothes, burying the old ones in the sand. He was very pleased with his new appearance as a young Uighur.

But he met no other Uighurs on the road, and the Uighur villages and dwellings he came upon were all burnt to the ground—obviously the good work of General Zhao Hui's army. He decided he was unlikely to meet any Uighurs on the main highway, so he cut off south, and headed into the mountains. In such desolate wilderness, there was little chance of finding any settlement, and after three days, his dry rations were finished. By pure chance, he managed to catch and kill a goat.

Two days further on, he met a number of Kazak herdsmen. They knew that the Uighur army had retreated westwards in the face of the Manchu force, but had no idea where it had gone. There was nothing for it but to continue west. Chen let his horse gallop on, and made no attempt to hold it back. For four days he covered more than a hundred miles a day with nothing but sand and sky before his eyes.

On the fifth day, the weather turned hot. The burning sun blazed down on both man and horse. Chen wanted to find somewhere shady where they could rest, but wherever he looked there was nothing but sand-dunes. He opened his water flask, drank three mouthfuls, and let the white horse drink the same amount. Despite a terrible thirst, he did not dare to drink more.

They rested for two hours, then started out once again. Suddenly, the white horse raised its head and sniffed at the wind, whinnied loudly, then turned and galloped off south. Chen let it go. Soon, sparse vegetation began to appear on the sand around them, then actual green grass. Chen could tell there must be an oasis ahead, and his heart leapt. The white horse too was in high spirits and its hooves flew along.

After a while, they heard the sound of running water and soon came to a small stream. Chen dismounted and scooped up a handful of water. As he drank, he felt a coolness reach deep into his lungs and noticed a slight fragrance to the water. The stream was full of little pieces of ice which jostled each other, emitting a crisp jingling noise, like the music of fairies. After drinking a few mouthfuls, the white horse gave a whinny and gambolled about happily.

Having drunk his fill, Chen felt relaxed and content. He filled his two leather water flasks. In the midst of the sparkling ice fragments, he spotted petals floating past and realized that the strange fragrance of the water must come from flower beds further upstream. By following the stream, he might come across someone who could tell him where Huo Qingtong might be. He remounted and started along the bank.

The stream gradually widened. In the desert, unlike elsewhere, most rivers and streams are in fact larger close to their source. Further downstream the water is gradually soaked up by the desert sands and eventually disappears. Having lived many years in Uighur country, Chen did not consider it strange. The trees along the banks of the stream also increased in number and he spurred his horse into a gallop. As they turned a bend in the stream round a hill, a silver waterfall came into view.

Chen felt greatly invigorated by the discovery of this gorgeous place in the midst of the barren desert, and was curious to know what further vistas were waiting for him above the waterfall. He led the horse round and up and, as they emerged from a line of tall fir trees, he stopped in amazement.

Before him stretched a wide lake fed by another large waterfall at its southern end. The spray from the cascade combined with the sunlight to create a glorious rainbow, while a profusion of trees and flowers surrounded the lake, their myriad colours reflected in the turquoise-green waters. Beyond was a huge expanse of verdant grass stretching off to the horizon on which he could see several hundred white sheep grazing. A high mountain rose into the clouds from the western bank of the lake, its lower slopes covered in the green foliage of trees, its upper slopes brilliant with pure white snow.

He stood staring at the scene for a moment. The song of small birds in the trees, and the tinkling of the ice in the lake, combined with the roar of the waterfall to create a symphony of sound. Looking down at the surface of the lake, he suddenly noticed a circle of small ripples. Then a jade-white hand emerged from the water, followed by a dripping-wet head. The head turned, caught sight of him, and with a shriek disappeared back under the water.

In that moment, Chen had been able to see that the head belonged to a young girl of extraordinary beauty. He was beginning to wonder if such things as water spirits and monsters existed after

all, and pulled out three of his Go-piece missiles and held them
ready in his palm just in case.

The ripples stretched across the surface of the lake northwards.
There was a sudden splash, and the girl's head re-emerged a little
further away, against flowering trees and bushes. Through a gap in
the leaves, he could see her snow-white skin, her raven hair splayed
out on the surface of the water, and her eyes, bright as stars, gazing
across at him.

'Who are you?' her clear voice asked. 'Why have you come
here?'

She spoke in the Uighur language, and, although Chen
understood what she said, he felt incapable of answering. He was
dazed, like a drunken or dreaming man.

'Go away and let me put my clothes on,' the girl said. Chen's
face flushed and he quickly retreated into the trees.

He was extremely embarrassed and wanted to escape
altogether, but he thought he should at least ask the girl if she had
any news of the lady he was seeking, Huo Qingtong. For a while
he was undecided. Then the sound of singing, soft but clear, floated
over from the opposite shore of the lake:

> Brother, brother, passing by,
> Please come back.
> Why have you run away so fast,
> Without a word?

He walked slowly back to the lake and, looking across, saw
the young girl dressed in a dazzlingly white gown, sitting barefoot
in a bed of red flowers by the water's edge. She was slowly combing
her long hair, which was still dripping wet. Flower petals drifted
slowly down from the trees onto her head. He marvelled that such
a beautiful girl as this could exist.

The girl smiled radiantly and motioned with her hand for him
to come over.

'I was riding this way and felt thirsty,' Chen said in the Uighur
language. 'I happened to find a stream and followed it here. I did
not know I would run into you. Please forgive me if I have offended
you in any way.' He bowed as he spoke.

'What's your name?' she asked.

'Ahmed.'

This was the most common name among men of the Muslim faith, and the girl smiled again.

'All right,' she said. 'Then my name is Ayesha.' This was the most common name among Muslim women. 'Are you looking for someone?'

'I have to find the Hodja Muzhuolun.'

The girl looked startled. 'Do you know him?'

'Yes, I do,' said Chen. 'I also know his son, Huo Ayi, and his daughter, Lady Huo Qingtong.'

'Where did you meet them?'

'They travelled to the central plains to recover the sacred Koran and I happened to come across them there.'

'Why are you looking for the Hodja?'

Chen detected a note of respect in her voice. 'Is he of the same tribe as you?'

The girl nodded.

'Your father's people killed a number of Agency guards while they were recovering the sacred Koran, and friends of the guards are now seeking revenge,' explained Chen. 'I want to warn them.'

The girl had had a smile constantly playing around her lips, but now it disappeared. 'Are the men that are coming to take revenge very terrible?' she asked. 'Are there many of them?'

'No, not many. But they are good fighters. As long as we are prepared, there is nothing to fear.'

The girl relaxed and smiled again. 'I will take you to see the Hodja,' she said. 'We will have to travel for several days.' She began to plait her hair. 'The great Manchu army came and attacked us for no reason and all the men have gone away to fight. The women and I have remained here to look after the livestock.'

As she talked, Chen gazed at her in wonder. He could never, not in his wildest dreams, have imagined such exquisite jade-like beauty in a human being. The whole scene, the young girl and the superb natural setting that surrounded her, belonged to another world.

When the girl finished combing her hair, she picked up an ox horn and blew several notes on it. A short while later, a number of Uighur girls on horseback galloped towards them across the pastures. She went over and talked with them while the girls weighed Chen up, very curious as to who he was. She then walked over to a tent pitched between the trees and came back leading a chestnut horse carrying food and other essentials.

'Let's go.' She mounted in one effortless bound, and rode off ahead of him heading south along the course of the stream.

'How did the Chinese people treat you when you were in their country?' she asked as they rode along.

'Some of them well, some not, but mostly well,' Chen replied. He wanted to confess to her that he was himself Chinese, but her complete lack of suspicion somehow made it difficult for him to do so. She asked what China was like. Chen chose a few interesting stories to tell her, and she listened enthralled.

The sky began to grow dark, and they camped for the night beneath a huge rock by a river. The girl lit a fire, roasted some dried mutton she had brought, and shared it with Chen. She was silent throughout, and Chen did not dare to speak, as if words would desecrate the purity of the scene.

The girl began telling him about her youth, how she had grown up as a shepherdess on the grasslands, and how she loved flowers more than anything in the world.

'There are so many, many beautiful flowers on the grasslands. As you look out, you can see flowers stretching to the horizon. I much prefer eating flowers to eating mutton.'

'Can you eat flowers?' Chen asked in surprise.

'Of course. I've been eating them since I was small. My father and my elder brother tried to stop me at first, but when I went out by myself to look after the sheep, there was nothing they could do. Later, when they saw that it did me no harm, they didn't bother about it any more.'

Chen wanted to say something to the effect that, considering her floral diet, it was no wonder she was herself as beautiful as a flower, but he restrained himself. Sitting beside her, he became aware that her body exuded a slight fragrance, more intoxicating than that of any flower. It made him quite light-headed. He wondered what kind of floral lotion she used. Then he remembered the rules of propriety and discreetly moved to sit a little further away from her. The girl laughed.

'Ever since I was young, I've had a nice smell,' she said. 'It's probably because I eat flowers. Do you like it?'

Chen blushed at the question and marvelled at her simplicity and frankness. Gradually, his reticence towards her faded.

The girl talked of her life as a shepherdess, of picking flowers, and of looking at stars, and of the games that young girls play. Chen had left home when still a boy, and ever since that time he had spent his life amongst the fighting community. He had long ago forgotten such simple, childlike matters. After a while, the girl stopped talking and gazed up at the Milky Way sparkling across the heavens.

Chen pointed up. 'That constellation is the Weaving Girl,' he said, 'and that one on the other side is the Cowherd.'

She was fascinated by the names. 'Tell me about them,' she said, and Chen told her the old story of how the Cowherd and the Weaving Girl fell in love but found themselves separated by a silvery river, the Milky Way, and how a stork built a bridge across the river to unite them once a year.

The girl looked seriously up at the stars. 'I've never liked storks before, but now that I know they build a bridge to bring the Cowherd and the Weaving Girl together, I've changed my mind. From now on when I see them, I will give them something to eat.'

'The Cowherd and the Weaving Girl may only be able to meet once a year,' said Chen, 'but they have done so every year for hundreds of millions of years. In a way they are much better off than we ordinary mortals, doomed to die after a short span of life.' The girl nodded.

The desert had grown very cold with the coming of night and Chen went to look for some dead wood and grass to build up the fire. Then they wrapped themselves in blankets and went to sleep. Despite the distance between them as they slept, it still seemed to Chen that he could smell the girl's fragrance in his dreams.

Early next morning they started out again heading west, and after several days arrived at the banks of the Tarim River. That afternoon, they chanced upon two mounted Uighur warriors. The girl went over and spoke with them and after a moment the Uighurs bowed and left.

'The Manchu army has already taken Aksu and Kashgar, and the Hodja and the others have retreated to Yarkand,' she reported to Chen. 'That's more than ten days' ride from here.'

Chen was very concerned at the news that the Manchu forces had scored a victory and penetrated so far into the Uighur lands.

'They also said that the Manchu troops are so numerous that our army's only option is to retreat and stretch their lines of communication. When their rations are exhausted, they will not have enough strength left to fight.'

Chen decided the Uighur force would probably be safe for a while using this strategy. Once Qian Long's order to halt the war arrived, General Zhao Hui would have to retire with his troops. Huo Qingtong would be with her father, and therefore far away from central China. She had the protection of a large army, so there was no longer any reason to fear the vengeful Devils of Manchuria, Teng Yilei and his two friends. With that thought, he set his mind at ease.

The two of them continued travelling westwards, riding by day and sleeping by night. They talked and laughed as they went and, as the days passed, they became closer and closer. Chen found himself secretly hoping that the journey would never end, that they could continue as they were forever.

One day, just as the sun was about to disappear behind the grasslands on the horizon, they heard a bugle note, and a small deer jumped out of a spinney of trees nearby. The girl clapped her hands and laughed in delight.

'A baby deer!' she cried. It had clearly been born only a short time before and was very small and still very unsteady on its feet. It gave two plaintive cries and then leapt back into the trees. The girl watched it go, then suddenly reined in her horse. 'There's someone over there,' she whispered.

Chen looked over and saw four Manchu soldiers and an officer carving up a large deer while the fawn circled around them making pitiful cries. The dead deer was obviously its mother.

'Goddamn it, we might as well eat that one too!' cursed one of the soldiers, standing up. He fixed an arrow to his bow and prepared to shoot the fawn which, ignorant of the danger, was moving towards him.

The girl gave a cry of alarm. She jumped off her horse, ran into the thicket, and placed herself in front of the fawn. 'Don't shoot!' she cried. 'Don't you dare shoot!' The soldier started in surprise and took a step backwards, dazzled by her beauty. She picked up the fawn and stroked its soft coat. 'You poor thing,' she murmured. She glanced hatefully at the soldier, then turned and walked out of the thicket with the fawn.

The five soldiers whispered amongst themselves for a moment, then ran after her, shouting and brandishing their swords.

The girl started running too and quickly reached Chen and the horses. The officer barked out an order and the five fanned out around them.

Chen squeezed the girl's hand. 'Don't be afraid,' he said. 'I'll kill these villains to avenge the death of the fawn's mother.' She stood beside him, the fawn cradled in her arms. Chen stretched out his hand and stroked the animal.

'What are you doing?' the officer asked haltingly in the Uighur tongue. 'Come here!'

The girl looked up at Chen, who smiled at her. She smiled back, confident that they would not be harmed.

'No weapons!' the officer shouted, and the other soldiers threw their swords to the ground and advanced. Strangely, despite the usual preference of soldiers for young maidens, they were perhaps cowed by her glowing beauty and made for Chen instead. The girl cried out in alarm, but before the cry was fully out, there was a whooshing sound and the four soldiers flew through the air, landing heavily on the ground some distance away. They grunted and groaned, unable to get up, for they had all been touched on Vital Points. The officer, seeing the situation was unfavourable, turned and fled.

'Come back!' Chen ordered. He sent his Pearl Strings flying out, wrapping them around the officer's neck, then sharply pulled him back.

The girl looked over at Chen, her eyes full of admiration.

'Why are you here?' he asked the officer in Uighur. The officer clambered to his feet, still dazed. He looked around, saw his four comrades lying motionless on the ground, and knew he was in trouble.

'We…we soldiers,' he stuttered, 'General Zhao Hui army…his orders…we…we never…'

'Where are the five of you going?' asked Chen. 'You'd better not lie.'

'Not lie! Not lie!' the officer said, shaking with fear. 'General orders…go Stellar Gorge…meet people…'

His stammered Uighur was almost incomprehensible, and Chen switched to Chinese. 'Who are you going to meet?' he asked.

'A deputy commander of the Imperial Guard.'

'What's his name? Give me those documents you are carrying.'

The officer hesitated then pulled an official document from his pocket. Chen glanced at it and noted with surprise that it was

addressed to Deputy Commander Zhang Zhaozhong—the Fire
Hand Judge. He knew that Master Ma Zhen had taken Fire Hand
Zhang away to discipline him, and wondered how he could be on
his way there. He ripped the letter open and read: 'I am delighted
to hear that you have received Imperial orders to come to the Uighur
country. I have sent these men ahead to rendezvous with you.' It
was signed by General Zhao Hui, the officer in command of the
entire Manchu expeditionary force.

If Fire Hand Zhang had come at the Emperor's command,
Helmsman Chen concluded, then surely he must have been
entrusted with passing on the order to retreat (the order Qian Long
had promised he would issue). It would be best not to interfere. He
gave the letter back to the officer, released the four soldiers' Vital
Points, then rode off with the girl without saying another word.

'You managed that so well!' she said. 'A man like you would
certainly be very well known amongst our people. How is it I have
never heard of you before?'

Chen smiled. 'The little fawn must be hungry,' he said. 'Why
don't you give it something to eat?'

'Yes, yes!' she cried. She poured some mare's milk from the
leather gourd into her palm and let the fawn lap it up. After a few
mouthfuls, the fawn bleated mournfully. 'She's calling for her
mother,' the girl said.

The Love-Match Party

They travelled on for another six days. On the morning of the
seventh day, they spotted dark clouds in the distance.

'Is that a storm brewing?' Chen asked.

The girl studied the horizon. 'Those are not rain clouds,' she
said. 'That's dust from the ground.'

'How could there be so much?'

'I don't know. Let's go and find out!' They spurred their horses
forward, and as the swirling dust cloud rose before them, they began
to hear the clashing sound of metal on metal drifting over towards
them. Chen reined in his horse.

'It's an army,' he said. 'We must get out of the way quickly.'
They turned and rode off east, but after a while, another dust cloud
arose in front of them and a column of mounted troops appeared.
Through the dust, Chen saw a huge flag inscribed with the name

of General Zhao. Having already clashed once with Zhao's armoured troops by night at the Yellow River crossing, he knew them to be formidable fighters, and he motioned to the girl with his hand and galloped off southwards. Luckily, both their horses were swift, and, after some hard riding, the armoured column had dropped far behind.

The girl looked anxious. 'I hope our army will be able to hold their own,' she said. Chen was just about to say something comforting when horns sounded in front, and rank upon rank of soldiers appeared over a rise. To the left, there was a thunderous ground-shaking roar and a vast carpet of cavalry moved across the hills towards them. With one sweep of his left arm, Chen swung the girl onto his horse and took out his shield to protect her.

'Don't be afraid,' he said. The girl was still hugging the little deer. She looked round at him and nodded. 'If you say there's no need to be afraid, then I won't be,' she said. As she spoke, her soft, orchid-like fragrance enveloped him, and despite the danger that surrounded them on all sides, feelings of tenderness stirred within him.

Enemy troops were advancing from the east, north, and south. Chen urged the white horse westwards, and her chestnut horse followed along behind. After a while, they spotted Manchu troops ahead of them once more. Now they were totally encircled. Chen spurred the horse up onto high ground to get a better idea of the Manchu positions and to look for a gap through which they could escape. But he could see at a glance that there was none. To the west, beyond the thousands of Manchu foot soldiers in close ranks protected on both flanks by cavalry, was the Uighur army, also an imposing force with a forest of spears and scimitars rising above the striped gowns of the warriors. The two sides had halted, obviously in preparation for battle, and Manchu officers rode back and forth making final preparations. The huge army gradually became deathly quiet. Chen and the girl had by this time been noticed, and several soldiers approached to question them.

'The gods have conspired to deliver us into the hands of the Manchus,' Chen thought. But the idea of dying with the girl beside him gave him a strange pleasure. He grasped the Pearl Strings in his right hand, the reins in his left, and shouted: 'Let's go!'

The horses galloped off towards the end of the Manchu lines, and in a flash had passed three companies of troops. Rank upon rank of armoured soldiers, bows at the ready, filed past them, and Chen knew that with one word from the Manchu commanders, he and the girl in his arms would immediately become the target for a thousand spears and ten thousand arrows. He pulled the reins in tightly and cantered steadily along, not even glancing at the soldiers.

The morning sun had just risen, and the troops stared in amazement at the girl's extraordinary beauty, her hair, face, arms, and gown splashed with pale sunlight. Each one of them, whether officer or trooper, found his heart thumping furiously. They watched as the two gradually rode off into the distance.

Even General Zhao, the Commander-in-Chief of the army, was overcome by an unaccustomed feeling of tranquillity when he beheld her. Somehow he was in no mood for killing. Looking round, he saw similar expressions of dazed serenity on the faces of all his officers and underlings. They had all already replaced their swords in their scabbards, and were obviously awaiting the general's order to retire.

'Return to camp,' Zhao said in a far-away voice. The order was relayed back, and the tens of thousands of soldiers turned and went back to their camp-site more than ten miles away beside the Black Water River.

Helmsman Chen had broken out in a cold sweat and his hands were shaking with fear, but the girl looked unconcerned, apparently unaware of the great danger they had just been in. She smiled at him and leapt over onto the back of the chestnut horse.

'There's our army in front,' she said. Chen put away his shield and galloped towards the Uighur lines. A small detail of cavalry rode out to meet them, shouting and cheering as they came. The riders jumped off their horses and bowed before the girl. The officer in charge walked over to Helmsman Chen and bowed before him too.

'Many thanks to you, sir,' he said. 'May Allah the true God protect you!'

Chen bowed in return and thanked him. The girl rode straight into the Uighur ranks of her people without waiting for Chen. She obviously commanded a great deal of respect, for wherever her chestnut horse went, the soldiers made way for it with cheers.

A brigade commander invited Chen to the barracks to eat and rest, and Chen told him he wanted to see the tribe's leader, the Hodja Muzhuolun.

'The Hodja has gone to observe the enemy's strength,' the commander replied. 'When he returns, I will immediately inform him.' Following the long journey and the tense encounter with the Manchu army, Chen felt worn out, and after he had been shown to a small tent, he immediately slept.

Some time after noon, the commander returned to say that the Hodja was now not expected to return until evening. Chen asked him who the white-gowned girl he had travelled with was.

The commander smiled. 'She is the most beautiful young woman in the world!' was all he would say by way of reply. 'Tonight,' he continued, 'we are having a love-match gathering. It is an age-old tradition among our people. Why don't you come along? You will be able to meet the Hodja there.'

Chen did not press him further. Towards evening, he saw the young warriors donning their finery, each face alive with excitement. The desert evening sky slowly deepened in colour and a thin crescent moon rose above the horizon. Chen heard the sound of music strike up, and soon afterwards the commander came into the tent.

'The new moon has risen,' he said, taking Chen's hand. 'Let us go!' The two walked towards a huge bonfire where the young Uighur warriors were gathering. All around, people were roasting beef and mutton, and preparing various delicacies, while their friends were playing music. A horn blew, and a group emerged from a large tent near the bonfire, among whom Helmsman Chen recognized the Hodja and his son, Huo Ayi. Chen decided he would wait until the official ceremony was over before revealing himself, and turned up the collar of his gown to hide his face.

The Hodja motioned to the crowd, and they all knelt down and prayed to Allah. When the prayer was ended, he spoke.

'I must now ask those men who are already married to go and stand guard,' he said. 'This evening the pleasure is reserved for your younger brothers.'

Three columns of warriors were formed. Huo Ayi, flourishing his sabre, led them off into the darkness.

Having lived many years in the Uighur regions, Chen knew that although Uighur marriages were arranged by parents according to various considerations of wealth and property, the procedure was still much more liberal than that of the Chinese. The love-match party was a Uighur tradition that had been passed down for many generations. It was an occasion for young, unmarried boys and girls to seal their romantic attachments and become engaged. The initiative was taken by the girl, who would place a belt round the neck of her chosen boy and lead him to dance.

After a while, the music became softer in tone. The tent door flaps parted and out came a large group of young Uighur girls who sang and danced their way towards the bonfire. They all wore colourful clothes and small caps laced with gold and silver threads which sparkled brightly in the firelight. Chen saw two beautiful girls walking over to the Hodja, one dressed entirely in yellow, the other in white. With a start, he recognized them as Huo Qingtong and the girl who had brought him to the Uighur camp. In the moonlight, they looked equally graceful and beautiful. The two girls sat down, one on either side of the Hodja.

A thought suddenly struck Chen. 'The girl in white must be Lady Huo Qingtong's younger sister! No wonder I kept thinking her face was familiar! It's the face on the jade vases, though the drawing does not do justice to her real beauty...'

His heart began to thump wildly. From the day he had first met Huo Qingtong, his love for her had been growing; but the intimacy that he had observed between her and Hidden Needle Lu's handsome young disciple had convinced him that she was already spoken for. Now, having spent the past days in the company of the white-gowned girl, his romantic thoughts had taken a new turn. He was captivated by her matchless beauty.

The music stopped, and the Hodja's voice rang out clearly: 'The prophet Mohammed teaches us in the Koran, chapter two, verse one hundred and fifty: "Fight in the cause of Allah those who fight you." And in chapter twenty-two, verse thirty-nine: "To those against whom war has been made, permission is given to fight because they are wronged. Verily, Allah is great! Allah will make them victorious!" We are oppressed, and Allah will surely assist and protect us.'

A thunderous cheer went up from the crowd.

'Brothers and sisters!' he shouted. 'War may be all around us, but tonight we celebrate love! Enjoy yourselves to the full!'

Singing and laughter erupted all about, accompanied by the music of the Uighur horse-head fiddle. Cooks distributed roast meat, honeydew melons, raisins, and koumiss among the throng. Everyone held a small bowl made out of rock salt, in which they rubbed the roast meat. As the new moon rose higher in the sky, the merry-making became more and more intense. One young girl after another jumped up and danced over to the boy of her choice, took the embroidered belt from her waist, and placed it round the boy's neck, then led him off to dance near the bonfire.

Chen had grown up in a traditional Chinese world of strict Confucian convention and had never before seen an occasion of such open and unrestrained merriment. With the singing ringing in his ears and emotions swirling through his heart, he found his face beginning to flush after only a few cups of koumiss.

The music stopped momentarily, then started up again, even faster than before. Everyone looked curiously towards the Hodja, and, following the direction of their gaze, Chen saw that the white-robed girl had now risen to her feet and was drifting gracefully towards the bonfire. A buzz of excited whispering rippled through the crowd. Chen heard the cavalry commander beside him say: 'The Lady Hasli has chosen a lover. But who could possibly be worthy of her?'

That his beloved younger daughter had found a boy she loved seemed to come as a great surprise and a great joy to the Hodja. He watched her intently, with glistening eyes. Hasli glided round and round the circle that had formed. In her hands, she held a brilliantly embroidered belt, and all the while she sang softly:

> Come here,
> You who picked the snow lily for me.
> I am searching for you,
> You who saved my little deer.

The words struck Helmsman Chen's ears like a clap of thunder. Then a white hand touched his shoulder and the embroidered belt fell around his neck. Hasli tugged gently and Chen followed her, scared out of his wits. The crowd cheered, and all around him people were bursting into song.

In the misty moonlight, the Hodja and Huo Qingtong had failed to recognize Chen, and they were walking forward to congratulate him along with the others, thinking he was an ordinary Uighur, when suddenly, they heard three blasts from a distant horn: this was the signal for danger, and the crowd immediately dispersed. The Hodja and Huo Qingtong also returned to their seats.

Hasli took Chen's hand and led him off to sit at the back of the crowd, which was now waiting expectantly. Chen felt her soft body pressed against his, and a light fragrance assailed his nostrils, intoxicating his senses. Was he dreaming? Or was he in heaven?

The Four Giants

Everyone was gazing intently in the direction from which the horn blast had come. Presently two Uighur guards rode up and reported to the Hodja: 'The Manchu General Zhao Hui has sent an envoy who requests an audience.'

'Very well,' replied the Hodja. 'Bring him here.' The two riders galloped off and returned with five other men on horseback, who dismounted about a hundred feet from the crowd.

The Manchu envoy was a robust man and walked up towards them with powerful strides. But his four attendants were veritable giants, a good two heads taller than most ordinary men, and heavily built. The Uighurs viewed them with alarm.

The chief envoy strode up to the Hodja and asked in an arrogant tone of voice: 'Are you the head of the tribe?' The Uighurs were outraged, and several of the younger warriors drew their sabres. The envoy ignored them.

'I am under orders from General Zhao Hui to deliver an ultimatum,' he announced loudly in the Uighur tongue. 'If you know what's good for you, you will surrender immediately, in which case your lives will be spared. Otherwise, our two armies will meet at daybreak the day after tomorrow and you will be completely annihilated. It will then be too late for regrets.'

The crowd of Uighurs sprang to their feet in rage, but the Hodja, with a wave of his hand, ordered them to be seated. He turned to the envoy. 'You Manchus have come here without reason or justification. You kill our people, and steal our property. The True God on High will punish you for your dishonourable behaviour. If you want a fight, we will give you one. We'll fight! Even if our army is reduced to one man, that last man will never surrender.'

The Uighurs raised their sabres and took up his words in unison: 'We'll fight!' they roared. 'We'll never surrender!' The mood was sombre but determined. The Uighurs knew perfectly well that the Manchu force was a mighty one and that in a battle to the finish, the chances were they would lose. But they were devout Muslims, they had faith in Allah, they loved freedom, and they would be no man's slave.

The envoy looked about him and sneered. 'Very well,' he said. 'The day after tomorrow, each and every one of you will die.' He spat savagely onto the ground. It was a calculated insult, and three young Uighurs leapt towards him. 'Today you are an envoy, so you will be allowed to leave safely,' one of them shouted. 'But just wait till we meet on the battlefield!'

The envoy's mouth twisted in anger, and his four giant attendants roughly pushed aside the three Uighur youths and took up their positions around him.

'You scum!' cried the envoy in contempt. 'What you need is a taste of our Manchu skill!' He clapped his hands. One of the four giants glanced round and strode over to a poplar tree nearby, to which several camels were tethered. He grasped its trunk in his arms and after a few rigorous tugs, pulled the entire tree bodily out of the ground. Then he snapped the reins of one of the camels and gave it a hefty kick on the rump, sending it racing away in great pain. When the camel had gone thirty or forty yards, another of the giants sprinted after it and caught up with it in a moment. He swung the huge beast onto his shoulders, ran back towards the bonfire, and set it back on its feet. Then he stood proudly beside it. The third giant muttered something in contempt, and punched at the camel's head with his fist. The animal swayed unsteadily, then crashed to the ground. The fourth giant now proceeded to grab hold of its hind legs, and swung it round and round above his head, then with a shout let it go. The camel flew twenty yards through the air before falling to the ground.

The giants, who were known as the Four Tigers, were four brothers, quadruplets. Their mother had died giving birth to them. Their father was a poor hunter living and working in the forests of Manchuria and, with his wife dead, he had found himself with no milk to feed the four babies. But not long after her death, he heard a mournful cry outside in the forest and found a female tiger caught in a trap. He and a companion were tying the animal up when he happened to notice three tiger cubs lying close by. In a flash of inspiration, he killed the cubs and took the tiger back to his hut where he looked after her, feeding her meat every day, and milking her regularly to feed his four sons. From the very start, they were uncommonly big and strong boys, and they became more so as they grew up into men. The only problem was that they were more than a little impetuous and stupid.

The Uighurs were overwhelmed by this amazing show of brute strength but, unwilling to appear weak before the enemy, they still continued to roar out their defiance.

'Why kill a good camel? What sort of men are you?' shouted one of them. The chief envoy curled his lips into another sneer. The crowd became even more incensed, and it looked as though he would be mobbed at any moment.

'So you're going to ill-treat an envoy, are you?' he shouted.

The Hodja restrained the crowd with difficulty. 'You may be an envoy,' he said, 'but you allowed your men to kill one of our camels, which is a great insult. If you were not my guests, I would have you punished. Now I would thank you to leave immediately.'

'Do you think we Manchus are afraid of scum like you?' shouted the envoy. 'I came with an ultimatum. If you have a reply, give it to me now and I'll pass it on. I'm sure you'd all be much too frightened to go and hand it to General Zhao personally.' Another angry roar went up from the Uighurs.

Huo Qingtong jumped to her feet. 'Is that what you think? Is it? None of us are afraid of your general, none of us, men and women alike!' The envoy looked taken aback for a second. Then he threw back his head and roared with laughter.

'Well I'll be damned! These girls would die of fright just to *see* General Zhao!'

'Don't underestimate us,' replied Huo Qingtong angrily. 'We will send someone back with you now. Pick someone yourself. Whoever you choose will go. You will see what spirit we followers of Mohammed have.' The Uighurs roared their approval. The cry went up: 'Choose me! Choose me!'

'As you wish,' said the envoy coldly. He planned to pick some weak creature, a young girl, who would immediately burst into tears. That way the Uighurs would lose face completely. His eyes roved over the crowd, searching back and forth, and suddenly lit up. He walked over to Hasli and pointed at her. 'Let her go!' he said.

Hasli glanced up at him and slowly rose to her feet. 'For the sake of my people,' she said, 'for my brothers and sisters, I would go anywhere without fear. Allah the true God will surely protect me.'

She spoke calmly, and with great dignity. Her stunning beauty caused even the envoy involuntarily to lower his eyes, and he felt a tinge of regret at his choice. The Hodja, Huo Qingtong, and the other Uighurs, although proud that Hasli had not displayed weakness, were nonetheless anxious. Huo Qingtong was particularly worried. Her sister knew no kungfu whatsoever, and it would be like walking unprotected into a tiger's lair.

'She is my sister,' she said. 'I will go in her place.'

The envoy laughed. 'I always knew the word of a girl could not be trusted. If you are too scared to let her go, why bother sending anyone at all? I can take the message for you. Do you want war, or will you surrender?'

'If we meet on the battlefield, and provided you don't run away first, I'll show you what we girls are made of!' said Huo Qingtong proudly. Anger had made the colour mount in her face.

'With a beauty such as yourself,' replied the envoy, smiling smarmily, 'I would naturally be merciful.' The Uighurs gnashed their teeth at his insolence.

'Sister,' said Hasli to Huo Qingtong, 'let me go. You don't need to be afraid on my behalf.' She pulled Helmsman Chen up by the hand. 'He'll come with me.'

In the light of the flames from the bonfire, Huo Qingtong suddenly recognized Chen and stared at him in shock. Chen made a subtle motion with his hand, indicating that she should not reveal his identity yet. Then he turned to the envoy.

'That is our reply. And we mean what we say. I will accompany this young lady to see your General Zhao. Unlike you, we won't be needing four useless giants to protect us.'

'You're the useless one!' retorted the envoy. 'You're just a little weed. Even supposing you were ten times stronger than you are, you would still be no match for one of my giants.'

Helmsman Chen decided this envoy needed to be cut down to size. It was time to save the face of the Uighurs. He stepped forward.

'I may be the weakest member of our tribe, but I am still better than you Manchus,' he said. 'Tell those four hulks of yours to come over here.'

By this time, the Hodja had also recognized Helmsman Chen. 'Daughter,' he cried to Huo Qingtong in surprise and joy, 'look who it is!' She did not answer. The Hodja saw that her eyes were brimming with tears. At that moment he realized that both of his daughters were in love with the same man. He wondered how Chen had come to meet his younger daughter, Hasli.

Beside the giants, Chen looked like a small child. He must have issued this challenge, the Uighurs decided, in a brave effort to defend the honour of the Lady Hasli and her people. But clearly he could be no match for the giants. Chen raised his hands to the crowd.

'My friends,' he said. 'These Manchus are nothing. Let me deal with them by myself.'

The envoy translated his words to the four giants, who angrily sprang forward to grab Chen. Chen stood firm, smiling faintly, and the envoy hurriedly restrained his four men.

'This gentleman evidently wants a contest,' he said to the Hodja, 'and we must agree that there will be no blame if anyone gets hurt. And it must be one against one. No one else is allowed to interfere.'

The Hodja reluctantly grunted his agreement.

'One against one is no fun!' protested Chen. 'Tell the four of them to come at once.'

'And how many will you have on your side?' asked the envoy.

'Why, just me of course.' A murmur ran through the crowd: surely he had gone too far this time?

The envoy laughed coldly. 'You Uighurs really think too highly of yourselves. Tiger One!' he called to the largest of the four giants. 'You go first.' Tiger One strode forward. 'The first round is to be strictly punching,' announced the envoy. 'Neither party is allowed to block or retreat. The first one to fall loses.'

'I repeat: one is not enough,' insisted Chen. 'If we are going to fight, let them all fight together.'

The envoy began to suspect that Chen had some plan worked out. 'Don't worry,' he said. 'If you manage to beat Tiger One, the others will come after you next.'

Chen smiled. 'All right. It's all the same to me.' The giant ripped off his upper clothing, exposing his huge, rippling muscles. Huo Qingtong glanced furtively at her younger sister and saw her gazing intently at Chen, her eyes full of adoration and love. Huo Qingtong heaved a sigh and then looked over at Chen. As their eyes met, he smiled warmly. She blushed and looked away.

'We will draw lots to decide who strikes first,' said the envoy.

'You are our guests. You may go first,' replied Chen. He took two steps towards the giant and thrust out his chest. 'Go on. Hit me!' he said.

'Please come over here,' the envoy said to Huo Qingtong. 'We two will act as judges. Whoever kicks with his feet, uses his arms to deflect a blow, bends, or dodges will be considered the loser.'

Huo Qingtong went to stand next to the envoy as Chen and the giant faced each other, less than an arm's length apart. The huge crowd stood silently about them, watching intently.

'The Manchu strikes the first blow,' the envoy called out. 'The Uighur will strike the second blow. If both survive the first exchange, then the Manchu will strike again followed by the Uighur. Right! The Manchu to strike!'

The silence was broken only by the sound of Tiger One taking a deep breath. All over his body his joints cracked loudly as he concentrated his strength. Suddenly, the right side of his chest bulged outwards and his right arm swelled to almost twice its normal size. Chen leant slightly forward. 'Punch me,' he said.

Several Uighur men moved behind Chen and prepared to catch him. The Hodja and Huo Qingtong silently prayed to Allah. Only Hasli seemed unconcerned. Chen had said that he was unafraid. So there was certainly nothing to be afraid of.

The giant crouched slightly, then with a mighty roar slammed his right fist at Chen's chest. But as it reached its maximum extension, the fist only lightly grazed the lapel of Chen's gown. The giant stared dumbfounded at Chen. At first he was too shocked even to withdraw his fist.

'Is that it?' Chen asked. The giant blushed deep red and hastily retracted his arm.

To the crowd, it looked as if the blow had struck home, and they were puzzled that Chen seemed unaffected. The Hodja and Huo Qingtong were the only ones who knew that he had made use of Inner Force kungfu (of which he was a master) to draw in his chest, following with precision the incoming movement of his opponent's fist. It was a classic move, brilliantly executed. Huo Qingtong smiled radiantly and breathed a sigh of relief. The envoy, who was himself something of a kungfu expert, scowled in annoyance.

Chen smiled. 'Now it's my turn,' he said.

'Punch!' roared Tiger One. He thrust out his hairy chest and Chen's fist shot forward and punched it lightly. At first the giant felt no pain, but then he became aware of a great force pushing him backwards. He put all his weight into countering it by leaning forward. Suddenly Chen withdrew his fist, and the giant, having no time to stabilize himself, toppled forward and crashed to the ground in a cloud of dust. All this took place in the blink of an eye. There was a stunned silence for a second, then the crowd erupted in applause and joyful laughter. The envoy rushed over to help Tiger One who was howling with pain. Blood was pouring from his mouth, and two of his front teeth had snapped off altogether as he hit the ground.

Seeing their fellow giant injured, the other three charged at Chen with a blood-curdling roar of rage. Chen skipped nimbly around behind Tiger Three and shoved him at Tiger Two. Tiger Four meanwhile lunged at Chen with his arms outstretched, but Chen ducked down and tickled his armpits as he passed. Tiger Four was extremely ticklish, and he immediately collapsed into a helpless ball, rolling and laughing hysterically on the ground.

Chen danced effortlessly amongst the four giants (Tiger One had by now succeeded in clambering to his feet and was back in action), making them all look utterly foolish without even so much as hitting them. The envoy could see that Chen was a transcendent Martial Arts master and tried in vain to stop the fight. But once roused, the Four Tigers were unstoppable. That was their nature. They closed in on Chen again, Tiger One coming from in front while the other three closed off his line of retreat behind. Chen waited until Tiger One was within arm's reach then toppled him over backwards with a push, grabbed him by the leg, and hurled him away so that he landed head first in the very hole where the tree he had uprooted had once stood.

Tiger Four roared and kicked out with his right leg, but Chen grabbed him by the trousers and shirt, lifted him up, and with a hefty kick sent him flying through the air. The giant landed with a thump on the corpse of the camel he had himself killed.

While Tiger Four was still in mid-air, Tigers Two and Three came charging at Chen from opposite directions. Chen waited until they were almost upon him before leaping out of the way, and the two giants smashed into each other and toppled to the ground like a great two-man pagoda. Before they could clamber to their feet,

Chen tied their two pigtails together, then, with a laugh, he walked back to Hasli's side. She clapped her hands in delight as the other Uighurs cheered and shouted.

The Four Tigers picked themselves up and the envoy rushed over and struggled to undo the knot in the hair of Tigers Two and Three. The four giants looked across at Chen, not with hate but with respect. Tiger One raised a thumb in Chen's direction.

'You good,' he said sombrely. 'You win.' He bowed, and the other three giants followed suit. Chen hurriedly returned the compliment. Seeing that they were no more than simpletons, he began to rather regret the way he had played with them.

Tiger Four suddenly ran over carrying the camel's corpse, while Tiger Three led their four horses over to the Hodja.

'It was wrong of us to kill your camel,' he said. 'We would like to give you these horses to make up for it.' The Hodja declined the offer with thanks.

The envoy was, needless to say, extremely embarrassed by this whole turn of events. 'Let's go!' he shouted to the Four Tigers. He turned to Hasli.

'Do you really have the courage to come too?' he asked.

'What is there to be scared of?' she replied, and bade the envoy wait for her. She walked over to the Hodja. 'Father, write out a reply and I will deliver it for you.' Her father hesitated. If she did not go, the whole tribe would lose face; but if he let her go, he would worry endlessly. He motioned Chen over, and led him by the hand into the tent with Huo Qingtong and her sister following behind. Once inside, the Hodja threw his arms around him.

'Helmsman!' he said. 'What happy wind is it that has blown you here?'

'I was on my way to Heaven Mountains on personal business, and heard some important news which I wanted to pass on to you. By coincidence, I met your daughter, who brought me here.'

Hasli was dumbstruck at hearing her father call Chen 'Helmsman' and, seeing the shocked expression on her face, Chen said: 'There is something I must apologize for. I haven't told you that I am Chinese.'

'Helmsman Chen is a good friend of our people,' the Hodja added. 'He recovered our sacred Koran for us. He has saved your sister's life, and recently he intercepted the Manchu army's rations which slowed their advance and gave us time to collect our forces.

The services he has rendered us are truly uncountable.' Chen modestly declined the compliments.

'I don't blame you at all for not telling me who you were,' Hasli said with a smile. 'I'm sure you did it because you did not want to bring up all the things you have done for us.'

'That Manchu envoy was unforgivably arrogant,' said the Hodja. 'It was fortunate that you intervened, Helmsman. You certainly deflated his pride. Now he has chosen my younger daughter to be our envoy. What do you advise us to do?'

Chen was reluctant to meddle in the affairs of the Uighur people. 'I come from China and know little of the situation here, sir,' he said. 'If you decide that she should go, then I will do my utmost to protect her. If you feel it would be better for her not to go, then we will think of some other way to deal with the envoy.'

'Father, you and my sister spend all day and every day worrying about our people's affairs,' Hasli interrupted. 'Let me do this one thing. Making one trip as an envoy is nothing serious. Let me do it. If I don't go now, the Manchus will laugh at us.'

'I am just afraid that they will harm you,' said Huo Qingtong.

'What about you?' replied Hasli. 'Every time you go out on the battlefield you risk your life. So it's only right that I should risk my life this once.' She looked at Chen. 'Anyway, he always knows what to do. If he goes with me I won't be the slightest bit afraid, not at all.'

Huo Qingtong could see how deep her sister's feelings were for Chen. An inexpressibly strong emotion swept through her heart.

'Father,' she said. 'Let her go.'

'Very well then. Helmsman, I entrust my young daughter to you.' Chen blushed and Hasli's eyes gazed up at him, as limpid as the water in an autumn pool. Huo Qingtong looked away.

The Hodja wrote out a formal reply to General Zhao's ultimatum, which said simply: 'We will fight. Allah will protect us.' Chen nodded his head in approval. The Hodja handed the note to Hasli, then kissed her on both cheeks.

'Allah will protect you too, sister,' said Huo Qingtong. 'Come back soon.' Hasli threw her arms around Huo Qingtong and thanked her.

A feast was organized to entertain the Manchu envoy, after which there was music and dancing to see off the guests; then the envoy raised his hand, leapt onto his horse, and galloped off, with

Hasli, Helmsman Chen, and the four giants following behind. Huo Qingtong watched the seven figures disappear into the darkness and felt a great emptiness inside. It was as if her heart had disappeared with them into the infinite depths of the desert.

'Your sister is very brave,' said the Hodja. She nodded, then suddenly covered her face and ran inside the tent.

Spellbound

They galloped for most of the night, and finally arrived at the Manchu camp at dawn. The envoy ushered Hasli and Helmsman Chen into a tent to rest, then went off alone to see General Zhao. As he bowed before the general, he noticed a newly arrived military official seated beside him, a bearded man wearing the uniform of a deputy commander of the Chinese Banner division of the Imperial Guards known as the Valiant Corps.

'My report, General,' he said. 'We delivered the ultimatum. They refuse to surrender and have sent someone to present you with their answer.'

General Zhao grunted. 'These people are incorrigibly ignorant,' he said, and turned to one of his attendants. 'Prepare for an audience,' he ordered. Horns blew and drums rolled and all the senior officers of the army gathered in the great tent. Then three hundred armoured troops formed two lines outside and the Uighur envoy was summoned.

Hasli walked fearlessly in ahead of Chen. The officers recognized them instantly, to their great surprise, as the two they had seen the day before galloping across their lines. General Zhao had planned to overawe the envoy with a show of military might, and was taken aback for a moment when it turned out to be a beautiful girl who appeared before him. Hasli bowed before the general, then took out her father's note and offered it to him with both hands.

One of General Zhao's personal aides moved forward to accept the letter. As he neared her, he was overwhelmed by her sweet fragrance and lowered his head, not daring to look at her directly. Then, catching sight of her flawless white hands, he stood there stock-still, too flustered to move.

'Bring the letter here!' shouted Zhao.

The aide started, then stumbled and almost fell to the ground. Hasli placed the letter in his hands and smiled at him. The aide gazed at her, oblivious of all else. Hasli pointed at General Zhao and gave the aide a slight push, and he finally managed to walk forward and place the letter on the table in front of the general.

It made General Zhao furious to see his man rendered so spellbound and helpless by this girl. 'Take him out and chop off his head!' he roared. Several soldiers ran forward and dragged the luckless aide outside the tent. A moment later, a bloody head was brought in on a plate and presented to the general.

'Put it on public display!' ordered Zhao, and the assembled soldiers began to retire. But Hasli was heartbroken at the sight of such cruelty and at the thought that the man had died because of her. She took the plate from the soldiers and gazed at the head, tears falling one after another down her cheeks and onto the floor.

The officers in the tent were by now completely mesmerized by the sight of this beautiful young woman. Any one of them would have willingly died for her. The soldier who had performed the execution was greatly distressed at the sight of her crying, and suddenly shouted: 'I did wrong to kill him. Don't cry!' He slashed his sword across his own neck and fell to the ground, dead.

Hasli was more upset than ever. Helmsman Chen was growing more than a trifle uneasy about the situation: an envoy should not cry in such a fashion. He leant forward to comfort her.

General Zhao was a hardened soldier, and a man of great cruelty and brutality; but even his heart softened at the sight of her tears. He gave orders that the two dead men should be properly buried, and then proceeded to open the letter. As he read it, he grunted.

'Right,' he said. 'We fight tomorrow. You may leave.'

'General,' the bearded officer sitting next to him suddenly interrupted. 'I have a feeling this girl may be the very one the Emperor wants.'

Chen's attention had until now been directed entirely at Hasli but, hearing the officer speak, he looked up and recognized him as none other than Fire Hand Zhang. At the same instant Zhang also recognized Chen, despite his Uighur disguise.

They stared at each other in total amazement.

'Well, Helmsman,' said Zhang, and laughed coldly. 'Fancy meeting you in a place such as this!'

Chen grabbed Hasli's hand and turned to leave, but as he did so, Zhang bounded over and struck out at him with all his might. Chen picked Hasli up under his left arm, deflected Zhang's blow with his right, and went running out of the tent with Zhang close on his heels. None of the other officers or soldiers intervened to stop Chen. They were all still too dazzled by the apparition of Hasli, and felt that this officer of the Imperial Valiant Corps was interfering in matters that should not have concerned him.

Helmsman Chen ran for their horses and, as Zhang closed in, he threw six Go-piece missiles at him. 'I'll keep him at bay,' he shouted to Hasli. 'You escape on your horse!'

'No, I'll wait for you to beat him.'

Chen had no time to explain. He deposited her on the saddle of the chestnut horse as Zhang dodged the projectiles and attacked again. Not daring to face him head on, Chen crouched down underneath the white horse and punched it in the belly. The startled horse kicked out with its back legs straight at Zhang, who only just managed to jump clear.

'Go!' shouted Chen as Zhang grabbed for Hasli. Her horse leapt forward in the nick of time. Chen knew what a deadly opponent Fire Hand Zhang was. He drew his dagger and lunged at him. Zhang caught him by the wrist and the two fell to the ground, rolling together, neither daring to let go of the other. The officers crowded out of the tent to watch, and the Four Tigers, who had acquired a healthy respect for Chen and were annoyed at the way he was being treated, even ran over to help him.

Chen's strength was fading as he grappled with Zhang, and when he saw the four giants running over he thought he was done for. But to his astonishment, instead of attacking him, the four grabbed Fire Hand Zhang and pinned him to the ground, shouting to Chen: 'Run for it!' For all his kungfu skill, Zhang could not counter the immense strength of the Four Tigers, and Chen was able to leap to his feet. He mounted the white horse and galloped off after Hasli. Zhang stared after them helplessly as they disappeared into the distance.

The two horses raced like the wind and were soon beyond the army's furthest guardposts. Helmsman Chen's fight with Zhang had been short but extremely intense and, after riding on for a while, he gradually felt his control slipping. Hasli could see that he was in difficulty, and noticed that his wrist was badly bruised. It was covered in black and purple stripes.

'They'll never catch us now,' she said. 'Let's dismount and rest for a while.' Chen fell off his horse and lay on the ground, shuddering and gasping. Hasli pulled a container of sheep's milk from her leather satchel and rubbed some onto his wrist. Chen gradually recovered, but just as they were getting ready to start out again, they heard the sound of galloping hooves and saw several dozen soldiers riding after them. They leapt onto their horses without bothering to pick up their belongings, and sprang forward. A moment later, Chen noticed a dust-cloud rising up ahead and, cursing their bad luck, galloped on ahead of Hasli. As they rode closer, he saw that there were only seven or eight riders in the group in front, and his anxiety eased. He reined in his horse and took out his Pearl Strings to prepare for the riders as they closed in.

Suddenly, one of the riders shouted: 'Helmsman, are you well?' Through the dust Chen could see that the speaker was a hunchback.

'Brother Zhang!' he yelled, overjoyed. 'Quickly!' As he spoke, the first arrow from the pursuing Manchu troops flew towards them.

Desert Cover

'Enemy soldiers are chasing us,' Chen shouted. 'Hold them off for a while!'

'Excellent!' exclaimed Hunchback Zhang. By now Leopard Wei had galloped up to join him, and the two charged at the Manchu horsemen. Chen watched in surprise as Rolling Thunder Wen, Luo Bing, Mastermind Xu, Zhou Qi, and Scholar Yu all galloped past him with cries of greeting, on their way to engage the Manchu troops. Xin Yan raced up behind, leapt off his horse, and kowtowed before Chen.

Wen and the others quickly killed or dispersed the Manchu troops, but in the distance they could see a much larger force heading their way. They rode back to Chen.

'Which way shall we go?' Wen asked.

Chen looked at the size of the pursuing enemy force and decided it would be a good idea to try and lead them away from the main Uighur army to the west.

'South,' he said, pointing with his hand. The others immediately set off in that direction. They were all riding good horses, and slowly drew away from their pursuers as they galloped across the featureless desert stretching out all around them. Chen wondered why General Zhao would want to send such a huge force after only two of them. Then he suddenly recalled Fire Hand

Zhang's remark: 'I have a feeling this girl may be the very one the Emperor wants.' So Qian Long was after the lovely Hasli! As Chen considered the significance of this, he noticed another column of soldiers riding round to head them off from the south. The Red Flower heroes reined in their horses, uncertain what to do.

'We must make for some sort of cover as quickly as we can, and wait until dark to escape,' said Mastermind Xu.

'Yes,' agreed Chen. 'Travelling across the desert in daylight is impossible.' They dismounted and used their weapons and bare hands to dig a large hole in the sand.

'You go in first,' Luo Bing said to Hasli. But not understanding Chinese, she simply smiled back and made no move.

The Manchu troops were gradually closing in upon them, so without further ado Luo Bing grabbed hold of Hasli and jumped into the hole. The rest followed close behind. Wen and the other heroes had brought bows and arrows with them and they quickly fired off a volley of arrows, downing a dozen or so soldiers. As one column of Manchu troops galloped up to the edge of the hole, Wen shot an arrow at the commander which hit him in the chest, passed right through him, and flew on for twenty or thirty yards further before falling to the ground. The other soldiers were so frightened by this demonstration of power that they turned and fled.

The first wave had been beaten back, but looking round them the heroes saw they were completely surrounded.

'The hole is deep enough, but we should start making it wider,' Xu said. Seven or eight feet below the loose sand was firm earth, and Chen and the others dug away at the sides, piling the sand up on top as a defensive wall.

Hunchback Zhang pointed to the dead Manchu soldiers lying just beyond the hole. 'Let's get their weapons,' he suggested to Xin Yan. The two clambered out of the hole and collected seven or eight bows and a large batch of arrows from around the corpses.

Only now did Chen have a chance to introduce Hasli to the Red Flower heroes. When they heard that she was Huo Qingtong's sister, they all welcomed her, but the language barrier made it impossible for them to talk to her. Chen rested for a while, and gradually his strength returned. He ordered the others to keep a close watch on the Manchu forces and told them they would try to break out after nightfall.

A Sinister Story, and Snow

Helmsman Chen had been greatly surprised to see Leopard Wei out in the desert. Wei had been sent along with Melancholy Ghost Shi to Peking to discover what was going on in the Manchu Court. 'What are you doing here, Brother Wei?' he asked. 'And where is Brother Shi?'

Wei jumped down from the edge of the hole.

'Brother Shi and I went to Peking as you instructed us to, but for a long time we discovered nothing,' he began. 'Then one day, we happened to see that traitor Fire Hand Zhang and Master Ma Zhen in the street.'

Chen nodded. 'So they went to Peking,' he said. 'I was wondering how Zhang managed to escape. Master Ma told us he would take him back to Wudang Mountain.'

'Have you seen Zhang recently?' asked Xu, who was listening.

'Just a short while ago. He is a very dangerous individual.' Chen told them what had happened at the Manchu camp.

'When we saw them,' Wei continued, 'Master Ma Zhen and Fire Hand Zhang were walking along talking animatedly, and they didn't see us. We suspected that they might have joined forces against us, so we followed them carefully to a house in an alleyway. We waited until after dark, but they didn't come out again, so we decided to go in and have a look. We two are no match even for Zhang by himself, let alone for him and his brother-in-arms together; so once we were over the wall into the courtyard, we lay dead still, not daring to even breathe. After a long time, we heard talking in a room nearby and went across to investigate. Through a crack in the window, we saw Master Ma lying on a kang while that traitor Fire Hand Zhang was pacing back and forth in the room. The two were arguing. We didn't dare look for too long and squatted down to listen. It seems Zhang had insisted he had to come to Peking to sort out a few private financial matters before he could go to Wudang Mountain, and Master Ma had agreed. A few days after they had both arrived in Peking, the Emperor had returned as well. Fire Hand Zhang was telling Ma that the Emperor had given him orders to go to the Uighur regions on important business.'

'What important business?' Chen asked quickly.

'He didn't say exactly, but apparently he had to go and look for someone.' Chen frowned when he heard this. 'Master Ma spoke

to him very sternly and told him he should immediately quit
working for the Manchus, but Zhang said he could not refuse an
Imperial edict. If he did, he said, he was afraid the whole Wudang
Mountain and its Martial Arts School would be trampled underfoot
by the Emperor's troops. Master Ma told him that with the whole
country under the heel of the Manchus, the destruction of Wudang
Mountain would be nothing to grieve about. They argued fiercely.
Eventually, Master Ma jumped off the kang in a rage, and shouted:
"I made a promise to our friends in the Red Flower Society!" To
this Zhang replied: "Those bandits! What do they matter?" Then
there was a clanging sound as if one of them had drawn his sword.
I had a look through the window crack and saw Master Ma, sword
in hand, his face black with rage. "Have you forgotten our Shifu's
last wishes?" he roared. "Do you know no shame, to run
whimpering to the Manchu cause? You are a most ungrateful
disciple! I will fight you to the death." Zhang appeared to soften.
He sighed and said: "Very well. If that's the way you feel, we'll
leave for Wudang Mountain tomorrow." Master Ma then resheathed
his sword and went to sleep on the kang. Zhang sat on the chair
nearby. He appeared undecided about something. His body kept
trembling. Brother Shi and I were worried he would discover us,
and wanted to wait for him to fall asleep before leaving. Almost an
hour passed, but still he didn't sleep. He got up several times and
then sat down again. Finally, he gnashed his teeth and muttered:
"Brother Ma!" Master Ma was by this time sound asleep and snoring
slightly. Zhang walked quietly over to the kang and—'

Hasli suddenly let out a scream. She didn't understand what
Wei was saying, but she could feel the dark, sinister tone in his
voice, and it terrified her. She took hold of Chen's hand and snuggled
up to him. Zhou Qi glanced at her resentfully.

Wei continued. 'Zhang went up to the kang. He lunged
forward at Master Ma, then sprang back again. Master Ma gave a
wail of agony and jumped up. There was blood pouring from his
eye sockets. Both his eyes had been gouged out by that dog of a
traitor!'

Helmsman Chen leapt up in a rage and slammed his fist into
the side of the pit, sending sand flying in all directions.

'I swear I will kill the traitor!' he said through clenched teeth.
Hasli had never seen him angry like this, and she tugged on his
sleeve in fear.

Wei's voice shook as he went on with his account: 'Master Ma went silent. His face was a terrible sight. He walked slowly towards Zhang, then suddenly kicked out with his leg. Zhang leapt out of the way, and Master Ma's foot slammed into the kang. Zhang looked a little shaken, and tried to get out of the room, but Master Ma made it to the door first and stood straining his ears to hear Zhang's movements. Zhang suddenly laughed, and Master Ma kicked out with his left leg in the direction of the sound. But Zhang had stuck his sword out in front of him and Ma's leg hit the blade. It was cut clean off.' Zhou Qi ground her teeth and drove her sword into the wall of the pit.

'By this time, Brother Shi and I could stand it no longer. We jumped through the window and burst into the room. We fought with Zhang, but he managed to escape. He was probably scared that we were not alone. We chased after him, but Brother Shi was hit by his Golden Needles, and I had to help him back into the house. I tried my utmost to staunch the flow of blood from Master Ma's wound, but he died in a matter of minutes. He only managed to say a few words.'

'What did he say?' asked Chen. A cold wind suddenly blew down on them and they all shivered.

'He said: "Tell my brother-in-arms Hidden Needle Lu and my disciple Scholar Yu to avenge my death!" Just then, some people outside who had heard the fighting started shouting, so I helped Brother Shi out and we returned to our lodgings. The next day, I went back to have a look and saw that Master Ma's body had already been taken away. Brother Shi had been hit by five Golden Needles, but I took them out for him and now he's recovering in Twin Willows Lane in Peking.

'Fire Hand Zhang said the Emperor wanted him to come to the Northwest to look for someone. I thought perhaps it could be your Shifu, Helmsman—Master Yuan. I remember you said that there were two important items relating to the Emperor in Master Yuan's safe keeping. So I came out with the others to warn him.'

'How is Brother Shi?' enquired Chen.

'His wounds are serious,' Wei replied, 'but luckily not fatal.'

By now, the cold wind was blowing hard, and thick, leaden clouds were gathering above them.

'It's going to snow soon,' said Hasli, and moved even closer to Chen.

Zhou Qi could control herself no longer. 'What did she say?' she demanded.

Helmsman Chen was surprised by her outraged tone. 'She said it's going to snow.'

'And how would she know?' She paused for a moment, then blurted out: 'Helmsman, just who is it that you actually *love*? Lady Huo Qingtong is a nice girl. I like her, and I won't allow her to be betrayed like this.'

'I agree,' Chen began. 'She is a nice person, and we all have a great deal of respect for her—'

'Then why did you forsake her the moment you met her beautiful sister?' Zhou Qi interrupted.

Chen blushed. It was Luo Bing who came to his rescue. 'The Helmsman, like the rest of us, has only met Lady Huo Qingtong once. She is a friend. You can't start talking about love.'

'Why are you sticking up for him?' Zhou Qi demanded, even more agitated. 'She gave him that precious dagger, didn't she? And the way the Helmsman looked at her, it was plainly a case of love at first sight...'

Hasli was listening to this animated discussion, and looking on with her big round eyes, full of curiosity.

'The truth is,' said Chen, 'Lady Huo Qingtong already had a suitor before she met me. Whatever my feelings may have been, I knew that I stood no chance with her.'

Zhou Qi stared at him in surprise. 'Is that true?'

'Why would I choose to make up such a thing?'

Zhou Qi's tone immediately changed. 'Well, that changes everything,' she said. 'You're a good man after all. I was wrong to accuse you. I'm sorry.' The others laughed at her frankness. Zhou Qi took Hasli's hand and squeezed it. Suddenly, they felt a gust of cold air on their faces and looked up to see snowflakes as big as goose feathers floating down from the sky.

'You were right,' she said. 'It's snowing!'

'If someone doesn't come and rescue us soon, we are going to die here,' said Luo Bing.

'The Hodja is sure to send out scouts to look for his daughter and the Helmsman when they fail to return,' Xu replied.

'I'm sure he will,' Chen said. 'But we have come so far south, I'm afraid they may have difficulty finding us.'

'Well then, we will have to send someone out to get help.'

'I'll go!' volunteered Xin Yan.

Chen thought for a moment and then nodded. He asked Hasli to write a note to her father, and Xin Yan gave her a writing-brush and some ink from his knapsack.

'Take Sister Luo Bing's white horse,' Chen said to Xin Yan. 'We'll create a diversion over there to the east, and you can make a break for it to the west.' He then gave him directions to the Uighur camp. On the signal, the Red Flower heroes leapt out of the pit and charged eastwards with shouts and battle-cries, leaving only Zhou Qi and Hasli behind. Xin Yan led the white horse out of the hole, vaulted onto its back, and galloped off westwards. The Manchu troops loosed a few arrows but none came even close to hitting him. Once the Red Flower heroes were sure that Xin Yan had got away, they retreated back to the pit.

By this time, the snow was falling heavily and the ground about them had been transformed into a vast white carpet. They settled down as best they could for the night, but all slept badly—except for Hasli; she was still fast asleep when dawn broke. Her hair and shoulders were covered in a layer of snow which rose and fell slightly as she breathed. Luo Bing laughed gently. 'This child is completely without fear,' she said.

Time dragged by. Mastermind Xu frowned deeply. 'Why is there still no sign of a rescue?' he asked thoughtfully.

'Could Xin Yan have met some trouble on the road?' said Wen.

'What worries me is something else,' replied Xu.

'What is it?' Zhou Qi demanded. 'Stop mumbling and get on with it.'

'Helmsman, who makes the decisions in the Uighur camp?' Xu asked. 'The Hodja, or his daughter Lady Huo Qingtong?'

'Both, apparently. The Hodja discusses everything with his daughter.'

'She may refuse to send out soldiers. Then…things would be difficult,' continued Mastermind Xu. The others began to see what he was driving at.

'How could you say such a thing about her?' Zhou Qi demanded, jumping up. 'Doesn't she already have a young man of her own? She may be jealous of her sister, but I know she would never refuse to save the man she once loved!'

'When women become jealous, they are capable of anything,' answered Mastermind Xu. Zhou Qi began shouting angrily, and

Hasli woke with a start. The Red Flower heroes had only met Huo Qingtong once. She seemed nice, but they knew very little about her. Xu's words did not seem altogether unreasonable.

The Wolf-trap

After breaking out of the Manchu encirclement, Xin Yan followed the route Chen had indicated, galloped to the Uighur camp, and presented the letter to the Hodja in person. The old man had been frantic with worry, and jumped up joyfully as he read his daughter's note.

'Assemble the troops!' he ordered.

'How many Manchu troops were there surrounding you?' Huo Qingtong asked Xin Yan.

'Four or five thousand altogether.'

She bit her lip and paced from one side of the tent to the other, deep in thought. Horns sounded outside as the Uighur soldiers began to gather, and the Hodja was just about to go out to join them when Huo Qingtong suddenly turned to him.

'Father, we can't go,' she said.

He looked at her in astonishment, wondering if he had heard correctly. 'What! What did you say?'

'I said we can't go.'

He was about to fly into a rage, but then he thought how clear-thinking and intelligent his daughter usually was. 'Why?' he asked.

'Zhao Hui is a very capable general. He would not dispatch four or five thousand troops just to capture our two envoys. It must be a trap.'

'Supposing it is a trap? Are we to stand by and let the Manchus kill your sister and our Red Flower Society friends?'

Huo Qingtong hung her head and said nothing. 'I am afraid that if we go,' she said finally, 'not only will we fail to rescue them, we will sacrifice several thousand more lives as well.'

Her father slapped his thigh in exasperation.

'But she is your own flesh and blood!' he cried. 'And we owe their Helmsman Chen and the others a great debt. Even if we died trying to save them, what would it matter? You...you...' He was both angry and hurt by his daughter's apparent ungratefulness.

'Father, listen to me. I have another idea. It may be possible to save them and win a great victory as well.'

The Hodja's expression changed immediately. 'Well, why didn't you say so earlier, child?' he said. 'How can we do it? I will do whatever you say.'

'In that case, give me the Command Arrow,' she said. 'I will command this battle.' Her father hesitated for a second. Then he handed the arrow to her. Huo Qingtong knelt to receive it, before prostrating herself on the ground and praying to Allah.

'Father,' she said, when she had risen to her feet again. 'You and my brother must follow my orders.'

'If you can save them and beat the Manchus, I will do anything,' he replied.

'All right, then it's settled.' She walked out of the tent with her father and made her way over to the troops, who were already waiting in ranks with their commanders.

'Brothers!' the Hodja called out to them. 'Today, we will fight the Manchus to the death. The battle will be commanded by my daughter, Lady Huo Qingtong.'

The soldiers raised their sabres and roared: 'May the True God protect her and lead us to victory!'

'Right,' said Huo Qingtong flourishing her Command Arrow. 'Here are your orders.' Everyone return to their tents to rest. That is all.' The commanders led their troops away. The Hodja was too stunned to speak.

They went back inside the tent. Xin Yan prostrated himself before Huo Qingtong and kowtowed frantically.

'My lady, if you don't send troops to save them, my master will surely die,' he pleaded.

'Get up. I didn't say I wouldn't save them.'

'But there are only nine of them,' he cried, 'and one of them—your own sister—doesn't know any kungfu. And there are thousands of the enemy! If we delay even for a moment, they'll be, they'll be— '

'Have the Manchu troops attacked them yet?' Huo Qingtong interrupted him.

'Not before I left. But I'm afraid they will have done so by now. And with their heavy armour, our arrows will be useless.' When she heard this, Huo Qingtong frowned. Xin Yan began to weep and the Hodja paced about the tent, uncertain what to do.

'Father,' said Huo Qingtong, 'have you ever seen a wolf-trap? A piece of mutton is fastened to a metal hook, the wolf bites on it and pulls, and the trap snaps shut. Zhao Hui sees us as the wolf and my sister as the mutton. She's the bait in the trap. No matter how brave the Red Flower fighters are, they could never stop four or five thousand determined soldiers. That means that Zhao Hui has deliberately decided not to order an attack.' Her father nodded. 'The Manchus let this young man out on purpose to put pressure on us to send a rescue force. Otherwise he would never have been able to make it alone through so many troops.'

'Well, in that case,' replied the Hodja, 'let us attack Zhao Hui's forces from the side and catch them unawares.'

'They have more than forty thousand troops to our fifteen thousand,' she pointed out. 'In a pitched battle we would certainly lose.'

'So from what you say, your sister and the others are bound to die!' the Hodja exclaimed. 'I cannot bear to abandon my own daughter to her fate! And I refuse to leave our friends in danger! Let me take five hundred men with me. If we succeed in rescuing them, it will be because of Allah's help. If we fail, then we will die with them.'

Huo Qingtong said nothing.

Xin Yan began frantically kowtowing before her once more, his forehead striking the ground heavily. 'If our master has done anything to offend you, my lady, please forgive him,' he cried.

Huo Qingtong realized he suspected her motives. 'Don't talk such nonsense,' she said angrily.

Xin Yan looked startled for a second. Then he jumped up. 'If you are determined to be so cruel, I will go and die with my master,' he said. He ran out of the tent, leapt on the white horse, and galloped away.

'We *must* go and help them!' pleaded the Hodja.

'Father, the Chinese have a saying: In warfare, planning is of more importance than bravery. We are outnumbered. If we are to gain victory, we must make use of surprise tactics. Zhao Hui has set a trap. We must counter with a trap of our own.'

'Really?' said the Hodja, only half believing her.

'Father!' she exclaimed, her voice shaking. 'Surely you don't suspect my motives too?'

The Hodja saw great tears brimming in her eyes and his heart softened. 'All right,' he said. 'We will do as you say. Now send out the troops immediately.'

Huo Qingtong thought for a moment, then said to an attendant: 'Strike up the drums.' The drums rolled and the commanders of each of the Uighur brigades entered the tent. By now, the snow was falling thickly outside the tent and was already several inches deep on the ground.

Huo Qingtong flourished the Command Arrow and announced: 'The First Brigade of the Green Banner will go to the western side of the Great Gobi Quagmire, and the Second, Third, Fourth, Fifth, and Sixth Brigades of the Green Banner will gather together the local herdsmen and farmers around the other sides.' She gave the commanders their orders and the brigades departed one by one. The Hodja was unhappy that some of their best troops seemed to have been sent off on a secondary mission, rather than to perform the rescue.

'The First, Second, and Third Brigades of the White Banner will go to the city of Yarkand and to the Black River, and will make various preparations as I will indicate,' Huo Qingtong continued. 'The First Brigade of the Black Banner and the Kazak Brigade will go up into the hills along the Black River. The Mongol Brigade will station itself on Yingqipan Mountain.' She gave each commander his individual orders, after which they all bowed and left.

'Father, you will command the forces to the east. Brother, you will command the forces to the west. I myself will command the Second Brigade of the Black Banner and coordinate things from the centre. The general campaign plan is like this—' She was just about to explain in detail when the Hodja stopped her.

'Who is going to rescue your sister and the others?' he demanded.

'The Third Brigade of the Black Banner will ride in from the east to save them. The Fourth Brigade of the Black Banner will do the same from the west. When you meet Manchu troops you must do as I indicate in these orders.' She quickly wrote out two notes and handed them to the commanders. 'Your units must have the best mounts available,' she added. The two Black Banner Brigade commanders bowed and retired.

'You have sent thirteen thousand of our best soldiers off on a trivial mission, and two thousand young boys and old men to effect the actual rescue. What is the meaning of this?' demanded the Hodja.

'My plan—' Huo Qingtong began, but he angrily cut her off.

'I don't believe you any more! The truth is that you are in love with Helmsman Chen, but you know that he loves your sister; so you plan to let them both die. You...you are heartless!'

Huo Qingtong almost fainted from the shock of hearing these words coming from her father's lips. The Hodja stared at her for a second, then stormed out of the tent shouting: 'I go to die with your sister!' He leapt onto his horse and, calling to the Third and Fourth Brigades of the Black Banner to ride with him, he galloped away into the desert, brandishing his sabre.

Her brother saw how distressed she was and tried to comfort her. 'Father is very confused,' he said. 'He didn't know what he was saying. Don't be upset.'

Xin Yan meanwhile had ridden back to where Helmsman Chen and the others were waiting, sobbing all the way. The besieging Manchu forces did little to stop him as he passed by, only loosing off a few arrows in a perfunctory fashion. Finally he jumped off the white horse and led it down into the pit. He sat down on the ground, still sobbing.

'Don't cry!' said Zhou Qi. 'What's the matter?'

Mastermind Xu sighed. 'Is there any need to ask? Lady Huo Qingtong refuses to send troops to rescue us.'

'I kowtowed before her... I pleaded...' sobbed Xin Yan. The others were silent.

Hasli asked Helmsman Chen why Xin Yan was crying. Not wishing to hurt her, he said: 'He couldn't break through the enemy lines to fetch help.' Hasli took out her handkerchief and gave it to him.

The morning of the third day dawned, and still the snow fell heavily. The Manchu forces continued to show no signs of attacking. Mastermind Xu was more and more puzzled. He turned to Xin Yan: 'What questions did Lady Huo Qingtong ask you?'

'She asked how many Manchu troops there were surrounding us, and whether the armoured cavalry had attacked yet.'

Mastermind Xu seemed greatly excited. 'Then we're saved! We're *saved*!' he exclaimed happily. The others stared at him uncomprehendingly.

'I was stupid ever to have doubted Lady Huo Qingtong,' he said. 'How small-minded of me! She is a much, much wiser strategist than I am.'

'What do you mean?' asked Zhou Qi.

'It's like this. If the Manchu armoured cavalry were to attack us, we wouldn't stand a chance.'

'Hm,' Zhou Qi replied. 'Yes, it's strange that they haven't.'

'And even if they didn't use armoured cavalry, if thousands of foot-soldiers charged at once, the eight of us could never hold them off. They would make mincemeat of us.' The others agreed that the Manchus had been remarkably restrained.

Helmsman Chen suddenly understood what Xu was driving at. 'Yes, that's it!' he cried. 'They've held back on purpose in the hope of luring the Uighur main forces in to try and rescue us. But Lady Huo Qingtong has seen through their trick!'

'Mind you, whatever the outcome, we're still finished,' commented Hunchback Zhang.

'No, we're not,' Chen replied. 'She is certain to think of a way out.'

Their spirits were suddenly revived, and, leaving two of the Red Flower heroes to keep guard, the others settled down to rest at the bottom of the pit.

CHAPTER 7

A Commander loses His Head; Quicksand and Furnace;
Snow Burial; A Sister Disappears; The Grey Tide;
The Sand Game; Circle of Fire; The Bent Coin;
Left Three Right Two; The Secret City

A Commander loses His Head

Many hours later, they heard shouting in the distance, the sound of galloping hooves, and the clashing of swords. The sounds steadily increased in volume until finally a man could be seen riding towards the pit, shouting: 'Daughter! Helmsman Chen! Where are you?'

'Father! Father! We're here!' called Hasli.

The Red Flower heroes clambered out of the pit and saw the Hodja, sabre in hand, galloping up to them with a ragged bunch of Uighur soldiers riding behind him, fighting bravely. Hasli ran to him crying, 'Father! Father!'

He took her in his arms. 'Don't be afraid,' he said soothingly. 'I have come to save you.'

Mastermind Xu jumped up and stood on a horse's back to get a better view of the situation. He saw a great cloud of dust rising to the east and knew the Manchu armoured cavalry were on the move.

'Master Hodja!' he called. 'We must retreat to that high ground to the west!' The Hodja immediately ordered his troops to comply. They started out from the pit with the Manchus close behind and, as they reached the hill, saw another force of Manchu troops moving in from the west.

'Huo Qingtong was right,' the Hodja thought glumly. 'She has a clever head for strategy. I should never have thought so badly of her. She must have been very hurt by what I said.'

They threw up temporary defences on the hilltop and settled down to wait for an opportunity to escape. With the Uighurs firmly established on high ground, the Manchus did not dare, for the moment, to attack.

Huo Qingtong had, in the meantime, stationed her unit about four miles away from the enemy forces. At noon, all the Brigade commanders came to report. She told the commander of the Green Banner's Second Brigade: 'Go with five hundred troops and take up positions along the southern bank of the Black River. The Manchu troops must not be allowed to cross the river. If they attack, do not engage them head on, but rather delay them as long as possible.' The commander bowed and retired.

She then turned to the commander of the White Banner's First Brigade. 'I want you to lure the Manchu forces westwards. If you clash with the enemy, your troops must not be allowed to win the engagement, but must continue to flee into the desert, the further the better. Take our four thousand head of cattle and goats with you and leave them along the road for them to seize.'

'We cannot give them our livestock! I refuse to do it!'

Huo Qingtong's lips tightened. 'You mean you refuse to follow my orders?' she asked quietly.

The commander brandished his sabre. 'If you tell me to win a battle, I will follow your orders. If you tell me to lose a battle, I would rather die than obey!'

'Seize him!' Huo Qingtong commanded. Four guards ran forward and grabbed the commander's arms. 'The Manchu forces are oppressing us. To beat them, we must work together with one heart. Will you or will you not follow my orders?'

'No!' cried the man defiantly. 'What are you going to do about it?'

'Execute him!' she commanded, and the officer's face turned pale. The guards pushed him out of the tent and sliced off his head with one stroke of a sword. The other commanders stood there quivering with fear.

Huo Qingtong promoted the assistant commander to take the dead man's place and repeated her instructions: he was to retreat westwards before the Manchu forces until he saw smoke rising from the east. Then he was to return as quickly as possible, avoiding battle with the Manchus. She ordered the other Brigades to gather beside the treacherous area of desert to the east known as the Great Gobi Quagmire.

Her work complete, she mounted her horse and drew her sword. 'First and Second Brigades of the Black Banner, follow me,' she shouted.

Quicksand and Furnace

The Hodja, Helmsman Chen, and the others were still trapped on their hill. The Manchu troops had attacked twice, but had been beaten back. The hill was ringed with piles of corpses. Losses on both sides had been heavy.

Sometime after noon, there was a movement in the Manchu lines, and a column of mounted Uighur soldiers could be seen charging through towards them. Amidst the flying snowflakes, they spotted Huo Qingtong at its head.

'Forward!' shouted the Hodja to his men, and went galloping down the hill towards her. Hasli also galloped up to her sister, and embraced her.

Huo Qingtong took her hand and shouted: 'Commander of the Black Banner, Third Brigade: lead your men west until you meet up with the First Brigade of the White Banner. Then follow the orders of its commander.'

The officer and his troops galloped off, and a column of Manchu cavalry broke away from the main force and chased after them.

'Excellent!' exclaimed Huo Qingtong. 'Commander of the Black Banner, First Brigade: retreat with your men towards Yarkand and follow my brother's orders. Commander of the Second Brigade, you retreat towards the Black River.' The two Brigades broke out of the encirclement, and disappeared into the distance pursued by two more columns of Manchu cavalry.

'Everyone else head east!' Huo Qingtong ordered, and the remaining Uighur soldiers along with the Red Flower Society fighters galloped through the circle of Manchu troops and away.

The Manchu cavalry, under the command of General Zhao Hui, closed in on the fleeing Uighurs, cut them off, and slaughtered them all, several hundred all told. Zhao was delighted. He pointed to the huge Crescent Moon banner near Huo Qingtong and shouted: 'Whoever seizes that banner gets a reward!' The cavalrymen surged forward, galloping flat out across the desert.

The Uighurs were riding good horses and the Manchu cavalry had difficulty keeping up with them. But after ten or fifteen miles, some of the Uighur fighters began to fall behind and were killed by the Manchu troops. General Zhao saw they were all either old men or boys, and exclaimed: 'Their leader has no crack troops with him.

After them!' They galloped on for another two or three miles and saw the Uighur force dispersing, apparently in confusion. Fluttering on the top of a large sand-dune ahead was the Crescent Moon banner.

Zhao Hui brandished his sword and personally led the charge towards the dune, with his guards following close behind. But as he reached the top and looked out ahead of him, he had the fright of his life. Beyond the dune, stretching north and south, he saw rank after orderly rank of Uighur warriors, waiting in grim silence. The Manchu force had originally been several times larger than the Uighurs, but so many units had been sent out in pursuit of the various breakaway Uighur columns that now he was left with only ten thousand of his armoured cavalry against the concentrated might of the Uighur army. Two more Uighur columns now appeared behind his troops. There were enemy forces to the north, south, and west. Zhao Hui had only one option left. 'Everyone forward! East!' he shouted. The Manchu forces surged forward as the Uighurs gradually closed in on them.

Suddenly, there was a chorus of cries from the cavalry unit in the lead. A soldier came riding back to Zhao and said: 'General! We're done for! There's quicksand ahead!' Zhao could see a thousand cavalrymen and their horses already flailing about as they sank into the soft mud.

Helmsman Chen and the others were standing on a nearby sand-dune, watching as the Manchu troops fell into the quagmire. The soldiers in the rear tried to escape, but the Muslims pressed relentlessly in behind them, forcing them into the mud. At first the air was filled with the screams of the hapless Manchu soldiers. But then the mud crept up their legs, and when it reached their mouths, the noise ceased. The dwindling numbers of surviving Manchu troops fought desperately, but in less than an hour, the whole army had been forced into the quagmire. Only General Zhao and a hundred or so guards managed to escape by carving a bloody path through the Uighur ranks.

'Everyone head west and gather on the south bank of the Black River,' Huo Qingtong ordered. Her entire force of more than ten thousand troops galloped off.

As they rode off together, Helmsman Chen and the Hodja talked of everything that had happened since they parted. The Hodja's heart was uneasy. He loved his two daughters more than anything in the world, and they had both fallen in love with the same Chinese man. According to Islamic law, a man could marry four wives, but in the first place Helmsman Chen was not a believer, and in the second place he had heard that Chinese men had only one proper wife, and that the second and subsequent women were treated more as concubines than as real wives. He wondered how the matter could be resolved. It might be best to wait until the Manchus were beaten, he thought. 'One of my daughters is wise, and the other is kind. A way will surely be found.'

Towards evening the great Uighur column arrived at the south bank of the Black River. A soldier galloped up and reported breathlessly: 'The Manchus are attacking hard. The commander of the Green Banner Second Brigade is dead, and the commander of the Black Banner Second Brigade is badly wounded. Our losses are heavy.'

'Tell the deputy commander of the Green Banner Second Brigade to take over. He is not to retreat a single step,' Huo Qingtong ordered. The soldier galloped off again.

'Should we not go to their aid?' her father suggested.

'No!' she replied and turned to her personal guards. 'The whole army will rest here. No one is allowed to light a fire or make a sound. Everyone will eat dry rations.' The order was transmitted, and the soldiers settled down silently in the darkness. Far off, they could hear the waters of the Black River and the cries and shouts of Manchu and Uighur fighters.

Another soldier galloped up with urgent news. 'The Green Banner Second Brigade's deputy commander has also been killed! We can't hold them back much longer!'

Huo Qingtong turned to the commmander of the Green Banner Third Brigade. 'Go and reinforce the Second Brigade,' she said. 'You will be in command.' He raised his sabre in salute and led his unit away. Presently, the sound of battle rose to a roar.

'The Green Banner Brigades will lie in ambush behind the sand-dunes to the east. The White Banner and Mongol Brigades will lie in ambush to the west,' Huo Qingtong ordered. 'The rest, come with me.'

She rode off towards the Black River, and as they approached it, the clang of clashing weapons became deafening. In the torchlight, they saw the Uighur fighters bravely defending the wooden bridge across the river in the face of ferocious assaults by the best Manchu cavalry.

'Give way!' Huo Qingtong shouted, and the fighters on the bridge retreated, leaving a gap through which several thousand Manchu mounted troops swarmed like bees. When about half of the Manchu troops had crossed, she gave the order to collapse the bridge. The Uighurs had earlier loosened the beams of the bridge and tied them with long ropes to horses on the bank below. The horses strained forward, a series of loud cracks rent the air, and the bridge collapsed, throwing hundreds of Manchu soldiers into the river. The Manchu army was thus cut in two by the river, with neither side able to assist the other.

At Huo Qingtong's orders, the mass of the Uighur army, hiding behind the sand-dunes, now emerged and overwhelmed the Manchu troops on the near bank. In a short time, they were all dead, while the Manchu force on the other side of the river was so frightened by the sight of the slaughter that it turned and fled westwards towards the city of Yarkand.

'Cross the river! After them!' shouted Huo Qingtong. A makeshift bridge was swiftly constructed with the remains of the former structure and the Uighur army charged off towards Yarkand. The citizens of Yarkand had long since evacuated their city. Huo Qingtong's brother, on her instructions, had resisted perfunctorily when the Manchus attacked, then led his troops in retreat from the city. Soon after, the Manchu forces fleeing from the banks of the Black River arrived along with General Zhao Hui and his hundred-odd battered guards. The walled city was now full of Manchu soldiers.

General Zhao was about to go to bed, when he received a report that several hundred of his troops had died of poisoning after drinking water from wells in the city. He sent a unit to collect some uncontaminated water from outside. Then the sky turned red. All over the city, fires had been lit by a small number of Uighur soldiers left behind. The city was turning into a huge oven.

Under the protection of his guards, General Zhao fought his way through the flames and smoke towards the west gate as the rest of the Manchu soldiers trampled each other in their haste to escape. Zhao's guards slashed at them with their swords, forcing them to make way for their general. But when they got to the west gate, they found that it had been blocked by the Uighurs. The fires were now burning more fiercely than ever, and the streets were filled with frenzied mobs of soldiers and horses. Through the confusion, a small group of riders came up shouting: 'Where is the general?'

'Here!' Zhao's guards shouted back.

'There are fewer enemy troops at the east gate,' replied one of the riders. 'We can force our way out there.'

Even in danger such as this, General Zhao remained calm and led his troops in the attack on the east gate. The Uighurs fired wave after wave of arrows at them, and several attempts to break out failed with heavy losses. But at the critical moment, Fire Hand Zhang led a troop of Manchu soldiers in an attack from outside the city and managed to snatch General Zhao away to safety.

Many thousands of Manchu soldiers had already been burned to death, and the stench of roasting flesh was sickening. The whole city was filled with cries and screams. Huo Qingtong and the others were watching from a piece of high ground.

'This is terrible! Terrible!' cried the Hodja. Huo Qingtong sent more troops down to help blockade the east gate of the city. With Zhao gone, the Manchu soldiers left inside were leaderless. They raced frantically about, but the four gates were blocked by the Uighurs, and they all died in the monster furnace.

'Light the signal fires!' Huo Qingtong ordered, and previously prepared piles of wolf droppings (which are known to produce the thickest and blackest smoke) were put to the torch, sending a huge column of black smoke up to the heavens. A short while later, a similar column of smoke arose five or so miles to the west.

The Uighurs had won three victories and wiped out more than thirty thousand of the best Manchu troops. The warriors embraced each other and sang and danced around the Yarkand city wall.

Huo Qingtong called her officers together. 'We will camp out here tonight,' she said. 'Each man must start ten fires. The fires must be spread out as much as possible.'

Snow Burial

More than ten thousand Manchu cavalry had chased westwards after the Third Brigade of the Uighur Black Banner. The Uighurs were riding the best horses, but the commander of the Manchu troops was under orders from General Zhao to catch them at all costs, and he urged his men mercilessly on. The two armies thundered across the desert. After thirty or forty miles, a herd of several thousand cattle and sheep suddenly appeared in the path of the Manchu army and the soldiers chased after them excitedly, killing as many as they could for food. This slowed their pace considerably. The Uighurs, meanwhile, galloped on, and were never once obliged to clash with the pursuing Manchu troops. Close to evening, they saw a pall of thick smoke rising from the east. It was the predetermined signal.

'Lady Huo Qingtong has won!' shouted their commander. 'Turn back east!' The warriors' spirits soared and they reined their horses round. Seeing them turning, the Manchu troops were perplexed. They charged forward to attack, but the Uighurs swung round them at a distance, obliging the Manchus to follow.

The Uighur Brigade galloped through the night, the Manchus always in sight. The Manchu commander wanted to gain great merit for himself, and many of his cavalry horses died of exhaustion. Towards midnight, they came across General Zhao riding in front of about three thousand wounded. Zhao's hopes rose slightly as he saw the Manchu column approach: it seemed to him more than likely that the enemy would be in a state of unpreparedness after their recent success. So if he was to attack now, he might be able to turn his own defeat into victory. He therefore ordered the troops to advance towards the Black River. After ten miles or so, scouts reported that the Uighur army was camped ahead. General Zhao led his commanders up onto a rise to view the scene. What they saw made them shudder.

The entire plain was covered in camp-fires which seemed to stretch endlessly before them. From far off they heard the shouts of men and the neighing of horses. They wondered how many warriors the Uighurs had mustered. General Zhao was silent.

'With such a huge army against us, no wonder…no wonder we have encountered some set-backs,' mumbled one of the senior Manchu officers, Colonel Herda.

General Zhao turned to his men. 'All units are to mount up and retreat south,' he ordered. 'No one is to make a sound.'

The order was received badly by the troops who had hoped to stop at least long enough for a meal.

'According to the guides, the road south passes along the foot of Yingqipan Mountain and is very dangerous after heavy snows,' objected Colonel Herda with some hesitation.

'The enemy's forces are so powerful, we have no choice but to head southeast and try to meet up with General Fu De,' replied General Zhao.

So the straggling remnants of the great Manchu army headed south, the road becoming more and more treacherous as they went. To the left was the Black River, to the right, Yingqipan Mountain (known to the Uighurs as Yangihissar). The night sky was cloudy and inky black, and the only light was a faint glow reflecting off the snow further up the mountain slope.

General Zhao issued a further order: 'Whoever makes a sound will be immediately executed.' Most of the soldiers came from Northeast China and knew that any noise could shake loose the heavy snow above them and cause a deadly avalanche. They all dismounted and led their horses along with extreme care, many walking on tiptoe. Three or four miles further on, the road became very steep, but as luck would have it, the sky was growing light. By now the Manchu troops had been fighting and running for a whole day and a night. Each one of them looked like death.

Suddenly, a scout shouted out, as several hundred Uighur warriors came into view on the road ahead, standing behind a number of primitive cannon. The Manchu troops were scared out of their wits, and thrown into utter confusion. Many turned and fled just as the cannon went off with a roar, spraying them with shards of metal and nails, and instantly killing more than two hundred men.

As the boom of the cannon faded, General Zhao heard a faint rumbling sound, and at the same moment felt a coldness on his neck as a small amount of snow fell down inside his collar. He looked up at the mountainside and saw the snowfields above them slowly beginning to move.

'General!' shouted Colonel Herda. 'We must escape!'

Zhao reined his horse round and started galloping back the way they had come. His guards slashed and hacked at the soldiers in their path, frantically pushing them off the road into the river below as the rumble of the approaching avalanche grew louder and louder. Suddenly, countless tons of snow—intermingled with rocks and mud—surged down onto the road with a deafening roar that shook the heavens.

General Zhao, with Colonel Herda on one side and Fire Hand Zhang on the other, managed to escape the catastrophe. They galloped on for more than a mile before they dared to stop. When they did look back, they could see that several thousand troops had been buried by snowdrifts dozens of feet deep. The road ahead to the south was also covered in thick snow. The present danger of their situation, and the loss of an entire army of forty thousand men in a single day, were too much for him. General Zhao broke down and wept.

'General, we must go up the mountain slope,' cried Fire Hand Zhang, grabbing hold of Zhao and racing off with him up the slope, with Colonel Herda following along behind as best he could.

Huo Qingtong was watching from a distant crest. 'Someone's trying to escape!' she shouted. 'Catch them quickly!' Twenty or thirty Uighurs ran off to intercept them. When they saw from their uniforms that the three were high-ranking officers, they rubbed their hands gleefully, determined to catch them alive. Fire Hand Zhang silently increased his pace and seemed to fly across the treacherously slippery slope, despite the weight of General Zhao. Colonel Herda could not keep up with him and was cut off by the Uighurs and captured after a spirited fight. Apart from General Zhao and Fire Hand Zhang, a mere thirty men had survived the avalanche.

Huo Qingtong led her Uighurs back to their camp, along with the prisoners. By now, they had taken the main Manchu camp, thereby acquiring huge supplies of food and weapons. The Four Tigers were among those taken prisoner after being found bound and gagged inside a tent. Helmsman Chen asked them why they had been put there, and the eldest of the four giants replied: 'Because we helped you. General Zhao said he would have us put to death after the battle.' Chen pleaded before Huo Qingtong to allow the four to go free, and she agreed.

A Sister Disappears

Mournful dirges were played as the Uighurs dug deep trenches and buried the bodies of their fallen warriors upright and facing west, according to their custom. Helmsman Chen was puzzled by this, and asked one of the nearby soldiers why the dead were buried in this way.

'According to Islam,' the soldier replied, 'if the body is buried upright, then the spirit will ascend to the heavenly kingdom. And west is the direction of the holy city of Mecca.'

When the burials were finished, the Hodja led the entire army in prayer to thank Allah for having helped them achieve such a great victory. Then a loud cheer went up from the ranks and the commanders of all the Brigades went before Huo Qingtong and presented their sabres to her in respect.

'Inflicting such a crushing defeat on the Manchus has also done us a great service,' remarked Leopard Wei to Mastermind Xu. But Xu was deep in thought.

'The Emperor made a pact with us,' he said. 'And yet instead of withdrawing his forces, he sent them into the desert. I wonder if he could have deliberately sent his troops to be destroyed?'

'I never have trusted this Emperor,' said Rolling Thunder Wen. 'How could he have known that Lady Huo Qingtong would win such a decisive victory? What's more, I'm sure he sent Fire Hand Zhang out here for some sinister purpose.'

As the heroes talked, they noticed Helmsman Chen gazing at Huo Qingtong in concern. She was seated apart, her face as white as a sheet, with a wild look in her eyes. Luo Bing went over to talk to her and, as Huo Qingtong stood up to greet her, she swayed unsteadily. Luo Bing caught hold of her.

'Sister, what's wrong?' she asked. Huo Qingtong said nothing, but fought to control her breathing. Hasli, the Hodja, Helmsman Chen, and the others ran over. Hasli led her into a tent and laid her down on a rug.

The Hodja knew his daughter was exhausted after the protracted battle, which she had both directed and taken part in alongside the other warriors. She had also had to bear the suspicions of her own commanders. But he was afraid that the thing affecting her most was the attachment between Helmsman Chen and her younger sister. Unable to think of anything to say to comfort her, he sighed and left the tent. He went for a walk round the camp, and from all sides heard nothing but praise for Huo Qingtong's brilliant strategy.

That night, he slept badly, worrying about his daughter. Early the next day before it was light, he went over to her tent to see how she was, but found it empty. He hurriedly asked the guard outside what had happened to her.

'Lady Huo Qingtong left about two hours ago,' the guard replied.

'Where did she go?'

'I don't know, sir. She told me to give you this letter.' The Hodja seized it and tore it open. Inside, in Huo Qingtong's delicate hand, was written:

'Father, the war is over. All that is necessary now is to tighten the encirclement and the remaining Manchu soldiers will be annhilated in a few days.' It was signed, 'Your Daughter, Huo Qingtong.'

'Which direction did she go in?' he asked. The guard pointed east.

The Hodja found a horse and galloped off immediately in pursuit. He rode for an hour far into the flat desert plain, where it was possible to see several miles in all directions, but found no sign of any living being. Afraid that she might have changed direction, he decided the only thing to do was to return to camp. Halfway back, he met Hasli, Helmsman Chen, and the other Red Flower heroes who were all anxious about her safety. Back in camp, he sent units out to the north, south, east, and west to search. By evening, three units had returned without finding anything, while the fourth brought back a young Chinese youth dressed in black.

Scholar Yu stared at the youth in shock: it was Li Yuanzhi dressed as usual in boy's clothing.

'What are you doing here?' he asked, hurrying up to meet her.

'I came to find you, and happened to run into these soldiers,' she replied, very happy to see him again.

Hasli was still frantic with worry about her lost sister. 'Whatever can have happened to her?' she asked Helmsman Chen. 'What can we do?'

'I'll go and find her,' he replied. 'Come what may, I'll convince her to come back.'

'I'll go with you,' she said at once.

Chen nodded. 'All right. Go and ask your father.'

'You all do just as you like anyway,' replied the Hodja angrily, stamping his foot. He knew that it was the intimacy between Hasli and the Helmsman that had upset Huo Qingtong in the first place, and that seeing them both together again would only make matters worse for her. But there was nothing he could do. Hasli looked up at her father and saw how bloodshot his eyes were. She took his hand and squeezed it.

Yuanzhi ignored the others, and was bombarding Scholar Yu with questions about what had happened to him since they had parted.

'*That's* the boy your sister likes,' Helmsman Chen said to Hasli, pointing at Yuanzhi. 'I'm sure he will be able to convince her to come back.'

'Really?' Hasli replied. 'Why has she never told me about him? She's so mean!' She walked over to Yuanzhi to get a closer look. The Hodja, who was equally curious, did the same.

Yuanzhi had met the Hodja previously and she bowed before him in greeting. Then she saw Hasli and was dumbfounded by her extraordinary beauty. Hasli smiled at Chen and said: 'Please tell this young gentleman that we are very pleased to see him, and ask him to come with us to help find my sister.'

Only now did Chen greet Yuanzhi. 'What are you doing here, my young friend?' he asked. 'How have you been since we last met?'

Yuanzhi blushed and laughed. She glanced at Scholar Yu, wanting him to explain.

'Helmsman, this is Master Lu's disciple,' Yu said.

'I know, we've met several times.'

Yu smiled. 'That makes her my sister-in-arms.'

'Your *what*?' Chen exclaimed in surprise.

'She likes wearing boy's clothes when she travels.'

Chen looked a little more closely at Yuanzhi and noticed for the first time what delicate eyebrows she had and what a small mouth, not at all like a man's. Chen had always been under the impression that there was a special relationship between this handsome 'youth' and Huo Qingtong, but he had never looked closely at 'him' before. He now stared in shock. So perhaps he had been completely wrong about Huo Qingtong and her feelings towards him. He remembered: she had once told him to go and ask Master Lu about his disciple, and he had never done so. 'Now she has most probably left the camp because of her injured feelings, because she cannot bear to witness the great love her sister has for me!'

To Luo Bing it was clear that Yuanzhi was besotted with Yu. She hoped and prayed that now, with such a beautiful girl in love with him, Yu would finally be able to stop torturing himself with his unrequited infatuation for *her*. But he looked as desolate and unhappy as ever.

'Where is Sister Huo Qingtong?' Yuanzhi asked. 'I have something important to tell her.'

'She's gone off somewhere,' replied Luo Bing. 'We're looking for her ourselves.'

'You mean she went off by herself?'

Luo Bing nodded.

'Where did she go?' Yuanzhi asked urgently.

'She left the camp heading east, but she may have changed direction. We don't know.'

'Oh, no!' Yuanzhi exclaimed, stamping her foot. They asked her what was on her mind. 'It's Three of those Manchurian Devils! They're looking for her to get their revenge. You know that already. But I met them on the road. They were behind me. If she's heading east, she might run into them.'

'We haven't a moment to lose,' said Chen. 'I'll go and find her.'

'Never underestimate the Devils,' Mastermind Xu warned. 'It would be better if some of us went too. Helmsman, you should go ahead with Lady Hasli. Miss Li, you also know Lady Huo, but it would be too dangerous for you to go alone. Perhaps Brother Yu could go with you. My wife and I can go too. The others can remain here at the camp to watch out for Fire Hand Zhang.'

'Very well!' said Chen. He borrowed Luo Bing's white horse and he and Hasli galloped off, with the others not far behind.

At about noon that day, Rolling Thunder Wen and the other Red Flower heroes were talking with the Hodja in his tent when a guard rushed in to report that the Manchu officer Herda had escaped and that the four Uighur soldiers guarding him had been killed. They hurried over, and found a dagger stuck in the chest of one of the dead soldiers with a note attached to it which read: 'For the heroes of the Red Flower Society, from Fire Hand Zhang.'

Wen angrily screwed the piece of paper up into a ball, and spoke to the Hodja. 'You keep the Manchu army encircled, and we'll go and find this traitor Zhang.' The Hodja nodded. Wen led the other Red Flower heroes off into the desert, following the tracks of the Manchu horses.

The Grey Tide

Huo Qingtong had left the camp feeling lonely and confused, thinking she would go to her Shifu's home on Precious Mountain and spend the rest of her days in the desert with her Shifu and her husband, Bald Vulture. She took with her the two large eagles that her Shifu had given her. She was weak and sick and, even though her kungfu training enabled her to keep going, after ten days travelling across the desert, she was absolutely exhausted. And she was still four or five days from the home of the Twin Eagles of Heaven Mountains, Bald Vulture and his wife Lady Guan. Finally, she stopped beside a small sand-dune and let her horse graze on the sparse, dry grass nearby.

She set up her tent and slept for several hours. In the middle of the night she was awakened by the sound of three horses approaching from the east. As they neared the dune, they slowed and headed for the same patch of dry grass that had attracted her mount. The horses were then unwilling to continue, so the three riders dismounted to rest. They did not see Huo Qingtong's tent, which was on the other side of the dune. She heard them talking Chinese, but she was still sleepy and did not bother to listen closely. Suddenly, however, she heard one of the men say: 'That damned bitch in the yellow dress! I'll skin her alive and rip out every tendon in her body, or my name isn't Gu!'

'Brother Yan's kungfu was excellent,' said another. 'I don't believe that a mere girl could kill him without using some sort of trickery.'

'Of course,' added a third. 'As I said, we have to be very careful. There are a lot of Uighurs around.'

Huo Qingtong realized in astonishment that the voices belonged to the three surviving Devils of Manchuria, and that they were talking about her.

'There's not much water left and we don't know how many more days we'll have to go before we find water again,' one of them said. 'From tomorrow, we'll have to drink even less.' Soon afterwards, they went to sleep.

Huo Qingtong was uncertain what to do. The desert was flat and empty for miles in every direction. If they found her, there was no way she could escape, especially as she was still sick. After some thought, she decided the safest course would be to reveal herself, and find some way to lead the three of them to her Shifu's home.

Early next morning, the Devils woke to find Huo Qingtong standing in front of them. She had examined them carefully. One was a tall man who looked like a member of the gentry. The second had a thick black beard, while the third was wearing Mongol clothes.

'Lady, do you have any water to spare?' asked the first man whose name was Teng Yilei, pulling out a silver ingot as he spoke. Huo Qingtong shook her head to indicate she did not understand Chinese. The Mongol, who was named Hahetai, repeated the request in Mongolian and she replied in the same tongue: 'I cannot give you any of my water. I still have far to ride. The Yellow-Robed Lady, Huo Qingtong, sent me on an important mission and I am now returning to report back to her.' She went back to her encampment on the other side of the dune, quickly took down her tent, and mounted her horse. Hahetai ran forward and grabbed hold of her horse's reins.

'Where is she, the Lady Huo?' he asked.

'Why do you want to know?'

'We are her friends. We have some urgent news to pass on to her.'

Huo Qingtong pouted. 'That's a downright lie! She is at Precious Mountain, but you are heading west. Don't try to fool me!'

Hahetai turned to the other two and said: 'She's on her way to see the bitch now!'

From her sickly appearance and the way she wheezed as she spoke, she did not look at all like someone who knew kungfu. So not suspecting her in the slightest, the Devils took advantage of her supposed ignorance of Chinese and loudly discussed how they would kill her when they reached Precious Mountain, and then go to find Huo Qingtong. The bearded man, Gu, could see that she was a very beautiful woman despite her worn-out air, and lust began to stir in his loins. Huo Qingtong noticed him constantly eyeing her. She knew that even though they had not recognized her for who she really was, travelling alone for four or five days with these three Devils would be too dangerous. She ripped a strip of material off her jacket and tied it round the leg of one of the two giant eagles. Then she launched the bird into the air. It spread its wings and flew off towards the horizon.

'What are you doing?' demanded Teng suspiciously. Huo Qingtong shook her head, and Hahetai translated what he had said into Mongolian.

'There are no more springs for another seven or eight days. You've got so little water, it will never be enough. I'm letting the birds go so they can go and find water for themselves.' As she spoke, she released the second eagle.

'Two birds wouldn't drink very much water,' Teng replied.

Hahetai mumbled oaths. 'Even in the deserts of Mongolia, you would never have to travel for seven or eight days without water. This is a cursed region!'

They camped that night in the middle of the desert. Huo Qingtong could see Gu's eyes constantly devouring her, and she started to become very worried. She went into her tent, drew her sword, and sat down beside the tent entrance, not daring to sleep. Towards midnight, she heard someone tiptoeing over. Suddenly, the tent flap opened and Gu crept inside. He began feeling about for her in the darkness. Then, an instant later, he felt an icy coldness on his neck as a sharp blade gently ran along it.

'If you so much as twitch, I will run this right through you,' Huo Qingtong whispered. 'Lie down on the ground!' He immediately complied. She placed the tip of the sword to the small of his back, then sat down, wondering what she should do next.

'If I kill him, the other two will certainly do me in,' she thought. 'It's probably best to wait for my Shifu to get here.'

A couple of hours later, Teng woke and noticed that Gu was missing. He jumped up and began calling for him.

'Answer him—now!' Huo Qingtong whispered fiercely. 'Tell him you're here.'

'Everything's all right!' Gu shouted back, well aware that he had no choice. 'I'm over here.'

Teng laughed. 'You horny old bugger! You never change, do you!'

The next morning, Huo Qingtong waited until the other two were up before letting Gu out.

'Hark at you!' Hahetai berated him as he emerged from her tent. 'We're here for revenge, not to fool around.' Gu was silently gnashing his teeth as he thought about the humiliation that the girl had inflicted on him. He didn't tell them what had happened. If he had done so, the shame of it would have followed him for the rest of his life. But his mind was made up. He would have the girl the following night, and then kill her.

The next night, at about midnight, Gu advanced on Huo Qingtong's tent again, a spear in one hand and a torch in the other. As he entered, he saw her crouching in the far corner and lunged at her triumphantly. Suddenly he felt something cut into his legs: he was caught fast in a rope noose hidden on the ground. Huo Qingtong gave it a tug and he overbalanced and fell heavily forwards, then rolled over onto his back.

'Don't move!' she hissed, holding the tip of her sword this time against his stomach. She didn't think she could stand another night like the previous one. But killing Gu was not enough. She had to finish off all three.

'Tell your tall friend to come over here,' she whispered. Gu guessed what she was planning and remained silent. She increased the pressure so that the sword cut its way through his clothes and into the top layer of skin. Gu knew a sword in the stomach was a particularly painful way to die. 'He won't come even if I call,' he whispered back.

'All right then, I'll kill you first,' she replied, and the sword moved again.

'Teng!' he gasped. 'Come here! Come quickly!'

'Now laugh!' ordered Huo Qingtong. Gu frowned and uttered several hollow laughs.

'Sound a *lot* happier!'

He cursed her silently, but the sword was already making its way into his flesh. He managed to produce a loud hysterical laugh. Teng and Hahetai had already been woken up by the racket.

'Stop fooling around, will you!' yelled Teng. 'Save your strength for tomorrow!'

Huo Qingtong could see he wouldn't come. 'Call the other one,' she hissed, and Gu shouted out again, this time to Hahetai. The Mongol may have been no more than a rough and ready sort of bandit, but he did not believe in taking advantage of women, and he was very unhappy about the way Gu was carrying on. Since they were sworn brothers, he just pretended not to hear.

Huo Qingtong knew she would have to kill all three of them if she was to save her honour. Holding the sword in her right hand, she wound the rope round and round Gu until he could not move. Then she leant against the side of the tent, but did not dare to fall asleep.

The next morning, as it grew light, she saw that Gu was fast asleep and angrily whipped him awake with her horsewhip. She held the tip of her sword to his heart and said: 'If you so much as grunt, I will skewer you!' She wondered again whether she should kill him, but decided that it would merely bring immediate disaster down on her own head. She estimated that her Shifu should reach them by that afternoon anyway, so she untied the rope, and pushed Gu unceremoniously out of the tent.

Teng looked suspiciously at the bloody welts on Gu's face. 'Who *is* this girl?' he asked in a low voice. 'What's she up to?'

Gu glanced meaningfully at him. 'Let's grab her,' he said. He and Teng started to walk slowly towards her, but she saw them coming and ran over to their horses. She pulled out her sword and punctured Gu's and Hahetai's water-bags, then grabbed the largest of Teng's water-bags and jumped onto her own horse. The Three Devils stood there watching dumbly for a second as the precious water drained out of the two bags and was instantly swallowed up by the sand; then they ran after her angrily.

She lay along the horse's back breathing heavily. 'Come one step closer, and I'll slash this bag too,' she gasped. The Three Devils stopped dead in their tracks. When she had recovered slightly, she spoke again:

'I agreed to take you to see Lady Huo Qingtong, and in return what do you do? Take advantage of me! From here to the next spring is six days travelling. If you don't leave me alone, I'll slash this bag too and we will all die of thirst.'

'We won't hurt you, we promise,' protested Teng.

'Very well then, let's go,' she ordered. 'You three first.' So they rode on across the desert, the three men in front, the girl behind. By noon, the burning sun was riding high in the sky, and their lips and tongues were parched. Huo Qingtong began to see stars before her eyes and had recurring dizzy spells. She wondered if she was going to die.

'Hey you! Give us some water!' she heard Hahetai shout. She shook herself awake.

'Get a bowl and put it on the ground,' she replied. Hahetai did as she said. 'Now walk back a hundred paces. All of you.' Gu hesitated suspiciously. 'If you don't, you won't get any water,' she added. They cursed her, but retreated. Huo Qingtong rode forward, undid the cap of the water-bag, and filled the bowl, then rode away again. The three men ran over to the bowl and took turns at gulping down the liquid.

They continued on their way. About four hours later they began to see green grass growing beside the road. Teng's eyes lit up. 'There must be water ahead!' he shouted. Huo Qingtong was worried. She tried to think of some course of action, but her head was splitting with pain. Suddenly, there was the long cry of an eagle from above and she looked up to see a black shape swooping downwards. Overjoyed, she raised her arm and the great bird alighted on her shoulder. She saw a piece of black material fastened to one of its legs and knew that her Shifu would arrive soon.

Teng could tell that something funny was going on, and with a flourish of his hand he sent a sleeve dart flying towards Huo Qingtong's right wrist, hoping to knock the sword from her grasp. But she blocked the dart with her sword, and with a wave of the reins, galloped around them and into the lead. The Three Devils began shouting and chased after her. After two or three miles, her legs and arms were totally numb, and she could hold on no longer. The horse reared into the air and she toppled to the ground.

The Three Devils spurred their horses on. Huo Qingtong struggled to get back onto the horse, but she was too weak. Then in a flash of inspiration, she slung the water-bag's leather strap over the eagle's neck and threw the bird up into the air. At the sight of their water being carried away, Teng and the others forgot all about Huo Qingtong and chased frantically after the eagle. The bag was almost full of water and the bird was too weighed down to be able to fly high or fast. The three men could just keep up with it.

A few miles further on, the eagle glided downwards just as two riders came into view in a cloud of dust up ahead. The bird circled twice and landed on the shoulder of one of the riders. The Three Devils spurred their horses on. One of the strangers was a bald, red-faced old man, the other was a white-haired old lady. 'Where's Huo Qingtong?' the old man barked, and the three stared at him in surprise. The old man removed the water-bag from the eagle's neck and hurled the bird back into the air. He gave a shrill whistle and the bird answered with a squawk and headed back the way it had come. The old couple—who were, of course, the Twin Eagles of Heaven Mountains, Bald Vulture and Lady Guan—took no further notice of the Three Devils but galloped on past them, chasing after the eagle. Teng saw that the old man still had the water-bag, and with a wave of his hand to the others, followed along behind.

When the Twin Eagles had ridden three or four miles, they saw the bird glide downwards to where Huo Qingtong was lying on the ground. Lady Guan leapt off her horse and grabbed the girl up into her arms. Huo Qingtong began sobbing.

'Who has been treating you so badly?' demanded Lady Guan, looking down at the girl's deathly appearance. Just then, the Three Devils rode up. Huo Qingtong pointed at them, then fainted away.

'Well, are you just going to sit there?' Lady Guan demanded angrily of her husband. Bald Vulture wheeled his horse round, charged at the three of them, and began fighting furiously.

Lady Guan slowly poured water into Huo Qingtong's mouth and the girl gradually regained consciousness. Only then did the old lady look round to see how her husband was faring. He was struggling to keep the three at bay, so she drew her sword and jumped into the mêlée. She struck out first at Teng, who swung round to counter the stroke, only to find that before he could do so her style had changed. Amazed that this skinny old woman could be such a formidable swordswoman, he concentrated completely on defence.

Huo Qingtong sat up and watched the Twin Eagles gradually gaining the upper hand. As she watched, she heard a strange sound floating faintly towards them on the wind from far off, a sound full of violence and dread, of hunger and evil, a sound as of hundreds of wild beasts howling in unison.

'Shifu, listen!' she cried. The Twin Eagles disengaged themselves from the fight and cocked an ear to listen. The Devils had been hard-pressed to hold their own, and did not now dare to attack the old couple.

The fearsome sound grew slightly louder, and the Twin Eagles turned pale. Bald Vulture ran over to his horse and stood on its back.

'Come and look!' he shouted. 'See if there's anywhere we can take cover.'

Lady Guan picked up Huo Qingtong and placed her on her own horse, then vaulted up onto her husband's horse and stood on his shoulders.

The Three Devils looked at each other, absolutely baffled. These strange opponents of theirs had broken off the fight when they had already as good as won, and were now building a human pagoda on a horse's back.

'What witchcraft are they up to?' Gu growled darkly. Teng had no idea what was going on. He only knew he must be prepared for anything.

Lady Guan gazed about in all directions. Suddenly she shouted: 'There! I think there are two big trees to the north!'

'Whether there are or not,' replied her husband, 'let's go!' Lady Guan jumped over to Huo Qingtong's horse, and they galloped off north without taking any further notice of the Three Devils.

Hahetai noticed that in their hurry to get away, they had left the water-bag behind, and he bent down to pick it up. By now, the terrifying howling sound was becoming even louder. Gu's face turned grey.

'It's a wolf-pack!' he cried.

The three leapt instantly onto their horses and galloped hell for leather after the Twin Eagles. Looking back, they saw large wildcats, camels, goats, and horses, all racing for their lives before a huge grey tide of ravening wolves. Fifty or so yards ahead of the fleeing multitude rode a man in a grey gown, galloping along as if somehow leading the flight. In a flash, his powerful horse raced up and passed the Three Devils, who were able to see that he was an old man. He turned back to shout at them: 'Faster! Do you want to die? Faster!'

Teng's horse was scared out of its wits by the mass of animals bearing down upon them, and it stumbled and threw him to the ground. As he leapt to his feet, a dozen wildcats rushed past him. He was sure that this meant the end for him, and began screaming at the top of his voice. Gu and Hahetai heard his screams and headed back to rescue him. The wolves were already bearing down upon them. One huge wolf threw itself at Teng, baring its snow-white teeth; Teng drew his sword to defend himself, knowing it was a useless gesture. Then suddenly, he heard the sound of horse's hooves behind him. It was the old man, who had galloped back and now grabbed Teng by his collar and threw him bodily towards Hahetai. Teng somersaulted through the air and landed in a sitting position on Hahetai's horse. The three riders then pulled their horses round, and fled for their lives.

The Twin Eagles had lived in the desert many years and knew only too well that even the most ferocious animal could not survive an encounter with a wolf-pack. They galloped on, and as they saw the two tall trees come into view, they thanked the Heavens that they had once again avoided ending up in a wolf's stomach. As soon as they reached the trees, Bald Vulture leapt up into the branches of one, and Lady Guan helped Huo Qingtong get up to him. The wolf-pack was approaching fast. Lady Guan whipped the backs of their two horses and shouted: 'Run for your lives! We can't help you!' The two horses galloped away.

Just as the three of them had found somewhere to squat in the branches, they noticed the grey-gowned rider galloping along ahead of the wolf-pack. As he passed by below, Bald Vulture seized him with his free hand and lifted him up. The old man was taken completely by surprise. His horse shot onwards, while he himself was left dangling in space, a host of animals passing beneath his feet. He performed a somersault, and landed on his feet on a branch higher up the tree.

'What's wrong?' said Bald Vulture. 'Don't say you're afraid of wolves too, Master Yuan?'

'Who asked you to interfere?' the old man replied angrily.

'There's no need to be like that,' Lady Guan interrupted him. 'My husband just saved your life.'

The old man laughed coldly. 'Saved me? You've messed everything up!'

This Master Yuan was in fact none other than Helmsman Chen's Shifu, Yuan Shixiao, known as the Strange Knight of the Heavenly Pool. He and Lady Guan had grown up together in central China and many years earlier had fallen in love. But they had argued constantly, and eventually Yuan had left and spent more than ten years travelling in the Northern Deserts. There had been no news of him, and Lady Guan had presumed he would never come back. Eventually, she married Bald Vulture. But shortly after the wedding, Yuan unexpectedly returned home. Both Yuan and Lady Guan were heartbroken at the way things had turned out, although they never spoke of the matter again. Bald Vulture was also very unhappy, and on several occasions went after Yuan to get revenge. But his kungfu was simply not good enough, and it was only Yuan's regard for Lady Guan's feelings that kept her husband from being seriously hurt. So Bald Vulture took his wife and travelled far away, deep into Uighur territory. Yuan, however, could never forget her. He too moved to the great range known as Heaven Mountains. He never visited them, but just living within reach of the woman he loved made him feel a little happier. Lady Guan did all she could to keep from seeing her former lover, but Bald Vulture would not let the matter drop, and the couple had fought and argued for decades since. All three were now old and white-haired, but not a day passed without their thinking of the entanglement.

On this occasion, Bald Vulture was very pleased with himself for having saved Yuan. His rival had always had the upper hand. Perhaps he might show a little gratitude towards him after this. Lady Guan was puzzled by Yuan's anger.

'What do you mean, "messed everything up"?' she asked. 'Messed what up?'

'This wolf-pack is growing bigger and bigger,' Yuan replied. 'It has become a real plague in the desert. Several Uighur villages have been completely wiped out already. The wolves eat people, animals, everything. So I prepared a trap and was just leading them to their deaths when you went and interfered.'

Bald Vulture could tell that Yuan was telling the truth. It was not like him to invent such a story. He now felt acutely embarrassed. Yuan saw the apologetic expression on Lady Guan's face and brought his anger under control. 'But no doubt you were doing what you thought was best,' he added. 'I thank you, anyway.'

'What sort of trap is it?' asked Bald Vulture.

'*Save them!*' shouted Yuan suddenly, and jumped down from the tree right into the very midst of the wolves.

Even as they had been talking, the Three Devils had been overtaken by the wolves. Their horses had already been ripped to shreds. The Devils were now standing back to back and putting up a furious fight. They had killed more than a dozen wolves, but more and more beasts continued to lunge at them. All three men were already wounded in several places, and it looked as if they could not hold out for long. Yuan raced over, and his fists flew through and smashed the skulls of two wolves. He picked Hahetai up and hurled him up into the tree, shouting to Bald Vulture, 'Catch!' Yuan hurled Teng and Gu up in exactly the same way, then killed another two wolves, grabbed one of the corpses by the neck and swung it round and round, opening up a path to the tree, and leapt up into the branches himself. The Three Devils, having been literally snatched from the jaws of death, showered the old man with thanks. They were astonished by the speed and strength he had displayed. He had made killing wolves seem as easy as catching rabbits.

Several hundred wolves now circled the base of the tree, scratching at the trunk, throwing back their heads and howling. A short distance away, a hundred or so of the motley crowd of fleeing animals had been cut off and encircled by the wolves. The air was filled with their cries as the animals leapt frantically about, and the wolves tore them in pieces and gnashed at their flesh. It was a horrible sight. In less than a moment, the animals had all been ripped apart and eaten. The spectators sitting up in the tree were all in their various ways brave fighters, but this was the first time any of them had witnessed such a terrifying scene at close quarters. They were very frightened.

Bald Vulture eyed the Devils suspiciously.

'Those three are not good men,' Huo Qingtong told him.

'All right, then,' he replied. 'In that case they can go and feed the wolves.' He was about to push them off the tree, when he looked down once more at the hideous scene below and hesitated for a split second. It was just long enough for Teng to shout 'Let's go!' and leap over to the other tree, Gu and Hahetai following him.

Lady Guan looked at Huo Qingtong. 'My dear, what do you say?' She was asking if the girl wanted them to chase after the three and kill them.

Huo Qingtong's heart softened. 'Let them go,' she said.

'I am Huo Qingtong,' she shouted to the Three Devils. 'If you want to get your revenge on me, why don't you come over here?' Teng and his two friends were astonished and angered by her words, but they did not dare return to the other tree.

The wolves had come fast, and they left with equal speed. They swirled around the trees for a while, howling and barking, then chased off after the remaining wild animals.

Lady Guan told Huo Qingtong to pay her respects to Master Yuan. Seeing her sickly appearance, the old man took two red pills from his bag and gave them to her, saying: 'Take these. They're Snow Ginseng Pills.' Made from the rarest medicinal herbs, these pills were well known for their ability to restore life even to the dying. Just as Huo Qingtong was about to bow and thank him, Yuan jumped down from the tree and ran off. In a moment, he had become just a black speck amidst the swirling desert dust.

The Sand Game

Lady Guan helped Huo Qingtong down from the tree, and told her to swallow one of the Snow Ginseng Pills. Soon after she had done so, a wave of warmth rose from the pit of her stomach, and she felt much better.

'You are very lucky,' Lady Guan said. 'With these wonderful pills you'll recover much quicker.'

'She wouldn't die even if she didn't take them,' Bald Vulture commented coldly.

'So you'd rather she suffered a bit longer, would you?' his wife snapped back.

'If it was me, I'd die rather than take one of his pills. But you, you'd take one even if there was nothing wrong with you.'

Lady Guan put the girl on her back, and started walking off north with Bald Vulture following behind, muttering ceaselessly.

When they got to the old couple's home on Precious Mountain, Huo Qingtong took the other pill, then slept peacefully. She felt much refreshed when she woke. Lady Guan sat on the edge of the bed and asked her what she had been doing travelling alone and sick through the desert. Huo Qingtong told her about how the Manchu army had been destroyed and how she had met the Three Devils on the road, but did not say why she had left the camp. Lady Guan, however, always wanted to get to the bottom of things, and pressed her for an explanation. Huo Qingtong respected her Shifu more than anyone in the world, and found it impossible to deceive her.

'He...he has become attached to my younger sister,' she sobbed. 'And when I gave the orders to the troops before the battle, my father and everyone thought I was only acting out of self-interest.'

Lady Guan jumped up. 'Is it that Helmsman Chen you gave the dagger to?' Huo Qingtong nodded. 'Then he's fickle-hearted and your sister has no sisterly feelings for you. They should both be killed!'

'No, no...' Huo Qingtong replied hastily.

'I'll go and settle this for you,' Lady Guan declared fiercely and rushed out of the room, almost bumping into her husband who had come to find out what the shouting was about.

'Come with me!' she cried. 'There are two heartless young people who need to be taught a lesson about gratitude! They must be killed!'

'Right!' he replied, and ran out after her.

Huo Qingtong jumped off the bed, wanting to explain, but she collapsed on the ground, and by the time she had recovered, they were already far away. She knew that together they would make light work of Helmsman Chen, and was worried they actually would kill him and her sister. So despite her weakness, she climbed onto her horse and galloped off after them.

As they rode along, Lady Guan talked at length and with considerable passion about how all the heartless men under heaven should be killed.

'That dagger she gave him is a priceless treasure,' she said angrily to Bald Vulture. 'She gave it in good faith, as a token of her feelings. But clearly it meant nothing to him! He casts her aside, and then decides he likes her sister instead. He should be carved into a thousand pieces!'

'And how could her sister be so shameless as to steal him away like that?' her husband added.

On the third day, the Twin Eagles spotted a dust-cloud in the distance and saw two riders galloping from the south towards them.

'Ah!' Lady Guan exclaimed. 'The very man!'

'What is it?' her husband asked, and then he too spotted Helmsman Chen. He moved to draw his sword.

'Not so fast,' said Lady Guan. 'Let's pretend we know nothing and take them by surprise.'

Helmsman Chen had also seen them and galloped over. He dismounted and bowed before them.

'I am so glad we have met you,' he said. 'Have you seen Lady Huo Qingtong?'

'No,' replied Lady Guan, secretly furious at the brazen way in which he still pretended to be concerned for her. 'Why, what's the matter?' Suddenly, her eyes opened wide as the other rider approached and she saw that it was a young woman of extraordinary beauty.

'This is your sister's Shifu,' said Helmsman Chen to Hasli. 'Pay your respects to her.' She dismounted and bowed before Lady Guan.

'My sister has often spoken of you both,' she said, smiling. 'Have you seen her?'

Bald Vulture was stunned by her beauty and thought to himself it was no wonder Chen had changed his mind—she was so much more beautiful than her sister.

Lady Guan was astonished that this innocent-looking young woman could be so cunning as to steal her own sister's lover. But her voice betrayed none of her feelings. She asked again what was wrong. Chen explained that Huo Qingtong was missing, and that they were looking for her, to warn her of the danger posed to her by the Three Devils of Manchuria.

'Let's go and look for her together,' Lady Guan said.

So the four started out together heading north. That evening, they set up camp in the lee of a sand-dune, and after dinner, sat around and talked. Hasli pulled a candle from her bag and lit it. The Twin Eagles looked at Chen and the girl in the candlelight, both so young and handsome, like figures in a painting. They wondered how they could be capable of such heartlessness and evil.

'Are you sure my sister is not in any real danger?' Hasli asked Chen.

He too was very concerned for Huo Qingtong's safety, but he comforted her, saying: 'Your sister's kungfu is good and she is intelligent. I'm sure she's all right.'

Hasli had complete faith in him and set her mind at ease. 'But she's ill,' she added after a moment. 'When we've found her, we must persuade her to come home with us and rest.' Chen nodded.

Lady Guan's face turned white with anger as she listened to the two of them engaging in what she thought was play-acting.

'Let's play a game,' said Hasli suddenly to Bald Vulture. He looked at his wife. Lady Guan nodded slowly.

'All right!' he said. 'What game?'

Hasli smiled at Lady Guan and at Chen. 'You two will play as well, won't you?' she asked. They nodded.

She brought a saddle over and placed it in the middle, then scooped a pile of sand onto it. She patted the sand down firmly, and planted a small candle on top.

'We pass the knife round and each take turns at removing a part of the sand-pile,' she said. 'The one who causes the candle to fall has to sing a song, or dance, or tell a story. You start first, sir.' She handed the knife to Bald Vulture.

The old man had not played a game like this for decades, and he looked embarrassed. Lady Guan gave him a push: 'Go on!' she said. He laughed and sliced away a section of sand. Then he handed the knife to his wife who did the same. They went round three times until the pile was reduced to a pillar only slightly bigger than the candle on top. Chen carefully made a slight indentation in the side of the pillar. Hasli laughed and made a little hole on the opposite side. The pillar began to sway slightly. Bald Vulture's hand shook slightly as he accepted the knife.

'Hold your breath!' Lady Guan hissed at him.

'Even one grain of sand counts,' said Hasli. When Bald Vulture touched the pillar with the knife, it collapsed, taking the candle with it. He gave a cry of frustration. Hasli clapped her hands in delight as Lady Guan and Helmsman Chen looked on smiling.

'Well,' said Hasli. 'What are you going to do? Sing a song for us, or dance?'

He could see it was impossible to refuse, so he said: 'All right. I'll sing a song.'

In a high-pitched voice he began singing:

You and I, dear,
When we were young, dear,
Life was like a play, dear,
And we cried…

He glanced over at his wife. As she listened, Lady Guan found herself remembering how good life had been just after they got married. If Master Yuan had not returned, they would most probably have been happy together for the rest of their days. She leaned over and lightly squeezed his hand. Bald Vulture felt quite dizzy at this sudden show of affection from his wife, and tears welled up in his eyes. Helmsman Chen and Hasli looked at each other knowingly, both aware of the love these two old people had for each other. They played the sand game a second time and this time Helmsman Chen lost. He told a story. The third time, Bald Vulture lost again.

As the night deepened, Hasli began to feel cold and edged closer to Lady Guan, who put an arm round her and carefully rearranged her wind-blown hair. The Twin Eagles didn't have any children of their own, and often felt very much alone in the great desert that was their home. Lady Guan sighed and wished she could have had such a daughter. She looked down and saw the girl was already asleep. The candle had been blown out by the wind, but by the starlight, she could see the hint of a smile on her face.

'Let's get some rest,' said Bald Vulture.

'Don't wake her,' his wife whispered. She carefully carried Hasli into the tent and covered her with a blanket.

'Mother,' the girl called faintly, and Lady Guan froze for a second in shock.

'It's all right, go to sleep now,' she replied softly. She crept out of the tent and saw Chen setting up his own tent a long way from the girl's. She nodded thoughtfully to herself.

'Well?' said Bald Vulture. 'Are we going to do it when he's asleep, or go over and give him a chance to explain first?'

'What do you think?'

The evening had filled the old man's heart with tender thoughts, and he had no stomach for killing at that moment. 'Let's sit a while and wait until he's asleep. That way he can die painlessly.' He took his wife's hand and the two sat silently together on the sand. Soon after, Chen entered his tent and went to sleep.

Normally the Twin Eagles were capable of killing without batting an eyelid. But for some reason tonight they found it difficult to deal with these two while they slept. The constellations slowly turned in the night sky, the wind grew colder, and the old couple hugged each other for warmth. Lady Guan buried her face in her husband's chest and Bald Vulture lightly stroked her back. Before long, both were asleep.

Circle of Fire

Next morning, when Helmsman Chen and Hasli awoke, they were puzzled to find the Twin Eagles gone.

'Look, what's that?' asked Hasli all of a sudden. Chen turned and saw several huge characters drawn on the sand: 'Your evil deeds cannot be forgiven. You will have to die.' The characters were five foot square and looked as if they had been drawn with the tip of a sword. Chen frowned, wondering what the message meant. Hasli could not read Chinese and asked him to explain what it said.

'They had some other business and went on ahead,' Chen replied, not wishing to worry her.

'My sister's Shifu and her husband are really nice—' She stopped in mid-sentence and jumped up. 'Listen!'

Chen had also heard the distant, blood-curdling howl. He had lived in the northwest many years, and instantly recognized it.

'That's a wolf-pack,' he said urgently. 'And it's coming in our direction. We must go!'

They hurriedly packed up their tents and provisions and galloped away just as the wolves closed in on them. Luckily, their horses were extremely fast and the pack was soon left far behind. But the wolves had been hungry for a long time and, having once glimpsed them, continued to track them, following the hoof prints in the sand.

After half a day of hard riding, they dismounted to rest; but just as they had prepared a fire to cook some food, the howling drew near once more, so they hurriedly re-mounted, and rode off again. Only when darkness had fallen and they estimated the wolf-pack to be at least thirty miles behind them did they stop and rest. Around midnight, the white horse began to neigh and kick about, waking Chen. The wolf-pack was closing in once more. With no time to pack their tents, they grabbed their rations and water-bags and jumped onto the horses. They travelled in a great arc through the desert, never managing to shake off the wolves. The chestnut horse could finally take no more and dropped dead of exhaustion. They had to continue with both of them on the white horse. The extra weight slowed the horse down, and by the third day, it was no longer able to outrun the wolf-pack. They spotted a clump of bushes and small trees and made their way over to it.

'We'll stop here and let the horse rest,' said Chen, dismounting. With Hasli's help, he built a low circular wall of sand and placed some dead branches on top. When they were lit, the branches became a protective ring of fire for themselves and the horse inside.

After a matter of moments, the wolf-pack raced up. The wolves were afraid of the flames, and milled around outside the circle howling, not daring to get too close.

'We'll wait for the horse to recover its strength and then try to break out,' said Chen.

'Do you think we'll be able to?'

'Of course,' he replied. But he had no idea how.

Hasli saw how emaciated and hungry the wolves were. 'The poor things,' she said. 'I wonder how long it's been since they last ate?'

Chen laughed shortly. The long, sharp fangs of the wolves gleamed through the flames, the saliva dripping drop by drop from their mouths onto the sand. They howled savagely, waiting for the slightest opening in the flames to leap through.

Hasli knew the chances of their getting out alive were very slight. She moved closer to Chen and took his hands.

'When I'm with you, I'm not afraid of anything,' she said. 'After we die, we will live happily together in heaven, for ever.'

Chen pulled her towards him and embraced her. She sighed, and was just about to close her eyes, when she noticed the flames were dying down in one section of the circle. She gave a scream and jumped over to add more branches, but three wolves had already slipped through. Chen pulled her behind him. The white horse kicked its hind legs in the air and sent one wolf flying back out of the fiery circle. Chen grabbed another wolf by the scruff of its neck and slung it bodily at the third, a huge grey beast, which dodged out of the way, then opened its mouth and reared up on its hind legs to go for Chen's throat. Chen picked up a burning branch and rammed it down the wolf's throat. The animal leapt back out of the circle, rolling about on the ground in great pain. Chen added more branches to the gap.

After a while, their reserves of wood were getting low, and Chen decided he would have to risk going to get more from some bushes about a hundred feet away. He took out his barbed shield and his weapon known as the Pearl Strings. 'Build up the fire a bit more until I get back,' he said to Hasli. She nodded. 'Be careful,' she said. She did not add any more wood to the fire. She knew that the branches kept the two of them alive, and that when the flames were extinguished, they would be too.

Chen leapt out of the burning circle and raced off, using Lightness kungfu, fending off the wolves as he went. They surged at him, but in three leaps he was already beside the bushes. He quickly reached for firewood with one hand while protecting himself with the shield. Twenty or thirty wolves surrounded him, snarling fiercely, but the flashing hooks on his shield kept them at bay. He collected a big pile of wood and was leaning over to tie the branches up when a large wolf lunged forward. He swung the shield, and the animal died instantly, cut to pieces by the sharp blades of the hooks attached to the shield's rim. Its carcass swung from the shield lifelessly in mid-air, and the other wolves barked even more frantically. When Helmsman Chen dislodged the body and flung it to one side, the wolves charged forward to rip it apart and devour it. He took advantage of this diversion to pick up the firewood and make his way back to Hasli in the ring of fire.

She ran to him and threw herself into his arms. Chen embraced her, and threw the firewood on the ground. He looked up, and started: there was a third person in the circle. It was a large man whose clothes had been ripped to shreds by the wolves. In his hand he held a sword. His whole body was covered in blood, but his face was calm. It was Chen's deadly enemy, Zhang Zhaozhong, the Fire Hand Judge.

The two gazed at each other in silence.

'He must have seen the fire and run over this way,' said Hasli. 'See how exhausted he looks.' She poured a bowl of water from the water-bag and handed it to Zhang, who grabbed it and slurped it down in one draught. He wiped the blood and sweat from his face with his sleeve, and Hasli gasped as she suddenly recognized him as the Manchu official Chen had fought with.

Chen rapped his shield with the Pearl Strings. 'Come on and fight!' he shouted.

Zhang's eyes glazed over and he fell forward onto his face.

He and the Manchu officer Colonel Herda had been tracking Chen and Hasli when they had met the wolf-pack. Herda had been devoured, but thanks to his superlative kungfu, Zhang had succeeded in killing thirty or forty of the ferocious creatures, and had then managed to escape. He had fled across the desert for a day and a night, but finally his horse had dropped dead under him. He'd had no alternative but to continue on foot and had kept going for another day without food or water. Finally, he had spotted the flames in the far distance and had fought his way over to the fire.

Hasli made a move to help Zhang up, but Chen stopped her.

'This man is extremely dangerous. Don't fall for his tricks,' he warned. He waited for a while to make sure Zhang really was unconscious before going closer.

Hasli moistened Zhang's forehead with some cold water, then poured lamb's milk into his mouth. Zhang slowly revived, drank half a bowl of the milk, then fell back onto the ground, sound asleep.

Chen wondered what sort of devil's emissary had delivered this traitor into his hands. Killing Zhang now would be as easy as 'blowing away a speck of ash', as the old saying had it; but to take advantage of another's hardship was not a manly thing to do. What was more, Hasli would certainly be displeased if he were to kill a defenceless man. He decided to spare Zhang once more. In any case, Zhang would be a great help in killing wolves. Perhaps the two of them together could save Hasli. He knew he would never be able to do it alone. He drank a few mouthfuls of lamb's milk, then closed his eyes to rest.

After a while, Zhang woke again. Hasli passed him a piece of dried mutton, and helped him to bandage several wolf-bite wounds on his legs.

'All three of us are in great danger,' said Helmsman Chen. 'We should temporarily put aside our differences and work together.'

Zhang nodded. 'Yes, if we fight each other now, we will all end up inside a wolf's stomach.' He had rested for more than two hours, and his strength had partially returned. He was already beginning to consider how he could kill Chen and escape with the girl.

Chen meanwhile was racking his brains for a way out of their present predicament. He saw the many piles of wolf droppings outside the circle of fire, and remembered how Huo Qingtong had used them earlier to fuel signal fires. Using his Pearl Strings, he dragged some of the piles over, made them into a heap, and lit it. A thick pall of smoke rose straight up into the sky.

Zhang shook his head. 'Even if someone saw it, they wouldn't dare to come and help us,' he said. 'It would take an army to chase away so many wolves.'

Chen also knew it would probably do no good, but it was better than doing nothing.

The daylight faded, and the three of them gradually added more branches to the ring of fire and took it in turns to sleep.

'Never forget that he's a very bad man,' Chen whispered to Hasli. 'When I'm asleep, you must watch him closely.' She nodded.

Towards midnight, the moon rose and the wolves began to howl mournfully. It was an eerie sound, and it made their skin crawl. Early next morning, they saw that the wolves were still pacing around outside the ring. They obviously had no intention of leaving.

'The only thing that would draw these monstrous creatures away would be if a herd of wild camels were to pass nearby,' said Chen. Suddenly they heard more wolf howls in the distance. Three riders could be seen galloping towards them in a cloud of dust, with several hundred wolves at their heels. The wolves round the ring of fire spotted them too, and surged forward, encircling the three men on horseback.

'Help them!' shouted Hasli, as the men tried desperately to fight the wolves off.

'Let's go,' Chen said to Zhang. They ran frantically out of the ring of fire, carving a path of blood through the wolf-pack, and led the three riders back into the circle. They noticed that one of the horses was carrying a second person, by all appearances a Uighur girl, lying limply across the saddle with her hands tied behind her back. The three riders jumped off their horses, and one of them pulled the girl down after him.

'Sister!' screamed Hasli, throwing herself onto the girl.

The Bent Coin

It was Huo Qingtong. She had run into the Three Devils once again while searching for Chen and her sister, and this time had lacked the strength to resist. Hahetai had wanted to kill her immediately, but Gu had overruled him. They had started heading back east, but after a day or so, they found themselves being chased by a wolf-pack. As they fled, they caught sight of the column of black smoke started by Chen and galloped towards it.

Huo Qingtong began to regain consciousness. Hasli looked at Chen beseechingly. 'Tell them to let my sister go,' she implored.

Chen turned to Gu. 'Who are you? And why have you seized my friend?' he asked. Teng strode in front of Gu and coldly sized up Chen and Zhang.

'We thank you two gentlemen for saving our lives,' he said. 'What are your names?'

Before Chen could answer, Zhang said, 'This man is the Helmsman of the Red Flower Society, Chen Jialuo.' The Three Devils started in shock.

'And you, sir?' Teng asked.

'My name is Zhang Zhaozhong.'

Teng gasped. 'The Fire Hand Judge! No wonder the two of you have managed to stay alive against this pack of wolves!' He told them his own name and those of his two colleagues.

With four tough opponents to deal with now, it would be even harder than before to escape, thought Chen, with ever mounting anxiety.

'We should forget our differences for the moment,' he urged. 'Do any of you have any idea how we might escape?'

The Three Devils looked at each other. 'We would welcome your suggestions, sir,' said Hahetai.

'What I know is this,' replied Chen. 'If we face the wolves together, we have a chance of survival. If we fight amongst ourselves, they will eat us all.' Teng and Hahetai nodded; Gu just glared at him angrily. 'I ask you to immediately release my friend. Then we can work out a plan together against our common enemy, the wolves.'

'And what if I *won't* let her go?' Gu shouted back. He had gone to considerable trouble to capture Huo Qingtong and he was extremely loath to give her up again.

'Brother Gu, if you refuse to let her go, you're on your own,' said Teng. 'I won't be able to help you.'

Hahetai decided to take matters into his own hands. He walked over and cut the bonds binding Huo Qingtong. As Chen went to her, Huo Qingtong suddenly shouted: 'Watch out behind!' He ducked down just as a wolf swept over him. It rushed at Hasli, but Chen grabbed it by the tail and, using all his strength, pulled it to a halt. The wolf whipped its head round, snapping and snarling. With a single blow, Chen broke its neck. Another wolf leapt towards him, and he quickly drew his dagger and thrust it at the beast, a huge, cunning animal which dodged the blade with ease.

Three more wolves now jumped into the ring. Hahetai grabbed one by the neck and slung it back out, Zhang cut the second in two with his sword, while Teng fought fiercely with the third. Hahetai stoked up the fire to stop other wolves from entering. On the other side, Chen feinted to the left with his dagger, to throw his attacker-wolf off guard, then plunged the blade down towards its head. Unable to avoid the stroke, the wolf opened its huge mouth and bit hard onto the dagger. Chen drove the blade home as hard as he could, but despite the pain, the wolf hung on desperately. Even when Chen tried to pull the dagger back out, the beast refused to yield. Chen mustered his strength once more and punched the wolf right between the eyes, smashing its skull. It fell back dead and the dagger finally came free, the blade glinting coldly as it reflected the flames.

The strange thing was, there was still a blade firmly lodged between the dead animal's teeth. They were all perplexed at this. The dagger was obviously in Chen's hand, and intact. It had not snapped in two. What had happened? Where had the second blade in the wolf's mouth come from?

Chen bent down and tried to pull the blade out of the beast's mouth, but although the wolf was dead, its teeth were still clamped tightly shut. He used the dagger to slit open the wolf's jowls, and the muscles and tendons of its face collapsed, freeing the second blade. Chen examined it closely. It was in fact hollow, like a scabbard. He thrust the dagger inside it. It fitted perfectly. Huo Qingtong had told him, when she presented him with the dagger, that it was said to 'contain a great secret'. If it had not been for this wolf and its strong teeth, he would never have guessed that there was a blade within the blade!

Hasli took the dagger from Chen and examined it, marvelling at the design of the 'scabbard' and the precision of the workmanship. She turned it upside down and a small white pellet rolled out. Chen and Huo Qingtong bent down to get a closer look and saw it was a small ball of wax.

'Let's open it,' Chen said. Huo Qingtong nodded. He picked the ball up and lightly squeezed it, cracking the wax open to reveal a small piece of paper inside, which Chen then spread out. On the paper was a map, as densely and finely drawn as a spider's web.

Zhang had seen them discover the piece of paper, and glanced at it stealthily. But he was disappointed to find it was covered in Uighur script, which he could not understand.

Chen knew something of the Uighur written language, but he couldn't decipher the meaning of the writing on the piece of paper. He handed it over to Huo Qingtong, who examined it closely for a long time, then folded it up and placed it in her pocket.

'What does it say?' Chen asked. Huo Qingtong did not answer, and her head was hung low.

Hasli knew her sister well and smiled. 'She is trying to puzzle something out,' she said. 'Don't disturb her.'

Huo Qingtong sat down on the ground and began to draw lines in the sand with her finger. She drew one diagram, then rubbed it out and drew another. After a while, she wrapped her arms around her knees, deep in thought.

'You are still weak. You should rest,' Chen said to her. 'You can work it out later. The important thing now is to think of a way of getting out of here.'

'I'm working on a plan to escape from hungry wolves and from hungry *human* wolves as well,' Huo Qingtong replied, glaring angrily at Zhang as she spoke. She continued her meditations for a moment, then said to Chen: 'Please stand on a horse and look to the west. Tell me if you can see a mountain with a white peak.'

Chen led the white horse over and did as she said. In the distance, he spied a range of mountains, but could see none with a white peak. He scanned the horizon carefully for a minute longer, then looked down at Huo Qingtong and shook his head.

'According to the map, the Secret City should not be far from here, and we should be able to see the White Jade Peak.'

Chen jumped off the horse's back. 'What secret city?' he asked.

'When I was young, I heard people talk about an ancient city that was buried in this desert,' she replied. 'The city was once extremely prosperous, but one day a great sandstorm blew up, and dunes as large as mountains buried it. None of the city's residents escaped.' She turned to Hasli. 'You know the story better than I do. You tell it.'

'There are many stories about the place, but no one has ever seen the city with their own eyes,' said Hasli. But then she corrected herself. 'Many people have been there, but few have returned alive. There are said to be piles of gold and silver and precious jewels there. Some people who lost their way in the desert found the city by chance and were overwhelmed by the sight of such wealth. Needless to say they started loading the gold and jewels onto their camels to take away with them. But no matter which way they went, they couldn't get out of the city.'

'Why?' Chen asked.

'The story goes that all the people of the city who were buried in the sand were turned into ghosts. These ghosts cast a spell on any visitors who try to take even the slightest part of the buried treasure away with them. But if you put down the jewels, every single one, then it's easy to find your way out.'

'I doubt if many people would be willing to do that,' said Chen.

'It's true, the sight of such riches is too much for most people! The story goes that if you take nothing away, and leave a few taels of silver in one of the houses, then the wells of the city will spurt clear, fresh water for you to drink. The more silver you leave, the more fresh water there will be.'

Chen laughed. 'The ghosts of this Secret City sound very greedy.'

'Some members of our tribe who were badly in debt once went to look for the city, but only those who didn't succeed in finding it ever returned,' continued Hasli. 'Once, a caravan crossing the desert came across a man who was half dead. He said he had entered the city, but had found himself going round and round in circles when he tried to get out again. Finally, his strength gave out and he collapsed, and the next thing he knew was the arrival of the caravan. The caravan leader asked him to lead them to the city, but he refused. He said he would never step into that haunted place again even if he was given all the riches of the city as a reward.'

'It may not have been ghosts that bewitched these people,' said Chen. 'If a man suddenly comes upon a huge treasure, it could easily affect his mind and make it difficult for him to think clearly. But if he decides he doesn't want the treasure after all, that might clear his head, and make it easier to find the way out.'

'Anyway, that's what the map hidden in the dagger is,' Huo Qingtong said quietly. 'It shows the way to the Secret City. According to the map, the city was built around the foot of a high snowcapped mountain. From the look of it, the mountain shouldn't be too far from here. We should be able to see it. I don't understand why we can't.'

'Sister, you're wasting your time,' said Hasli. 'Even if we could find the mountain, what use would it be?'

'We could hide in the city. There are houses and fortified buildings there, and our chance of escaping the wolves would be much greater than it is here.'

'That's right!' Chen said. He stood on the horse's back once more looking west. But all he could see was a hazy white sky stretching to the horizon.

Zhang and the Three Devils couldn't understand a word they were saying, but they watched suspiciously as Chen twice stood on the back of his horse, and wondered what sorcery he was up to.

Hasli took out some dry rations and divided them up amongst all of them. As she sat eating, she gazed out beyond the flames at the horizon. Suddenly, she jumped up, calling: 'Sister! Look!' Huo Qingtong followed the direction of her hand and saw a black spot in the sky, stationary.

'What is it?' she asked.

'It's an eagle,' Hasli replied. 'I saw it fly over. But why has it suddenly stopped in mid-air?'

'Yes, it must be an eagle,' said Chen. 'But see how completely motionless it is! It's not even hovering in mid-air. How strange!' The three watched the spot for a while, then saw it moving and becoming larger, until a large black bird of prey swept directly over their heads.

Hasli raised her hand to tidy her hair, which had been blown about by the wind. Chen looked at her snow-white skin against the white material of her dress, and suddenly understood the 'eagle mystery'.

'Look at your sister's hand!' he said excitedly to Huo Qingtong.

'Yes, I know: her hands are very pretty,' she replied absent-mindedly.

'Of course her hands are pretty. But there's something else. Don't you see? Her skin is so white, it's difficult at a glance to tell where the hand ends and the dress begins.'

'So?' asked Huo Qingtong, puzzled.

'The eagle was actually *perched* on top of a white mountain!'

'Yes! You're right,' Huo Qingtong exclaimed. 'The sky over there is white, the same colour as the peak, so from a distance, the two can't be told apart.'

'Exactly,' said Chen.

'So *that's* where the Secret City is,' said Hasli. 'How do we get there?'

'That is what we have to work out,' replied Huo Qingtong. She pulled out the map again and studied it carefully for a while. 'When the sun starts to go down, we'll be able to tell if there's a mountain there or not by its shadow.'

'We mustn't give ourselves away,' said Chen. 'We don't want the others to work out what we're doing.'

'Yes. Let's pretend we're talking about that wolf,' suggested Huo Qingtong.

Chen pulled the wolf across and the three sat around it, now pulling out one of its hairs and examining it closely, now opening its mouth to look at its teeth. The sun gradually sank in the western sky and the mountain's shadow did indeed appear, stretching out longer and longer across the desert horizon like some recumbent giant. Huo Qingtong drew a map on the ground, estimating the distances.

'From here to the mountain must be about twenty or thirty miles,' she said, turning the wolf over.

Chen picked up one of its legs and played with its sharp claws. 'If only we had another horse apart from the white horse, the three of us could make that in one go.'

'So we have to think of some way to get *them* to allow us to go,' Huo Qingtong replied.

'Yes.' He picked up his dagger and slit open the wolf's stomach.

'What's so interesting about that dead wolf?' Zhang shouted, annoyed at not being able to understand what they were saying. 'Are you planning some big wolf-funeral, or what?'

'We are discussing how to get out of here,' Chen said. 'Look, the wolf's stomach is completely empty.'

'Do you have a plan?' Zhang asked.

'When the firewood has all been burned,' said Chen in Chinese, 'and there is no more to collect, then we are all going to die. Wouldn't you agree?' Zhang and the Three Devils nodded. 'But if one of us was willing to sacrifice himself and ride out of the circle, the wolves would swarm after him like bees from a hive. Once the beasts were drawn off, the others could escape.'

'But what about the one who goes?' asked Zhang.

'If he comes across either the Manchu or Uighur armies then he stands a chance. Otherwise he will die. But it is better than us all dying here together.'

'Not a bad idea,' said Teng. 'But who's going to lead the wolves away? I'd say it's certain death.'

'Who do you suggest?' replied Chen.

Teng was silent. 'I suggest we draw lots,' said Hahetai. 'Whoever loses, goes.'

'Yes, let's draw lots,' Zhang said eagerly. Chen had wanted to offer himself and then break out with the sisters. But he could not suggest it without arousing their suspicions, so he said: 'Very well. Just the five of us will draw. Let's keep the two young ladies out of this.'

'We're all human,' Gu protested. 'Why should they be left out?'

'I'd rather die than be saved by a girl!' said Hahetai, who consistently showed a more developed sense of honour than his two Chinese friends.

'I think that if we're going to draw lots, we should *all* draw,' said Teng, wanting to lessen the chance of himself being chosen.

They all looked at Zhang, waiting to hear his opinion. Zhang had already worked out his plan, and he knew he could not lose. Moreover, one of the girls was wanted by the Emperor and he fancied the other for himself.

'I will not allow a lady to save my life,' he said proudly.

'All right, then,' said Gu. 'In that case we'll let them off.'

'I'll collect some sticks to use,' said Teng, but Zhang stopped him.

'No,' he said. 'It's too easy to cheat with sticks. We'll use copper coins instead.' He pulled a dozen or so coins from his pocket and selected five. 'Four of these are Emperor Yong Zheng coins and the fifth is from the reign of Emperor Shun Zhi. Please examine them. They are exactly the same size.'

'And whoever picks the Emperor Shun Zhi coin will be the one to lead the wolves away,' Teng added, as he carefully examined the coins.

'Exactly,' said Zhang. 'Put them in your bag for the draw.' Teng did as he was told.

'Now, who will draw first?' asked Zhang. He looked at Gu and saw that his hands were shaking. 'You are afraid,' he said with a smile. 'Life and death are governed by fate. I will go first.' He reached his hand into Teng's bag and pulled out an Emperor Yong Zheng coin.

'Oh, what a pity!' he exclaimed. 'I won't be able to be the hero.' He opened his fist and showed the coin to the other four. The five coins were the same size, but the Shun Zhi coin was about eighty years older than the others and therefore slightly smoother and thinner, although not enough to be immediately obvious.

Chen's turn was next, and to his disappointment he too chose a Yong Zheng coin. Zhang turned to Gu: 'You next, please.' Gu drew his sword and flourished it threateningly.

'This is a trick!' he shouted. 'You already decided that it would be one of us three.'

'What do you mean, a trick?' Zhang demanded.

'They're your coins, and you had first choice. How do we know you haven't marked them in some way?'

Zhang's face went white. 'Then what do you suggest instead?'

'One of those Yong Zheng coins in your pocket is lighter in colour than the others. Put that in with four dark ones. Whoever picks the light one goes.'

Zhang hesitated for a second, then smiled. 'Just as you say. But I fear you will still be the one to feed the wolves.' He surreptitiously bent the light-coloured coin slightly before placing it with the others.

'If neither you nor I lose, I will fight you afterwards,' Gu said threateningly.

'It will be my pleasure,' replied Zhang. He put the five coins in the bag. 'You three gentlemen choose first, then myself, and lastly the Red Flower Helmsman. Is that to your satisfaction?'

The Three Devils did not object. 'Brother Hahetai, you go first,' said Teng.

Just as Hahetai put his hand in the bag, Huo Qingtong shouted out in Mongolian: 'Don't take the bent one!' He started in fright. The first coin he felt was indeed slightly bent. He chose another one and pulled it out: it was dark coloured.

Huo Qingtong had seen Zhang bend the coin. She had warned Hahetai because he seemed the most human of the Three Devils.

Next was Gu's turn. Hahetai told him in the thick, unintelligible dialect of northeast China not to take the bent coin. Gu and Teng both glanced angrily at Zhang and pulled out dark-coloured coins. Chen looked questioningly at Huo Qingtong.

'Don't take the bent one,' said Hasli.

Chen knew Zhang would be sure to take the unbent coin, thereby giving Chen both the light-coloured coin and the chance to escape with the girls. But as Zhang put his hand into Hahetai's bag, Chen saw Gu eyeing Huo Qingtong, and realized they would never let him take the girls with him. Uncertain what to do and with no time left to think, he suddenly blurted out: 'Take the bent one! Leave the other one for me!'

Zhang started in shock and drew his hand back. 'What do you mean, the bent one?' he demanded.

'You bent one of the two coins in the bag. I want the one that's not bent.' Chen put his hand in the bag and pulled out the dark coin. 'You've caused your own funeral,' he said to Zhang with a smile.

Zhang's face darkened and he drew his sword. 'We'd agreed that I would choose first,' he said, and swung the blade at Chen's neck. Chen ducked and thrust his dagger at Zhang's stomach. The two fought closely for a moment. Suddenly, Zhang threw his sword at Huo Qingtong. Chen was afraid she would be too weak to dodge it and raced over to intercept the weapon. But it was just a diversion. As Chen ran towards Huo Qingtong, Zhang jumped over to Hasli and grabbed her.

'Go!' he shouted to Chen, who had stopped in his tracks and was staring dumbly back at Zhang. 'Go now, or I'll throw her to the wolves!' He picked the girl up and swung her about above his head. Chen's heart pounded and his brain whirled in confusion.

'Ride out and lead the wolves away!' Zhang shouted again.

Chen knew that Zhang would do what he threatened. He slowly untied the white horse's reins and mounted up.

'I'll count to three. If you're not out of the circle by then, I'll let her go. One...two...three!' On the count of three, the white horse bounded out of the ring.

Chen landed in the midst of the wolves. He grabbed the first two that attacked him by the scruffs of their necks, then wheeled the horse round, soared back into the ring of fire, and flung the wolves at Zhang.

With two such ferocious animals flying at him, Zhang was forced to drop Hasli in order to protect himself. Chen threw two of his Go-piece missiles at him, scooped Hasli up, then leapt out of the circle of fire once more. Another horse was close behind: Huo Qingtong had taken advantage of the fight to cut the reins of a horse and mount up without the Three Devils noticing.

She and Chen ploughed through the wolf-pack, slashing right and left with their weapons as if they were chopping vegetables, and in a moment the two horses were out in the open and galloping off westwards with the wolf-pack chasing behind. The horses were much faster than the wolves, and before long they had left the pack far behind. But Chen knew the hard part would be staying ahead of these tireless, ravening beasts.

Left Three Right Two

As the three of them rode along, the land about them gradually became more rocky, and a crooked path appeared. It grew dark, and White Jade Peak began to tower over them.

'According to the map, the Secret City was built around the base of the mountain,' said Huo Qingtong. 'It shouldn't be more than three or four miles from here.' The three dismounted and gave their two horses some water. Chen stroked the white horse's mane lovingly knowing that, without it, he would never have been able to rescue Hasli. He also knew he would not have left without her.

They rested for a while until the horses had recovered some of their strength and then continued on, the cries of the wolves already vaguely discernible in the distance. Chen rode the chestnut horse alone and the two sisters rode together on the white horse.

The night was cool and the snow on the peak glistened brilliant white under the moon; it looked almost close enough to touch. The track became rough and treacherous, suddenly splitting into a dozen or so different paths, with no indication of which was the correct one.

'It's not surprising people get lost,' said Chen. Huo Qingtong pulled out the map and examined it in the moonlight.

'It says, "left three right two",' she said.

'What does that mean?'

'It doesn't explain.' In the distance, they could hear the wolves howling in unison.

'It's about midnight,' Huo Qingtong said. 'They must have stopped to howl at the moon. When they've finished, they'll be after us again. We must choose our path and go quickly.'

'There are five paths on the left here,' said Chen pointing. 'The map says left three right two, so let's take the third.'

'If it's a dead end, we won't have time to come back again,' replied Huo Qingtong.

'In that case, the three of us will die together,' said Chen.

At his words, Huo Qingtong felt a sudden warmth in her breast and tears welled into her eyes. She raised her horsewhip and led them down the middle path. It soon narrowed into a stone-walled corridor which had obviously been hacked out of the mountainside by human hand. After a while, they came to another crossroads from which three paths branched out to the right.

'We're saved! We're saved!' Huo Qingtong shouted with joy, and they spurred their horses up the middle path with renewed energy. But the track had not been traversed for many years. In some places, it was completely entangled with grasses which grew over their heads, while in others it was blocked by sand-drifts. They all had to dismount and lead the horses over the obstacles. Chen also heaved rocks up onto the top of the drifts to slow the wolves' pursuit.

Less than half a mile further on, they came upon three more paths forking to the left. Suddenly, Hasli gave a scream and pointed to a pile of white bones at the beginning of one of the paths. Chen dismounted to investigate. They were the remains of a man and a camel.

'He must have been unable to decide which path to take and ended up dying here,' he sighed.

They took the third path. It suddenly rose steeply before them. The cold and darkness became oppressive. A short while later they came upon another skeleton by the side of the path, with jewels glistening amongst the bones.

'He was rich but he couldn't get out,' Huo Qingtong said.

'But at least it means we're on the right path,' replied Chen. 'There must be even more skeletons on the wrong paths.'

'When we leave, none of us must take a single jewel. Is everyone agreed?' said Hasli.

'You're afraid the ghosts won't let us go,' said Chen with a smile.

'Promise me!'

He heard the pleading tone in her voice and hurriedly replied: 'I won't take anything, don't worry.' He suddenly found himself thinking that all the jewels in the world could not equal having the two sisters as companions, and then felt ashamed. What had made him put the two of them together in his mind in this way?

They continued up the twisting path the whole night, and by morning, they and the two horses were exhausted.

'Let's rest a while,' said Huo Qingtong.

'We must find shelter first,' Chen replied firmly. 'Then we can all sleep easily.'

The Secret City

A short way further on, the path opened out into a wide, flat valley of extraordinary beauty. By now the sun was just rising and before them the white mountain soared straight up into the sky from the valley floor. Around its base was a city that had clearly once known great prosperity. But now, the thousands of houses that they could see, although magnificent in scale and design, were all in various stages of ruin and collapse. Not a sound was to be heard, not even the twittering of a single bird. None of them had ever seen a place that was at once so beautiful and so terrible. They stood for a moment, overawed by the crushing silence, hardly daring even to breathe; then Chen urged his horse forward and they entered the city.

The place was extremely dry, so dry that there was virtually no vegetation at all. The contents of the houses seemed to have stayed undisturbed for countless years, and most of the things appeared to still be in good condition. They entered the first house they came to and Hasli noticed a pair of ladies' shoes on the floor. Their colour was still fresh, but as soon as she touched them, they disintegrated into dust. As they continued through the streets, they found skeletons everywhere and swords and other weapons scattered about at random.

'It doesn't look as if the city was really buried in a sandstorm as the story says,' Chen commented.

'No,' Huo Qingtong agreed. 'It looks more likely that there was a big battle and that all the people were killed.'

'But there are so many paths outside the city,' objected Hasli. 'How would the enemy have been able to find their way in?'

'There must have been a traitor,' Huo Qingtong replied.

They went into another house, and she spread the map out on a table and leaned over to examine it. Despite its apparent sturdiness, the table was completely rotten, and it collapsed under the weight of her arms. She picked up the map and studied it for a moment. 'I'm afraid these houses wouldn't withstand an attack by the wolves for very long,' she said. She pointed at a place on the map. 'This is the centre of the city, right at the foot of the mountain. There are a lot of markings around it, which probably means it was a place of importance. If it's a palace or fortress, it's bound to be very sturdily built, so let's go there.'

'Right!' said Chen. They continued on their way, following the path indicated on the map. The roads in the centre of the city were a veritable maze, twisting and turning this way and that in a dizzying fashion. If they had not had the map, they would surely have lost their way.

After an hour or so, they came to the place marked on the map as the city's centre, but were disappointed to find no sign of any palace or fortress. From close up, White Jade Peak looked even more beautiful than from a distance. It was completely white— pure and shining. A jade carver who found even a small piece of this highly valued white jade would never go hungry for the rest of his life. But here was a whole mountain of the precious stone! They looked up at the towering peak and felt spiritually uplifted. Their cares and worries dispersed and they reflected on the wonderful mystery of creation.

But not for long! Amidst the silence, they heard from far off the howls of wolves drifting towards them.

'They're coming!' cried Hasli. 'Do you think the wolves have got a map as well?'

'Their nose is their map,' Chen replied. 'We've left our scent wherever we've gone and all they have to do is follow it.'

Huo Qingtong pointed at the map. 'Look,' she said. 'There is the mountain, but there are all these roads marked inside it.'

'They must be tunnels,' he said.

'Yes. Now how do we find them?' She read the instructions on the map and slowly deciphered them. 'To enter the palace, climb the tall tree and call out "Ailongabasheng" three times towards the sacred mountain.'

'What's Ailongabasheng?' asked Hasli.

'It must be the password,' Huo Qingtong replied. 'But where is the tall tree? And could this really be a magic spell?'

'Of course it could,' said Hasli, who had always believed in spirits and fairies.

'Once, there might have been people in the mountain who would have moved a handle when they heard the password, opening a cave entrance,' said Chen. 'But after so many years, everyone in there is certainly dead.'

The howls of the wolves sounded closer. 'Let's go and hide in one of the houses,' Huo Qingtong suggested.

They turned and ran towards the closest of the buildings. As they ran, Chen tripped on something sticking out of the ground. It was the stump of what must once have been a huge tree. 'This must be the tree!' he called.

Hasli examined the sheer face of the mountain looming above them and pointed. 'That must be the cave mouth there. Look, aren't those footholds?' Chen and Huo Qingtong looked up and saw to their great excitement that there were indeed notches in the rockface.

'I'll go up and have a look,' said Chen. With the dagger in his right hand, he bounded up the cliff. He made it up a few yards, then used his Inner Force kungfu to lodge the dagger in the rockface for an instant and race up further. Finally, he reached the point where the footholds began. The two girls cheered from below, and Chen waved to them before turning his attention to the cliff above. Over the years, the cave mouth had become blocked by sand. Chen grabbed an outcrop of jade rock with one hand and started to shift some of the sand with the dagger. He pulled broken slabs of rock out one after another and let them drop to the ground, and in a short while had made a hole large enough to wriggle through. He crawled in and sat down. Then, pulling his Pearl Strings from his pocket, he undid them all and tied them together, end to end, making them into a rope which he dangled down the cliff face to the girls waiting below.

Huo Qingtong tied the rope round her sister's waist and Chen slowly pulled her up. She screamed as she reached the cave mouth, and Chen quickly helped her inside, saying: 'Don't worry, you've made it.'

Her face was deathly pale. 'Wolves!' she cried.

Chen looked down and saw that seven or eight wolves had already reached the base of the cliff. Huo Qingtong was valiantly fighting them off with her sword. The white horse shook its mane and neighed loudly then galloped off through the streets of the ancient city.

Chen hastily grabbed some large rocks from around the cave mouth and threw them down, forcing some of the wolves to back away. Then he dropped the rope down again. Huo Qingtong was afraid that she would be too weak to hold on long enough, so she transferred the sword to her left hand and tied the rope round her waist as she continued to fight off the wolves.

'Pull!' she yelled. Chen tugged on the rope and she flew into the air just as two wolves threw themselves at her. One of them bit deeply into her boot and refused to let go. Hasli screamed in fright as Huo Qingtong bent over in mid-air and chopped the wolf in half across its belly. The top half of its body accompanied her up to the cave mouth.

Chen helped her inside and tried unsuccessfully to pull the half-wolf off her boot.

'Did it bite into you?' he asked quickly.

'I'm all right,' she replied. She took the dagger from his hand and cut open the wolf's mouth. They could see that both rows of teeth had sunk deep into her boot. A small trickle of blood oozed out of one of the holes in the leather.

'You're wounded!' said Hasli. She helped her sister remove the boot, and ripped a strip of material off her own gown to bandage the wound. Chen turned his head away, not daring to look at her bare feet, considered the most erotic parts of the female anatomy.

When she had finished the bandaging, Hasli looked down at the thousands of wolves now gathered amongst the buildings down below, and shook her finger at them angrily. 'You bad, bad wolves,' she scolded them, 'biting my sister's foot like that! I'll never feel sorry for you again!' Chen and Huo Qingtong smiled.

They turned to look into the cave, but all they could see was pitch-blackness. Huo Qingtong took out her tinder-box and lit it. She immediately jumped in fright: they were sitting on a thin ledge and next to them was a drop of nearly two hundred feet down to the floor of the cave, which looked even lower than the ground at the foot of the mountain.

'There's been no fresh air in here for a long time,' said Chen. 'We can't go down yet.' After a while, when he thought most of the stale air would have dissipated, he said: 'I'll go down first to have a look around.'

'Once we're down it won't be easy to get back up again,' said Huo Qingtong.

Chen smiled. 'If we can't, we can't,' he said. Huo Qingtong blushed and looked away.

He tied one end of the rope round a rocky outcrop and started to slide down into the abyss; but when he reached the end of the rope, he was still a hundred feet from the bottom. Abandoning the rope, he climbed down the cliff face for a way, and then jumped lightly to the floor.

'Throw down the tinder-box!' he shouted, and Huo Qingtong did so. He struck a light and, in its glow, he saw he was in a chamber carved entirely out of white jade furnished with several sets of wooden tables and chairs. Chen looked up and saw the two girls peering down from the ledge, and shouted: 'Come on down!'

'You go down first, sister,' Huo Qingtong said. Hasli took hold of the rope and slid slowly down to its end. She saw Chen standing beneath her with his hands opened wide, so she closed her eyes tightly and let go. Almost immediately, she felt his strong arms catch her and place her lightly on the ground. Huo Qingtong jumped down in the same fashion and as Chen embraced her, she flushed deep red with embarrassment.

By now, the howls of the wolves outside had become faint. Chen looked at the shadows of the three of them dancing on the white jade walls, and then at the two beautiful women beside him. In the glow of the reflected light, they looked even more exquisite than ever. Here they were, in the bowels of a mountain, not knowing what was in store for them. Of all the strange things that had happened to him in his eventful life, this was the strangest.

Chen snapped off a chair leg and lit it with the flame from the tinder-box to make a torch. Hasli exclaimed at the beauty of the chamber they were in and, taking the torch from Chen, began walking about. He broke off a number of chair legs and the three began walking down a long tunnel which turned out to be a cul-de-sac. Chen was wondering how they would get out when, in a corner of the tunnel, he noticed something sparkling in the torchlight. He walked over and saw that it was a gold suit of armour containing a pile of old bones. The suit of armour was exquisitely made, and the three marvelled at the fine workmanship.

'This man must have been a nobleman,' said Hasli. Huo Qingtong noticed that there was a winged camel engraved on the breastplate and added: 'He may even have been a king or a prince. I've heard that in ancient times, only kings could use winged camels as their emblem.'

'It's the same with our dragon in China,' replied Chen. He took the torch from Hasli and began to examine the end wall of the tunnel for some trace of a door or an opening mechanism. Raising the torch, he saw a huge ringed door knocker with a long-handled axe lodged in it.

'There's a door,' Huo Qingtong exclaimed with relief. Chen passed the torch over to her and tried to pull the axe away, but it had rusted onto the iron ring and was immovable. He took out his dagger to scrape away the rust then, with an effort, managed to pull the axe free. He found it very heavy.

'If this was his weapon, then His Highness was a strong man,' he said with a smile.

On closer examination, they found there was an iron ring fastened to all four corners of the stone door. Chen took hold of each of the rings and one by one gave them a mighty tug; but the door did not move even a fraction. He tried pushing it instead. With a series of loud squeaks, it slowly began to swing open. It was at least ten feet thick. Solid stone. In fact, it was more like a huge boulder than a door.

Chen raised the torch high and, with the dagger in his other hand, led the way through. One step inside, and something crunched under his foot. He looked down and saw a pile of bones on the floor. Ahead, there was a narrow tunnel leading off into the darkness, just big enough for a single person to walk along. Skeletons and swords lay scattered all about them.

Huo Qingtong pointed to the back of the great stone door. 'Look,' she said. By the torchlight they saw deeply scored lines that had clearly been scratched out of the surface of the door with swords.

'These people must have been locked in here by the king,' said Chen. He sounded shaken. 'They tried their best to get out, but the door was too thick and the jade rock too solid.'

'Even if they'd had ten blades as sharp as your dagger, they would still never have broken through that door,' replied Huo Qingtong.

'They must have considered every alternative, and finally, as hope faded, they died one by one...'

'Don't! Don't go on,' Hasli pleaded. It all sounded too tragic. She could not bear to hear any more.

'Why did the king—or whoever he was—stand guard on the other side of the door, instead of escaping?' Huo Qingtong asked. 'I can't work that out at all.' She pulled out the map and studied it for a moment. Her face brightened. 'At the end of this tunnel there should be a great hall, and a lot of other rooms,' she said.

Slowly, they walked forward, treading on human bones as they went. They turned two corners, and emerged into a cavernous hall, just as Huo Qingtong had predicted. They stood at the entrance and looked about. The entire floor of the great hall was covered with skeletons and weapons lying about at random, evidence that a furious battle had been fought here.

As they walked into the hall, Chen's dagger suddenly shot out of his hand and fell with a clatter to the floor. At the same instant, the belt supporting Huo Qingtong's sword around her waist snapped, and the scabbard fell heavily to the floor. The three of them started in fright. Huo Qingtong bent down to pick up her sword, but as she did so, the darts in her pocket flew out with a whoosh and dropped to the ground in the same manner.

Chen grabbed the two girls and leapt backwards several paces, steeling himself to ward off any attackers. But there was not a sound from the hall. He wondered what kind of kungfu it was that could snatch their weapons from their hands and even suck Huo Qingtong's darts from her pocket.

'We have come here only to escape wolves and with no other purpose,' Chen shouted into the darkness in the Uighur language. 'Please forgive us if we have offended you in any way.'

There was no answer other than the echo of his own words returning from the far side of the hall. As Huo Qingtong's initial fright receded, she walked on and stooped to pick up her sword. But it was stuck to the floor as if nailed in place. She tried again using all her strength and finally she managed to free it. But a second later, it flew out of her hand again and hit the ground with a clang.

It suddenly dawned on Chen what was happening.

'There must be a magnet under here,' he said.

'What's a magnet?' asked Huo Qingtong.

'Sailors say there is a big mountain in the far north which attracts things made of iron, and makes them point north to south. When they're on the ocean, sailors rely on something called a magnetic compass to find their direction.'

'So you think this is another magnet mountain, and it's attracting our weapons?' asked Huo Qingtong.

'I think so. Let's try it.' He prized his dagger from the ground and placed it and a wooden chair leg flat on his left hand with his right hand on top to hold them in place. When he took his hand away, the dagger flew to the ground but the chair leg remained motionless.

'So as you see, the magnet is powerful,' said Chen, picking up the dagger again and gripping it tightly.

Huo Qingtong walked on a few more steps. 'Come here!' she called. Chen hurried over and saw a skeleton which was still standing. A few tattered pieces of clothing hung on the frame, and its right hand was holding a white-coloured sword which was stuck into the skeleton next to it.

'It's a jade sword!' Huo Qingtong exclaimed. Chen carefully extracted the sword from the grasp of the skeleton, which, with its support gone, collapsed to the floor in a heap.

The jade blade was very sharp, but fragile enough to shatter if it ever clashed with a metal blade. Looking round, they saw there were many other jade weapons of all sizes lying about the hall.

'I know!' Huo Qingtong suddenly said. 'I've understood it! The master of this mountain certainly planned things very carefully.'

'What do you mean?' asked Chen.

'He used this magnet to draw the enemy's weapons away, and then his guards finished them off with the jade swords.'

Hasli pointed to a skeleton wearing a metal breastplate. 'Look! Some of the attackers were wearing armour. They'd have been sucked to the ground. I'll bet they couldn't even get to their feet.'

'But what I don't understand,' Huo Qingtong continued, 'is this: if the guards with the jade weapons killed all the attackers, why did *they* die here as well?'

Chen had also been considering this question. He could think of no explanation.

'Let's go further in and explore,' said Huo Qingtong.

'No,' said Hasli. 'Let's not.'

Huo Qingtong saw the anguished expression on her face and squeezed her arm. 'Don't be afraid. Perhaps there are no skeletons over there.'

They walked to the other side of the hall and looked into a smaller chamber. But the scene there was even more terrible than in the first hall. There were dozens of skeletons piled about the room, most of them standing there as if they were still alive. Some had weapons in their hands, some didn't.

'Don't touch anything!' said Chen. 'There must be some strange reason for them dying like this.' They continued on, and passed through the chamber into another tunnel. After a couple of bends, they came to a small swing door. As they pushed it open, their eyes were assailed by a bright light. Sunlight poured in from a crack in the ceiling hundreds of feet above them into an exquisite jade room which had obviously been carved out of the mountain at this spot to take advantage of the natural lighting.

It was only a single shaft of sunlight, but it had the effect of immediately raising their spirits. The room they found themselves in contained a jade bed, a jade table, jade chairs. Each item was beautifully carved. A skeleton reclined on the jade bed, while in one corner of the room, there were two other skeletons, one large and one small.

Chen extinguished the torch. 'We'll rest here,' he said. They pulled out their dry rations and water and had a small meal.

'I wonder how long the wolves will wait outside the mountain for us?' said Huo Qingtong. 'This has become a contest between us and them. We will have to make our food and water last as long as possible.'

For several days, Chen and the two sisters had not had a moment's rest. Now, in this silent jade room, an immense exhaustion came over them and before very long they fell into a deep, deep sleep.

CHAPTER 8

Verbal Sparring; Dumb Donkey; Mami's Last Testament;
The Saucepan and the Chicken; Duel at Jade Pool; Vengeance;
Warm Jade

Verbal Sparring

Zhang and the Three Devils had watched the wolves swarm after
Helmsman Chen and the two Uighur sisters with great relief,
although they felt a twinge of regret at the thought of two such
beautiful girls being devoured by the animals. The four men sat
down to rest for a while, then roasted and ate one of the dead
wolves left behind. Gu noticed that the supply of branches was
almost exhausted. He was too lazy to go and get more, and instead
threw piles of wolf's dung onto the fire to stoke up the flames.
Before long, a column of thick, black smoke began rising up into
the sky.

Just as they had eaten their fill of wolf meat, they noticed a
dust-cloud approaching from the east. Assuming it to be another
wolf-pack, they hurriedly jumped up and ran for the horses. Only
two horses were left, both of which had been brought by the Three
Devils. When Zhang stretched out his hand to take the reins of one
of the mounts, Hahetai lunged in front of him and grabbed them
first, shouting: 'What do you think you're doing?'

Zhang was about to attack him when he saw Teng and Gu
with weapons in their hands closing in. 'What are you getting so
excited about?' he protested. 'That dust-cloud has got nothing to
do with wolves. It's something quite different.'

The Three Devils turned to look and, as they did so, Zhang
vaulted onto the horse's back. Only then did he see that what he
had said as a lie was in fact the truth: the dust-cloud arose from a
large herd of camels and goats. He galloped off towards the herd,
shouting: 'I'll go and have a look!'

After riding only a short way, he saw a rider coming towards
him. The rider, an old man dressed in grey, raced forward and then
reined in his mount at regular intervals with a tug on the reins.
Zhang marvelled at his display of horsemanship.

The rider could see that Zhang was wearing a somewhat tattered Manchu uniform.

'What happened to the wolves?' he asked in Chinese. Zhang pointed west.

By this time, the herd of camels and goats was upon them and Zhang noticed a bald-headed, red-faced old man and a white-haired old woman riding hard towards him in the midst of the dust and noise and confusion. He was just about to ask who they were when the Three Devils came walking over and bowed respectfully before the old man in grey.

'We are indeed most honoured to meet you again, sir,' Teng said obsequiously. 'How fares it with you?'

The old man grunted and mumbled: 'Nothing to complain about.' He was in fact the Strange Knight of the Heavenly Pool, Master Yuan.

Zhang knew nothing of this old man, but he noted the respect with which the Three Devils treated him. Yuan examined the four of them for a moment, then said: 'We are off to catch the wolves. You will all come with me.'

They were completely taken aback by this and wondered for a moment if he was insane. The Three Devils knew his kungfu was formidable and did not dare to refuse. But Zhang gave a 'humph' of protest and turned to leave, saying: 'Sorry, I want to live a few more years. I won't be able to accompany you.'

Bald Vulture grabbed furiously at Zhang's wrist, crying: 'So you refuse to heed Master Yuan's orders! Do you wish to die?'

Zhang deflected his hand deftly with the move known as Dividing the Clouds and Moon, and the two fought closely for a while, neither gaining the upper hand. Then they leapt apart, both surprised to have come upon such a skilled practitioner of the Martial Arts in the middle of the desert.

'What is your name, friend?' shouted Zhang.

'What makes you think *you* can call me friend? Will you obey Master Yuan?'

Zhang knew his opponent was as good a fighter as himself, and yet he still respectfully referred to the other old man as Master Yuan. This indicated that Yuan's kungfu was probably superior to both of them. He wondered who this Master Yuan could be. 'What is your full name, sir?' he asked Yuan. 'If you are my superior, I will naturally respect your orders.'

'Ha! So you think you can start asking me questions, do you?' Master Yuan exclaimed. 'I do the questioning here. Tell me: just now, you used the move Dividing the Clouds and Moon. But what would you have done if I had replied with Descending the Mountain to Kill the Tiger on your left while going for your House of the Spirit Vital Point on your right?'

Zhang thought for a second. 'I would have kicked out with an Arrow Shooting the Hawk, and grabbed your wrist.'

'You obviously belong to the Wudang School,' Yuan replied, to Zhang's evident surprise. 'Once when I was in Hubei, I sparred with Master Ma Zhen.' Zhang went deathly pale. 'So: if I used a Secret Hand move to counter your attempt to seize my wrist, and then struck at your face with my left hand, what would you do? Master Ma Zhen was defeated by this move. Let's see if you can work it out.'

Zhang thought deeply for a while. 'If you were fast, I would naturally be unable to avoid the blow,' he said finally. 'Instead I could aim a Mandarin Duck kick at your left ribs, and force you to retract your hand and defend yourself.'

Yuan laughed. 'Not bad. Of all the fighters in the Wudang School, you are one of the best.'

'Then I would aim at your Ultimate Profundity point,' Zhang continued.

'Good! A master always attacks if he can. But I would then move into the Marrying Maiden position and attack your lower body.'

'I would then retreat to the Conflict position and strike out for your Heavenly Spring point.'

Gu and Hahetai listened in bewilderment to this high-flown Martial Arts sparring match. Hahetai gave Teng's gown a tug. 'What's this secret language they're speaking in?' he whispered.

'It's not a secret language. They're using two lists of terms: one is made up of the names of the Sixty-Four Positions, based on the Sixty-Four Hexagrams of the *Book of Changes*; the other is made up of the names for moves, based on some of the Vital Points on the human body,' Teng replied.

'I advance to the Darkening of the Light position and attack with a Gate of Anticipation move,' Yuan said.

'I retreat to the Inner Truth position and counter with a Phoenix Eye move,' replied Zhang.

'I advance to the Before Completion position and go for your Circular Jump point.'

The pressure was beginning to show on Zhang's face, and there was a pause before he answered: 'I retreat first to the Thunder position and then to the Return position.'

'How come he keeps retreating?' whispered Hahetai, but Teng waved him to silence. The verbal sparring continued, Yuan smiling and obviously at ease, Zhang beginning to sweat and sometimes taking a long time to come up with a response. The Three Devils knew that in a real fight, he would have had no time for such thinking, and would have been beaten long before.

After a few more moves, Zhang said: 'I attack with a Taming Power of the Small move and then strike at your wrist.'

'That's not good enough,' Yuan replied. 'You lose.'

'Please explain,' said Zhang.

'If you don't believe me, allow me to give you a demonstration. Watch out!' Yuan kicked up at Zhang's knees with his right leg.

Zhang jumped away shouting, 'If you touch me—'; but before he could finish, Yuan's right hand had shot out and touched a Vital Point on his chest. Zhang felt a surge of pain and immediately began to cough uncontrollably.

Yuan smiled at him. 'Well?' he asked.

The others were amazed by this nonchalant display of such advanced kungfu skill. Fire Hand Zhang, looking deathly pale, did not dare to continue his intransigence. 'I will do as you say, Master Yuan,' he replied.

'But your kungfu is of the first rank,' said Bald Vulture. 'What is your name?'

'My surname is Zhang, my given name Zhaozhong.'

'Ah, so you are the Fire Hand Judge,' Bald Vulture replied. Then, to Master Yuan, he said: 'This man is a brother-in-arms of Master Ma Zhen.'

The Strange Knight grunted. 'He's a better fighter than his brother-in-arms. Let's go.' He galloped off.

There were several horses in amongst the camels and goats. Once the Devils and Zhang had chosen another couple of horses and all four men were mounted, they began helping to herd the animals after Master Yuan. As they galloped along, Zhang said to Bald Vulture: 'How do you intend to catch all these wolves?'

'Just do as Master Yuan says,' Bald Vulture replied. 'What's so terrifying about a few little wolves?' Lady Guan, riding nearby, smiled to hear her husband boasting like this to Fire Hand Zhang.

They rode on. Suddenly Yuan wheeled his horse round and shouted: 'The wolf droppings are very fresh. The pack passed here not long ago. From the look of it, we'll catch up with them in another ten miles or so. We'll ride another five miles and then all pick fresh horses. When we catch up with the wolf-pack, I'll lead the way. The six of you divide up, three on each side, to make sure the animals don't escape, otherwise the pack will split up.' Just as Teng was about to ask a question, Yuan wheeled round again and galloped off.

The wolf droppings around them became increasingly moist as they galloped forward.

'The pack must be just ahead,' said Lady Guan. 'Our camels and horses make such a noise, it's surprising they haven't turned back to attack us already.'

'Yes, it is strange,' her husband replied. A couple of miles further on, the topography began to change and they saw a cluster of hills ahead with a high white mountain in their midst. The Twin Eagles had long lived in the desert, and had heard many stories about this beautiful mountain, and how it sparkled in the bright sunshine.

'The wolves must have gone into the maze!' Yuan shouted. 'Full speed ahead!' They raised their horsewhips and began lashing the camels, goats, and horses. A great roar went up as the beasts snorted and neighed in pain and anger. Before long, a large grey wolf came running towards them from the hills. Yuan whirled his long whip about his head and cracked it sharply in the air. Then with a shout, he wheeled his horse round and galloped off south, with the Twin Eagles, Zhang, and the Three Devils driving the herd after him. After a couple of miles, the howls of the wolf-pack could be heard from behind. Bald Vulture glanced back and saw the grey tide moving towards them across the desert. He spurred his horse on and caught up with the others. Zhang, Gu, and Teng appeared to be having difficulty keeping their terror under control, but Hahetai the Mongol was shouting and whistling crazily, driving the animals on and intercepting strays. He was a herdsman by birth and he made sure not one was lost.

The wolves were ferocious and persistent, but they lacked stamina. After four or five miles, they had already been left far behind, and another five miles further on, Yuan shouted: 'Let's rest for a while!' They all dismounted and ate some food while Hahetai herded the animals together. When the wolves began to close in, they started off again. They continued south in this way, stopping occasionally to rest. Later in the day, two Uighur riders came galloping towards them.

'Master Yuan,' they shouted. 'Did it work?'

'They're coming, they're coming!' he shouted back. 'Tell everyone to get ready.' The riders turned and galloped back.

A short while later, they spied a huge circular fort-like wall rising up out of the desert, at least forty feet in height, with only one narrow entrance. Yuan rode through the opening with the herd of animals close behind him. The Twin Eagles and the others drove them through the gate and then veered off to either side just as the first of the wolves arrived. The huge wolf-pack charged into the enclosure and the wolves threw themselves at the animals. When the last wolf was inside, a horn sounded and several hundred Uighurs sprang from trenches on either side of the entrance, each man carrying a bag of sand on his shoulders. They raced for the opening and, in a moment, the gap was completely blocked.

As they clapped and cheered, Fire Hand Zhang wondered what had happened to old Master Yuan inside the fort. He saw thirty or forty Uighurs standing on top of the wall, and jumping off his horse, ran up a flight of steps, reaching the top just in time to see Yuan being pulled up by a rope. He glanced down into the pit and shuddered with terror: down below were the hundreds of camels, goats, and horses, and thousands upon thousands of hungry wolves sinking their teeth into them and tearing them apart. The noise was terrifying, and streams of blood flowed freely about the floor of the pit. The fort was built with bricks of sand; it was more than a thousand feet in circumference, and its walls were coated with a smooth layer of mud to make them unscalable. Yuan stood with the Twin Eagles on the top of the wall laughing heartily, obviously very pleased with himself.

'This wolf-pack has been terrorizing the Heaven Mountains range for hundreds of years, but you have now destroyed it, Master Yuan,' said Bald Vulture. 'You have done the people a great service.'

'It needed everyone to work together. I could never have done it by myself,' he replied. 'It took three thousand men half a year to complete the fort. You have also been a great help today.'

'I'm afraid it will be a long time before all these wolves finally die of hunger,' said Lady Guan.

'Of course, especially after they've feasted on all those animals down there.'

A cheer arose from the crowd of Uighurs below and several of their leaders came up to express their thanks to Yuan and the others. They brought goat meat and koumiss for them to eat and drink.

'Huo Qingtong defeated the Manchus at Black River, and we have defeated the wolves here,' said one of the leaders. 'Now that the wolves have been caught, we can go and look for her and—' He stopped as he spotted Fire Hand Zhang, wearing the uniform of a Manchu officer, standing close by.

'Master Yuan, I have something important to discuss with you,' Bald Vulture said later. 'Please don't take offence.'

'Ha! I see you've learned some manners in your old age,' Yuan replied drily, surprised by his formality.

'It's about your disciple. He's got no morals, he needs to be severely disciplined.'

Yuan looked startled. 'Who are you talking about? Chen Jialuo?'

'Yes.' Bald Vulture told him how Chen had first won Huo Qingtong's heart, and then shifted his affections to her sister.

'I know him to have a loyal and devoted heart,' Yuan said firmly. 'He would never do such a thing.'

'We have seen it with our own eyes,' said Lady Guan, and related how they had met Chen and Hasli in the desert. Yuan stared at them for a moment, then his anger exploded.

'I agreed to be his foster father!' he exclaimed. 'I raised him from when he was small, and now this happens. How can I ever face Old Helmsman Yu in the other world? We must go and find Chen and question him about this face to face.' He leapt off the wall and mounted his horse: 'Let's go!' he roared, and galloped off, with the Twin Eagles following behind.

Dumb Donkey

Fire Hand Zhang's spirits rose as he saw his enemies departing. The Emperor had sent him on this secret mission to find Helmsman Chen and the Uighur girl Hasli. Before he returned to the Court, he wanted to know for sure if they had both been eaten by wolves. If they had, there was nothing more to be done. But if they were still alive, he would have to capture them. Helmsman Chen's kungfu, he knew, was only marginally inferior to his own, and if Huo Qingtong joined forces with Chen against him, he would be sure to lose. This was why he had decided to invite the Three Devils along as well. He gave Gu's sleeve a tug and the two walked off a few paces together.

'Do you miss that beauty?' he whispered.

Gu thought Zhang was making fun of him. 'What's it to you?' he replied angrily.

'I'll tell you what. I have a score to settle with that fellow Chen, and I want to go and make sure he's well and truly dead. Come with me. If she's still alive, the girl is yours.'

Gu hesitated. 'They've probably already both been eaten by wolves,' he said slowly. 'And anyway, I don't know if Teng would be willing to go.'

'If they've been eaten, then you're out of luck,' Zhang replied. 'But you never know. As for your friend Teng, I'll go and talk to him.'

He then went over to Teng and said: 'I'm going to look for that fellow Chen to settle accounts with him. If you'll help me, that dagger of his is yours.'

What student of the Martial Arts would not have coveted such a precious weapon? Even supposing Chen *were* already inside a wolf's belly, Teng thought to himself, the dagger wouldn't be! He agreed immediately. 'Let's go!' he shouted to Hahetai, who was standing on the wall of the fort, animatedly discussing the wolf-pack with the Uighurs. 'Where are we going *to*?' Hahetai shouted back.

'To look for Chen and the others. If their bodies haven't been completely devoured, we can give them a proper burial. We owe them that much!'

Hahetai respected Chen, and he immediately agreed. The four obtained some food and water from the Uighurs, then mounted up and headed back the way they had come, northwards.

At about midnight, Teng protested that he wanted to stop for the night, but Zhang and Gu insisted that they keep going. The moon was high in the sky, and by its silver rays the desert scene around them looked just like a painting. Suddenly, a figure darted from the side of the track and into a stone grave nearby.

'Who goes there?' shouted Zhang, reining in his horse.

A moment passed, and then the laughing turbaned head of a bearded Uighur appeared from a hole between the flagstones. 'I am the corpse of this grave,' he said. To the great surprise of Zhang and the others, he spoke to them in Chinese.

'What are you doing out here if you're a corpse?' Gu shouted.

'Just having a little stroll.'

'Corpses don't go for strolls!' cried Gu angrily.

'Yes, yes, you're right. I'm wrong. So sorry.' The head nodded and disappeared back into the hole.

Hahetai burst out laughing, but Gu was furious. He dismounted and stuck his hand into the grave, wanting to pull the cheeky Uighur out. But he felt about inside without finding anything.

'Don't take any notice of him,' said Zhang. 'Let's be on our way again.'

As the four men turned their horses round, they spotted a small, skinny donkey by the side of the grave, chomping grass.

'I'm sick to death of dry rations,' said Gu gleefully. 'A bit of roast donkey meat would go down nicely.' He jumped off his horse again and was about to take hold of the donkey's reins when he noticed the animal had no tail.

'Someone seems to have cut off the donkey's tail and eaten it already,' he observed with a smile.

There was a whooshing sound and suddenly the bearded Uighur appeared on the donkey's back. He laughed and pulled a donkey's tail from his pocket and waved it about. 'My donkey's tail got covered in mud today, which didn't look very nice, so I cut it off,' he said.

Zhang looked at the man's great bushy beard and generally crazy appearance and wondered who on earth he was. He raised his horsewhip and rode towards the donkey, striking out at the Uighur's shoulder as he passed. The Uighur dodged to one side, and Zhang suddenly found himself holding the donkey's tail in his own hand. It was indeed covered in mud. He also noticed a certain coolness on his head. His officer's cap had disappeared.

'So you're a Manchu officer,' said the Uighur, twirling the cap about on his finger. 'You've come to attack us, I suppose. This is a very pretty cap of yours.'

Startled and angry, Zhang threw the donkey's tail at the Uighur, who caught it easily. Zhang leapt off his horse and faced him. 'Who are you?' he shouted. 'Come and fight!'

The Uighur now placed Zhang's cap on the donkey's head and clapped his hands in delight. 'A dumb donkey wearing an officer's hat!' he exclaimed. He squeezed his thighs and the donkey trotted off. Zhang began to run after him, but stopped as a projectile came hurtling towards him. He caught the cold, glittering object deftly in his hand, and with a surge of fury recognized it as the sapphire off the front of his own cap. By now, the donkey was already a long way ahead, but he picked a stone off the ground and hurled it at the Uighur's back. The Uighur made no effort to avoid it, and Zhang was delighted, certain that this time he had him. There was a loud clang as the stone struck something metallic. The Uighur cried out in despair: 'Oh no! He's killed my saucepan! It's dead for certain!'

The four men looked at each other dumbfounded as the Uighur and his donkey disappeared into the distance.

'Was that a man or a demon?' Zhang asked finally. The Three Devils silently shook their heads. 'Come on, let's go. This place is evil beyond belief.'

They galloped off, and early the next morning they arrived outside the Secret City. The paths (as we have already seen) were many and confusing, but the trail of wolf droppings was a perfect guide which brought them unerringly to the base of White Jade Peak. Looking up, they saw the cave mouth that Chen had excavated.

Mami's Last Testament

Having slept for several hours in the jade room carved out of the mountain, Helmsman Chen woke towards midnight, his strength revived. By the light of a moonbeam that shone down through a crack in the roof of the cave, he could see Huo Qingtong and Hasli leaning against one another on one of the jade seats, fast asleep. In the silence, he heard their breathing and inhaled the delicious fragrance, even more beautiful than that of fresh flowers or musk, emanating from the younger sister.

He wondered again what the wolves outside were doing and whether the three of them would ever be able to escape. And if they did, would his brother the Emperor keep his word and overthrow the Manchus?

'Which one of them do I really love?' Over the past few days, this was the thought that had been constantly on his mind. 'Which one of them really loves me? If I were to die, Hasli would not be able to go on living. Huo Qingtong would. But that doesn't mean Hasli loves me more.'

The moonbeam slowly shifted onto Huo Qingtong's face.

'Hasli and I have declared our love for each other. But although Huo Qingtong has never spoken a word, her feelings towards me are clear,' he thought. 'And why did I come so far to give her a message if it was not because I loved her? My mission is to restore the Dragon Throne to the Chinese people. That will involve immense trials and tribulations. Huo Qingtong is a superb strategist, better even than Mastermind Xu. Her assistance would be invaluable.' He stopped himself, ashamed of his own thoughts. Did he just want her because she might be useful to the cause?

'Ah, Chen Jialuo,' he whispered under his breath. 'Are you really so calculating?'

Time passed and the moonbeam moved across onto Hasli.

'With her, life would be pure happiness,' he thought. 'Nothing but happiness.'

His eyes opened wide and he stared up at the crack of light in the rock high above them for a long, long time. Slowly, the moonlight faded and the first rays of the morning sun began to fill the room with the pure light of dawn. With a yawn, Hasli woke. She looked over at him through half-open eyes and smiled, her face like a newly opened flower.

Suddenly she sat bolt upright. 'Listen!' she whispered.

Footsteps could be heard distantly from the tunnel, gradually moving closer. In the silence of these old caverns, each step could be heard clearly. Their flesh crept as they listened. Chen shook Huo Qingtong's arm to wake her and the three of them ran quickly back down the tunnel. When they reached the main chamber, Chen picked up three jade swords and gave one to each of the two sisters. 'Jade wards off evil,' he whispered.

By now, the footsteps were audible just outside the chamber. The three of them hid in a corner near the entrance, not daring to move. They saw the flickering light of torches and four men walked in. The two in front they instantly recognized as Fire Hand

Zhang and Gu. There was a series of clanging sounds as the magnetic force exerted its power and the weapons of the intruders flew out of their hands to the ground. Helmsman Chen knew this was an opportunity not to be missed and, as the four of them stood staring at the floor in dumb surprise, he gave a shout and leapt out, knocking their torches to the ground and plunging the chamber into complete darkness. Zhang and the Three Devils turned and raced back down the tunnel. They heard a dull thud followed by a sharp curse as one of them bumped into the wall. The footsteps gradually receded.

Suddenly, Huo Qingtong gave a scream of panic. 'Oh no! Quick! After them!'

Chen immediately realized what she had in mind and raced out of the chamber into the tunnel. But before he reached the end, he heard a creaking sound followed by a heavy bang, and he knew the stone door was closed. Huo Qingtong and Hasli ran up behind him. He felt around for a piece of wood and lit it, then looked again at the scarred surface of the stone door, the relic of the death struggle of the skeletons around them.

'We're finished!' Huo Qingtong said, despairingly.

Hasli held her hand tightly. 'Sister, don't be afraid!'

Chen forced a smile. 'It would be strange if we three died here.'

For some reason, he felt a sense of relief wash over him. It was as if a great weight had been taken from his shoulders. He picked a skull off the ground and began speaking to it: 'Well, my friend, it seems you have three new companions.' Hasli gasped in horror, and then laughed out loud.

Huo Qingtong looked at them both. 'Let's go back to the Jade Room,' she said after a while. 'We must calm down and think things through.'

They walked back the way they had come. Huo Qingtong pulled out the map once more and pored over it, desperately searching for a way out. Helmsman Chen knew that if they were to escape it was more likely to be because of outside help or because Fire Hand Zhang returned to look for them. But how could rescuers ever hope to find them? And Zhang, after the fright he had just received, was unlikely to dare to come back.

'I feel like singing a song,' announced Hasli.

'Please do,' replied Chen.

She sang for a while then stopped, concerned about Huo Qingtong who was still staring hard at the map, her head resting on her hands.

'Sister, you should rest for a while,' said Hasli. She stood up, and went over to the jade bed. This time it was her turn to begin speaking to the skeleton lying on it: 'Excuse me, I wonder if you could move over a bit? My sister needs to lie down and rest.' She carefully pushed the bones into a pile in a corner of the bed. 'Oh!' She picked something up. 'What's this?'

Helmsman Chen and Huo Qingtong looked up and saw that she was holding what appeared to be a blackened parchment scroll of great antiquity. In the sunlight, it was just possible to see that it was covered in writing, all in an ancient Uighur script. Huo Qingtong glanced through it, and pointed at the skeleton on the bed.

'It was written by this girl with her own blood just before she died. Her name was Mami,' she said.

'Mami?' asked Chen.

'It means "beautiful". I'm sure she *was* very beautiful when she still had flesh on her bones.' Huo Qingtong put down the scroll and went back to examining the map.

'Does the map show some other way out of here?' Chen asked.

'There appears to be a secret tunnel somewhere, but I can't work out where.'

Chen sighed. 'Would you read out Miss Mami's last words to me?' he asked Hasli. She nodded, and began to quietly recite:

'The people in the city, thousands upon thousands of them, are all dead. The Guardians of the Mountain and the Warriors of Islam are all dead. My Ali has gone to meet Allah, and his Mami will be going soon too. I will write our story out here, so that the children of Allah will know that, victorious or defeated, our Warriors of Islam fight to the end, and never surrender!'

'So this lady was not only beautiful, but courageous too,' commented Chen.

Hasli continued to read:

'Baojunlonga oppressed us for forty years. In those forty years, he forced thousands of his subjects to build this Secret City and to carve out the chambers and halls within the Sacred Mountain. Then he killed them all. After he died, his son Sanglaba proved to be even more cruel. Of every ten goats raised by the Uighur people during the year, four had to be given to him; of every five camels, he claimed two. We all became poorer and poorer each year. Any beautiful daughters from Uighur families were taken into the city and, once there, not one of them ever came out alive.

'We are the brave children of Islam. We could not tolerate this oppression, we could not allow these pagans to go unpunished! Over a period of twenty years, our warriors attacked the city five times. But each time they were defeated, because they could not find their way through the maze. On two occasions, they fought through into the Sacred Mountain, but Sanglaba used some devilry to take their weapons from them, and they were all killed by his guards.'

'That's the magnet,' said Chen. Hasli nodded and continued reading aloud from the parchment scroll:

'In the year that I turned eighteen, my mother and father were killed by Sanglaba's men and my elder brother became the chief of our tribe. That spring, I met Ali. He was a hero of the tribe. He had killed three tigers, and wolf-packs scattered when they saw him. He could beat ten ordinary men, no, a hundred. His eyes were as soft as those of a deer and his body was as beautiful as a fresh flower, but he had the strength of a desert hurricane—'

'The lady is exaggerating, I think,' Chen said with a smile.

'Why do you say that?' asked Hasli solemnly. 'Are there not such people in the world?'

She continued reading: 'One day, Ali came to our tent to talk to my brother about launching another attack on the Sacred City. He had obtained a copy of a book about Chinese kungfu and had studied it for a year. He said he now understood the rudiments of the Martial Arts, and was convinced that even without weapons, they could kill Sanglaba's men. He took five hundred fighters and taught them what he knew, and they practised for another year. By then, I was already Ali's. I was his from the moment I first saw him. He was my heart, my blood, my very self. He told me that as soon as he saw me, he knew that this time we would win. But although they had mastered kungfu, they still did not know the way through the maze of the city, much less the secrets of the Sacred Mountain. Ali and my brother talked for ten days and nights, but could find no solution.

'Finally, I said to them: "Let *me* go." They understood my meaning. Ali was a brave warrior but he began to cry. I took a hundred goats and went to graze them outside the city. On the fourth day, Sanglaba's men seized me and took me to him. I cried for three days and three nights before letting him have his way. He liked me very much and gave me everything I wanted.

'At first Sanglaba would not let me take so much as one step outside. But he grew to like me more and more. I thought about our people every day and of how I used to sing while I tended goats on the grasslands: that was real happiness. But most of all I thought about Ali. Sanglaba saw me becoming more thin and haggard each day and asked me what I wanted. I said I wanted to go out and wander round everywhere. He flew into a great rage and hit me, so for seven days and nights I didn't smile or say a word to him. On the eighth day, he took me out, and after that on every third day. At first, we only travelled about the city, but later we went even to the very entrance of the maze. I memorized clearly every single street and path until I could have found my way through the maze blindfold.

'This took almost a year. I knew my brother and Ali would be getting impatient, but I still did not know the secrets of the Sacred Mountain. Soon after, I became pregnant with Sanglaba's child. He was delighted of course, but I just cried and cried every day in loathing of him and of myself. He asked me what I wanted, and I said: "You have made me pregnant but you don't love me at all."

'"*I don't love you?*" he replied. "There is nothing I would not give you! Do you want red coral from the bottom of the sea, or sapphires from the south? They are yours."

'"I have heard that you have a jade pool which makes beautiful people who wash in it even more beautiful and ugly people even uglier," I said.

'His face drained of all colour and in a shaky voice, he asked me where I had heard this. I told him a fairy had whispered it to me in a dream, but in fact I had heard about the pool from the servant girls who said that Sanglaba had never let anyone see it.

'"You can go and wash there," he said, "but you must know something: whoever sees the pool must have their tongue cut out afterwards to prevent the secret being revealed. That is a rule decided by the ancestors." He begged me not to go, but I insisted. I said: "You must think I am very ugly and do not wish me to become even uglier." In the end he took me there.

'I took a small knife with me, planning to stab him to death by the pool, since it was the only place in the palace where there were no guards. But the knife was snatched away by some magic under the floor of the great hall. After I had bathed in the Jade Pool, I don't know if I really became more beautiful or not, but he certainly seemed to love me more than ever. He still cut out my tongue, because he was afraid I would reveal the secret. Now I knew everything, but had no way of telling my brother and Ali.

'Every day and every night, I prayed to Allah, and Allah finally heard the cries of his poor daughter. He gave me wisdom. Sanglaba had a small dagger which he kept on his person at all times. The dagger had two scabbards, and the inner scabbard was formed exactly like the blade of a knife. I asked him for it, then I drew a map of the city, with all the paths and tunnels in it, sealed it inside a ball of wax, and placed it inside the inner scabbard. In the third month after the birth of the child, he took me out hunting. When no one was looking, I threw the dagger into Tengbo Lake. When we returned to the palace, I released several eagles with "Tengbo Lake" written on pieces of paper tied to their legs.'

Huo Qingtong put down the map and started listening intently to her sister's recitation of the ancient scroll.

'Several of the eagles were shot down by Sanglaba's men, but I knew that at least one or two would be caught by people of our tribe and that my brother and Ali would go to Tengbo Lake and search the waters of the lake thoroughly. They would find the knife and know the way through the city.

'Ah! I never thought it possible that they would find the dagger, but not discover its secret! I never thought that they would fail to see that there was a scabbard within the scabbard! My brother and Ali decided that the dagger must be a call for them to attack. So they attacked. Most of the warriors lost their way in the maze. My brother, who was stronger than two camels, died in this way. Ali and some of the others caught one of Sanglaba's men and forced him to lead them in their attack on the Sacred Mountain. In the Great Hall, Sanglaba's men fell on them with their jade weapons. But Ali and his warriors had learned their kungfu lessons well and though unarmed they held their own, even if in the end many of them lost their lives. Seeing his guards being slaughtered and Ali pressing in closer all the time, Sanglaba ran into the Jade Room. He wanted me to escape with him to the Jade Pool, and then run away with him altogether—'

Huo Qingtong jumped to her feet. 'The Jade Pool!' she exclaimed. 'That's it!'

'Suddenly Ali ran in, and I flung myself into his arms. We embraced, and he called me many beautiful things. I had no tongue and could not answer him, but he understood the cry of my heart. Then that despicable Sanglaba, ten thousand times more evil than a thousand devils, hacked him down with an axe from behind—'

Hasli screamed and threw the scroll back onto the bed, an expression of horror on her face. Her sister gently patted her shoulder, then picked up the scroll herself and continued to read it out loud:

'—with an axe from behind. He split my Ali's head in two. His blood spurted out all over my body. Sanglaba picked our child up off the bed, placed it in my hands and shouted: "We must leave quickly!" I raised the baby high above my head and threw it to the ground with all my strength. The baby died bathed in Ali's blood. Sanglaba was deeply shocked to see me killing his son. He raised his golden axe, and I bowed my head, offering my neck to him. But then he heaved a great sigh and rushed back out into the Great Hall.

'Ali has gone to Allah's side and I will soon follow him. Our warriors are many and, with all his soldiers dead, Sanglaba will certainly not survive. He will never again be able to oppress us followers of Islam. I myself killed his only son, so we will be free of oppression from his descendants, because he has none. In the future, our people will be able to live peacefully in the desert and on the grasslands, our young girls will be able to lie in their lovers' arms and sing. My brother, Ali, myself, we are all dead, but we conquered the tyrants. Even if their fortress had been stronger than it is, we would still have broken through eventually. May Allah, the True God, protect our people.'

Huo Qingtong slowly rolled up the ancient scroll. The three of them sat for a long time without saying a word, deeply moved by Mami's tale of courage and virtue. Finally Hasli, her eyes full of tears, sighed.

'To relieve the oppression of her people,' she said, 'she was willing to leave her loved ones, to have her tongue cut out, and even to kill her own child.'

Chen thought with shame of his own conduct, which seemed so selfish by comparison. Faced with the task of recovering China for the Chinese people, he had thought only of his own affairs of the heart. Hasli noticed the sudden change in his expression. She pulled out her handkerchief and went over to wipe the beads of sweat from his brow, but Chen pushed her away impatiently. She stepped back, startled by his hostile behaviour, and Chen's heart softened towards her. Taking the handkerchief from her, he made up his mind that while the great endeavour of the Restoration remained unfinished he would pay no further attention to his romantic affairs, and would treat both sisters purely as friends, as his own sisters.

Huo Qingtong, meanwhile, was once more poring over the map and pondering phrases in the ancient scroll.

'It says here that Sanglaba came to this Jade Room and wanted her to escape with him to the Jade Pool,' she murmured. 'But this room is a dead end… Afterwards, he returned the way he had come. He must have been extraordinarily strong. The Muslim warriors failed to stop him and he forced his way through to the stone door and locked them all inside, condemning them to death. But the map clearly indicates another tunnel leading to the pool…'

'Then it must be in this room,' Chen replied. He lit another torch and began to examine the walls closely for cracks, while Huo Qingtong looked at the jade bed. Chen remembered how Rolling Thunder Wen had been captured at Iron Ball Manor and wondered if the tunnel could possibly be under the table. He placed his hands beneath the round tabletop and tried to lift it, but it did not budge.

'There's something strange about this table,' he said, with renewed interest. Huo Qingtong brought the torch over to give him more light.

'Oh, look!' exclaimed Hasli. 'There's a design carved on the surface.' They looked closer and saw that it was a herd of winged camels. They had not noticed it before because the carving was in very low relief. But strangely, the heads and bodies of the camels were not joined. They were more than a foot away from each other. The heads were carved on one circular section of the table, the bodies on another, and two sections were not properly aligned. On an impulse, Hasli grasped the table edge and pulled it from left to right in an attempt to line up the heads and bodies. It did indeed move an inch or so. Chen and Huo Qingtong joined her and they slowly moved the rim round until the camels were whole again. Just as the carving was complete, there was a grinding sound and a panel beside the bed slid back to reveal a row of steps leading downwards. The three of them gave a cry of joy.

Chen led the way down, torch in hand. The passage twisted and turned for a while and then ran straight for more than a hundred feet. Then they rounded a corner, and burst out into the daylight. Looking around them, they saw that they were in a small natural hollow surrounded by high mountains. In the centre was a circular pool, filled with water of a luminous green jade colour. It was a scene of magical beauty.

'The scroll said that if beautiful people washed in the pool they would become even more beautiful,' Huo Qingtong said to her sister with a smile. 'You should go and wash.'

Hasli blushed. 'You are older than I am, you go first,' she replied.

'But that will only make me more ugly,' Huo Qingtong protested. 'Are you going to wash or not?' Hasli shook her head.

Huo Qingtong walked to the edge of the pool and put her hands in the water: it was intensely cold. She cupped her hands and scooped up some water and saw that it was very clear: the water appeared green only because it reflected the colour of the green jade. She took a sip and found it extraordinarily cool and fresh-tasting. They all drank their fill. The white peak towering above them was reflected in the pool. Hasli lazily moved her hand about in the water, unwilling to leave such an enchanting place.

'What we must do now is think of a way to avoid those four devils outside,' said Huo Qingtong.

'First, let's bring Mami's remains out and bury them beside the pool,' Chen suggested.

Hasli clapped her hands in delight. 'It would be best if we buried her and Ali together,' she said.

'Yes. I expect the skeleton in the corner is Ali's.'

They returned to the Jade Room. As they were collecting what they imagined to be Ali's bones, they found amongst them some bamboo strips of the sort used in China in ancient times for writing. Chen picked them up, and saw that they were thickly covered with Chinese characters written in red ink on a black background. Glancing through them, he recognized the writings of the ancient Taoist sage, Zhuangzi. He had thought it might be some very special sort of book and was rather disappointed to find it was instead something he had read and memorized as a child.

'What is it?' asked Hasli.

'It's an old Chinese book, but it's not much use except to historians.' He threw the strips back on the ground, and as they scattered he noticed one which looked slightly different from the rest. Beside every character there were circles and dots and lines of writing in Uighur script. Chen picked the strip up and saw that it was the section entitled 'Butcher Ding' from Zhuangzi's chapter, 'The Secret of Caring for Life.' He pointed to the Uighur characters written alongside.

'What does this say?' he asked Hasli.

'"The key to smashing the enemy is here",' she replied.

'What can that mean?' he wondered out loud, greatly surprised.

'In her last testament Mami said Ali got hold of a Chinese book and learned kungfu from it. This could be it,' Huo Qingtong suggested.

'Zhuangzi taught a philosophy of enlightenment, serenity, and harmony with nature,' said Chen. 'That has nothing to do with kungfu.' He threw the strip back down again, then picked up the pile of bones and walked out. They buried the remains of Mami and Ali beside the Jade Pool and bowed respectfully before the graves.

'Let's go now,' said Chen. 'I wonder if the white horse managed to escape the wolves?'

'What is the section of that book about?' Huo Qingtong asked.

'It's about a butcher who was very good at his job. The movements of his hands and legs, the sound of his knife chopping, were all perfectly coordinated. The sound had the rhythm of music, the movements were like dancing.'

'That sort of skill could be useful when facing an enemy,' Huo Qingtong commented.

Chen stared at her in surprise. Every word of the passage from Zhuangzi was familiar to him, but suddenly he felt as if he had never read it before. The words of 'Butcher Ding' ran through his mind: 'When I first began cutting up oxen, all I could see was the ox itself. After three years, I no longer saw the whole ox. And now—now, I do it with my spirit, I don't look with my eyes. Perception and understanding have come to a stop and spirit roams where it wills.'

'If my kungfu were really like that,' he thought, 'I could kill that traitor Zhang with my eyes closed, just with a slight movement of the knife…' The two sisters were staring at him, wondering what he was thinking about.

'Wait a moment,' he said, and ran back inside. A long time passed and still he did not re-emerge. The two sisters were worried and went in as well. They found him prancing about among the skeletons in the Great Hall, his face wreathed in smiles. He danced around a pair of skeletons for a moment and then stood stock-still staring at another pair. Hasli glanced at her sister in fright, afraid that perhaps he had totally lost his mind.

Huo Qingtong took her sister's hand. 'Don't be afraid, he's all right,' she said. 'Let's go and wait for him outside.'

The two returned to the Jade Pool. 'What do you think he's doing in there?' asked Hasli.

'I think he's worked out some new kungfu moves after having read those bamboo slips, and now he's practising them by copying the positions of the skeletons. I think we'd better not disturb him.'

Hasli nodded. After a while, she sighed and said, 'Now I understand.'

'What?'

'All those people in the Great Hall must have been very good fighters. Even after their weapons had been snatched from them, they still fought on against Sanglaba's guards.'

'Yes, but they weren't necessarily very good at kungfu,' Huo Qingtong replied. 'I would guess they just learned a few really formidable moves which allowed them to take their enemies with them.'

'Ah, they must have been so brave! But what is *he* learning them for? Does he want to die with his enemies too?'

'No, a true Martial Arts master would not be killed along with his opponent. He is just studying the finer points of the moves.'

Hasli smiled. 'Well I won't worry any more, then.' She looked out over the surface of the pool. 'Let's bathe in the water.'

'Don't be ridiculous. What if he should come out?'

'But I really want to go and bathe,' Hasli replied. She stared out at the cool water once again and said softly, 'Wouldn't it be nice if the three of us could live here together for ever!'

Huo Qingtong's heart jumped. She blushed, and quickly turned her head away towards White Jade Peak.

A long time passed and still Chen did not emerge. Hasli took off her leather boots and put her feet in the water. Resting her head on her sister's lap, she gazed up at the white clouds in the sky and slowly fell asleep.

The Saucepan and the Chicken

Scholar Yu and Li Yuanzhi understood why it was that Mastermind Xu had sent them out together to look for Huo Qingtong. Yu was greatly moved by Yuanzhi's obvious love for him, and by the fact that she had saved his life several times. But the more infatuated *she* became with *him*, the more *he* shrank away from *her*, for reasons which he himself didn't understand. As they travelled, she laughed and chattered with him, but he remained cool to her advances, to her great disappointment.

One day towards noon, they spied a skinny little donkey hobbling towards them across the desert, its rider nodding from side to side as if he was snoozing. As they got closer, they saw it was a turbaned Uighur with a large saucepan slung across his back and a donkey's tail dangling in his right hand. The donkey, they noticed, was tail-less and was wearing the official cap of a Manchu officer from the Imperial Guard, with a plain stone in the place of its original sapphire. The rider looked about forty years of age and had a big bushy beard. When he saw them, he smiled warmly.

Scholar Yu knew that Huo Qingtong's name was known across the length and breadth of the desert. 'Excuse me, sir,' he said, reining in his horse, 'have you seen a lady by the name of Huo Qingtong?'

The man laughed, and replied in Chinese, 'And why would you be looking for her?'

'There are several bad men after her and we want to warn her. If you see her, could you give her the message?'

'I suppose so. What sort of bad men?'

'Two of them are big Chinese, and the third is a Mongol,' answered Yuanzhi.

The man nodded. 'Yes, I know all about that lot: they *are* bad. I've met them. And there was a fourth. He was bad too. He wanted to eat my donkey, but I stole his cap. But who are you?'

'We are friends of the Hodja Muzhuolun,' replied Scholar Yu. 'We must stop these men from finding Lady Huo Qingtong. Take us to where you met them and we will give you some silver.'

'I don't need any of your silver,' replied the Uighur. 'And first I'll have to ask my donkey if he's prepared to go.' He leant over close to the donkey's ear and mumbled into it for a while, then placed his own ear near the donkey's mouth, and nodded repeatedly. Yu and Yuanzhi grinned at his clowning. The man listened intently for a moment and then frowned. 'This donkey has had a very high opinion of himself ever since he started wearing his official cap,' he said. 'He's rather contemptuous of your horses and he says he doesn't want to travel with them for fear of losing face.'

Yuanzhi looked at the skinny, lame animal, its body covered in mud, and burst out laughing.

'You don't believe me?' exclaimed the Uighur. 'Well then, let's give my donkey a chance to compete with your horse.'

Scholar Yu and Yuanzhi were riding two of the Hodja's best horses, infinitely superior to the donkey.

'All right,' said Yuanzhi. 'But when we've won the contest, you must promise to lead us to the three bad men.'

'It's four, not three. But what happens if you lose?'

'We'll do whatever you say.'

'If you lose, you have to wash my donkey clean.'

'All right,' Yuanzhi agreed. 'What sort of contest is it to be?'

'You can decide.'

The Uighur seemed supremely confident of victory and Yuanzhi began to feel suspicious. 'What's that in your hand?' she asked.

'The donkey's tail,' he replied, waving it about. 'After he started wearing the official cap, he thought it didn't go with his dirty tail, so he decided he didn't want it any more.'

'Let me have a look,' she said.

He threw the tail across. She caught it, then pointed with it to a small sand-dune some distance away. 'We'll race from here to that sand-dune,' she said. 'The winner will be the first to get there, your donkey or my horse.' The man nodded. 'You go over there and be the judge,' she added to Scholar Yu. He slapped his horse and galloped off toward the dune.

'Go!' shouted Yuanzhi, and with a lash of her whip, her horse leapt forward. After a few hundred feet, she glanced back and saw the donkey, limping along far behind. She laughed and spurred her horse on even faster. Then all of a sudden a black shape shot past her. She almost fell off her saddle in shock when she saw that the man had slung the donkey around his shoulders and was running with long strides. He was already a good distance ahead of her. She pulled herself together, and tried to catch up with him again, but he ran like the wind and stayed ahead all the way to the finish. Just before she reached the dune, Yuanzhi threw the donkey's tail back behind her. 'My horse was first!' she shouted.

The Uighur and Scholar Yu looked at each other in puzzlement.

'Young lady!' the Uighur protested. 'We agreed that whichever got here first, the donkey or the horse, was the winner, isn't that right?'

Yuanzhi tidied her hair with her hand. 'Yes,' she replied. 'But only *part* of the donkey got here first.'

The man pulled on his beard. 'I don't understand. What do you mean, only part of the donkey?'

Yuanzhi pointed to the tail she had thrown far behind them. 'My horse arrived in one piece, but only a *part* of your donkey made it. His tail didn't!'

The man laughed heartily. He clearly had a highly developed sense of humour. 'Yes, you're absolutely right!' he exclaimed. 'You win. I give in. I'll take you to find those four bad men.' He went over and picked the tail up and brought it back. 'You stupid donkey!' he said to the animal. 'You may be wearing an official cap, but you still need your dirty tail.' He leapt onto its back.

Scholar Yu had been greatly impressed by the Uighur's immense strength, and his ability to run faster than a horse even with the donkey slung over his shoulders. He knew he must be a Martial Arts master and bowed before him.

'If you will just tell us the direction, we will go and find these men ourselves,' he said respectfully. 'We don't wish to trouble you, sir.'

'But I lost,' the Uighur replied, smiling. 'I can't possibly back out now!' He swivelled the donkey round, pointed him in the right direction, and shouted to the two of them: 'Follow me!'

And so they travelled on. When Scholar Yu asked the man for his name, he simply smiled and answered with more crazy jokes. The lame donkey made very slow progress, and in half a day they covered only ten miles. They saw riders approaching from behind, and soon Mastermind Xu and Zhou Qi came galloping up. Scholar Yu introduced them saying: 'This gentleman is taking us to find the Three Devils.' Xu dismounted and bowed.

The Uighur simply smiled in response. 'In the state she's in, that wife of yours should be at home and getting some good rest,' he said to Xu. 'What's she doing, gallivanting about like this?'

Xu stared at him, not understanding. Zhou Qi, however, blushed red, and galloped on ahead.

The Uighur was very familiar with all the tracks and paths of the desert, and towards evening he led them to a small village. As they approached, they saw that a Manchu military unit had also just descended on the village. The Uighurs were fleeing in all directions, dragging their children after them.

'Most of the Manchu forces have already been wiped out, and the survivors have all been rounded up, so where did these soldiers come from?' Mastermind Xu wondered aloud.

A group of about twenty Uighurs dashed towards them with a dozen soldiers on their heels, shouting and brandishing their swords. When the Uighurs caught sight of the man on the donkey, they began to call out his name ecstatically: 'Afanti! Afanti! Save us!'

'Everyone must flee!' shouted the man they addressed as Afanti. He himself raised his whip and headed off at full speed into the desert (his donkey had apparently now regained his momentum), with the Uighur and Manchu troops following behind.

After a while, several of the Uighur women fell behind and were captured by the soldiers. Zhou Qi could not bear to abandon them. She drew her sword, wheeled her horse round, and charged at the Manchu troops. With a swish of her blade, she sliced off half of one soldier's head. The other soldiers now surrounded her. Mastermind Xu and the others came galloping up to the rescue. Suddenly, Zhou Qi felt a wave of nausea and, just as one of the soldiers was leaping forward to grab her, she vomited all over his face. While he was frantically trying to wipe the mess off, Zhou Qi killed him with her sword. Then her legs and arms went all rubbery and she swayed unsteadily in the saddle. Mastermind Xu rushed over to support her.

'What's the matter?' he asked.

Scholar Yu and Yuanzhi had by now killed or chased away the rest of the soldiers. Mastermind Xu caught one of the fleeing troops and interrogated him as to where the column had come from. The soldier threw himself down on the ground and begged for mercy, gabbling incoherently. Finally they extracted from him the fact that he was attached to a relief force that had arrived from the east. Mastermind Xu chose two strong young men from amongst the group of Uighurs and sent them off immediately to inform the Hodja, so that he would be prepared. He gave the soldier a kick on the behind and shouted, 'Now, go to hell!'

Xu turned back to his wife. 'Are you all right?' he asked. 'What's the matter?'

Zhou Qi blushed and turned her face away.

'The cow is going to calve,' Afanti said.

'How do you know?' Xu asked, surprised.

'It's strange. The bull didn't know the cow was going to calve, but my donkey did.'

They all laughed, then continued on their way. As evening approached, they stopped and set up tents for the night.

'How many months pregnant are you?' Mastermind Xu quietly asked his wife. 'How is it that I didn't know?'

'How would my stupid bull know?' Zhou Qi replied, smiling.

'You must be careful from now on,' said Xu. 'No more sword-fighting.' She nodded.

The next morning, Afanti said to Xu: 'Your wife can stay at my home while we go and look for those men. It's another ten miles further on. I have a very beautiful wife there—'

'Really?' Yuanzhi interrupted. 'I'd like to meet her. Why would she like a bearded fellow like you?'

'Aha, that's a secret,' Afanti laughed.

They arrived at a village and Afanti led them to his house. Raising his saucepan in the air he began to bang it loudly, and a woman in her thirties came out to greet him. Her features were indeed beautiful and her skin white and delicate. They could tell she was overjoyed to see Afanti, but from her mouth issued a stream of curses in the Uighur tongue: 'Where the hell have you been, Whiskers? I shouldn't think you even remember who I am after all this time!'

'Enough of your racket,' replied Afanti, with a good-natured smile. 'I'm back, aren't I? Bring me something to eat. Your Whiskers is starving!'

'Isn't it enough just to look at my lovely face?' countered the wife, also smiling.

'That's very true, your beautiful face is delicious, but if I had some bread or something to go with it, it would be even better.'

She reached over and gave his ear a sharp twist. 'I'm never allowing you to go off again,' she said. She went back inside, and reappeared soon after with piles of bread, watermelon, honey, and roast lamb. Yuanzhi didn't understand a word Afanti and his wife said to each other, but she could see from their teasing that they loved each other dearly, and felt a renewed sense of loneliness.

While they were eating their lunch, two people walked into the house, one a young boy and the other a labourer.

'Old Hu says that you should give him back the saucepan you borrowed,' said the boy.

Afanti glanced at Zhou Qi and smiled, then said to the boy: 'You tell him that the saucepan is pregnant and is about to give birth to a baby saucepan. It can't possibly be moved at the moment.'

The boy looked puzzled, but he turned and left.

'And what are *you* here for?' Afanti asked the labourer.

'Last year, I went to an inn in the village and ate a chicken. Before I left I asked the innkeeper for the bill, but he said: "We'll settle it next time, there's no rush." I thought at the time that he was just being nice, so I thanked him and left. Two months later, I went back to pay. He started counting his fingers and mumbling away as if he was trying to work out a very complicated account. I said: "How much was that chicken? Just tell me and I'll pay!" The innkeeper waved his hand at me and told me to be quiet.'

'A chicken, even the fattest chicken in the world, couldn't be more than a hundred copper pieces,' said Afanti's wife.

'That's what I thought too,' said the labourer. 'But he went on mumbling away to himself for ages, and then asked me for *twelve taels* of silver!'

'Ai-ya!' exclaimed Afanti's wife. 'No chicken could cost that much! You could buy hundreds of chickens for that much money.'

'Yes, that's what I said. I said there must be a mistake. But he said: "There's no mistake. If you *hadn't* eaten my chicken, how many eggs do you suppose that chicken would have laid for me? And how many of those eggs would have become little chicks? And when those little chicks grew, how many eggs would *they* have laid?" The price kept on getting higher, and in the end he said: "Actually twelve taels of silver is very cheap!" Naturally, I refused to give him the money, so he dragged me over to see Old Hu for him to settle the dispute. Hu accepted the innkeeper's story, and told me to pay up. He said that if I didn't settle the account quickly, there would be even more eggs (that were never laid) that would hatch into even more chicks, and I wouldn't have a hope of *ever* settling up. Afanti, tell me who is right?'

Just then, the boy returned.

'Old Hu says a saucepan can't be pregnant! He doesn't believe you and says you must give him back the saucepan.'

Afanti went into the kitchen and brought out a small saucepan which he gave to the boy. 'This is clearly the son of a saucepan,' he said. 'You give it to Old Hu.'

Uncertain whether to believe him or not, the boy took the small saucepan and left.

Afanti turned to the labourer and said: 'You go and tell Old Hu you want to hold a meeting to settle the matter of the chicken.'

'But if I lose, I'll have to give him double, won't I? That'll be twenty-four taels of silver!'

'Don't worry,' said Afanti. 'You can't lose.'

After another hour or so, the labourer returned and said: 'Afanti, Old Hu has called the meeting, and they've already started. Please come.'

'I'm busy at the moment,' Afanti replied. 'Come back in a little while.' He sat laughing and chatting with his wife and the others. The labourer started fretting and pleaded with him and finally Afanti got up and accompanied him to the meeting.

Mastermind Xu and the others went along too to see the fun, and they found seven or eight hundred people gathered in the village square. A fat man wearing an embroidered fur-lined gown sat in the middle. He, they decided, must be Old Hu. The crowd had become very restless waiting for Afanti.

'Afanti,' called out Old Hu. 'This labourer says you're going to speak for him. Why are you so late?'

Afanti bowed before him. 'I'm sorry, but I had some important business to attend to,' he said.

'How could it be more important than settling this dispute?' replied Old Hu.

'It was much more important,' said Afanti. 'Tomorrow, I am going to plant some wheat, but still I hadn't fried the seeds or eaten them. I fried them three times and it took me a long time to finish them up.'

'Nonsense!' roared Old Hu. 'You can't possibly plant seeds that you have already eaten!'

The crowd laughed heartily, but Afanti just stroked his large beard and smiled. After a while, the hubbub died down, and he said: 'You say that wheat seeds that have been eaten can't be planted. Well, how can the chicken that the labourer ate lay any eggs?'

The crowd thought for a second, and then cried out: 'Yes, that's right, how can a chicken that's been eaten lay eggs?' Everyone began shouting and laughing and lifted Afanti up onto their shoulders.

Seeing the crowd's reaction, Old Hu had no alternative but to announce: 'The labourer should pay one hundred copper pieces to the innkeeper in return for the chicken he ate.'

The labourer happily handed over the string of copper coins to the innkeeper, commenting, 'I'll never dare eat one of your chickens again!'

The innkeeper took the money and walked silently away. The crowd laughed at him and some small children threw stones at his back.

Old Hu went over to Afanti. 'So, the saucepan I lent you has given birth to a son. That's excellent. When will it be giving birth again?'

An expression of deep sadness appeared on Afanti's face. 'Old Hu,' he said. 'Your saucepan is dead.'

'How can a saucepan die?' replied Hu angrily.

'If a saucepan can give birth to a son, then of course it can die.'

'You charlatan!' cried Hu. 'You just don't want to return my saucepan!'

'All right,' Afanti shouted back. He pointed to the crowd: 'We'll let *them* decide.'

But Old Hu remembered that he had already accepted the small saucepan, and decided he had lost enough face. He waved his hand to indicate that the discussion was over, and walked off through the crowd.

Afanti was extremely pleased with himself for having managed to make a fool of Old Hu, who was himself a master at cheating the poor. He threw back his head and roared with laughter.

Duel at Jade Pool

Suddenly, a voice behind him said: 'Well, Whiskers, what idiocy are you up to now?'

Afanti turned and saw that it was the Strange Knight of the Heavenly Pool, Master Yuan. He jumped up happily and grabbed him by the arm.

'Aha! So you're here. Come and see my wife,' he said.

'What's so special about your wife that you keep showing her off like a monkey would a jewel—' Before Yuan could finish, Mastermind Xu and Scholar Yu came forward and kowtowed before him.

'That's quite enough of that!' protested Yuan. 'I'm not your Shifu! Where is your Helmsman Chen?'

'The Helmsman came on ahead of us,' Xu began. Suddenly, he noticed behind Yuan the Twin Eagles of Heaven Mountains— Bald Vulture and Lady Guan. He bowed to them. He was surprised to see that Lady Guan was riding Chen's white horse.

'Where did you find that horse?' he asked.

'We found him running free in the desert. It took the three of us quite a while to catch him,' she said.

Xu was shocked. 'Do you think the Helmsman could be in danger?' he exclaimed. 'We'd better go and find him.'

They finished lunch quickly and bade farewell to Zhou Qi. Afanti's wife was furious that her husband was leaving again after only a few hours at home, and grabbed his beard, wailing and screaming as she did so. Afanti laughed and tried to comfort her.

'I've found a young lady to keep you company,' he said. 'In fact, there's a baby inside her, which means there will soon be two people to keep you company, which will be much better than just having me.' But his wife wailed even louder.

Yuanzhi rode the white horse, and let it lead the way back to Chen. Afanti again rode his donkey, but the animal was much too slow. By nightfall, they had still gone only ten miles, and everyone was getting anxious.

'We'll go on ahead,' Xu finally said to Afanti. 'We are afraid that our Helmsman may be in trouble.'

'All right, all right!' Afanti replied. 'When we get to the next village, I'll buy a better donkey. This stupid thing thinks he's something special, but really he's useless.' He urged the animal on and caught up with Yuanzhi.

'Young lady, tell me, why are you so unhappy all the time?' he asked.

Despite his apparent silliness, Yuanzhi knew that this strange Uighur was very wise, and she decided to ask his advice.

'Afanti,' she replied. 'How would *you* deal with someone who was completely unreasonable?'

'I would cover his head with my saucepan and skewer him with a sword.'

Yuanzhi shook her head. 'No, that won't do. What if it was someone who was very…very dear to you, and the nicer you were towards him, the more stubborn he became—like your donkey.'

Afanti pulled at his beard, fully understanding her meaning. 'I ride this donkey every day,' he replied with a smile, 'and I've learned a trick or two. I know how to deal with his bad temper.'

They entered a village. As they approached the village square, the white horse suddenly whinnied and galloped forward. Yuanzhi pulled desperately on the reins, but could not control him. The villagers scattered in front of the apparently crazed animal. It galloped up to a group of people and stopped dead in its tracks. Yuanzhi dismounted and saw, standing before her, Luo Bing, Rolling Thunder Wen, Leopard Wei, Hunchback Zhang, Xin Yan, and the white-bearded Hidden Needle Lu.

Scholar Yu ran over to Lu, knelt down before him, and began to sob. Lu helped him up, tears glistening in his eyes too. 'I started out as soon as I heard the shocking news about your Shifu, Master Ma Zhen,' he said. 'I met these friends on the road. They are also after that traitor, Fire Hand Zhang. Don't worry. We will avenge your Shifu's death.'

The Red Flower heroes found somewhere to rest briefly while Afanti went off to buy a fresh donkey, Yuanzhi quietly following him. He found and purchased a strong animal, twice the height of his tail-less animal, which he sold to the donkey merchant for a small sum.

'The official's cap was the undoing of this stupid creature,' he said, and laughed. He threw the cap on the ground, and trampled it into the dust. Yuanzhi led the new donkey for him as they walked back.

'I once raised a donkey that was most terribly stubborn,' Afanti said. 'If I wanted him to move, he would stand still. If I wanted him to stand still, he would walk round in circles. One day, I wanted him to pull a cart to a mill a few hundred feet away, but no matter what I said, he wouldn't budge. The more I pushed him, the more determined he was to stay put. I shouted, I hit him, it made no difference. So, guess what I did?'

'I'm sure you thought of something.'

'The mill was to the east, so I pulled the donkey round to face west and then urged him to move forward. He retreated one step at a time, backwards, all the way to the mill!'

'You mean you wanted him to go east, and he insisted on doing the opposite,' Yuanzhi said thoughtfully. 'So you tried making him go west instead.'

Afanti stuck up his thumb. 'That's right. That's the way.' Yuanzhi smiled. 'Thank you for your advice,' she said.

She decided he was right. The nicer she was to Yu, the more he avoided her. So she decided that from now on she would do the opposite: she would ignore him instead. She lost no time putting this into practice. Luo Bing and Mastermind Xu were surprised by her sudden change in attitude, but Afanti just stroked his beard and smiled.

With Afanti riding his new donkey, they made much faster progress. The white horse led them straight to White Jade Peak, but it was still afraid of the wolves and stopped outside the maze of paths leading to the Secret City, refusing to go any further.

'The wolf-pack went in here,' said Master Yuan. 'We should be able to find our way easily by following the trail of wolf droppings.' Their anxiety for Helmsman Chen's safety increased with every moment that passed.

The path twisted back and forth for a long time. Suddenly, they heard footsteps ahead and four men appeared round a corner. The first was instantly recognizable as Fire Hand Zhang. His face turned pale at the sight of the Red Flower heroes, and particularly his former brother-in-arms Hidden Needle Lu. Scholar Yu gripped hold of his Golden Flute and was about to charge forward when Master Yuan touched him lightly on the shoulder, and stopped him dead in his tracks.

Master Yuan pointed at Fire Hand Zhang accusingly. 'When we met several days ago, I called you a Master of the Wudang School. I did not know then that you were capable of killing your own brother-in-arms. Why not end it cleanly and quickly yourself?'

Fire Hand Zhang had already assessed the situation. He knew that at least five of his opponents were his equal at kungfu or better. He would gain nothing from a head-on confrontation. With one swift, smooth movement, he drew his sword, and flung a large handful of Golden Needles at the Red Flower heroes. They ducked, and as they did so he grabbed Hahetai and squeezed a Vital Point on his right wrist. 'Run!' he shouted.

Hahetai was no longer master of his own movements. He ran with Zhang back along the path towards the Secret City, with Teng and Gu following along behind. By the time the Red Flower heroes had picked themselves up, the four men had disappeared around the bend. Master Yuan and Afanti were furious, and shot after them at high speed. Master Yuan was particularly fast, and in a moment he had caught up with Teng. He grasped him by the neck and lifted his tall frame up off the ground. Unable to see his attacker, Teng kicked out backwards with his foot, but a huge force propelled him through the air, smashed his head into the rock-face, and killed him instantly.

Master Yuan ran on and, rounding the next corner, found himself confronted by three paths leading off the main track. Mastermind Xu soon caught up with him. He looked carefully at the ground. 'Someone trod in this pile of wolf droppings,' he said, pointing. 'They must have been following the trail of droppings back.'

'Very good. Let's go,' Master Yuan replied. They too followed the droppings all the way to the base of White Jade Peak, without seeing any sign of Fire Hand Zhang and the other two surviving Devils. But then they noticed the cave mouth above them. Master Yuan and some of the others went speeding up the cliff while the rest were hauled up one by one by Hidden Needle Lu and Rolling Thunder Wen.

Master Yuan pushed open the massive stone door, and ran on ahead of the others down the tunnel. When they entered the Great Hall, their weapons were snatched away from them by the magnetic force. It was a rude shock. But they had urgent business, and pressed on, picking up their swords and other weapons without bothering to work out what had happened and running on to the Jade Room, where they saw the tunnel mouth beside the bed. The further they went into the bowels of the mountain, the more astounded they became. Suddenly, they emerged once more into bright daylight. They saw six people standing around the luminous Jade Pool, three on one side and three on the other. On the far side were Helmsman Chen, Huo Qingtong, and Hasli; on the near side were Fire Hand Zhang, Gu, and Hahetai.

'We're here, master!' Xin Yan called out excitedly to Helmsman Chen.

'Child! Are you all right?' cried Lady Guan to Huo Qingtong.

'I'm fine!' she called back. Then she pointed at Gu and added: 'But please kill that foul creature quickly.' Bald Vulture drew his sword and sprung at Gu, while Lady Guan began to fight with Hahetai. The other Red Flower heroes quietly surrounded Fire Hand Zhang.

Gu and Hahetai fought for their lives, but could not hope to win against the Three Part sword style of the Twin Eagles. As their swords clashed, Bald Vulture gave a mighty roar and blood could be seen pouring from Gu's chest. Bald Vulture followed up with a swift kick, and Gu fell backwards into the pool, sending fountains of water spraying out in all directions. A stream of blood rose to the surface. A moment later, there was another splash as Gu surfaced and began swimming slowly towards the bank. Hahetai threw down his sword and helped him out of the water. Gu was badly wounded and had swallowed a large quantity of water. Hahetai lay him down on the bank, and rubbed his chest.

Fire Hand Zhang watched helplessly as Gu and Hahetai were overcome. Then Scholar Yu lunged at him. Zhang swept his left hand across and, as Scholar Yu dodged to avoid the blow, Zhang grabbed him with his right hand and hurled him at a nearby stone wall, with a ferocious roar. Horrified, Yuanzhi jumped forward to grab Yu, but Zhang's strength was too great and the outcome was that the two of them slammed into the wall. There was a sharp 'crack' as Yuanzhi's left arm snapped.

The Red Flower heroes' anger flared once more. Master Yuan went over to Yuanzhi and put a Snow Ginseng Pill in her mouth to ease her intense pain, while the others surrounded Zhang.

'The Fire Hand Judge will die a hero!' he shouted defiantly. 'Well, are you coming altogether or one at a time?'

'I'll fight you first!' Bald Vulture shouted back.

'This traitor has done me too great a wrong,' Rolling Thunder Wen interrupted him. He wanted revenge for the relentless way in which Zhang had hounded him. 'Let me go first.'

'He killed my Shifu!' shouted Scholar Yu. 'I may not be as good a fighter as him, but I want to be first. Brother Wen, you can take over from me if I exhaust my strength.'

'We should draw lots,' suggested Helmsman Chen.

Fire Hand Zhang addressed Chen directly: 'We agreed in Hangzhou to meet at a later date for a duel. Does that agreement still hold?'

'Yes,' Chen replied. 'As I remember, we postponed the meeting because your hand was injured. Now is an excellent time to settle the affair.'

'Then you and I will compete first and the others will wait their turn. Are we agreed?' Fire Hand Zhang had fought with Helmsman Chen on several occasions and knew he could beat him. If he could capture him, he might be able to find some way to escape. And if he could not capture him, he would at least have the satisfaction of killing the Red Flower Society's leader.

'If you think you are going to escape with your life today, you are deluding yourself,' said Chen. 'We spared your life in that dungeon in Hangzhou, and we spared it on Lion Peak. Only a few days ago, I saved you once again from the wolves. But now the Red Flower Society has run out of mercy, as far as you are concerned.'

'Well, come on then,' Zhang replied impatiently. Chen leapt at him, his two fists aimed straight at Zhang's face. Zhang ducked, and then jumped up out of the way. Chen followed with a sweeping kick, timing it to strike Zhang as he fell back to the ground. Surprised, Zhang had to thrust his sword at Chen's chest to extricate himself. Chen moved back as fast as lightning, and Zhang struck out again.

Hidden Needle Lu was shocked by Zhang's speed. He was even faster than their Shifu had been in his prime. He drew his sword and watched the battle carefully, ready to help Helmsman Chen if necessary.

Meanwhile, Scholar Yu and Luo Bing were looking after Yuanzhi, who had fainted from the shock and pain of her broken arm. Yuanzhi opened her eyes and pointed to the east with a gasp of surprise, but when Yu looked round he could see nothing but the sun shimmering on the hills about them.

'What's that?' Yuanzhi asked. 'Are we back in Hangzhou?'

'It's just the sun,' Yu said softly. 'Close your eyes and rest.'

'No, I'm sure that's Thunder Peak Pagoda in Hangzhou,' she replied. 'I've been there with my father. Where is my father? I want to see him.'

Scholar Yu lightly patted the back of her hand. 'We'll go there together after this, and I'll see your father with you.'

A smile lit up her face. 'Who are you?' she asked. Scholar Yu saw her staring at him, her face completely drained of colour, and fear struck him.

'I'm your brother-in-arms. I promise I'll look after you from now on.'

'But in your heart, you don't like me, I know,' she cried, tears beginning to course down her cheeks. 'Take me back to see my father. I want to die.'

On a sudden impulse, Scholar Yu embraced her. 'I truly love you,' he whispered. 'You won't die.' She sighed. 'Tell me you won't die,' he repeated. Another wave of pain from her arm struck her and she fainted away.

Fire Hand Zhang and Helmsman Chen had all the while been fighting, moving round and round. At first, Chen was able to contain his enemy with the Hundred Flowers kungfu style. But as Zhang gradually came to grips with it, he became more daring and forced Chen onto the defensive. He swept his sword across at Chen forcing him to jump away, and then with a quick double movement of his sword, struck out at Leopard Wei and Hunchback Zhang, wounding them both. Rolling Thunder Wen roared with anger and was about to leap forward when Chen slipped past him and hit out at Zhang's face with his open hands. There appeared to be no force behind the blow, but there were two sharp claps as his hands made contact with Zhang's ears. Surprised and angry, Zhang retreated.

The Red Flower heroes were astonished by the effortless way in which Chen, who had seemed to be losing the fight, had managed to box Zhang's ears.

'Brother Yu,' Chen called out to Scholar Yu. 'Play me a tune.'

'What do you want me to play?' asked Yu, putting the flute to his lips.

Chen hesitated for a moment. 'Play me "The Ambush",' he replied.

Scholar Yu did not understand what he was getting at, but, having received an order from the Helmsman, he complied immediately and began to play with all the skill he could muster. The tune was a martial air written originally for the bamboo flute. Played on the Golden Flute, it sounded more rousing than ever, and conjured up the image of armoured troops on the march.

Helmsman Chen looked Fire Hand Zhang straight in the face and challenged him. 'Come on!' he cried, then turned around and kicked out into thin air as if dancing. Seeing his opponent's back undefended, Zhang thrust his sword at him, and the Red Flower heroes gasped in fright. But Chen suddenly turned again, grabbed Zhang's pigtail with his left hand, and pulled it over the edge of the sword, slicing it clean in two. With his right hand, he gave Zhang's shoulder a sharp blow. Zhang had now been struck three times, and although he had not yet been badly hurt, he was obviously baffled by Chen's kungfu style and had had to suffer the shame of having his pigtail cut off. But he was a master of self-control. He carefully retreated several steps, staring fixedly at his enemy all the while. Helmsman Chen moved forward slowly, his feet following the rhythm of the tune Yu was playing.

'Look!' Huo Qingtong said to her sister excitedly. 'It's the kungfu style he learned in the Great Hall.'

Chen and Zhang whirled round each other, Zhang keeping his sword strictly on the defensive, striking out only when Chen got too close.

'Master Yuan,' said Bald Vulture, 'I have never had so much respect for you as I do today. You should be proud of your disciple.'

Master Yuan was greatly perplexed: he himself was probably the leading Martial Arts master in the land and yet he had never seen anything remotely like the kungfu style Chen was using. 'I didn't teach him this,' he replied. 'I wouldn't know how to.'

Yu played his flute ever more spiritedly. At first, Helmsman Chen had felt a little hesitant with his newly learned kungfu style. But by now he was using it smoothly, advancing and retreating with great precision until Fire Hand Zhang's clothes were drenched in the sweat of fear. The flute hit a high note, then the melody came cascading down like a shooting star falling through the night sky. Zhang gave a cry as Chen touched the Vital Point on his right wrist, forcing him to drop his sword. Chen followed quickly with two blows to Zhang's back, then jumped away, laughing. Zhang stumbled forward a few steps, as if drunk, and collapsed on the ground. Jubilant, the Red Flower heroes rushed forward to tie him up. Zhang's face was deathly white. He made no attempt to resist.

'Shifu,' Chen said, addressing Master Yuan. 'What should we do with this traitor?'

'Feed him to the wolves!' cried Scholar Yu. 'First he killed my Shifu and now he... now he's...' He looked down at Yuanzhi's broken arm.

'Good idea!' said Yuan. 'We have to go and see how the pack is doing anyway.'

Hidden Needle Lu carefully set Yuanzhi's broken arm and bound it tightly with a cloth. Master Yuan slipped another Snow Ginseng Pill into her mouth and felt her pulse.

'Don't worry,' he said to Scholar Yu. 'She'll pull through.'

'Put your arms round her, and she'll get better much quicker,' Luo Bing whispered to him with a smile.

Huo Qingtong, meanwhile, was examining her map again, looking for a path from the Jade Pool out to the Secret City, when she heard shouts and turned to see Gu running crazily towards her screaming: 'Kill me! Kill me!' Shocked and angry, she raised her sword and ran it through his chest. As she pulled the blade out again, a stream of blood spattered her yellow robe and Gu collapsed on the ground. Hahetai knelt over him and tried to staunch the flow of blood, but to no avail. Gu gasped in pain.

'Do you have any affairs that need settling?' Hahetai asked him.

'I just want to touch her hand, then I can die happy,' whispered Gu, looking up at Huo Qingtong.

'Young lady,' Hahetai pleaded. 'He's about to die. Take pity on him!' Huo Qingtong turned without a word and walked away, her face deathly pale. Gu gave a long sigh, and his head fell to one side. He was dead.

Holding back his tears, Hahetai jumped up and pointed his finger accusingly at Huo Qingtong.

'You have no heart!' he shouted. 'You know no mercy! I don't blame you for killing him, but you could at least have given him your hand to touch, so that he could have died in peace. What difference would it have made to you?'

'Shut your mouth!' cried Hunchback Zhang angrily.

Hahetai made no reply. He picked up Gu's body and strode away. Yu led over a horse for him.

'Brother Hahetai,' he said. 'I respect you for being an upright man. Please take this horse.'

Hahetai nodded and slung Gu's body over the horse's back. Yu filled a bowl with water and drank half of it, then presented it to the Mongol.

'This water can take the place of wine,' he said. Hahetai threw back his head and drained the bowl at one draught, then rode away without looking back.

Vengeance

The Red Flower heroes made their way in high spirits to the round fort in which the wolves were trapped, singing and laughing as they went. Master Yuan questioned Helmsman Chen about the origin of the strange kungfu style he had used, and Chen gave him a detailed account of his discovery.

'What an extraordinary coincidence,' said Master Yuan with delight. 'It's the sort of secret one stumbles upon only by chance. If one set out to discover such a thing, one would never find it in a million years!'

After several days' travel, they arrived at the fort and climbed up onto the parapet to look inside. The wolf-pack had long since eaten the entire herd of animals and were now fighting over the carcases of their dead comrades, barking and snapping at each other. The scene was a gruesome one, and even the hardened Red Flower heroes were shocked by it. Hasli could not bear the sight, and went back down to talk with the Uighur guards.

Scholar Yu pulled Fire Hand Zhang to the edge of the wall, and began to mumble a prayer: 'Oh, spirit of my benevolent Shifu, we have today avenged your death.' He reached over and took the knife Mastermind Xu was holding, cut the rope binding Zhang's hands and feet, and kicked him off the edge.

Fire Hand Zhang had been seriously injured by Helmsman Chen's last two blows, but his Inner Force kungfu was profound, and he had recovered much of his strength by the time they reached the fort. As he fell downwards, he knew he had no chance of survival, but he still had to fight one last time. The wolves threw themselves at him just before he hit the ground. He grabbed two of the beasts by their necks and whirled them round and round, forcing the others to back off while he slowly made his way to the wall of the fort.

They all knew he would die. Despite their hatred for him, Helmsman Chen, Luo Bing, and the others with weaker stomachs could not bear to watch to the end and walked back down from the parapet.

Warm Jade

That evening, they set up camp, and Helmsman Chen told Master Yuan about his meetings with Emperor Qian Long. Master Yuan was amazed by the twists and turns in the story. When it was finished, he pulled a small, yellow bag from his inner pocket.

'Last spring,' he said, handing it to Chen, 'your foster father, Old Helmsman Yu, sent the Twin Knights to see me and asked me to look after this, saying there were two important items inside. They didn't say what they were and I have never opened the bag to see. But I imagine this must be the evidence the Emperor wants.'

Chen opened the bag and found a small parcel tightly wrapped in three layers of waterproof oilpaper. Inside the layers of paper was a tiny box made of redwood. He opened the lid, and took out two plain envelopes yellowed with age. The first envelope contained a sheet of paper on which was written in a confident cursive hand: 'Excellency Minister Chen: send someone over with your newborn son for me to see. Yong Di.'

Master Yuan read it, but could not grasp its significance. 'What does it mean?' he asked. 'Why would your foster father have considered this note to be so important?'

'It was written by Emperor Yong Zheng,' replied Helmsman Chen.

'How do you know?'

'There were many examples of calligraphy by various Emperors around our home when I was young, so I can recognize the different styles easily. But there is more to it. This note was obviously written before he became Emperor. Yong Di was the name he used before he ascended the Throne, when he was just a prince. Also, after he became Emperor, he would not have referred to my father as "Excellency".'

Yuan nodded. Helmsman Chen proceeded to count off the years and months on his fingers. 'I was born after Yong Zheng became Emperor, and so was my other brother. My *sister* was born at the time the letter was written, and yet this letter says "your newborn son". This is irrefutable evidence!'

Master Yuan begged him to explain.

'What happened was this,' replied Chen. 'Emperor Yong Zheng, who was still a prince at the time, needed a son: he only had a daughter. So he arranged for his newly born daughter to be exchanged for my newly born brother, who then grew up to be a Prince, and ultimately became the Emperor Qian Long.'

'Qian Long!' gasped old Master Yuan. Chen nodded.

He opened the second envelope and took out a letter. As soon as he saw the writing, tears sprang to his eyes.

'What is it?' Yuan asked.

'This is my mother's writing,' he replied. He wiped away his tears and began to read the letter:

'Dear Brother Yu, our destiny has run its course. What more is there to say of my ill-fated life? All I am concerned about now is the troubles I have brought upon you. You are a brave and upright man but, because of me, you have been rejected even by your own school of Martial Arts. Of my three sons, one is now buried in the heart of the Imperial Palace, the youngest has gone off into the desert, and the one left behind to keep me company is both stupid and wicked. It makes me very sad. My youngest son is very intelligent and has been put under the care of an excellent teacher. I love him and miss him, but I am not worried about him.

'My eldest son is playing the role of Manchu Emperor and knows nothing of his true origins. Brother Yu, dearest Brother Yu, can you enlighten him for me? Tell him he has a bright red birthmark on his left buttock, and he will have to believe you.

'My strength is gradually failing. Day and night, all I think and dream of is the times we had together when we were young. If Heaven has pity on us, we will meet after death and spend the rest of eternity together as man and wife.' The letter was signed 'Chaosheng'.

Chen was deeply shocked and moved as he read it.

'Shifu,' he said, his voice quavering. 'Is…is the Brother Yu in the letter my foster father? Is he the former Red Flower Helmsman, Yu Wanting?'

'Who else could it be?' replied Master Yuan sombrely. 'He and your mother fell in love when they were young, but things did not go as they wished, and they were separated. As a result, he never married.'

'Why did my mother want me to go and live with him? Why did she want me to treat him as my real father? Could it be…'

'I was Yu's closest friend,' replied Yuan. 'But I only know that somehow he broke the regulations of the Shaolin School and was expelled. He would never raise such a humiliating matter himself and it was difficult for others to ask him about it. But he was a good man, and I'm certain he would not have done anything to be ashamed of.' He slapped his thigh. 'When he was expelled, I felt sure he had been falsely accused and I got together some fighters with the idea of going to the Southern Shaolin Monastery and demanding an explanation. It nearly created a serious split in the fighting community. But your foster father disagreed strenuously, insisting that the expulsion was his own fault and that he deserved it. In the end, I did nothing. But I still don't believe he would have done anything shameful. I don't know what it could have been.' It was clear from his tone of voice that he felt indignant at the way

Yu had been treated. 'After he was expelled from the Shaolin School, he went and lived as a hermit for several years. Later he founded the Red Flower Society.'

'But why did my foster father and my mother want me to leave home? Do you know?'

'I never found out. When he stopped me from confronting the Shaolin School and forcing them to explain their actions, he brought disgrace on me too,' Yuan replied angrily. 'After that I refused to have anything to do with him. He sent you to me, and I taught you what you know of the Martial Arts, so I don't owe him anything.'

Helmsman Chen could see there was no point in questioning his Shifu any further. But the key to the restoration of a Chinese Emperor to the Dragon Throne lay with Qian Long. It lay with this well-kept secret of his elder brother's true origins. He had to be completely sure of the truth. Even the slightest error, and all their efforts could be rendered useless. So he made his mind up: he himself would go to the Shaolin Monastery. He told Yuan of his plan.

'That seems to me to be a good idea,' the old man replied. 'But be forewarned: the monks there are a strange lot. I'm afraid they won't tell you anything.'

'We shall see,' said Chen.

Yuan looked at his disciple thoughtfully. 'Both of those Uighur girls are very nice. Which one do you want?' he asked.

'The famous Han dynasty general Huo Qubing once said: "How can I think of marriage until the barbarians are defeated?" I feel the same way.'

Yuan nodded. 'That's very commendable. I will speak to the Twin Eagles so they won't accuse me again of being a bad Shifu.'

'Why? Have they said something about me?'

'They have accused you of fickleness, of abandoning one sister for the other.'

Chen remembered how he and Hasli had met the Twin Eagles in the desert, and how they had departed without saying farewell, leaving their message in the sand. With a shock, he now realized what they had meant.

The next day, Helmsman Chen informed the Red Flower heroes of his decision to go to the Southern Shaolin Monastery in Fujian Province, and then bade farewell to Master Yuan, the Twin Eagles, Huo Qingtong, and her sister.

Hasli wanted to go with him, and Chen felt very bad about leaving her behind. He had no idea when they would meet again. But with Heaven's help, the Grand Design of driving the Manchus out of China would one day succeed and they would be reunited. If it did not succeed, he and his Red Flower Brothers would probably die and be buried in China, far from the Uighur lands.

'You must stay here with your sister,' Helmsman Chen said to Hasli, steeling himself to leave.

'You must promise to return!' Hasli was weeping, tears streaming down her face. He nodded. 'If it takes ten years for you to come back,' she continued, 'I'll wait ten years. If it takes a lifetime, I'll wait a lifetime.'

Chen wanted to give her something. He felt around in his bag and his hand touched on something warm: it was the piece of Warm Jade the Emperor had given him in Haining. He took it out and placed it in her hand.

'When you look at this jade, imagine you are looking at me,' he said softly.

'But I must see *you*,' she replied tearfully.

'What's all this crying about?' he said. 'When the Grand Design is completed, I will take you to see the Great Wall outside Peking. I promise.'

Hasli stared at him for a moment, then the trace of a smile appeared on her face. 'You must never say anything you don't mean,' she said.

'When have I ever lied to you?'

Only then did she agree to stay behind.

As they rode away, Chen found himself constantly looking back at the two sisters. Their silhouettes gradually faded and finally merged with the desert horizon.

The Red Flower heroes travelled on slowly because of Yuanzhi's injuries. Now that his Shifu's death had been avenged, Scholar Yu was in high spirits and looked after the girl with loving care and attention.

After several days, they arrived back at Afanti's home. Zhou Qi was delighted to hear that Fire Hand Zhang was dead. Helmsman Chen wanted her to stay with Mastermind Xu in the Uighur lands until their child was born and she had fully recovered, but she would have none of it. Apart from the boredom, she did not want to miss a chance to travel to the Shaolin Monastery, where she knew her own father was staying. The Red Flower heroes finally agreed, and Xu rented a carriage for his wife and Yuanzhi to ride in.

By the time they reached the Jade Gate and were on the road to central China, the weather was growing warmer and the first signs of spring were apparent.

CHAPTER 9

The Five Halls; Confession; A Bigger Desert; Broken Glass;
The Setting Sun; Muslim Fat or Chinese Fat?; Eternal Hell;
Fresh Blood; Trickery at the Lama Temple; Metallic Vest,
Baby Hostage; Butterfly Spirit

The Five Halls

The day the Red Flower heroes crossed the provincial border into
Fujian, the hills were covered in flowers and dancing butterflies.
Chen thought of Hasli and how she would have loved the sight.

They were met at the Shaolin Monastery by Zhou Qi's father
Lord Zhou, who had come south to Fujian with his wife and servants
some time before to meet the Monastery's abbot, Heavenly
Rainbow. Zhou had a great reputation in the fighting community,
and the Shaolin monks of the Southern Shaolin Monastery, which
was closely affiliated to the Northern Monastery in Henan Province,
were more than happy to exchange Martial Arts knowledge with
such a renowned northern master. Heavenly Rainbow had insisted
that Zhou stay in the temple, and by the time Chen and the others
arrived, he had already been there for several months.

The Abbot led his assistants, Great Insanity, Heavenly Mirror,
Great Hardship, and Great Idiocy, into the Great Hall to meet the
visitors. After everyone had been introduced, the Abbot led them
to a quiet antechamber where tea was served. He asked the reason
for their visit.

Helmsman Chen prostrated himself before the Abbot, tears
glistening in his eyes. Greatly surprised, Heavenly Rainbow moved
quickly to help him up.

'Helmsman,' he said. 'What need is there for such formality?
Please say whatever you wish.'

'I have an embarrassing request to make that according to the
rules of the fighting community should not even be uttered,' Chen
replied. 'But, Venerable Sir, for the sake of millions of my fellow-
countrymen's souls, I make bold to speak.'

'Please do so freely,' the Abbot said.

'The former leader of our Red Flower Society, Helmsman Yu Wanting, was my foster father...' Heavenly Rainbow's expression changed immediately as he heard the name, and he raised his white eyebrows.

Chen told him in detail about his relationship with Emperor Qian Long and about the plan to restore the Chinese Throne and overthrow the Manchus. Then he went on to ask the questions that had been so much on his mind: why his foster father had been expelled from the Shaolin School; and whether this expulsion had been in any way connected with the Emperor's identity.

'I beseech you, Venerable Sir,' he concluded, his voice almost choked with sobs. 'Think of my fellow-countrymen...'

Heavenly Rainbow sat in silence, his long eyebrows trailing over his closed eyes. He was deep in meditation and no one dared disturb him.

After a while, his eyes sprang open, and he spoke.

'For several hundred years, it has been the practice of the Shaolin School not to reveal to outsiders information on members who have offended in any way against the School's disciplinary regulations. Helmsman Chen, you have travelled a great distance to our Monastery to enquire into the behaviour of our expelled former disciple, Yu Wanting. According to the Monastery's rules, it would *ordinarily* be out of the question to give you an answer...' At the word 'ordinarily', the faces of the Red Flower heroes lit up with anticipation. 'But since, to use your own words, this affair involves the fate of millions of your fellow-countrymen, I am willing to make an exception. Helmsman Chen, please send someone to the Vinaya Hall to collect the file.'

Helmsman Chen bowed to the Abbot in thanks, and another monk led the Red Flower heroes away to their guest-rooms to rest.

Helmsman Chen was congratulating himself on his success when he detected a worried expression on Lord Zhou's face. 'What is troubling you?' he asked.

'The Abbot has instructed you to send someone to the Vinaya Hall to collect the file,' replied Zhou. 'But to reach the Vinaya Hall, you have to pass through five other halls. Every hall is guarded by a formidable kungfu master, each one of whom is stronger than the last. It will be extremely difficult to make it through all five.'

'We could try and force our way through together,' suggested Rolling Thunder Wen.

Lord Zhou shook his head. 'No. One person, unaided, must make his way through all five halls. If anyone helps him, the monks themselves will come to the assistance of the guardians of the halls and it will turn into a free-for-all. That wouldn't do at all.'

'This is an affair involving my family,' Chen said quietly. 'Perhaps Buddha will be merciful and let me through.'

He took off his long gown, picked up a bag of his Go-piece projectiles, tucked the antique dagger that Huo Qingtong had given him into his belt, and let Lord Zhou lead him to the first hall.

As they reached the hall entrance, Zhou stopped and whispered: 'Helmsman Chen, if you can't make it, please come back and we'll think of some other way. Whatever you do, don't try and force your way through or you may get hurt.' Chen nodded.

'We are ready!' Zhou shouted, and then stepped to one side.

Chen pushed open the door and walked inside. By the bright candlelight, he saw a monk seated on a mat and recognized him as one of the Abbot's chief assistants, Great Hardship.

The monk stood up and smiled. 'So you have come yourself, Helmsman Chen. That is excellent. I look forward to learning a few Martial Arts moves from you.'

Chen saluted him with his fists. 'Please,' he replied.

Great Hardship bunched his left hand into a fist and swung it round in a great arc while his right palm swept up. Chen recognized this as the Drunken Boxing kungfu style. He had once studied the style, but decided not to reveal the fact by using it now. Instead he clapped his own hands together and countered with a move from the Hundred Flowers kungfu style. Great Hardship was taken off guard and only avoided being struck by dropping to the floor. He rolled away and stood up, and the two continued to fight closely, each exhibiting total mastery of his own style.

Great Hardship now aimed a blow at Chen's legs. Chen leapt into the air, and, as he landed, hooked his right leg round, tripping the monk up neatly. As fast as lightning, Chen bent over and stopped him from falling. Great Hardship's face flushed red with embarrassment and he pointed behind him.

'Please proceed,' he said.

Chen saluted once more and walked through into the second hall, seated in the middle of which was the senior monk, Great Insanity. As Chen entered, the monk rose and picked up a thick staff lying beside him. He casually tapped the floor with its tip.

The impact shook the very walls of the hall, bringing a shower of dust down from the rafters. The monk then lightly flipped the staff from his left hand to his right, and attacked using the Crazy Demon staff style of kungfu. Chen knew it would be folly to underestimate the power of this opponent, and he drew his dagger. Great Insanity swept his staff across; Chen ducked down to avoid it, then countered with a thrust from his dagger. The two fought round and round inside the hall, their weapons apparently greatly mismatched.

Rather than attack, Chen concentrated instead on trying to tire the monk out. But Great Insanity's Inner Force kungfu was profound and, as time passed, Chen could discern not the slightest slowing of the monk's actions. On the contrary, his staff seemed to whirl and dance with ever-increasing speed, finally forcing Chen back into a corner of the hall. Seeing that Chen could not escape, Great Insanity grasped the staff in both hands and swung it down at his head with all his strength. Chen stood stock-still until the staff was no more than two inches from him, then grabbed its end and gouged a deep cut across the very middle of it with his dagger, snapping it clean in two.

Great Insanity was furious, and charged at Chen again. But with his staff only half its former length, he wielded it with much less dexterity. A moment later, Chen snapped another piece off the end, then dodged past the monk and ran towards the rear of the hall. With a roar of anger, Great Insanity threw what was left of his staff to the floor, making sparks fly in all directions.

At first, when he went on into the third hall, Helmsman Chen was dazzled by the combined light of so many candles, burning at both ends of the hall. Then he saw the monk Great Idiocy, standing in the centre.

'Helmsman Chen,' he said, a big smile on his face. 'Let us compete using projectiles.'

Chen bowed. 'As your Reverence wishes,' he replied.

'There are nine large candles and eighty-one incense-sticks at each end of the hall. Each of us takes one end. Whoever can extinguish all the candles and incense-sticks on his opponent's side is the winner.' The monk pointed to the altar-table in the centre of the hall. 'You will find darts and projectiles of all kinds on the altar. When you have used up whatever you have brought with you, you can go and help yourself to more.'

Chen pulled a number of Go-pieces from his pocket, wishing he had spent more time in the past learning the finer points of dart kungfu from the Red Flower Society's dart expert, Buddha Zhao. 'After you,' he said.

Great Idiocy smiled again. 'Guests first,' he replied.

Selecting five of his Go-pieces, Chen threw them simultaneously at the opposite wall and extinguished five incense-sticks.

'Excellent kungfu,' exclaimed Great Idiocy. He took a string of prayer-beads from around his neck, snapped the chord, and let five of the beads fall into his palm. With a single movement, he sent them whizzing through the air, snuffing out five incense-sticks at Chen's end of the hall.

Chen quickly extinguished another five sticks of incense. Great Idiocy replied by knocking out all nine candles at Chen's end. In the ensuing darkness, the burning tips of the incense-sticks became much easier targets for the monk.

'Of course, why didn't I think of that?' Chen thought. He selected nine Go-pieces and threw them three at a time at the candles at the monk's end of the hall. But the flames continued to burn. They had not been touched. He had heard a series of clicks coming from somewhere in the centre of the hall and realized that Great Idiocy had intercepted each of his nine projectiles with his prayer-beads. Chen gaped in amazement at this superlative skill. The monk went on to extinguish another four incense-sticks. Chen waited for the monk to launch another wave of prayer-beads, and then aimed his Go-pieces to intercept them. But with the candles on the opposite side still burning he found it difficult to spot the small beads clearly and only managed to hit two out of the five. The other three beads struck home.

Great Idiocy was now nine candles and two incense-sticks ahead. He had decided to concentrate on protecting his own candles, while extinguishing more of Chen's incense-sticks whenever the opportunity arose. In a short while, he had snuffed out another fourteen, while Chen, putting his all into the task, only managed to extinguish two of his opponent's candles. Suddenly, he remembered one of Buddha Zhao's tricks, known as the Silver Shuttle of the Flying Swallow. He hurled three Go-pieces with great force at the side wall of the hall. They ricocheted off the wall and two of the three struck their targets. Great Idiocy, who had thought the throw was merely a show of childish petulance on Chen's part, let out a cry of surprise. Even he could not intercept them.

'Excellent kungfu!' he cried, unable to stifle his admiration.

Chen continued in this way, bouncing Go-pieces off the side wall. Great Idiocy, though he now had no way of protecting his candles, was already many incense-sticks ahead, and so, taking little notice of his opponent, he redoubled his efforts to knock out the rest of Chen's. As the last of the monk's candles went out, the hall was plunged into total darkness. Chen counted seven incense-sticks burning at his own end, while the monk's end was still a mass of red dots, perhaps thirty or forty. Just as he was coming to the conclusion that he had lost, he heard Great Idiocy shout: 'Helmsman Chen, I've used up all my projectiles. Let's stop for a moment and get more from the altar-table.'

Chen felt in his bag and found that he too only had five or six Go-pieces left.

'You go first,' the monk added. Chen walked over to the altar-table and, with a flash of inspiration, swept all of the projectiles into his bag. He jumped back to his place and Great Idiocy ran over to find the tabletop empty. Chen then threw a shower of projectiles at the remaining fiery spots, and in a moment had extinguished them all.

Great Idiocy let out a hearty laugh. 'I have to hand it to you, Helmsman Chen,' he said. 'That was more of a battle of wits than a trial of strength. You win. Please continue.'

'I apologize,' Chen replied. 'I had already lost, and only resorted to such a low trick because of the importance of the matter. Please forgive me.'

'The masters guarding the next two halls are my own Shifu's brothers-in-arms. Their kungfu is of the highest order. You must be careful.'

Chen thanked him and went on to the fourth hall. This hall was also brightly lit with candles, but it was much smaller than the previous three. Two rattan mats were spread on the floor in the centre of the hall, and the senior monk Heavenly Mirror was sitting on one of them. As Chen entered, the monk stood up in greeting.

'Please be seated,' he said, gesturing to the other mat. Chen wondered how he wanted to compete, but took his seat in silence.

Heavenly Mirror was an extremely tall man and very formidable to look at. Even seated on the mat, he almost reached the height of an ordinary person. His cheeks were two deep hollows. There appeared to be no flesh on his body at all.

'You have passed through three halls, which is greatly to your credit,' he said. 'But you are still junior to me, so I cannot compete with you on equal terms. Let us do this: if you can complete ten moves with me without losing, I will let you through.'

Chen stood up and bowed to him. 'Thank you for your kindness, Your Reverence.' He sat down again.

'Now parry this!' grunted Heavenly Mirror.

Chen felt a mighty force moving irresistibly through the air towards his chest and raised his hands to counter it. Their palms met and Chen was forced to rise to his feet and make use of his full strength to keep from falling backwards. The shock of the impact set off a dull ache in his left arm. He sat down once more.

'Now for the second move!' called out Heavenly Mirror. This time Chen did not dare to counter directly with his hand. He leant to one side, then hit out at the monk's elbow. Heavenly Mirror should have responded by withdrawing his arm, but instead he swept it across in attack, and Chen only just managed to parry it. At this moment, a bell close to the hall began to chime, and as it resounded, Chen had an idea and leapt to his feet. He switched to the kungfu style he had learned at White Jade Peak, whirling around the hall and synchronizing his movements to the sound of the bell. Heavenly Mirror gasped in surprise and fought back carefully. When the bell ceased, Chen withdrew his hands and sat down. 'I cannot continue,' he said.

'That is quite enough!' exclaimed Heavenly Mirror. 'We have already exchanged more than forty moves. Your kungfu is superb. Please pass.'

Chen stood up, and was about to leave when he suddenly swayed and stumbled, and had to hurriedly lean against the wall for support. Heavenly Mirror helped him to sit down again.

'It was just that very first blow of mine,' he said. 'Rest here for a moment and catch your breath. It won't affect matters.'

Chen closed his eyes and did as the monk said.

'Tell me, where did you learn that style of kungfu?' Heavenly Mirror asked. Chen told him the story.

'I am amazed that such a superb style of kungfu has ever existed out there in the west, on the border. If you had used that style from the start you would not have hurt your arm.'

'But I am hurt,' Chen said, 'and I'm sure I won't be able to make it through the last hall. What does Your Reverence suggest I do?'

'If you can't make it through, then turn back now.'

Chen's Martial Arts training made it impossible for him to accept defeat so easily. He stood up and bowed to Heavenly Mirror, then strode on bravely towards the fifth and last hall.

He was surprised to discover that the last hall was in fact no more than a tiny meditation chamber (far too small for any normal sort of kungfu contest), and he was dismayed to see, seated cross-legged on a couch in the centre of it, the Abbot of the Shaolin Monastery, Heavenly Rainbow himself. Helmsman Chen could not imagine what sort of contest it was going to be, and how he could possibly stand any chance of overcoming the best kungfu fighter in the Shaolin Monastery, when the Abbot's junior, Heavenly Mirror, had already proved so formidable.

The Abbot rose to his feet and bowed. 'Please be seated,' he said. Chen sat down on one end of the meditation-couch. A steady stream of sandalwood-scented smoke rose from an incense brazier on a small table between them. On the wall opposite hung a scroll of those two crazy monks, Cold Mountain and his side-kick Shi De. Although executed with only a few bold brush-strokes, the painting was full of the unmistakable vitality of Zen.

Heavenly Rainbow meditated for a moment, then said: 'There was once a man who was very successful at herding goats. He became very rich, but he was by nature very miserly...'

Chen was greatly puzzled to hear the Abbot launch into a story, but he tried to concentrate on what the old man was saying: 'An acquaintance of the goatherd knew that he was very stupid, and also that he badly wanted to find a wife. So he cheated the goatherd, saying: "I know a girl who is very beautiful. I can arrange for her to marry you." The goatherd was delighted and gave him a large amount of money. A year passed, and the man said to him: "Your wife has given birth to your son." The goatherd hadn't even seen the woman, but hearing that he had a son, he was more pleased than ever and gave the man another large sum of money. Later, the man came to him again and said: "Your son has died!" The goatherd cried uncontrollably. He was utterly heartbroken.'

Chen was well enough read to know that the Abbot was quoting from the *Hundred Parables Sutra* of the Mahayana School of Buddhism.

'All worldly matters are like this,' the Abbot continued. 'Rank and wealth are like the wife and child of that goatherd: illusions. Why waste effort for the joy of obtaining them when losing them will only cause sorrow?'

'There was once a husband and wife who had three cakes,' Chen replied. 'They ate one cake each, but could not decide who should eat the third. Finally, they agreed that whoever talked first would be the one *not* to eat the cake.'

It was another story from the *Hundred Parables Sutra*. Heavenly Rainbow nodded.

'The two stared at each other in silence,' continued Chen. 'Soon afterwards, a thief entered and ransacked the house for the couple's valuables but, because of their agreement, the couple continued to stare at each other and neither said a word. Seeing them thus silent, the thief became bolder still and proceeded to rape the wife in front of her husband's eyes. The husband made no complaint at all about what was happening, but in the end the wife could stand it no longer and cried out. The thief grabbed the valuables and fled, while the husband clapped his hands and shouted triumphantly: "You lose! The cake is mine!"'

Heavenly Rainbow could not help but smile, even though he was already familiar with the story.

'The husband turned a blind eye to great suffering for the sake of some minor personal satisfaction,' commented Chen. 'He allowed the thief to steal his possessions and rape his wife merely in order to satisfy his appetite for cake. This was wrong. The Buddhist faith teaches us to try to help all living things and not think only of ourselves.'

Heavenly Rainbow sighed, and himself began quoting from the Buddhist scriptures: 'There is no Permanence in human actions; in all of Dharma there is no self. All obstacles spring from pre-existing Karma. Let there be no desire, and no untoward thoughts will arise.'

'Life for sentient beings is full of hardship,' Chen replied. 'The monk Zhi Daolin once said: "The Tyrants of Old were cruel by nature. One cannot stand idly by and watch such evil being done."'

The Abbot could see Chen's determination to carry out his duty and help ease the burden of his fellow-countrymen, and was full of respect for him.

'Your enthusiasm is commendable, Helmsman Chen,' he said. 'I will set you one more question, and then you can have your way.'

Chen bowed his head in acknowledgement.

'An old woman was once lying under a tree, resting. Suddenly, a huge bear appeared, and wished to eat her. She jumped up and ran behind the tree to escape, and the bear stretched its paws round either side of the tree to grab her. Seizing the opportunity, the old woman pressed its paws down onto the tree trunk. As a result, the bear could not move, but the old woman did not dare to let go either. Some time later, a man passed by and the old woman appealed to him for help, saying they could kill the bear together and share the meat. The man believed her and took her place holding down the bear's paws. The old woman then fled, leaving the man in the same predicament she had been in.'

Chen knew the moral of the story: 'Never regret helping others, even if you suffer yourself as a result,' he replied.

Heavenly Rainbow swished the long-haired duster he was holding—a symbol of his own renunciation of the Red Dust of the world. 'You may go through,' he said.

Chen stood up and bowed before him. 'Please forgive me for disturbing the tranquillity of this sacred place,' he said.

The old Abbot nodded. As he walked out of the room, Chen heard him sigh.

Confession

Helmsman Chen passed along a covered pathway and into yet another hall lit by two massive, flickering candles and filled with row after row of wooden cabinets, each one marked with a piece of yellowing paper stuck to the side. He picked up one of the candles and began his search. Before long, he located the cabinet he was looking for. He opened it and found inside three parcels wrapped in yellow cloth. The parcel on the left was inscribed in vermilion ink with his foster father's name: 'Yu Wanting'. Chen's hands shook slightly and several drops of candlewax spattered on the floor. Then, with a silent prayer, he opened the parcel.

It contained a thick file of yellowing papers, a man's embroidered waistcoat, and a woman's white undergarment which was badly ripped and speckled with black spots that appeared to be bloodstains. Chen opened the file and began reading from the beginning:

'I, Yu Wanting, a twenty-first generation disciple of the Shaolin Monastery of Putian, Fujian Province, do hereby respectfully confess in full my misdemeanours.

'I was born into a peasant family and spent my youth in great poverty and hardship. I knew the girl Xu Chaosheng, who lived next door, from when we were very young. As we grew, we came to love one another dearly...'

Chen's heart began to thump wildly. Could it be that his foster father's misdemeanour had something to do with his mother? He continued reading:

'We secretly agreed to remain faithful to each other for life, and to marry no one else. After the death of my father, there were several years of drought, and, with nothing in the fields to harvest, I went out into the world to find a life for myself. Thanks to the compassion of my benevolent master, I was taken in by the Monastery. The embroidered waistcoat enclosed was given to me by the girl Xu when I left home.

'Before I had been fully initiated into the higher skills of the Shaolin Martial Arts School, I left temporarily to return to my home village. Because of the girl Xu's warmth and kindness towards me, I was unable to abandon worldly emotions and went back to see her. By now she was a woman. I was shocked to find that her father had married her into the family of the local landlord, to a man named Chen. In my extreme anguish, I entered the Chen mansion one night to visit her. Using Martial Arts skills I had learned from the Shaolin School, I trespassed on the property of an ordinary citizen for personal reasons. This was my first breach of discipline.

'The woman Xu moved with her husband to Peking and, three years later, having failed to renounce my love for her, I went there to visit her again. As it happened, that very night, she gave birth to a son. I was outside the window and managed to catch a glimpse of the child. Four days later, I returned once more and found the woman Xu looking very pale. She told me that her son had been taken away by the Princess Rong Zhang, and had been replaced with a baby girl. Before we had a chance to talk further, four assassins entered, obviously sent by the Princess to kill the woman Xu. In the heat of the fight, I received a sword wound on my forehead, but I killed all four assassins before myself losing consciousness. The woman Xu bandaged my wound with the enclosed undergarment. I heard an Imperial secret, and I was seen by others to use Shaolin kungfu; I thereby risked bringing great trouble upon the School. This was my second breach of discipline.

'For the next ten years, although I was in Peking, I did not dare to go and see the woman Xu again, but submerged myself in the study of kungfu. Finally Emperor Yong Zheng died and his son Qian Long succeeded him to the Throne. I worked out the dates and realized that this Qian Long was in fact the son of the woman Xu. Knowing how cold-blooded a man the Emperor Yong Zheng had been during his life, I was afraid that he might have left orders for her to be killed, in order to silence her and safeguard the secret of Qian Long's parenthood. I therefore entered the Chen mansion again. One night, two assassins did indeed come. I killed them both and found Yong Zheng's written order on one of them. I enclose the document.'

Chen flipped through the rest of the pile of papers and found at the very end a note on which was written: 'If, when I die, Minister Chen Shiguan and his wife are still alive, they must both be speedily killed.' It was unmistakably the calligraphy of Emperor Yong Zheng. Yong Zheng must have known that the Chens would not dare breathe a word while he was still alive; but he suspected that they might try to make use of the information after his death. Helmsman Chen continued reading.

'The young Emperor Qian Long apparently knew nothing of the matter, for no more assassins were sent to the Chens. But I could not rest easy, so I decided to dress as a commoner and obtain employment in the Chen mansion, where I chopped firewood and carried water. This I did for five years. Only when I was certain there would be no further repercussions did I leave. I acted with great recklessness and, if I had been discovered, it would have caused great embarrassment to the Shaolin School, and would have damaged the School's honour. This was my third breach of discipline.'

Now Chen understood why it was that his mother had wanted him to go away with Yu, and why Yu had died of a broken heart after his mother's death. He thought of Yu working for five years as a lowly servant in his own household to protect his mother. What an expression of true love! What an overwhelming sense of duty! He wondered which of the many servants around the house when he was young was Yu.

After a while, he wiped his eyes and read on: 'I am guilty of three serious breaches of discipline. Full of apprehension, I hereby present the full facts to my benevolent Shifu and plead for leniency.'

Yu's submission ended at that point and was followed by a comment written in vermilion characters: 'Yu Wanting has committed three misdemeanours. If he is truly willing to reform and follow the teachings of the Buddha, why should we not forgive him, just as the Buddha was willing to forgive the Ten Sins? But if he still hankers after worldly passions and refuses to use his intelligence to break the bonds of emotion, then he should immediately be expelled. It is up to him.'

So Yu was expelled from the Shaolin School because he could not renounce his worldly passion for Chen's mother... As the Helmsman reflected on his foster father's fate, he looked up and saw that the stars on the western horizon were beginning to fade, while in the east day had already broken. He blew out the candles, wrapped the papers and other items up in the yellow cloth, and picked up the parcel. He closed the cabinet doors and slowly walked back out to the courtyard where he found a statue of a laughing Buddha gazing down at him. He wondered what his foster father must have felt after his expulsion, confronted with this Buddha in the courtyard. He walked back through the five halls, all of them now deserted.

As he passed through the last doorway, Lord Zhou and the Red Flower heroes came forward to greet him. They had waited anxiously for half the night and were delighted to see him returning safely. But as he came closer, they saw his weary look, and his red, swollen eyes. Chen gave them a brief account of what had happened, omitting to tell them only about the relationship between his foster father and his mother.

'Our business here is finished,' he said. The others nodded.

Lord Zhou accompanied Chen back inside to bid farewell to the Abbot, then the Red Flower heroes collected their belongings before starting out.

Just as they were leaving the Monastery, Zhou Qi went pale and almost fainted. Her father quickly helped her back inside to lie down, and the Monastery physician announced after examining her that she was in no condition to travel and would have to rest at the Monastery to await the birth. Zhou Qi could only smile bitterly and agree.

The others discussed the situation and decided that Lord Zhou and Mastermind Xu should both stay behind to look after Zhou Qi, and join them in Peking after the birth of the child. Lord Zhou rented some cottages a couple of miles west of the Monastery for them to live in, and Chen and the other Red Flower heroes started off north.

A Bigger Desert

They arrived in the town of Tai'an in Shandong Province, and were met there by the local Red Flower Society Lodge Master who informed them that Melancholy Ghost Shi had also just arrived from Peking. The Red Flower heroes were delighted and went to see him. Xin Yan ran on ahead, shouting, 'Brother Shi! The traitor's dead!' Shi looked at him blankly. 'Fire Hand Zhang!' Xin Yan shouted.

Shi's face lit up. 'Zhang is dead?'

'Yes, he was eaten up by wolves!'

Shi bowed before Helmsman Chen and the others.

'Brother Shi,' said Chen. 'Have your wounds fully healed?'

'Thank you for your concern, Helmsman. Yes, they are completely better. You and the others must have had a long, hard journey.'

'Is there any news from the Capital?'

Shi's expression turned grim. 'No, none from the Capital. But I have hurried here to report that the Hodja's entire army has been destroyed.'

'What?' Chen's face went white.

'When we left the Uighur lands, General Zhao Hui and the remains of his army were competely surrounded,' said Luo Bing. 'How could the Manchus have managed to score another victory?'

Shi sighed. 'Reinforcements suddenly arrived from the south. According to those Uighurs who managed to flee, the Hodja and his son fought to the death. Lady Huo Qingtong was ill at the time of the attack and was unable to direct the defence. No one knows what happened to her.'

Helmsman Chen slumped down into a chair.

'Lady Huo Qingtong has an excellent command of kungfu,' said Hidden Needle Lu. 'She would not come to any harm at the hands of the Manchu troops.'

They all knew he was just trying to ease Helmsman Chen's anxiety. It was difficult to see how a sick girl could protect herself in the confusion of battle.

'Huo Qingtong has a sister called Hasli,' said Luo Bing. 'Did you hear any news of her?'

'None at all,' Shi replied. 'But she is well known. If anything had happened to her, there would be bound to be reports circulating in the Capital. I heard nothing, so I presume she is all right.'

Helmsman Chen was embarrassed by the extent of their concern for his feelings. 'I'll go inside and rest for a while,' he said, and walked to his room in the inn where they were staying.

'Go and look after him,' Luo Bing whispered to Xin Yan. The boy ran after his master.

After a short while, Chen thrust aside the curtain to his room and strode out again. 'We must eat quickly, and move on to Peking as quickly as possible,' he said.

The new note of determination in his voice surprised the Red Flower heroes. Rolling Thunder Wen raised his thumb in agreement and tucked into his food with increased gusto.

It was not long before they were on the road again. Helmsman Chen forced himself to smile and chat with the others along the way, but his expression became more and more drawn as the days went by. Before too long, they arrived in Peking. When he was in the Capital before, Melancholy Ghost Shi had rented a large residence in Twin Willows Lane: Father Speckless, the Twin Knights, Buddha Zhao, and Iron Pagoda Yang were all there waiting for them.

'Brother Zhao,' Helmsman Chen said to Buddha Zhao. 'I want you to go with Xin Yan to see the commander of the Emperor's Guard, Bai Zhen. Take the lute that the Emperor gave me, and the jade vase that Luo Bing stole, and give them to him to pass on to the Emperor. That way he will know that we are here.'

Buddha Zhao and Xin Yan left and returned several hours later.

'We went to Bai Zhen's home to look for him and he happened to be there,' Xin Yan reported. 'We gave Brother Zhao's name card to one of his servants, and he rushed out to greet us. He dragged us inside and insisted on us drinking several cups of wine before letting us go. Extremely friendly.'

Chen nodded.

Early the next morning, Bai Zhen paid them a visit in person. He chatted with Buddha Zhao for a while about the weather, then asked respectfully if he could see Helmsman Chen.

'The Emperor has ordered me to bring you to the Palace,' he whispered to Chen when he appeared.

'Good,' replied Chen. 'Please wait here for a moment.'

He went back inside to discuss the situation with the others. They all thought he should exercise the utmost caution. Several of the Red Flower heroes accompanied him into the Forbidden City, while Rolling Thunder Wen and the rest stationed themselves outside the Palace walls to await their return. With Bai Zhen leading the way, Chen and the others walked through the Palace gates, past rows of guards who respectfully bowed to them. They were overawed by the imposing atmosphere of the Palace: its huge walls and impregnable defences. They had walked for a good while when two eunuchs ran up to Bai Zhen.

'Master Bai,' said one. 'The Emperor is in the Precious Moon Pavilion, and orders you to take Chen Jialuo there to see him.'

Bai nodded, and turned to Chen. 'We are now entering the Inner Sanctuary of the Palace. Please instruct all your men to leave their weapons here.' The Red Flower heroes were uneasy at this, but they knew they had no alternative and did as he said, placing their swords on a nearby table. Bai led them through countless halls and across countless courtyards, until they finally stopped in front of a large, richly decorated pavilion, built in the manner of a pagoda and reaching several storeys into the sky.

'Announcing Chen Jialuo!' he called out. Chen straightened his cap and gown and followed an old eunuch into the pavilion while Father Speckless and the others were forced to remain outside.

They climbed up the stairs to the fifth floor, and entered a room in which they found Qian Long, seated and smiling. Chen knelt down and kowtowed before him respectfully.

'You've come at last!' exclaimed Qian Long. 'Excellent. Please be seated.' With a wave of his hand he dismissed the eunuch. Chen remained standing where he was.

'Sit down and let us talk,' Qian Long repeated. Only then did Chen thank him and take a seat.

'What do you think of this pavilion?' the Emperor asked.

'Where else would one find such a fine building but in the Imperial Palace?'

'I told them to build it quickly. From start to finish, it took less than two months. If there had been more time, it would have been even more elegant. But it will do as it is.'

'Yes,' replied Chen. He wondered how many workers and craftsmen had died of exhaustion during the construction.

Qian Long stood up. 'You have just returned from the Uighur lands. Come and see. I want your opinion. Does this look like a desert scene?' Chen followed him to a window and, as he looked out, started in surprise.

To the right was a classic Imperial Chinese garden, filled with purple and red blooms, pergolas and bowers, and twisting paths, a sumptuous scene of the sort with which he was familiar. But looking left, towards the west, the view was entirely different. For about a third of a mile, the ground was covered in varying shades of yellow and arranged into small sand-dunes. Looking closely, Chen could detect signs of previous pavilions having been knocked down, water pools filled in, and trees and bushes uprooted. The scene naturally lacked the natural majesty of the endless desert, but it was a good likeness.

'Does Your Majesty like desert views?' he asked.

Qian Long smiled. 'Tell me, what do you think of it?'

'A lot of work has certainly been put into it,' Chen replied. There were a number of Uighur tents staked on the sand, with three camels tied up nearby; with a sudden heartache, Chen thought of Hasli and her sister. Looking beyond, he saw hundreds of workers busy demolishing yet more buildings: the Emperor had obviously decided he wanted a bigger desert.

Chen wondered why on earth Qian Long would have had a piece of dry, desolate desert constructed in the Palace grounds. Placed in the middle of such a lush Chinese garden, it looked incongruous, even ludicrous.

Qian Long walked away from the window and pointed to the antique lute he had given Chen, which was now lying on a small table.

'Why don't you play me a tune?' he said.

Chen could see the Emperor did not wish to discuss the important business at hand, so he sat down and began to pluck the strings. As he played, something caught his eye. He looked up to see the jade vases decorated with Hasli's image smiling at him across the room. She was smiling at him, and yet at the same time there were tears in her eyes. With a twang, one of the lute-strings broke.

'What's the matter?' Qian Long asked. He smiled. 'Are you feeling a little nervous, here in the Palace?'

Chen stood up and replied respectfully: 'Your humble servant has disgraced himself in front of your Celestial Majesty.'

Qian Long laughed. He seemed amused by this. Chen lowered his head and noticed that Qian Long's left hand was bound with a white cloth as if it had been wounded. Qian Long's face flushed red and he hurriedly put the hand behind his back.

'Did you bring the things I wanted?' he asked.

'They are with my friends downstairs,' Chen replied.

Qian Long picked up a small hammer and rapped the table with it twice. A young eunuch ran in. 'Tell the gentlemen accompanying Chen Jialuo to come up,' the Emperor ordered. The eunuch returned a moment later with the six Red Flower heroes.

Chen stood up and shot them a glance. They knew at once that they had no option but to kneel down and kowtow before Qian Long.

'You stinking Emperor!' thought Father Speckless to himself as he did so. 'We almost scared you out of your wits that time in the pagoda in Hangzhou, but you're still just as damned arrogant as ever. If it wasn't for the Helmsman, I'd kill you this instant.'

Chen took a small, sealed wooden box from Buddha Zhao and placed it on the table. 'The items you requested are in here,' he said.

'Good. That will be all,' Qian Long replied. 'When I have looked at them I will send for you.' Chen kowtowed again. 'And take the lute with you,' he added.

Chen picked up the lute and handed it to Leopard Wei, then said: 'I know that Your Majesty has already subdued the Uighur lands. Your servant pleads with you to be merciful and to order that there be no indiscriminate killings there.'

Qian Long did not answer, but simply waved them all away with his hand. Bai Zhen led them to the Palace gate where Rolling Thunder Wen and the others were waiting.

Broken Glass

When Helmsman Chen had gone, Qian Long dismissed the eunuch and opened the small box. He read Emperor Yong Zheng's note and the letter written by his natural mother, which was correct in saying that he had a red birthmark on his left buttock. He sighed. There could no longer be any doubt about his true origins. He ordered a eunuch to bring him a brazier and threw the documents one by one into the fire. As the flames leapt up, he began to feel more at ease, and on an impulse, threw the small wooden box into the flames as well, filling the room with heat and smoke.

He stared for a moment at the jade vases on the table, then said to the eunuch: 'Send her up.' The eunuch disappeared. When he returned, he fell to his knees and reported: 'Your slave deserves to die. The lady refuses to come.'

Qian Long laughed shortly and glanced at the jade vases again. Then he stood up and went downstairs. Two eunuchs followed, carrying the vases.

One floor down, a maidservant pulled aside a curtain and Qian Long walked through into a room full of fresh flowers. Two other maidservants took the vases from the eunuchs and carefully placed them on a table. A girl wearing a white gown was sitting facing the wall. With a wave of his hand, Qian Long now dismissed the maidservants. He had just opened his mouth to speak when the door-curtains parted and two guards came in and stood quietly by the entrance.

'What are you doing here? Get out,' he said angrily.

'Your slaves have orders from the Empress Dowager to protect Your Majesty,' said one of the guards.

'I'm fine. Why do I need protection?'

'The Empress Dowager knows that she…that the lady is not…that she is strong-willed. Her Imperial Highness is afraid that she will inflict injury on Your Majesty's precious self.'

Qian Long glanced down at his bandaged hand, and shouted: 'I don't need you! Get out!'

The two guards kowtowed frantically but did not retire. He knew that no matter what, they would not dare to disobey the Empress Dowager's orders, so he took no further notice of them, and turned back to the girl in the white gown.

'Turn around, I have something to say,' he said, speaking haltingly in the Uighur tongue. The girl took no notice. In her hand was a dagger. She gripped it even tighter.

Qian Long sighed. 'Look at what is on the table,' he said. The girl ignored him for a moment, but finally her curiosity got the better of her. She glanced round and saw the pair of jade vases. At the same moment, the Emperor and the guards were dazzled by her beauty: it was Hasli, or to give her the title by which she was known in the Palace, the Fragrant Princess.

She had been finally captured by General Zhao Hui's army and sent to Peking under special guard to the Emperor. Some time before her capture, Qian Long had already decided that it would be more interesting to be able to talk to the girl directly, so he had called for a teacher to teach him some Uighur. He was an intelligent man and had studied diligently. After a few months he could talk in a fashion.

But Hasli's heart was already tightly bound to Helmsman Chen. Furthermore, Qian Long had been responsible for the death of her father, which made her all the more adamant in her rejection of his advances. Several times she had been forced almost to the point of suicide, but each time she thought of Chen and restrained herself.

'It's just like when I was surrounded by the wolves,' she thought. 'The large wolf wanted to eat me, but *he* finally saved me.'

Qian Long watched her becoming more pale and drawn day by day. He was afraid she would die of melancholy, so he called for the Capital's best craftsmen and had the Precious Moon Pavilion built for her to live in.

But the Fragrant Princess took not the slightest bit of notice of the new building. She studiedly ignored the priceless treasures decorating the pavilion, all except for the murals covering the walls, which were painted by the Italian Jesuit priest Giuseppe Castiglione. These depicted scenes of the Uighur lands, and she would stare at them endlessly, glassy-eyed, reliving over and over the days she and Chen had spent there together.

Sometimes Qian Long spied on her secretly and saw her staring into the distance, the trace of a smile playing around her lips. One day he could contain himself no longer and had come bursting in, stretching out his hand to grasp her by the arm. There was a flash of steel, and only the Princess' ignorance of kungfu and his own sprightliness had saved him from her dagger. But his left hand had been badly cut and in a moment was covered in blood. He was so scared by the incident that, from that moment on, he never risked provoking her again. When the Empress Dowager heard of the matter, she ordered the eunuchs to take the dagger off the girl, but the Princess pointed it at her chest and threatened to commit suicide whenever anyone came near her. So Qian Long ordered them to stay away from her and not to interfere.

The Princess was also afraid they would put something in her food or drink so, apart from fresh fruit she had peeled herself, she would touch nothing. Qian Long had a Uighur-style bath constructed for her, but she refused to use it, and stitched up her gown so that it could not be removed. After many days of not bathing, her body fragrance became even more pronounced. She had always been such a naïve, romantic girl, ignorant of worldly affairs. Now, surrounded as she was in the Palace by evil and danger, she was obliged in a very short space of time to grow stronger and more determined.

She was shocked when she spotted the vases, and quickly turned back to face the wall, gripping the hilt of the dagger ever more tightly and wondering what Qian Long was up to.

He sighed. 'When I first saw your image on the vases, I was certain that such a beautiful person could not exist in this world,' he said. 'But now I have seen you, I know that the greatest of craftsmen could not capture a ten-thousandth part of your beauty.'

The Princess ignored him.

'If you continue to fret and brood like this all day, you are going to make yourself ill,' he continued. 'Do you miss your home? Go and look out of the window.' He ordered the guards to open the shutters.

The Princess looked at the two guards and Qian Long standing near the window, pulled a face, and turned away. Qian Long understood; he walked to the other side of the room and ordered the guards to do the same. Only then did the Princess slowly walk over to the window and look outside. She saw the expanse of sand, the Uighur tents, the little mosque, and her heart twisted in pain. Two tears rolled slowly down her cheeks. Then, in a sudden fit of anger, she picked up one of the vases on the table and threw it with all her strength at Qian Long's head.

One of the guards shot forward and intercepted the vase, but it slipped from his grasp and shattered on the floor. Then the second vase came flying after it. The other guard tried to catch this second one, but it too slipped through his hands and ended up in pieces beside the first.

Afraid that she would try some other way of harming the Emperor, the guards sprang across the room at her. The Princess put the dagger to her own throat.

'Stop!' Qian Long shouted, and the guards halted in their tracks. The Princess retreated several steps, and as she did there was a clinking sound as something fell from her dress to the ground. The guards were afraid it was some new kind of weapon and quickly retrieved it. Seeing it was a piece of jade, they handed it to the Emperor.

Qian Long took hold of it, and his face drained of colour. He recognized it instantly as the piece of 'warm jade' he had given to Helmsman Chen on the breakwater at Haining. When he had presented it, he remembered having told Chen to give it to his chosen sweetheart.

'Do you know this man?' he asked, flustered, almost as if he was talking to himself. He paused for a second, then said: 'Where did this piece of jade come from?'

The Princess put out her hand. 'Give it back to me,' she said.

Qian Long's jealousy flared. 'Tell me who gave it to you and I will return it.'

'My husband gave it to me.'

Qian Long was greatly surprised by this reply.

'I didn't know you were married already.'

'I'm not, but my heart has long been his,' she answered proudly. 'He is the kindest and bravest person in the world. I know he will rescue me from you. He is not afraid of you and neither am I, even though you are Emperor.'

'I know the man you are talking about,' he said, his voice full of hatred. 'He is the Helmsman of the Red Flower Society, a man called Chen Jialuo. He's nothing more than a bandit leader. What's so special about him?'

The Princess' heart leapt for joy at the mere sound of Chen's name and her face lit up.

'So you know of him too. It would be better for you if you let me go.'

Qian Long looked up and caught a glimpse of his own face in her dressing-table mirror. He thought of Helmsman Chen, a man of handsome, cultured appearance, a man equally versed in the refinements of scholarship and in the manly Martial Arts. He knew he could never be a match for him. Full of jealousy and hatred, he threw the piece of jade at his own reflection, smashing the mirror, and covering the floor in broken glass. The Princess rushed forward to pick up the jade, which was unharmed, and wiped it lovingly, which made Qian Long angrier than ever. With a stamp of his foot, he stormed out of the room and down the stairs.

He went to the study where he usually read and wrote poetry in peace and quiet, and spotted a half-written poem on the desk entitled 'Precious Moon Pavilion'. He had been working on two lines:

> *The Fairy Princess is in the Pavilion,*
> *A vision from the Son of Heaven's dreams of former days.*

In a flash of anger, he ripped up the poem, and sat there in silence for a long time.

Slowly, his temper cooled. 'After all,' he thought to himself, 'I am the Son of Heaven, I am supposed to be all-powerful. I could never understand why this barbarian girl kept holding out against me. Now the truth has finally come out: it's all the fault of Chen Jialuo. Her stubbornness is simply the result of his meddling.

'He appealed to me to drive the Manchus out of China, and set up a Chinese dynasty. It seemed a good idea. But things might not go as planned; the affair might end in failure, and my life could end as well. I've been turning this whole thing over and over in my mind for months now, and I still can't come to a decision! What should I do?'

Another thought came rushing into his mind: 'The way things are at present, I can do whatever I like. If Chen's idea *were* successful, I could end up being controlled by him and his people. I couldn't allow myself to become a puppet! Why should I abandon what I have for the sake of uncertain future glory? This girl thinks of nothing but him. Very well, we'll settle these two matters together.'

He seemed to have reached a decision. He ordered a eunuch to call for Bai Zhen, who appeared shortly afterwards. 'Station four top-ranking guards on each floor of the Precious Moon Pavilion and another twenty outside,' he ordered. 'There must be no slip-ups of any kind.' Bai Zhen bowed. 'And call for Chen Jialuo again. I have important business to discuss with him. Tell him to come alone.'

The Setting Sun

When Helmsman Chen received the Imperial Command, he went to discuss the situation with the others. Hidden Needle Lu and

Rolling Thunder Wen were both concerned that the order to go alone could indicate a trap.

'The fact that he has called me back so soon after receiving the evidence I gave him must mean he wants to talk about it,' argued Chen. 'This could be our big chance to recover China for the Chinese. I have to go, no matter what dangers are waiting for me. Brother Wu,' he added, turning to Father Speckless. 'If I don't return, please take over command of the Red Flower Society and avenge me.'

'Set your mind at ease, Helmsman,' replied the priest, deeply moved.

'There's no need for you to wait for me outside the Palace this time,' said Helmsman Chen. 'If he means to harm me, there is no way you could help me, and trying would just cause needless casualties.'

By the time Helmsman Chen re-entered the inner sanctuary of the Palace with Bai Zhen, it was already dark. Two eunuchs carrying lanterns led them to the Precious Moon Pavilion through the webs of moonlight and shadow cast by the branches of trees. This time, they went up to the fourth floor and, as soon as the eunuchs reported Chen's arrival, Qian Long ordered him to be sent in. The Emperor was seated on a couch in a small room, a far-away look in his eyes. Chen knelt and kowtowed and Qian Long told him to be seated. He was silent for a while. Chen looked around him and noticed a poetic couplet on the wall written by Qian Long himself.

'What do you think?' Qian Long asked, seeing him reading it.

'Your Majesty has high aspirations. You have the spirit of an Emperor of great courage and intelligence. When our Grand Design is successfully accomplished, and the Manchus have been driven from China, your merit will far exceed even that of the Han-dynasty Emperor who expelled the Tartars or the Ming-dynasty Emperor who threw out the Mongols. You will be remembered for ten thousand generations.'

Qian Long was delighted to hear such praise. He smiled and stroked his whiskers. 'You and I may be servant and master, but in spirit we are brothers,' he said after a moment's contemplation. 'In the future, I shall need you by my side.'

Chen was overjoyed to hear these words. From his tone, Qian Long did not appear to be planning to go back on his oath. His doubts dispersed, Chen knelt down once again and kowtowed.

'Your Majesty's wise decision is truly a great blessing for the people,' he said.

Qian Long sighed. 'I may be the Son of Heaven, but I am not as blessed by fortune as you are,' he said. Chen wondered what he could be referring to. 'Do you remember,' continued Qian Long, 'in August last year, when we were in Haining, I gave you a piece of jade? Do you still have it with you?'

Chen was taken completely unawares by this. 'Your Majesty told me to pass it on to someone else,' he replied, 'and I have already done so.'

'I know how high your standards are. The person to whom you gave it must be one of the world's most beautiful women.'

Chen's eyes reddened. 'Unfortunately, I do not know if she is dead or alive, or where she might be. When our business here is concluded, I will search to the ends of the earth to find her.'

'You obviously love this lady deeply.'

'Yes, I do,' said Chen quietly.

'The Dowager Empress, the woman the outside world calls my mother, is a Manchu, as I am sure you are aware.'

'Yes.' Helmsman Chen wondered where this was all leading.

'She has looked after me for a long time and is a very virtuous and devoted woman. If we go ahead with this plan of ours, she will certainly fight it to the death. What do you think should be done?'

Chen was unable to answer. 'Your Majesty's opinions are sacred,' he finally said. 'Your servant would not dare make any reckless suggestions.'

'I cannot allow the nation to be split in two. This consideration has made me very uncertain of late. Also, at present I have a personal problem which unfortunately no one can help me with.'

'I will do whatever Your Majesty orders.'

'One gentleman should never snatch a prized possession from another,' replied Qian Long. 'But this is something decided by Fate. Ah! When a man's love is concentrated on one person, to the exclusion of all else, what can that man hope to do? Go over there and take a look.'

He pointed to a doorway on one side of the room, then stood up and walked out.

Helmsman Chen was greatly confused by Qian Long's strange and rambling words. He calmed himself and pulled aside the thick door-curtain, then walked slowly through into what he saw was an extremely sumptuous bedchamber. A red candle burned in the corner, and a girl in a white gown sat staring at its flame.

The shock of seeing Hasli in the depths of the Imperial Palace was almost too much for Helmsman Chen. He swayed unsteadily on his feet, and was unable to speak. Upon hearing the footsteps, the Princess had grasped the hilt of her dagger tightly. Then she looked round, and saw before her the very person she had been dreaming of day and night. Her angry glare immediately melted into an expression of blissful delight. She cried out and ran across the room to throw herself into Chen's arms.

'I knew you would come and save me!' she cried. 'All I had to do was wait patiently, and you would be sure to come!'

Chen held her warm body tightly. 'Are we dreaming?' he asked. She looked up and shook her head as tears began to course down her cheeks.

Chen's first thought was that the Emperor had found out that Hasli was his sweetheart, and had brought her from the Uighur lands so that she could be with him. He put his arms around her waist and then unselfconsciously kissed her on the lips. In the sweetness of the long kiss, they became oblivious to everything around them.

After a long, long time, Chen finally looked at the pink flush on her cheeks. Behind her, on her dressing-table, he noticed a broken mirror, and in it he saw the fractured image of the two of them embracing.

'Look,' he whispered. 'There are one thousand pieces of me, and each one of them is holding you.'

The Princess glanced at the broken mirror, and then pulled the piece of warm jade from her pocket.

'He stole my jade and broke the mirror with it,' she said. 'Luckily it wasn't damaged.'

'Who?' Chen asked, startled.

'That evil Emperor.'

'Why would he do that?' Chen asked, even more astonished.

'He tried to have his way with me again, but I said I wasn't afraid because I knew you would come and rescue me. He got very angry and tried to grab me, but I have this dagger.'

'Dagger?' he repeated in a far-away voice.

'Yes. I was with my father when they killed him. He gave me this dagger of his, and told me to kill myself if one of the enemy ever tried to violate me. People who commit suicide are sent to Hell, but Allah makes an exception if they are girls dying to protect their virtue.'

As she said this, she handed him the dagger. Helmsman Chen looked at her and wondered how many times this weak, naive girl had come close to death in the past few months. His heart was filled with love and pain and he embraced her again. After a while, he steadied himself and began to consider the situation more carefully.

He now realized the truth, that Qian Long had had the Princess brought to Peking because he wanted her for himself. He had obviously ordered the construction of a desert in the Imperial Gardens in order to please her. But she had been true to her own love. He had threatened and cajoled her in every way he could think of, all without effect. That must be why Qian Long had said that he was not as blessed by fortune as Chen was.

He looked down at the Princess as he held her and saw that she had closed her eyes. She seemed to be asleep. He wondered why he had been allowed to see her like this. Why had Qian Long raised the problem of the Dowager Empress and her opposition to the Grand Design? Did Qian Long mean that he himself would have to make a choice between family and country? And that Chen would have to make a choice too? Yes, that must have been his meaning. Chen was beginning to understand. He shivered and broke into a sweat. He felt the Princess press herself slightly against him, and heard her sigh. A smile spread across her face, like a flower bursting into bloom. His thoughts ran on:

Should he break with the Emperor for her sake? That would mean abandoning the Grand Design for the sake of their love. Or should he do the opposite, and ask her to give in to the Emperor, for the sake of the cause?

The very thought shot through his brain like a bolt of lightning. He could feel himself recoiling from it.

After all, she loved him so deeply. He knew that. Somehow she had succeeded in preserving her virtue for his sake. All along she had firmly believed that one day he would come and rescue her. How could he possibly bring himself to abandon her now, to betray her into the enemy's hands? But if he were to think only of the two of them and of their love, then it followed that he would have to set himself against his brother the Emperor. And then this rare opportunity to recover the Throne for the Chinese would be lost for ever. If he were to do that, he and Hasli would surely be cursed by generations to come! His mind was in turmoil. He simply did not know what he should do for the best.

The Princess opened her eyes. 'Let's go,' she said. 'I'm afraid of seeing that evil Emperor again.'

'Wait here for a moment. I'll be gone for a while, then I'll come back.' She nodded trustingly, and took the dagger from his hand. Then she watched him leave the room, following him with smiling eyes.

He went up the stairs and found Qian Long on the next floor sitting on a couch, stony-faced and motionless.

'Affairs of state are of more importance than private concerns,' announced Helmsman Chen. 'I have made up my mind. I will urge her to give in to you.'

Qian Long jumped up off the couch in delight. 'Really?' he exclaimed.

'Yes, but in return you must swear an oath.' Chen stared at him as he spoke.

'What oath?' asked Qian Long, avoiding his gaze.

'That you will do all in your power to drive the Manchu barbarians out.'

Qian Long thought for a moment, then said: 'I swear. If I break my oath, then no matter how glorious a life I may lead, after my death let my grave be dug up and let my skeleton be smashed to pieces.'

The grave of an Emperor was a sacred and inviolable thing. Such an oath was extremely serious.

'Very well,' said Helmsman Chen. 'I will talk to her. But I will have to do it outside the Palace.'

'Outside?' said Qian Long, taken aback.

Chen nodded. 'At the moment, she is consumed by her hatred for you. Here, she won't be able to listen quietly to what I have to say. I wish to take her away from here, to the Great Wall, to explain things.'

'Why do you want to go so far?' said Qian Long suspiciously.

'I once promised to take her to the Great Wall. When I have fulfilled that promise, I will not see her ever again.'

'You will definitely bring her back?'

'We members of the fighting community consider our word to be worth more than our lives. I will stand by my word.'

Qian Long was uncertain what to do. He wondered how he would ever find this beautiful young woman again if Chen decided to escape with her. But on the other hand, he knew the girl would never give in to him unless Chen could convince her to do so. He was sure that Chen was being sincere. He was committed to their Grand Design, and would not abandon it just for the sake of a girl.

'All right,' he said finally, slapping the table. 'Go, both of you.'

He waited until Chen had gone, then spoke to someone concealed in the curtain behind him: 'Take forty guards and follow him the whole way there. Whatever you do, don't let them get away.'

Chen went back down to the Princess and took her hand, saying: 'Let's go.' The two walked together out of the pavilion and out of the Forbidden City. The guards had already received their orders and made no attempt to stop them. The Princess' heart was full of joy. She had always believed her hero was capable of doing whatever he set his mind to, and she was in no way surprised that they could just walk out of the Palace gates unhindered.

Outside, the sky was already growing light. Xin Yan was standing close by keeping watch, the reins of the white horse in his hands, and when he spotted Helmsman Chen, he rushed over. Seeing the Uighur Princess at his master's side, he was even more surprised and delighted.

Helmsman Chen took the reins from him. 'We are going on a trip out of the city for the day,' he said. 'We won't be back until late evening, so tell the others not to worry.'

Xin Yan watched the two mount up and ride off north, and was about to leave when he heard the sound of galloping hooves behind him and thirty or forty Palace Guards thundered past. He recognized the frail old man leading the troop as Bai Zhen, and returned quickly to Twin Willows Lane to report.

As the white horse left the city, it galloped faster and faster. The Princess, snuggling into Chen's arms, watched the trees on either side of the road flash past, and all the misery of the past few months evaporated. The horse's strong legs carried them quickly through the small villages to the north of Peking, and as they approached a crossroads, Chen said: 'Let's go and see the tombs of the Emperors of the Ming dynasty.'

The horse galloped on. Just past Jade Stone Bridge, they came upon a huge stone monument inscribed with the words 'The Sacred

Tombs of the Great Ming.' On the right-hand face of the monument were several lines of poetry in Qian Long's hand.

'What is it?' asked the Princess.

'It's a poem written by the Emperor.'

'He's vile and horrible. Don't look at it,' she urged. The two of them dismounted, and she took his hand. Soon they found themselves walking along an avenue flanked by stone lions, elephants, camels, and strange mythical creatures. 'I have only this one day left to spend with her, so I must make sure she enjoys it,' Chen thought. 'After today, we will neither of us ever pass another happy day together again.' So he roused his flagging spirits and smiled.

'You'd like to ride on a camel, wouldn't you?' he said. He lifted her up onto the stone camel's back and sat behind her. With shouts and calls, they urged the camel forward. The Princess was doubled up with laughter. Then after a moment she sighed.

'If only this camel could really run and carry us back to Heaven Mountains,' she said.

'What would you want to do there?'

She looked into the distance. 'Oh, I'd be so busy! I'd pick flowers for you to eat, and I'd look after the goats and feed the small deer. And I'd visit the graves of my father and mother and brother to keep them company, and think of some way to find my sister—'

'What happened to her?' he asked.

'She was ill the night the Manchus attacked. We were split up during the battle and I've heard no news of her since.'

Helmsman Chen was silent as they remounted the horse and continued on their way. The road wound upwards and before long they arrived at Ju Yong Pass and caught sight of the Wall, writhing like a long snake through the clusters of hills.

'Why did they waste so much effort to build this thing?' the Princess asked.

'It was to stop the northern enemies from invading,' Chen replied. 'Countless people must have died on either side of this wall.'

'Men are so strange. Why don't they all live happily together and dance and sing instead of fighting? I really can't see the point of it at all.'

'If you ever get the chance, you must tell the Emperor not to make war on the poor peoples who live in the border areas. Will you do that?'

'But I'll never see that evil man ever again!' she replied, puzzled by his suddenly solemn tone of voice.

'But supposing you ever *were* able to make him do your bidding, you must urge him not to do bad things, and to do some good for the people. You must promise me!'

'What a funny thing to say. You know I'd always do anything you asked me to do!'

'Thank you,' said Chen, and she smiled.

They walked along a stretch of the wall hand in hand.

'I was just thinking...' said Princess Fragrance.

'What?'

'I am very happy today, but is it because of this beautiful scenery? No. I know it's because I'm with you. As long as you're there by my side, I'd think even the most ugly place on earth was beautiful.'

The happier she was, the more uncomfortable Chen felt. 'Is there anything you'd like me to do?' he asked.

'Oh no! You've done everything already! You've always given me everything I wanted, even without my having to ask for it.' Then she added with a smile, 'There is only one thing you refused to do, and that is to sing me a song.'

Chen laughed. 'It's true,' he said. 'I've never sung you a song.'

The Princess pulled a face. 'Well, I'm not going to sing for you any more either.'

'I remember my mother's maidservant singing several rhymes when I was young,' said Chen. 'I'll sing one for you now, but you must promise not to laugh.'

She clapped her hands in delight. 'All right! Sing!'

He thought for a moment, and then began:

The light rain falls
So mistily;
The wind blows in squalls
So fitfully;
Down below a voice calls
Sweet nothings;
'Tis my love, I think,
And softly curse his name.
But then I look again
And see it's not

My darling man,
And I start to tremble
With fear…

After he had finished, Chen explained the words of the Chinese song to her in the Uighur tongue, and the Princess laughed.

'The lady's eyesight was not too good, apparently,' she said.

They explored the top of the wall, which consisted of battlements on the northern side, a stone handrail on the other, and a walkway in between. Every three hundred feet or so, there was a watchtower. They came to a beacon tower, and Chen thought of the time when her sister Huo Qingtong had lit fires with wolf-dung as part of her plan to destroy the Manchu army. He wondered again if she was alive or dead, and his sadness increased.

'I know what you are thinking,' said the Princess.

'Do you?'

'Yes. You are thinking of my sister.'

'How did you know?'

'When the three of us were in the Secret City together, I could see how happy you were in spite of the danger. Oh, you mustn't worry so!'

He took her hand, 'What do you mean?' he asked.

She sighed. 'In the old days, I was just a child. I didn't understand anything. But every day I have spent in the Imperial Palace, I have thought about the times we were together and realized many things that had not occurred to me before. My sister loved you all along. And you love her, don't you?'

'Yes. I should never lie to you.'

'But I know you love me too. Truly. And I know that without you, I cannot live. So let's go and find my sister quickly and we can all live together happily forever. Don't you think that would be lovely?'

Her eyes and face radiated happiness. Chen squeezed her hand. 'You have thought it all out perfectly,' he said softly. 'You and your sister are the sweetest and best people in the world.'

The Princess stood looking out into the distance, and noticed the sun glinting off a body of water to the west. 'Let's go and have a look over there,' she said.

They made their way across the hills, and came upon a clear spring bubbling out of a crack in the rocks.

'I'll wash my feet here, if you don't mind,' said the Princess.

'Of course,' Chen replied with a smile. She took off her shoes and socks and stepped into the crystal-clear water, relishing its coolness as it flowed around her milk-white feet. Chen caught a glimpse of his own shadow on the water, and realized the sun was already sinking into the west. He reached into his bag and pulled out some food for them. The Princess leant against him and wiped her feet dry as she ate.

Chen gritted his teeth. 'There is something I must say to you,' he said. She turned and put both her arms round him, resting her head on his chest.

'I know you love me,' she said quietly. 'I understand. You don't have to say it.'

He cringed, swallowing what he had been about to say. After a while, he tried again: 'Do you still remember Mami's last testament that we read inside White Jade Peak?'

'She is living in Heaven now with her Ali. That's the way it should be.'

'You Muslims believe that after good people die, they live forever in paradise, is that right?'

'Of course that's what happens.'

'When I return to Peking, I will go and find one of your Imams, and get him to teach me so that I can become a good follower of the Muslim faith,' said Chen.

The Princess was overjoyed. She had never in her wildest dreams guessed that one day he would be willing of his own free will to become a Muslim. 'Oh my dear,' she said, looking up at him, 'will you really do that?'

'Definitely.'

'You'll do it just because you love me. I never dared to hope for such a thing.'

'I'll do it,' Chen continued slowly, 'because in this life, after today, we won't ever be able to be together again. So I want to be sure that after death, I can be with you every day.'

The words struck the Princess like a thunderbolt. After a moment's silence, she said in a shaking voice: 'You…what are you talking about? What do you mean? We can't be together?'

'No. Not after today. We'll never be able to see each other again.'

'Why?' Her body quivered and two large tears fell onto his gown.

Chen embraced her tenderly. 'If only I could be with you, I'd be happy even if I had to go without food or clothing for the rest of my life, even if I had to be beaten and humiliated every day. But do you remember Mami? She made the choice to leave her true love Ali so that her people would no longer be oppressed and bullied by the wicked Sanglaba. She even chose to let him have his way with her...'

The Princess' body went limp. 'You mean you want me to give in to the Emperor?' she whispered. 'And then you want me to kill him, like Mami did?'

'No, not that. You see, the Emperor is actually my blood brother.'

Helmsman Chen then told her all about his relationship with Qian Long, and about the Red Flower Society's plans, about the oath sworn in the Six Harmonies Pagoda, and of Qian Long's demand earlier that day. As he spoke, the Princess realized that what she had been longing for day and night, the happiness she thought she had finally achieved, had slipped suddenly from her grasp. She was overwhelmed by a sense of total despair, and fainted away.

When she came to, she felt Chen holding her tightly, and was aware that his tears had soaked a damp patch on her dress. She stood up.

'Wait for me here,' she said softly. She walked over towards a large flat rock in the distance, and there she prostrated herself in prayer, facing towards the west. She appealed to the True God, Allah, for guidance on what she ought to do. The setting sun shone on her white dress, and her silhouette was a picture of melancholy and tenderness. After a while, she walked slowly back.

'Whatever you want me to do, I will do,' she announced.

Chen jumped up and ran to her, and the two embraced each other tightly.

'If I had known we had only today, I would have wanted you to hold me the whole day rather than come here,' she whispered. Chen kissed her, unable to answer.

A long time passed. Then suddenly, the Princess said: 'I have not had a bath since I left home. I am going to have one now.' She began to take off her outer gown.

Helmsman Chen stood up. 'I'll go over there and wait for you,' he said.

'No! No! I want you to watch. I want you to see me. The first time you saw me, I was bathing. Today will be the last time. After you have seen me, I want you to never forget me.'

'Do you really believe I could ever forget you?'

'Please don't go,' she pleaded. There was nothing for Chen to do but to sit down again. She removed all her clothing piece by piece and stepped naked into the gurgling mountain spring. The golden rays of the evening sun shone on her flawless body. The sight dazzled Chen. He hardly dared look directly at this vision. But he could not fail to notice her innocent, guileless expression, and suddenly thought of her as simply a naked three or four-year-old child. She was so beautiful and so pure.

'There must surely be an all-knowing, all-powerful God in heaven,' he thought, 'to have created such incomparable beauty.' His heart was filled with a sense of reverence and gratitude.

The Princess slowly wiped the pearls of water from her body, and then put her clothes back on.

'I will never again be able to show my body to the man I love,' she thought, not without a touch of self-pity. She rubbed her hair dry and then returned to sit in Chen's embrace.

'I once told you the story of the cowherd and the weaving maid, do you remember?' Chen asked.

'Yes. I remember you saying that although they met only once a year, they still saw each other countless times more than ordinary people.'

'Yes. We cannot be together now in this world, but the True God will make sure we meet again eventually. In the desert, and here, we have been very happy. Our time has been short, but perhaps we have had more happiness than many couples who live together for decades.'

She listened to his soothing voice as he tried to comfort her. The sun slowly sank towards the hills, and her heart followed it. Suddenly she jumped up and wailed: 'No! The sun is disappearing!'

Chen's heart felt as if it would shatter into a thousand pieces. 'I've asked so much of you!' he cried, taking her by the hand. She continued to stare at the point where the sun had gone down. 'If only it could rise again, even for just a moment,' she said quietly.

'It is right that I should have to suffer for the sake of my people,' murmured Chen. 'But why you? You have never even seen them, let alone loved them.'

'I love you,' she replied, 'so they are my people too. You love all of my Uighur brothers, don't you?'

The sky was growing darker. The sun did not rise again, and a wave of coldness touched her heart.

'Let's go back,' she said. 'I am very happy. My life is fulfilled.'

They climbed onto the back of the white horse and started back the way they had come. They were both silent and neither turned back to look at the beautiful scene they had just witnessed.

Less than an hour's ride later, they heard the sound of many galloping hooves ahead and thirty or forty riders emerged out of the evening mist with Bai Zhen in the lead. His face lit up as soon as he saw Helmsman Chen and the Fragrant Princess, and signalling to the others to stop, he leapt off his horse and stood by the roadside. Chen did not even glance at him, but urged the white horse on even faster. Soon after, more horses' hooves sounded up ahead, and the Red Flower Society heroes came into view.

'Helmsman!' shouted Leopard Wei. 'We're all here!'

Muslim Fat or Chinese Fat?

That morning, Qian Long had watched the sun rising in the east and the sky gradually growing light as the eunuchs laid out his Imperial breakfast. It consisted of a great many exquisite delicacies, but he had found it difficult to swallow a single one of them. With Helmsman Chen and the Fragrant Princess gone, he felt extremely ill at ease.

That day, he did not grant his ministers an audience, and spent his time napping fitfully. On several occasions, he sent guards out to find out what was happening, but evening came, the sky grew dark, and the moon sailed up over the Palace walls, and still none of them had returned to report. He started to become very anxious and tried to calm himself by staring fixedly at the Castiglione desert murals on the walls of the Precious Moon Pavilion.

'If she likes him, then she will certainly like Chinese clothes,' he thought. 'When they return he will already have convinced her, so I'll take off these Manchu clothes and put on something Chinese to give her a surprise!'

He ordered his eunuchs to bring him some, but it proved almost impossible to find Chinese clothes in the heart of the Manchu Palace. Finally, one bright young eunuch ran over to the Palace opera troupe and brought back a theatrical costume, which he helped Qian Long put on. The Emperor examined himself in the mirror. At first he seemed delighted by his dashing appearance as a Chinaman. Then he noticed a few white hairs amongst his whiskers and urgently ordered the young eunuch to fetch a pair of tweezers and pull them out.

Just as he was sitting with bowed head to allow the eunuch to remove the offending hairs, he heard the patter of light footsteps behind him and another eunuch announced the arrival of Her Highness the Empress Dowager. Qian Long started in surprise. He looked up and saw the reflection of his 'mother' in the mirror, her face stern and pale and full of anger.

'I trust you are well, Madam?' he said, hurriedly turning to face her. He escorted her to the couch, where she took a seat. She dismissed the eunuchs with a wave of her hand. There was a moment's silence.

'The servants say you have not been well today,' she began in a deep, almost booming voice. 'They say you did not hold court this morning and haven't eaten, so I have come to pay you a little visit.'

'I'm better now thank you,' he replied. 'It was just that I ate something fatty which made me feel a little uncomfortable. It was nothing. I would not have presumed to bother Your Highness about it.'

'Hah! Was it Muslim fat or Chinese fat?' she said, to Qian Long's consternation.

'I think some roast lamb I ate last night disagreed with me,' he replied.

'That is one of our Manchu dishes. Hah! You seem to be tired of being a Manchu.'

Qian Long did not dare to say anything.

'Where is that Uighur girl?' asked the Empress Dowager.

'She was in a bad mood so I sent her out with someone who can talk some sense into her.'

'She has a knife. I am sure she would prefer to die rather than give in to you. What use is there in getting someone to talk to her? Who did you send?'

Qian Long noticed anxiously how close her questioning was becoming.

'An old officer of the Palace Guard, named Bai,' he replied.

The Dowager looked up and let the silence hang for a moment. Then she laughed coldly. 'You, my son, are the Emperor, you are the master of All under Heaven. You can do whatever you like, and concoct whatever lies you like, too.'

Qian Long knew the eyes and ears of the Dowager were many and guessed he probably would not be able to deceive her about this affair. 'There was another person I sent with the girl,' he answered quietly. 'He's a scholar I met in the south, a very learned man—'

'It's someone from that Chen family of Haining, isn't it?' the Dowager's voice rasped out sharply.

Qian Long hung his head, unable to utter a sound.

'No wonder you've put on Chinese clothes. I'm surprised you haven't killed me yet!' Her voice was becoming harsher and harsher. Qian Long fell to his knees and began kowtowing fearfully.

'May I be damned by Heaven and Earth if I have been unfilial in any way!' he protested.

The Dowager flicked up the long sleeves of her gown and walked out. Qian Long rushed after her, then stopped when he realized he was still wearing the Chinese costume. To be seen wearing such clothes would not do at all, so he hurriedly changed back into his usual Imperial dragon-gown and rushed out after the Dowager. He found her in a side room of the Martial Hero Pavilion.

'Please don't be angry, Madam,' he pleaded. 'If I have made some errors, I am more than willing to accept your criticism.'

'Well, for a start, why have you summoned that man Chen into the Palace several days running?' she asked coldly. 'And what happened between the two of you in Haining?' Qian Long hung his head and was silent.

'Do you really intend to restore the Chinese style of dress?' she shrieked. 'Are you going to kill every one of us Manchus?'

'Please don't listen to the nonsense spouted by servants,' he replied, his voice shaking. 'How could I plan to do such a thing?'

'How do you intend to deal with this man Chen?'

'His Society is large and widespread and many of his followers are Martial Arts masters who would die for him, so I have been polite to him throughout while waiting for an opportunity to deal with them all at once. I want to destroy them root and branch.'

The Dowager's expression softened slightly. 'Is this true?'

Qian Long knew the secret had leaked. He knew he had no room left to manoeuvre, and decided he had no choice but to swear to destroy the Red Flower Society.

'I will see to it that Chen is beheaded within three days,' he said.

The shadow of a smile appeared on the Dowager's grimly forbidding face. 'Good,' she said. 'That will show that you want to fulfil the wishes of our Ancestors.' She stood up. 'Come with me,' she added.

She walked over to the main hall of the Martial Hero Pavilion with Qian Long close behind. As they approached, a eunuch gave a shout and the huge doors were opened. Inside the brightly lit hall, two files of eunuchs stretched away from the entrance towards a row of eight princes, all of them kneeling on the floor to receive the Emperor. The Dowager and Qian Long walked over to two chairs set on the dais in the centre of the hall and sat down. Qian Long saw that all eight princes were of the immediate Imperial family. They included his own brothers. He wondered uneasily what the Dowager was plotting.

'When the late Emperor passed away,' she began slowly, 'he left orders that the command of the Imperial Banner troops was to be divided amongst eight members of the Imperial family. But because of the constant dispatch of forces to the Uighur border regions in the past few years, it has never been possible to act on the Emperor's last wish. Now, thanks to the blessed protection of the Ancestors, the Uighurs have been pacified. From today, the leadership of the Banners will be divided amongst the eight of you.' The princes kowtowed and expressed their great gratitude.

The Empress Dowager had decided to undermine Qian Long's military strength.

'Please proceed, Your Majesty,' the Dowager said to him. 'Assign each prince to be in command of a Banner.'

Qian Long knew he was in a losing position, but he decided that as long as he did not attempt a revolt, a temporary dispersal of military power would be of no great consequence. The Dowager, he could see, had been very thorough, and he guessed that she had also made preparations in case he refused.

Meanwhile, the eight princes were thinking to themselves: 'According to the wishes of the founder of our dynasty, three of the Banners should be under the direct command of the Emperor, and the other five should be indirectly subordinate to them. By dividing the Banners among us in this way the Dowager is seriously violating the rules laid down by the Ancestors. She is obviously doing it in order to weaken the Emperor's power.' None of them dared to openly refuse the Dowager's command. But they all decided it would be highly advisable to return the command to the Emperor the following day if they wanted to keep their heads on their shoulders.

The Dowager signalled with her hand and one of the princes came forward holding a tray on which was placed a small iron box. He knelt before her and she picked the box up and opened it, taking out a small scroll. Qian Long glanced at it out of the corner of his eye and saw that the inscription at the head of the scroll, written in Emperor Yong Zheng's hand, read 'Posthumous Edict.' Next to this was a line of smaller characters: 'In the event of a national crisis, the eight princes who lead the Banners must gather together and open this.'

Qian Long's face drained of colour. So his father had long ago taken precautions to guard against what might happen if the secret of his true parenthood were ever revealed. If he now dared to alter in any way the instructions of his Ancestors, let alone attempt to overthrow the Manchus, the eight Banner commanders would be required to dispose of him and set up a new Emperor. Helmsman Chen's Grand Design had been cleverly anticipated. He steadied himself.

'My father the late Emperor was indeed far-sighted,' he said. 'I only hope I can live up to a thousandth of his abilities, Madam.'

The Dowager passed the scroll to the most senior of the eight princes and said: 'Take this Edict of His Majesty the late Emperor and have it placed in the Lama Temple. Assign one hundred guards to keep watch over it day and night.' She hesitated for a moment, then added: 'They are not allowed to leave their posts for a second, even if ordered to do so by His Majesty Qian Long.'

The prince left with the scroll for the Lama Temple. The temple was in the northern part of the city near the Gate of Serenity, and had been used by the Emperor Yong Zheng as his home before he ascended the Throne. After he died, Qian Long had had the residence expanded and turned into a Tibetan Lamaist temple in memory of his father.

Now that her arrangements were complete, the Dowager yawned lazily. 'The *Grand Design* of our Manchu Ancestors must at all costs be safeguarded,' she sighed. Her point was not lost on Qian Long. She knew everything.

Eternal Hell

Immediately after seeing the Empress Dowager on her way, Qian Long called for his guards. Bai Zhen came forward to report.

'Chen Jialuo has escorted the young lady back to the Palace, and she is now awaiting Your Majesty in the Precious Moon Pavilion,' he said.

Qian Long was delighted with the news and walked briskly to the door of the Martial Hero Pavilion. Then he stopped and turned. 'Was there any trouble on the road?' he asked.

'Your slaves came across a large number of Red Flower Society fighters at one point, but luckily Chen Jialuo intervened and prevented an incident.'

When Qian Long arrived at the Precious Moon Pavilion, he found the Fragrant Princess seated there as before, facing the wall.

'Did you have fun at the Great Wall?' he asked happily. She ignored him. Qian Long decided to deal with more pressing matters first before questioning her further. He went into the adjoining room and gave orders for his favourite, Fu Kangan, to be summoned.

Before too long, Lord Fu came hurrying in and Qian Long ordered him to lead a troop of Imperial Guards and lay an ambush around the Lama Temple. After he had departed, Qian Long instructed Bai Zhen to take his men and hide near the temple too.

'I intend to hold a great feast in the Lama Temple tomorrow evening,' he added. 'Tell Chen Jialuo and all the senior members of the Red Flower Society to be there.'

Bai Zhen immediately guessed that the Emperor intended to deal with all the Red Flower Society leaders at one stroke. He shuddered at the thought of the slaughter that would take place.

'Also,' Qian Long added, 'summon the Abbot of the Lama Temple immediately.'

A short while later the old Abbot kowtowed his way into the Imperial presence. 'How many years is it since you came to the Capital?' asked Qian Long.

'I have served Your Majesty for twenty-one years.'

'Do you want to go back to Tibet?'

The Abbot kowtowed again but said nothing.

'There are two Living Buddhas in Tibet, the Dalai Lama and the Panchen Lama,' Qian Long continued. 'Why isn't there a third?'

'Your Highness, that has always been the way, ever since—'

Qian Long silenced him with a wave of his hand. 'If I made *you* the third Living Buddha and gave you an area to govern, no one would dare to defy the order, would they?'

The Abbot's heart leapt. He kowtowed furiously, unable to believe his luck. 'Your Majesty's benevolence will be difficult to repay,' he said.

'I want you to do something for me right now. Go back to the temple and gather together all your trusted lamas. Then prepare gunpowder, firewood, and other materials for lighting a fire.' He pointed at Bai Zhen. 'When he gives you the signal, you will put the temple to the torch.'

The Abbot began frantically kowtowing again, this time in fright. 'But our temple is the former residence of his late Majesty,' he protested. 'Many of his possessions are still there. I could never—'

'Do you dare to disobey me?' Qian Long roared, sending the old Abbot into a cold sweat.

'I...I will do as Your Majesty commands,' he replied in a quavering voice.

'If even a hint of this leaks out, I'll have you and every single one of your eight hundred lamas executed.' After a moment, he added in a more friendly tone: 'There will be a lot of Banner troops guarding the Suicheng Pavilion in your temple, so you'd better be careful. When the time comes, I want those troops trapped inside and burned to death. When all this has been successfully completed, you will be made the third Living Buddha of Tibet. Now go!' He waved his hand and the Abbot left with Bai Zhen, thanking the Emperor for his benevolence as he went.

His preparations completed, Qian Long considered how his plan for the following evening would enable him to kill two birds with one stone—to destroy both the Red Flower Society and the soldiers loyal to the Dowager. His own position would be secured, and he would be able to continue his reign in peace. He felt very satisfied. Looking round, he noticed a lute lying on a table and went over and started playing a martial air on it. After a few measures, his playing grew increasingly strident and aggressive. Then suddenly there was a twang, and the seventh string broke. He started in surprise and laughed loudly. Then, pushing the lute aside, he stood up and walked back to the other room.

CHAPTER 9

483

The Fragrant Princess was sitting at the window staring up at the moon. As she heard his footsteps, there was a glint of light. She had pulled the dagger out again. Qian Long frowned and sat down at a distance.

'When you and Chen Jialuo were at the Great Wall, did he tell you to kill me?'

'He told me to obey you in everything.'

'And are you going to disobey him?'

'I would never do that.'

Qian Long was at the same time delighted and jealous. 'Then what are you still carrying the dagger for? Give it to me!'

'No, I'll wait for you to become a good emperor first.'

So that's how Chen hoped to control him! Anger, jealousy, lust, and hatred flared up within Qian Long all at once. He laughed harshly. 'But I am already a good emperor,' he replied.

'Is that so? That's not what it sounded like to me. I heard you playing the lute just now. You're planning to kill people, you're going to kill many, many people. You're... you're evil.'

Qian Long realized that his bloodthirsty intentions had indeed revealed themselves through his playing. 'Yes,' he replied. 'It's true. I *am* going to kill people. I've already caught your Chen Jialuo. But if you do as I say, I can release him. If you don't do as I say...' He laughed again. 'Then you're right. Then I'll kill many people.'

The Princess was shocked. 'You'd kill your own brother?' she asked in a trembling voice.

Qian Long's face went white. 'So he told you everything?'

'I don't believe you've caught him. He's much cleverer than you.'

'Is he really? If I haven't got him today, I'll get him tomorrow!'

She said nothing. 'I advise you to forget this idea of yours,' Qian Long went on. 'Whether I'm a good emperor or a bad emperor, one thing is for certain: you're never going to see that man again.'

'But you promised *him* that you'd be a good emperor,' she protested. 'You can't go back on your word!'

'I can do whatever I want!' he roared. 'No one tells me what to do!' All the pent up anger from his humiliating audience with the Dowager came spilling out. His words struck the Princess like a fist-blow to the chest. 'So the Emperor *is* planning to betray Helmsman Chen after all,' she thought to herself in anguish. 'Our sacrifice has been in vain! If only we had both known earlier! Then

I would never have had to come back here.' She almost fainted at the shock of this realization.

Seeing her face suddenly go pale, Qian Long immediately regretted having been so harsh. 'Treat me well,' he said, 'and of course I won't harm him. In fact, I'll make him an important official, I'll make him rich and powerful.'

But the Princess was no longer listening. She was trying to think of a way of letting Helmsman Chen know of the Emperor's treachery, a way of saving him from falling into the deadly trap that had clearly been set for him. She frowned, deep in thought, and her concentrated expression deepened the seriousness of her face. Qian Long stared at her, mesmerized by her beauty.

'Everyone in the Palace is the Emperor's servant,' she thought. 'I can't trust anyone to deliver a letter for me. There's only one way to do it.'

'So you promise you won't harm him?' she said aloud.

Qian Long was delighted. 'I promise, I promise,' he replied without hesitation. The Princess could not detect the slightest trace of feeling or sincerity in his voice. She looked at him in hatred.

'Early tomorrow morning, I want to go to a mosque,' she said calmly. 'I want to pray to Allah. Then I will do as you say.'

Qian Long smiled. 'Very well,' he replied. 'But there is to be no more delay after that.'

The Fragrant Princess watched him leave. There was a smile on his face. Then she found a pen and paper and wrote a letter to Helmsman Chen, warning him of the Emperor's intentions, and telling him that the whole plan to overthrow the Manchus, the Grand Design, as he had called it, was just an empty dream. He must think of a way of coming to her rescue yet again. When she had finished, she wrapped the letter in a blank sheet of paper and wrote on it in the Uighur script: 'Please deliver speedily to the Helmsman of the Red Flower Society, Chen Jialuo.' She knew the respect and sense of devotion that all Muslims felt for her father and his family, and felt certain that if she just had a chance to pass the letter on to any fellow-Muslim in the mosque, they would find a way to deliver it.

Having written the letter, her heart felt much easier. She was confident that Helmsman Chen could do anything. He would easily find a way to rescue her. A sense of indescribable warmth and sweetness swept over her, and, tired out from the day's exertions, she fell fast asleep.

She became dimly aware of bells chiming around the Palace, and opened her eyes to find the sky already growing light. Hurriedly, she arose and washed herself, then combed her hair. The maidservants sent to look after her knew she would allow no one near her and watched from a distance. She carefully secreted the letter in her sleeve and then left the pavilion. Eunuchs were already waiting outside with a palanquin, and they carried her to the mosque on the western stretch of the Avenue of Eternal Peace. Palace Guards crowded round her as she went.

Seeing the round dome of the mosque as she descended from the palanquin, she felt both happiness and anguish. She walked through the entrance with head bowed and noticed two men walking next to her, one on either side. They were dressed as Muslims, and she was about to pass the letter to one of them when she stopped herself. The man's features and manner were not at all those of her people. She glanced at the other man and saw that he was the same.

'Were you sent by the Emperor to guard me?' she asked quietly in the Uighur tongue. Both men nodded, but clearly they had not understood a word of what she had said.

Dismayed, she turned round and looked behind her. She could see another eight Palace Guards dressed as Uighurs. All the real Muslims were being kept at a safe distance. She walked over to the chief Imam of the mosque and said to him: 'Please make sure this letter is delivered no matter what happens.' The Imam started as the Princess pushed the letter into his hand. A guard rushed forward and snatched the letter away, giving the Imam a heavy push on the chest, which caused him to stumble and almost fall to the ground. The other worshippers looked at each other in surprise, wondering what was going on.

'What do you think you're doing?' the Imam demanded angrily.

'Mind your own business,' the guard hissed at him. 'We are from the Palace.'

The Imam was too frightened to say another word, and turned to lead the gathering in prayer. The Princess knelt down with the others and tears came gushing from her eyes like water from a spring. In the midst of her pain and sorrow only one thought remained: 'I must warn him! I must let him know of the danger, even if I have to die in the attempt! But how?'

The realization struck her like a flash of lightning. 'That's it! I can do it by dying! If I die here, word will get out and he will hear of it. There's no other way!'

Then the Prophet's words sounded in her ears like a clap of thunder: 'Those who take their own life will fall into the eternal fires and will never escape.' She herself was not afraid of death. She believed that people who died could ascend to Paradise and be reunited with their loved ones for eternity. But with suicide, there was nothing to look forward to but never-ending pain! A violent shiver ran through her and she suddenly felt extremely cold. She listened for a moment to the congregation reciting the words of the Koran. For a true believer there was nothing more terrible than the thought that the soul would be consigned to eternal Hell. But she could see no other way. Love overcame the greatest fear of all.

'Most Sacred and Holy Allah,' she whispered. 'It is not that I don't believe you care for me. But there is no other way. Only with my own blood can I save him.'

She took the dagger out of her sleeve and on the paving-stone in front of her she scratched the words, 'The Emperor is not to be trusted!' Then, murmuring the name Chen Jialuo, she thrust the blade of her dagger into her breast—the purest, most beautiful in this world.

Fresh Blood

That morning, the Red Flower Society heroes were in their quarters in Twin Willows Lane discussing the situation, when a servant appeared to announce the arrival of the captain of the Emperor's Guard, Bai Zhen. Helmsman Chen went out alone to meet him. Bai Zhen passed on the Emperor's invitation to all the leading members of the Red Flower Society to attend a banquet in the Lama Temple that evening to be hosted by the Emperor himself. He explained that the banquet was being held outside the Palace in order to avoid raising the suspicions of the Empress Dowager and the Manchu nobles. Chen expressed his thanks. He assumed that things were progressing according to plan. The Fragrant Princess had already fulfilled her part of the agreement: she had already done what had to be done, she had given in to the Emperor. He felt an inexpressible mixture of emotions. After having seen Bai Zhen out, he returned to discuss matters with the others. They were very excited that the Emperor was keeping his part of the bargain, although they were also painfully aware of the personal sacrifice Chen had made for their plan to go ahead.

They passed the rest of the morning performing Martial Arts exercises. Helmsman Chen showed the others some of what he had learned inside White Jade Peak. When they were still busy practising, they heard wailing and mournful singing outside. At first, they took little notice, but the noise gradually increased in volume, as if thousands of people were gathering in a state of extreme grief.

Xin Yan had lived in the desert for a long time and he soon recognized the song as a Uighur funeral dirge. His curiosity aroused, he ran out to find out what was going on, and returned a while later, unsteady on his feet and ashen-faced. He walked over to Chen. 'Master!' he exclaimed, his voice shaking.

The Red Flower heroes stopped their kungfu training, and Chen turned to his page-boy. 'What is it?' he asked.

'She...the Fragrant Princess...she's dead!'

The heroes blanched. Everything went black before Helmsman Chen's eyes and he collapsed to the ground. Father Speckless dropped his sword and helped him up.

'How did she die?' asked Luo Bing.

'The Uighur man I talked to said she stabbed herself to death while praying in the mosque,' Xin Yan replied.

'What else did he say?'

'That the Empress Dowager would not allow her body to be carried back into the Palace, and insisted that it should be handed over to the authorities at the mosque. They are just on their way back from burying her now.'

The Red Flower heroes all cursed the Emperor bitterly for his cruelty in driving such a pure, innocent young girl to her death. Luo Bing broke down altogether and started to cry. Helmsman Chen was silent for a while. Then all of a sudden he said to Father Speckless: 'I haven't finished showing you all the moves yet. Let's continue.'

To their amazement, he walked back out into the middle of the courtyard. Father Speckless decided it would be a good idea to help distract the Helmsman from his grief, so he raised his sword and gave the signal to resume the training session. The Red Flower heroes could see that Helmsman Chen's footwork was just as sure as before, and that his hands moved with his usual skill. It was as if the news had had absolutely no effect on him. They commented on this quietly amongst themselves.

'Men have no hearts,' Yuanzhi whispered into Scholar Yu's ear. 'All he thinks of is his great cause. He doesn't care at all that the woman he loved is dead.'

Yu said nothing. But in his own mind he silently praised Chen for his self-control. If it were me, he thought, I would be insane by now.

In view of the circumstances, Father Speckless did not dare press Chen too hard. A few moves, and Chen had easily gained dominance. As the priest retreated, Chen's hand suddenly shot out and touched his hand. The two leapt apart.

'Good! Excellent kungfu!' exclaimed the priest.

'You weren't really trying,' Chen replied, and he laughed. But before the laugh was finished, he had vomited a mouthful of blood. The Red Flower heroes rushed forward as one to help him, but Chen waved them away with a wan smile.

'It's nothing,' he said. He walked back into the house, supporting himself on Xin Yan's shoulders.

Chen slept for more than two hours. Upon waking, he thought of all the important things he had to do, including seeing the Emperor that evening. He knew he had to look after himself. But as soon as he thought about Hasli's tragic death the pain was such that he wanted to end it all. He wondered why she would suddenly commit suicide, after clearly agreeing to their plan. Could it be that she had changed her mind? Could she have decided she could not renounce her love for him? But she knew that it was for a great cause. He was convinced that something untoward must have happened. But what? He brooded on the problem for a while but could come to no conclusion, so he took out some Uighur clothes he had brought back with him from the northwest and put them on, then darkened his face with some diluted ink.

'I'm going out,' he said to Xin Yan. 'I'll be back in a while.' Xin Yan quietly followed him. Chen, who knew he was simply acting out of loyalty, did not try to stop him.

The streets were full of people and noise, and thronged with many carriages and horses. But Helmsman Chen saw none of this. He hurried to the mosque on the Avenue of Eternal Peace, walked straight into the main hall, and threw himself down on the ground to pray. 'Wait for me in Heaven,' he said quietly. 'I promised you that I would become a believer, and I will make sure that you do not wait for me in vain.'

When he raised his head, he noticed what looked like some writing on the floor about five feet in front of him. He went forward to have a closer look. Several words in Uighur had been scratched into the stone with the point of a knife: 'The Emperor is not to be trusted.' There was some colour in the scratched lines, and Chen started as he saw it. Looking around, he saw that a part of the floor nearby was slightly darker in colour. 'Could this be her blood?' he thought to himself. He bent down and caught the sharp odour of fresh blood. In that moment, he was overcome with grief and threw himself sobbing on the ground.

After weeping for a while, he felt a light tap on the shoulder. He leapt to his feet ready to fight, but to his astonishment he discovered that it was Huo Qingtong, dressed as a Uighur boy. She had arrived that day with the Twin Eagles in the hope of rescuing her sister, but had heard almost immediately that she was dead, and had come to the mosque to pray for her. As they were talking, Helmsman Chen noticed two Palace Guards enter the mosque, and with a tug on Huo Qingtong's sleeve, he pulled her down to the ground where they prostrated themselves in prayer.

The guards walked over. 'On your feet!' they barked. Helmsman Chen and Huo Qingtong did as they were told and walked over to a window. Behind them, they heard the sound of hammering as the guards prised up the flagstone with the Princess' message on it. Then they carried the stone out of the mosque and rode away.

'What was that?' asked Huo Qingtong.

'If I had arrived one moment later,' replied Helmsman Chen, 'I would never have seen the words your sister wrote with her very life-blood. I would have missed the warning she sacrificed her life to give me.'

'What warning?'

'There are too many eyes and ears here,' Chen replied. 'Kneel down on the floor again and I'll tell you.' So they prostrated themselves once more and Chen whispered a brief account of all that had happened.

'How could you be so stupid as to trust the Emperor?' Huo Qingtong declared angrily.

Chen was mortified with shame. 'I thought that because he was Chinese, and because he was my blood-brother—' he began.

'What if he *is* Chinese? Do you think Chinese are incapable of doing bad things? And what does he care for brotherly love? He's the Emperor!'

'I am responsible for her death,' Chen sobbed. 'How can I go on living without her?'

Huo Qingtong saw how heartbroken he was. She felt she had been too hard on him. 'What you did was for the good of your people,' she said softly to comfort him. 'You mustn't blame yourself.' After a moment's silence, she asked: 'Are you going to go to the banquet in the Lama Temple this evening?'

Chen gritted his teeth in rage. 'The Emperor will be there. I'll kill him and avenge her death.'

'Yes,' Huo Qingtong agreed. 'And my father's death and my brother's death, and all the other thousands of my people who have been killed!'

'How did you manage to escape when the Manchu troops attacked?' he asked.

'I was very sick at the time,' she replied, 'but luckily I had my own guards with me who managed to get me out and took me to my Shifu's home.'

Chen sighed. 'Your sister said that even if it meant travelling to the ends of the earth, we had to find you.' The tears began to stream down Huo Qingtong's face.

They walked out of the mosque and Xin Yan came up to meet them. He was astonished to see Huo Qingtong with Chen.

'My lady! How are you?' he exclaimed. 'I've been thinking of you.'

'I'm well thank you,' she replied. 'You've grown taller since I last saw you!'

They returned to Twin Willows Lane to find the Twin Eagles of Heaven Mountains in the middle of a heated argument with the Red Flower heroes. Helmsman Chen swallowed his tears and told them of the bloodstained words he had seen scratched on the floor of the mosque. Bald Vulture slapped the table.

'Didn't I tell you?' he demanded. 'Of course that Emperor means us harm. She must have got definite proof of it in the Palace, and decided to sacrifice her life to let us know.' The others agreed with him.

'When we go to the banquet this evening,' said Helmsman Chen, 'we won't be able to carry swords, so everyone must prepare daggers or darts. The food and drink may be poisoned so don't allow anything to touch your lips. We must kill the Emperor tonight and have our revenge. But we must also plan our escape route.'

'None of us will be able to live in China again,' said Bald Vulture. 'We should all go to the border country, to the Uighur lands.'

The Red Flower heroes had long lived in the south of China, and the idea of leaving their home was not easy to accept. But the Emperor was evil and dangerous and bitterly hated by all of them. They were willing to do whatever was necessary.

Chen ordered Leopard Wei to go to the west gate of the city with several of the Red Flower heroes and to be ready to kill the guards at the right moment, so that they could all escape. He then ordered Xin Yan to arrange for horses to be waiting outside the Lama Temple. Turning to Scholar Yu, he told him to immediately inform all the Red Flower Society's members in Peking and in the various provincial Lodges to go to ground in order to avoid being arrested.

The arrangements complete, Helmsman Chen turned to the Twin Eagles and to Hidden Needle Lu. 'I would like to ask you three elders for suggestions on how the assassination should be carried out,' he said.

'I should have thought it was simple,' replied Bald Vulture. 'I go up, grab his neck, and give it a good twist. That should finish him off.'

Lu smiled. 'I'm afraid you'll never get close enough to grab his neck with all the guards he is bound to have around him.'

'Buddha Zhao should attack him with poisoned darts,' suggested Father Speckless. 'We only need one to hit its target.'

Lu turned to Luo Bing and said: 'You could dip your throwing knives in some poison too, and I'll do the same with my Golden Needles.'

Luo Bing nodded. 'If we all let loose our weapons at once, one or two are bound to hit him no matter how many guards he has.'

Chen watched the heroes as they dipped their various weapons into a pot of bubbling poison on the stove. He still had nagging scruples about what they were planning. The Emperor was after all born of the same mother as himself. But then he remembered the cruelty and deviousness of the man, and his rage flared up again. He drew his own dagger and dipped it for a moment in the pot of poison along with the other weapons.

Trickery at the Lama Temple

That afternoon, the Red Flower heroes ate a hearty meal and then waited until it was time to leave. At about four o'clock, Bai Zhen arrived with four guards to accompany them. The Red Flower heroes put on formal gowns, and rode to the Lama Temple. Bai Zhen noticed with relief that none of them were carrying swords.

At the temple gate they dismounted, and Bai Zhen led them inside. Three tables had been prepared in the temple's Hall of Tranquillity, and Bai Zhen solemnly invited the heroes to be seated. Chen sat at the head of the middle table while Bald Vulture and Hidden Needle Lu took the head seats at the other two tables. Underneath the statue of the Buddha, a fourth table had been set up with a single large chair covered with satin and brocade. This was obviously the Emperor's seat. The heroes began secretly calculating distances in preparation for the assassination attempt.

Dishes of food were brought out and placed on the tables and the Red Flower heroes quietly awaited the arrival of the Emperor. After a while, footsteps sounded outside and two eunuchs marched into the hall with a senior military official whom the heroes all immediately recognized as Li Kexiu, the former Commander-in-Chief of Zhejiang Province. Yuanzhi gripped Scholar Yu's hand and almost cried out in surprise at the sight of her father. She had no idea he had been transferred to the Capital.

'Hearken to the Imperial order!' one of the eunuchs shouted, and Commander Li, Bai Zhen, and the other officials present immediately knelt down. Chen and the rest of the Red Flower heroes had no alternative but to do likewise.

The eunuch unrolled a scroll and began declaiming: 'On the orders of the Heaven-ordained Emperor, the following proclamation is made: "Whereas We nurture benevolence and encourage talent, and whereas it is good that Our ministers and the common people should strive for merit in order to gain rewards; whereas Our subject Chen Jialuo and certain of his colleagues have been loyal citizens and deserve to be fitly honoured; accordingly, we bestow upon Chen Jialuo the title of Doctor of the Imperial Civil Service Examination *summa cum laude*. His various associates are to be given positions of appropriate rank in the Boards of Rites and War. We invite all of them to dine at the Lama Temple. The Commander-in-Chief of the Imperial Forces in Zhili Province, Li Kexiu, will host the banquet."' The eunuch looked up from the scroll and shouted: 'Express your humble thanks for this act of Imperial benevolence!'

The Red Flower heroes suddenly realized that the Emperor had cheated them. He was not coming.

Commander Li walked over to Helmsman Chen and bowed before him.

'Congratulations, Doctor Chen. You are indeed honoured to have been so highly favoured by His Majesty.' Chen received this with a self-deprecating remark.

Yuanzhi and Scholar Yu rose to their feet and stood before Li. 'Father!' said Yuanzhi quietly.

Commander Li turned and saw his long-lost daughter standing before him. It was as if she had suddenly dropped from nowhere. He grasped her by the hand, tears welling into his eyes.

'My child!' he said, his voice shaking. 'Are you well?' She nodded. 'Come, come and sit with me,' he added, and pulled her over to a side table.

The two eunuchs, obviously kungfu experts, walked over to the central table and stood before Helmsman Chen. One of them saluted with his fists, then turned and shouted: 'Boy!'

Two young attendants entered carrying a tray on which was placed a pot of wine and several cups. The eunuch lifted the pot and filled two cups. Then he raised one of them to his own lips. 'I drink to you!' he said to Helmsman Chen, and drained the cup at one draught. He picked the other one up and offered it to Chen.

But Chen had been watching intently, and had noticed two small holes on the side of the wine pot. The eunuch had placed his thumb over the left hole when he poured the first cup of wine, but had moved it to cover the right hole as he poured the second cup. Chen guessed that the pot was divided into two inner compartments, and that the flow of wine from each could be controlled by covering one or other of the holes. He glanced at the eunuch in distaste, knowing that if it had not been for Hasli's warning, he would have drunk the cup down.

He saluted with his fists in thanks, and lifted the cup as if to drink. Expressions of delighted anticipation lit up the faces of the eunuchs. But then Chen put the cup down again, picked up the wine pot, and poured out another cup. This cupful he drank, then offered the cup originally meant for himself to the second eunuch.

'You drink a toast as well,' he said.

The eunuch realized that Chen had seen through the trick, and turned deathly pale. His right foot shot up and kicked the cup out of Chen's hand. The other eunuch shouted: 'Get them!' and several hundred Imperial Guards sprang into view from every side.

'If you gentlemen don't wish to drink, then don't,' said Chen with a smile.

'His Imperial Majesty decrees,' shouted one of the eunuchs, 'that since the Red Flower Society has engaged in rebellion and continues to harbour evil intentions, its members must be immediately seized and killed.'

Helmsman Chen waved his hand and the Twin Knights leapt at the two eunuchs, paralysing each with a swift blow to the neck. The Red Flower heroes brought out their weapons from under their gowns, and Father Speckless charged for the door with the others close behind. He seized a sword from one of the guards and killed three others as he passed.

Commander Li grabbed his daughter's hand and dragged her after him as he directed his men to stop the heroes. But Yuanzhi pulled herself free and ran off shouting: 'Save yourself, father!'

Commander Li stared after her for a moment, then called out urgently: 'Yuanzhi, come back!' But she had already left the hall to join Scholar Yu, who was fighting fiercely with five or six guards in the courtyard outside.

Flames were licking up towards the sky from a nearby hall. There was apparently another battle taking place simultaneously, and the noise was deafening. Helmsman Chen and the other heroes broke out of Tranquillity Hall into the open, and were surprised to find twenty or thirty lamas fighting with a group of regular Manchu soldiers outside the burning hall. From the look of things, the lamas would not be able to hold out for much longer. But even as they watched, Bai Zhen led some of the Imperial Guards into the courtyard, and helped the lamas force the Manchu troops back into the hall. Chen had no knowledge of the struggle that was taking place between the Emperor and the Empress Dowager, but he immediately recognized the fight as an excellent diversion and quickly ordered the Red Flower heroes to escape over the temple walls.

As their feet touched the ground, they involuntarily sucked in their breath: in front of them stood rank upon rank of Manchu troops, all with bows taut or with swords in hand. The scene was brightly lit by several thousand torches.

'He has thought it all out,' Helmsman Chen reflected bitterly. Father Speckless and Bald Vulture charged into the Manchu ranks, killing as they went, and a hail of arrows descended on them.

'Everyone try and make a break for it!' shouted Huo Qingtong.

The Red Flower heroes fought like demons. Father Speckless noticed seven or eight Manchu soldiers attacking Hunchback Zhang, and leapt over to help him. He stabbed three of them in the neck. The rest howled and retreated.

'Brother Zhang, are you all right?' he cried.

Hunchback Zhang looked up at him and dropped his Wolf's Tooth club. 'Brother Wu,' he gasped, 'I'm finished.' By the light of the flames, Father Speckless saw that he was badly wounded and spattered from head to foot in blood. He could not support him with his one arm.

'Get on my back and hold on,' the priest gasped between clenched teeth. He squatted down, and Zhang threw his arms round his neck. Father Speckless felt the warm blood spurting out of the Hunchback's wounds, but he rose to his feet and charged off again with sword raised to continue the killing.

Helmsman Chen could see that things were going badly for his men. He ordered the Red Flower heroes to return to the temple wall to regroup.

'All right, Brother Zhang, you'd better get down now,' said Father Speckless as they reached the comparative safety of the wall. But Zhang did not move. Luo Bing went over to help him down. But his body was stiff and his breathing had already ceased. She threw herself onto his corpse and began to sob.

Just as the Manchu troops moved in for a final attack on the heroes, over thirty Shaolin monks could be seen fighting their way through the ranks, their yellow robes glowing in the firelight. Leading them, his long white beard dancing and shaking, was Lord Zhou.

'Come with me, all of you!' he shouted to the Red Flower heroes. They charged after him through the encircling Manchu ranks, where Heavenly Mirror and the other Shaolin monks were battling fiercely.

Huo Qingtong surveyed the situation with dismay. The Red Flower heroes were killing large numbers of the enemy, but no matter which direction they went in, they were always surrounded. She looked around for some possible solution and spotted a dozen or so people standing on the nearby Drum Tower.

'One of those men must be their commander,' she shouted to the others, pointing at the tower. 'Let's seize him.'

The Red Flower heroes immediately saw the wisdom of her words.

'Let's go,' roared Father Speckless. Rolling Thunder Wen and the Twin Knights ran after him. In no time they reached the foot of the Drum Tower, and leapt up onto the terrace just as thirty guards moved to intercept them. Wen, however, dodged nimbly past them and charged straight for an officer standing in one corner, a man wearing a red cap signifying senior rank. As he caught sight of the officer's face in the firelight, he almost called out 'Helmsman!'— the man was very nearly Chen's double. Wen remembered his wife telling him about the resemblance of Qian Long's favourite, Fu Kangan, to Chen, and decided this must be him.

It was indeed Fu, who was the Peking Garrison Commander. Wen deftly dodged the swords of two surprised guards and lunged at Fu, with Father Speckless close behind. Down below, the Manchu troops ceased their attack and stood watching the drama on the terrace above them.

Fu knew no kungfu whatsoever and he cringed in fear as Wen lifted him bodily into the air. A gasp went up from the Manchu troops down below. By this time, the Twin Knights had killed the last of the guards on the Drum Tower terrace and had run over to Wen. Fu raised his command flag and shrieked: 'Stop, all of you! Return to your units!'

Three men charged bravely forward, but Father Speckless held the tip of his sword at Fu's throat and smiled at them. 'Come on!' he said. 'Come on!'

The men hesitated, glanced at each other, then withdrew.

Wen squeezed Fu's arm and he screamed in agony. 'Retreat! Back in position, all of you!' The Manchu troops did not dare to disobey their commanding officer's orders and immediately retreated and lined up at a distance.

Helmsman Chen now gathered the Red Flower heroes and the Shaolin monks together on the Drum Tower terrace. He counted up the casualties and found that apart from Hunchback Zhang who was dead, eight or nine of the others had been wounded, only one of them seriously. He surveyed his followers in the light of the flames from the still burning temple.

'Let's attack the Palace and kill the Emperor to avenge Brother

Zhang!' he shouted. The heroes roared their approval, and the Shaolin monks joined in.

'He destroyed our Shaolin Monastery,' added Heavenly Mirror. 'Today, I make a special dispensation: we are allowed to kill!'

'What?' asked Helmsman Chen, shocked. 'The Shaolin Monastery is destroyed?'

'Yes, it's been burnt to the ground. Our Abbot, Heavenly Rainbow, died protecting the sacred scriptures.'

This news compounded Chen's anger. With Commander Fu as their hostage, the Red Flower heroes marched through the ranks of Manchu soldiers encircling the Lama Temple. Finally, they saw Xin Yan and a number of the Red Flower Society followers standing at a distance with twenty or thirty horses. They ran over and mounted up, one or two to each horse, and, with a defiant shout, galloped off towards the Imperial Palace.

Metallic Vest, Baby Hostage

Mastermind Xu rode up alongside Helmsman Chen. 'Has an escape route been planned, Helmsman?' he shouted.

'Brother Wei has gone with some of the others to the west gate to wait for us. What are you and the monks doing here?'

'Those Manchu monsters!' replied Xu, his voice full of hatred. 'They came one night and sacked the Monastery. Father Heavenly Rainbow would not leave and was burned to death. They even kidnapped my baby son! We have been looking for the officers responsible ever since, and the chase brought us to Peking. We went to Twin Willows Lane and they told us you had gone to the Lama Temple.'

By this time, they had arrived at the Forbidden City with the Manchu soldiers pressing in on them from behind. Even if the soldiers lacked the courage to attack, they were still loth to leave them alone.

Xu looked over at the Twin Eagles. 'If the Emperor gets wind of this and hides somewhere in the depths of the Palace, we'll never find him. You two go on ahead and investigate.'

The two old people were delighted to have the opportunity to show their worth, and immediately agreed. Xu took four flares from his bag and gave them to Bald Vulture.

'When you catch sight of the Emperor, kill him if you can, but if he is guarded too closely, signal us with these,' he said.

The Twin Eagles leapt over the Palace wall and ran swiftly across the courtyard inside and then up onto the rooftops. As they raced along, they saw the heavy Palace gates and the endless courtyards and pavilions, and wondered how they could ever hope to find the Emperor in such a huge and well-guarded enclosure.

'Let's grab a eunuch or someone and question him,' said Lady Guan.

'Good idea!' replied her husband. They jumped down to the ground and hid themselves in a dark corner. After a while, they heard footsteps approach and two figures walked quickly by.

'The thin one knows kungfu,' whispered Bald Vulture.

'Let's follow and see where they go,' Lady Guan replied.

The Twin Eagles silently shadowed the two figures, one very thin, the other fat and much slower on his feet. The thin man had to constantly stop to wait for the other to catch up, and at one point said: 'Faster! Faster! We must report to the Emperor as soon as possible.'

The Twin Eagles were delighted to hear this. They followed them through doorway after doorway and courtyard after courtyard, until they finally arrived in front of the Precious Moon Pavilion.

'You wait here,' the thin man said and disappeared upstairs, leaving the fat man standing alone by the front door. The Twin Eagles crept round to the side of the pavilion and climbed up onto the roof. Then, with their feet hooked onto the eaves, they hung down over a balcony smelling of fresh paint and flowers and saw a row of windows, one of which glowed with the faint light of a candle. They slipped onto the balcony, just as a shadow passed across the window-paper. Lady Guan carefully wet the paper with her finger, making a hole, and then looked through to see Qian Long seated in a chair, a fan in his hand, and the thin man kneeling before him: it was Bai Zhen.

'The Hall of Tranquillity in the Lama Temple has been burned to the ground and not one of the soldiers guarding it escaped,' he said.

'Excellent!' exclaimed Qian Long, very pleased.

Bai Zhen kowtowed. 'But your slave deserves to die. The Red Flower Society bandits eluded capture.'

'What?'

'They saw through the attempt to poison them with the wine, and they escaped while I was dealing with the Manchu soldiers sent by Her Highness.'

Qian Long grunted and hung his head, deep in thought.

Bald Vulture pointed at Bai Zhen and the Emperor, indicating to his wife that *he* would attack Bai Zhen while *she* killed Qian Long. The two were just about to burst through the window when Bai Zhen clapped his hands twice and twelve guards slipped noiselessly out from behind cupboards and screens, each one carrying a sword. The Twin Eagles knew they were no match for so many expert fighters and decided to summon the other Red Flower heroes first. Bai Zhen whispered something to one of the guards who left and brought the fat man back with him.

The fat man, wearing the yellow robes of a Lama priest, kowtowed energetically before the Emperor.

'You have done well,' Qian Long said. 'Are you sure you left no clues?'

'Everything was done according to Your Majesty's wishes. Nothing is left of the Hall of Tranquillity or what was in it.'

'Good, good! Bai Zhen, I promised that this Abbot should be made a Living Buddha. Go and see to it.'

'Your Majesty,' Bai Zhen replied with a bow.

The Abbot kowtowed again.

As they walked away from the pavilion, Bai Zhen stopped the Abbot. 'You show your gratitude to His Majesty, Reverend Father,' he said.

The Abbot looked at him in some surprise, but unwilling to disobey an order from the captain of the Imperial Guard, he knelt down again and kowtowed in the direction of the Precious Moon Pavilion. As he did so, he felt an icy coldness on his neck. He started in shock.

'What... what's happening?' he asked, his voice shaking.

Bai Zhen laughed coldly. 'His Majesty said I was to make you a Living Buddha. So I'm sending you to Heaven to be one.'

He twitched his hand and the blade did its work. Two eunuchs brought a carpet over, wrapped the corpse in it, and carried it away.

Suddenly Bai Zhen heard shouting in the distance. He turned and ran back into the pavilion.

'There seem to be bandits outside causing a disturbance, Your Majesty,' he said. 'Please retire to the Inner Palace.'

Qian Long immediately assumed they must be Red Flower Society fighters. He had seen them in action in Hangzhou and knew that his guards were no match for them, so without questioning Bai Zhen further, he stood up to go.

Just then, Bald Vulture released a flare. With a 'whoosh' it scrawled a path of white light across the night sky.

'Where do you think you're going?' he roared as he and Lady Guan burst through the window into the room. 'We've waited a long time for this!'

The guards around the Emperor stared for a moment in disbelief at the red-faced old man and white-haired old woman who had suddenly appeared in their midst, then rushed at the intruders. Bai Zhen lifted Qian Long onto his back and, with four guards protecting them to the front and four to the rear, ran for the stairs. But Lady Guan forced the guards back with a fistful of projectiles and lunged at Qian Long with her sword. Bai Zhen leapt backwards in fright.

Meanwhile, Bald Vulture was fighting with three guards simultaneously. Bai Zhen gave a whistle and four other guards joined the fray, completely surrounding Bald Vulture. But he fought like a demon and kept all seven at bay for a while, until one of the guards lashed out with a whip which cracked loudly against his right arm. In great pain, Bald Vulture switched his sword over to the left hand and forced the guards back.

Seeing her husband wounded, Lady Guan went over to help him, and the two retreated towards the second floor of the pavilion. Bald Vulture knew they could not keep so many top-class kungfu fighters at bay for much longer, so he slipped over to the window and shot off another flare. He and his wife blocked the stairs, and began retreating downwards a step at a time. The pressure was great, but luckily the staircase was narrow and only three or four guards at most could attack at one time. Even so, the strain of having to fight against an enemy which always had the advantage of coming from above was very wearing.

Bai Zhen saw the need to extricate Qian Long from the danger. He ordered one of the guards to put the Emperor on his back. The guard squatted down and the Emperor climbed on. Bai Zhen gave a shout and charged at Bald Vulture. The two began to fight, and Bald Vulture cursed his bad luck. The longer he fought, the more painful the wound to his right arm became. Bai Zhen by himself was as much as he could manage, let alone the other four or five guards who also surrounded him. Bai Zhen's hands moved with lightning speed, every move accurate and deadly, and Bald Vulture, completely absorbed in fending him off, was unprepared for the cold-blooded attack that came from behind: a guard thrust his sword deep into Bald Vulture's back.

Bald Vulture knew instantly that he was dying. He swung his elbow back with all his strength and smashed his attacker's skull; then, with a huge roar, he raised his sword and threw it forcefully across the room at Qian Long. The guard who was carrying the Emperor saw the blade flying towards them and, with no time to dodge out of the way, put his hand up to stop it. But this was a throw by a man on the verge of death, propelled by incalculable reserves of strength and outrage. The sword sliced off half of the guard's hand, then plunged through his chest and out the other side.

Bald Vulture was content, assuming that the sword must have entered Qian Long: exchanging his own life for that of an Emperor made death seem worthwhile. Lady Guan ran to her husband as Bai Zhen hurriedly picked Qian Long up off the floor, crying: 'Your Majesty, are you all right?'

Qian Long was scared out of his wits, but he was still alive. He struggled to control himself. 'At least I was well-prepared,' he replied with a wan smile.

Bai Zhen could see the tip of Bald Vulture's sword extending six inches out of the guard's back. He also saw a long rip down the front of Qian Long's gown. He wondered in awe how it was the Emperor had avoided injury.

'Your Majesty is very fortunate,' he said. 'Truly, the Son of Heaven has the protection of a hundred gods.'

What he did not know was that Qian Long had been so fearful of an assassination attempt as a result of his decision to break his pact with the Red Flower Society that he had decided to wear a metallic vest at all times. It was this that had saved his life.

Bai Zhen looked round and saw that there was no longer anyone blocking the steps. He lifted Qian Long onto his back, the guards fell in around him, and they all ran straight downstairs. But just as they were about to pass through the pavilion's main entrance, Qian Long gave a shout of alarm and struggled free of Bai Zhen's grasp: standing in the doorway was Chen Jialuo. Behind him, their torches dancing and swords glinting, were thirty or so kungfu fighters. The Emperor turned and ran straight back up the stairs. The guards swarmed after him with the Red Flower Society heroes on their heels. Two of the guards who were slightly slower than the rest were intercepted by the Twin Knights and instantly killed.

Chen and the other heroes had had to fight their way through the Palace to the Precious Moon Pavilion, and were delighted to find that, in spite of the delay, the Emperor had not yet escaped. With a loud cry, the Red Flower heroes galloped up the stairs. Chen assigned men to watch the various exits. Father Speckless stood with his sword at the ready at the head of the stairwell on the third floor, while the Twin Knights went back down to guard the bottom of the stairs. Buddha Zhao and three of the Shaolin monks took up positions by the windows.

Huo Qingtong saw her Shifu Lady Guan in a corner embracing Bald Vulture, whose blood was welling forth in great surges from the gash in his back. She went over with Hidden Needle Lu who took out some ointment. Bald Vulture smiled bitterly and shook his head.

'I'm sorry I've made you unhappy all these years,' he said to Lady Guan. 'When you return to the border country you must marry...marry old Yuan...and then I will be content in the afterworld. Brother Lu, you must make sure that this happy event takes place...'

Lady Guan's eyebrows flew up in outrage. 'Do you mean to say,' she demanded, 'that you do not know how I have felt towards you in the past few months?'

Hidden Needle Lu was just about to suggest it would be better for her to say a few comforting words to her dying husband rather than start another argument, when she jumped to her feet and shouted: 'Well, I'll set your mind at ease!' She raised her sword and drew it firmly across her throat. Hidden Needle Lu and Huo Qingtong were standing at her side, but neither was quick enough to save her. Bald Vulture let loose a dying wail of grief. Huo Qingtong threw herself onto their corpses and sobbed uncontrollably.

Chen pointed his dagger at Qian Long. 'Even forgetting the pact we made in the Six Harmonies Pagoda, we agreed on the dyke at Haining never to harm each other. And yet you used poisoned wine to try and get rid of me. What do you have to say?' He stepped forward and pointed the blade of his dagger, glinting coldly, directly at Qian Long's heart. 'You have decided to throw in your lot with the Tartars. You have cruelly oppressed the common people. You are the enemy of all good men under heaven!' He spoke with a formal severity. 'Our fraternal bond is broken forever. Today, I will drink your blood to avenge all those who have been killed in your name.'

Qian Long's face turned deathly pale and his whole body quivered with terror.

Heavenly Mirror strode forward. 'We of the Shaolin Monastery led a simple life,' he cried. 'We had no quarrels with the world. What was your reason for burning our Monastery to the ground? Today, I will disregard our own sacred commandment against the taking of human life.'

Helmsman Chen helped Huo Qingtong to her feet and placed his dagger in her hand. 'Your father, your brother and sister, and countless members of your tribe died at the hands of this man,' he said. 'You kill him.'

Huo Qingtong took the dagger and walked towards Qian Long. One of the guards moved to intercept her, but Rolling Thunder Wen stopped him in his tracks and, with eight or nine swift blows, broke his ribs and cracked his spine in two, so that he fell limply to the floor in a heap. A hubbub of voices rose from outside. Buddha Zhao looked out and saw a sea of torches and faces around the pavilion.

Rolling Thunder Wen walked over to the window. 'The Emperor is here,' he called. 'If anyone dares to come up, I will kill him myself.' He spoke in a forceful, commanding tone. A hush fell over the crowd below. The Red Flower heroes in the Precious Moon Pavilion also fell silent, and stared fixedly at the gleaming blade in Huo Qingtong's hand as she advanced step by step towards Qian Long.

Suddenly, a figure darted into the room and stood in front of Qian Long. Huo Qingtong stopped in surprise. It was a Manchu officer holding a baby—a white, chubby baby which was sucking its little fingers.

'My baby! Give me back my baby!' screamed Zhou Qi, and lunged forward.

'Come on, then,' the man shouted. 'If you want a dead baby, come and get it.'

Zhou Qi stopped in her tracks and stared at him in a daze.

The officer, a man named Fang, was commander of the troops sent by Qian Long to destroy the southern Shaolin Monastery in Fujian. He knew that the Emperor wanted to eradicate the Red Flower Society and, during the night attack, his men had, on his orders, snatched Zhou Qi's baby son. Fang had thought that this would be considered an achievement of great merit and had made his way to Peking for an audience with the Emperor.

Qian Long had questioned him closely earlier that evening, wanting to ascertain for certain that no evidence relating to his Chinese origins could have survived at the Shaolin Monastery. When the Twin Eagles appeared, Fang had dodged behind a curtain, but he now saw an opportunity to use the baby to gain even greater merit.

'All of you leave the Palace at once,' cried Fang, 'and I will give you back the child alive.'

'You monster!' Huo Qingtong shouted at him. 'This is just a trick!' In her excitement the words came out in the Uighur tongue, and Fang looked at her uncomprehendingly.

The Red Flower heroes had thought they finally had the Emperor in their grasp. But now one man, a man clearly ignorant of kungfu and holding a baby, had rendered them powerless to act. They turned to Helmsman Chen, waiting for his decision.

Chen looked at Huo Qingtong and thought of how Qian Long had driven her sister Hasli, the Fragrant Princess, to suicide. Were the deaths of her father, her brother, and her sister to be left unavenged? Looking round, he caught sight of the corpses of the Twin Eagles of Heaven Mountains. Then he saw Mastermind Xu's face, full of fear for his son, and glanced back at the child in Fang's arms. It was only two months old and was gurgling happily, stretching out its little fingers to feel the rough soldier's hand. Chen looked at the others: Father Heavenly Mirror's eyes radiating compassion, Hidden Needle Lu sighing, and Lord Zhou's white beard shaking backwards and forwards as he trembled. As for Zhou Qi, she was standing with her mouth wide open, a crazed expression on her face.

Helmsman Chen knew that Lord Zhou's son and heir had died as a result of the Red Flower Society and that this baby before them now was the sole surviving hope for the continuation of his family line. But if they did not kill the Emperor today, they were unlikely ever to have another opportunity to gain revenge. So what was he to do?

Huo Qingtong turned and handed the dagger back to Helmsman Chen. He nodded. 'Very well,' he said to Fang. 'We will not harm the Emperor. Give the child to me.' As he spoke, he replaced the dagger in its sheath and stretched out his hands.

'Huh! Why should I believe you?' Fang replied darkly. 'I'll return the child only after you have left the Palace.'

Chen was furious. 'In the Red Flower Society, we hold to our word,' he said. 'We don't cheat. Perhaps that's something scum like you wouldn't understand.'

'I still don't believe you.'

'Very well,' Chen countered. 'In that case, you leave the Palace with us.' Fang hesitated.

Qian Long was ecstatic when he heard Chen say that his life was to be spared. He did not care less what happened to Fang. 'Go with them,' he said. 'You have gained great merit today. I will not forget it.'

Fang shivered as he heard the Emperor's words and strange tone of voice. He was clearly talking about awarding him some sort of posthumous honour. But all he could bring himself to say was: 'Thank you, Your Majesty, for your benevolence.' Then he turned to Helmsman Chen. 'If I leave the Palace with you, what are my chances of staying alive?' He wanted Chen to promise to spare him.

'You've already done enough evil,' Chen replied angrily. 'You should have been consigned to Hell long ago.'

Qian Long, worried that other complications could arise, and that Chen might change his mind, urged Fang on: 'Quickly, leave with them now.'

'But I'm afraid that once I've gone, they will try and harm Your Majesty,' said Fang.

'So what do you suggest?' asked Chen in exasperation.

'That you allow his Imperial Majesty to leave first. Then I will accompany you out of the Palace.'

Chen could see they would have to let him go. 'All right,' he said to Qian Long. 'Leave.'

Qian Long was beyond considerations of Imperial dignity. He bolted for the door as fast as his feet could carry him. Suddenly, Chen stretched out his right hand, grabbed him as he ran past, and slapped him sharply several times on the face. The sound rang out crisp and clear. Qian Long's cheeks immediately began to swell up.

The Red Flower heroes were taken by surprise, and there was a brief silence before they roared out their approval.

'Do you still remember that oath you swore?' asked Helmsman Chen, but Qian Long lacked the courage to reply. With a contemptuous wave of his hand Chen dismissed him, and the Emperor stumbled out of the room and down the stairs.

'Pass me the child!' Chen shouted.

Buddha Zhao was holding his poisonous darts and looking out of the window, waiting for the right moment. As soon as Chen had hold of the child, and Qian Long appeared down below, he would fire off a stream of projectiles at the Emperor's body. Fang, meanwhile, was frantically looking around, trying to think of some way out for himself. 'I want to see with my own eyes that His Majesty is out of danger before I hand over the child,' he said, shuffling slowly towards the nearest window.

'You filthy turtle!' snarled one of the Twin Knights. 'You're a dead man!' They shadowed him, waiting for an opportunity to strike.

Qian Long emerged from the main door of the pavilion, and the guards waiting down below surged forward.

'Traitor!' Buddha Zhao muttered to himself. 'Traitor!'

Fang saw the guards gathered below. He could not simply do nothing and die where he was. With a sudden movement, he threw himself out of the window, the child still in his arms. The Red Flower heroes were taken completely unawares. They let out a cry of surprise. One of the Twin Knights flicked out a Flying Claw and hooked it round Fang's left leg, then tugged with all his might. Fang flew up into the air, the baby flew out of his hands, and the two of them began to fall again. Buddha Zhao crouched down and launched himself like an arrow out of the window. As he flew head first through the air, he stretched out his left hand and grabbed hold of one of the child's tiny legs while at the same time throwing three of his poisonous darts at Fang, hitting him squarely on the head and chest. It was a stunning feat of acrobatic kungfu. A shout went up both from the Red Flower heroes in the pavilion and from the guards who were watching down below. Zhao braced himself, hugged the baby to his chest, and landed firmly on his two feet. The Twin Knights, Lord Zhou, and some of the other heroes jumped down from the pavilion and surrounded Zhao and the baby. Zhao looked down at the child in his arms. It was kicking and waving its arms about, chuckling away in delight. It obviously thought the flying descent that had almost ended its life had been great fun, and wanted to do it all over again.

Helmsman Chen pushed their hostage, Lord Fu Kangan, to the window and shouted: 'Do you want this man to live?'

Qian Long, once more under the protection of his guards, caught sight of Fu in the torchlight. 'Stop! Stop!' he shouted. The guards turned and waited for his directions.

Fu was in fact more than Qian Long's favourite. He was his illegitimate son. His beautiful mother had been spotted by Qian Long when she had come to the Palace one evening to pay her respects to the Empress. He had had illicit relations with her, and the result was Fu. Qian Long had many sons, but for some perverse reason he loved this illegitimate one more than all the rest. The striking physical likeness between Helmsman Chen and Fu was therefore the result of the simple fact that they were uncle and nephew.

Chen knew nothing of this, but he was well aware that the Emperor doted on Fu. He and the other Red Flower heroes escorted their hostage downstairs. Zhou Qi ran over to Buddha Zhao and took the baby from him, beside herself with happiness.

On one side were the Red Flower Society heroes and the Shaolin monks; on the other, the Palace Guards and the elite corps of the Imperial Guard. Commander Li knew that his forces vastly outnumbered the enemy, but he also knew how the Emperor felt about Fu.

'Helmsman Chen,' he shouted. 'Let Lord Fu go and we will allow you to leave the city peacefully.'

'What does the Emperor say?' Chen shouted back.

Qian Long's cheeks were painful and badly swollen like overripe peaches as a result of Chen's blows, but seeing his beloved son in the hands of the enemy, he could only gesture and say: 'Let them go, let them go.'

'Lord Fu will see us out of the city,' said Chen. Then, looking Qian Long straight in the eye, he announced in a loud voice: 'All the common people under Heaven would be happy to eat your flesh and make a quilt of your skin. If you live another hundred years, may they be a hundred years of days filled with fear and torment, a hundred years of sleepless nights!' He turned to the Red Flower heroes. 'Let's go,' he said.

The Red Flower heroes pushed Fu forward and made their way towards the Palace gate, carrying with them the bodies of the Twin Eagles and Hunchback Zhang. The Manchu guards stared at them fixedly as they passed, but did not dare to stop them. Soon after they had passed out of the Palace, they spotted two horsemen galloping after them, one of whom was Commander Li.

'Helmsman Chen!' he called as he got closer. 'There is something I wish to discuss with you.'

The Red Flower heroes reined in their horses and waited for Li and his lieutenant, Zeng Tunan, to catch up.

'His Majesty says that if you allow Lord Fu to return safely, he will agree to any conditions,' Li said.

Chen's eyebrows shot up. 'And why should I believe a single word the Emperor says any more?'

'Please. I ask you to express your wishes so that I can return to report.'

'Very well,' said Chen. 'Firstly, I want the Emperor to rebuild the Shaolin Monastery with his own funds. The golden statues of Buddha must be even larger than before. And the Monastery must never be harrassed again in any way.'

'That is easy to arrange,' said Li.

'Secondly, the Emperor must not increase the military burden on the common people in the Uighur lands, and all Uighur prisoners must be released.'

'That is not difficult either.'

'Thirdly, the Emperor must not persecute the Red Flower Society or seize any of its members no matter where they may be.' On this point, Commander Li was silent. Chen continued. 'If you really did try to seize any of us, do you think we would have cause to be afraid? I believe our Brother Wen spent some time as a guest in your own military headquarters, didn't he?'

'All right. I suppose I have no choice,' said Li finally.

'Exactly one year from today, if all three of these demands have been fully met, Lord Fu will be released.'

'I accept your terms,' replied Li and turned to Fu. 'Lord Fu, Helmsman Chen is a man of his word. Please set your mind at ease. His Majesty will certainly issue orders to see that all three requests are met. I will not allow a moment to pass without thinking of your safety, and will make sure everything is done as quickly as possible in the hope that Helmsman Chen may see fit to release you early.'

Fu was silent.

'Commander Li, we must take our leave of you,' announced Helmsman Chen, and saluted with his fists. 'When you are promoted and become rich, take care not to oppress the common people.'

Li saluted in reply.

Yuanzhi and Scholar Yu dismounted and walked over to Li. They knelt down in front of him. Li realized to his sorrow that he would never see his daughter again.

'Look after yourself, child,' he said quietly. He stretched out his hand and stroked her hair, then turned his horse round and rode back to the Palace. Yuanzhi began to cry as Scholar Yu helped her onto her horse.

The Red Flower heroes galloped to the city gate where Pagoda Yang and Leopard Wei were waiting for them. Fu ordered the city gate to be opened. The huge bell in the Bell Tower above sounded, ringing out the fourth watch of the night.

Butterfly Spirit

As they left the city, the Red Flower heroes rode past an expanse of reeds growing beside the city moat. The reeds swayed in the pale moonlight. A little further on, they came upon a graveyard, and noticed a crowd of people there wailing and singing a Uighur funeral dirge. Helmsman Chen and Huo Qingtong rode over to investigate.

'Who are you mourning for?' they asked the crowd.

An old Uighur man raised his head, his face streaked with tears, and said: 'Princess Hasli.'

'You mean the Princess is buried here?' Chen asked.

The old man pointed at a new grave, the yellow earth not yet dry. 'There,' he replied.

Huo Qingtong began to cry. 'We cannot allow her to remain buried here,' she said.

'You're right,' Chen replied. 'She loved that Jade Pool in the heart of White Jade Peak. She said how much she would like to live there for ever. We should take her remains and bury them there.'

'Yes,' said Huo Qingtong, swallowing her tears.

'Who are you?' the old man enquired politely.

'I am the Princess' sister,' replied Huo Qingtong.

Another of the Uighurs excitedly shouted out this news to the other mourners.

'Let's open up her grave,' Huo Qingtong said. Chen and the Red Flower heroes, helped by several of the Uighurs, shifted the earth as fast as they could and, in a moment, had uncovered the stone slab placed over the grave. They raised the slab and a perfumed fragrance emerged. But when they looked inside, they found that the grave itself was empty.

Helmsman Chen took a burning torch from one of the mourners and held it over the opening. On the very floor of the grave he could see a small pool of congealed blood, and beside it the piece of 'warm' jade that he himself had given her. Even the blood itself had taken on the jade-green tint associated since time immemorial with the blood of martyrs.

'We brought Princess Hasli's remains here and buried them ourselves,' said the Uighurs. 'We have not left this spot since. How could her body have disappeared like this?'

'Such a beautiful lady must surely have been an immortal spirit descended to earth,' Luo Bing suggested. 'She was a fairy being. Now she has simply returned to her home in Heaven. Don't be distressed.'

Chen bent down and reached into the grave to pick up the piece of jade. Suddenly, he began to weep, the tears running down his face like rain. She had been so beautiful, so pure. Perhaps it was true. Perhaps she had always been a spirit.

The people sighed and covered up the grave once more. Just as they finished the work, a large butterfly the colour of green jade appeared in the air and began fluttering to and fro above the mound.

Helmsman Chen turned to the old man. 'I want to write a few words,' he said. 'Please ask a master carver to put up a stone on this spot, engraved with the inscription.'

The old man nodded, and Xin Yan gave him ten taels of silver to cover the costs. Then he took writing implements from his bag and handed them to Helmsman Chen.

Chen raised his brush thoughtfully, and wrote the two words 'Fragrant Tomb' in large characters. Then after a moment's thought, he wrote:

Oh vast, vast sadness!
Oh boundless, boundless loss!
The song has ended,
The moon has waned.

In the mournful city
The jade blood of a martyr
Has been shed.
Jade is exhausted,
Blood runs dry,
But your fragrant spirit
Lives for ever—
A butterfly!

The Red Flower heroes stood there for a long time in silence. Only when the eastern sky was already light did they mount up and ride off westwards.